WARLORD

DOC SPEARS

WARGATE

An imprint of Galaxy's Edge Press
PO BOX 534
Puyallup, Washington 98371
Copyright © 2022 by Doc Spears
All rights reserved.

This is a work of fiction. Any similarity to real persons, living or dead, is coincidental and not intended by the author.

No part of this publication may be reproduced, stored in a retrieval system, or transmitted in any form or by any means electronic, mechanical, photocopying, recording, or otherwise without the prior written permission of the publisher and copyright owner.

Paperback ISBN: 978-1-949731-75-0
Hardcover ISBN: 978-1-949731-76-7

www.wargatebooks.com

✣ ✣ ✣

BENJAMIN COLT IS A SOLDIER DAMAGED BY CIRCUMSTANCE. WHILE others have stumbled into honor, each time the prize of combat is dangled in front of him, it's snatched from his grasp. There's nothing for a professional warrior to do except keep getting up, no matter how many times he's knocked down, hoping that the next time will be the one that brings him his day of days. At last, a real Green Beret on the most select of Special Forces A-Team, he's poised to get his wish.

So, of course, it's just then that the universe plays another practical joke on him.

Aliens are real, and come bearing gifts that are secretly sending the world back to the Stone Age.

Using the alien's technology to beat them at their own game, he and his team are catapulted not into a future Earth, but onto a world not their own. An ancient and dying world of a dream.

Ben Colt fights battles perilous and personal, against barbaric aliens and the twisted hearts of men, surrounded by the tragic remnants of a once great civilization—one slowly withering from the galaxy's memory to return to the red dust from which it came.

Air cars and ray guns, four-armed giants and eight-legged cavalry, miniguns and 40-mm grenades. A captive princess needs a hero to save the world. And Ben Colt needs a princess to make him—a Warlord.

✣ ✣ ✣

01

My name is Deacon Benjamin Colt.

By giving me such a grandiose name, I think my folks hoped to inspire me to do something great. I like to think I've lived my life in a way that's put something substantial behind that manly moniker. But nobody could live up to such a name. My dad was overcompensating for a lack of success in his own life. I just go by Ben. Deacon sounds too much like I'm a preacher, and I never liked Deke.

See, there's form, then there's substance. Like my name, and my life. Someone once said about General Curtis LeMay—the man who firebombed Japan in World War II and who formed the nuclear air forces that made the Cold War so very hot—that there were men who were all form and no substance. So, for a student of all-things-war like myself, that a colleague of the great air warrior said about the man—"LeMay is all substance and no form"—it makes you think.

LeMay was a hard man, all about the business of war—not for parade show. He led from the front. Flew the lead bomber on every mission until they forced him to stop. No matter that he was right, won wars—one hot, one cold—and kept us safe, people hated him for being brash and unkind with his words.

That's why you read history. To learn from someone else's mistakes. Like LeMay's. His thanks for service? He was put out to pasture. What would the history of our first lost war have been if he hadn't been made to sit it out? What I learned from his life was that so often it's the form by which something's said that makes it objectionable. The actual substance, not so much—especially if the thing had only been said kindly or at least without venom.

What she'd said to me that night in her apartment was all poison, meant to rot me from the inside. Like a snakebite necrosing the deepest tissue first.

"I don't need you."

It was the cruelest thing I'd ever been told. Even if it was true. Whenever I thought of her, I always pictured Curtis LeMay's scowling face hovering over her like some kind of guardian angel. Maybe she was a distant relative of his.

"You know, I don't *need* you."

As much as I like to think time had rendered that deepest stab into a barely remembered prick, the memory was just another pocket of decay hidden under my tough outer layers. And I hid them all from the world very well. But I was the one to always peel my apple to the core to find the worm at the rotten center of myself. No one else had been able to do it. I'd never broken, never failed, never quit. I've come to think that it's these little vignettes of pain that have driven me, pushed me, helped me to be better.

But sometimes they were a distraction. Like now.

The aircraft vibrated and groaned, and I dug my fingers around the jump seat straps to steady myself. I pushed the image of her and General LeMay from my mind. There were real things to worry about, things much more important than the betrayal of a girlfriend whom I should've kicked to the curb much sooner than she did me.

It felt like we were going down. Been there. Done that. It was an occupational hazard when you spent a lot of time around planes and helicopters—things that weren't meant to defy gravity permanently. I wasn't in the mood for a repeat.

Still, I couldn't let the images go just yet, and there was not much else to occupy my mind besides the thought of the impending death that awaited me when this shuddering behemoth of a C-17 lost its battle to stay airborne. And why the memory of those last words from her came to me just now, I guess things must've sparked it. The nagging doubt that I wasn't the warrior I thought I was, and the other woman's voice coming from the cockpit.

"Terrain. Terrain. Bank angle."

There was a pause and she repeated, "Terrain. Terrain. Bank angle."

"Yo, brah." Dave's voice vibrated as though he were being roughly massaged, but it was the airframe shaking like a roller coaster on a tight turn that disrupted his usually laid-back tones. "Whoever said man wasn't meant to fly was dead-nuts on."

"You're saying we picked the wrong profession?"

The life of a Special Forces operator meant you were bound in marriage to the machines that carried you aloft. And from your very first parachute jump, you would forever have more takeoffs than landings, a kind of cheating in the rules of aviation marriage. So maybe one final landing—a fiery crash—was the karmic way of punishing our infidelity.

"DOL, brah," Dave spouted back. *De Oppresso Liber.* Our motto. Latin for "to liberate the oppressed." When you said those three little letters, you said it all. See, most soldiers have job-type-jobs in the military. They were the gray, four-door Olds-mo-Buicks driving bumper to bumper on six lanes in a sea of other nondescript conveyances, chugging along on the highway of life. For those like us, the low-to-the-ground, wide-tire, racing-spoiler, supercharged models, the possibility of death in all sorts of nasty ways was on the list of standard factory options.

Being in Special Forces was everything to me. And now that I was finally here, on a real mission—as crazy a one as it was—Heather's scowl and bitter voice were there again to punish me for my hubris about finally getting my wish of being selected for the most special, the most secret, the most fantastic mission of all time.

Whenever I confided in her my pride at being in SF—those few moments of honesty and vulnerability—she used my pride against me like she was the dragon tattooed on her shoulder. The claws may have been curled around the red rose, but the teeth were sharp and ready to kill.

"I think all that Green Beret stuff is twisted. You're just begging to be killed in some sick male heroic fantasy. It's all stupid."

And like a starving man whose stomach needed to be filled, I'd swallow the spoilt meal, ignore the ill it caused me, then hold my plate up for more. And I wouldn't just feast on the meal heaped on my table, I'd replay it in excruciating detail, right down to the sour taste of each bite. Why didn't I dump her sooner? Most people wouldn't tolerate that, right? But I'm not most people.

One of the other things that makes me special—besides my enduring hope-springs-eternal attitude—is that I'm cursed with a good memory. I carry all the bad with me, never to be forgotten. And sometimes it bubbles up and seeps into the good, staining it. Ruining it. Or, like now, when there are other things that I should be focusing on, some tidbit of regret from my past replays like a surreal movie with its most particularly cringeworthy scene—like when you finally learn Luke and Leia are brother and sister. Every time you see them kissing, for the rest of your life—cringe. How'd Luke ever look Han Solo in the eye again?

I've never talked to anyone about my sometimes intrusive thoughts. I just assume everyone has those memories that haunt them at inappropriate times. But maybe it's just me.

Before I get too far, let me set you straight on something.

I'm a winner.

Whatever mistakes I've made, whatever crummy memories haunt me, they haven't held me back. I've made good things happen in my life because I have the right stuff. Here's proof: I'm among the most respected group of warriors to walk the earth. If there's a weakness in you, the process to get where I am exposes and destroys the person with those flaws, like a flood flushes furry rodents from the safety of their holes and up to the surface to be eaten by the predators.

So, as we're tossed about inside a C-17—which, if it fails to remain airborne, is really just an ultra-expensive metal coffin—hurtling into the future to rebuild our mutagen-plagued country in the most totally unbelievable, half-assed plan imaginable, I'm still proud. The sour cherry on that cake is that I'm haunted by thoughts of a failed relationship and a cigar-chomping general as we're about to mimic a bug on a windshield—complete with searing flames and flying metal debris—when I light upon the answer why I'm pestered with these unwanted images.

I still have something to prove. If not to myself, then to the men around me.

Or maybe to just one man.

I stole a glance at where the Chief was belted in. Chief Bryant is our team executive officer—a warrant. His silver hair's brushed back and held in place with some kind of gel product. I hope he brought plenty of it with him, because I doubt where we're going there'll be more of it. More like, *when* we're going.

More on that later. If we survive.

The Chief made it clear from the start he didn't want me on the team. Whenever he could get away with it, he let it be known. I wasn't intimidated by him. He was big and thick, but not bigger or thicker than me. He'd tried to get the occasional cheap shot in when we sparred. And in turn, I punished him for it. Mildly. I could've hurt him, but that's not the right thing to do when you're the better fighter. Not in training, and not to a teammate. He didn't reciprocate. He just knew he was better than me, and just like when I held back sparring with him, he used every opening I allowed him to take a passive-aggressive swipe at me. He had all the tabs and badges, but so did I.

All but one, that is.

The rifle and wreath. The Combat Infantry Badge. The CIB. The universal symbol that means you've been there and done that, that you're forever in the fraternity, that you've been on the two-way shooting range, and you know what it's all about. And it was because of that, or the lack of it in my case, that he made it known I wasn't worthy.

It was, "I don't need you," all over again.

That little blue-and-silver badge doesn't mean you're Audie Murphy. Far from it. But it does mean something. And its importance to me made it sting even more that it was so conspicuously absent on my chest. It was the difference between Chief Bryant's acceptance—which I badly wanted—and his contempt.

It wasn't my fault. I'd been swindled of my chance to go to war, over and over again. I suppose I wasn't alone, but it didn't make me feel any better about it. I'll save that tale for later, along with how we came to be time-traveling guinea pigs—provided we wouldn't be crispy cinders soon.

At first, the Chief was loud about it. "We don't need any unproven elements on this team, Top," he said in the team room not thirty seconds after Master Sergeant Williams brought me in to introduce me to his team.

I'm not shy about defending myself. I was just about to tell him I had his unproven element hanging, when Mike cut him off.

"Sergeant Colt's not unproven, Chief. And the matter's already settled. He's our new O-and-I." I was fresh out of Operations and Intelligence school, and just arrived back at Group—a unit I'd only been a part of on paper. I'd never spent so much as a real day on a team there. Sergeant Williams's A-Team was truly legendary. To get pulled to the best team in Group at his personal request had done more for my self-confidence than most anything I'd ever experienced. If I'd been a victim of one cosmic joke after another since I'd been in the Army, then this was the universe sending me good karma in exchange for so many years of suffering and insults to my manhood. It was a warmth that swelled my chest with warm embers and made me feel bulletproof.

It lasted exactly as long as it took for Chief Bryant to quench the brazier of my self-esteem with ice cold water in front of all my new teammates.

"He's never been in combat. That's no good. Not for this team."

Sergeant Williams gave the team commander, Captain Nelson, a secretive eye dart, and the captain returned a slight nod. I took that to mean the captain would be pulling the Chief aside for what I sensed would be a private moment. In Special Forces, the team commander and the executive officer—a warrant officer like Chief Bryant—they may command the team, but the team sergeant is the de facto potentate who rules the team with an iron fist, drives the team like pack animals, eats the ones that die, protects the team like a mother bear defending her cubs, and makes the train run on time.

It's a very complex dynamic. Officers have been transferred off teams at the say-so of a team sergeant for the inability to conform to the way things are done in SF. Officers come and go. NCOs are on a team forever. The captain may command, but it's the team sergeant's team. It's always been that way in SF.

The nylon harness was digging into Chief Bryant's shoulders like it was mine, the jump seats bouncing like pews in a wicked temple trying to expel its heretics. The rest of the vast space was stuffed with our implements of war, stacked like that warehouse in *Indiana Jones*. Our death machines—our GMVs and the Stryker—and of course, Baby Blue. The Minecraft box that could make anything.

Like the time slipstream conduit we'd flown through, Baby Blue was on the upside of the coin toss we got when the aliens landed. The flip side—the plague that was wiping out Earth.

The Chief must've sensed me eyeing him. He squinted, giving me a tight-lipped look of disapproval. Why did I care what he thought of me? I didn't like him. I didn't dislike him. Being on this team was a dream come true, but like most of my dreams, there was something that stained it, that kept it from being the perfect movie in my head. The dancing dwarf talking backwards while the beautiful girl in the chair smiles at you with sad, secret eyes. I was the second-ranking NCO on the team. I was every bit the operator he was, even if I didn't have combat under my belt to prove it. So why then did I need his approval of me as a warrior so badly?

It was because, in some small way, I feared he was right.

I tried to block his bad vibes aimed at me, but they penetrated my defenses like an electromagnetic pulse and released all the zombies submerged beneath the surface of the black pool of my hard drive. The twisted mouths of the unkillable wrecks and their confidence-destroying groans rose out of the tar, ruining my mind's nice white carpet with their sticky black trudges as they intruded into my consciousness. Always at the wrong time.

But I'd learned to turn their desecrations into advantage in my internal war. All they did was drive me to get the carpet cleaned again. Bad thoughts of bad things that couldn't be erased from my memory, but could be hidden under a new, clean layer of pristine white carpet.

Tabs and badges were new white carpet. Running five-minute miles was new white carpet. Fifty pull-ups was new white carpet. Getting pulled to *the* team was new white carpet. And this mission would be the whitest, most luxurious carpet of them all. Whatever stain there was on my honor for not having combat on my resume would be gone forever.

I would prove it. To the Chief. To the world. To myself.

So that was number one of the two things I figured that had hit the on-switch to the projector in my mind and made me remember *her*. The other was the woman's voice from the cockpit. This woman's voice was nothing like *her* voice. This voice had no malice or poison. It was almost pleasant. But it was a woman's voice. I guess that was enough.

Though here was a case where it wasn't *how* she said what she was saying that filled me with dread. It was very much *what* she said.

"Terrain. Terrain. Bank angle."

The automated warning from the cockpit of the C-17 made its way down to us in the cargo bay. The squeals of the straining airframe pierced through the *whomp, whomp, whomp* that came with the shuddering of the wings. G-forces pushed me deeper into the smooth nylon jump seat, the engines whining behind it all like a bass and drum rhythm section. The chains securing our vehicles to the aluminum deck looked thin and flimsy to me just then. Baby Blue sat forwardmost in the bay, all six thousand pounds of it. At least it was not on wheels. Maybe it would stay in place when we crashed. Maybe it would break free and smash us all into pink meaty pancakes.

I'm an operator, not aircrew. I care nothing about aircraft or about flying them. The Air Force are all bus drivers to me. Get me to altitude and I'll jump or land and go get my mission on. Either way, I don't really care. To me, it's all about the guy on the ground with the rifle in his hands, not how you got him there. But you didn't have to have aviator wings or have spent as much time in and around aircraft as I have to know the words she kept repeating were bad. Very bad. It didn't matter that the nice computer lady saying them sounded cool, calm, and slightly alluring. What she said was the stuff you heard right before you crashed into a mountain or something equally unmovable. Stuff I'd rather not be hearing.

So, I gave her an A-plus for form—sexy. But an F for substance—bad news. But that wasn't her fault. She was just the messenger. Something had gone very wrong. And anyway, computer lady was just a line of code, not even the recording of a real person. You can't blame her.

"Look." Dave nudged me, pointing out one of the tiny windows across the bay from us.

"What?" I wasn't really in the mood for playing doggie in the window just now. I couldn't see what he saw, my view blocked by a GMV—one of our souped-up, heavily armed trucks. If Dave saw something interesting that would enlighten me as to our situation, I wish he'd just tell me. At the moment, I had two handfuls of nylon, and the pilots were doing a fine job of turning this into a combination roller coaster–slash–capsizing boat, and making my usually cast-iron stomach do flip-flops.

It also didn't help that we'd flown through the time slipstream conduit so we could perform a recon into the future and try to take back our disintegrating world. You know. That. My eroded sense of reality combined with the C-17 trying to pull my stomach out through my anus, and no, I was not in a mood to play looky-loo games with Dave.

"We must still be in Nevada. Looks like the Grand Canyon."

I didn't feel like wheedling over details. Dave was from Hawaii, so Arizona and Nevada were close enough to make his point—that we hadn't ended up too far from where we took off through the gate from Groom Lake.

The Grand Canyon? That was a spot of good news—we were still in the southwest. The bright flash at the end of the takeoff as we'd flown through the slipstream was like passing through a mirrored waterfall of static. It hadn't whisked us to never-never land—which the scientists admitted was a remote possibility. Coming out of the gate to be flying over land and not in some black void of nothingness—pure bonus. And, it hadn't transported us to some other part of the globe. And to Dave, the southwest of the future looked the same as the one we'd left. But it was dark out, so I couldn't confirm or rebut what Dave saw as we banked and bobbed.

"Terrain. Terrain. Bank angle."

A real human voice came over the speaker. "We've got to put her down. There's a primary problem with the engines. We're having trouble keeping altitude. I'm getting us out of this canyon to a better potential landing zone. Hang on."

Dave swore. "Crashing in the desert. Great. Not much of a start to this mission."

A calm but stern voice, tainted slightly by an east coast accent, shut down the negativity. "Yo. Survive crash first. Mission, later." Karlo was our medic. We only had one. His usually erudite manner and perfect diction had defaulted to his upbringing before MIT. I took a little comfort that the too-perfect mix of genius and death-dealer was not above showing the same stress Dave and I felt.

I kept my eyes fixed on the tiny window across from me. There was just enough starlight for me to make out the terrain. What I saw made no sense. The walls of this canyon were taller than any mountain. Any mountain anywhere. The engines screamed as the pilots pushed them like rented mules to make our giant flying anvil climb.

The pilot came back. "We're going to push on. We're maintaining altitude better. As soon as we find the runway, we'll put down. Stay belted in."

The bucking stopped. We flew on, maybe it was an hour. Then it got real quiet.

"Crash, crash, crash," was the last thing I heard. My impression of what a glide should be, wasn't this. We dropped at the rate of the pure acceleration of gravity, which I know from military freefall school is ten meters per second per second. The last thing I saw before we hit and every tendon and ligament in my body screamed at the limit of their elastic stretch as they struggled to keep me connected—I filed away.

Because I didn't know what to make of it.

In the distance, just at the edge of the far horizon of a vast desert.

I only saw it for a flash. It looked tiny, but that was because it was so far away. That simply meant it had to be huge and sprawling. Sharp spikes pierced the sky. Round domes and right angles.

All lightly glowing in the reflected light of a pair of red hunter's moons.

02

I READ A BOOK ONCE THAT SUMMED UP THE ARMY EXPERIENCE PERfectly. It was by that guy who wrote the book about fighting super-arachnids in powered armor—the good guys had the suits, not the bugs. The movie by the same name is cool, but it has nothing to do with the book. We all love it and it's a staple, even though we all agree that co-ed showers aren't ever going to happen in the U.S. Army. Ever.

The other book of his I read, he used someone's observation about something dead-nuts-on that describes how the Army works. The Army consists of three bureaucracies: a Surprise Party Department, a Practical Joke Department, and a Fairy Godmother Department. The first two handle most personnel matters, and the third is a very, very small office run by one elderly female GS-5 clerk who every so often puts down her knitting and does something nice. Mostly she's out on sick leave.

My career had mainly been the purview of the first two. I've shared some of my deepest, most personal thoughts, so before the wet concrete of bad impressions I've given about me dries completely, my career so far will explain why anyone should think less harshly of me.

When I joined the Army, I didn't have grandiose plans. I just didn't want to be where I was, doing the same stuff everyone else was doing back on the block. Towards the end of infantry training, they asked for volunteers for the Airborne. My hand shot up. Jumping out of airplanes was just the sort of thing that I knew would separate me from the rest of the ants in the green machine. Feeling special about myself was very important. I hadn't found that *thing* in civilian life that was supposed to anchor me, to give me drive, to make me excited to get out of bed every morning. Jumping out of airplanes would do.

Outside the recruiter's office was a poster of soldiers under big, square, puffy canopies. It was impossible not to feel the wind on my face and the sensation of floating as I stared at it. That's what got me in the door. I'd wanted jump school as part of my contract, so I was disappointed when it didn't happen.

News flash: recruiters lie.

So maybe when I look back on it, there was a little bit of the Fairy Godmother thing happening for me early on.

I was in the 82nd Airborne Division for about eighteen months. Not just a rifleman—an Airborne infantryman. Think there isn't a difference? You'd be wrong. Here's an insight into my first unit of assignment. In the 82nd, we refer to our unit as Division. Capital D. Not the 82nd, not the 82nd Airborne, not even as *the* division.

The Army has lots of infantry and armor divisions. When someone asks you where you're from, if you're from the 82nd, you say one word. Division. As if it's the only division in existence. You say Division; the rest is assumed. And only a dirty leg (a non-Airborne soldier) wouldn't understand.

So, when the opportunity to try out for Division I&R came up, I was down. I was already in my battalion scout platoon—my PT and GT scores making me a standout early on—but Division Recon was a whole different level of cool. Division Intelligence and Reconnaissance Company was badass. Once upon a time, they'd been LRRPs, then Intelligence and Security, then Strategic Reconnaissance Company. The names came and went. If you just said Division Recon, everyone knew who you meant.

They got all the cool schools, just like guys in SOCOM. Scuba, freefall, Ranger. Amongst ourselves, we joked about how Hollywood Division Recon was, about how they were just pampered pets of the division commander, and mocked them for all their badges and tabs. Secretly, we all wanted to be there. I say secretly, because the sure way to get a reputation as a malcontent in Division was to mention there's somewhere else you'd rather be other than the unit you were currently in. My request went up the chain from my squad leader to the platoon sergeant, the first shirt, then the sergeant major. And while they might've been partially resentful that I had somewhere else I wanted to be other than right where I was, my request was approved.

"See you back when you bolo out, Colt," my platoon sergeant told me. "I'll save your spot."

"All the way and then some, Sergeant, Airborne," I answered like one of Pavlov's dogs.

Long story short, soon enough I was back, packing up and heading to Division HQ. I'd made it.

I know it seems like I complain about the Army, but I'll tell you one thing about the green machine that I think is squared away. As an institution, it does not discourage you from improving yourself. It does not prevent you from taking on challenges to become a better soldier, not even from trying out for the elite. The needs of the Army to have someone doing your job right there, right now, aren't an obstacle. They'll find another body to fill your spot when you move out and up.

I've known several Marines who, after a hitch with the Corps, transferred to the Army. And to an individual, it wasn't because they didn't love the Corps or being a Marine. It was because they were held back from being anything more than what they were wherever they first landed in the Corps. I went through the Q course with a former Marine. His story was like the others I'd heard. One night on Robin Sage, lying on a perimeter with our student guerillas, he told me his story in whispers as we rubbed Copenhagen spit in our eyes to stay awake.

"I was a wheeled vehicle mechanic. That's what I drew as an MOS out of boot. I wanted infantry. I was told, 'That's where the Corp needs you, Marine. Oorah.'

"I was up for enlistment. I wanted to go to jump school, go to Recon—I don't know, do something, anything, other than just PT and be a motor dog. It was, 'The Corps doesn't need you anywhere but where you are, Marine. Sign the dotted line. Oorah.'

"If they'd let me just do that one thing for myself, I'd still be there. I went and talked to an Army recruiter off post. They had me a service transfer and a slot to jump school and to SF selection so fast I don't even remember saying yes. But I was a traitor. It was a tough few months, waiting to get sworn in to the big green. Screw 'em. The Corps was never going to let me do anything like that. Not in twenty years of reenlistments."

In the Army, any challenge you wanted to take on was only a 4187 Request for Personnel Action Form away from letting you at least try. Oh, there's more to it than that, but you get the idea.

Once I met an Air Force guy, a clerk, who'd been to a dozen Army schools. When I say clerk, I mean the clerkiest stereotype of clerks. His job involved inventory. Never so much as the chance of getting a hangnail in the job. When I saw him in his Air Farce uniform with all those skill badges, I thought it was some kind of stolen valor thing. What he told me blew my mind, almost as much as what was about to happen at the end of our roller coaster ride through the time slipstream conduit. The portal to our mission into the future to save the world. Or something like that. Anyway, when I tell you more about it, you'll have the comparison for my scale of amazement. The slipstream was a ten out of ten. What this zoomie told me still sits at about an eight.

"My wife was having a bad pregnancy. She had to go home to be with her folks. There was an Army base nearby. The Air Force transferred me to the Army base so I could be with her. They sent me to a bunch of schools, one after another, to justify my being there." His wife's family was in Georgia, next to Fort Benning. Guy had been to Airborne, Ranger, Pathfinder, Jumpmaster, heck, you name it. Sure, he'd been out in the boonies, most of the time doing very hard stuff. He was no wimp. You don't make it through even jump school by accident, much less those others. That airman found out something about himself during that time. He had to have. But when his wife had their baby and everything was all right, the Air Force sent him back to his cushy job in an office, never to use one of those skills again for the rest of his career—and with enough action-man badges to make every blue-uniformed zoomie turn Army-green with envy.

The Army would never do something like that. It would be, "The Army didn't issue you a wife. Besides, first marriages don't work out. If your kid lives, you can see him on FaceTime." Maybe in another life, I'll join the Air Force. The Navy? No thanks. I've never heard a story about the Navy that made me fancy that as a respawn option.

Division I&R was a dream I didn't even know I'd missed out on having. There was no pining for it. It was there, it seemed right for me, and I raised my hand. I'd skipped the fantasy of someday being rich and famous, jumped past being in a bunch of crappy sitcoms, and gone straight to the Hollywood A-list. For me, so far, the Army had been like the farmer who turned up gold nuggets with his plow instead of turnips. That's how I felt about it, anyway.

As you can surmise, it didn't last.

I was four years into the Army, a buck sergeant in the most elite unit in Division, the only division in the Army, when Venezuela One was cranking up. Yeah, there was the other one, just before the world started falling apart, but this was the first. This was going to be a big one. We hadn't had a real live shooting war since I'd been in. Sure, the SOCOM guys were always off somewhere doing this and that. You'd see them at Bragg, combat patches and CIBs. Always looking like they'd been there and done that, because they had.

The older guys in Division had been to combat, or the best our country had that counted as combat, and now it was going to be our turn. Or so I thought. We were still at Bragg, not quite at the point where we were spinning up to deploy—though we all knew it was coming—when our carnival ride came to a screeching halt with no brass ring at the end. Instead of shipping off to war and all the spoils of combat, we ended up in the train wreck of all train wrecks, with explosions and twisted metal, bodies ground to hamburger, and lots and lots of flames.

And what caused the locomotive to run off the rails and crush us in a fiery death?

Pride.

Pride and a mouth. Those things go together a lot. My platoon leader had them both. Lieutenant Cummins was a stud. First looies command the recon platoon, and he'd been the one out of hundreds who'd gotten the spot. West Pointer. And not just a West Pointer. A football West Pointer who'd won the Army Navy game his senior year. Now, I am virtually unsmokeable in PT. I can stick it out with the very best of them. At the start of any PT session he conducted, I wondered if I'd still be hanging with him by the end. I always did, but only after pushing so hard that I, as they say, "went black." You can do a lot and not be conscious, trust me.

The LT was a beast. He'd spent all his young life being the best, being told he was the best, and getting all the rewards for it. Know what I've learned over the years? No one can be humble who's never failed. I learned it from the LT. Maybe you get where I'm going with this.

Division HQ, of which we were a part, was having its monthly PT competition as a unit. We'd been doing this thing that had been borrowed from SF—the run, swim, ruck, shoot. It was a nice break from our usual training as a platoon, and gave the rest of division HQ a challenge, though it wasn't much of one for us. The rest of HQ was division staff offices and the like, mainly clerks and jerks, and very heavy with high-level officers. The commanding general himself participated once in a while, and as we always won the competition, it was one of those points of pride he maintained about his personal platoon of supermen. Us.

The event had gotten kind of routine, to tell the truth. We ran the ten miles out to the SF compound at Mott Lake. We swam the lake, where our rucks, gear, and weapons were waiting for us. Soaking wet, we jocked up and marched the twelve miles to the range, where we shot a qualification with M4 and M17. No biggie. Just another day of what was otherwise pretty sedate training for Division Recon. There were individual paratroopers in Division HQ who could keep up with us. One of the ops officers who'd been in our unit was one, but it was a team event. And as a team, no one came close to our scores.

Afterward, all gathered as usual in the theater for the payday activities speech by the HQ commander, in front of the division two-star general and all his staff, and it was time for him to announce the winner of the competition. It was always us. So, when he announced the team from S-1 as the winners, there was a bit of a buzz in the room. The personnel office. The finance clerks. Don't get me wrong. All good soldiers and, like all paratroopers, hard as woodpecker lips. But not possible. More buzz went up in the seated crowd and soon a few laughs as the S-1 captain, a rail-thin paratrooper—known to us as Pee-Wee Herman—took the stage to accept the certificate.

The muscles rippled under Lieutenant Cummins's jaw skin as he ground away in disbelief. I smelled a rat, too, but I was more curious than mad. Not the LT. He looked ready to murder.

Pee-Wee took his seat to applause and cheers.

"Lieutenant Cummins, front and center. We have an award for you and I-and-R platoon."

Our platoon sergeant urged the LT, "Be cool, sir." He'd said it quietly, but we all heard it.

On the stage, with the Division commander and all his staff in the front row, the company commander couldn't hide his delight. The captain had a bit of a gut. He was a man in charge of clerks. He wasn't in the operational chain of command for Recon. Orders came straight from Division Ops to us. The captain was the nerd ready to embarrass the jock who dated the head cheerleader, reading out the exam scores for the final, hoping to score points with her by knocking the big man down in public. The general beamed in anticipation and the sniggers from the front row started again.

"For I-and-R, we have the award for the last-place team."

Someone produced a rubber chicken, which he took and thrust out with a stupid grin. LT Cummins was about to protest when the captain explained.

"Per the rules, all team members must pass through each event checkpoint to certify there was no cheating. I-and-R didn't abide by the rules."

We were first in every event. By the time we were out of the water and rucking, which we did at a run, the rest of the teams were just entering the water. There wasn't anyone at the mid-course checkpoint by the time we blew past it. It had happened before. Some specialist detailed to run the checkpoint took the opportunity for some sham time and was at the PX getting dip and energy drinks before he posted up with his clipboard.

"Your team average is zero. Congratulations. Better luck next time." He thrust the floppy award out to more laughs, jeers, and applause.

"Don't say it!" I whispered like a suppressed M4, just loud enough that no one a few rows away knew where it came from, but everyone heard it. "Don't."

I should have yelled it.

The LT snatched the joke award and growled, "This thing's just like your anatomy, Captain. I'll think of you every time I look at it."

The commanding general frowned. He was an older man. You didn't get to be a two-star general at thirty. That only happened in ancient history. The general was probably more fit than any man his age, but he was still an older man. He had a gut.

The LT hadn't just committed suicide. He'd locked us all in the garage with him and started the car.

03

I've seen the aftermath of a couple of helo crashes. The biggest thing left to find at the sites were the pilot seats and the transmissions. Every other bit was no bigger than a crushed beer can, including the people. It can't be much different crashing an airplane. They're made of aluminum, too. So, I suppose we didn't crash-crash, because we were mainly in one piece. Mainly.

I've had parachute landing falls like the way the pilots landed this bird. On a nighttime full locker jump—meaning wearing all your combat equipment and weapons—I've done many a three-point PLF. Feet. Knees. Face. This is how we landed in the C-17. But we were down, and in one piece. Sort of.

Every cell in my body had been pounded by a power hammer. Instead of forging me into hard steel, it snapped every little spicule of bone and stretched every cord of muscle. I hurt. The first thing you worry about in an aircraft crash is fire. No matter that my bells were wrung and I was seeing double, if I was alive enough to feel like I'd fallen off a building, it was time to get up and out before I became a crispy critter.

My teammates struggled out of their harnesses, some hanging awkwardly above jump seats snapped away from the fuselage on impact. Our massive rolling hardware in the chasm of the C-17's enormous cargo space was still in place. Thank God. As was Baby Blue. We hadn't been crushed by the behemoths in our midst, but there was still a wonderful opportunity to get roasted.

"Ben, we have to get everyone out." Karlo was already free and moving. He hauled Dave to his feet and took off forward. Cabin lights flashed erratically making the bay a bad disco studio, but there was no smoke. Yet.

I pointed at Dave. "Don't wait for the loadmaster. Get that ramp down. I'm going forward with Karlo." The three of us had been aft in the bird, everyone else spread out to take advantage of having one of the world's largest transport aircraft all to ourselves. Those poor Ranger kids back at Area 51 were stuffed into theirs like sardines. It had been a sight, that many C-17s lined up on what was billed as both the most secretive and longest runway in the world, waiting their turn to take off for the short flight through the slipstream.

A lot had happened in the year since the existence of honest-to-God ETs had been made known. The government had been leaking hints about such for years. But when it was revealed that aliens had traveled to Earth and that the hair-lips had set up shop in Kazakhstan, it was finally real.

It was more than the cleft palates that made them believable as aliens. I scrutinized the news clips and the few YouTube vids of them. Oh, from the back, you could mistake one for a human. But no one could ever confuse one of those scrunched faces for homo sapiens, not even one with every known birth defect and too many plastic surgeries. That, of all places, the aliens had made Kazakhstan the site for their interplanetary embassy should have sent up a dozen red flags.

The name of their race was unpronounceable. They preferred to be called "the Guests." At first, we were all excited. They promised to share their technology, introduce us to space travel—all the stuff from *Star Trek* that violated the Prime Directive. Every day, the news had an item about some advance the Guests were sharing with the world's scientists, from ways to improve energy production, to agriculture, and medicine, until it all became routine and expected. The hair-lips weren't any kind of a threat. Life went on like normal, especially in the Army.

Then it started. The rumors about technology literally coming apart.

From remote parts of Asia, videos popped up on social media and disappeared off the net as fast as they appeared. Flat-screen TVs melting. Electric vehicles catching on fire. Smart refrigerators, cell phones, laptops—sporadically crapping out for no reason. The most spectacular of all the clips, though, the only one that really made me take it seriously—as if this wasn't just some kind of internet attention-seeking fake—was the clip from the machine shop.

I recognized it for what it was. I've always been fascinated by machinery, probably why I love guns and trucks. A very large and complex milling machine was doing some kind of Transformer thing. But instead of it turning into a Camaro and going for a beer run, it disassembled itself into a pile of components. It seemed like more of the fake conspiracy theory kind of stuff that was always out there, especially because it was all from unidentified urban sprawls in China or India, and none of the videos were really that clear or coherent. This one made me question, though.

The news had snippets of it all for a day, debunked by government experts as fake, as well as denying whether the Guests had something to do with it all. The aliens were peaceful and had brought with them amazing tech they were willing to dole out. There was an election coming up and the news cycle was full of candidates promising to secure closer ties with the Guests to ensure the US of A wouldn't be stuck behind Russia in the alien welfare line. Then it was the usual about cleaning up Washington once and for all. This from politicians who'd spent their entire lives in Washington. Takes one to know one, I guess.

A few planes fell out of the sky. The war broke out in northern India, and we weren't sure if it was that or all the other stuff that was responsible for us getting moved to readiness level 1. All military personnel to remain on base. Locked. Down. That's about the time the manbearpig video hit. That's what we called it. It was only around for a day before the censors killed it, and then like the others, it disappeared as though it had never existed. Which only made the rumors and conspiracy theories spread like a grass fire in a drought, until they killed all those too.

It was another cellphone video set in some crowded market.

"It's a goof. Totally fake," Dave said as he looked over my shoulder at my phone after a PT smoke session.

Dripping in sweat like you can only do in a Florida summer, I plopped onto a chair in the team room to check my phone, and the short clip was on all the sites. A misshapen, lumpy face too bizarre to be anything but a mask sat on top of an equally deformed body, hair in all the wrong places. The curved claws tore at a prostrate form on the ground as panicked mobs scattered, blocking much of the photographer's subject. I wiped the screen. The sweat dripping like rain onto my expensive new phone was not making it any easier to judge if the images were plausibly real or not. There had been a lot of bizarre stuff going on lately, and as much as I was a skeptic at heart, there's only so much you can shrug off until you wonder if you're missing bigfoot for the moose.

"China," Dave grunted. "It's always China. They're not getting first dibs on all the stuff the hair-lips have to share, so they're doing some kinda psyops."

"What purpose would it serve, though?" I couldn't figure out how their government faking boogeymen tearing folks limb from limb helped their cause to dominate the world economic stage.

"I dunno. You're the O-and-I guy. You tell me. They're creeps." Dave was Japanese-Hawaiian. He was born and raised on Oahu. He didn't like mainland China for personal reasons. Growing up, he'd suffered hordes of nouveau riche Chinese tourists invading his personal paradise. "Bad enough Hawaii's full of haole trying to kook-out in all our best surf holes. Now there's Chinese buying everything in sight. Pretty soon, there won't be room for any of us real Hawaiians."

Dougie was from south of LA and was the other ardent surfer on the team. In perpetual competition with each other for surf-supremacy, Doug was on him.

"You're Japanese, Dave. And when the hair-lips figure out Oahu is a better camp site than Kazakhstan, you won't have to worry about the Chinese. Plus, I thought you said you were never going back. That Hawaii was 'the rock.'"

Dave told me what a lot of guys from the islands told me. By the time you were out of high school, everyone you were ever going to know, everything you could ever do, had been established a dozen times over. It was an island. The Army was a way out of boredom, unemployment, or drugs.

"Yeah, yeah," he dismissed Doug. "Whaddaya say, Karlo?"

The too handsome, dark-haired medic grunted, shrugged, and moved to his locker. As our only 18D busied himself without answering, Dave kept scolding.

"He knows something. He just ain't saying. As usual. You know, Karlo, there's a fine line between quiet professional and stuck-up brainiac, brah."

Karlo sighed. "I don't have enough information to say anything intelligent, Dave. So rather than follow your example and remove any doubt about my ignorance, I'll keep it shut."

Our team sergeant's voice came from the next room. "Doc's the only one who could rightly spout off about anything and everything and not be wrong—but doesn't. You, on the other hand, Dave, never cease to hang it out there like a target. High time you follow Karlo's example. What say you rekey all our radios before we head out? Shouldn't take much gabbing."

Mike had been an Echo once upon a time. He kept a close tab on Dave and our junior commo, Mitch, and Dave delighted in proving there was no aspect of commo in which Mike could show him up, despite the team sergeant's many years as an Echo himself.

"Yes, Top." Dave grinned. It was all in fun, especially Mike gruffly telling Dave to shut his piehole. The few months I'd been with the team, I'd gotten closest to Dave and Karlo. Dave was no less an intellect than Karlo, though he hid it behind his pidgin—but Karlo had the pedigree to prove it—though he never let on he had the sheepskins he did.

I'd had to drag it out of him. Karlo was an X-ray. He entered the Army with a ticket to go straight to Special Forces selection—rather than slog out years in the regular Army like most of us—because he had standout qualifications in the civilian world.

He had an engineering degree. I think several. He was a national-level tri-athlete. The Army recognized that they had something special in Karlo and offered the patriotic Poindexter who could run a marathon without breaking a sweat the opportunity to go SF right out of entry-level training.

The other standout thing about Karlo? He didn't opt to be an 18 Charlie, an engineer. That would've been too easy for him. He went for 18 Delta, SF medic. Which most people, including myself, thought was the most difficult way into SF.

During that getting-to-know-you phase on a new team, which was a lot like the dance you did with a blind date—except if you didn't like what you heard, you couldn't swipe left and try again—I coaxed Karlo into telling me how a *real* engineer came to be a medic.

"I would've learned a lot in Charlie school, but I knew it would be tougher as a Delta." He left it at that. In that way, Karlo was like all of us. Always looking for the hardest challenge. Not needing to explain the why of it any further to those who thought the same way. Besides, our engineers let me know that Karlo had pretty much taught himself the Charlie course in his spare time.

So, when we went into isolation in Nevada to prep for our jump through the slipstream and it came time to get acquainted with the Subatomic Matter Mill, it was Karlo and not Chucky or Doug—our engineers—who got pulled to learn how to run what we were told was a bottomless well of creation, an actual horn of plenty that would make whatever we needed. A self-contained factory to keep our shelves stocked on the other side of our rapidly collapsing present, where it was predicted that the mutagen-plague that was tearing the world apart would be burned out in a few years. Our job—take a little hop into the future. Do an end run around the Guests. If there were any left, bring the hate to them. Stabilize the human terrain that had survived the breakdown of all things comfortable. Squash any domestic disturbances to tranquility (which is really where we came in). Let the brains going with us reestablish the government if need be.

We were the safety net for the Constitution. And the massive mechanism known as the Blue Fairy was a critical part of the plan to win back the future.

"How's it work?" I wasn't alone in wondering. We gathered around the massive machine like it was an unfrozen caveman lawyer before a jury. We didn't know much; we just knew it made stuff. And for our pain and suffering, we deserved all the compensation it could give us.

Karlo's explanation said a lot and said nothing. The supremely smart and educated often forget that you don't know what they know. But sometimes, dumbing it down for the simpletons isn't possible.

"The Guests shared the principal tech. The laws of thermodynamics prevent transmuting matter from one element to another. The physicists think it uses a stabilized infinite mass to tap into tachyon emissions that capture subatomic matter and bring it to the present. It's also the basis for how the slipstream's going to let us jump into the future. The Guests figured out a side step around the physical laws of the universe."

Complete silence.

Chuck was our senior engineer. "Infinite mass? Is that why it's so heavy?"

Karlo was good about not groaning. "It duplicates what you could think of as a black hole."

More silence.

When he'd demonstrated the mill in action, it made a pleasing otherworldly blue light leak from inside it. "What's the blue glow about?" I asked.

Karlo seemed grateful for a simple question. "Cherenkov radiation. It's more of an 'on' indicator than anything else. But that's why the DARPA guys call the subatomic matter mills the Blue Fairy."

"You mean like Pinocchio? If we're good, it'll grant us wishes and make us real boys?" Dave asked.

"Radiation? Dangerous radiation?" Doug cupped a sensitive area. "Do I have to worry about my boys when it's making stuff?"

"No. But if you stand close enough, it'll keep you tan, Dougie."

He took his hands away. "Then Baby Blue's alright with me."

"So, it'll make whatever we need?" Chuck tried to clarify. "Can it make itself?"

"All I care about is keeping us in ammo," Marky-Mark, our senior weapons man said. "With enough ammo, you can always get anything else you need." It was a simple philosophy and like most worldviews based on basic truths, he was mostly correct. Provided there were still things worth getting on the other side of our ride through the stargate.

Doug's name for the mill stuck. Karlo stayed blasé about his inability to enlighten us with a condensed explanation about how Baby Blue worked. He was used to the fact that even if there were people near his intellectual ability, there were few who had as much knowledge as he did. Captain Nelson was a very educated man, but I could tell even he was falling short in the comprehension department when it came to the physics of the two technologies that were about to dominate our future. Karlo patiently continued after the assault of questions petered out.

"Like a lot of tech, it's not necessary to understand how it works at the finite level to take advantage of what it offers. I spent the last two days with the DARPA and Caltech folks. They don't even really understand what makes the clock tick. Point being, we can produce basic and even some very advanced material for our mission sustainment, and once we've established a security zone, the multitude of subatomic matter mills together can start producing en masse the fundamentals of what'll be needed to restart society, outside the control of the Guests."

Had Baby Blue survived the crash?

Top and the captain were organizing getting us off the bird with whatever essential gear we could. There were tears and gaps in the skin of the C-17, more of the creepy dim red light seeping in. It was moonless when we'd loaded at 51. One of those small things my mind processed to subconsciously tell me that Elvis had left the building. I followed Karlo, who held up to give Baby Blue a quick once-over. It was still on its pallet, but the whole thing was skewed out of its rolling tracks.

The crew cabin bulkhead was smashed. The ladder leading up was twisted and the door to the flight deck was crushed like a dixie cup. I'd grabbed the breaching tool off the back of my plate carrier when I came to enough to get into action, and pushed ahead of Karlo to jam the pry into the cabin door. I didn't have my gloves on and immediately cut myself as I wedged both hands into the crack I'd formed.

Karlo had his light out, flooding what looked like an upended kitchen drawer stuffed with useless old electrical cords and parts for gadgets long since replaced. He aimed the flashlight at each of the crew, letting the blinding beam settle long enough to feed him the data he needed before saying, "No good."

Remember what I said about the Air Force being little more than bus drivers to me? That was just me being a jerk. I wasn't a medic, but I knew he was right. The crew cabin was so much junk. The two pilots and the loadmaster were dead. It was obvious. I'd always been taught that you can fill a bad guy full of as many holes as a spaghetti strainer, but that didn't mean he still didn't have enough juice to give you what for one last time before he was totally lights-out.

Dead soon don't mean dead right now.

But sometimes, you just know. The horrible angles of bent body parts not meant to be bent and the lack of movement made me know better than to argue with our expert. "They did their best," I said by way of agreement and eulogy. Whatever decision the crew had made in the air about where to put down, they'd made to give us the chance to survive. They just couldn't save themselves in the process.

See, there's two kinds of risk. There's individual risk, and there's team risk. The team is the component necessary to accomplish the mission. The individual may have to risk himself for the benefit of the team so that the mission is completed. The aircrew made a decision about how best to put down to give *us* the chance to survive. And therefore, the mission. As they say, no greater love. To me, that elevated those men to god-like status.

"We'll recover them later, Ben. Come on."

I may talk smack about other services and other units, but I'd fight anyone who said the same as if they really meant it. If I had to do it alone, I would come back and cut our comrades out of their metal graves and give them a real resting place.

No one gets left behind. Ever.

Guys were tearing apart pallets. We each had our first-line gear and weapons with us in our jump seats, but if the bird did start burning, there were some very critical things we needed to get off here before we said goodbye to them forever. We weren't sitting level. It had been a lean-forward trudge up to the front of the bird. I pictured the tail so low that the ramp wouldn't have room to open all the way. To balance the load of Baby Blue sitting all the way forward, the Stryker was near the aft end. The tailgate wasn't down yet. If something prevented getting the Stryker off, nothing sizeable other than the two four-wheelers on the ramp would be coming off, provided we could get the tailgate even partially down.

The jump doors were open on both sides, and I joined the daisy chain to start tossing gear out.

Dave yelled, "Stand clear. Stand clear."

Motors whirred, stopped, and started again with the flickering lights. The ramp gapped open a little more, then a little more—just as all the power went out. The ramp was frozen halfway down.

"I think we're okay," the captain yelled. "There's a fire suppression system in these C-17s. Inert gas pumps through the fuel tanks in a crash. If we were going to flame up, it would've happened."

"Negative, boss," Mike said, and yelled a little louder to make clear he was countermanding the captain's assessment. "Keep shagging ass, guys. A fire can start at any time. Get everything you can away from the aircraft. Go."

Before diving out to follow Top's order, I did the salmon swimming upstream and made my way to the back of the Stryker. I'd strapped the hard case with my Mark 22 inside for safekeeping. I wanted it very badly. Baby Blue or no, nothing could duplicate it. It was the best rifle I'd ever had, and I felt psychologically impotent without knowing that it was at least available when I wanted it. I popped the hard case, relieved to see the soft case within. I'd chosen the 300 Norma Magnum barrel to leave on her, ready for me to grab and run. I could get the rest of the kit later if it was not in an inferno. If it only ever had the one barrel again, I'd be missing nothing. 230 grains of sweet boat tail copper could do anything I ever asked of the best sniper rifle ever made.

I hit the ground with feet and knees together, not knowing if the landing would be hard or soft. I hit and bounced, lost my balance, but came down at the base of one of the hills of stuff we'd tossed to safety. I grabbed the first two things nearest my touchdown, a rucksack and a hard case full of something fragile, and almost started off, but hesitated and grabbed two more rucks. Something felt off, but what was bad about feeling strong? Adrenaline always kicks in during stress, so it was time to take advantage of it and take a double load. I trotted. New piles were growing a few hundred feet away off the tail, far enough away that the impending fuel explosion should avoid turning our salvage into so much melted plastic.

I passed unencumbered guys heading back for more, running in bounding leaps. Yes, it seemed odd, but who would've believed the why of it just then? I dropped everything, then carefully set my girl down to take her place of honor on top of the new pile, hoping the case itself would scream "respect." The rifle was a rock. The optic on top of her was not.

It was getting light out. Our C-17, a marvel of aviation engineering and military logistics, reminded me of a beached fishing trawler I once saw. Deposited on a sandy point after a hurricane, bow up, rigging snapped like used chopsticks, its grounded stern was lapped by waves, simultaneously teasing and beckoning it to return to the sea that had held it aloft.

We were at the top of the world, on an enormous escarpment. I imagined the canyon we'd materialized in on the other side of the slipstream was the sharp horizon, a drop-off at the very edge of the world where the map said, *here be dragons.*

The front of the aircraft had run head-on into a rocky island jutting from the landscape. There were buckles and rents in the fuselage. The wheels were buried above the sponsons. It didn't take much of an analysis to know it was never going anywhere again, the bright starry sky laughing at our shipwreck.

"Where've you been?" The Chief appeared from around the half lowered ramp of our ruined ride to the wherever/whenever we now were. "I thought you must've run for the hills." The aspersion he cast wasn't subtle enough to let me ignore it, and my internal thermometer spiked. I was about to tell him how Karlo and I had run *toward* danger and deeper into the bird to rescue the aircrew, when Dave sounded off with a deep diaphragmatic, "HEY," from the back of the ramp, saving me the wasted effort of defense.

"We've got company. Ground recovery party moving this way. Help's arrived." Dave had his helmet on and NODs down. He owned the night and I'd be renting from him until I could get my own night vision goggles out of my ruck.

"Where?" Mike appeared beside him.

I followed Dave's outstretched knife hand and squinted. Movement caught my eye. Dark shapes breaking up the otherwise barren terrain. Subtle, but enough to remove doubt that it was more than imagination. If they were rescue vehicles, where were the lights?

"Uh-uh," Mike said, putting into words the same doubts I was having. "No one's our friend until they are. Let's get it on."

04

I was telling you about what got me to where I am now, and why it explains so much about me and my demons. It wasn't long after the rubber chicken incident that we spun up for Venezuela. As you know, we staged on Grenada for the invasion. It was a place that had a lot of history for Division. I got really familiar with it. Because when D-Day came, Division Recon was left behind on the beach. Literally.

The unit that was supposed to lead the invasion for our division was left behind. On. Purpose.

Message received.

Even the HQ company jumped in with the rest of the division. The clerks and jerks of the staff. We, on the other hand, stayed behind. The elite of the division. We watched as the C-130s loaded with our fellow paratroopers jocked up in T-11 chutes and full combat equipment, flew off sortie after sortie. I wasn't the only one who wiped at tears of frustration. We should've HALO'd in. Done a recon. Led the way for the rest of Division. Instead, we were told to stand by for follow-on missions. And every day that passed, I knew that the call would never come.

This was punishment.

Back at Bragg, the gold stars on jump wings, CIBs, and combat patches were handed out. Soon, the entirety of Bragg was full of 10,000 maroon beret–wearing paratroopers even more full of themselves than normal, and rightly so. The SOCOM guys weren't the only ones to be wearing the ultimate badges of soldierly accomplishment.

Like I said, having that stuff isn't a testament to you being another Audie Murphy. Venezuela wrapped up quick. The vast majority of those guys never fired a shot. But that's not how it works. You've got the jewelry, you're in the club. And if you don't, you're not. For the first time in my life, I was embarrassed to be seen in uniform. All my badges and tabs suddenly didn't disguise the real me, the guy who secretly felt unsure of himself, the guy who wanted to be special.

And we got mocked. Get a load of recon. Not so special now, are you? Where'd all your scuba diving and freefall get you? A guy would tap his CIB or gold star and laugh. It happened to me more than once. The Hollywood platoon that all of Division was secretly jealous of, had gotten their comeuppance.

I wanted to die.

The LT resigned his commission shortly thereafter. No one ever goes on to be completely anonymous and hidden, no matter how hard they try. Even if you cut ties and run, it doesn't erase your trail. The bloodhounds always find you in the end. I later heard that he became a drug addict and was found dead. Homeless. I know, it's hard to imagine, but I believe the story. It was a tale to rival any Greek tragedy and a morality lesson about humility as harsh as any ever put to page by all the playwrights who ever plucked a quill.

If you piss off the gods, they will destroy you. The favored son who forgets to be grateful doesn't get to become king. Not when there are so many other worthy sons to choose from.

I wasn't ready for the same. But like the LT, I wasn't going to stick around.

I'd gotten to know some SF guys, going through all the courses I did since most of them were run by the SF school house. I liked all of the green-beanies I met. They were all laid-back, but you could tell. They felt no need to throw their weight around about where they'd been and what they'd done. They showed it by their competence. And their quiet. So, if Division was going to treat me like a redheaded stepchild and keep me from going to the ball, I was going to go where all you did was go to the big dance. And those guys down the road from Division, they lived in a world where their dance card was full, and it was always open bar. Or so it seemed to me.

I was at almost five years in, on the E-6 list, and it was nearing time for my first re-up. Division couldn't stop me from going to selection if they wanted. Remember when I said the Army is cool about you bettering yourself? Temper that with what I also told you about Division. To some, Bragg is a Mecca you never make a pilgrimage away from.

There are literally third- and fourth-generation paratroopers in the 82nd. Guys who are born at Womack Army Hospital, join the Army to be in Division—just like everyone in their family before them—retire after their twenty or thirty, stay right there in Fayetteville, and become the guy who delivers your mail or sells you your house, cranking out another generation of paratrooper after another to feed the Airborne machine.

Cult? Tradition? Call it what you will, the label you get if you want to go elsewhere is *defector*. Maybe apostate's a better term for it. They do bad things to sectarians who want to leave their clan. With the humiliation of what happened to me and Recon during what should have been our grand entrance into confirmed warriorhood, I wasn't going to give anyone else the chance to kick me while I was down. Everyone knew of guys who tried to do what I was doing who got jumped, even one guy who got pummeled and then painted in the dye they used to mark cattle with. He was purple from head to toe. That stuff didn't come off.

Mainly, I didn't want hassle, and I didn't want to get held up by a CID investigation for murder if anyone tried that kind of stuff with me. I kept mum about my plans until it was a reality. Until you have the orders in your hand, they're just wisps of smoke you can't do anything with, but they make you hope there's a fire that's going to dry you and stop your shivering after falling through the ice. I wasn't close enough to reenlistment time, so there was a small administrative extension to my first enlistment to allow me time to make it through the Q-course and go to a team. If I made it through, I'd definitely re-up. If I didn't, I'd only have a short time left in the Army as a bolo, and I'd weather it out and go try being a civilian.

I told you I'm a winner. My self-doubts and recriminations don't ever keep me from turning on the juice when it's go time. Like I said, I've come to think of all my shame as a force that propels me to be better. I've read a few books. There's a healthier way to do it, and I've tried it. I've just accepted this works for me.

I was a first pass at selection, and was straight on into the Q-course, destined for my green beanie. I'll tell you about the Q. It goes on forever. I've read the books about BUDS, and God knows there's no book from a SEAL that doesn't mandate a blow-by-blow of their BUDS class. Yawn.

I'd gotten slotted for the Special Operations Weapons Sergeant course as my MOS. 18B. The backbone of SF. It was relatively shorter than the other MOSs, way shorter than SF medic, but still, by the time I put on my new headgear, it was over a year. And sometimes, it was a real mind game to stay motivated with the end so far away. I've been through all the other schools. You can do most anything knowing the end is at most a couple months away. The Q? Rome was built in less time than it takes to train an SF operator.

I learned a lot. About the job of being an unconventional warrior and about myself. And that feeling of accomplishment returned. Having been through all the other schools most of my classmates had not yet been to, when I reported to Eglin to join my first A-Team, I felt assured I'd be going right to one of the best.

There were all kinds of rumors about teams that did all the coolest, secret squirrel stuff you could imagine, and they all required operators who had checked the HALO/Scuba/Ranger boxes already. I was more than a little hopeful that I'd be a shoo-in. If there were actually such a thing as those kind of teams. I was sure there was. The history books were full of the declassified stories about them. Of course, all told thirty or forty years after the fact. SF are the quiet professionals, unlike some other groups I could mention. If those special teams had existed then, they must exist now, I told myself. And there was a good chance I'd be headed for one.

Enter the Practical Joke Department.

Day one, I was in the Group sergeant major's office. He sat me down and explained the situation as the world disappeared from beneath my feet and I fell headfirst into a pit of broken glass.

"Sergeant Colt, every once in a while, a sacrifice is demanded." He was very fatherly. I could tell he took no pleasure in what he was telling me. He was like a doctor breaking the news to the patient with incurable cancer. "As much as Special Forces is a priority for personnel, the Army is the Army. And they demand we play along with the rest of the Army in all their games."

It was as simple as this. Department of the Army demanded that the Special Forces Regiment provide one E-6 for assignment. For a term of three years, that individual would have a choice. Drill instructor or recruiter. They didn't care which. And I was to be the sacrificial virgin, offered to please the gods and ensure a good harvest of melons and corn for the coming year.

I'd rather I was a real sacrifice, and they carved my heart out on the top of that stone pyramid. I was so close to redemption.

There was no way out of this. It would never have happened if I'd been a medic or a commo man. There were no overstrength MOSs in SF, but a weapons sergeant or engineer came close. I could stay for another six months until my term of service was over, be on an A-Team for no longer than it took to get acquainted with how things were really done in SF before putting on the civvies forever, or take the assignment with the promise that when it was over, the regiment wouldn't forget my sacrifice.

"There's no way out of this, son."

I knew he was telling me the truth.

Think I'm making this up about this part of my career? Think I'm hiding some foul-up to justify how I ended up being a drill instructor? Screw you. You know nothing. Even I wish there was a better explanation for what had happened to me.

I didn't even unpack. I was shipped straight to Fort Jackson, South Carolina, ready to begin drill duty. The choice was easy. I didn't want to be a recruiter, and I didn't want to be a civilian. Somewhere in my hazy future, there was still the possibility of touching that distant shore where sparkling waters touched white sands, and honor waited for me like a girl's brown body wrapping me in her arms. Yeah, I like that old "Tales of Brave Ulysses" song. I sang along with it the whole drive up to Jackson, telling myself this was just one more challenge, just one more finish line waiting over the next hill for me to cross, another pain that would disappear once I could drop my ruck and rest.

That's the trick for getting through anything. Lie to yourself. Just get around the next bend, just see the next hill, just make it until the end of the day. Then it'll be better. All I had to do was get through this, one day at a time. Three years' worth of one day at a time.

It wasn't quite three years that I was exiled away from the possibilities that got me out of bed every morning. It was two and some change. It was during this time that she came into my life.

I was kind of the big man around town. Those tabs, all the other doodads on my uniform. The average joe at Fort Jackson did not have such a pedigree to show for their time in service. It made me stand out. In a military town like Columbia, such things are known, even by the civilians. It was kind of fun being the big man on campus. The other drills who had CIBs didn't even really care that I didn't. They all just figured I was some kind of secret squirrel. That maybe what I'd done was *too secret* to let me be awarded something so mundane, that maybe it was different for SF guys.

I never got close to anyone. I never talked about it. It was a tough time.

Heather was a waitress. A strip club waitress. I should've known better, but to tell the truth, she came after me. Hard. It should go without saying that she was beautiful. Hers was the first key to a girl's apartment I'd ever gotten. If the blow of being so close to greatness only to have it snatched away from me so cruelly was my lot, then the comfort of a real girlfriend was at least a consolation prize.

I wasn't around a lot. The hours were long, the work of turning civilian children into soldiers was difficult, and, if I'm honest, had few rewards. It's got to be the toughest job in the Army. But if I was being punished for some essential sin I didn't even know I'd committed, at least I had Heather.

You know how that ended. Badly.

The how of it was this. It was my fault. What did I know about being a boyfriend? The Army trained me to be a killer. What I knew about building a relationship with a woman wouldn't fit inside a thimble. When I look back on it, I can see with the crystal clarity of hindsight what I did wrong, but had I known those things, I still would've been powerless to change them. I'm not making an excuse; I'm telling the truth. You can't spend eighteen to thirty-six hours straight at a time yelling at dumb recruits who can't lace their boots properly and not find fault in the world and the people around you. When your job is to be critical of others, it tends to seep into other areas of your life. They warned us about it during drill instructor training. About what how we had to separate our persona as drills from the rest of our lives. That for the average person, it would erode and damage our family life.

And I am that average person. I am not the superman I pretended to be, that I thought all my little costume jewelry made me. I couldn't leave my BS where I hung my round brown when I came to her place. Words hurt. Even when you don't mean to be derisive or critical. I'd always apologize when I knew I'd hurt her, when she'd withdraw, the look of disappointment on her face, but it was too late.

She was always looking for her car keys. She was always late. She never knew what she wanted at the restaurant. I'd sigh or groan. It was enough to chip away at the mortar that held us together, which was never really much of a bond to begin with.

The final straw for her came when I left my platoon of recruits one night in the care of one of the other drills and showed up at her place late. I knew she'd be working, or out with friends, and she knew my schedule could be erratic. I'd left her high and dry many times because of some problem at work. Recruits are stupid. Young people do stupid things. That's what they do. Our job was turn them into soldiers. To give them a better way of doing things. To make them responsible individuals. In a society where personal responsibility was rare and entitlement was the norm, turning those lumps of mushy clay into marble was a challenge.

The platoon wasn't ready for company inspection the next morning? Then the cadre stayed all night, hammering our babies to make them live up to the standard. Bye-bye, a night at home catching up on sleep. A recruit had a breakdown? It was all hands on deck, making sure some kid didn't lose it and kill himself. It had happened.

Anyway, things were smooth, and I was able to get away and spend a night with my girl, ready to forget my troubles as the most overworked babysitter in existence, when I got to her apartment door and fished out my key, one of the most special possessions I'd ever had that fit in a pocket. The door was ajar. She hadn't locked it.

It pissed me off. Physical security is basic. You lock your wall locker. You close a door. You check these things. A recruit who'd failed that basic task would do push-ups until South Carolina was moved to Georgia. I pushed the door open with irritation. This was not what I expected. Coming from her bedroom was some hairbag I'd never seen before. He was scrawny and zit-faced, greasy and stupid-looking. A typical civilian.

Was she cheating on me? The thought passed quickly and a more urgent fear entered my mind. This dirtbag had broken in, and my girlfriend was in the other room, a victim of this scumbag. Raped, beaten, dead. I launched at him.

"Where's Heather?" I yelled as I laid him out. He hit the ground cold before he could answer. I stepped over him and checked the apartment. Heather was nowhere to be found. Relieved but still worried about her, I checked mister hippie. Still out cold. I called 911.

"My girlfriend is missing and there's some stranger in her apartment."

I explained who I was and in no time, two officers were at the door. I had the intruder pinned and was ignoring his protests about looking for someone named Trudy.

They were leaving with this idiot in custody just as Heather showed up. She'd had a couple of beers and gone out with some girlfriends to a bar, where she'd had a few more. She'd left the door unlocked. The turd I'd decked was some fool who'd had a few himself, who was confused, probably a mental case to begin with, who'd been checking doors in the apartment complex looking for "Trudy" when he found Heather's door. I'd caught him just as he'd come from the bedroom to find no Trudy. At least, that was the story he told. There'd already been complaints called in about the guy trespassing on the property, but no unit had responded to the calls just yet.

It would've been better for him if they had. His face was swelling and the EMTs were checking him out before they gave the all clear to haul him away. The police took all my information and a statement. They let me know I'd likely be called as a witness at dummy's trial, if there was one, and assured me there was about zero chance I was in any trouble. Soon, it was just me and Heather alone. I exploded.

"What were you thinking? You left your door unlocked! What the hell's the matter with you?" I'd just blurted it out and now it was too late to explain what I'd really meant. I'd thought she was in that bedroom, the place where I'd felt safe and happy for a few hours out of my life, with someone caring and kind, now bloody and assaulted. I'd felt fear like I'd never felt before, picturing her tiny body broken and mutilated. She gave it right back to me with the words I still hear like a torturer's laugh as he flays the skin off my back, the point of the session having nothing to do with any secrets I could give up.

"I don't need you. I don't need you to protect me. I don't *need* you for anything!"

And there it was.

I wasn't needed. Not by her. Not by the world. I wasn't special. I wasn't going to be a hero. I was a cog. I was just a guy in a suit they gave to anybody who signed the dotted line. In an Army that conspired to keep me from the honor it threw to men who hadn't worked nearly as hard as I had. And a girlfriend who didn't need a hero to protect her.

"I don't need you."

05

On a natural berm, I pushed my rifle in front of me. It was beginning morning nautical twilight—BMNT—that time when the first morning light makes outlines visible but dark enough so that it was worth attaching my clip-on night vision device in front of my day scope. Behind my true love once more, I was a werewolf. The darkness was my ally. Anyone who thought themself hidden under its cloak was now powerless. Everything before me was prey. The world was sharp and bright.

And just as instantly, confusing.

Mitch, our junior commo, hit me over the intra team radio. "Ben, I don't even know what I'm seeing. What do you make of it?"

As snipers we would normally work in teams, one spotting, one on the big gun. We opted to each grab our smoke poles and split up. Marky-Mark and his junior weapons, Matt, grabbed their Mark 48s, belts of 7.62 copper death pills over their shoulders, as they likewise spread out with the rest of the team and their lightweight Mark 46s or M4s. We could hold off a battalion of light infantry. And if our visitors meant to test us, I would kick it off by making someone dead from so far away, it would be almost two full seconds before anyone heard the sound that killed their friend.

What I was looking at now, I didn't know how to classify.

"Maybe we stumbled into a cosplay gathering. Some kind of *Star Wars* convention."

"Is Burning Man still a thing?"

"Snipers, give me a read on what you've got." The captain was correctly impatient. We'd been on our optics for minutes, and should've already updated him. Instead, both of us had been too unsure to even ask what the other thought, much less report in. I ranged the massing figures.

"Sir, at 1300 meters, we have a couple of squad's worth of troops mounted on horses. They've remained stationary since we first spotted them. No one's broken off the main party."

There wasn't much terrain to hide behind for anyone to flank us.

"Horses, huh?" the captain repeated. "Guess they still don't have things running again."

"They've got rifles," Mitch added.

He was right. Some had weapons slung on their backs, some in hand. I dialed up the magnification, and right at 16 power, the image became too grainy to be useful. I backed down. It was the trade-off of night vision. At higher magnifications, the image was useless.

"What's your call, snipers?" Mike asked.

I kept it simple. "They're not doing anything obviously aggressive, but they've got their attention on us. They seem to be waiting. Maybe for sunup."

"Are we just ignoring the too many arms and legs thing?" Mitch broke in.

"What?" the captain quizzed back.

Mike ignored the nonessential. "Heavy weapons?"

"Negative," I replied. "They're all still mounted. I don't see anything looks like tubes or crew served coming out." Mortars or heavy machine guns would get the party started earlier.

There was a pause, and I knew Mike and the captain were making chitchat. "Stay on the ball, team," Mike said after a minute. "Chief, run the play. Give us an update if something changes. The captain, Dave, and I are getting this jam in our parking lot cleared so we can get something heavier ready to work."

"Roger," Chief Bryant replied.

I tuned out the chatter in my ear. I was busy running sniper math in my head, checking my initial calcs again, and getting a sense of what the winds were doing. I stayed immersed in the sea of variables and didn't break the surface for air until Mitch spoke.

"Getting light. How 'bout you stay on the gun? I'm going to pull off my clip-on."

"Do it." I kept eyes on the stationary mob, swaying slightly as their animals shifted from side to side beneath them on… how many legs? It was more than four.

"Ben, get yours off and tell me what you see."

Mitch was doubting himself, or was wanting me to be the first one to say the outlandish. I'd play his game. With my clip-on off, now I could crank up the magnification up to 35 for a good look.

"The horses aren't horses. They've got eight legs and heads like reptiles. The men have four arms and are green. Tell me you see the same, or you better get Karlo to pull me off the line and tranq me."

"Nailed it," Mitch confirmed. "This is unreal. You better let the Chief know."

I hit the team channel instead, wanting everybody, especially the captain and Mike to hear. "We've got an update on our observers." I described what I saw.

The Chief immediately fired back, hotly annoyed.

"Colt, this isn't any time for screwing around."

Mitch took up the cause for me. "I see the same, Chief. Someone's playing us. I don't know what else to make of it."

I heard motors revving behind me. Mike broke in.

"We've got the ATVs on the ground. The GMVs aren't coming off until we get the Stryker off, and the ramp's still frozen."

Our best mobile firepower was on our war wagons. The M134s were on the GMVs, our hot-rodded Gatling guns, with M240s on the side pintle mounts. Deadly, but not really armored. The Stryker mounted a fifty and a MK 19 grenade launcher and was our best and only "real" armor as well as the mothership for our other vehicles.

"Hold tight. Captain and I are coming up on the ATVs. Chucky and Doug, get ready to pull back to the bird. You two and Dave are going to get our rides out of there if you have to tear what's left of that bird apart."

"No problemo, Mike," Chucky replied. "All we've been waiting on is your green light to break stuff."

"Heads up, team," I broke in. "We've got movement."

The freak show cavalry was ambling toward us.

"They're riding up. Slowly. Looks like they've decided on a closer look."

"We're outta time," Mike said. "Chief. Protect Baby Blue and our equipment at all costs. Nothing comes closer than five hundred meters. Captain and I are going out to meet whoever it is."

The Chief beat me to it.

"I'm not liking that plan, Mike. We should have more muscle going to meet them."

I agreed but said nothing.

Then the captain laid it out for us.

"Those locals haven't shown any aggression. They're the people we're here to save. They just don't know it yet. A big bird fell out of the sky in their backyard. They probably haven't seen anything flying in some time. They gotta be curious. We need to learn their intentions and get oriented. If it had gone up in flames, it'd be easier, but seeing as it hasn't, protecting Baby Blue is a mission priority."

The C-17 holding the mill that was our bottomless well of goodies and the rest of our irreplaceable combat power was still intact. It was everything to our ability to project force and conduct our mission. And it was still vulnerable. I understood the captain's decision.

I broke in. "There's something funky, sir. Mitch and I both see it. Too many arms and legs."

The captain chuckled. "A better reason to get a closer look. It's just a meet and greet."

Making contact with the local human terrain was the specialty of the detachment commander. Mapping it out was mine. It was a critical part of unconventional warfare, and why there were A-Teams on Task Force Elon Musk.

The potential breakdown of all things more advanced than a manually operated can opener, coupled with the absurdity of the tech behind the slipstream and Baby Blue, as well as the mind-bending plan itself to launch us into the future, all combined to make our task force name apropos. It was thought up by a newly promoted major. Someone still close enough to the troops, but so far away from stars on their collar that the levity was worth the risk to a future career. And someone big signed off on it. Imagination and humor condoned in the Army? Who'd've thunk it?

Then there was the Navy. We'd all watched the first element, Trident One, fly through the slipstream yesterday. It was always Neptune, or

Trident, or Poseidon. Mako, or Thresher, or Hammerhead. It was never anything subtle or quiet or deceptive or imaginative. That would defeat the purpose. The SEALs always wanted who they were to be known. SEALs were a type, similar as they were different from guys who gravitated to SF. If they'd wanted to do things how we did them, they wouldn't be with the hair gel crowd. Oh, Naval Special Warfare has some very capable clandestine elements, but the average SEAL platoon was not of the same mindset.

I shouldn't be busting their stones. We were all getting whisked away through some barely tested gizmonic device on a mission that was the result of someone's epically half-baked idea. "Hey, let's jump ahead two years to fix the unfixable problem, no matter we don't have a fix. We'll just figure it out as we go along." The best assurances that the mutagen plague would be burned out by then rang hollow to all of us, considering the brain trust behind this plan. When I took all that into consideration, staring into the void that swallowed the first of a long line of us to come, what did it matter if the Navy element insisted on a name as subtle as a bumper sticker with their Budweiser Trident on it?

"Why's a SEAL platoon going first?" Dave asked me as we witnessed the giant C-17 become tiny as it went airborne off the impossibly long airfield at 51. It had barely leveled off when it disappeared through a wall of void. It wasn't black. It wasn't any color. It was just a big patch of nothing.

Karlo tsk-tsked. "If it was about securing an LZ on the other side, wouldn't it be more sensible for the Ranger elements to go first? That's kinda what they do."

"Don't go interjecting common sense or this house of cards will come falling down," I said. "Maybe the master plan will all come together for us after it's our turn."

And now, here we were. I backed off to a lower magnification again and was tracking the biggest of the riders as they meandered closer.

The captain capped off his op plan. "Be ready to bring the smoke show if we get into trouble." It didn't need to be said, but when you're the one working with a hot wire, things that go without saying bear repeating, over and over. If the electricity starts arcing, shut off the power. I'd turn off the lights, all right.

Mike hurried things along. "We'll stay on hot mic, kids."

The two ATVs grew louder as they passed me. I stayed focused downrange. Our visitors reacted by halting and spread out. I kept my firing hand where it was and hit my mic. "They're taking a defensive posture, but no muzzles coming up yet." Mike and the captain took a serpentine route to where the reception committee waited, following level ground between swells of terrain, until after ten minutes of cautious navigating they pulled up side by side in front of the still mounted party. The banter between our team sergeant and detachment commander came through loud and clear.

"This is some kinda joke," Mike said, the growl of the engine competing with his own. He was struggling to make sense of the freak show, same as Mitch and me. Now they saw what previously only we'd been able to. Too many arms on the people. Too many legs on the critters.

Plus, everyone was the wrong color. Beasts and riders.

"There's an explanation, Mike. We just gotta play it cool. Let's parley." The captain raised an open hand and spoke loudly. "Good to see you. We had a rough landing this morning. Thanks for coming to help us."

"I'm on the big guy getting off his horse," I told Mitch. "Pick the next closest."

The lead greenie took a few steps forward, and it was now I saw he had tusks sticking up from his lower jaw. A chest plate broke up the green skin. A curved sword hung sheathed at his side.

"I'm on the mounted guy with a rifle across his lap," Mitch replied.

"First hint of trouble, take the shot," the Chief said to us.

Mike heard. "I'll be the one to tell you if you need to get into this, boys. Let the captain work."

The captain dismounted, and Mike followed. They stopped a few meters short of where the lone standing freak towered over them. Both Mike and the captain were over six feet. The waist of the leader came up to their shoulders and his four arms were unmistakably visible—the lower set folded across its abdomen, an upper pointing at the captain with an outstretched finger.

"I'm not catching good vibes, boss," Mike said.

Things happened suddenly. The monster drew his sword in one motion and sliced at the captain in a rising draw stroke. Mike's rifle came up, and the party started. My world became very focused just then. In a process that took all of one-and-a-half heartbeats, I touched the face of the trigger, laid the reticle on the gold-armored chest, pushed the reticle three tics right into the wind, checked my cant bubble, and pressed.

My optic settled again with the recoil, and I watched a vapor trail cruise over top of the sword-wielding reptile-man. Way over the top. I swore. Mitch did the same in my ear. He'd either seen the vapor trail left by my way-too-high shot or had the same thing happen himself. Auditory exclusion to gunfire was at full effect. I didn't know if Mitch had fired as I was shooting, and there was a full-on gunfight happening downrange. I worked the bolt and told myself to trust what I saw. Trust my equipment. For whatever reason I'd missed, it was time for me to make a correction and send another one. The tall geek with the sword maybe heard the round pass over him, maybe heard the report from my rifle, but only momentarily paused. Now he was going for an overhand slash at my captain.

I saw where the path of my first shot had gone, held the same amount lower, gave it the same wind, and pressed the trigger. I definitely heard the report of Mitch's rifle off to my side. He was in it, too. My face stayed with the recoil of my gun and the scope settled right back onto the scene I'd left a millisecond before. I followed the trace to the tiny spot of darkness I'd selected on the shiny breast plate. Maybe it was a dimple, a dent in the armor, maybe a stain. I'd always been taught to find some tiny target—the inside corner of a pocket, the tiny fold at the inner eye—to see as the target. Never the whole thing. *Aim small, miss small* is a real thing.

He dropped his pig sticker and stared at the neat hole. That told me what I needed to know.

I'd just brought mister lime-green swordsman the good news.

I had proof that my answer to the deadly math equation I needed to kill them all was correct. A second shot and he dropped. In the bottom of my scope, Mike was moving and shooting and the mounted troops were firing back, flashes coming from the muzzles of their rifles in bright white discharges. I transitioned to a rider. As he moved to my right, I added a lead to the wind hold and sent it. I watched him fall off his mount and hit my push to talk.

"Captain and Mike are down. Light 'em up."

As the riders split to get out of the kill zone, it took them farther away from where the captain and Mike lay. It was the worst decision they could've made. The *chug-chug-chug* of machine-gun bursts thawed my chilled heart. I found another rider and was about to shoot when I noticed that for all the noise coming from my left and right, there wasn't a lot of effect downrange. They were shooting over their heads, same as I'd done, vapor distortions filling the air overhead of the chaos happening at 1300 meters.

It hadn't just been me.

"Marky-Mark, Matt. Come down five mils. Come down five mils. You're shooting over them." It was a huge correction. One that they'd likely balk at. I didn't know why my first round had gone so high, but the machine gunners were having the same problem.

"The hell you say," Marky-Mark spat back.

I kept my voice calm. "Trust me. Do it."

I'll try to explain. The hardest shot to correct for is one that's too high. I'd gotten lucky by seeing the trace of my first round, the vapor trail wake of disruption left by the bullet as it cut the air. It's what we look for as snipers. Catching the wisp of the trace so high had been luck, because it was so unexpected.

One shot, one kill is the sniper's motto, but it's not a reality at really long distances. It's more like, one shot, make a correction, get him on the next one. A shot where you've underestimated the range, the bullet strikes low. That's easy. Even if you miss the trace, the dirt kicking up short of the target is a pretty big clue you blew it, and it gives you something very definite to make a correction from. Dirt kicks up, you get a terrible feeling, but you get back at it, confident that the next shot will be on the money.

When you've overestimated the range and the bullet takes a path way over the head of your target, unless there's a big hill behind your target where the miss impacts, it's almost impossible to correct for—unless you see the trace. It most commonly happens when you've lost awareness of which revolution the elevation turret of your scope is on. Everyone's done it once. But that wasn't happening here. I was sure as sure can be of what I'd dialed in on.

And we hadn't blown the range to our target. Both Mitch and I had lazed the group several times and were in close agreement. So had

Marky-Mark as he helped direct the gun teams to get them dialed in with the correct elevation.

Tracers, you say? Couldn't the machine guns see the trail of their tracers going high? We don't use tracers. They work two ways, telling the world where you're firing from. That's not a thing for us, giving an enemy friendly hints as to how to find us.

Back on my optic now, my weapons men were making hay. Marky-Mark directed the rest of the team's fire as the 48s and 46s rained copper into the left and right flanks. I had my attention back on the center and found another target, a dismounted greenie leveling his rifle to where the captain lay. A gentle press, the pleasing break of the glass rod trigger, then the push of my rifle relaxed and I came back with it to see green splatter from the unripe melon that was its head.

The machine-gun fire stopped, and for the moment, nothing moved.

There had been a lot of commo traffic. You can be aware of it, and tune it out all at the same time. They say the human mind can only focus on one thing at a time. That multitasking isn't really a thing. The proof of that is the natural human reaction when searching for a new address while driving. The radio always gets turned down.

All I knew was, I heard and received all the traffic running through my skull while I was working to kill the green attackers, I just couldn't talk while I was doing it. The Chief spoke up.

"Mike, talk to us. Mike, come back. Captain, talk to me." The Chief repeated the call to our two friends. No answer.

The Chief was on his feet. "We gotta go get 'em. Chucky and Doug, get with Dave and get that Stryker moving. Now. Rest of us, let's move."

I left my MK 22 where she rested on the bipod, picked up my M4, and took off. To both sides, the team was with me on the move. Karlo was trying to get the captain or Mike to respond as we trotted. Nothing. The terrain was rolling, and uneven. It was a kilometer to where the melee happened. I was numb. Was this combat? One-sided, yes, but it seemed so. It wasn't that much different from anything I'd ever done. A small gulley was in front of me and I took a leap. I cruised to the other side and landed softly. I was moving all out to make it to our teammates, and didn't pause to think about how effortlessly I'd jumped, or how far.

"What the hell happened back there, Colt?" The Chief was running next to me, yelling as we ran. "You blew it. You missed by a mile. I saw."

"And so did everybody else." It wasn't adding up for me just then, and it sure wasn't for him as he blamed me for what had happened. "Didn't you see, Chief? We were way over on the range."

"Later," he grunted. "Move it. We've gotta save them."

We covered the distance in no time and spread out as Karlo made a beeline for our guys. I trotted past where our medic dropped to tend to the captain as Mitch and Matt ran to where Mike lay a dozen meters away. Four-armed bodies were strewn about, red and yellow eight-legged horses—some dead, some making agonizing screeches in the throes of death—lay scattered.

Marky-Mark, the Chief, and I pushed out farther, sweeping the kill zone, looking for any threats that might still exist, when Karlo yelled from behind us.

"Cap and Mike are dead. They're gone, brothers."

Marky-Mark fired a single round from his M4 into a green body at his feet, the head rebounding off the sand with the impact. "Now you're a good ape, aren't you?"

"Find us a wounded prisoner," I told him. "We still need answers. Mitch, go with him."

The Chief was next to me again, in my face. "Who are you to start giving orders, Colt? You blew it. You got the captain and Mike killed. You shanked that shot by a mile. I saw. I said you've got no business on this team, and I meant it. Mike fought for you, and you got him and the captain killed."

"Whoa!" It was Mitch putting himself between us, prying us apart, putting his back to me to push the Chief away. "That's not what happened, Chief. Not even close. We both missed. And so did everybody else until we figured it out."

"Figured what out?" the Chief hammered back.

It was Karlo who said it.

"We're all ignoring the obvious. We're not on Earth anymore."

06

The last phase of my career that led to me fighting four-armed green giants came quickly after Heather told me off and sealed my self-image for a long time to come. At two years and some change, the Army decided I didn't need to push recruits anymore, and I was returned to SF. I had a new badge, Drill Instructor, and before I packed them away for my trip back to Eglin, that day I cut the patch off all my uniforms. I was trying to shed my bitterness and resentment at being hijacked for drill duty, and that little badge would always be a reminder of that period of my life, and I just wanted to forget it. My round-brown drill sergeant campaign hat? It went into the dumpster.

There was a new command sergeant major back at Group. While he didn't know me personally, he knew what I'd been through. He renewed my faith that my sacrifice hadn't been forgotten. He had a good news/bad news situation for me. That's how he said it. "I've got good news and bad news." He didn't make it sound like there was a punch line coming, but for a moment, I felt the earth open up, ready to swallow me again. The bad news part of it wasn't really all that bad.

I'd just been promoted to E-7, sergeant first class. I was now a senior NCO. But it meant that in SF, I was a little behind the power curve. The required schooling I would have been otherwise receiving while I was Shanghaied to leg-land? I now needed to do it all. No A-Team for me just yet.

(Parenthetical comment number one about the military. My sincerest apologies to any non-airborne personnel reading this. The military instills pride. In the Airborne, that pride is on display sometimes a little too fragrantly and carelessly. Putting someone down is usually a sign of insecurity. I truly have respect for anyone who serves honorably.

Every job in the military is important. As much as I try to not be, at my core, I'm still that insecure teenage paratrooper. You buncha legs!)

It was back to Bragg for me. There was the SF senior leader course. I'd kept up with the online portions of SF NCO development while I was stuck teaching kids how to march, but there was no avoiding having to go do the live attendance course. I was always working or studying, even as long as the hours were on drill instructor duty. When I wasn't seeing she-who-shall-no-longer-be-named, I had my nose hovering over a computer screen.

(Parenthetical comment number two about my breed. I don't know what you think about the military. It isn't like the movies. You think we sit around the barracks, waiting for someone to come tell us what to do? That scenario might exist, but I'd never been in a unit like that. SF operators especially have the equivalent of a PhD in the skill sets they acquire, and work like obsessed demons to maintain them. It's a long road of schools, practical application, adding more skills, maintaining old ones, and it never really ends. I'll keep bursting your bubble about how wrong some Hollywood writers get it. It's not about who has the biggest muscles. It's about who has the biggest brain that drives those big muscles, plus who's going to treat every day like it's the only day to prepare yourself for the real deal. That means schools and training. Until you die.)

I'd never been on a real A-Team and here I was, off to study how to be a "senior leader" on one. After senior leader, there was the Operations and Intelligence school. It was necessary training to be able to take the number two NCO spot on a team someday—the O&I slot, which was also known as the assistant team sergeant spot. An 18 F. I hadn't even served as a Bravo, and here I was getting teed up to be a Foxtrot. It was a gateway as magical as the slipstream. It was the how-to guide of all the secret squirrel stuff. I'd be inducted into the very select society of O&I. Again, kind of weird as I'd never been anything on an A-Team, but there it was.

Military Freefall refresher, static line jumpmaster refresher, might as well throw in HALO jumpmaster while I was getting schooled up. In other words, though it was a reward, I was going to be in schools for a very long time before I ever got to a real team. I was assigned to one as soon as I hit Eglin, but I was gone just as fast as I met the guys.

It was one of those teams the group had that filled just such a purpose. Spare bodies came off that team to fill in where operators were needed on other teams for missions, and where guys like me got parked for notional purposes while we were going to be at Bragg for long stints.

It was very much good news, bad news.

If you don't know the military, much less SF, this all probably sounds like nonsense. Like I'm some chump nobody wanted, so they just kept shuffling me around to keep me away from a place where I could cause trouble for a real team. You could think that, despite all I've told you, but I swear it's true.

I knuckled down. Bragg is a place you always return to. It was always a stop on any journey in SF. Like going to your mother-in-law's for Thanksgiving. Love it or hate it, you're going back. Forever. No matter it held some bad memories—the shame post-Venezuela—it was also the place of my greatest achievements. The Special Warfare Center was the Jedi academy. It was the finishing school for all supermen. The schools I was attending were the most prestigious in SF, and it meant I was finally headed for a place that would once and for all let me do the real work of a soldier.

I won't bore you with the details. But to wrap it up, I'll tell you about the wonderful, life-changing event that steered my tale away from being a less elegant version of *Grapes of Wrath* or *Les Miserables* to something more like an Ian Fleming novel. I was about to ship out to Yuma for MFF refresher, jumpmaster, and advance tactical infiltration, when I had a visitor. You guessed it. Master Sergeant Mike Williams. He was in civvies. His hair was long and he had a big droopy mustache. In O&I, I'd been read into some of the special programs that operate within Special Forces. Mike ran one of those teams out of Eglin. I won't say the name here, but maybe someday if it's declassified and someone wants to talk, you'll know what it is. Maybe wherever and whenever you are, there might even be e-books and Audible again. But it won't be me who squawks first. Not for a million dollars or all the beach babes in Destin.

Mike and the CSM were good buddies. If there's any proof I can offer you that I'm not a leper who's been shunned to some cave at the edge of town to slowly rot, here it is. The team sergeant of the most high-speed special project team in SF wanted me as his number two.

When I made it back to Destin, there would be a home waiting for me. A team with the choicest mission in all of SF and thereby, all the world. Did I want the job?

Did Icarus wish he'd used superglue instead of wax?

"I wish it was tomorrow, Sergeant Williams."

If he wanted me to pack up right now and follow him, I would. I didn't need more than one run in the vertical wind tunnel to be ready to jump again. I didn't care about being a freefall jumpmaster more than I cared about what was waiting for me in that team room. I tried to imagine it.

"I'm Mike," he corrected me. SF was a place of professionals, and there was an informality on a team that went along with that.

"Thank you, Mike. I won't let you down."

The other thing about me you don't know. I've never been in a school where I wasn't the honor grad or the distinguished honor grad. And it was no different this run. I told you—I'm a winner. Even if I beat myself up on the inside too much. I landed this amazing fairy godmother opportunity because the Regiment didn't forget me and because on the outside, I'm sterling. On the inside, well, you get the idea.

Mike was everything I'd ever dreamed about in a team sergeant, and I'd only known him a few minutes. He was Charlton Heston as Moses, only he wasn't playing the role. Wise. Grizzled. Fatherly. Powerful.

"You got crucified. I know your story. Even the Venezuela stuff."

My face turned red.

"The word on what happened to you guys in Division R&I spread like tuberculosis. You can't keep that kind of biblical proportion smackdown under wraps. It shouldn't have happened. I was never in the eighty-deuce, but that's the kind of petty vindictive big-green weenie crap that drives guys out, or up. If you've endured all that *and* then getting fed to the sharks at the Department of the Army and are still here, it isn't because you're worried about hitting your twenty and retiring to the beach. You're all warrior. That's what I want. I know you'd die before you let us down, Deke."

I winced. He saw it.

"Isn't Deke short for Deacon?"

"It is. I usually go by Ben, but you and the team can call me anything you like if it means I've got a spot."

He laughed. "Ben, it is."

And that's how I knew more than ever that SF was where I was always meant to be.

They needed me.

So of course, it wasn't too long before the world started to disintegrate around us.

✣ ✣ ✣

"This isn't Area 51. It's the Nevada Test Range." With his knife hand, Karlo threw a tomahawk chop toward a mountain range like he was casting a fishing rod. "51 is over there somewhere."

I'd never been here, but a lot of the team had. New Mexico Tech and Sandia ran special schools here. Chemical and nuke warfare (how to survive, not how to conduct), advanced energetic materials manipulation (read that as *blowing stuff up*), and all kinds of Homeland Security topics were taught at the test range.

"To think, the whole world believed they had aliens here. If there were hair-lips hiding out when I was here, I never saw them," Chucky said.

"Probably weren't. If they'd gotten to Vegas, no way they'd have made Kazakhstan their interstellar vacation destination," Dave said.

Doug had been here, as well. "They say it doesn't, but I'm on the side that says the whole place has enough latent radiation to maybe grow you an extra head or arm. They tested about a thousand nukes here back in the day."

Karlo countered, "You receive more background radiation at altitude in the Rocky Mountains or in a Pittsburgh basement bleeding radon than where we are."

Pure Southern Cali born and raised, Doug Knoblock was a standout on a team of very bulky men. He was known as Thor to other teams, but he hated the name. Dougie was his preference. Out of uniform, the most accommodation he'd make for the frosty winter mornings in the Florida panhandle was to wear jeans with his flip-flops instead of board shorts. He'd been raised in the cold waters of the Pacific. When the locals put on down jackets whenever the temp dipped below 60, Doug was in the water with Dave on any stormy day, trying to catch what waves there were in the generally calm Gulf near Eglin.

"Might not have been aliens here, Ben, but it is true that there're tunnels underneath the desert that go on for miles," Dougie added for my benefit. "They let us see, dude. My class had one of the original Manhattan Project engineers give us a history lesson. I'm just saying I came away knowing some stuff. Stuff I knew as rumors turned out to be true, which means maybe some of the other wacky stories are, too. Like there being aliens here, and their spaceships."

Karlo as usual got the last word in. "The test range is secret and controlled for a lot of reasons. It's where they built and tested the first nukes. It's exempted from EPA and other agencies' regs and inspections, and it let us develop technology ahead of our enemies without a bureaucracy and endless regulations hampering them. And yes, it's where experimental aircraft are trotted out in secrecy. Other than the toxic waste stored in some areas, that's all there is to the rumors. Besides, since the site's become so well known, the really secret stuff is somewhere else now."

"Ah ha!" Doug stuck a finger in the air. "You admit the possibility that the hot rods of the gods *could've* been hidden here? Otherwise, why would they have to move it all somewhere even *more secret* once the History Channel started blabbing, dude?"

Karlo was used to being naysaid after he dropped a logic bomb. But Doug's insistence about the ridiculous was as futile a counter as someone you'd knocked to the ground saying he'd kick your ass, all while spitting out teeth. Karlo never so much as rolled his eyes. His silence lent him the dignified contempt of the noble champion standing victorious over his vanquished foe.

Around us they were assembling an invasion. For what, we didn't know. The tent city was growing rapidly as more and more troops and equipment were flying in by the hour. We'd seen a lot of 75th troops, a much smaller number of Navy types and other services represented, and A-Teams like ours—whose designation and mission I can't tell you—one from each of the Groups. That night while we stood under the stars, one by one speakers took the stage and told us what was going on in the world and why we were here.

All of a sudden, Doug's insistence that Area 51 was a place where real mysteries had been hidden didn't seem so outlandish.

The first briefer was a four-star I'd never seen on any chain of command picture wall. She came to the point quickly. There was something happening in Asia. A contagion of some kind. What was happening to machinery and technology was just the start. DNA was vulnerable, too. What we'd been witnessing around the world was real.

"The caveman in the video," Dave nudged me.

Then, for the first time, I knew we were in trouble. Because when they tell you the truth, it's never because they feel like sharing. It's because they have to. And that only happens when things are very, very bad. The scientists had identified a cause. It was a type of infective particle that could only be the result of a very advanced technology.

The general took off her hat and rubbed the back of her neck. "We believe the Guests are responsible for this. They're the Trojan horse for our subjugation and domination."

Doug whispered. "Kazakhstan, here we come. Time to kill hair-lips."

Karlo shushed him, but Doug wasn't alone in voicing a guess about our destination.

The general continued. "Russia is not in agreement that the Guests are the cause of this plague. But the national command authority has decided that the US cannot wait on the formation of a coalition to fight this threat. As we speak, the air-land invasion of Kazakhstan is mounting. The goal is to capture the ET visitors and shut down their plans for this planet. To learn the cause of the plague and how to counter it. It will result in large-scale warfare between us and other nations in the region. It may incite attacks on the homeland.

"But the scientists agree. While our forces fight the epicenter of the known threat, it is inevitable that the plague will spread across the planet."

I was getting the sense that we weren't headed for central Asia.

Next, a civilian lady in a dark suit took over. She was out of place the way a Louis Vuitton purse is out of place on a shrimp boat, or a Rolls Royce sticks out in a Walmart parking lot. She was to the point as well, but in a way that made me feel she wasn't just being concise. It was thinly disguised revulsion. She spoke to us as underlings. She was accustomed to ordering house staff, not explaining to butlers why she wanted dinner served an hour early. And we were the menial providers of her will. After some short and insincere remarks about what an honor it was to be the civilian leadership of this "grand adventure and you wonderful boys"… Yeah. I'm not making that up—"boys"… she got down to it.

"Top government scientists estimate the plague will cross the globe in weeks, leaving a wake of destruction that will throw us back to a time before modern civilization. If our forces can defeat the Guests before that happens, then this nation has a chance at a future. But what kind of future will that be? One where all the building blocks of our civilization have been rendered to dust? It will require the work of our best and brightest to rebuild a future worth having."

It was unsaid that those on the stage were those best and brightest. And that she was the bestest and brightest of them all.

"The mutagen causing this plague was designed for a specific effect. Like most virions, it is self-limiting. The scientist estimate that the mutagen will have run its course in two to three years. Which brings us to why you are all here today."

Another speaker took the lectern. This one struck me as the scientist type. Without a white lab coat on, he seemed undressed, his ill-fitting suit hanging off his cadaverous body. His chest may have been underdeveloped, but the might of his intellect came through like he was the Arnold Schwarzenegger of brainbuilding. Every voice tells a story about its owner. His said he was a soldier as much as we were.

"The Guests' mistake was in underestimating us. The technology they teased us with they thought beyond our understanding. Instead, it was quickly recognized as the bridge to many possibilities the physics and engineering community had considered for decades."

That's when we first learned about the slipstream and the Blue Fairy. Then the general took the podium again.

"We're going to take a jump into the future. A future where if the Guests are still on our planet, we'll finish the fight. And if our brothers and sisters have already won, then we go straight to work rebuilding the United States of America. Either way, that's our job."

We were the cavalry, arriving not from over the hill, but from a hole in the sky.

The energy in the crowd had been building. We were outnumbered by the Rangers around us. Most of them were younger than us by seven or eight years, or much more. Not a big difference if you're forty looking to date a thirty-year-old, but a big difference in the world of special operations. It was the difference between being a green, trusting, and—even in the Army—innocent youth, and being jaded, skeptical, and numb. I was a lot of the latter, the youngest of the Rangers the former. They couldn't help but be who they were. Deadly youngsters fueled by testosterone, caffeine, and dip, kicked in the nuts by a bunch of suits and people wearing stars who had never existed for them until today, but whom they had to obey.

"What'd she say?"

"Time travel's all bullshit."

"I'm short. This is just a way to keep me from ETSing next month."

"I just bought a truck."

The four-star ended the preamble to our impending trip through the looking glass. "This is a good stopping point. We're done for tonight. D-Day is in seven days. If we can hold off that long. Units are dismissed."

Rangers were in the front-leaning rest before she'd left the stage, and Mike made an overhead loop several times before shooting an azimuth out of the mass formation toward our tents.

Back in our team quarters, Dave plopped down next to me on my cot. "Crazy stuff, huh brah? Still glad you came to the team?"

Some of the guys were dazed and silent with the thousand-yard stare that said their minds were fixed on possibilities too grim to put into words. It was the married guys. Chuck, Marky-Mark, and Matt had young families. I caught Dave's eye and made a nod in the direction of our hurting brothers. The news had been dropped on us with all the subtlety of an atomic bomb. Dave picked up on it and nodded in understanding. He mouthed, "This is messed up."

Mike took charge. His kids were adults, but he was very much a married man. "I know what you're all thinking. Because I'm thinking it, too. We've been asked to leave our families behind, maybe to die. And we haven't been given a choice." He let it hang.

"Because there isn't a choice. The Guests are here to wipe out the world. You heard the lady. Know how I know it's real? Because there wouldn't be so many suits ready to jump through this tunnel in the sky with us if there was even a remote possibility that they could stop this thing here and now. They'd send all of us to die, every one of us, and do it without regret, if it could keep them here running the show and in Italian shoes and Starbucks for one more day.

"And that means, we really are the best chance for our country and our families to survive this plague. I'm saying that if we love our families, and if there's a tough job waiting for us on the other side, we're the only ones who can do it. We have to do this. Because we're the best there is. It's us, or no one."

"Mike." It was Marky-Mark. Our senior weapons man was a tank. He was unemotional, gruff, never made small talk or pleasantries. He was all business. And his business was killing in big numbers. "We've got to be able to say goodbye to them. We can't do this and leave them without knowing what happened to us." Besides the outright hostility of the Chief toward me at all times, it was only Mark who hadn't shown me any gesture of comradery. I figured it was just his personality and didn't take it personally. Now I saw a different side of him. He was hurting.

"We can't leave them thinking the worst of us."

We'd deployed sterile, meaning we'd stripped all our personal items, any identifying material, and our cell phones, and left them at home.

Mitch rolled his eyes. "Pfft. I saw one of those Air Force pukes texting on an Iridium while the briefing was going on. Not everyone came sterile, Top. I saw a Navy guy doing the same."

"Some SEAL probably contacting his agent," Doug said.

Dave hopped up. "Say the word, Top. Mitch and I'll get commo up with the B-Team in Eglin so everyone can call their families."

Mike gave the captain the final word. "Sir?"

Captain Nelson didn't hesitate. "Do it. But no satellite. And nothing encrypted. This place is crawling with counterintel. Let the secret police listen to you ask your kids how ballet lessons went today. Let them hassle the real leaks. Let's be smarter, as usual."

Dave was chomping at the bit. "We'll have a clandestine antennae rigged for AM commo in no time. No sense advertising what we're doing. No FaceTime, but the B-Team can link our audio to everyone's cell phones."

"Keep it in the clear," Captain Nelson reminded. "No location or what we're doing." We all knew the drill. But it was one of those things that didn't hurt to repeat. "It won't help your families for you to tell them it's the end of the world. Just tell them you love them."

Matt looked grim. "I'm going to tell my wife to take the kids and go to her folks in Iowa. If what they say is true, I'd feel better if they were at the farm."

I spoke up. "Matt, that might not be the best idea this late in the plague. Planes are dropping out of the sky in Asia. Cars are dying mid-drive. If this thing hits the US soon, it'd be awful if your family got hurt trying to get all the way to Iowa. Eglin might be the best place for them. At least the base will have security and medical help."

"I think Ben's right," Karlo added. "Plus, OPSEC. The more anyone says about what's going on, the closer it might take you to having to deny what you know." Operational security was second nature to a team.

"You do what you think's best," Mike put a cap on it. "That goes for everyone. Tell your families whatever you want—except for the obvious part about where we are and what we're doing. The captain and I will take the heat if anyone wants to give us shit about it. They should've already had a plan in place for us to communicate with our families, instead of treating us like disposable commodities. You can bet they've got their people in deep bunkers somewhere in the mountains and they've told them everything about what to expect. Screw 'em. Besides, what are they going to do at this point? Leave us behind?"

✣ ✣ ✣

My eyes were wet with sadness and rage as we carried the captain and laid him next to Mike, Karlo carefully arranging their broken bodies with dignity. Our team leader and our team sergeant. They were friends and brothers to each other and to us all. And they were gone.

"What's the move, Chief?" Marky-Mark asked. "It's you and Ben running the team now. What's next?"

The Chief said the first thing I'd agreed with almost since I'd known him. "Find out where the hell we are and kill anyone who screws with us."

07

Breaching saws and cutting charges sheared metal in the background while we worked the kill zone many hundreds of meters away from the wreck.

"Over here," Mitch said over comms. "This guy's alive."

I trotted with Karlo, curiosity competing with my instinct to keep my attention out for more greenies. What he was, I didn't know. Other than full of holes, that is. The blood on his green skin made for a bizarre pallet like some kind of ancient black light poster still hanging in Grandpa's basement bar.

Mitch's menace had little effect. His muzzle was pointed at the soldier's head. "Stay where you are. Keep your hands where I can see them. All of them."

His four arms failed to support his attempted crab walk, betraying his weakness from blood loss with each collapse, but still he kept trying, a stepped-on spider making a half-hearted getaway.

"I said don't move."

"I'm hands," I said, meaning for Mitch to stay on cover, ready to put one in his brain if he got sufficiently testy.

How do you restrain a prisoner with four hands? One set of them at a time. I grabbed an outstretched arm, locked his elbow, and put him on his face. Some things were still the same. Karlo helped me get flex cuffs around his wrists and ankles, and we rolled him on his side. Karlo went to work to patch his many holes.

"You got your prisoner, Ben," Mitch said as he relaxed his rifle. "He's not the biggest of them, but he's plenty big."

I'd grappled with platoons of guys bigger than me, but as I manhandled the green soldier, I couldn't help but be thankful he was shot to hell. This fella had to have outweighed me by a couple hundred pounds. I knew he was on his way to wherever green apes go when they bleed out their last drops, because he had no fight left as I rolled him onto his side for Karlo to start his survey of injuries. Greenie was just along for the ride. I watched Karlo work as Dave pulled up in the Stryker.

"What is he, Karlo?" Mitch asked.

"I'm busy. If I can save him, we'll ask him later," Karlo said dispassionately as he dug into his aid bag for more dressings.

The Chief broke us out of our gawking.

"Let's get loaded and back to the bird. That's our firebase, for now."

Still there was no discussing the elephant in the room. The first grumble was when Dave trotted over with a litter to help us with our wounded prisoner.

"Ben-Dog, what's happening? We stumbled into a Stone Age village in the Balkans one time. The sandbox was full of crazy places and people you didn't think could exist in the modern world. But this? This is just too strange, brah."

"Guess the hair-lip's mutagen did a number on the hillbillies," Mitch said.

We helped Karlo heft the litter up the ramp and crowded in. The bodies of Top and the captain lay up front.

Even with hatches open, it was crowded. I climbed up top to perch behind the Chief standing in the TC hatch, Dave back in the driver's hole. Marky-Mark was below in the gunner seat, the .50 and the MK 19 pivoting beside me to his remote control. When we were loading out for the mission, Mark had told me, "I was born in a Stryker." I took it to mean as a young soldier he'd been in a Stryker Infantry Brigade. It was one of the few tidbits he'd ever shared about himself.

SF was full of every background and skill. Karlo was the exception, the only one on the team to have not suffered through at least one hitch in the regular Army before coming to SF. Many's the time I'd wished I'd been special enough to do as he'd done and skip the whole experience, as they say, taking the green weenie. But then you had guys like Mark who had invaluable experience from their time in the regulars. For me, what I brought to the team from all that time? Hunger. Hunger to do it right.

The Chief motioned me to lean close as we rolled. I put my ear next to his mouth. "Security first. Chucky and Doug have the GMVs in play. I want Marky and Matt in the Stryker, Mitch and Doug in one of the GMVs to give us a perimeter. The other GMV stays with us at the plane, ready to roll out if needed. The rest of us, we work."

I reversed the arrangement so he could hear me. "I'll get the drone up. We need eyes out. Before we went down, I'm pretty sure I saw something that looked like a city. Way the heck out there. If that's where these clowns came from, we need to know. And get some early warning about any more of them coming at us."

"Agreed."

For a moment, I thought we were simpatico. But it was that moment you ignore experience and touch the paint to see if it's dry. I should've known better. The print on the wall was proof of the bad assumption, as he left his on me.

"Colt. I need you to step it up. No more screw-ups. Got me?"

We were back to our former state of interpersonal affairs. Him finding fault, me on the defensive. The heat in me rose. I wasn't going to be silent this time.

"Screw-up? Is this why you don't want to talk about it in front of the whole team? I got us on the kill zone. The foul-up is where we're at. Karlo's right. We're not on Earth, or is that somehow my fault, too?"

He waved me off. "I don't want to hear it right now. Do your job. We'll get to the bottom of this."

I leaned back and tried to think calm thoughts. I'd do my job. As if my performance should even be in question. I'm the one that figured out the problem on the fly and got us rounds on target. I had to put it aside. In a minute, we were close enough to the C-17 that what had just gone down between us took a back seat.

Chucky and Doug had done a number on the tail of the C-17. Masterful destruction at its finest. The ramp was lowered as far as it could go given the angle of how it landed, and the top cargo door had been removed with violent finesse. It lay in pieces below. For the next eight hours, we didn't surface for air from our deep dive into the work.

The sun got higher, but never really high. It was more like a winter sun in the far north. Low on the horizon and dim. The landscape grew redder as the day went on and a heat rose to match it. The faintest wind came up at times, not enough to dry our sweat, and I started to think about our water supply. The Chief pulled the five of us together in the shade of the cargo bay and spoke over comms so everyone could hear.

"Karlo, you're first. Go."

"No one's wounded or injured. The prisoner's stable, or at least his vitals haven't changed. I don't know anything about his physiology, but he's nonhuman. He's got a pair of two-chambered hearts. I think. He's unconscious and lost a lot of blood. There's no way for me to replace it. He's restrained and littered up front. He's not getting into any trouble.

"Chucky and I checked on the water situation. We've got three hundred gallons of bottled, most of which survived the impact, and another two hundred seventy-five in the tote tank. We're good for a while, but not indefinitely. We'll need a water source that I can purify."

Chucky added, "I don't know if the JP-8 in the wings is recoverable. I mean, I can pump it out and transfer it to the bladders, I just don't know if it'll be useable. It didn't torch off, which is good, but it's because the fire suppression system worked. I don't know much about it. It's an inert gas that pumped through the fuel into the tanks. All I can do is test a batch, see if it's ignitable. If it is, I can purge one of the vehicles, try some of the tainted fuel. If it doesn't run, I can reverse the process."

Karlo looked thoughtful. "If it's a nitrogen system, it shouldn't affect the fuel. It prevents fuel vapor from igniting in the tanks. If we pump some of the fuel out and leave it exposed to the air, it should de-gas on its own. But you're right. We test some and go from there."

"What about Baby Blue?" the Chief asked the obvious. "If it's running, we might not need to mess with it."

The plan was to use the plane's JP-8 to run our fleet of vehicles and spare Baby Blue for other necessary items.

All eyes went to Karlo again.

"Between caring for our prisoner and helping Chuck with sustainment, I haven't gotten too detailed a check on Baby Blue. It seems to be fine. I'll only know once I get it printing something."

"Ammo." Marky-Mark's single word, a command. "I want more fifty. We didn't bring enough."

We started with ten thousand rounds. That was enough to take on a tank battalion. I agreed, though. More would be good.

"First, we'll try simple molecules. Water's a good test. Then we'll try more complex things. The analyzer will tell me how far we can go based on the fidelity of the output. Then we can set a priority for production. Once Chuck and I get it producing, we'll know in a couple of hours if it was worth hauling with us, or if it's just six thousand pounds of junk."

The Chief gave a quick thumbs-up. "That's medical and sustainment. Commo?"

Dave shook his head. "I've got satcom, FM, and AM running. Nada. No satellite pings. No traffic."

The Chief frowned. "No response to the common mission bands?"

"Negative. If there's anyone from the task force here, I'm not picking them up, and no one's responding to my blind transmission with our mission identifier."

"Keep trying. I want you or Mitch on it, twenty-four seven. Intel?"

The Chief already knew what I did, as he'd helped me prep a drone and watched over my shoulder as it flew, or rather, struggled to. I had a couple of Ravens and one Puma UAV. The only difference was the range on these small tactical drones. Both could operate at an altitude of at least 500 feet and should give us some info about what lay over the horizon in all directions. I checked out the Puma, satisfied it was juiced up, and gave it a heave. Turns out, it didn't matter which I'd chosen. It struggled to maintain even a few feet of altitude before nosing into the ground a dozen yards away.

"Nice going, Colt," the Chief criticized. "You've got to let the engine high rev before you toss it." This time I had him.

Silently, I ran to retrieve it. It wasn't broken. I ran back. "Be my guest." He harrumphed. I let him hold it as I started the engine again. It sputtered, came to life, and he raised it over head for a toss. I knew what the outcome would be before he grunted with extra effort to launch the UAV farther than I had, only for it to repeat the same disappointing nosedive.

"That's why we dropped like a rock in the C-17, Chief. We're above a maximum operating altitude. It has to be." I held back my other suspicions for now. "These fixed wing UAVs are too heavy. Just a minute."

I trotted to where the piles of some of our stuff were still stacked and selected the case with fragile contents I'd dropped earlier that day.

The quadricopter was the lightest drone we had. After a few minutes I had it ready, and what I showed to the team now were the results from its anemic flight.

I turned the laptop so the others could see the screen. I'd pushed the little copter as high as it would go and did a spot turn, panning around in one complete circle before it petered out and came down again.

"Whole lotta nothin'," Dave said.

"Here." I switched to a still taken in the opposite direction. At the very edge of the horizon was what I had seen from in the air. Tiny. Just the tops of the shapes above the horizon, concealed by the backdrop of jagged mountains behind them.

Karlo moved closer to the screen, stooped, and squinted. "There's nothing in nature domed or right angled. That's a city."

The others crowded in and did the same. I'd already stared at the images for too long.

"What is it?" Matt said over comms.

"Ben found a city with the drone, brah. It's way the heck out there, though. I don't even know. Forty, fifty klicks maybe. What do you think, Ben?"

"No good way of knowing. Most importantly to our immediate situation, though it's not much of a recon of the area, I don't see anything closer that indicates people."

"People?" Mitch said from on the perimeter. "You mean the green four-armed variety or people-people like other Americans? Where the heck is everybody?"

The dam that had been holding back our fears broke.

Chuck was chanting, "There's an explanation."

Marky-Mark was loudest. "Why the hell didn't we go back in time and kill the hair-lips when they showed up? That woulda been a better mission."

Karlo shook his head. "Time travel to the past is impossible, Mark."

"But stealing matter from the future to build shit in Baby Blue is?" Dougie yelled.

In front of me, Chucky was still chanting. "There's an explanation. It's time to interrogate the prisoner. Or snatch new ones. We're just in the dark, is all." He said it again, begging for one of us to agree with him.

What Dave said, I won't repeat. He was a master of compound obscenities.

"At ease, at ease," the Chief said, reverting to basic Army speak, hoping to get control again.

"HEY!"

It was Karlo. Karlo never yelled. He never raised his voice. He was always in control. We all froze.

"Watch."

He pushed Dave and Chuck back from either side of him, squatted slightly, and jumped. Karlo touched the ceiling of the cargo bay, touched down with a slight cushioning bend to his knees, then stood erect.

"Whaa?" Dave gasped.

"How far up was that, guys?" he queried us like Socrates.

I was as stunned as the others at Karlo's demonstration.

"Twelve feet," Chucky answered. "The cargo bay is twelve feet high. I know from working with the loadmaster."

"Right. Twelve feet. And I touched the ceiling without breaking a sweat. I still have my plate carrier on, too. Step outside with me."

Karlo strode through our center, down the ramp, and outside. The light was dimming and the night sky was peeking through, a blanket of stars appearing to make the isolation of our position away from any light pollution agonizingly apparent.

"Who else has been through open water celestial navigation?" he asked.

Matt answered over comms. "I have, right after small boat school."

"Good. Step out of your vehicle and take a look at the sun. What's that above it? About a hand's breadth higher. Tell me what you see."

I looked to where the sun was low on the horizon, then up.

"Venus," Matt answered.

"You sure?" Karlo quizzed him.

"I don't have my wheel with me, but—"

"What color is that planet?"

I saw it now, too. I hadn't been through the schooling Karlo and Matt had, but I knew fundamentals. I said it out loud.

"It's blue. Not silver, like Venus."

Blue. Blue as the only planet that it could be.

"Knock it off, Karlo," Chuck said. "That's not Earth, that's impossible."

"See that small bright dot a little higher? That's the moon. THAT—" he pointed, "is Earth."

"Where the hell are we then?" Matt asked.

Karlo remained silent as he so often did when making a point. It was his signature move. It was sometimes annoying, but right now, he was challenging us like a good professor, waiting for us to take the deductive step to enlightenment. I was ready to be the first to embarrass myself in front of the class.

"Mars. We're on Mars."

08

From the second we'd appeared through the slipstream, we'd all known there was something majorly wrong. With every new oddity we encountered, we'd refused to put the pieces of the puzzle together. Survival has a way of prioritizing your data analysis. No one thinks about the chicken or the egg in the middle of a fist fight. Now that we'd overcome the existential problems caused by crashing one of the largest airplanes ever made, combatting aliens, and losing our friends, we were diverting processor power to analyzing our situation.

Marky-Mark was first to sound off. "There's no air on Mars, brainiac. I know you're the smartest guy in the room, Karlo, but that's stupid."

"There's no such thing as four-armed greenies either, Mark," Karlo retorted without malice. "But your 7.62 chewed up a couple dozen of them and we've got one on a litter to remind us."

Mitch ticked off items from the list running through his head. "The plane couldn't keep altitude. Or the drones. There's air, but it's too thin. We were off on the dope for our guns by a friggin' mile. I'm making Olympic quality long jumps while carrying twice as much gear, all without tearing something. It has to be because the gravity's not the same. It makes sense. Sorta."

"How much lower is the gravity on Mars than Earth?" Chucky asked Karlo.

"This much," Dave said, and mimicked Karlo's demonstration by compressing into a crouch and springing up, his arms leading the effort like a kid on the playground going for the monkey bars. He peaked at about twice his own height, came down gently, but not quite as gracefully. I suspected Karlo had practiced a few times to test his early theory while the rest of us had been occupied.

Matt's disgust was undisguised even over comms. "Yeah, it makes sense. All except there being air we can breathe and green aliens for us to shoot. What's the explanation there?" He was following suit with Marky, also not an early convert to Karlo's theory.

The only one yet to say anything was the Chief. I prompted him.

"What do you say, boss?"

"We're tabling this discussion. Security, security, security is all that matters right now. I'm pulling everyone outside back in for some downtime. The rest of us are going on perimeter. Except Karlo. You stay with your patient, work Baby Blue, and get a little shut-eye when you can."

"I'm staying out, Chief," Marky said. "I ain't sleeping. Why don't you come to the Stryker and rack out? I'll let you spell me when I need it."

"M'kay. Dave, you stay back. You and Mitch split radio watch. Ben and Chuck—swap out with Mitch and Dougie. Get your kit together and meet me at the GMV in ten."

We drove quietly until we dropped the Chief off at the Stryker.

"Go fifty-fifty and get some rest. It's going to be a long time before we get any real sleep."

I waited for him to throw a jab my way, but he let it go to fist-bump Matt as they passed on the ramp.

From inside the Stryker, Marky-Mark said sternly, "I don't have an explanation."

It was the answer to no one's question. Was it the last word to a heated discussion with Matt, or did he mean it for me? We got our passenger and took off.

✢ ✢ ✢

I had my NODS down as I drove, the white phosphor tubes making everything bright and clear with the rising night sky. There were too many stars. More than I'd ever seen from the highest mountain or the middle of the ocean. We rolled a few hundred meters around the nose of the crashed bird, and I thought about my promise to recover the aircrew.

"Tomorrow, we bury everyone," I said aloud.

"Yes, we will," Matt said from the back. "I'll start right after stand-to."

I thought about this morning and when the first useable rays of light had appeared. If more of the greenies came, would they do the same and hold off until the sun was up?

I pulled up to our other GMV where it sat hull down behind a gentle bump in the landscape. Mitch and Dougie were on the door-mounted guns, the truck nosed just high enough for the guns to clear the top of the berm. Mitch was seated, but like a kid on tiptoes trying to be big enough to ride the roller coaster as he struggled to peer higher. Dougie was half in, half out—one cheek on the seat, a leg out, otherwise at full height so his head cleared the top of the door. Cramming Dougie into a GMV wearing full battle rattle was like an iron maiden torture. He was just too big for most vehicles, and it was worse in the Stryker. In the Army, the larger the vehicle was on the outside, the smaller it was on the inside.

I left our war wagon running and hopped out.

"Anything to report?" I asked as I came around to the driver's side.

Mitch shrugged. "There's some kind of small rats or something playing around out there. Nothing of any size." Mitch was like me, a sniper. He was an excellent observer.

"Roger. Get some Z's."

I dropped my gear and extended a hand to pull him out of his seat. He groaned with the effort. Standing, he lifted his plate carrier by the shoulder straps and shifted underneath the momentary freedom before releasing it.

"I love putting it on because it feels so good getting it off."

Sitting for hours in full gear is a kind of torture all its own, a kind of self-imposed straight jacket. No matter all the gear was as much a part of you as your own skin, I'd call anyone a liar who didn't admit to the pleasure of shedding.

Chuck was moving to the passenger side. "I'm going up on the minigun. I'd rather stand than sit." It was the first thing he'd said to me in a while.

Doug came round the other side. "Whole lotta nothing so far, dudes. When they do show up, make it plenty noisy, 'cause I don't wanna miss out on all the fun. I'm going to be deep in dreamland with visions of bikini bottoms and rip curls in ten. Later."

Mitch picked up his pack, but hesitated. "Ben, I wanted to tell you—it was one hundred percent you who figured out what was happening out there with those first shots. Everyone who was on a machine gun knows it, too. If I didn't step up hard enough to make that clear to everyone, I'm sorry. The Chief's coming from left field. I'm not talking behind his back, but he's just flat-out wrong. If it comes up again—"

"Mitch's right, dude," Dougie joined. "Sorry 'bout not having your back."

"Forget about it, man. There's too much happening to worry about piddly stuff."

I made it sound like I was blowing off the Chief's accusation I'd blown the shot and gotten the captain and Mike killed. It still stuck in my craw. Living in my head so much I think I've become a decent amateur psychologist. The Chief had wronged me, and kept wronging me. If you want to wrong someone, accuse them of something they didn't do. Paint them for having a view they don't hold. Incorrectly judge them. I know there's a bunch of fancy names for it. Attacking a straw man and all those logical fallacies. I learned about them in a lot of courses, O&I being one.

(What someone else got in college studying basket weaving on their way to unemployment, I got in a finishing school whose ultimate goal was to make me deadly. You can judge which teaches it better. I already know.)

I once read something like, "Resentment is the deadliest emotion. It's swallowing a poison, hoping it will harm your enemy." Okay, lest you think it was from a self-help book, I saw it in a meme. Anyway, just because I understood how harmful it was to hold on to my indignation at being treated unfairly by the Chief, it didn't mean I was good at letting it go. My point is—with a few words, they gave me the antidote to the poison I'd been swallowing.

And that's the amazing thing about being on a team. And no matter what else had happened, I was on a team. A real team. This was the proof.

"Thanks, brothers."

He and Dougie peeled off with Matt in the rear, head tilted back, lightly snoring. Everyone was feeling the letdown. Except me. I was refreshed and already thinking about my next view to a kill.

I'd brought my MK 22 and pulled a padded mat off the side of my day pack. My plan was to lay out on top of the GMV next to the M134. It'd be crowded, but like I've told you, behind my sniper rifle is where I preferred to see the world, especially a strange one. Chucky was standing up through the gunner's hatch and busying himself with the minigun. I gave him my favorite non sequitur.

"Groovy times."

"What that gun is to you, this is to me," he said somewhere between a whisper and theater conversation.

What I did with a single round from my weapon of choice, the minigun made happen at 3,000 rounds a minute. Pure Rube Goldberg magic, six barrels turning by electric motor, dragon fire if there ever was such a thing.

"One shot, one kill. Pfft. If you're a werewolf, I'm a dragon."

I'd let it slip—my imaginary avatar.

We were quiet for some time as we acclimated to the environment. I alternated between my NODs for a while, flipped them up and used the magnification behind the PVS-27 on my rifle to scan our sector, Chuck between his and a handheld thermal. It was more than just changing between devices—it was breaking up the mental grind that was observing. Watching. Processing. Interpreting. Mostly, waiting.

After an hour or so, I asked Chucky, "You wanna flake out for a while? I got this."

"Nah. I'm wired."

He felt like me. It'd be pointless to try to close my eyes—removing other stimuli would just be flipping the switch to the curio cabinet light, forcing me to examine each of the little figurines of the day's puzzles more closely. More silence passed. There were few noises to pay attention to. Most anywhere there'd be insects, animals, vegetation moving in the wind to catch your attention—something. Instead, there was a whole lot of nothing. And there could never be nothing. Not in a place where giant sword-wielding four-armed aliens wanted to slice you from stem to stern. If there was nothing to see, you weren't looking hard enough.

The guys had a tarp strung over the permanently open ramp of the C-17 far behind us, and very little light or noise escaped to even provide me a background to ignore, like Mom banging pans in the kitchen while I was trying to watch my show. I was droning, starting to fuzz out with the blandness of it all, when Chucky half startled me.

"You know, the Chief's a good guy."

I kept quiet. Soon enough, he continued.

"We were the pilot team for Venezuela two."

I knew that. Their team was the first on the ground. Clandestine. They were there for months building human networks, doing target analysis, and all the sneaky Pete stuff expected of a special team.

"Marky and the Chief were running the urban recovery. The Chilean embassy rescue that kicked off the invasion. We established the route in for the rescue team. Those two were traveling it one last time. The last eyes on the ground before the big show started. Got made by State Security. Chief made Marky drop him off, and while he stayed with the vehicle, Chief led the secret police down an alley on foot. Killed both of them by himself. With his knife. Silent. When he was done, he called Marky in, and they put the bodies in the van and cleaned the site. One of them was a woman."

I played the movie in my head to go with the scene. Where his script was lacking wordy detail, the picture he painted was nonetheless rich with color. He didn't say more. Until he did.

"The Bolivar Pride crowd were nasty. True believers. Real fanatics. Their secret police made anyone else's secret police look like nuns doling out charity to the downtrodden." The next pause was shorter. "Just remember, Mike picked the Chief. Same as he picked you. Same as all of us."

I tried to picture it again. The Chief going wet, as close as you can get, one on two. The integrity of the mission riding on him. Making the decision. Carrying out the act. Alone. How would I fare in the same situation? Enemy or no, would I kill a woman?

He took a swig from his canteen. "I don't know where we are. This Mars thing Karlo thinks is going on? No way. This is Earth. The hair-lips took over after the whole mutagen plague thing did its job. And Chief's the one to make 'em pay. For Mike, and the captain. For everything. I'll follow him all the way."

I was about to tell him I agreed when something caught my eye. Sweeping back across my sector was something new. A dark blob where I didn't remember seeing one earlier. It wasn't moving. Maybe it was only now visible as the starlight got even more spectacular as the night went on.

"I got something. Check it on thermal." I directed where I wanted him to look. "Need me to paint it?" I could hit it with my invisible laser as a reference he could see under his NODs, then he could check the same spot again under his thermal. Thermal saw differences in heat. It was the best tech to ID if something was living, and not just some green-to-black blob of a tumbleweed under night vision. You can't see lasers by thermal, so the process was a little cumbersome, switching between the two.

We had one set of magnified fusion binoculars that overlaid thermal on infrared. It would've let us see what was going on out there at the thousand-yard mark where the blob was, but I didn't have it. We could jump through time and print grenades from thin air with the same voodoo, but we didn't have a full complement of the latest, greatest night vision tech. Something about "cost."

"No. Don't," he said. "I got it. It's hot. There's something hot behind it, too. Moving."

I saw it. These weren't the rodents Mitch described earlier. Unless they were the size of the greenies, and I was certain Mitch would've mentioned that.

"I'm getting everyone up." I hit my PTT. "We've got movement." I gave a description, location, and range.

Marky-Mark came back. "Same here. Infiltrators checking over the kill zone."

The Stryker was positioned to watch over yesterday morning's battle. We'd swept the kill zone, collected weapons, and left the bodies. The weapons were piled up by the bird. They were unlike anything we'd seen before, but it was another mystery that had to stay on the back burner for daylight to return.

"What's the word, Chief? Light 'em up?" Mark's voice had a little lilt at the end, like talking to a puppy into it when it was time for walkies.

"Burn it all down. Weapons free."

I dropped off the side and came up behind the 240. I hit the aiming laser and let loose. The minigun flashed above me and became an artificial sun, one chainsaw burst at a time. *BRRRT. BRRRT. BRRRT.* Chuck ran his gun along the horizon, his green laser obscured during each burst before reappearing again. I did the same from my side, the *CHUG CHUG CHUG* of the 240 a musical section distinct from the 134.

I stood erect again and waited a second for the haze in my NODS to clear. To our right, the Stryker was laying down fire with the .50, the MK 19 lobbing 40mm HE, the *WHUMP WHUMP WHUMP* of its impacts blocked to my vision by the GMV. Another spread of grenades went out, then splashed in a different impact zone.

"Check fire," the Chief said. "What do we have?"

I scrambled back topside and got behind my MK 22. My heart pounded and my breath fogged the lens of my scope. I blew out through twisted lips and in a second it cleared.

"See anything, Ben?" Chucky asked.

"No. You?"

Chucky got on the radio. "Nothing moving over here, Chief."

"I want that other GMV rolled out. Light up the Hellfighters if you need them." The huge infrared lights on the big guns would blast invisible light into every dark nook and cranny out there. "If the enemy can see infrared, I don't care anymore. We're well past staying dark and avoiding active emissions. Anything pops up short of a white flag of surrender waving, use everything we've got and bring the pain to them."

"Roger, Chief," we all answered. No matter that some of his words to me were hurtful, the Chief was always well spoken. Like now. Clear, concise, educated. After what Chucky told me about my critic, I made the vow to double my efforts to prove myself to him.

Chief Bryant gave his last order of the night.

"One hundred percent security until after sunup. In the morning, we go hunting."

09

Karlo was staying behind to tend his patient, with Mitch and Doug to pull security close to our grounded bird. The rest of us saddled up for a vehicular patrol. I stuck my head in to check on Karlo as I grabbed an energy bar and more batteries for all my gizmos. I kept a little container in my ruck where I had 123s, double, and triple-As sorted into small sandwich bags, each clear packet a night's worth of juice for all my devices. I tossed two bags in my day pack. I was sure we'd be back well before dark, but I wouldn't be found wanting if we didn't.

"He come around yet?" I asked.

Our prisoner was supine, lashed to the litter hanging on the fuselage. Karlo looked the opposite of how I felt. He was clean-shaven and fresh, bright-eyed and bushy-tailed. I itched from dried sweat in all my creases and wished I had some coffee.

On cue, the stimulus of my voice the alarm, the greenie's eyes shot open and it lifted its head, the black irises cold and menacing.

"Easy there," Karlo soothed, his hands open. "You're okay. No one's going to hurt you."

The greenie's response? "Blicka blarg. Fuss." Whatever it said, it said weakly. It laid its head down, not testing its restraints. A deep exhale, its eyes closed, and it was out again.

"Pretty sure it understood you as much as we did it. Congrats, Karlo. You made first contact with an alien."

"Pretty sure the captain got the distinction of first, Hoss," Marky-Mark said behind me. He strode between us to look down at the bound patient. He was a modern knight, a one-man infantry squad, loaded and ready for war. "Colt goes down as the first to center punch a greenie. I got the record for the most one-day kills. Maybe I beat my own record today. Watch yourself, Karlo. It might have a set of those telescoping jaws that'll pop out and bite you if you get too close. Know what I mean?" He chuckled at his own reference.

Karlo didn't see the humor. "No. I checked its airway. It has a tongue. And teeth, not too different from a man's. And it is a man. Male, that is."

"Yikes, Karlo. You medics always get down to the nitty-gritty, don't you? What do you say, team daddy?" Mark said while still looking at the prisoner. "Ready to go find their nest and burn it down?"

It took me a split second to realize he was talking to me.

"Be right there."

"And maybe print us up some more fifty while we're gone," Marky said over his shoulder. "I got a feeling I'm coming back light today."

I let Mark get out of earshot before I spoke. "Marky thinks these things are mutated people."

Karlo sighed. "I don't know that he's wrong. I do know we're not on Earth."

I was divided on the issue. I'd been the first to follow his logic trail. Karlo's case that we were on Mars was well laid out, like everything he ever said. It was still too fantastic.

"How can that be?"

He checked one of the dressings on the thing's abdomen. "Time travel's witchcraft. I asked the Caltech guys about it while they were familiarizing us with Baby Blue. Three dimensional space plus a fourth dimension of time—it's all conceptual. And like a lot of engineering based on theoretical mathematical constructs—" He saw me glazing over. "It's just that, most people don't even know how a magnetron works, much less a refrigerator."

He had me.

"What's a magnetron?"

Karlo was always patient as a nursery school teacher. His sigh proved he was tired, too.

"It's what makes a microwave heat your coffee."

"Oh." I felt stupid.

"Sorry, Ben. My point is, physicists try to understand the nature of what makes the universe tick. Engineers make the physical universe *do* work. And sometimes we don't know why something works. We just know it does.

"What makes that work," he thumbed at Baby Blue, "the longhairs were adamant they didn't fully understand. They just took the tech the physicists adapted and made it do something useful. When I asked them about the slipstream, since it uses some of the same physics, they rolled their eyes. Some of them looked downright scared.

"I pressed them about it. They doubted the ability of the slipstream team to accurately predict the when and where any of us would end up on the other side of the temporal portal. What physicists call success, an engineer would call a crapshoot."

"Did you say anything to Mike or the captain about it?"

My question made him slump with fatigue.

"Yes."

"And?"

A gray cloud appeared over him. "I told them both what the gearheads told me. They asked me to keep it to myself. And I agreed. What choice did Mike and the captain have? What choice did we have? I know we like to think of ourselves as different, smarter, but we're just soldiers, too. The guys in the landing craft ready to hit Omaha Beach knew the odds were bad. And off they went. Our D-Day was the same. What could I have done differently, Ben?"

I hadn't meant it as an accusation.

"Sorry, Karlo. We all depend on you for a lot, but I didn't mean to sound like I thought you should've done something to prevent this. Not what I meant at all."

Chief Bryant's voice came from down the cargo bay. "Colt. Let's get a move on."

"Moving," I hollered.

Karlo laid a hand on my shoulder before I could turn away. "Ben, there's something else."

"What?"

"I'll say it again. I know this isn't Earth. Period. I've proved it to my own satisfaction. But why we're breathing? I've got two theories. One, the slipstream dropped us across a time period so fantastically huge that Mars grew an atmosphere. The other—" He looked scared to say. "We're in a different universe all together." His brow furrowed with angst.

Both theories had the opposite effect on me. I burst out laughing. Not a sardonic or ironic laugh. But a snorting, full belly laugh.

"Glad I was able to cheer you up, Top." Now he smiled, too.

"Knock it, off."

Top was what you called the team sergeant. Not me.

"You're the team sergeant now. So, anything I think's important, I'm telling you first."

"Thanks, Karlo. We'll send postcards."

"See that you do."

I tightened my M4 to my chest, shouldered my pack, and grabbed my MK 22 in its soft case and took off. I thought about Karlo's theories. Were we on a future terraformed Mars? Would we find some kind of NASA remnants somewhere? Or had we gone through the looking glass to another dimension? Either way, his conjectures—as wild as they were—were no wilder than what was slapping us in the face every time we turned around.

What had made me laugh was thinking about an old cartoon my dad had stuck to the refrigerator with fruit magnets. It was two guys in a fishing boat with lines in the water. On the horizon was a huge mushroom cloud. Dad had grown up when the fear of a nuclear war destroying the world was a thing. The cartoon summed up what he thought about the possibility.

The caption was: "I'll tell you what this means, Norm. It means no size restriction and screw the limit."

If what Karlo thought had happened to us really happened, then maybe our mission didn't matter anymore, and we might as well find a fishing hole.

✢ ✢ ✢

Marky and the Chief were having a close talk that stopped abruptly as I came down the ramp. "If you're ready," the Chief said abrasively. I remembered my personal vow to squelch any sense of indignation and work to keep winning him over. I took a cleansing breath.

"Set, Chief."

He gave a quick op order, and we were off. Conspicuously absent in his brief, a review of the chain of command. Maybe he felt it went without saying. Maybe not. He hadn't recognized me as team sergeant, which, if we had to split up, would make me in charge of one of the elements. I let it go, but when I thought about him and Marky spending so much one-on-one time together, and the close confab they'd just had, it made me uneasy.

"Mount up," Chief Bryant said, and we were rolling.

First, we would check yesterday's kill zone and then where Chucky and I had concentrated fire. Then we'd start our reconnaissance of the general area, sweeping out in successively farther distances, trying to pick up sign of where our attackers were coming from, all the while ready to respond to an ambush.

Dave drove and I let Chucky take the M134 again. Chief rode with Matt and Marky in the Stryker. Mark let it be known he wasn't going to give up the gunner station.

"If anyone were better than me, I'd switch off with you. But you ain't. So, the king keeps his throne."

We tried for a staggered column as we patrolled, but the terrain channeled us into a single file in some places. The ground was decently hard, but it was best for the GMVs to test the path before rolling the Stryker in. If we stuck it, there was no recovery vehicle to tow it out. How long would it take Baby Blue to print us a new one? A looong time.

A mounted patrol is not so very different from one on foot. Posting far side security at danger areas, selecting rally points, bounding to expected contact, coming on line to fire. It's all pretty common sense stuff. With two vehicles, it was simpler than moving a full-sized mechanized unit, but also left us wanting.

The third vehicle was an important part of our maneuver force. The other GMV was needed to protect our command post and Baby Blue, which Karlo reported was in fact cranking out more fifty-cal at Marky's request.

"First rounds are coming off the assembly line," Karlo confirmed. "Or I should say the dispenser, since Baby Blue doesn't assemble anything, it creates it whole."

"Keep it coming, Karlo," Marky answered. "No matter how much you make, I want more."

"Good commo check," Dave replied as he drove. "Mitch, let's keep to a radio check every fifteen."

"Copy," Mitch answered.

"Coming up to the kill zone," Matt said.

The Chief directed us. "Chucky and Mark stay on the guns. Rest of us, dismount."

We spread out on line, taking a cautious walk through the carnage left by two fights on the same soil. Dave lifted his shemagh over his nose. "Whew. Smells like somebody died around here. Especially those dino-horses."

Matt raised a fist. "Here's a fresh one."

"How can you tell?" Chief asked. He was close to me on the far left flank of the battle remains.

"We cleaned this site yesterday. This one's got a rifle. That plate armor the greenies wear? Not this guy. He's in some kind of ghillie." A ghillie was a bulky camouflage suit used for stalking and stealth, meant to blend in with the environment. With good camo and trained movement techniques, it was possible to stalk slowly and undetected into an area of enemy observation to gather intelligence or deliver deadly sniper fire. "Nothing fancy. It's just a big poncho with a hood. These guys learned it wasn't in their best interests to pull a cavalry charge on us and went all sneaky Pete."

"It was recon for a larger force in wait," I said.

"Ditto," Marky said from in the Stryker. "Colt's right. I bet we're being watched right now."

Dave was farthest out on foot. "Got more of them over here. The 40mm made a mess of things. What's the math on this? Based on the number of arms, if I divide by four, it's a half dozen more."

I arrived with the Chief to examine what Matt had found.

"That's too many for a recon," I said. "Too many to keep the risk of compromise at a minimum. They were building up an attacking force."

"They look like what we chewed up last night, Ben?" Chucky asked.

"Mos' def."

Chief had heard enough. "Back to the vehicles, men. Let's check Ben and Chuck's sector from last night, then we'll push out our perimeter sweeps and make sure we don't have any still out there, waiting to try again tonight."

I've spent a great deal of my life working in the dark. When normal people are heading for their beds, I'm just starting work. By my math, I have the hours adding up to a solid year or more under night vision. Which is to say, day and night are pretty much the same to me. My brain had long ago erased any of the misperceptions you feel early on between night and day. But now as we approached the spot where last night Chuck and I had hammered the greenies, I felt the déjà vu of a newbie return.

Last night, it had seemed like Chuck and I were pulling a *Beau Geste*—miles away from the lone desert fort and on our own. I felt foolish as we pulled around the nose of the C-17 and a few hundred meters away rolled over where we'd posted only a few hours before. "Head over there, Dave." I pointed. On the far horizon was a pair of sharp peaks I remembered as a landmark during the fight.

"They must not've been too sneaky," Dave said. "You spotted them a long way out. A good five hundred meters."

I tried to analyze what this told me about our enemy. It was dangerous to underestimate their abilities. Yes, we'd detected and repelled their attack easily. They rode animals for transport. They wore metal armor, carried swords, but also had weapons of advanced technology. We tested one, Marky insisting he be the one to try one of the captured rifles. It was crude, with rudimentary sights, but the sizzle and smell of ozone that followed the flash of the white energy blast was just one more incongruity too strange to reconcile.

"I'd say they've learned not to underestimate us, at least. Stop here," I told him as we neared where we'd halted the enemy advance. We repeated the dismounted search and farther out from where Chuck and I had first spotted the creepers were more bodies, properly aerated by our lethal gardening.

Matt was crouched, fixated on the ground. He stood, took cautious steps from side to side, his eyes moving near to far and back again. "There are trails in, and trails leaving," Matt said, confidently. "We didn't get them all." Matt was our tracker. He'd been to all the schools. Anytime he wasn't working, he was in the woods or the swamps of Florida, alone with nature. It was his thing.

"But if we drive over everything, I may lose all the good sign."

"What do you need?" I asked.

"Time on the ground."

"Chief, I'll stay on foot with Matt while he works."

Chief Bryant came back. "Don't make it a career, guys. Find us a general direction where their objective rally point most likely was. We need to secure as much of this ground as we can during daylight."

The infiltrators who'd tried to get the drop on us last night had staged from somewhere before making their stalk to spy on us. If they'd come on the same huge beasts as their buddies, they couldn't have ridden to within several klicks without us having detected them.

"I'll keep eyes out, Matt. Go to work."

"Thanks."

He went back into his trance, taking a careful assessment of the ground ahead before moving. At first, he moved slowly, repeating the same high/low, side-to-side assessment before taking a few steps. This repeated for another hundred meters, and I stayed quiet, not wanting to disturb his concentration, though I was curious about his process. He pointed.

"Look, Ben. That's where they decided it was time to haul ass out of the hate zone we laid on them."

He made a bound and I followed. If the atmosphere was so thin it wouldn't keep an aircraft up, surely my lungs would tell me they were starving for O-two. But the burn in my lungs I thought would come, didn't.

Matt took another long jump and stopped. Now he smiled.

"Three pairs of tracks. Running. Sticking to the low ground, but definitely heading there." He pointed to a rise a few klicks away. "See, you don't have to follow a track step by step, sign by sign. If you know the terrain or have a map, it makes tracking pretty easy. An enemy will channel themselves based on the terrain. When you're in pursuit, you can predict where your quarry is likely going. River fords, tight bends over danger areas like roads. You just think like they would. We don't have a map, but know our enemy travels on those huge critters. That rise is the only terrain for miles they could've hidden behind. And I bet there's a canyon or arroyo on the other side. We can make a straight shot for it."

He choked. "My five-year-old could follow this. I was teaching him. He loved the woods, Ben. Just like me."

Matt got a faraway look, and I knew he was lost with thoughts of his family.

"He loved the stars, too. I put posters of the planets all over his room. And a night sky on his ceiling."

I thought tears would fall when he broke out of his reverie and chuckled.

"Did I ever tell you how I got to be in the Army?"

It was the most Matt had ever said to me. Maybe it wasn't the best time or place to get to know him better, but I could tell he had some purpose in mind. I let him continue.

"I always wanted to be an astronaut. Or do something with space."

He didn't take my look of surprise as an insult. I thought of him as the quintessential mountain man. He was from Montana. His wife was from Iowa farm stock. They were a cute couple and didn't seem to fit into the beach vibe that most everyone adopted being on the Gulf coast.

"I know. It's okay. I'm not the knuckle dragger I play most of the time. But you're a weapons man, too. You know how it is."

It was true. On a team, the weapons specialists did enjoy a reputation, mostly self-perpetuated, for being the least intellectual of those in SF. It wasn't true.

"But it's easy to follow Marky-Mark's lead."

His senior wasn't acting, though, of that I was sure.

"I had a trap line as a kid and used the money I made to buy a telescope, that's how crazy I was about space. I kept saving and when everyone else was on their way to the oilfields or trying to rodeo, I left for college. I tried to be an engineer, like Karlo is. Well, maybe not like Karlo. It was a struggle for me. Anyway, it was getting clearer and clearer that I wasn't cut out for NASA. But then I thought, how about the Space Force?"

Space Force was a long way from the Army. I was curious how we would weave the tale to its conclusion, explaining how he got to SF.

"Long story short, the recruiters were all in the same building in Helena. I saw a poster about SF. You know, the one with the team under canopy, doing a HAHO?"

High Altitude, High Opening was a freefall insertion method where you jumped so high, you had to use supplemental oxygen, then immediately opened your chute and glided stealthily for miles under canopy to land silently and undetected behind enemy lines.

"I can relate."

"When I saw that, all of a sudden I forgot about satellites and rockets."

But like me, Matt had come to SF by the traditional route, after his first hitch.

"Going to 75th was about the farthest you could get from Space Force," I said, knowing Matt had been a Ranger before coming to Special Forces.

"True. But in the back of my mind, I always thought that if we started doing the space thing for real, like real military ops in space, an SF scuba team would be the naturals for it."

"Not the SEALs?"

"Well, them too."

The Chief's voice interrupted. "What'd you get for us, Matt? Daylight's burning."

Matt took a deep breath. "I have a good bearing on what was most likely their staging point. It's a few klicks ahead. Somewhere they could assemble below our line of sight."

"Roger. You two stay put. We're moving to you."

I had my binos out and scanned the route ahead.

Matt hurriedly said, "The reason I was telling you all this, Ben. Marky and I have been talking. I know what he thinks. But I know Karlo is right. That ginormous canyon we barely flew out of? That's the Valles Marineris. I've shown those images to my boy a thousand times. Watched the simulated flights on YouTube. It was one of his favorites. There's only one place like that. We are on Mars."

Just then the vehicles pulled up. Matt's face changed. For a few minutes, he'd been a man seeking my understanding, almost pleading for me to follow his train of thought, to convince me with his conviction that Karlo was right. Now he was grim again. Moving to the Stryker and ready to go back to war.

Before he got out of earshot, I had to ask him something. I might be of above average intelligence, but there was nothing in my experience that so far had let me fill in any of the blanks on my questionnaire.

"So how did we end up here, Matt? How are we even alive?"

Matt shot around. "I don't know, Ben. But it doesn't matter. My family's gone. Marky's no Karlo. Or Chief. But he's right, you know? These freak shows know who's responsible. And we need to burn them all down."

✠ ✠ ✠

I took the front seat next to Dave.

"What was that about, brah? You piss Matt off or something?"

"He's remembering he's got a family somewhere. And that we're supposed to be saving them."

We stuck to the low ground. The terrain was rolling, climbing, but still flat enough to qualify as open all the way to the rise. I kept waiting for white ray gun blasts to suddenly ambush us. The sun was halfway above the horizon, reminding me again of a winter season where the sun never peaked directly overhead. The mountain peaks in the distance never drew any closer.

Dave was trying to raise Mitch back at the C-17 as we rolled. "Chief, we're out of comm range with the CP already."

We couldn't be more than ten straight-line klicks away from where the rest of the team waited. If I looked hard, I could still see the reflection and mirage from the bird far behind us.

"I've raised the GMV antenna, switched to AM transmission, I've got nothing. Last trick I've got is to string a hundred-foot longwire."

"Don't bother," Chief replied. "We'll deal with it later. Let's keep moving."

I told Dave about my conversation with Matt.

"Karlo got it right, brah," Dave said to me alone. "Know how I know this isn't Earth? I can make commo from anywhere. I can't raise Mitch from a rock's throw away. This is grade-A messed up."

I laughed. "You are the quintessential commo man, Dave. Low gravity, aliens, ray guns… none of that's important evidence. But test the ionosphere and prove there's not enough for you to bounce a radio wave off, and you're convinced we're on Mars."

"It is what it is. And no magnetic bearing for a compass, don't forget that."

"Hold up, Dave," Matt said from behind us. "I can see from back here. There's multiple trails heading low around this rise. There's an arroyo or a small canyon on the other side. What do you think, Chief? Let me scout this."

"Enough pussyfooting around," Chief Bryant fired back. "Recon by occupation. Ben, you guys go high. We're heading low to block the mouth of whatever's on the other side."

Marky-Mark gave a whoop. "Hell yeah, boss. Good call. I'm ready."

"Me, too," Chucky said, standing right behind me on the minigun.

There was a time to discuss alternatives, and there was a time for sudden explosive force. Whether this was one of those times or not, the wheels were in motion, so to speak.

"Punch it, Dave."

After a couple of hours of crawling at a snail's pace, the slight acceleration pushed me back into my seat and jolted away the drowsiness hanging over me. We took off uphill.

Chucky had the best view from up top and cheered Dave's driving like a dad at his kid's soccer game. "Keep on it, Dave. Almost there."

A sharp drop off revealed a flat basin below. Dave braked suddenly and we slid toward the edge. I was moving as he did, pouring out to get directly behind the 240, when I saw it, too. Instead of greenies and dino-horses, a fountain sat below us, bubbling water into a wide stone pool.

10

We stayed up top as the Chief, Matt, and Marky roamed below.

"This is where they staged," Matt assured us. "There's sign of their mounts everywhere, and it's all fresh."

"What's all this? Some kind of ruins?" Marky said on comms.

I stole a glance at Dave whose eyebrows were raised in interest. The fountain alone was evidence of something substantial. Ruins? I wanted to know more.

"It leads back under the overhang. Keep an eye on it," Chief said. "Matt, with me."

I ached to see what they were seeing, but kept covering their six o'clock from above. It didn't take a trained man tracker—or eight-legged horse tracker—to figure out that the signs on the basin floor were fresh. Around the fountain were deep gouges left by so many huge animals. There was nothing substantial that could hide even one of the greenies, so it was time to look for work. I mounted my spotting scope on the open door and began dissecting the specimen of new ground beyond. It was the highest ground we'd yet occupied and for the first time, I held the kind of commanding view I liked best as a sniper. I was suddenly reminded of a buzzed haircut private I once knew and the mystery of his many tailored suits.

He'd been one of my first squad mates as a kid back in Division. Deshawn was a peacock. Most privates spend their paychecks on a high interest car loan, booze, a girl, or all of the above. This guy spent it on clothes. Whenever he was out of uniform, he looked like a cover for *GQ*. Like he was trying to imitate a celebrity on one of those award shows. While most of us when out of uniform were content in jeans and T-shirts, Deshawn lived waiting to be discovered by a casting agent, the star of his own movie wherever he went.

Whenever someone made fun of him overdressing for a night on the town at Fayetteville's finest establishment, the Flaming Mug, he always said the same thing: "You see the world, the world sees you."

I made sure the honeycomb anti-glare filter was on the objective lens. Tracks led off through dips between the hills before I lost them. I searched farther and farther away, expecting to see a swaying line of dino-horses and green riders cantering off in a single file, but was disappointed. Instead, I became fixated by the farthest things on the skyline.

Ever been fooled by the kind of clouds so low in the sky they shot up to look like mountains in the distance? The ones that made you momentarily question your reality? That made a place as flat as Florida a fantasy landscape from some kind of Frazetta painting? Just like that, were the tallest mountains I'd ever imagined. But they were real.

Below them, I focused on the spot I'd seen twice. Once from the C-17 as we crashed, and the other captured by the pathetic hop of our quadricopter drone. The tiny blotch of pale color and shapes that screamed civilization.

"YOU! DON'T MOVE! HANDS UP!"

Someone had yelled it. Matt. The commands spilling up to us from below and over the lip to where we stared at desert and mystery.

"Punch it, Dave," I said as I piled back in. "We're rolling on your six," I said, hitting my PTT.

"Let's rock," Chuck hollered. "Time to meet the neighbors."

We barreled into the basin and around the Stryker and stopped on the far side of the surreal fountain, bubbling from its center and sending ripples out in circles, tiny swells lapping at the sides. Our three teammates were aimed in on a deep opening cut into the canyon wall below where we'd been perched a moment before. Ornate shapes and symbols were carved out of the rock. A pair of strange animal figures like elephants on their hind legs, too many of them, holding aloft a craggy roof with their stubby flat skulls and more limbs, a tunnel leading into the darkness.

"What do you have?" I said loud enough for them to hear me over their chatter as Dave and I moved on line with them. Chuck remained on the minigun, ready to rain minigun pain over our heads.

Matt was keyed up, his voice closer an alto I was unused to hearing. "I didn't imagine it, Chief. It was that Monty Python guy. The one at that always starts the show."

"Make some sense, son," Marky growled.

"That hermit guy. With the long white beard. Scrawny Gandalf in a toga."

"You saw a human?" I asked.

"Sure as hell did," Matt answered. "He popped out, saw me, and took off back there."

"Anyone else see it?" Dave asked.

"No," the Chief said. "YOU IN THE CAVE. COME OUT WITH YOUR HANDS UP."

I moved nearer to the Chief, M4 up, and hit my white light. Useless. I was adding clean water to muddy water and getting the same muddy water, penetrating no farther into the depths beyond the arch formed by the strange animal statues. You don't know unless you try.

"Grab a bang off my back, Chief." I had a nine-banger on my back. I'd filled the pouch before we left this morning, cursing my decision as we rode, the flash bang causing me to sit cocked to one side in the already uncomfortable seat.

"Bang out." Chief Bryant gave an overhand pitch, sending the flash bang on a long arcing sail into the deep dark. The bang ignited in successive loud explosions, magnesium fireworks flashing in strobe mode with them.

We were moving. Gliding forward, four abreast into the maw of the rock face, to find—an empty hole.

"I swear to God, there was an old man here," Matt blurted. "He strolled out with a hand raised, saw the SWAT team was here, and took off. It was like he was about to invite us in for tea and crumpets, realized we weren't family, and freaked."

The tunnel made a slight left-hand curve and ended abruptly in a stone altar. More of the strange carvings and glyphs lined the interior. We moved in pairs and searched.

"I saw what I saw," Matt insisted as he took a hand and pushed against hard rock. "I swear."

Marky harrumphed. "It's okay, junior. You're ragged. We all are. In Ranger school, I once tried to stick a rock into a pine tree. I thought I was putting a quarter into a soda machine."

"You didn't see him, Marky?" Matt implored.

"No, Matt."

I aimed my weapon down and swept side to side, looking for footprints as my light splashed wide over the rocky surface. It was rough, but level. There was no sign of foot or boot print.

"Check this out," Dave said from the dark. I let my rifle hang with the light flooding our legs and moved to where he had a handheld light painting the walls. Tiny alcoves were cut into the surface here, each filled with a tiny figurine. I leaned in with Dave to get a closer look. A four-armed greenie, with the head and beak of a bird, sat cross-legged. Dave reached for it.

"Don't," I said reflexively, not even sure why.

"Whaa?" He hesitated.

"Hmm. Nothing, I guess."

Dave grabbed it, turned it side to side, and tucked it in his cargo pocket.

"You're sure, Matt?" the Chief was asking Matt again.

"Positive," Matt said with a mix of anger and frustration.

"What do we do, boss?" Marky prompted.

Chucky commed from outside. "I've got charges. We can make sure there's no place to hide."

The Chief seemed to consider it.

"I don't think so, Chief," I cut anyone else off before they could give an opinion. "We don't know what we're dealing with here. If Matt did see someone, it's the first person we've found. Not a good precedent for a meet and greet. I'd hate to make new enemies before we need to."

"I saw him, alright," Matt reiterated.

"Make another secondary," the Chief said.

I pulled the small tablet from its folded position on my chest. The GPS function was useless, but it had a camera. I took pictures and some video we could examine later. I scanned over more of the carved figures. More greenies morphed with animal shapes. I paused to hover over a change in the theme they all seemed to follow. This one was a human. Feminine in every way the artist could capture, arms spread wide like a mother beckoning children to receive her warmth and protection.

"Anything?" the Chief asked after several minutes.

We all stayed silent.

"We leave it for now." Without acknowledging my opinion, he echoed what I'd said earlier. "Best not to make enemies where we don't have them. We've done what we came to do. It was a valuable first patrol. RTB, team."

I took more images of the exterior and the fountain as I made my way to the GMV.

The Chief spoke over the team channel. "Stryker will lead heading back. Colt, take trail and make sure no one's following us home. Stay in comms range."

"Roger."

I directed Dave to take us back up to the top of the ridge and waited while the rumble of the Stryker's engine faded as it lumbered back the way we'd come. I got my spotting scope out again and let the image settle on the city far away.

"How far you figure that is, brah?"

"My scale is way off, man," I replied. "It could be a hundred klicks. More."

"Tomorrow Mitch and I can set up a repeater here. It'll give us some line of sight for FM at least. It'll be better than what we have now, anyway."

"Hmm."

A repeater was a good idea. If we were going to remain in this location. As I searched the skies over the city for some indication of life, I wondered if staying here was the right move.

"Hey, why'd you spaz when I wanted to pick up the statue?" Dave held the small carved figurine, turning it in his hand. "You think it was going to release some kind of booby trap or something, Doctor Jones?"

I went back to my spotting scope. Nothing moved that I could see. As far as the desert revealed, we were the only animate things on this barren world. Yet we knew that not to be true. The city had to be our destination if we were to do anything other than wait for this world to reveal itself to us on its own terms.

"Remember that *Brady Bunch*? The one when the family goes to Hawaii and the kids pick up that statue and get cursed? You of all people should know better."

He gave the groan of all groans. "Stupid haole."

✢ ✢ ✢

We gathered outside and gave the rest of the team the rundown on what they'd missed.

"Dude, you saw a human? Like a real-life person, not a hair-lip or some other biped alien?" Dougie was still convinced about Area 51 ETs.

Matt frowned as Marky answered for him. "Thinks he did."

I pushed the video and pics to a laptop and narrated while the others crowded around the screen.

The Chief continued. "We patrolled out almost ten klicks, and that's all we found. We can't call the AO secure, but we can drop to fifty percent security tonight."

The sun was getting low, and it would be time to get back on the perimeter.

Mitch straightened up and looked at me. "What's next then, Top?"

I saw the Chief bridle, but went ahead and answered.

"We can't stay here."

The Chief snorted. "Hold on there, Colt. You're getting a little ahead of yourself."

"We can't stay here," I said again. "Not long term, Chief."

I'd run the options over and over again as we patrolled back to the C-17. Yes, I'd wanted to pull the Chief aside and have a strategy meeting, but he'd deliberately dodged my previous attempts to have a sit down. So far, he hadn't sought collaboration with the team, much less me. Yes, it was an extreme situation, but now that we had a semblance of security, it was time to utilize all our resources. And the collective brains of an A-Team are its greatest strength.

An A-Team is a different kind of military organization. The mission is the mission. But how that's accomplished is drastically different with us than most anywhere in the entire military. Someone once said that what's wrong with SF is that same stuff that's wrong with the whole Army. But what's right with SF, the Army couldn't begin to comprehend. We allow the best ideas to float to the top. The leadership solicits those ideas. Demands them. Prizes them. Being a team leader is supposed to be one of the easiest jobs in the Army—because the NCOs on an A-Team are the most proficient at their tasks of any individuals on the planet.

The operators on an A-Team are experts in their fields. When there are problems to be solved, those experts work the problem like a blue-ribbon panel. They determine a course of action. They implement it. Whether it's ambushing a column of enemy tanks while leading stick-wielding savages, or delivering a nuclear bomb behind enemy lines, it's done with input from everyone on the team. It's not a top-down hierarchy.

If I was the team sergeant, then it was time for me to exercise my role and start setting the tone for how the team was run. As Mike had done. With the captain gone, the Chief was undeniably the team lead. But however he felt about me, I wasn't going to let it change how this A-Team would be run—as much as he seemed to be trying to run things by himself.

My go along, get along time was coming to a close.

I folded my arms across my chest. "Our security situation here is untenable."

"I agree." It was Karlo.

Chief had been about to silence me, but he took a breath and closed his mouth. Even the Chief respected him. Karlo to the rescue. Chief gestured me to go ahead.

"Say your piece."

I'd worked out the problem and a bare bones course of action. "Staying here's not an option. Leaving Baby Blue is not an option. Dividing our force is not an option. We have to move—lock, stock, and barrel—and make for the city."

If we'd been under a roof, it would've come off.

"Move on an enemy stronghold?" Marky yelled, rolling his eyes.

"What do you mean, we're not secure here? We haven't even begun to build a camp," Chucky added.

There were lots of grumbles, save Dave—who was a study in still life—and Karlo who, unbeknownst to me, had been working the problem as I had.

"Ben's got the rudiments right, guys. Here's why."

Everyone quieted to let our one-man science team make his case.

"I'm sure Chuck and Dougie can design us a defendable camp. Of course you can," he said, giving the engineers their props. "We can print HESCOs and spend months filling them."

The wire mesh fortifications made to hold sand that would become the walls of a perimeter fortification weren't the issue. He was right that without front-end loaders, we'd wear ourselves down with labor to fill them.

"And if we do, what then? We can use Baby Blue for perishables sustainment. Maybe the water source you found is useable. Still, it'll be a bleak, bare-bones survival for us here in the desert."

Chucky came back. "But it is defendable. It's not high ground, but we do have huge kill zones around us. We can put the drones out as ground surveillance to feed us visuals for early warning along the likely routes in."

"True," I admitted. "And it's a good short-term bolster to our security. I'll get to work on it, ASAP. Go ahead, Karlo. Continue."

"So, we build an A-camp around the wreck and Baby Blue. And then what? We sit tight and wait for more of the local residents to wander into our AO? We make some long-range recons to find if there's something better? The problem is that while we're spending the time making this location defendable, Baby Blue may not be the infinite resource we hope it is. It's working now. If it goes down for any reason, I have doubts I can repair it."

Chief's eyebrows shot up. "What do you mean?"

The rest of the team stopped their mumbles.

Karlo sighed. "The plan for our reappearance into the future was to link the joint capabilities of all Baby Blues so we'd be able to build back the necessary tech to restart society. That plan included the necessity that all the super brains who built Baby Blues would be with us. Those engineers were spread out amongst the other sticks that took off with us from Area 51—and there weren't a ton of them to begin with. I got the quickie immersion in how to run Baby Blue and troubleshoot some of its idiosyncrasies. But I'm not confident that I can fix any major malfunction. Which means if our strategic planning is in any way based on my ability to keep Baby Blue running indefinitely—I'm saying that I'm pretty sure I cannot."

My stomach seized. All of a sudden, the consolation prize we'd taken by theft of the Guests' intellectual property, an honest-to-goodness cornucopia better than a Star Trek replicator—wasn't so consoling.

We were on a world we still knew little about. One that so far had been purely hostile. I'd already come to the same conclusion about Baby Blue, but hearing Karlo voice my fears was the bad news I hoped wouldn't be confirmed by our expert. I desperately wanted him to tell me that Baby Blue was a rock-solid 1950s refrigerator that would keep running forever. My team of hard-core killers looked like the kid whose folks forgot and left him home alone for Christmas vacation. Everyone else seemed to understand my doubts about our odds of survival in the long term here in the literal middle of nowhere and nothing, without a 7-11 in sight.

Karlo concluded. "Which means we're going to have to find help."

11

"Make friends with the greenies?" Mitch asked.

"Or find someone else to buddy up with," Dougie said. "If there is such a thing."

They were getting it. I spread my palms. "That's how I see it."

"Okay, Colt," the Chief continued. "What's your suggestion for a COA?"

"Our best course of action is to pack up, take Baby Blue with us, and make for greener pastures."

Chucky tilted his head. "Can Baby Blue be moved?"

Karlo's pensiveness held us silent. "Baby Blue eventually had to be de-planed. The library holds the plans for a towable flatbed. I've been doing the math. It'll take at least a week of 24-7 printing to make the components and assemble, roller it up with come-alongs, a GMV, and a lot of muscle. But it can be done."

"We can do it, dude," Dougie said, nodding to Chuck for agreement, who seemed unsure.

"It's pretty fragile, isn't it, Karlo? Can it tolerate being hauled?"

"It's in a hardened and cushioned housing. It survived the impact of the crash. I think it can handle a ride over hill and dale."

"Or it stays here where we know it's working and don't chance it," Marky said. "We need it to keep cranking out ammo. Everything else we can improvise."

"Leaving it behind isn't an option," I stated flatly. "Say we do find other sticks who've made it here like we did. We still have a mission, and Baby Blue is part of it. And if not, we need it for our sustainment. We could leave a split team to guard it while another team goes on a recon, but we're already too small to mount a decisive defense. A few of us to guard it, separated by a great distance from help if it's attacked, doesn't seem sound. Same with leaving it or caching it—we'll most likely only come back to find it destroyed or gone."

"Agreed," the Chief allowed, for the first time admitting that he was seeing things as I did. "But taking it overland, we're potentially exposing it to kinetic damage. We get fired on, it's going to come out of a firefight as useless as a dead houseplant."

"Can you print us some armor for that carriage?" Marky asked.

Karlo nodded. "Ceramic plating should do as well against the weapons we've encountered as it would against bullets. We can do some testing."

"Can do," Matt volunteered for the task.

"So, we just pack up, and go for a caravan?" Mitch asked the group. "We round up the wagon train and head for parts unknown?"

I shrugged. "I've worked this a few ways. We can keep working up a better plan while we get things in motion, but eventually, that's what's got to happen. Chief?"

I turned the attention back to him. I'd done my job as team sergeant. I'd gotten the crew to bail out all the rain, and the ship was righted, ready to steer the course our captain set for us.

"Chuck, Doug—pitch in with Karlo and start the work to get Baby Blue mobile. Colt, Marky, let's get a security and work plan set."

The stars were coming out and the last rays over the red landscape were fading.

I passed Dave as I moved to where the Chief and Marky-Mark were already in conference. "You've been pretty quiet, Davey-Dave. Nothing to add?"

"Remember what Mike told me to do—follow Karlo's example? When you've got nothing smart to say, don't confirm it by opening your mouth. I'm going to run a check on the repeaters. We've only got two, and it doesn't sound like we've got space in the schedule to make any more in the immediate. I doubt we can get a forty-klick coverage range out of them. C'mon, Mitch." The two trod off up the ramp, lost in common-man lingo I wasn't privy to understanding.

I'd worked until I finally allowed myself a whole hour's sleep and an MRE. I toyed with a tripod, makeshift lashing one of the drones to it with 5-50 cord. In the right spot, it should be high enough off the ground to give us the ability to use the cameras for surveillance. The engineers had power strips connected in series to a generator, and we had every rechargeable device plugged in, looking like a fire marshal's wet dream of safety violations.

I passed out on the deck with my head propped on my day pack until my watch buzzed me awake thirty seconds after I'd closed my eyes. "Our turn on the perimeter. Let's roll." I pulled Doug to his feet from his relatively dark spot in the bay, sprawled on what looked like a heavenly row of soft jump seats.

"Movin', Ben. I'm movin'. I got cheated, dude. No bikinis or surf that movie time."

I drove us to the Stryker, positioned where it had been the night before. Chief and Marky met us as we pulled up.

"Go on ahead, Doug," Chief said to him as he and Marky drew close to me. "Colt'll be right behind you."

"Good to go," he said a little less drowsily than before. He slugged a tall can of energy drink on the ride over and belched loudly as he crushed the can into the sand with his foot. "I don't think we have to worry about sterilizing the area. I'll hop on the gunner station, Top."

"Sure, Dougie," I said. The vibe coming off the Chief and Marky told me something was up. "Anything to report?" I asked to get the ball rolling.

"I'll just come out and say it, Colt." Chief Bryant's smirk I could see in the dark. "You're not team sergeant. Mark is."

"Huh?" I don't know what I was expecting, but it wasn't that.

Mark had his hand on the pistol riding on his hip. It wasn't uncommon for any of us to rest a hand there. It was a kind of a check, unconsciously making sure it hadn't fallen out. The way Marky stood made me sense it wasn't that.

"It's like this. I should've nipped it in the bud earlier. I didn't. My fault. But now it's time to set things straight."

I was fully awake now, not sure what was coming next. "Okay, Chief. Let's hear it."

"Marky's senior to you. He has more time in grade. He'd have had O&I and senior leader if the op tempo hadn't been what it was, even before we got spun up for this. You getting the early shot at those, well, it was a gift to you. You understand that, right? You didn't have the team time you should've had before getting the keys to the kingdom."

"Okay," I was too numb from the shock to light the fire I should be feeling right now.

"You're doing a decent job, given the circumstances. But the circumstances are critical. And the team needs the most experienced NCO as team sergeant. And that's Marky."

Marky kept his hand on his piece. "Is that going to be a problem, Ben?"

And for a moment, I was transported away from the desert and the starlit sky, meteors streaking overhead, to the tiny apartment and its mismatched furniture, the hateful scowl of a face I'd once found so beautiful, saying the words I couldn't ever seem to silence.

"You know, I don't need you."

✣ ✣ ✣

It was a long night. We traded off watches and I greedily took my turns sleeping, counting down to the minute until it was time to wake Dougie to spell me. Replaying the Chief's verbal assault on my confidence lulled me to sleep, only to dream the exchange over and over again. But in my sleep, he and Marky morphed into something different. Transformed into amalgams of the men I'd sworn loyalty to and creatures from our new reality. With each word, curved incisors sprouted like weeds from their lower jaws.

"You were right about some things, Colt," the Chief said between tusks dripping blood. "But you should've hammered them out with me alone first, not undermined me in front of the whole team. That was unprofessional."

"Live and learn, Ben," Marky said. "You'll get the dynamic down. We've all been there. It takes time. And Mike wasn't there to show you the ropes. Not your fault."

The Chief's tusks were suddenly gone, but his eyes were the size of saucers, the same black pools of dead as the greenies. "We can't divide the team, but we also can't take the risk your COA would expose us to and go exploring as a single unit. The team sergeant and I've taken all factors into consideration, and we've decided this is how it's going to go down.

"I'm sending you to recon the city. Dave'll go with you. You're going to assess the situation. Maybe it'll be appropriate to make contact with the residents. Dave sounds like he thinks he can establish a commo trail to keep in touch with us. You evaluate the scene, and we'll keep working here.

"It's putting you two at risk, but it's necessary to protect the team and the overall mission."

His face changed again, split into an evil smile, too wide for a human mouth, his tongue sharp and forked as it darted in and out as he hissed his words.

"It's the best use of your skills. And if you get into trouble, then we know we can't risk taking the team into the greenies' sphere of influence. We'll strike out elsewhere to find a better base of operations."

"It's a good mission, Ben," Marky-Mark said. His skin was the same carved stone as the ruins of the fountain. His face, but not his. He had a long curved beak that clicked as he spoke. "You'll be on your own. Like only SF operators can be."

My watch buzzed and I opened my eyes. The night sky was a shade lighter. The images in my dreams were conjured by my subconscious, but the words had been real.

"Take a break, Doug. You catch an hour, then we'll put the early warning out, and get back in time for breakfast."

By the time Doug and I rolled back into camp, the whole team would have been given the lowdown on Chief's new world order. I felt the shame burning my face already. But first, I was going to put the drone out on a suitable spot and let it be our unblinking eye, the software set to alert with any motion. It would let as many of us as possible work on the plan. My plan.

Doug yawned. "Okay, Ben. No argument here." He swapped out of the gunner's seat. "I don't know what to say, man. I don't think the Chief's making the right call."

"Maybe not. But his plan to recon the city before we roll en masse for it makes sense."

"I s'pose. Dave'll be good company. He's the man, you know? I don't think the rest of the team's going to let it go without a fuss, though. Dude, I'm spent. Wake me when the sun's up."

✤ ✤ ✤

"Great job, brah. Stellar work. Demoted and exiled on the same day. Can't begin to tell you how grateful I am to be banished from the tribe with you."

Dave was mostly kidding. Mostly.

"Think nothing of it, my Hawaiian brother."

"The only good part about the shunning was giving us a full night's sleep as consolation for being sentenced to death in the wastelands."

"See? Stick with me, and it's nothing but five-star living from here on out." A full night's sleep had done wonders for my mental outlook, and I answered Dave's sarcasm with like, as though it was my second language. "How's our guest?"

I was driving while Dave rode shotgun. It was my idea to take the prisoner along. I pitched the idea as we worked to get ready for our mission.

"If we do make contact, it could be a major sign of goodwill, returning him to his people," I'd argued.

"Then I should go with you," Karlo insisted.

Bryant shut him down immediately. "No. You're critical. The prisoner isn't. He'll make it, or he won't." I could tell the Chief was enthusiastic about getting rid of the wounded greenie. "You said he's stable. And too weak to be much of a security risk."

The greenie was strapped to the litter and still unconscious while we talked about his fate.

"Is he eating?" I was curious as well as planning for the practical.

"He comes out of his coma every so often and will sip some water. He rejects MREs. Guess I can understand that. This morning he chewed some skittles and kept them down. He spits out the red ones like my dog does a pill wrapped in cheese."

The guys helped Dave and I load our GMV, pump JP-8 from the blivets to fill all the gas cans we could strap on—same for water—and cram ammo and essentials in and on every possible space. A poncho rigged with bungee cords stretched over the back to shade our litter patient.

"Our war wagon looks like the Clampetts' jalopy loaded for the move to California," Dave said.

It did.

"Bel Air, here we come." I was about to mention cement swimming ponds when I thought about the stone fountain and the ruins. We'd see them again soon.

Mitch and Dougie worked as though they were the ones going. I've come to believe there's a simple test to know if someone's a true friend. One more valuable than gold or diamonds. You'll know you've let a person into your close circle that you can trust with your money, your property, or your life by this—delegate a task to them. If they do the job as well as you'd do it yourself, you've found that most precious gem. In the military, you're taught how to perform all tasks with attention to detail. That no matter the job, it has to be done correctly. Even so, Mitch and Doug poured themselves into making sure we were ready. If I felt conflicted about anything, it was not about how lucky I was to have friends and teammates like these.

"Not happy about this, Ben," Mitch whispered next to me. Marky and Matt were just a stone's throw from us on top of the Stryker doing maintenance on the fifty. The Chief was in and out of the C-17, making the rounds and checking on everyone's progress.

I mumbled back, "There's nothing for it, Mitch. Chief's right. This needs to happen."

"Not like this, though. It just seems wrong. For a minute, I thought there was going to be a mutiny. Karlo looked like murder. He never gets riled. I think if he'd have taken a stand, most of the rest of us would've, too."

"Then I'm glad he didn't," I said.

"Mike wouldn't have liked this."

"Maybe not. But here we are."

Dave and I worked out our movement plan, wrote up an abbreviated Op order—with a lot of "per SOP" to move things along—and we briefed the team back. "We'll head out at 1500." We'd set our watches arbitrarily to mine, and today I'd selected the highest peak of the sun as noon. I'd pay attention to sunup and sundown and start keeping a log. So far, my sense was that we had a twenty-four-hour day. "Our first waypoint will be the ruins. We can move at least that far unobserved. From there, we'll wait until dark, then start our course toward the city. We anticipate easy conditions, but will be taking it slow. We'll find a lay-in site to conceal ourselves during the day, until we get close enough to human activity to select a hide for further observation and collection."

Matt grunted, "Inhuman activity," after I said it.

Dougie bristled. "Dude, we're sending them out there with no ass behind them if they get into trouble."

Marky-Mark knife handed him. "That negativity isn't appreciated. It is what it is. Ben and Dave volunteered for this mission. It's dangerous. It's necessary. End of discussion. We've got the best plan we're going to have. It's time to make it happen."

Dave angled so just I could see him and mouthed, "I didn't volunteer."

We followed our tracks, and at a cautious pace, in a couple of hours we were in sight of the rising slope that concealed the ruins below.

I idled to a stop and shut it off. "Let's go."

We'd discussed this at length, weighing options and go-to-hell plans. It would be difficult, but not impossible, for a spider-hole concealed enemy to reach our GMV while it was out of our sight. A quick investigation into the arroyo, retrieve the vehicle, and make another detailed search of the ruin. If we didn't come upon the Robinson Crusoe recluse Matt swore he'd seen, we'd creep up the slope and get eyes on our route until it was dark and we could move out.

"The coast is clear," Dave said as we stopped our foot advance far enough into the sheltered terrain to make sure there were no surprises of a green variety or otherwise waiting for us.

"Hold tight. Be right back." I hoofed it back to the truck and pulled up to let Dave hop behind the minigun.

"Hit it, brah."

I punched it and this time came to a sliding halt, nose aimed into the maw of the ruin. We waited. The fountain bubbled as placidly as it had before, a hidden oasis whose purpose was clear. Providing life in the desert to any who passed.

"No time like the present," Dave said as he hopped down. This time without the flash bang as our herald we burst into the darkness, our lights mimicking the headlights of a car blasting around a blind curve.

Dave lowered his M4. "You think Matt saw what he thinks he did? I've had some pretty real hallucinations, dead on my feet like we were."

"I'm ready to believe, man."

We each wandered off, drawn to a separate part of the chamber and the chiseled works that covered the walls. I scanned one by one the recessed niches and the figures within. I was searching for the one that stayed with me. The strange Madonna, beckoning the injured and frail to seek her comfort.

"Uh..." Dave drew out from behind me. "Brah?"

"Whaa?" I turned away from my search.

Dave held the figurine he'd swiped in one hand, his flashlight in the other.

"What is it?"

"Brah. Check me on something." He swept his light again, row by row, from left to right, up and down.

"What?"

"Ben, you're stupid haole crack about the Brady Bunch thing got me to thinking. I was gonna put this back, seeing as I cursed us and all..."

I hadn't thought about my prophetic joke since, but it did make me chuckle. Part of it was embarrassment from all the cultural detritus I had taking up space in my brain. I bet a guy like Karlo had differential equations coursing through his subconscious, not plots from TV shows that went off the air before I was even born.

"Okay. And?"

"I can't find where it goes."

"Sure. I'll help. Where'd you nab it from?"

"That's just it. I'm sure it was from here. D'you see an empty one?"

I brought my carbine up with its lumen spouting head that was an accessory sun rivaling a supernova. I sought the empty recess left by his plundering. It wasn't there. Every tiny cave had a figure within. It was cool in the cave, but a chill much colder than the air temp made me shiver.

"Let's get out of here, Dave."

He laid the piece on the stone altar and backed away.

"Bad juju, brah. Bad juju."

12

After three nights of cautious travel and days of fitful sleep tucked beneath the camo net draped over our war wagon, we arrived. Expecting encounters with roving patrols, small settlements, or any brush with the aliens, the absence of all didn't serve to relieve us but only made what we were sure was the greenies' domain even more mysterious. Each night, pinpoint lights taunted us from the direction of the city, guiding us like lost wanderers pulled toward a warm candle flicker in the dark.

Our last successful radio check with the team had been a day ago.

"I don't know if the solar cells can't produce enough juice in this weird light to keep the repeaters working, or if we just don't have the range, but there's no sense wasting batteries," he said, turning off the radios, silencing the comforting noise of the faint background crackle I was accustomed to hearing in my earpiece.

Through optics we were at last close enough to examine the magnificent city on the edge of the grand desolation of this desert. The emptiness to our rear made me want to retreat back to its safety. My skin tingled and we whispered involuntarily, the eeriness of the alien architecture, the ghost town vibes, the insanity of the incomprehensible heights of the mountains behind combining to make us fearful for the first time.

We were truly on our own.

There'd been no encounters with wandering shepherds or remote outposts, none of the massive eight-legged horses, or signs of their presence. We found a suitable dip behind a dune in which to stash the GMV, and once again rolled the camo net over its irregular shape. The net was woodland pattern. Not a good match at all for our environment. Another SNAFU of planning and supply availability when we'd loaded out back at Area 51. At the time, it had seemed unimportant. Now, I cursed whenever we rolled it out from its perch on the roof. It served to break up our outline, but to any eye—black or otherwise—it would attract attention like a turd floating in a punch bowl. No matter. Even a smorgasbord of the correct desert tans of Earth would be out of place in the reds and yellows of this sandy landscape.

We each wore our urban ghillie tops as we hastily fashioned a hide in a small depression overlooking the plain fronting the city. We picked dry vegetation to supplement our camo, and I draped another net over my MK 22 and settled in, waiting for daylight to come. I stared through my binos mounted on a short tripod.

"These guys must be confident. No sentries out. No patrols. This is home sweet home for them," I said with the tiniest breath I could use yet still be sure he heard me.

"If there's really anyone home, they're late sleepers," Dave agreed, propped on his elbows next to me.

We kept our silent vigil as the sun broke, and at last caught glimpses of movement between the buildings, the nearest of them 1500 meters away, the sharp spires of the glimmering towers and the dull domes of roofs both massive and small interspersed within. City dwellers were going about the business of what I assumed was everyday life. Too soon, mirage lifted off the ground, making everything a wavy, blurry mess. Surrendering to the unwinnable battle against light itself, I was considering telling Dave he should take a turn at sleep when the curtain dropped on my inner monologue.

"SHWEE. SCREEE. SHWEE."

"What the hell's that?" Dave said as one word.

It came from behind us.

"Oh no," I realized. "It's the greenie."

More of the whistling screeches pierced my soul.

"Why didn't we gag him?" Dave scolded.

"I was afraid we'd kill him."

"We should've chanced it. Shit. Let's back out of here and make for the GMV."

We low crawled backwards, then sprung up for a crouched retreat, naturally breaking into the effortless bounds we'd learned. I'd quickly become accustomed to how my muscles and motions extolled the unnatural virtues conferred on us here. But minor Superman or not, if regret were a yoke, I wore the heavy weight of it. We hustled to where the war wagon lay under the drab drape of green and brown tones clashing with the palette around us. Minutes seemed like hours as we reversed the long course of our stalk, all the while the tornado siren blaring from behind the dune. Right now, every sense I possessed screamed failure at me. The cacophony from the bed of the GMV silenced as I rocked the vehicle, vaulting onto the rear bumper. The greenie was wide awake, straining to break its restraints, black eyes accusing me as it saw my surprised face.

"Easy, buddy." I made all the usual gestures of non-harm and grabbed a water bottle. "How about a drink? You like water, yes?"

The greenie snorted, its nostrils flared as it sniffed the air. "Blick blarga flish. Kow plank. Kow toe."

"We're in it now, brah." Dave was beside me. "We've got riders forming up at the edge of the city. They're not charging to the rescue. Yet. Maybe they didn't hear him. Maybe it's just a morning patrol."

"Fat chance, that."

The greenie made fish lips at me.

"Okay. Good. Have a drink."

He took a sip then drew in a breath.

I dropped the bottle and pulled the shemagh out of my pocket to tie in its mouth as it fought me. "Sorry. You're gonna have to suck on this for a while."

"What's the play?" Dave asked as I took the binos and climbed onto the roof to look for myself. "Do we run for it, or play the hand we're dealt?"

"Try to make contact?" My voice broke a little, heart lodged in my throat.

"How'd we think this was going to go down? I mean, really?"

It was true. We'd made all the contingencies. Running into a patrol on our way here. Breaking contact and making a fighting retreat back to base. How we'd deal with a compromise while in our hide. But when it was in your face like the proverbial brick wall, the most detailed plans never seemed as prepared as what you'd imagined. Especially since all of our plans and contingencies hadn't really addressed the ultimate end game—making contact.

SF's forte is working behind enemy lines with unconventional forces. Guerillas and irregulars. Fighting a fifth column war without support. Swimming through a hostile sea while disguising ourselves amongst the fishes and sharks, until we wreaked havoc using our own pelagic predators from the same waters. We'd spend years studying, planning, and practicing the secret ways of entering into the first and most dangerous step that was meeting potential allies. Never trusting that our new friends would ever truly be reliable comrades. Anticipating that at any moment, if we were unprepared, betrayal and torture awaited us.

Dave and I'd come to the conclusion that the gurus of special warfare hadn't left detailed blueprints for this oddest of situations. But they had taught us to improvise.

I climbed down. "Time to wing it."

✢ ✢ ✢

We rolled out from behind the dune and crept ahead. I drove, Dave behind the minigun. Through the ground mirage was a band of mounted greens, much as we'd encountered—was it really just a few days ago? Our time here blurred into a run-on of fuzzy red days and blue and purple nights.

Our reception committee waited in two ranks on horseback. I call them horses, because what else could I call them? Dino-horse was too awkward. There was a better name, but it didn't matter. A whole lexicon of alien nouns waited to be coined as we focused on survival. Minutiae would be settled later. If we had a later.

I eased us forward until we were within easy M4 distance—a couple hundred meters. It was also what I judged to be the limit of what I thought their lightning bolt guns could reach. Matt showed me what he'd learned after tinkering with the captured rifles. They were of a technology both advanced and crude. Novel yet inadequate compared to our slug throwers.

Matt demonstrated, the rifle tucked under his armpit, the stock too long for him to mount on his shoulder and still reach the trigger analogue—a kind of switch. Regardless, as he peppered a few blasts into a safe direction, the lack of recoil made it a moot point. Electric jolts cooked the air, but didn't noticeably disturb the surface of the slope he aimed at a few hundred meters away. A bullet would've visibly kicked up dirt. He walked discharges closer and closer, selecting random backstops, until at a hundred meters or so, the ground smoked from a blackened spot left by the bolt's impact.

"I can't find how it's recharged. Other than the trigger mechanism, there aren't any moving parts. I'm not ready to risk one cooking off by prying at it with a screwdriver. As you see, the range seems limited, but I guess it could affect a person farther than where it causes obvious damage. I'm not saying I want to be hit with it, certainly not up close." Matt tossed it to me as he concluded. "But all in all, color me unimpressed."

If the mounted warriors decided to go kinetic on us, from here Dave could burn them down at three thousand rounds a minute with impunity. Unless they had gadgets more deadly than the ones we knew about.

It was a distinct possibility.

I put us in park and waited. I watched the greenies, focusing on their hands, waiting for one of them to raise a rifle. Instead, they stayed in place, as frozen as their mounts would allow. Occasionally, one of the horses would take more than a step, and its rider delivered a hammer blow to the side of its massive head, the animal naturally responding in pain, dipping its head and crying out in submission.

"They ain't moving, Ben," Dave said from above me. I thought about how the captain approached the aliens, and how he and Mike were cut down. If this was a contest to see who would blink first, it wasn't going to be us.

"They're going to make the first move, Dave. We're in no hurry."

"I'm content to wait them out. But if this is some kind of diversion and they send more out to try to surround us, I'm going hot, brah."

"Agreed."

Finally, after an interminably long freeze that made the Ice Age short by comparison, three riders advanced. Splitting the distance between us and their formation of riders, the three halted in line. The one I took to be the boss man—he had a headpiece of the same gold armor as their chest plates—spoke. I couldn't understand him, of course, but his words were commanding and clipped. In response, the rider at his left dismounted and stepped forward with authority. He planted his spear into the sand and let his shield hand drop.

"What do you think?"

"Stay on the gun, Dave. I'm going to make likewise."

I stepped out of the vehicle and tried not to think about how the captain had been cut down in just this way. Staying out of Dave's way, I stepped ahead, expanded to be as tall as possible. I kept a hand on the grip of my M4, but otherwise mirrored the alien like a statue. The boss man spoke to the mounted rider beside him. Even on horseback, he was a half a meter taller than the huge one who seemed to be giving the orders. He was a magnificent specimen. He wore less armor than his companions, and a red sash crossed his torso. They were pointing at me as they spoke.

"What's next?" Dave said.

The boss man grunted, "TOKRA."

The standing warrior dropped his shield and spear. He stepped in my direction, shedding his armor as he advanced. Halving the distance to me, he stopped, dropped his sword belt into the sand, and spread wide his four arms and bared his tusks.

His meaning was clear.

"I've seen this movie play out already, Ben," Dave yelled.

"I don't think so. It's not how it went down with the captain. Something's different," I yelled over my shoulder at him.

"So what? Don't play their game. Get back here."

My opponent had come forward unarmed. He was clearly waiting for me to do the same. To do what? Meet for a handshake? I didn't think so. These characters were warriors. If it was to be anything other than a test by combat, I couldn't conceive differently. You may not believe me, but I'm telling you true. I wanted this. My anxiety and feelings of being exposed and in peril evaporated. This was something I comprehended, down to my bones. I took my helmet off and dropped it.

"No way, Ben!"

I imitated the greenie's actions and cast off my weapons and accoutrements as I strode. "If I go down, Dave—make your best way out of here. Lay waste to everything, break contact, and leave me."

"Don't do it, Ben!"

I didn't bother to answer his appeal. I was building a fire in my furnace, stoking the energy I needed for combat ruthlessness. I watched the cruelty the greenies dealt to their animals, the merciless way they'd cut down the captain and Mike. If they wanted to see what hard was, I was ready to show them.

I'd imagined what this meeting would be like, evaluating what I'd observed about our aggressors since I'd first laid eyes on them. They were hugely muscled. But what I'd seen of them through the optics of my MK 22 when I dropped them one by one, they struck me as clumsy. Slow. As I stopped at spitting distance and looked up at my opponent, the steam pressure in my arteries pumped lava into my muscles as I ached to start the war.

"Bahh!" the greenie spat as he simultaneously crouched like a linebacker, his intentions clear. That's when I sprung.

Letting the other guy make the first move is stupid. This wasn't a boxing match. This was war. And the side that hits the hardest with the mostest wins. The speed I used to close our distances made me a blur. My feet landed just as he started his lunge. Too late for him. His arms moved to close around me as I uncoiled and drove an open hand uppercut into his outstretched chin and exploded up like a geyser with my newfound power. His head snapped back, and I felt and heard bone disintegrate. I returned to the ground, weight forward, projecting my deadly intent at my enemy, ready to follow the felled monster to the ground, but I already knew it was unnecessary.

The greenie hit the sand limp. A lime-colored skinsack of soft meat.

I drove my glare to where the mounted observers waited. If I could interpret their faces, then surprise was my guess. I was anticipating more stoic stillness. Maybe acceptance that I'd met the challenge. I was wrong. The boss man commanded with a shout that I bet they heard back at the city. Two riders responded from behind to gallop out of the formation.

"Going hot!" Dave yelled.

"NO! Hold tight!" I yelled back.

The two riders stopped short and leaped off their mounts to attack. They were bare handed, but still in armor. Both moved with deadly intention. I took a cross step and launched, covering meters at the speed of an arrow sent by the tautest bowstring. My foot caught the first in the face before his arms could deflect, and I sailed past him. I turned as I landed and used the rotation to unwind with a fist into the other one's mid-back, driving off my rear leg with all the force I could steal from the ground and sending it through my body, focused like a penetrator round, my fist the tungsten core. I don't know if the greenie's kidney was underneath the thick flank, but there was bound to be something of value there.

The beast sailed off its feet, four arms flailing as it folded, legs somersaulting overtop of him. The one I'd connected with my side-kick looked like my first opponent. Dead on arrival like a day-old fish delivered to market.

I pointed to the mounted boss man and raged, "Knock it off, or you're next!" I left no doubt to whom I was speaking.

"Enough!" Dave yelled. A quick burst from the minigun, fire spitting, bullets kicking up a cloud of dirt at the flank of the two chiefs and sending spall and skipping bullets, hundreds of them, just past the cavalry to their rear. Horses jumped and riders were thrown as the ejecta passed close enough to them to communicate lethal promises.

"You don't want to test us!" I yelled again. For a time I stood there, fists clenched at my sides, daring the greenies to challenge us further. For the first time I could recall, my lungs burned and my chest heaved. Oxygen or not, I was ready for more. The gold-capped alien met my eyes.

And laughed.

I know a laugh when I hear one. It sounded like a dog choking on a chicken bone. But his shoulders shook, his head was thrown back. He turned on his mount, encouraging his troops to do the same. Soon, they all joined in and a chorus of hacking guffaws swept the ranks. All except the red sash next to boss man. I met his eyes and what struck me was only this. Dignity. Not hostility. Nor contempt. Certainly not fear. He dipped his head to me in a curt nod, and I returned the same.

Now boss man turned on his mount, aiming back to the city from which he'd come, and made another gesture, too clear for me misinterpret. With four arms, he turned all palms up and cast them at the towers and walls of the city. At last, before me was the source of the beckoning flicker that only a few days ago teased through the tiny window of an asphyxiating C-17. Just before the light of hope—that we could save America—was doused. All there was left to do was follow the trail of smoke to seek the source of a different beacon to guide a new meaning for us.

13

Dave outdid himself in a tirade of compound and uniquely joined expletives as I dressed next to the truck. "What made you think you could win a fight against one of those things?" he ended with a loud exhale.

I know I've given some mixed impressions about me. Sharing my innermost doubts about myself like a schoolgirl confessing to her secret journal. What can I say? I'm a frustrated psychologist. Or maybe it's because I never learned how to get the angst out of me through poetry or songs like those in the haunting music I listen to when I'm alone and certain no one else can hear. I love a sultry feminine voice singing about hurt and pain, cruel love, and betrayal. The whine and distortion of electric instruments speaking the same language of torment as the singer. I can admit that most private thing about me right now, in the post-high of combat, as I still feel invulnerable and bulletproof after my victory.

I'd risk permanent injury or death for the buzz I get from physical violence. Does that make me psycho? Not to my way of thinking. Not if you have it under control like I do.

Know what always burned me up so badly about the Chief judging me for never having been in combat? Because I have been. Not in a shooting war (not until now, that is), but I've fought all my life. Wrestling, boxing, MMA, you name it. When other teenagers were tossing balls around or trying to get up the courage to talk to girls, I was on the mat or working the heavy bag.

If I can thank my dad for anything, it's that he started me on the road, teaching me how to wrestle from as early as I can remember. At first, it was just roughhousing and fun. But the spark he ignited lit my fuse, and from middle school on, if it involved any kind of combat sport, I was a fanatic. I learned to box at the local Y. I learned some judo and in the Army was introduced to MMA and jujitsu. I have to say, after wrestling and boxing for so many years, I could learn a new move or combination in minutes. It didn't matter what you called it. When a buddy in the 82nd took the time to show me the mechanics of kicking that he'd learned in Korean martial arts, I became as well-rounded a fighter as there was. I know because I've never felt outclassed or threatened by another opponent since. And I've never backed away from a challenge in the ring, no matter how big the other guy was.

I was also lucky. My dad and my teachers all inspired me to use my skills honorably. Nobly. And to never be a bully. Between my size, strength, natural aggression, and training, I could've been a walking time bomb. Could've ended up in prison for murder. If I allowed the narcotic of bloodsport to rule over my intellect. That's why I didn't kill the guy who surprised me in my girlfriend's apartment that night. I'd learned early that control and discipline were powers as vital as your muscles.

No, combat sports aren't the same as warfighting. But if there's another way of building fighting spirit, you can't prove it by me. Fear and pain are the enemy. Overcoming that by getting your nose smashed in, choking on blood and snot as someone grinds you into the mat, pummels your body, your muscles screaming for respite as you do the same to him—it is the way. Deep in my soul, I'd just known I could give one of these greenies a fight like they'd never had. Or die trying.

"Some things you just know, Dave," I boasted. "But I'm glad it worked out," I added, hoping I sounded a little humble. "Nice work with the 134. You preempted them trying to dogpile me."

"They went pretty quickly from letting it be a one-on-one thing to jumping you like it was a cage match with the ref knocked out."

I took a drink. "Yeah. We can't expect they have anything like fairness or honor in their culture. Not that we can relate to, anyway."

SF beat into you the differences of working with other cultures. I hadn't experienced it first-hand, but in training, they throw you into situations with role players that make you challenge your own conceptions of what's right and wrong. Like when in Robin Sage—the guerrilla warfare graduation exercise—when the guerilla chief executes one of his men for cowardice. Or offers teenage girls from the village to your team in thanks for a successful ambush patrol, and takes it as an insult when you refuse. Maybe it wasn't so different with the greenies, and we weren't totally navigating without a star to steer by.

Dave whistled. "The guys aren't going to believe this. Wish I had it on video. The Chief would turn as green with envy as one of these chumps. He's intimidated by you. You dig that, right? All this stuff about you not being combat proven? He's trying to prove something, too. He's no Bob Howard."

Dave was referring to one of the legends of SF. I'd say to look him up, but that's a stupid thing to say now.

I clenched. "Chuck told me about Venezuela."

"That?" Dave recoiled. "I bet he did. There're other stories about how that went down, you know? The Chief and Marky keep each other's secrets. That I can tell you. Don't believe everything you hear. You know there was an Article 32 investigation into that?"

"Say what?"

"After the dust settled, there were accusations that they'd killed two innocent civilians, just in the wrong place at the wrong time. There were no bodies, but a local who saw it go down brought it to the Red Cross good-niks crawling all over afterwards. Of course, nothing got thrown at the Bolivar Pride goons, just us. Anyway, it all got dismissed."

"What do you think?"

Dave shrugged. "Maybe they went savage. Maybe what they did really was for the integrity of the mission. We'll never know. I just know, I don't like being alone with those two. Ever." He shaded his brow and checked ahead. "They're holding fast. Waiting. Do we follow?"

"What else are we going to do? Go home?"

✢ ✢ ✢

I drove as Dave talked.

"How'd you navigate that first contact?" he asked.

How we'd gotten to this point with the greenies intrigued me, as well.

"Luck. I dunno. I tried to learn from what I saw go down with Mike and the captain. You were trying to get the ramp open in the

C-17 while I watched the whole fiasco. It was a nightmare. Maybe there was just something about the sequence of events that sparked the bloodshed. They expected us to know the rules, and we didn't play according to Hoyle." Mores. Formalities. Ceremony. Manners. Any could be the reason why the first contact had ended in slaughter. Or none of the above. "Who's to say we're not stepping into a slaughterhouse now?"

"I'm not getting off the minigun until I'm good and reassured. And that might not be for a long time, brah. Newsflash for you—no more disarming. You're done with that. We are officially in the lion's den now."

"Agreed."

Our entrance into the city was met with notice but little fanfare. We followed the riders through wide streets deeper and deeper into the city, citizens stopping to stare, but quickly returning to business. Most notably, there was no sign of hostility. Only mild curiosity then indifference.

The riders spread and halted at the footsteps of a palace, towers and white onion domes indicating it was a place of importance. I pulled into the center of their midst and dismounted.

As promised, Dave stayed behind the minigun. "What about our buddy here? Time to give him back?"

"High time," I said. I gestured to the nearest in the crowd to follow me. "We have one of your men."

Some of the greenies followed me around the GMV, and I released the tarp to reveal their wounded man. I pulled off the gag and released his restraints. I pointed at his bandages. "We took care of him as best we could. Hope you can see that."

Our prisoner attempted to rise, said something, and I bent to help, draping one of his arms over my neck. I passed him to pairs of arms as they hauled him to his feet and walked him into the gathering. The boss man was the last still mounted. He watched attentively until the wounded man was brought before him. Their leader questioned him as he was held on either side, and our captured guest answered. In my head, I anthropomorphized the conversation, hoping that our humane treatment was revealed.

Boss man dismounted and moved to stand before the weakened soldier. He barked, and the two attendants stood the wounded greenie up tall. He bolstered himself straight and his friends stood aside as boss man drew his sword.

"No!" I sprang, placing myself instantly between them, startling everyone. "We didn't bring him all this way for you to execute him. He was wounded. We cared for him. End of story."

Dave groaned. "You sure about this, brah?"

"Yup," I said from my diaphragm.

"Ready to go hot," Dave reassured me.

I locked eyes with the boss man. Without breaking our mutual stare, he said something to his men, sheathed his sword, and the same attendants carried the wounded man away. Fixing me again with his demon black eyes he spoke, then pointed up the steps.

"Dave. It's time."

Dave looked grim from behind the 134, and shook his head. "Time for the sit-down. It's why we came, I guess. Tea and the peace pipe."

I waited so we could ascend side by side behind the boss man. Around us, his retinue of warriors kept a distance.

"I'm not catching bad vibes. They seem pretty chill," Dave muttered sideways.

"Maybe it's time for some alien hospitality?"

Through a grand arch and into a room adorned like something from the Arabian Nights, we followed to a room of soft rugs and pillows piled beneath a vaulted ceiling adorned in sparkling gems. Boss man took a seat and laid his sword beside him then indicated for us to sit. I mimicked by laying my M4 beside me as Dave did the same. Cross-legged, we waited. The red-sashed greenie took a spot across from us, and more of the crew filled in, some taking seats, others standing behind, arms cradling rifles over broad armored chests.

"If they hose us down at this range, we're cooked, brah," Dave said, eyeing the armed giants towering around us.

"True dat."

"Time for diplomacy, 'member? Don't go all Conan the Barbarian."

"Yeah, yeah. Got it. We're cool if they are."

Boss man spoke to the gathering. One of his lieutenants barked and servants appeared. The female of the species was obvious. I thought the greenies were perhaps reptilian in some way, but the mammalian features were clear, making me discard my earlier biases. We were offered containers with narrow spouts holding a liquid. The boss man eyed us as I hesitated. If it was some greenie moonshine, it might be more like anti-freeze to us than Tennessee mash.

"Take it, brah," Dave whispered. "You know the drill."

We each took a container, then the servant dipped her tray and provided the rest to the gathering. The greenies all tipped their heads back and drank without waiting. I sniffed, and gingerly tilted the bottle to my lips. It was water. Clean and odorless.

"Good to go, Dave. Chilled agua."

Our wounded guest had done well with the water we'd provided from our stores, and I supposed it would be the same with roles reversed. I took another drink, deeper this time.

Dave made the universal "ahh" and smacked his lips. "We've got that in common at least. Guess we won't die of thirst here."

The boss man leaned forward and spoke. My frustration made me shake my head, hoping he understood.

"I regret we can't understand each other," I put as much empathy into it as I could, self-conscious about my overacting.

The boss made a very human nod. He pointed at the silver band that sat at the dip above one of his multiheaded biceps, then pointed at the other greenies seated around us, indicating they wore the same.

"Yes. Yes. Nice jewelry," I said, pointlessly and feeling stupid.

"Don't know how we're going to make any headway here, Ben. This is going to take forever."

A servant appeared at the boss man's beckon. He knelt before us, offering a pillow on which were two silver armbands.

"Maybe we're being inducted into the tribe?" Dave said.

"Forward progress, I'd say. We didn't bring gifts," I said. "Stupid of me. Maybe I'd better give him my flashlight."

I took a band off the pillow. It was sized for the massive greenies and could have easily fit my thigh. But putting it there might be some kind of insult. Besides, it would never stay up. I placed the band over my left arm. Almost instantly, it constricted. I jumped.

"What kinda magic's this?" Dave said, as surprised as I was.

The boss man spoke again. His gruff utterances mellowed to my ear.

"What was that?" I coaxed.

He tried again. Something had changed. His voice softened. The syllables of his words not a jumble of grunts anymore. He spoke again, slower.

"Understand to speak now. White of north people, not care speak with Tarn. Strong. But not respect."

"Ben, I got some of that! I understood him!" Dave said amazed. "Harry Potter Lord of the Rings wackadoo magic."

I too was shocked. I replayed our host's words and caught the essence of the broken accusation.

"We respect you, Chieftain. You and your people. You are warriors, like us. We want to be friends. We want your help." I enunciated and spoke slowly, with all the unconscious idiosyncrasies of a stranger in a strange land asking directions.

The boss man stayed silent, and I maintained the quiet and resisted saying more as he likewise pondered my words. Was it the translation or what I'd said that caused him to hesitate before speaking again?

"Friends. White not red. White not yellow. White just legend."

"What's he mean? I'm not a whitey like you," Dave whispered.

"Shh," I hushed. Idle banter was a comfort between comrades. A thing you learn in the Army. A way to support a brother, defuse tension, let a buddy know he wasn't alone. Sometimes the gravest circumstance produced the best humor and raised morale at a critical time. This was not one of those times.

"Let me work, Dave." I kept my eyes on the boss man as I rebuked my partner through muffled tones. I cleared my throat. "Chieftain, I do not understand. We desire friendship with your people. We do not seek war. We want to work together."

The boss man again stared blankly as he absorbed my words. He bared his tusks then raised a hand to halt me. He barked a rough order, but I understood none it. He again extended a single palm to me, as if asking me to wait. He took his bottle and sipped, indicating I should do the same. We waited. I tried to suppress my thoughts, wondering what would be next, and lost focus for a moment as I composed my next pleas for cooperation. Behind me, I heard footfalls.

A pair of towering green thighs broke into the circle, the lower hands above them dragging a vision. Beneath bounteous raven locks was a deeply red tanned face. Though I saw it for only a flash, it was long enough to launch a thousand ships. Then her savage captor cast her down. She stumbled and collided with the stone floor, her gossamer dress billowing then falling to drape her curvaceous form. A green female scurried to join the woman in collapse, displaying the cowed attendance of one anguished at the rough treatment. My hand shot to my rifle as I sprang to a knee. Though her skin was the deep red of Santa Fe adobe, she was human. With her head bowed and eyes downcast, she extended her chained arms to me and sobbed.

"I beseech you, White lord of the north, to aid me, a princess of the west. I am Talis Darmon Sylah, daughter of King Osric Darmon and his kingdom's emissary plenipotentiary. I am in great need and beg for my life. Pity me."

14

I understood her as clearly as though she spoke my own language, yet I knew she did not.

Dave's hand was on my forearm. "Easy, brah. Easy."

I fought the red clouding my vision.

"What's the meaning of this?" I yelled, every cell in my body focused, ready to protect the helpless woman that had been deposited at my feet like chattel. The vision of beauty and femininity captured my soul, and her treatment insulted my honor and manhood. Every sense of guardian and protector I'd imagined of myself my entire life was ignited.

"Please, my lord." Getting up, her face met mine, and my heart leaped. Through lips parched and cracked, she said, "I beg of you not to abandon me."

The guard who'd dragged her into our presence with all the manners of a slave master snarled and struck her with a backhand, knocking her to the floor again.

Without thought, at the speed of light, I launched. My fist smashed the square green face, and he flew over the heads of the seated clanmates behind him, colliding with the standing rank of smirking giants laughing at her degradation.

The red-sashed giant rose to rush me. I exploded from beneath to heft him overhead and threw him without effort at another unprepared rank of soldiers, wrecking them in the collision like so many dead stalks in a field struck by gale force winds.

Dave's expletives gushed. He was on his feet. "Drop your weapons. Drop them!" he yelled, his weapon menacing their chieftain.

The chained woman's green attendant shielded the assaulted woman with her own body, and I turned toward the boss man on the pillow where he sat. Frozen.

"We'll all die together if you don't order them to stand down."

Boss man scowled, but spread four arms wide and dipped his head ever so slightly.

"Offense has been given. Offense is regretted. Peace. Peace, White lord of the north."

"Over there," Dave commanded the greenies, herding them with his muzzle to move from behind us. The chieftain spoke, and the soldiers obeyed his command and moved to stand where we could see them all. I knelt to the woman and gently pried the servant from her.

"I will not abandon you. Come. Are you hurt?"

She allowed me to help her up, and I guided her to take my place on the cushion as Dave continued his vigil. She sat and her attendant knelt at her side, wrapping her with affection in the armor of her many arms.

"My name's Ben."

She looked at me with bewilderment, perhaps still senseless from the blows. She averted her eyes to the ground again and meekly said, "I have given you my name, lord. Talis Darmon Sylah. Will you not trust me with yours?"

I'd committed some grave error.

"Colt. Deacon Benjamin Colt."

She raised her face again, her beauty not diminished by her desperate state. She repeated my full name. "A White lord of the north has not appeared from beneath the mountain since the time of my father's father's father. The journey of all Vistarans, human and Tarn alike, end where the River Blix enters your kingdom to reach the afterlife. Is the time at hand for the end of all things?"

While I understood her speech as though it were our own, her meaning was lost to me.

"I don't understand. But I promise to protect you."

"The emissary from the Reds is prisoner," the boss man said, his speech becoming less foreign to my comprehension, his words gradually forming into a language in my head without accent or error. "I produced her in hopes of easing our parley."

The red-sashed giant rose from among the rubble of bodies, rubbing his head with two hands as he staggered back into our midst beside the chieftain.

Boss man made a short barking laugh. "No Tarn has ever thrown Khraal Kahlees in contest, much less a human. Let us be at ease. I vow no hostility. You have the oath of Domeel Doreen, Chieftain of the Mydreen Desert. You have safety here in my capital of Maleska Mal and with all my people."

The red-sashed greenie plopped onto his cushion, made rapid turns of his head like a dog shaking water off his coat. I'd done the same many times in my life. I'd rung his bell.

"Let's ease back, Dave."

"You are one crazy haole," Dave said. "How about some warning next time? Or better yet, chill, man."

The boss man—chieftain—awaited my answer. "Do you accept my oath, lord of the north?"

"Yes. I accept."

Domeel Doreen waved his arms at his men. "Leave. Assurance has been accepted. Honor is met. Oaths bind us now. Depart."

Greenies—Tarns—helped others to their feet. The one who'd struck the princess was carried away. His head flopped limply like a dead man pulled from a car wreck.

The chieftain laughed again. "You killed with a single blow yet another Tarn warrior. When first I witnessed this, I should have known that you are a lord of the underworld. Forgive me for not realizing sooner. All know of the kingdom beneath, ruled by the White clan. The princess speaks true. None have witnessed a White lord in an age, save those who have traveled the River Blix to join you in the next life. Our ancestors await us all in your kingdom beyond Temple Farnest—forgive me, your name again?"

"Deacon Benjamin Colt." I stuck with my full name.

"Lord Deacon Benjamin Colt."

This was too much.

"Your appearance is consecrated in my house. I am ashamed to have shown ill hospitality. You must rest. My servants will take you to proper chambers. We will speak later. All courtesy is given." He rose and a pair of attendants rushed to his side. "Escort our bonded friends to quarters."

The woman, Talis, stayed with her legs folded beneath her, held in place by the many armed embrace of her Tarn friend. Both kept their eyes averted, awaiting to be commanded. "And her?" I asked.

Domeel Doreen bared his tusks. "She is our enemy. And my prisoner. She returns to her captivity."

Both women sobbed.

They were big on the long form of everyone's name here. Chieftain Domeel Doreen was the proper address. I used it. "I have given you our oath and it has been accepted. I promise I will obey your will in your house. But parole them to my custody. There are many questions I have of them. It will aid our mission here to your kingdom."

The chieftain grunted and turned away abruptly. "Then it is the pleasure of Domeel Doreen that you take them."

✣ ✣ ✣

We found ourselves in an apartment of many rooms and were left with a pair of female attendants. "We will bring food and water. What else do you require?"

I turned to the freed women. "Is there anything you need?"

The princess's attendant spoke for the first time. "Bring clean clothes for the princess, at once."

The attendants bowed and left, and the guards closed the ornate doors from outside. I was about to speak, when the princess staggered and started to fall. I caught her and lifted her off her feet, cradling her like a bride.

"Lead us to a bed," I said. "What is your name?"

"Dosenie Beraal of Pardoo. I am companion and guardian to the princess," she said, giving her name in a manner different to what I'd only just become accustomed.

I followed her through halls and a sitting area similar to where I'd fought and learned to speak with our hosts just minutes before, and into a bedchamber. I laid her down gently and was pushed back as her attendant wedged herself between us.

"You must rest as well, my lords. I will attend to the princess and then yourselves."

Dave waited in the doorway, guarding my back. He was searching the space, gaze intense as he scanned our new surroundings with suspicion.

"C'mon, Ben. Let's give everything a once-over."

I hesitated to glance back at the princess. Talis Darmon Sylah. I said her name several times in my head, then out loud. "Is she okay, Dosenie Beraal of Pardoo?"

The Tarn girl didn't look away from her charge as she soothed the brow of the unconscious woman before covering her.

"I am properly called Beraal, as I have no family name. And Talis Darmon is as strong as a mountain gazraal. She will be fine. The Tarn of the Mydreen desert are vicious and cruel, and Domeel Doreen is their beacon."

She spat.

"Our captivity has been harsh. She needs rest. Please go."

I joined Dave and we retraced our steps back to the main room of the suite. Dave faced off with me.

"Look at you, man," my teammate scolded. "Get your head straight."

He wasn't joking or jibing me. I was caught off guard, not expecting his ire. He was serious as cancer.

"I know a guy in lust when I see one. We've got to lock this situation down. We're floating in shark-infested waters on a flimsy inflatable life raft, brah. We've allowed ourselves to get separated from our firepower. Right now, those greenies could be shagging our gear. And you! Sacrificing our safety and our mission to protect some strange woman!"

He clenched his fists and glowered at me.

"You through?" I asked him.

Dave seethed at me but remained quiet.

"I'm not saying you're wrong. But you're not right, either. We've come a long way in a short period of time, and we did it without any help. What do you think the Chief and Marky intended to happen to us, anyway? You think they sent us out here by ourselves on a milk run? I've thought about it a lot." My finger shot out and I pointed at him angrily. "And the more I think about it, the more I think they really did exile us, maybe to get rid of us on a one-way trip."

"Don't I know it!" Dave shot back. "And I got sent along for the rotten luck of being your friend. I wish Mike was alive. I wish you'd never come to this team."

I scrunched my eyes shut, wincing at the blow. A tiny voice started to break the surface of the pool where I drowned my bad memories, but I pushed her words back down with all my might.

Dave's sigh let me know it was safe to open my eyes again.

"I didn't mean that. God, I swear I didn't mean that, brah. I'm just exhausted. I'm on the ragged edge. I know you are, too. Look, I just mean we're in a deep, deep mess."

I relaxed. "We are." I shook my head. "But what could I have done differently?"

Dave blew out a deep breath. "Nothing, man. It is what it is. Question is, what do we do now? Lord Benjamin. Hah!"

He laughed, and I joined him. It was all absurd. Beyond anything I could have imagined in my wildest dreams.

Dave looked around again. "C'mon. Let's make sure there aren't any greenie assassins hiding behind the drapes at least, then we need to get some rest. I'm starving. I don't remember the last time I ate."

"Yeah. It was so long ago, I don't even feel hungry, that's how long ago it was."

"If their water's good, maybe their food is too, brah. If it passes the sniff test, I'm going for it."

✤ ✤ ✤

I awoke. My rifle was across my chest. I'd nodded out, reclined on a pile of pillows facing the doorway where guards stood watch on the other side. Beraal had assured us that the chieftain would honor his oath and that we would not be molested.

"Once the oath of protection is made, it cannot be broken. If word of such reached other clans, Domeel Doreen would be ostracized, and similar would be forbidden to him and his whole clan from others. We are safe. For now. And we have you to thank for that."

We'd found the food was edible and more than palatable, and decided for the time being we were safe under the protection of the oath the chieftain acknowledged. Dave snored lightly beside me. The light through the balcony window was dimming and I checked my watch.

I lay there for a moment, feeling sharp again, and concentrated. Dave had remarked about our surroundings before we succumbed to sleep, and I reexamined the room where I lay.

Dave had been first to put it into words. "Everything looks worn and aged, like an old trailer park. You notice the doors?"

"What about them?"

"The proportions are off. They're cut for heights of people, not Tarns."

It struck me suddenly. "None of this was built for Tarns." As I played back our entrance into the city, I remembered the disrepair of the buildings and walls, the crumbling and dirty surfaces, the cracks in the streets we traveled. The allure and grandeur I'd imagined I'd find once inside the mysterious city was tainted by the atmosphere of decay.

Beraal's head peered from the hall. "I did not want to disturb you, lord," she whispered. "If you wish, the princess is awake and begs to see you and give thanks."

I rose silently and followed her, leaving Dave to rest. Beraal stood aside to let me pass into the bedchamber first. A small stone glowed a warm bronze on the table beside her. Talis Darmon lay reclined on the bed, her mane of thick black hair draped like a hood around her. She hid a smile but did not avert her gaze as I met her eyes and approached.

Her eyes. How to describe them? Seas of blue turquoise with glints of gold reflecting in the light.

"I'm glad to see you awake, Princess Talis Darmon Sylah. Beraal tells me you're much improved."

Now the princess smiled. Her teeth were the whitest pearls framed by her ash-rose lips. "I am. And I thank you, lord, for your service."

Behind me, Beraal set a stack of cushions and I balanced myself on top of them at the bedside.

"How come you to be here from the undying lands of the underworld, lord, or is it forbidden for me to ask?" She shrunk slightly, and the welcoming beam of a smile she'd melted me with faded.

It was time to come clean.

"I don't know what you mean. I don't know where the undying lands are, and I am no lord. I'm from somewhere far from here, and I'm hoping you can help me figure out where I am so I can get back home."

15

We stood at the edge of the city. I shook Dave's hand as he mounted up. After two days and nights, we agreed that he should be the one to travel back to within radio range and report to the team all that had happened. We were both well rested and, equally welcome—we were clean. Beraal sniffed and scolded that since we were better than "desert Tarns," we must "resist the call of the savage." We bathed and were provided clothing, and Beraal gave strict instructions to our attendants to wash our stained uniforms as we spent the first day awaiting a summons for an audience with Domeel.

The princess remained in her room, and we spoke for only short periods, her strength fleeting. I asked Beraal about their treatment at the hands of the Tarns, whom she was quick to point out as inferior to her own people of the western mountains.

"They are little better than the roamak that swarm to bring down an aged gazraal. We were ambushed by Domeel Doreen's clan on our way to offer terms for the king's peace. The Mydreen disregarded the yellow light of discourse, and slaughtered the princess's contingent and guard. Not without giving as good as they took, I promise!

"Domeel tortured and killed the rest of our party before us, one by one. They threw us in cages with the animals, starved us, and ignored our thirst as we baked in the sun by day and shivered at night."

I smoldered at the thought of their treatment by the smug chieftain. "How long have you been captive?"

"Many, many days and nights have run together, lord."

"Will the king send his army to rescue you?"

"I don't know that he hasn't. We heard sounds of battle many, many nights ago. The next morning Domeel forced us to watch as he skinned alive the last of the diplomats and boasted that he had repelled an attack by King Osric Darmon."

Our second meeting with the chieftain followed our day of rest and refit. I explained that the rest of our clan was awaiting us.

Without prompting, Domeel Doreen offered his hospitality and rose to dismiss us. "I have the business of war to attend to. We will speak more of this later and how we may find a common enemy. Is your pet, the princess, well? Do not believe everything the sorceress tells you."

Before I could protest, he departed and we were escorted back to our apartments. Dave and I spent the rest of the night arguing how to best accomplish the next part of the mission.

"I'm concerned that if we both leave, Domeel Doreen will mistreat the princess again. We're protected by his code of conduct, but she's an enemy prisoner."

"And you don't want to abandon your crush."

I bristled. "It's not like that. She's our connection to a *human* presence here. I don't trust Domeel. I'd say our peace with the Tarns is fragile at best and partly based on their assumption we're some kind of angels from their version of an afterlife. Anyway, my goal is to get us to Talis's people. We need her."

"Just busting your shells, brah. She is something, though."

It wasn't necessary for me to agree. An obvious truth doesn't need to be restated. The sun warms us. Adversity forges us. Talis's beauty and aura of grace—even as weakened and frail as she was—were as otherworldly as the planet we rested on, the aliens we had a tentative friendship with, and the city we took refuge in.

"I'll commo check with you hourly. Maybe we get lucky and I'm able to find a spot where I can relay between you and the base."

"That'd be good."

"Tarns. Vistaran," he recited. "It's a lot to keep straight."

"Karlo will get it if no one else does."

"Daylight's burning." Dave gave my arm one last pump. "I'm going straight through. Shouldn't take me more than a day or two since I'm not trying to avoid attention."

We'd made all the usual contingencies for losing commo. The priority was him getting the team informed of the situation. What happened after that would be in the hands of the chief. If the initial plan hadn't changed, then it meant the whole team making the exodus to shelter here with the Tarns. In the meantime, I was going to keep working to get a more complete picture of the geopolitical picture of our new world. I was already organizing an area study of Vistara—the name of this world.

"Slow and steady, man. Don't screw the pooch and get stuck in a sandpit."

He scowled. "That your version of break a leg? Thanks."

"Sorry." It was one of the dangers we'd discussed. We'd taken it slow on our way here and more than once had investigated a potential route on foot in the dark, testing the ground as best we could before cautiously driving over it. We'd spun wheels a few times while praying loudly. "Following our tracks back'll be easy, especially in the day."

"And with that, I'm outta here. On the flip side, brah."

I stayed and watched him go until he dropped out of sight. I'd be able to receive him for longer than he could me, the powerful radio in the GMV having many times the range of my MBITR. He might be able to hear my squelch if nothing else, but we both realistically anticipated losing contact with each other after a short while, despite our optimistic plan.

Looking back into the city, you might think I was anxious about being on my own, surrounded by aliens. If anything, I felt anxious for Dave. For myself, I felt exhilarated at the opportunity to learn more about the world I now inhabited. And of course, I'd be lying if I didn't confess that I felt the urge to hurry back to our quarters and see the princess, to hear her voice, and feel the warm glow of her smile.

But besides her undeniable allure, I was restless to continue our conversation. She accepted that I was not who she thought I was.

"I see that it is so, lord, that you are not one of the Whites. Forgive me, but though your strength is great, perhaps you are not so transcendent a being as I believe a lord of the undying lands ought to be. You are very—"

I was hoping she would say sympathetic. Kind. Heroic, even.

"—coarse."

I laughed.

She did, too. "Forgive me. I did not mean that poorly. I mean you are hardy. And genial. As a warrior should be. Not like a custodian of the afterlife."

Hardy. Genial. I'd never been called either. Though I'd certainly been called worse.

"But you flew here. Why do your companions not fly to us now?"

I explained in as much detail as she could absorb about our arrival and crash.

"Your craft must have been great indeed. To travel so far and carry such mass. Our airships are not so great and can carry only a small party and not for such distances."

When she faded despite her best attempt at staying engaged, I left her to Beraal's care. Interrogations didn't yield a full picture of someone's knowledge from a single session. And this was far from that. I was depending on her being my guide to an entire world of which I knew next to nothing. One thing I desperately wished to revisit was her revelation about Vistara and the existence of other worlds with human life. Later, Beraal retrieved me to let me know the princess felt up to speaking more.

"Lord, are you Thulian? Hyborian? If your science is so great that you have ships to cross the ether between worlds as you describe, then you must have arrived here accidentally—flown off course."

"I'm sorry, Talis Darmon Sylah, those names mean nothing to me." I kept using the full name she'd proclaimed, but got a weird vibe this time as I said it.

"Lord, it is not necessary to use family *and* maternal dynasty names at all times. Now that I understand you are from elsewhere, I see I must educate you. It is proper to call me Talis Darmon, as we are acquainted."

"Talis Darmon, then. But please stop calling me 'lord.' I've told you, I'm not who you think. I'm a soldier."

"Then you have a rank? Is it General Benjamin Colt?"

I winced inside. I'd read about generals I'd admired, but I'd never met any to make me wish I was one. "I'm a sergeant. But I'd prefer you call me by my name. Ben." At that she frowned.

"You trusted me with your name. Deacon Benjamin Colt. Is it not then proper that now announced, I should drop your dynasty as a given, and call you Deacon Benjamin?"

It was sickly to my ear and reminded me of a scolding by my mother. Not an association I wanted to have when the princess spoke my name.

"It's different where I come from. If it's not acceptable to use a single name, then I'd prefer if you called me Benjamin Colt."

"Lord Benjamin Colt, it is."

✣ ✣ ✣

In his absence, Domeel Doreen had left me free run of his capital city of Maleska Mal, but the princess was not to be afforded the same courtesy.

She was in the main room for the first time, drawn to the object I'd left sitting atop a short column. The flat begged for some adornment. I'd perched my helmet on the bare stone stump, and she traced the camo patterns over it with a gentle finger.

My heart jumped when I saw her and the way she examined my belongings with such curiosity and care. It was like a promise of no winds on the drop zone and the anticipation of the thrill of the jump without the pain of a hard collision at its end.

"Talis Darmon, I'm glad to see you on your feet. Are you better?"

She radiated life itself with her smile. All the mysteries of the universe lay behind it, and I wanted to explore them all.

"I am much better, Benjamin Colt. Beraal has gone with the attendants to fetch a meal. She's used your status to demand finer service from the kitchens. I'm afraid the offerings have been poor. She's used to running my affairs and takes great pride in perfection."

"I have so many questions. Beraal is a Tarn, yet she's very devoted to you."

"And I to her."

"But your people are at war with the Tarns."

"With the Mydreen. Once we warred with our cousins of the Yellow dynasties to the south, and with all Tarns, but no more."

"Hmm."

I'd have to get her to help with a basic map and lay out the major polities in some kind of primer. From macro to micro, I wanted to understand this world, but she'd awakened a hunger that she hadn't yet sated for me when mentioning humans from other worlds—and assigned us as having come from one of them. It meant my knowledge of Vistara wasn't all that was lacking. The very planets in the night sky above us were part of a much bigger mystery. I asked her to please explain.

"Nearly all the worlds around us are home to those of our kind, Benjamin Colt. Come." She stood and led me to the balcony.

"There is Thulia." She pointed to the bright blue dot in the sky that Karlo had identified as our Earth, and the tiny dot near it, the white moon I spent a life patrolling under like a midnight sun.

"Hyboria." The silver planet I knew as Venus.

"Sarkasia." She identified a bright orange pinhole in the curtain of night. Maybe it was Saturn or Jupiter. "But the Sarkasians live on the moons that circle above it, too small for us to see on such a dim night."

"You're in contact with other worlds and their people?" It was incredible.

Her face became sad. "No. The means and the knowledge we once had has been lost for all the recorded ages. Our scientists tell us of a time when we traveled between worlds, when Vistara was a garden paradise, before the age to which we were born and our inherited struggle to keep our world alive."

I listened in awe as we ate, and she told me more of the history of Vistara.

"The Tarn are not native to this world," the princess said as Beraal joined us at the table after the attentive perfectionist insisted on proper placement of the feast she'd returned with. Only after shooing the attendants away and serving us did she accept the princess's encouragement to join us.

"Our people came from the place of dreams, lord," Beraal said. "But the Tarn are practical. We do not cultivate sages and tinkerers. All Tarns are warriors. We spend little time fretting over that which can't be changed or does not matter."

Talis Darmon gave a tiny smile of sympathy. "Which is partially why we struggle to keep Vistara living. The Mydreenian Tarns, especially the clan of Domeel Doreen, refuse to act as the proper custodians of the very machinery that keeps them and all Vistara alive."

Vistara was once a green world. As green as my own as she described it, with oceans and life of myriad forms I did not understand by the names she used. Over eons, it slowly withered to the become the barren desert it now was. Water and even the air we breathed was manufactured. The race between production and consumption was a constant war to keep the planet life-sustaining for all its inhabitants.

"My father's counsel of science produces the last guardians of the atmosphere plants. Their sect maintains the ancient foundries that keep the world alive. Domeel Doreen and his fellow chieftains have allowed the works in his control to become derelict and refuse help from my father's scientists to maintain them. The one here in Filestra, I mean Maleska Mal, is a perfect example."

"Filestra?" I asked.

"This grand city was once known as Filestra and was home to many thousands. Now, it is little more than a blighted ruin that the Mydreen claim as capital to their clan. Besides the atmosphere plant, it holds little value."

"You say the Mydreen are neglecting the atmosphere works in their city?"

"The atmosphere works are sturdy and have operated for thousands of years. They run virtually independently and the mechanisms can self-repair. For the most part. Their processes are mysterious and have defeated the efforts by the offices of the devisers to recreate, no matter how they have toiled to do so. In my lifetime, the forges of our air have become frail. The sect has succeeded in keeping most of them operating. But they are failing. Domeel Doreen refuses to allow my father's scientists to enter his territories, no matter how we have attempted to bribe and placate him and his fellow clan leaders.

"We are reaching the most desperate time in the life of Vistara. When I saw a White lord appear, my heart told me we were too late, and that it was at last the end of all things, as has been foretold, and we would all soon sail on the River Blix. That our toil and efforts to save Vistara have been the futile acts of our hubris, as warned."

Tears trailed down her cheeks, and she buried her face in her hands. I wanted to reach across the terrible distance between us to comfort her, but I was restrained by the gulf between us. It would be a tiny stretch of my hand to hers across the table, but to me it was an immeasurable canyon, plunging insanely deep to keep me from her. Because what she told me was all so incredible, I was helpless to comfort her.

I found my courage to try.

"Talis Darmon, I've told you I am not a lord from your undying lands. I can't be the messenger you fear."

Sometimes, the first step is the hardest. The pain you dread that will consume you, that will taunt your body to quit, you learn it can be silenced by will alone—if you're determined that you will not be stopped. Not by pain. Not by death. That determination is the first step to becoming the hero you imagine yourself to be. I used what I knew and steeled myself to try where I'd so often failed—to use intellect instead of force. And in this moment, a dazzling energy swept over me.

I'm not the most educated person. I know what the word epiphany means. In the abstract. Like maudlin stories about robots seeking humanity and by some miracle are granted emotions. Or maybe in my case, a beast of burden who's learned that the pain of the whip can only be avoided through exhausting labor. A revelation came to me. A moment of clarity and purpose like maybe Joan of Arc experienced. Was this what writers meant when they painted some tragic yet heroic figure as touched by a supernatural power? It was a measure of my conviction that I didn't feel absurd as I spoke.

"Princess. I left a dying world. I don't know how I came to be here. But I swear to you my oath. My purpose in life is to serve. To serve a greater good. I must protect those around me or my life has no meaning."

I had her attention, and she met my eyes. Everything I said became branded on my soul by a searing red iron.

"If I cannot save my own world, then there can be only one reason I have been sent here. To save yours. To serve you by my life or my death as I would my homeland. If there is a way I can save Vistara, I promise I will find it."

16

As more days passed, I made it my task to learn all I could from her and Beraal. The tragedy of Vistara and Talis Darmon weighed on me. The shoe was on the other foot, and I was now the one who had to stop our sessions when I could process no more. I overloaded with tales of Red, Yellow, and ghostly White human Vistarans. My head swam with dizziness as though I were ill with a building fever. The realization had become final for me that Vistara was my permanent home. Robinson Crusoe on Mars! But not alone with only a monkey for company.

What does it say about me that I think of things in terms of movies and not literature? If it were up to me to record the great cultures of the Earth, then our posterity would be only the best lines of all the sitcoms and thrillers I'd been raised on. And dialogue from the best NPCs. Sad, I know.

The world that had produced that entertainment no longer existed. I didn't know if I was in the past, the future, or even on the same plane of reality I'd come from. The ridiculous assertions of the suits at Area 51 about the slipstream were so much useless syntax now.

If you think you'd fare better in such circumstance, then you judge yourself too lightly and me too harshly. I'd lost an entire world, and myself with it. As much comfort as I took from being near Talis Darmon, there were moments by myself in the dark when I felt the terror of abandonment. Should something happen to her, I would be truly alone. I imagined the worst. There'd been no radio communication. The team had left me to search elsewhere. Even worse, some horrific tragedy befell them outside of my knowledge.

In SERE school—survival, evasion, resistance, escape training—I was taught how important hope was. Prisoners of war overcame the harshest conditions of torture and deprivation to survive and return home. Sometimes years kept in isolation was part of their confinement. Belief—in America, in their faith, in themselves—got them through. As well as the hope that someday their imprisonment would be at an end. That their country and their families never forgot them, and would welcome them home.

There was no home for me to return to. I accepted that now. And I evaluated my situation.

This was a one-way trip. That it had ended on this alien world, well, was it really worse than if I'd arrived as planned in future America? What if the mutagen plague hadn't abated like the experts prognosticated? They'd been wrong about the slipstream. Would they have been any less wrong about anything else? Would we have been in a kind of *Mad Max* universe, fighting hair-lip invaders in a post-apocalyptic world that was the stuff of every doom-predicting TV show? Or would we have become the enforcers for a new protected class of feudal lord? In fortresses where we doled out the magic of Baby Blues like gods to the desolated population that remained.

Karlo and I had kicked around all those possibilities, and many more, as we lost sleep in isolation at Area 51, sharing our worst fears with each other about the terrible future that might await us.

"It is what it is," I concluded inadequately. The saying was our refuge of both wisdom and ignorance anytime words failed.

"I'll tell you one thing, Ben. I may be a soldier and under obligation to obey the orders of those appointed over me, but I'll never forget it's the *lawful* orders of our leaders. And I'm not going to let anyone else forget it, either. These Washington types are working under their own authority. Say they do get rid of the hair-lips, but in three years the whole world is in a Stone Age. I'm pretty sure their plan for what's on the other side of this cockamamie stargate isn't covered by the Constitution. You think they're going to govern by consensus? It's all emergency powers gobbledygook that they've granted themselves. No one's talked about it yet, but I'm sure the captain and Mike would agree. I'm not going to be some stormtrooper for these beltway geeks to set themselves up as rulers in the future."

"Amen to that," I agreed.

Karlo was inferior to no one in the intellect department. He was humble. Humble for real, whereas I only pretended to be. His distaste for the civilian leadership of this mission incubated my misgivings about them, as well. My slight exposure to their presence had confirmed what I'd always believed about them. We were the serfs and they were the landed gentry. We were the chess pieces and they were the players. We'd been spared having any of the suits accompany us in our stick. They'd apparently felt it wisest to surround themselves with the greatest numbers of armed protectors, and had divided out among the many C-17s stuffed with Rangers. More guns ready to die in their service than what was on a tiny A-Team. And that had suited us just fine.

As I thought about it in the darkness, I was regretful that all the C-17s hadn't come out together on the other side, if for no other reason than so I could be a foil in the egotistic plans Karlo and I predicted the suits would default to.

I missed Karlo. And Dave. If they had been there, my fears and doubts would've evaporated. There would've been no obstacle to my boastful and grandiose vow to the princess. I made my decision and committed myself completely to my new reality. This was home. I would find a way to make my mission the team's mission. Because I had faith the team would come for me. And together, we would make everything right.

The next morning, I felt at ease and confident again. Just the sight of the princess made me forget my insecurities by thinking of her welfare instead of my predicament. "I'll be back," I assured her. Each day I explored the city. From its center I chose new destinations each day, never wandering far, but choosing a distant spire to follow to its base while turning frequently to identify the return path I'd take to find my way back to her. Along the way, I would pause to observe the goings-on and architecture of the city.

It was much like any populace I could imagine. Women and children seemed to perform familiar functions. Animals roamed the streets. All seemed to follow the convention of having multiple sets of legs. I catalogued the cats and dogs by size, the smallest being what I took as rodents that the cats chased. What I called dogs were anything but. Massive beasts whose shoulders came up nearly to my chest. When one yawned, it exposed a wide maw of teeth and tusks in its square, stout mouth.

They reminded me of dogs mainly in their demeanor. They were most always napping. On my first excursion, I'd stumbled on one sleeping. I reflexively brought my rifle up, but quickly returned it to my side when after it woke with a growl, shrank back, and whined as if awaiting harm.

As I observed further, it became apparent that the Tarns here were most unlike Beraal. The cruelty they showed each other and their animals was difficult to ignore. Females herded children with slaps and shoves. Tarns went out of their way to kick or abuse an animal within reach. Warriors tussled often in the streets, sometimes with bloodshed the result.

The Mydreen Tarns mostly ignored my presence. What attempts I'd made at communicating with them had been met with indifference. I was not bothered nor was I made to feel welcome. None of it deterred me in my task to gain more information about the terrain I occupied, both physical and native. I could learn only so much talking with my only two companions, and my firsthand observations would be necessary if the team needed to develop a strategy for working with the Tarns. I was evaluating their people and their culture for that possibility. The Tarns as our indigenous forces. I was still an SF operator, no matter I was on Mars.

Today, as I explored a new avenue between the massive buildings, I came across one of the sprawled forms of the biggest of the domesticated animals in my way. Coming the other way was a Tarn and her children. She viciously kicked the sleeping animal from behind, and it woke with a yelp to flee down an alley.

"Was that necessary? You could've gone around," I said irritably at the passing Tarn, receiving no reply as she pushed her curious children ahead of her and away from me.

My trepidation at the size of the animal was overcome by my pity and desire to make a friend. I loved animals. I'd always wanted to have a home where someday I could have pets like I'd had as a child. The life of a soldier, especially one like me, had made that an impossibility.

I peered down the narrow alley. The dog sat on its haunches, scratching itself with multiple feet.

"Hey boy, are you alright?"

The dog stopped its activity and lowered its massive chest to the ground. I knew an animal preparing for a charge when I saw one. I tried again with my best Steve Irwin imitation.

"You're a big fella, aren't you? What a beauty you are."

I dropped to a knee, but kept one hand on my rifle, just in case. Soon enough, the beast took a few steps forward, sniffing ahead as it did. Finally, it was close enough that I ventured to extend a hand. If it chose to snap at me, I'd lose a hand for sure.

It sniffed. It extended its tongue, and I let it taste me. Next, I brushed the thick hide of its jaw with the back of my hand. It lay down and rolled over. A few belly pats and more gentle compliments, and soon I had a companion that followed me wherever I went. The Tarns gave notice as the dog kept pace with me on the rest of the day's exploration and returned with me to the center of the city and the palace of Domeel Doreen.

A Tarn I had not seen in some time descended the steps of the palace. It was the red-sashed warrior I'd tossed in the melee, the one Domeel called Khraal Kahlees. He'd left with the chieftain, and I wondered if his return meant the chieftain had also.

I hailed him. My new friend was still with me, and he growled as the hugest of Tarns came near.

"Easy, boy. Sit."

The beast obeyed as though he understood me and panted happily.

"Deacon Benjamin Colt," the Tarn said, towering above me. I was taken aback that he'd remembered my name. He noted my companion. "Gadron of the desert are not like those of the mountains. They hunt in packs and avoid habitation. The ones in the city are tolerated in small number to kill other pests. You need but strike it to let it know its place."

"Do your kind not keep animals as companions? Like the beasts you ride?"

The Tarn grunted. "We of the Korund do. The gadron are, as you say, companions."

I searched my memory of things Beraal had tried to educate me about. "You come from the mountain region to the west?"

He said nothing but did not depart. It was as much of a conversation as I'd had yet with any Tarn besides Beraal and Domeel.

"Beraal has told me about your clan."

"She is of my kin."

"Talis Darmon Sylah tells me in the west, the Korundi Tarn and the Vistaran humans are not enemies. That your kin work and live among her people, and many of hers among yours."

He again remained silent and stoic. I was undeterred.

"What are you doing here so far from home?"

"Do you wish to know more of my people? Then come."

Without explanation he departed. His strides were enormous, and I took one of my sailing bounds and caught up with him. The warrior was indifferent to my presence at his side and continued his journey. My eight-legged companion squealed and followed. I decide to play the silent warrior as well and kept pace. We traveled around the palace through a sloping passage between buildings to end up in the large courtyard that stretched beneath the apartments I occupied with my parolees. Military-style barracks and stables lay on the far side, and beyond that were the pens where Talis and Beraal had been kept. The field had been where her people were murdered in front of her in ritualistic fashion, and I assumed it was no coincidence that Domeel housed his enemy in full sight of the slaughterhouse to continue her torture.

I stayed at his side as he marched to where more red-sashed Tarns waited with their mounts. I'd not seen other Korund Tarns in the city. They appeared to be loading out for a journey.

"Are you departing the city, Khraal Kahlees?"

I took a backhand across my chest and flew backward, the wind knocked out of me as ingrained instincts took over and I rolled back on my feet. A train hitting me at full speed would've left me less stunned.

"Of Vistara or not, I demand combat. Domeel Doreen's protection does not extend to matters of honor. Offense was given, and offense was taken."

There's no more certain way to flip my switch than by what he'd just done. The familiar red glasses of aggression tinted my vision. The drums of belligerence pounded in my ears. There'd been no anticipation before his sneak assault, so there was no pre-fight anxiety to quell.

Fear didn't exist in me once a fight started. He'd thrown the first blow. So it was on.

"You're going to regret that, just like I made you regret attacking me once before." I closed with him, judging my best opening when he launched at me. He was faster than the other Tarns I'd fought, but not fast enough. I slipped his lunge and threw some rapid blows at his flank as we passed each other. I hurt him, his winces and stagger proof.

Some of his men moved in but before I could react, an enormous gray hide hurtled between us, growling and snarling with an ear-piercing snarl I'd not heard before. My attention returned to my opponent who sent a back kick at me as all four arms braced off the ground. I ducked and tackled his planted leg and drove, heaving him onto his chest.

I scrambled to mount the massive back and shot an arm around his neck and began my naked choke. He reared off the ground and clawed at my back with his uppermost limbs. His nails tore into my flesh and white pain seared me. Instead of trying to escape, I squeezed even harder against both sides of his tree trunk neck. He flailed and dropped to his knees. He flung onto his back. I splinted and braced as he drove his mass into me, my tiny figure trapped between him and the hard soil.

He ground me like a massive stone crushing wheat to flour, and I doubled my efforts. My legs found their way around his trunk and I wrapped them around his lower arms. I'd learned by experience they were weaker than the upper set on a Tarn. He pulled at my arms with his upper limbs, and I felt the life start to go out of him. My lips were next to his ear. Instead of biting it as I'd considered, I spent some of my precious oxygen.

"Yield or die, Tarn. Or mine will be the last voice you ever hear before you sail the River Blix."

He gave a last attempt at breaking my choke, but it was brief and faded quickly. With what I judged to be the last of his consciousness, he furiously tapped my arms. I took that to mean he surrendered. I cautiously released my hold and pushed him off me onto his stomach. My pistol was still on me, and I reached for it as I anticipated being rushed by his men. My companion was still engaged in my defense, viciously darting from side to side and holding the other red-sashes at bay. My rifle lay behind me and I bounced to retrieve it.

"Stay your hand and call off your beast," Khraal Kahlees coughed. "Korundi, withdraw!"

"Come here, boy, come here. Come to me."

My feral guardian gave a howl that could curdled fresh milk on a cold day, then trotted to my side.

Khraal Kahlees rubbed his neck and moved to where his men waited as commanded. One rode forward leading a mount and passed the reigns to his lieutenant. He took them, and in one motion swung onto the beast. He glared, jaw thrust forward to bare tusks.

"Beraal has told me. You are no White lord of the underworld. I do not know what manner of human you are, but Domeel Doreen does not yet know, either. Pray he does not learn otherwise, or you and your princess will surely be on this field together for his pleasure." The tusks retreated. As they did, his scowl did as well.

"If you live and ever find yourself in the Korund Mountains, the name Khraal Kahlees will bring you protection. You have bested me twice. I owe you the honor that goes with that as my better. For now."

He galloped off with his cavalry, leaving me alone.

"OOF."

An overwhelming force pushed me to the ground, and I instantly had a face of rough tongue lapping at me. My adopted puppy, who was the size of a small horse, was crushing the wind from me all over again.

"It's okay, boy, it's okay. You did good. What a good boy you are!"

His short stubby tail wagged in glee.

"I suppose you need a name." I squinted as I searched my brain, patting his side heartily.

"Warthog? Like an A-10—a tank buster. Nah. Apache! Like the helicopter. A deadly angel watching over me. Apache, it is."

If he disliked his new name, it wasn't apparent to me.

"C'mon, boy. Let's get you a bone. Better find you a place outside the palace, though. I don't think Beraal will let you in the house."

Apache trotted alongside, rubbing against me in assurance to the point he drove me off course as I tried to steer us back to the path.

"Deacon Benjamin Colt!" Talis called to me with urgency from the narrow balcony above, Beraal at her side as always. She cried my name again, loudly, and with even more distress.

I tensed. Had she seen? Or was she in danger?

"Are you alright, Princess?"

From even this far away, I perceived her shift from concern to anger.

"Am I—alright!" she exclaimed. She pounded fists on the railing as she stammered, "I stood ready to throw myself from this height if you failed to rise. I pray—no, I *order*—don't leave me without your protection again!"

17

She was a queen on her throne of cushions, poised again and awaiting my return. She sat stiffly. Unapproachable and aloof. Beraal, the constant by her side, also giving me the steely eyes of disapproval. Two different species, the same look—but the new element of tusks fully bared thrown in to emote greatest displeasure. I was expecting a different ambience in the air of our apartments at my triumphant return. Maybe concern for my well-being? Adulation? A little hero worship? I'd just kicked the snot out of a towering four-armed juggernaut with a rep as El Numero Uno in the bad-ass department among his peers.

"Your oath to serve me cannot be fulfilled if you are distracted by the need to prove your martial courage at every opportunity."

My jaw dropped. Khraal Kahlees pulled a punk move on me, and I punished him for it. I was the victim! Or, would-be victim, if things had gone differently. I reconsidered my impression of double-K. Had I thought the Tarn dignified at our first meeting? It was trust misplaced, based on an erroneous perception and my foolish attempt to build a bridge. It'd almost cost me my life. The bluest waters are the most inviting, but until you've plumbed their depths, you find they conceal the greatest dangers. I'd violated a basic principle of survival in a hostile environment, and let myself drop from condition yellow to condition dumbass.

But being wrongly accused by my solitary—friend? Crush? Charge?—it stung. You can guess how that affected me, since I've so embarrassingly shared my insecurities. I was ready to launch into a defense of my innocence when her anger sublimated straight into tears. Blistering dry ice becoming mist. She sniffled, the waterworks started, and my defensive strategy failed as if she'd pulled a knife in the middle of a fistfight. Then I remembered—she'd blurted she was prepared to kill herself if something had happened to me.

I was a heel.

"My princess, I—"

"Do not speak to me so!"

Now what? What could I have said to earn that rebuke? My mistakes were piling up rapidly, and I swear I didn't know how I'd angered her now. I fumed in frustration. I thought of Dave's rule of conduct—if you keep your mouth shut, you don't confirm the proof of your ignorance. But this was more than my lack of experience with women.

There was more at play than I understood.

Foreign cultures are foreign. If you believe all people are basically alike, then you've fallen for one of the great lies so commonly foisted upon the minds of those educated in the land of plenty I grew up in. If by saying that all people are basically alike, you mean they desire to not be hungry, to not die from exposure to the elements, to be spared physical abuse by those more powerful than them—then I agree. If you mean we all want a little house with a picket fence, a spouse and a family, the liberty to self-develop, intellectual freedom, a say in how we're governed, blah, blah, blah—then I do not agree.

The farmer in the middle of Waste-a-Stan wants to drink the blood of the other tribe because they worship on Saturday instead of on Sunday. There are a thousand examples of inhumanity by one group on another whose justification is every bit as ridiculous and factually real in human history—current, not ancient.

My tribe is trained in those realities. We're taught how to navigate those obstacles when immersed in foreign cultures. Were even taught how to leverage some of those beliefs and to exploit them to our advantage.

Here I was, not only in a foreign culture, but a truly alien one if ever there were a definition of the word. Maybe the Chief was right. I didn't have the necessary time in SF. This was my first actual mission. I'd not had a single overseas operation with even the tamest elements of foreign culture to learn in. I wished the team were here and tried not to give life to my fears that they wouldn't come.

But a lesson learned came to mind. The short version of how I learned this fantastically crucial precept is like this. I had a friend in the

82nd. Very accomplished at judo. He was kind enough to teach me. He'd trained in Japan when his dad was stationed there. Once when I'd missed a session with him, at our next he chewed me out because he thought I'd flaked on him. I tried to explain that my squad leader had pulled me for extra duty, but he stopped me abruptly, then told me something that helped me succeed for the rest of my career.

"The Japanese may be screwy in some ways, but my coach taught me more than just technique. He taught me attitude. The Japanese are all about face. I knew that. But it's way more complex.

"I was late to training once and my coach chewed me out. It wasn't my fault. I tried to explain, but it infuriated him more. But I hadn't pissed him off too badly, and though he didn't like most Americans, he apparently thought I was worth the effort. He took pity on me and explained. 'To not accept a rebuke is poor character. To make excuses is impudent,' he told me. 'To accept a minor accusation and to admit fault—whether deserved or not—shows good character. To Japanese people, an apology is accepted as sincere. And the slate is wiped clean. Knowing this, then to take responsibility whether just or not, face is kept. Americans don't know this.'"

My buddy's advice to me—that if it was for anything less than a UCMJ offense—accept the rebuke. Apologize if it's appropriate. Only explain if someone demands an explanation. And according to him, if I knew that pearl, then the world would be my oyster. I scoffed. Every stupid boot learns to snap to parade rest and that there only three appropriate responses. Yes, Sergeant. No, Sergeant. No excuse, Sergeant.

But a few days later, a similar situation happened to me with my platoon sergeant. Something minor, but absolutely not my fault. I was getting chewed out because my squad mate hadn't properly set the timing and headspace on the fifty. I tried the tidbit out, but with a new attitude. With remorse and sincerity.

"Yes, Sergeant."

He accepted my taking responsibility. "Do it right." And he moved on. I knew that he knew it wasn't my fault. He just wanted it done and done right. It had been a test. And I'd passed. Success breeds habit, and it was one I took to heart that has served me since. And the profoundness of what and how I'd learned the lesson was no less a moment of transformation for me than the connectedness of a Zen awakening.

It's just that mine occurred not in kneeling meditation, but with a tongue stung by drips of sweaty camo paint and nostrils full of burnt gunpowder.

When I was in the Q-course, I'd heard the rumor that my judo buddy went to the big show. Yes—all the way to dreamland. That unit where only the big dogs ran. It didn't surprise me. It was much more than his physical abilities. One of those myths you heard about the supersecret unit was they didn't necessarily want the *best* guy. They wanted the *right* guy. I knew that my buddy was that guy. It was his character. And he'd taught me something important about how to show it. I'm certain that his advice helped get me where I am today, by teaching me about pride and attitude. Even though sometimes I sucked at it.

Would it work with her?

"Yes, Talis Darmon Sylah. I apologize." I remained still and awaited her next rebuke.

She sniffed and dried her eyes, and as quickly transformed back to the radiance that continued to stun me into singlemindedness. My mission was her. But, damsel in distress or not, I was flying over a landscape of surface-to-air missiles hidden beneath dense camo nets while enjoying the serene natural beauty of the view from 10,000 feet.

"Then let us proceed. How will you free me from this captivity?"

The doors opened abruptly and a guard entered.

"The Chieftain summons. Your clan is sighted outside the city."

My heart jumped. I ran to grab my plate carrier and checked my radio. Dead. I'd let the batteries die. I cursed as I changed them.

"Now," the guard grunted.

I kitted up. Before I left, there was something I had to know.

"Beraal. Khraal Kahlees said that you and he spoke about me. He knows who I am and my origin. What else did you tell him?"

The princess pivoted. "Have you done this?"

Beraal fell to a knee. "It is so. I have said that much to Khraal Kahlees."

"But why?" I asked.

Beraal kept her eyes turned down as she answered. "Khraal Kahlees is my kinsmen of the Korundi. But, more. He is my father, though he knows it not."

✠ ✠ ✠

"Good to hear your voice, Dave. I'll meet you where we first met the Mydreen welcome party. I'll escort you into their lines from there. Everyone knows the situation? First link up and all that. There's a full contingent with the chieftain."

"Copy that, Ben."

I was elated and accepted the hands up for a ride behind one of the mounted guards. I'd have preferred my own, but they hadn't offered. And, I might not be able to control one of their horses. Something to add to the list of new skills to learn.

Formed up outside the city was a gathering similar to the one that had met Dave and me days and days before. The chieftain sat in the center of the mounted warriors and my driver halted beside him. A full squadron flanked either side of his contingent of personal guards. They struck me as fresh from the field.

"Chieftain Domeel Doreen, I did not know you had returned. I'm pleased you're here to receive the rest of my clan."

My radio squelched. I had the speaker on.

"Colt, we have you in sight. How us?"

It was easy to spot the top of the Stryker in the distance.

"I see you, Dave. Wait one." I returned to my parley. "Chieftain, may I tell my people to approach?"

"No closer than the last flats of the plain, Benjamin Colt. There I will meet your kinsmen."

I expected as much. Though he hadn't admitted it during our brief palavers, his people who'd escaped our kill zone around the C-17 would've given him the benefit of intel about our capabilities. His intentions were to feel us out as allies for his war against the Reds. He wasn't ready to bring a bunch of white underworld warriors from the north and their killing tools into the middle of his home ground. He didn't get to be a chieftain in a world of savagery and craven brutality without expecting some kind of treachery on our part. I'd have been very suspicious had he simply wanted us to parade through his city and up to the steps of his palace to receive the keys to his kingdom as a welcome. Plus, we wouldn't have taken such bait.

"Dave, meet in the middle. I'll be waiting."

I dismounted. "Chieftain, I will go ahead on foot to meet my kinsman."

"Go with him," he said to the riders nearest. "Deacon Benjamin Colt. You have my oath, and I yours. If there is falseness in your intentions, remember I have the princess paroled to you."

I'd expected that. "My kind live or die by our word, Chieftain. And you have mine."

"Very well."

I walked as riders flanked me. The convoy of the Stryker and a GMV rolled. Halted far back from near the spot where Dave and I had made our stalk, was the other GMV. In tow behind it, a new piece of hardware. The large wheeled flatbed and Baby Blue.

The Chief's voice was familiar, and not the least bit sour to my ears. "Colt, we're coming in. Can you talk?"

"Affirm, Chief."

"Threat level?"

"Minimal. They don't have any heavy weaponry I've been able to discover. This group's just like they seem. On horseback, swords, spears, and their ray guns."

"Dave's given us the sitrep. Any changes since he's been out of the scene?"

"Negative. We're under their code of safe conduct and the chieftain's ready to parley and feel us out."

"Good work, Colt."

I won't kid you, the praise meant something to me.

"We're excited about the news there's real honest-to-goodness people here. Even if they are Martians. Looking forward to meeting your princess. Heard quite a bit about her."

"Roger, Chief. We've got a lot to go over about the ground situation."

"First things first. See you in a few."

Then began a long day of courtship rituals for the first date—potentially deadly instead of awkward if we messed up. It was hard to suppress my elation at seeing everyone, and quick fist bumps and mumbled greetings had to suffice. Missing were Karlo, Matt, and Mitch. They'd be with the other GMV guarding us and Baby Blue. Mitch, I knew was somewhere on his MK 22, watching over us from afar. Matt would be on the M134, and Karlo behind the wheel, ready to join in on the door gun. We were under the magnifying glass of the Tarn potentate's attention, and we were trying not to get burned like ants. There'd be time for catching up later.

Under a canopy, we met with the chieftain, me acting as translator, with Dave ready to act as secondary, his translator brace still in place. The chieftain's guard were a shield to their leader's back and were also interspersed with the rest of the team outside the shade of the tarp the guys had spread between the vehicles as a meeting place.

Our folding camp chairs were too tiny for a Tarn, and instead, a stack of ammo crates were his position of honor. Bottled water spewed out like a geyser from the chieftain's first grasp, but the taste of what remained seemed to please him, and Dave offered him another, which he accepted gingerly with his lower hands.

I made introductions. It was cumbersome, translating. After everyone saw the magic of the brace in action, Marky-Mark made the request for one for themselves. "Tell him we're glad to offer what we can in trade."

The chieftain made us wait before replying. "They are precious."

"I need yours then, Dave," Chief Bryant pointed.

"Once mated, they serve no other," Domeel Doreen said, after I dutifully repeated what had been said, making sure no comment went without repeating it for his comprehension.

I hadn't been aware that the braces were a single-user item. The princess told me that what tech the Tarns possessed came from her people. I wasn't going to offer that bit of knowledge just yet as there was no way for me to conceal from the chieftain anything I said. And such a weakness might be taken as a slight if I revealed as much so abruptly. There was much that would have to wait till when I was alone with the team.

"But perhaps it can be arranged," Domeel added. "Eventually."

After much negotiating, it was decided the team and our war wagons would remain outside the city, but that the Chief and Marky could accompany us into the city for further dialogue in the palace. It was a start.

Dave came with us, and we guided our team leadership into the city, out of earshot of the Tarns as they'd ridden ahead without us. I narrated for our visitors, as awestruck as I'd been my first time experiencing the dream-like architecture and the alien denizens within. We reached the palace and, when seated and served water, we started again with me acting the terp'.

"Deacon Benjamin Colt has proven himself honorable and capable."

I was a little embarrassed to relay the praise, but hey, I rolled with it.

"He has bested fine warriors as would an accomplished Mydreen lieutenant with many wars under his saddle. If the other Whites of your clan are such fighters, I am honored to also offer my oath to you."

Marky bristled and I took note of it while remaining stone faced myself. It was a side I hadn't seen to Mark before—not that I'd ever really gotten to know him. His choice. It struck me just then, because I'd thought the Chief was the sole personality on the team to have such a flaw. The need to have someone else do worse so they could do better. It was like Robin Hood economics. You had to steal from the rich to give to the poor because the amount of wealth was fixed. Only it was honor instead of coin. At their core, they didn't like others to do well. And his true self was being exposed under a red Martian sun.

Whatever grudge he held against me it must've been big if he couldn't hold it in. When I got the chance, I'd make it clear that if he had beef with me, it was one-sided, because I absolutely did not give a shit about the Chief's decision to demote me on the team. And if he thought me being complimented by the chieftain was a threat to his position, I was oblivious as an aardvark to taxes about it. There were way more important things to care about than either of our prides. Attention was still on me, and with the chieftain's permission, I explained how their code of conduct worked.

Chief Bryant grunted. "Colt is my junior, Chieftain, but he has been allowed to speak for me as my representative. It is my wish as chieftain of my clan to be friends with you and to offer our assistance. We do not want hostilities, but cooperation."

"And what help can you offer? What cooperation do you seek?"

I faithfully translated the Chief's offers of mutual support. He'd briefed me his plan on the way over, and I'd given what recommendations I could. We weren't ready to blindly make the chieftain's enemies our enemies or anything like that. We knew so little about the nature of the conflict here. It was bad luck on top of bad luck that we'd first encountered the Tarn instead of any human Vistarans.

The Chief kept at it to make the standard promise of friendly—but noncommittal—support. "As we learn more, we can offer more. We ask for shelter and the chance to become friends. For now, that is all. And I give our oath we mean no harm against you or your people."

The chieftain was a cautious Tarn. He kept his own counsel while considering everything we said. He knew how to play his cards close to his metal-plated chest. After an interminably long wait, he stood. "You are welcome to remain where you are outside the city. I offer sustenance to you, as is expected from those of us who are suckled in the desert. I will send for you when it is time to speak more."

"Domeel Doreen," I asked before he left. "May I take them to speak with the princess?"

"He may accompany you, Deacon Benjamin Colt." He used two hands to indicate the Chief. "And as you have taken her parole, you will continue as her bailiff. It is my pleasure that you remain in the palace."

"What'd he say?" the Chief asked after the chieftain and entourage departed.

Dave replied for me. "The chieftain wants Ben close. He's a kind of a hostage, too."

"But he agreed to let me take you to the princess, Chief."

Dave snickered. "This you'll want to see, Chief. Just don't get suckered in like Ben, though. Marky and I will wait for you outside."

18

"So she's a prisoner. From the Red Vistarites?" Chief asked as I led.

"Vistarans."

"Red. Yellow. White," he recited. "Mountain Tarns, desert Tarns. What else?"

"C'mon. We can talk about it with the princess."

I made the formal introductions and the Chief bowed deeply, though I hadn't coached him to do so.

"More like her at home?" the Chief whispered from bended waist. The princess caught wind of the Chief's remark and pinned me down to translate.

"My chieftain wants to know about your people, Talis Darmon," I replied as diplomatically as I could, hoping the Chief caught the hint about his faux pas. He should've known better.

We spoke for an hour, as I showed the Chief the crude global map I'd drawn, laying out the major polities as the princess and Beraal had instructed me like an elementary school student learning continents on a desktop globe. He asked about the conflict, and I clarified where I could, putting into terms appropriate to our needs.

"Cultural and geographic aspects to the dispute. The utilization of vital resources is what I take as the linchpin to the Red part of the dispute. The Tarns are seminomadic and tech-poor. I don't have a good read on minority versus majority relationships, but the Red Vistarans live integrated with the mountain Tarn subculture, whereas the Mydreen isolate themselves from non-Tarn."

Our radios crackled with Marky-Mark's gravelly voice.

"Boss. It'll be dark soon. I should be back to oversee the security plan. I think you should, too."

"Roger, Top. Moving now. Colt, I need to get back."

"I'll escort you out."

The Chief thanked the princess and promised to return.

From her rigid-backed posture on the cushions—how she maintained the regal pose this entire time was impressive—she halted us. "Brandon Bryant. You have not yet made apparent how you intend to free me."

The Chief shot me a sideways glance before he answered her. "For now, ma'am, Colt here'll continue to be your bodyguard. The rest, I'll work out as I can. I have the responsibility for my entire team's safety to consider. I'll let you know."

She was about to say more when he ducked out. I followed on his heels, her exasperated groan a stone cap to seal off the Chief's deep well of unnerving disregard.

"She's used to bossing people around," the Chief said as we walked.

I kept my tongue.

"Her father's supposedly a king with a half a dozen major cities and most of the northern hemisphere his domain, yet she sits here a captive. Where's their army? That doesn't jibe with me. Not even Jimmy Carter sat on his hands so long before he got the balls to try for a hostage rescue. There's a lot to figure out here, Colt. We're here for the long haul, that's blindingly apparent. Karlo's got us all seeing how it is. We are on our own and in a situation like nothing we planned for. Unless we learn something drastically different to alter what we know—and so far, you haven't found anything to contradict our new truth—we're on Mars. Vistara, she calls it. And all our past troubles are so much water over the dam."

"It is that."

Marky and Dave were on the street, looking anxious. "Ready to roll, Chief?"

"Yes." The Chief gave me a hard look. "You're doing okay, Colt. But don't get ahead of yourself here. Don't forget you work for me. You may be camping in the sultan's tent, but you don't start acting like a free agent. You run everything past me first. Got it?"

"Of course, Chief. I'm just working on the intel part of things, not making any decisions for us, and certainly not committing us to anything. The only promise I've made is what it took to start the ball rolling to build trust with the chieftain."

"Oh?" he accused. "How about making promises to your new girlfriend? I've heard all about your little one-man war with the Tarns. That could've ended very badly and endangered the whole team. And offering yourself and us as her personal hostage rescue team. If it wasn't for the sultan's insistence that you stay behind, I'd jerk you back into place and have you digging foxholes, mister."

I kept my cool. "I did what I thought right, Chief."

"Chief, take it easy," Dave said. "It wasn't like that. He had to act. Everything Ben's done, I can't see how it could've been done different. Or better. It is what it is."

"At ease, Sergeant," Marky said. "This isn't a free-for-all. What the Chief says is law. Period."

"S'alright, Top." The Chief seemed to think better of his admonishment. "We'll get it worked out. For now, we're in a better position than we were. Colt and Dave did alright. I'm just letting it be known in a way that can't be misinterpreted—don't go off script. Got me?"

"Yes, Chief," I answered with my best humility and remorse, though I didn't mean it. I've never had an acting lesson, but I know that the most important thing an actor must do is be sincere. And if you can learn to fake that, you're gold.

"If the security situation pans out, we'll get the rest of our gear and supplies moved here from the crash site. We cached most everything that wasn't junk. We'll get oriented, keep building trust. We'll offer help, see what Karlo, Chuck, and Dougie can do in the way of health and infrastructure improvement—these people look like they need the help—and broach military assistance. And just keep going from there. This may become our new base and these our allies. One step at a time. It's what we have to do to stay alive and viable. That's the priority. Anything else, ain't even secondary. It's tertiary. Good to go?"

We all answered in the affirmative.

"See you tomorrow, Colt."

Dave gave me a look as if to say, "Sorry, bro." Maybe he'd played a little loose with his retelling of how things had gone down here. Maybe he just saw it differently than I did. But we were cool. He stood up to the Chief when it counted, so I was willing to cut him some slack. We'd work it out when we could.

I was anxious to talk to the rest of the guys, especially Karlo. Our one-man voice of reason and science had apparently kept at the guys with his logical analysis of our predicament, so much so that I didn't have to spend any energy convincing the Chief that we were where we were. Small victories.

"The code of conduct is solid," I said as the guys dropped into a three-man wedge to leave. "No one will start any crap with you."

"Good to know," Marky said as he opened the breach of his 203 to make sure there was a grenade still in the pipe. "But sometimes you have to educate the stupid ones with a lesson they can't fail to understand."

Back in the apartment, I interrupted the princess nervously pacing, her face riddled with anxiety. It hurt me. "Benjamin Colt," she hugged herself. "I do not like that man. I do not trust him. I fear that my situation has worsened rather than improved with the arrival of your friends. Please tell me it isn't so."

Like reflex, I was about to tell her everything was going to be all right. That I wouldn't let anything bad happen to her. That I'd find a way. I stopped before I even started, because my assurances rang hollow in my head as they came to me. They were empty platitudes. As useless as a politician's promise before an election. She'd put into words what I didn't want to, and her fears were my fears. The appearance of my backup hadn't resulted in their instantaneous shift to my worldview on the temperature of politics in the city. And if the Chief wasn't going to do the right thing in regards to the princess, then there were very tough times on the horizon for me.

She shivered and Beraal covered her with a shawl.

It was unclear to me why there wasn't an army surrounding the city, demanding her release.

"Princess, why do you suppose your father's army hasn't marched on Maleska Mal? For what Domeel Doreen has done, I'd think a war would be underway by now."

Beraal's words were an accusation. "The king is a soldier but also a dedicated man of peace. His advisors are infirm. And I suspect that there is another who uses the princess's predicament to his advantage."

The princess placed a hand over Beraal's resting on her shoulder. "My brother is not to blame for this, Beraal. We must have faith. Benjamin Colt, our predicament is caused by the distances that separate us and our inability to conduct discourse or carry messages except at the rate which we can physically cross these distances. With messengers the only means of communication, the true nature of our distress here is still likely unclear to my father. If he has sent a rescue as I suspect, and Domeel Doreen has silenced them, then that in itself will communicate much to my father's generals."

"On my world, we speak effortlessly over distances. Around the world, even. Our technology doesn't work here, though. Do you not have a means of instant communications across distances on Vistara?"

"No. It is another part of our lost knowledge. What a boon that would be! To know as things transpired at their occurrence. How Vistara has fallen!"

She'd lamented their once great past before.

It was hard to imagine. But there were examples right up until the twentieth century where battles had been fought, only for the survivors to learn that a peace treaty had already been signed. That the dead would be alive if only for that knowledge come too late.

The telegraph was a huge leap forward from hand carried message, but even that was crude compared to the radio we take for granted, not to mention the truly instant extension of its use by microwave and satellite relay. I remember watching a documentary about how diplomacy between the struggling American colonies and Europe took months or more to bear fruit because of the hamper to discourse caused by communications. A storm could sink a ship and prevent a message from arriving. It could add weeks to a process that already took months for a simple exchange. Which is why ambassadors were trusted with special powers to speak with the full force of their government.

"You have the ability to make treaties on your own, is that right, Princess?" I trusted that the decipher had translated "plenipotentiary" in the correct way.

"Yes. Though my authority to negotiate my own release for any ransom on behalf of my kingdom has been disregarded entirely by Domeel Doreen. He is a barbarian in every sense."

"Princess, I see the hand of your brother in this."

The princess didn't object and seemed lost in her own thoughts. Both told me there was palace intrigue involved.

Beraal spoke softly to the princess. "Lord Benjamin Colt deserves to hear all, Talis Darmon. He has risked much on our behalf."

The princess nodded but kept her injured repose. There was pain. Beraal took that as the sign to proceed.

"The Prince Carolinus Darmon is the firstborn of the princess's siblings. He is not of sound character. He seeks the throne before his time. His weakness is such that he cannot hide his ambition. The king has given his eldest son a position of limited sovereignty over the westernmost city of Pyreenia, the grandest in all the kingdom—after Shansara, of course."

Here, the princess took up. "It is both test and placation, by my father's hand. Because Pyreenia lies farthest west in the kingdom, it has traditionally always had a royal presence, whereas the nearer Thoria and Clymaira do not. An administrator and council conduct the business of each, even in Shansara, but all in the name of the king."

Beraal scowled. "It was a reward for bad behavior. Better the king had kept his mischievous son close to be kept aware of his maneuvers. In Pyreenia, who knows what treachery is plotted—against the king and you! It is known the whole of the kingdom favors you as successor. Why your father hesitates to name you vexes all."

"I do not seek the throne!" Talis Darmon spat. "We will speak no more of it!"

Beraal dipped her head in obeisance.

"Forgive me, Princess. I know your feelings on this matter. But for our sake, I thought it best that Lord Benjamin Colt be made aware. You have enemies without and within the kingdom. If I do err, I would be glad, but if your brother knows of your captivity, I fear he makes play to hinder your emancipation. It would benefit him most of all."

The princess dropped face to hands and wept.

✤ ✤ ✤

More days passed and a way forward with our hosts took root. The Chief was now the owner of his own silver adornment, after which he and Marky spent more time in the company of Domeel Doreen—without me.

But it was good medicine for me to reconnect with the team. I spent the days with them, allowed to take two or three of them at a time for tours of the city, getting everyone oriented, and generally shooting the breeze about any and every thing the way buddies do.

But I learned the most when Karlo, Dave, and I took a jaunt through the maze of Maleska Mal. Like witnesses to the discord of Baghdad, the ancient center of a great civilization, it was now a remnant of its former glory, the current occupants as unharmonious as a badly tuned orchestra playing in a storm ravaged Hollywood Bowl. The hints of past greatness were all there, but that's all they were. Clues to what once was, but lived no more.

Karlo was his usual pensive self, absorbed by his own thoughts as I did my tour guide routine to acclimate everyone. After doing this a couple of times, I'd worked up pithy comments on what I'd thought about the touches of beauty, style, and artistic flair I saw in the architecture, and about how it was all now "just a neon sign flashing the message it was property condemned and posted for demolition." I especially thought that one would impress Karlo. We plopped on what was once the edge of a fountain to admire the attraction they'd most wanted to see.

The atmosphere plant.

It's not like you could miss it. The tallest spire in the city center rose from a gargantuan square base. We'd walked around the entire perimeter, hands running along the smooth seamless metal wall, curious children trying to learn by touch as we searched for a feature to indicate a way in. The base rose for many stories before the spiral tower grew from it, like the walls of a castle. The surface of the tower was wrapped with vines of tubular conduits twisting over each other, some entering, some exiting the face of the tower. The topmost tip was capped by a dense calliope of pipes of different heights rising into the sky. Nothing visible came from them and we detected no vibrations, heard no noises of life from inside.

"Is it dead?" Dave asked. "Must be an underground entrance. We can play tunnel rat sometime, or let the engineers do it. What do you think, Karlo?"

"The atmosphere is manufactured—it's fantastic."

A Tarn dumping a bucket of refuse on the street distracted us. Children wrestled nearby.

"I'd like to have seen it in its prime," Karlo continued. "Disregarding any human-centric bias, I'm curious to see if the other cultures of Vistara fare any better. What you tell me about the planet's ancient history and the lost technology paradigm at work here, I wonder if it's just the Tarns who are the lone children playing in the garden of the gods."

"Jeez, Karlo. I meant like, where to next? But please, don't hold back with the professor stuff." Dave changed tempo. "Marky says he and the Chief think they'll have us camped in the city soon and we'll start being able to venture out with the tribe and do some exploring. So maybe we get you your wish."

Dave swigged a plastic bottle refilled from the local water source, an intact fountain closer to the team encampment. "Do we need this much chlorine in the water, Karlo?"

"I don't trust it, and neither should you."

"Food's been doing fine with my system. Is it agreeing with everyone else?"

"Yes. It tells me Tarn and human digestive systems are similar, but I still want everyone taking the vitamin mix as a precaution. Our dietary needs and theirs may be vastly different. It's another thing I'll prioritize so we don't run out. We've a lot to be thankful for, but we're a long way from having enough of a track record with the environment to be certain that we're going to be able to sustain ourselves here without additional accommodation. We don't know what we don't know."

"Baby Blue working okay then?" I wondered.

"None the worse for wear. So far. Chief and Marky are all about cranking out more

Class V, but we've got a good surplus of ammo and boom-boom. I should be getting more basic rations and electrolyte replacement stocked, just in case. In fact, I need to be getting back to check on it."

"You're really doing double duty, Karlo," I said with admiration. "Thank God you're here."

"We're all double or triple hatted, brother. It's not just me." Karlo was quick to deflect praise. "But I'm seeing signs that it's taking a toll, and between us, I'm worried."

"Burn out? Sleep deprivation? Fatigue-type stuff?" I asked. "Once we get inside the city, we can drop our security profile and start to get people rested and repaired physically and mentally."

"Hmm. That'll help." He took a deep look over one shoulder then the other—which was usually the international sign language for, *I'm thinking about committing a war crime.* Instead, he drew us closer and spoke with a candor I knew indicated more than just another one of his dissertations was coming. "Between us, the married guys are having a bad time of it. Chuck and Matt are becoming withdrawn. Marky-Mark is even more Marky-Mark. Angry and pissed off more than usual. He doesn't even seem to confide in Matt anymore, who's like his little brother."

I understood his concern and his precaution about sharing it. The Chief and Mark would often appear unannounced, or we'd see them watching one of us like a squad leader looking to catch a Spec 4 shamming. Not the kind of behavior you'd expect from the top rung of a team of hard-charging operators. I tried to be understanding. Chief and Marky were carrying a lot of weight making sure we survived this, but it was a little off-putting.

"Yeah. The family men gotta feel awful," Dave said with the kind of sympathy I felt, too. "They ain't alone. I'm a little messed up myself, bros. I'm never going to see my folks again. And I'll never know what happened to them. We get settled somewhere, then what? We live here the rest of our lives? Alone?"

I'd had similar feelings. "I know, Dave. I try not to think about it."

Karlo wasn't joining in with Dave or I in our admission of loss and instead curiously watched a tiny segmented purple insect writhe past his feet.

"You okay, Karlo?"

He was always a rock and never, ever burdened anyone with the kind of bitches and complaints most anyone throws around just as small talk. It's too hot, it's too cold, my feet are killing me. That kind of stuff. It was like some vow of priesthood he seemed to hold himself to. Or maybe that was just him. But no one was a rock. Or an island. Or whatever the saying was.

"You always hear everyone's problems, but you never share yours. We can't have you go down, brother. I want to know, are you alright?"

Karlo thought. "Yeah, Ben. I'm fine. I made peace with our situation pretty quickly. I'm just that way. If this is how it's going to be, then it's onward and upward. There's no other option for me."

"Ranger on, is that it?" Dave said with a little disbelief.

Karlo nodded in the tiniest way. "It's just how I am. But since it's just us, I'll tell you." He took a deep breath. "I don't mind."

"Don't mind what?" I asked.

"Being here."

"Say what?" Dave's voice shot up.

"I'm cool with it. What's happened to us has me buzzed. My brain's never been more fine-tuned and clear. I can't sleep for thinking about all the puzzles there are to solve. For the first time in a long time, I'm excited."

Dave liked busting Karlo's stones. "You never act like you're excited about anything, man."

It was true, Karlo was always the even-Steven, take-it-all-in-stride guy. In a profession that mainlined the juice all thrill-seekers and tough guys needed—with near daily opportunities to shake hands with death—Karlo was unfazed by the roller coaster ride that was every day on an A-Team.

"I'm energized. It's like the first time I realized I could tackle any subject. Learn it, apply it, build, create, solve real problems—whatever. If I'm honest, I haven't felt challenged in a while. I was thinking about getting out. Going back to school. Mining diamonds in Africa. Starting a company. I dunno. This—" He waved a hand around. "I'm Edmund Hillary. I'm Leif Erickson and Neil Armstrong rolled into one. I'm Champollion translating the Rosetta Stone. I'm Oppenheimer testing the first atom bomb. I'm an alchemist, making things out of nothing with a quantum singularity."

"Glad our predicament's provided you with a new path to personal enrichment, dude."

Dave was a little exasperated, but I was profoundly amazed at what Karlo told us. I already thought he was superhuman. Now I'd heard it straight from the horse's mouth—he was. In SF, I was in the company of the most stellar guys I'd ever imagined. The most average operator was head and shoulders above anyone I'd ever known in civilian life. And Karlo sat at the top of my list of guys I wanted to be more like.

"You asked. I told," Karlo said flatly.

Dave's sarcasm was back. "Thanks for a glimpse into the enigma that is Karlo."

Karlo took umbrage. The first time I'd seen such from him. "You're taking this the wrong way, Dave. Even if I'm sad like everyone else, I feel a kind of gratitude. I'm grateful that I'm needed. Grateful that I can do something valuable. Something that no one has ever had the chance to do before. And if it had to happen, then I'm grateful we're going through this together, brothers."

I assured him I felt the same.

Dave's eyes rolled. "Yeah, yeah. Me too. Scumbags."

That was how Dave let someone know he thought highly of them. And it meant that Karlo had snapped him out of the temporary funk about his family.

"How do you rate the team's functionality, Karlo?" I wanted his assessment because where I thought he was going when he told us about how the other guys were doing—before I'd led us into a health and welfare check like a good leader should—was informing us that he had concerns about our team.

Karlo again made a once around to check our environment. "Dave, have you told him?"

Dave shook his head. "You go."

"Okay. I'll catch you up on what was in the papers while you were gone. Mike and the captain getting wasted gutted the team. Chief's an asshole. Always has been. But he's the kind of asshole you can depend on. Consistent. Reliable. But difficult. Like a good XO, he was the hatchet man on the team. The bad guy—ready to drop the hammer and make sure things got done. XO's a tough job, but he's always liked being a dick about it. Mike and the captain kept him in check."

He waited.

"Everyone had an issue with Chief bumping Marky past you. I love Marky. But he's—he's not Mike, and he sure isn't you. Just sayin'. While you and Dave were gone, there were words. It was a team-room-door-closed throwdown. Let's just say it didn't go well. Ever since, Marky's had his nose out of joint, and Chief's been a lot less friendly. Mitch especially got confrontational when he defended you, and those two came down on him hard. And since, they haven't made the effort to make things right. We may be in the shit, but, you know, we're still a team. Chief and Marky have been way more heavy-handed than Mike and the captain. My opinion—we have no confidence in them, and they feel the same about us."

"By a mile, they've been more like little Saddams instead of our new Mom and Dad," Dave joined in.

I was simultaneously heartened and bummed. I respected Karlo and Dave greatly. To have my friends tell me that what went down bothered the rest of the team—it comforted me. But to also have it confirmed that I wasn't alone thinking things were funky—it worried me. The dynamic developing inter-species would be best managed if the dynamic intra-team was solid.

"I'm glad you told me, guys."

Dave asked the obvious. "What do we do about it, though?"

Sometimes it was just this way.

"Chin tucked. Teeth clenched. Guard up. Ready to take what flies at us," I said. "We just keep doing our jobs and hope things settle out. Chief and Marky will calm down if they feel we're supporting them. Same as any leader. I've been going out of my way to make 'play along, get along' my game face. Show those two that I'm only concerned about the team. Right now, that's all we can do. I'll try to spend some solo time with each of the guys. Let them know I'm cool with Chief and Marky. Maybe that'll help. You able to help the guys hurting because they lost their families? Antidepressants?"

Karlo flashed a thumbs-up. "I'm going to offer. I've held off, but if I coax them that it's the right thing to do to get them over this hump for the good of the team, I think I can convince them. Well, not Marky, but the other guys. And as our official grief counselor, the rest of it's reinforcing we all understand what they're going through. And time."

19

I was making the rounds under the dense starlit sky. We'd progressed to a level of trust that permitted the team and all our stuff to now occupy a part of the open grounds behind the palace, situated closer to the Tarn barracks, the stables, and animal pens. Apache went wherever I did and had quickly become a team mascot. He no longer stayed in the pens, but whenever I returned to the palace and the princess, he whined like a toddler going down for a nap. Loyal friend he may be, Beraal put her foot down he would remain outside after the first time he gassed out the apartment.

I pictured the princess in her humiliation and degradation, stuffed into one of the small boxes that held the rat-like creatures the Tarn raised as a delicacy. It was difficult to imagine they could taste different from how they smelled. I didn't want Apache near there. Not even back in the horse pens where the Tarn had allowed me to keep my loyal friend. Now he was a happy camper, responding to the kindness and attention we all paid him like an affection-starved lover. Whenever he was around the team, he was all gooey licks and stubby tail wagging like a wheat thresher. It left a bruise if he hit you with it just right.

Mitch had taken to coddling the monstrous beast, who seemed to understand English or at least the word "treat" whenever Mitch used an MRE to soothe Apache's hurt feelings at being left behind. Further proving he was one of us, not even the gadron would eat the veggie omelets. Karlo had gotten his marching orders by unanimous team consensus to tweak Baby Blue's stored templates and erase the disgusting concoction from the standard table of production when it came time to make more.

We had a GP medium tent as a base, our war wagons fanned out in a semicircle toward the pens, overlooking the low roofs of the city behind the palace. We'd adopted that lower security profile, and one of us took turns at a roving guard so the others could sleep. Karlo and the engineers tackled the problems of water and sanitation. The chieftain had been slowly won over by our efforts, but without admitting the demerits we helped correct had needed any remedy. And as it had worked with many an earthly host, it was an inroad to getting closer to the Tarn army.

Dave and the Chief were with a patrol of Tarn cavalry now, with Mark left in charge. The commo relays had been retrieved with the rest of our stores. Dave had been able to keep in communication with Mitch for several days as he and the Chief rode with the Tarn on a patrol into the eastern lands, until eventually they'd dropped out of range.

I passed near a pair of Tarn sentries outside their quarters, and they hailed me over to their animal dung fire. "Show us, Deacon Benjamin Colt." With four arms they both urged me to entertain their curiosity, indicating their desire by pumping their palms upward several times. I obliged and from a standstill made a leap over their heads, turned in midair to land behind them. They startled to their feet to face me, coughing their coarse laugh.

"Tomorrow I want to grapple with you, White," one said.

We'd taken the offer to wrestle and play games with the curious Tarn soldiers once confirming that we were forbidden to fight to the death or cause harm to the Tarn under the code of tribal protection—and expected the same in return.

"Your besting Khraal Kahlees was but luck. You won't fare so well against a real Mydreen."

I'd learned that boasting was a necessity with the Tarn, and I played along, knowing it was their version of comradeship. "And I'll gladly teach you the error in your false pride." This brought laughter again.

Apache's hackles raised as he watched, but calmed as I waved him down. He reluctantly obeyed, eyes fixed on the like of his abusers.

The other Tarn waved me to a spot by their tiny campfire. "I witnessed you go through three of my clan like a cyclone, Deacon Benjamin Colt. Kasz Kardon was foolish to have underestimated you. He died a fool's death."

The Tarn had a philosophic outlook about their comrade whom I'd killed with a single blow at our initial meeting on the plains of the city. Both his death and that of the Tarn I'd killed in the throne room had not been held against me in any permanent way. If anything, by accidental necessity, it had earned me respect.

"A warrior now walks with his glorious ancestors in the underworld," I'd observed was the correct response whenever the dead were mentioned.

My hosts thrust their tusks forward in grunting approval.

"You're not yet a true Tarn and you have yet to learn all our ways, but it is honorable to learn from a skilled warrior. Only a roamak flees when without the tusks of the pack behind him. We welcome—"

Both Tarns snapped around. In the distance was a sound strange to the quiet night. A faint hum.

"The Reds attack!" He produced a curved horn and blew. "Alarm. Alarm."

I hit my PTT. "Stand to. Everyone up. The Tarn say the Reds are attacking."

Just then, I saw oval dark shapes blotting the stars, further betrayed by the white bolts that shot from them to impact the city below.

The chaos started. I bounded to the camp and landed just as guys poured out of the tent in ranger panties and kit.

"Where?" Marky asked, first out.

"Air assault."

"Everyone, get to a gun mount!" Marky yelled as he took two bounds and landed deftly on top of a GMV and dropped into the gunner hatch behind a minigun. I dropped my tubes over my eyes and took a course to the other GMV and landed behind a door mounted 240 as Matt yelled at me from the roof.

"Do we engage?"

Mark answered with a burst from his 134. His Hellfire was lit and the copper rain looked like a meteor shower streaking across the sky. Now every gun opened up. All our IR floods were on, and the sky looked like the lot over a new car dealership on its first night of a sale. I tracked one of the floating decks, tracing the origin of the spread of energy bolts pulsing in a regular rhythm back to the deck, and drove the aiming laser there as I started my own music of short bursts. The ships were slow, and I laid the splash of the laser on the leading edge of the craft and kept it there as I mashed the trigger repeatedly. The ship flared in a bright flash and pitched over.

In the tiny sunburst of my mind's eye, figures hurtled off it. Human figures. A voice in the distance reached my consciousness from the depths of my concentration on the mayhem, and I pivoted. From the dark balcony I knew so well, tiny in my green night vision, the aura of her two arms flailing over the head of her heated outline, confirmed for me the identity. The princess.

"NOOO! My father's army comes to my rescue. NOOO! Benjamin Colt. Where are you? You must stop this!"

The city was a vista of fireworks trailing back and forth from the ground and the air. The Tarn fired their energy rifles into the sky, the range inadequate to reach the airborne assault. The team mercilessly picked off the floating armada like waterfowl from a blind.

"Check fire! Check fire!" I yelled repeatedly, and when there was no response, I hit my PTT. "It's the princess's people. We're lighting up her rescue party. Check fire."

"Shut up, Colt!" Marky came back. "Ignore that order. I didn't give the check fire. Keep on them." After what had been a tiny pause in our barrage, all guns but mine opened up again.

I reached up to Matt. "Matt, we've gotta stop!"

"Marky says to light 'em up, Ben. What am I supposed to do?" He swung the minigun and sent more flames dancing in a chainsaw rip. I took a crouched run to where Marky was still running his 134 like a revving dirt bike and hopped up behind him. "Marky, we've got to stop." His fist caught me square between the eyes, and I toppled off.

He clocked me good. I landed onto my back, my helmet bounced and rebounded my chin to my chest and I saw stars. I was on my feet and Marky was in front of me. "You done messed up now, A-Aron," he mocked and kicked me, and it was a wrecking ball smashing into my midsection. I rolled with it and was on my feet again. He was immediately on me. I got hands on him and shut down his fist by crowding him as he tried to knee me. He broke my grasp and leaped back as he drew his pistol midair.

"Stand down, Colt, before I have to kill you."

Someone from behind hit me at the base of my neck above my plates. I knew the sharp force of a buttstock. I crumpled. As I curled up to shield myself from bootheels stomping and toes kicking me from all sides, I faded away. Above the ringing in my ears and the churn of automatic fire, I heard her shrieks.

"Traitor! Oath breaker! I wish you a painful death, Deacon Benjamin Colt!"

I died.

✠ ✠ ✠

I came to. I wasn't dead, but I was in total blackness. I felt my face. My orbits were swollen shut and my face crusted with blood. I don't know how long I'd been out, but I sensed much time had elapsed since I last remembered anything. Vertigo overcame me as I tried to sit, and I fell over onto a cold hard surface and retched acidic vomit, leaving me gasping for air. I went out again.

After some time, I awoke to my own groaning and forced myself to try to sit once more. I was naked and cold. I pried an eye open but was still blind. I felt my surroundings. I was on a rough stone floor. I shivered and wrapped my arms around my knees.

I stayed like this for some time until a grating door creaked open, and I turned only to be repelled like I'd hit an electric fence as the pain between my shoulder blades stopped me short. I fought through it to see the fuzzy form of a Tarn set something on the floor of my cell and retreat, returning me to the black void. I crawled toward the ghost image and found a bottle. I sipped cautiously at it, retched, then tried again. Exhausted from my effort, I lay on the floor. Pain washed over me, and I mercifully was out again.

Time passed. I knew neither night nor day. I judged the time by how often food and water were brought to me.

"Where are my companions? Why am I here?" I croaked whenever the guards opened my cell. They couldn't understand me nor I them. My jailer barked something and I understood the word "vereen."

Vereen were the foul burrowing animal they raised for food. He'd called me a rat. My own stench reminded me of one, as well.

My cell was a few meters on all sides. A hole in the floor for waste. I assessed my injuries and carefully tried to move more of my body with each wakening. It hurt to breathe. I had broken ribs. My arms and legs were swollen at all the joints, as was my face. Some of the crust on my face was surgical adhesive. Karlo must've doctored my injuries. My teeth hurt and my tongue tested several loose ones, and I comforted myself that at least they were all there. I had good teeth and had never needed braces as a kid. I hoped in time they'd firm up.

I'd been given a hell of a beating. I've taken more than a few, but on the Richter scale, this was as different as the trembler that knocked a few paintings off the wall and the one that dropped the roof. I was dealing with the tsunami and its lingering aftermath, and I was anxious for what would be left of me when the water receded. Only then would I know if I'd be whole enough to get justice from my abusers. My own teammates.

It'd been Mark and Chucky who doled out the punishment. They cursed me while they worked me over, holding back nothing as I received the manifestation of their resentment. I thought I remembered Karlo's harried voice as he pulled them off me, but maybe it was my imagination. If so, he saved me from death.

I felt every square centimeter of my cell and imagined myself the blind swordsman from those movies my dad watched with me on Saturday mornings, trying to find anything I could use as a weapon, searching for a crack around the door that didn't permit a photon of light to pass through. I pushed against it with all my might and when I was stronger, beat against it with my fists. On this world, I was stronger than a massive Tarn. I could defy gravity and leap huge distances. But I wasn't really Superman. Materials and their tensile strengths didn't care about gravity in that way. I conserved my strength and massaged my limbs back into function, and waited.

One day, I startled awake to the door of my prison opening and the blinding light that came with it a white dawn. Bile rose in my throat. The torture sessions were about to begin. They weren't going to take me without a fight to my death. This was my Zulu Dawn. My Little Big Horn. I was building up to ramming speed. I pushed myself up and stumbled, ashamed and frustrated that I was still too weak to make a proper last stand.

Karlo's voice quavered from the threshold. "Dammit, Ben. I'm so sorry. Everything's gone to hell. I can't fix it."

He pressed, probed, and tested. I winced wherever he touched as he spoke. "I don't have much time. Bryant made me shed everything and had Chuck search my aid bag." He pushed pills into my hand. "Swallow them. It's just some Toradol and Tylenol. It'll help for a while."

I swallowed them greedily.

"What's happening?"

Karlo was flustered. "I don't even know where to begin."

"Try. What happened after I got taken out?"

"Marky took charge and helped the Tarns finish repelling the Red attack. Chief and Dave got back in time to help us clean up the last of the ground forces. We impressed the chieftain so much that we're bonded brothers to the Tarns now. There was a big ceremony."

"Makes sense."

"No, Ben, it's worse than that. We're going to war against the Reds. The Chief and Mark made us all swear oaths to them. Loyalty oaths. The Chief's new plan is—"

"The new plan, Colt, isn't going to include you."

The Chief was in the threshold with a pair of Tarn warriors.

"It just isn't going to work out. Even if you come around to my way of doing things. Too many Tarns saw your Benedict Arnold act. It couldn't be explained away. The chieftain got the full report from his warriors, and it was all I could do to convince them not to pull you apart then and there. You alienated our allies and there's no way forward for the team with you around. Tribal laws are absolute, and we need the Tarns if we're going to make our place in this world. You can take off, Karlo. I'll finish."

"I'm not done treating his injuries, Chief."

"He looks alright to me. Nothing a little R&R won't fix. You can check up on him when we get back."

Karlo gave my shoulder a squeeze. "I'll be back, Ben. Promise. I'll see about getting you some clothes and whatever I can. There's no need to keep him like this, Chief," Karlo said angrily.

"Sure, Karlo. No need. Take off, Sergeant, and we'll talk about it later."

Karlo stormed out and the wake of his anger made the room warm for a moment, then faded as the Chief's icy speech resumed.

"It's gonna be okay, Colt. I'm not going to let them put you in the fires, which is what they do to traitors. You're going to stay put here until I can figure out what to do with you. Banish you, probably. But right now, this is the safest place for you. Trust me."

"Where's the princess?"

"She's on ice, too. She's got quite the temper. Domeel Doreen considered killing her and sending her head to her father, but I convinced him that wasn't how we like to do things. She's quite devoted to you. She insisted on seeing you, but with the state you're in, I don't think that's a good idea. Once we've gotten some tactical leverage over her father, she'll be useful as a bargaining chip. I think I can convince her to act as a negotiator on our behalf and help us avoid as much bloodshed as possible, so I prefer to treat her decently. But first, we're going to secure ourselves a position of strength."

"What the hell are you talking about, Bryant?"

"No more addressing your superior by rank, is that your new move to show remorse?"

"Remorse for what?"

"You screwed up, Colt. Mark should've killed you on the spot. But I'm glad he didn't. I like that you're going to be around to see how we put things in order. We're going to be kings, Colt. Warlords, at least."

My vertigo came back and I woozily sat.

"Yeah, you might want to sit for this. The conclusion I came to is this. I owe it to the team to secure the best life I can for us. The rules are different now. They have to be. The United States? It doesn't exist anymore. And neither does the legal basis for our service. But our duty to each other is still there, even without the law. We only have each other. I've made everyone a promise and in turn asked that they promise me—if we stick together, there's no reason for us to be hat in hand, trying to eke out a place to survive. Not when we're the most powerful force on the planet."

Karlo said the Chief and Marky had made everyone take an oath to them. It was crazy. Bryant—I'd stopped thinking of him as "the Chief"—took on more of a lecturing tone, like he was briefing me back on a mission plan.

"I've reconned one of their major cities and gotten a good assessment of the Red Kingdom, their organization, and capabilities. What I saw makes this place look as run-down as the pyramids. The Vegas strip compared to Detroit. And it was only one of their population centers. Militarily, they're as underwhelming as a troop of cub scouts. The big attack on the Tarns? They threw their best at us. Pathetic tactics. Their plan was infantile at best. Armaments and weapons? They're better off than the Tarns, but not by much. We're going to fix that for our Mydreen allies.

"Everything we knew is gone, Colt. And if the universe decided to hand us the shitty end of the stick, we don't have to take it. This is a whole world, and we can be the ones running it. We're the most powerful unconventional warfare force there's ever been. We've spent our lives destabilizing regimes and making enemies collapse from within. The Tarn are a natural group for us to exploit for that purpose, and their goals are completely aligned with ours.

"So, I'm taking the fight to the Reds. Once we've gotten their attention, they'll understand we're taking charge or they're going to be toppled like one of the tinpot dictators we've taken down. Then we can establish a new peace." He paused as if to wait for some compliment from me at the revelation of his masterful strategy.

"I can't believe the team is with you on this."

He bobbed his head side to side. "I'll throw you a bone, Colt. Not everyone is in perfect lockstep. But even Karlo and your buddy Dave understand what needs to happen here. And in order to get their cooperation, in return, I promised to make sure you were protected. They've all come around that it has to be this way, even if there're some small sticking points.

"You're the only one who doesn't get it. The muzzles are off. We're not dogs on a leash anymore. We control our own destiny. We're responsible for ourselves. No more orders from petty politicians who only want to enrich themselves and stay in power while they whittle away at our rights day by day. This is our chance to make something better. We don't have to be the enablers for a bunch of pedophiles and traitors anymore."

"You're conflating a lot of stuff."

"You feel the same way, Colt. You just don't want to admit it. If we'd made it where we were supposed to, this exact same scenario was going to play out eventually. No way we were going to let the Foggy Bottom crowd and the Georgetown idiots start up a new America for their own benefit. The military would've had to take charge to reestablish order for the common good. The captain and Mike and I had discussed that very possibility. I know most of the team had, too. You and Karlo grumbled about the same thing. Don't deny it."

"I won't but, this isn't the way."

"Yeah, it is. We have to take the initiative. Baby Blue is key. And it's still functional. But Karlo's right. We can't plan like it's always going to be. We're going to arm and train the Tarns just like we would some oppressed freedom fighters, and we're going to help them secure their future and ours. And put ourselves where we deserve to be. If our future's gone, then we're going to take back from the universe everything it took from us and more. Anything less is a waste of our capabilities. And we're going to do it right. This is a full military campaign, and the rules of war will apply. I won't have any civilian massacres or revenge killings. The Tarn army will grow under our guidance and leadership, and when it's over, we're not going to turn our backs on them like America's done to most of its allies. We're the good guys."

I coughed an ironic laugh and my ribs hurt. "I'm glad you've got it all figured out, Lawrence of Arabia."

"You can laugh, Colt. But you'll be laughing from here." He turned to go. "I'll have them bring you some amenities. There's no need to treat you worse than you deserve."

The door swung to close, and Bryant paused it to get his last digs in where I could just see his face mock me from the crack.

"You won't be seeing us for a long time. The campaign starts in a week. Don't know how long we'll be on the march, but I'm not stopping until we've won. Maybe by then I can get you a better deal for a parole somewhere safe. It's not personal, Colt. Maybe it was. But seeing you in your place makes me feel a little more noble, like I should be charitable in victory. See you around."

The door swung the last few degrees shut.

I wept in the dark.

20

Every day I got stronger and the pain subsided. I remembered all my SERE training. I knew my brain was going to be fine as I recovered the dusty files of lessons buried deep in the back of the rusty metal cabinet that held all my many years of training. The key to it all was to keep hope alive. And I had to be ready for the opportunity of escape. I exercised and built myself up. It was important not only to my physical but my mental well-being. My conditions improved. I had clothing, a mat to lie on, and a small amber stone to provide light. And as much as anything, it was that which gave me hope.

It was the same warm light that had bathed the princess on her recovery bed as I sat beside her each night during our first days together. The memories of those happy times alone with her on this alien world. I held them as dearly as would a man shipwrecked on a deserted island, imagining her companionship and inventing conversations to ease the silence of my isolation.

Bryant said she'd wanted to see me. That she'd shown her temper. Had she forgiven me? Or was it to scold me for my failure to protect her. I transcribed his words onto pages in my imagination and ran my finger over them as I read, so many times that the ink smeared and faded. Every time I rewrote them, the sentences were slightly different until I was unsure what had been actually said. It was a solitary game of telephone, each retelling warping the details until my imagined tale was unrecognizable from the original. But in my deepest heart, I prayed I would see her again—though a part of me lived in terror that it was a foolish, impossible dream. But maybe, I could live to get my hands around Bryant's throat. He just had to open the door again.

All the while, I kept the rage inside me simmering just beneath the top of the pot.

I was doing handstand push-ups, the gravity not enough to let me get much of a workout otherwise, when I felt a rumble on the other side of the door. I folded back to standing and when the door cracked, a Tarn I'd never seen before peered in cautiously. The door opened wider, and beside him was Beraal. She spoke, though I could not understand her. She beckoned me to come to her and my pulse raced. She thrust at me a thin silver band.

"Deacon Benjamin Colt, we must hurry. We are in grave peril."

In the last phase of SERE school—the POW camp—the end of the ordeal comes as the prisoners are assembled on the gravel of the prison yard. The sound of footsteps on the rocks was enough after a few days to seize you with fear. It meant the guards were coming to pull you from your cell for interrogation. With head bowed and the movement of the cadre all around, suddenly, the order to come to attention is given. As the Stars and Stripes raise to full height and the national anthem blares over the loudspeakers. I defy anyone who's gone through the same to tell me they didn't have hot, sweet tears running down their face. I felt the brief elation again, and immediately strangled it.

"Wait." I removed the sword scabbard from the unconscious guard and, grabbing his leather harness, tossed him into the cell. It was the first real test of my strength and the power my muscles generated was therapy complete. I eased the thick door closed until it clicked. On the ground was a rifle. It wasn't one of my own, but any rifle was better than no rifle.

And with a rifle in my hands, all things were possible.

"Beraal, who is this?"

Her Tarn conspirator faced down the dim corridor with a rifle of his own. The bands worked at a partly telepathic level. We spoke in sub-vocalizations but heard each other clearly.

"Fel Fargas. He is not of my clan, but his people once were."

I wasn't looking a gift horse in the mouth, but it was important I know how he came to be her compatriot in my escape. The risk of discovery and death were highest the first minutes of an escape. I wasn't about to be a lemming following the herd out of here without some vital information critical to my survival.

"Why is he risking his life to help us, Beraal?"

The Tarn answered for himself. "I owe you a life, Deacon Benjamin Colt." He was thicker than when last I'd seen him, but I recognized the chipped tusk. I'd placed myself between our wounded prisoner and his fellow Tarns and had not thought about him again. Now here he was.

"A pup raised even distantly in the ways of the Korund can never turn back on the true warrior code, no matter how long mixed with the Mydreen," Beraal said. "But more important than our distant kinship, the honor he learned from his maternal dynasty lives."

"It is true," Fel Fargas said. "Yet there is no time. We must hurry."

"Where are we going? Where's the princess?"

"We free the princess now, Benjamin Colt."

"Where is she? How?"

"Talis Darmon is close by. Mounts are waiting. We flee the city for the Korund Mountains."

I had a million questions but for now, it was enough. I trusted Beraal.

"Karlo Rinaldo Columbo gave me your decipher. He knew of my plan but was unable to smuggle further help to me. His clan watch him closely."

"Are they gone?"

"Your war clan has been departed for many days, the chieftain and his army with them. Who knows when they may return? The time is now."

That was language I understood like a commandment.

"Where is Talis Darmon?"

Fel Fargas pointed. "The dungeon is deep. We are in the lowest cavern. Come. We must move stealthily. There are checkpoints at the many descents. Long empty the dungeons have been. My people do not take prisoners or jail our own kind. I have used the guard's indolence to our advantage, but my submission of them could be discovered at any moment."

I moved with him, ready for war.

We ascended and came to a natural cave, where a Tarn lay. I recovered the rifle propped against the wall and slung it on my back. I thought about taking his sword also, but instinctively discarded the notion, imagining the long weapon bouncing noisily against the extra rifle on my back as we stalked.

Another level, another subdued guard lay undiscovered. We followed more turns and ascended until our path began to level and Fel Fargas held me back with two arms. He straightened and strode boldly around the bend and hailed. "Gol Garin sends me to relieve you."

"About time," the voice echoed my way. "It's dull duty and a waste. The puny Red prisoners don't need such. Have you seen the White demon? I hear he's as weak as—"

The pulse of Fel's rifle fizzed and I was on the move.

"What's the ruckus?" a voice from deep around the curving tunnel yelled and loud footfalls grew louder. I leaped past Fel and charged. The Tarn appeared in front of me as though materialized Baby Blue–style from nothing, and I buttstroked him in the face. I followed him to the ground and finished him, his skull spilling its contents.

Beraal was behind me. "Here!"

My heart pounded in my ears. "How do we open the door?"

Fel Fargas was beside me with a faceted gem and placed it into a recess. I reached over him to fling the door aside.

As stunning as the radiance of a topaz crystal, my princess waited. Realization brought her face to life and she gasped. "Deacon Benjamin Colt! I never dared to hope."

She was in my arms at last.

✣ ✣ ✣

The most dangerous part of our escape waited. The guard at the ground level entrance lay propped against a wall on a cushion, posed as though sleeping with his rifle across his lap. Fel Fargas covered the exit door. "There are two more guards below us on other paths. They can appear anytime. We must move." Beraal produced cloaks and draped them over us. The hood fell over my face, and I fought with it to stay in place. Beraal had a rifle, and I pushed my spare into Talis Darmon's hands.

"Can you use this, Princess?"

She grinned. "With pleasure."

"Don't fire unless I say. And don't shoot one of us by mistake. Keep your finger away from the trigger until you mean to shoot."

"Not to worry, Benjamin Colt. I have skills beyond your knowledge of me."

"We go now," Fel Fargas said. "Follow closely." He opened the door slowly, moved from side to side as he pierced the darkness ahead, then motioned. We stepped out onto the street. We were in a part of the city indistinct from any other to my recognition.

"Where to?" The moons had not risen and the streets were equally dark between the walls and towers that blocked the stars above.

"I have mounts waiting in the old temple square. It's a deserted area of the city, but we must be alert and cautious. We move slowly, not with haste. If we go quickly, it will bring attention, especially at this time of rest."

"How long until sunrise?"

"Two segments at most."

It's a difficult thing to remain calm and stroll like a tired man coming off a night shift at a factory while your heart hammers in your chest like an engine missing a cylinder. I followed at my new best friend's shoulder as he wove our course through the eerily silent city. We transitioned into a part of the city I'd never visited, the buildings little more than rubble around us. The second hand on the stopwatch in my head sped as I counted down the minutes until our darkness evaporated.

We came into an opening where a small Tarn stood by three of the giant arkall.

"This is where I leave you."

"You're not coming with us, Fel Fargas?"

"No. If I am found missing, it will be known it was I who assisted you. My kin would forfeit their lives in the torture fires to reveal what they knew."

"You have my eternal thanks, Fel Fargas."

"My debt to you is repaid."

"And mine to you owed."

The women were already mounted. I moved to the riderless beast and swung onto its wide back. It grunted and shifted under me as the Tarn passed me the reins from its collar.

"Go now," Fel Fargas said. "Keep a cautious pace until you're out of the city, then flee for your lives. Go."

"My kin will welcome you if you choose to leave," Beraal replied. "Your bravery and honor will be sung when the legend is composed."

"GO!" Fel Fargas urged a final time before departing with the youth who'd watched the mounts. I let my beast take its own course after Beraal and Talis Dorman as they led our way. We rode through more neglected streets and remnants of once grand structures until we were outside the city, and I took deep breaths again. Ahead were the featureless dark peaks of the mountains whose heights of proportion were insane to my eyes though they beckoned safety in the distance.

"Hold tight," Beraal said over her shoulder and with her middle arms slapped the hind quarters of her beast on both sides. Talis Darmon followed, and without command, my own broke into a run after them.

We fled.

✠ ✠ ✠

The ride was smoother than I anticipated, the eight legs of my arkall working in syncopated coordination as it coursed over the desert like a sailboat over calm waters, my motion reminding me of riding tiny swells on a gentle lake. Beraal drove us at a blistering pace, never slowing, and I looked behind us for pursuers like a guilty man, dreading the inevitable sunrise.

By the time the world took on the faintest red colors, we were closer to the first foothills, and when we rounded a draw between spurs, Beraal halted. The sparse dim twinkles of the city were behind us, but not far enough away that I felt any great comfort.

Atop her arkall, Beraal spoke. "We can continue mounted for a while longer. We will take a route through the bottoms where we can. It will be circuitous and slow, but we must evade observation. By now our escape will have been discovered. The gadron will be tracking us, not that they'll need them. We must push into the steep country and abandon the arkall. Then we push with all our might into the wilderness."

"Agreed. Princess, are you well?" There hadn't been a moment to speak to her beyond what had to be said to get us this far.

"I am now, Benjamin Colt. If our freedom is short, then I'm alive while it lasts, and I am with you again. I—" she stammered. "I ask your forgiveness for cursing you and condemning you an oath breaker. I don't know if you even heard my anguished spell against you, but I promise I did not mean it. I knew you were a man of honor and courage. I never once thought your promise to me was idle. And my faith in you is as firm as the mountains themselves. I swear."

"I never doubted, my princess."

She flustered slightly. "Not now, Benjamin Colt. Not now."

"Follow," Beraal commanded.

We climbed through gentle gullies and steep valleys until we leaned forward in the saddle to stay mounted. Finally, Beraal halted and dismounted. "We can go no farther as riders, and there's no point in leading the arkall with us. The way ahead is treacherous. It is best if we kill them. They will eventually take path back to the city. Perhaps rapidly. It is the best option."

Without hesitation, Talis shot her mount behind its skull and deftly rode its collapse and leaped off. Beraal did the same, and I had no choice but to follow. It was a foul thing to do, and I felt dirty as I completed the deed. The dumb beasts had gotten us far, and it was the unkindest way to repay them for their service. The women gathered satchels off the saddles, and I took mine.

"We have water and food, but it will not last long. I'm a city Tarn, but I was raised Korundi. I know the mountains and its ways since the first day of my hatching. Come."

We climbed. The sun was high by the time we left the safety of channeled cuts between jagged peaks and reached natural contours ringed by scree that became our new trail, ever higher. I plodded along behind Beraal with Talis Darmon between us. We stopped to sip precious water and I scanned the expanse at our shoulders. I squinted. Tiny dots of movement were on the plains near the city but soon dropped below our line of vision behind the sharp ridgelines we'd left below. I wished I had my spotting scope. I wished I had my MK 22. From the right spot, I could hold off an entire army of Tarns on such high ground.

"They're on us."

"Yes," Beraal said with a tactical detachment I admired. "A small party. I've watched larger parties head westward."

I squinted at the far plains where I was once deposited like a hail stone. Clearly, Beraal had amazing eyesight, well beyond the capabilities of my own twenty-fifteen vision.

"They suspect we flee to the safety of the kingdom of King Osric Darmon. Which is why we take the harsh path to the Korundi. It will be a long journey and will take many weeks. It is desperate, and I apologize there was not time to seek your assent."

"I trust your judgment, Beraal."

Talis Darmon beamed. "As you should, Benjamin Colt. Beraal has guarded and taught me since I was a hatchling, all these many years. None are wiser, none more loyal. It was her courage that brought us together again."

"Thank you again, Beraal. I don't doubt your reasoning. What lies ahead?"

"The Mydreen will pursue. If we can reach any Korundi, they will shelter us without fail. The desert Tarns lie to themselves that they do not fear the mountains and heights, but it will not deter them completely. The promise of what awaits their failure on Domeel Doreen's return will drive them to death itself rather than return without us. They will be slower than us by far, but they will still follow. We must press our advantage. We climb."

The air was thinner as we climbed, and the sun dropped beneath its zenith. I felt fatigue, as on any long march, but enjoyed the burn as we went. Talis Darmon tried to conceal her building exhaustion but the farther we went, the more her groans and grunts of effort were revealed. I'd long past taken her rifle and pack, but it seemed to do little to ease her struggle. "I can carry you, Talis Darmon," I told her during a break to sip at our precious water supply and to take a few bites of the sweet, starchy stalk from our packs. She didn't waste breath to answer.

Beraal returned the water decanter to her satchel. "Soon we should find a pass and the way will be easier for a time as we descend deeper into the mountains."

It was impossible to tell how high up we were. The face of the mountain wall we climbed against hid from me the enormous peaks behind them, which I knew reached beyond the atmosphere itself to practically touch the celestial bodies hidden by the sunlight. Had Karlo mentioned Edmund Hillary? The mountains of Mars made Everest a Kentucky molehill by comparison.

"I have some medicine for you, Princess." Beraal produced a small vial. "Take only a little on your tongue. You as well, Benjamin Colt."

Talis Darmon did as she was told and passed it to me.

I sniffed it. "What is it?"

"It will aid vitality and respiration."

The princess had to take deep breaths between words. "The air of Vistara is poor, even in the depths of the Furrow of the Creator's Hand. The atmosphere factories struggle. Is there enough air to sustain us as we go higher, Beraal?"

"Yes, Princess. Just enough. You should soon feel ease, and once we crest the pass, we will climb no higher and the air will improve much, I assure you."

I capped the vial and passed it back. "I'm fine. Save the medicine for the princess."

"As you say," Beraal said and put the tiny vial away. "We go."

The princess stood and swooned, but I reached out and caught her.

"I've got you," I said, scooping her up.

"No, Benjamin Colt. You cannot. I must not injure you by my weakness."

"Impossible, my princess."

There was no wind just then though she scrunched her eyes tightly as if a gust had come up. "Please. I have told you. Do not speak to me so. It is not proper." Was she in pain? Or had my attempted endearment hurt for reasons I couldn't comprehend?

I hefted her anyway. "I don't understand, Talis Darmon. Wrap your arms around my neck. I'm carrying you."

She did not fight me, and once I started moving, she lay her head against me. In my arms, she was as light as the air in my lungs.

21

The temperature fell as the direct rays of the weak sun disappeared. The way had gotten easier on the other side of the pass, and we continued until it was almost too dark to see. Beraal guided us into a rocky hollow at the base of a reverse sloped wall and stopped. "The princess must rest. We go no farther until early light. The cold will bite hardest then and force us to move." Of every hardship and lesson I'd endured, the mountains of Dahlonega, Georgia, were my sole experience in the environment. Jungles and urban ops had been my forte. Until now. Beraal's expert knowledge had gotten us far, and I thanked her again.

I guided the princess to the back of the tiny overhang and placed our supplies in one satchel and laid the others as a barrier to the heat thief that was the ground. "I'll take watch, Beraal. Warm the princess, if you can."

"Thank you, Benjamin Colt. Wake me and I will guard us, as well."

"I will," I lied. Sleep deprivation was a way of life for me. For today's exertions, I needed no sleep. I'd slept to keep sane during my imprisonment, praying for the narcotic of dreams that would ease the time spent in lonely captivity. But they never came. Only harsh nightmares that tortured me with the failures that led to me being betrayed by everyone I'd called brother. My helplessness compounded the pain of solitude and brought back the intrusive flashes of all the barbs, insults, and embarrassments of my life to haunt my waking hours in my cell. They hadn't plagued me since Talis Darmon had so startlingly been thrust into my life and with her near, they once again evaporated from my pool of regrets.

However desperate our situation, mentally, I was in a good place. Sleep? I'd get all the sleep I needed when I was dead. And the only dream that mattered to me now lay wrapped in Beraal's embrace. I laid my back against our Tarn pathfinder to try to shield them both from the cool night.

At some point, I dropped into the twilight awareness between awake and true sleep, a meditative state every predator learns from which they can snap into action—soldiers most of all among their kind in the kingdom of both animal and man. My eyes snapped open. I'd become perfectly tuned to our environment and something new had entered the domain. A hunter moved in the darkness, sniffing our trail. I brought my rifle up but too late. It was on me. Fetid breath blew on me and its slobber sprayed my face as I pushed with all my might, bench-pressing the rifle I'd jammed sideways into its maw. It wouldn't release its clench and I pushed it away with explosive extension. With my legs underneath me, I finished by pushing us both out into the open only to tumble down the slope. I came to rest with a slide, my death grip on the rifle matched by the beast's. On my back and straddled by the beast, I released a hand to punch and gouged its nearest eye. It let go of the rifle and snapped at my head. I shielded my face with my forearm and brought my knees to my chest. My feet found the thing's center, and with all my might, I launched it off me.

I was on my feet with the rifle. I'd hurled the damn thing farther down the slope, but its intent was sealed. On its own feet once more, hunched low to the ground, it paused only a moment before charging. I brought the rifle up and pressed the trigger. Nothing happened. The sword was not with me but lay on the ground where I'd guarded. I dropped, feeling for a rock to defend myself with, when—with a guttural snarl—another beast, a black behemoth the size of a moose, dove past me to intercept the night stalker, mid-leap.

I scurried back up the slope, losing my footing and stumbling as I crab-walked backward. The snarls of a fight to the death deafened me.

"Rifle, rifle, rifle!" I yelled.

Whatever had given me a reprieve from becoming a meal would do the same to me. This new entrant in the hierarchy of the food chain was a killer whale ramming a lesser shark off the school of mackerel. We were the tasty fish they both wanted. The carnivore I'd fought to a temporary standstill was shaken by its neck from side to side and, when limp, was discarded like a torn rag doll. We were next. Beraal was on her feet with rifle raised when a piercing howl froze us both. It was the howl of a gadron.

"Wait!" I yelled as I pushed her muzzle away.

The gadron trotted uphill, whining with bowed head as it did.

"Apache!"

At my recognition, he yelped in delight, raised two front paws to playfully push me down and suddenly I had a lap full—six hundred pounds of muscled lover, licking and squealing, as he shook with joy.

"Impossible! Oh my good boy! How did you find me?" I pounded his back and stroked his neck as he cried and nuzzled me.

"It cannot be!" Beraal exclaimed. "A gadron could not be so driven. Are you sure he is one and the same?"

"I'm sure," I said as I forced him off me.

"I recognized your pet beast loose on the streets after your imprisonment. He came close many times to sniff at me but retreated from my touch."

"Kindness has saved all our lives, Beraal," Talis Darmon said as she appeared from the shelter. "Repaid first by Fel Fargas and now by his bewitched gadron. I could have done no better."

There were many things Beraal and Talis Darmon sometimes said that were simply syntax to my ear. I gave no mind to her statement as I patted Apache firmly, praised him more, and chuckled. I always spoke so formally, trying to equal the regal way those on Vistara spoke and fearful that my words would not translate otherwise. But I dropped into the speech of my mother's people.

"Mawmaw always said, 'Above all else, Benjy, be kind.' More'n once she had ta drill it in to me with a slap upside the back of muh head. Thanks, Mawmaw—wherever you are. You was right."

✣ ✣ ✣

At early light, I skinned the dead critter with the sword and fashioned a sling out of sinew to join two haunches together so I could carry them around my neck. Apache watched me patiently and whined as I worked. I laid the meat aside then carved large bits off the other shoulders and tossed them to Apache who gulped them down as I did.

"Surviving the attack of even a small gazraal is a miracle," Beraal said from above. Behind her, Talis Darmon stomped feet and rubbed her arms beneath her cloak.

"Small?" I questioned her.

"It is a young one. Not more than two annuals, freshly weaned from its mother. The smell of a Tarn should have deterred it. Your strange scent, combined with its inexperience, meant it did not know to keep its distance from the danger we pose."

"Do we have to worry about more of them in the future?"

"The scent of your pet will make even the fiercest gazraal stay hidden. The Mydreen allow the beasts to roam the city out of fear of a weakened gazraal, too old to hunt, wandering into their midst and making easy prey of a young Tarn. It has happened. All Tarn have heard the tales. Only desert Tarn have been the victims of such. Korundi know no such fear."

"I thought we could use the extra food. We can dry the meat or maybe there'll be the chance to cook small pieces of it at some point."

Beraal bared tusks. "You show wisdom, Benjamin Colt."

With Apache in our party, we departed. For many days, we traveled between the frighteningly tall and hurtling mountain heights, up and down trails a goat would have difficulty traversing, deeper and deeper into the barren mountains. I offered Apache drops of water in my palm. He lapped it gratefully, but Beraal scolded. "Waste no water on your gadron. He can go far longer than us without it, and I nearly as long as he." We were on the last of our water, but I was thankful that we'd had no more wildlife encounters and that no sign of Tarn pursuit had reached us.

We camped again in a small redoubt. The princess's lips were dry and cracked, as were my own. She slept as Beraal and I assumed our usual position of protection around her. Apache lay at my feet, dozing, every so often stirring and sniffing the air before trotting off into the darkness, only to return with the wagging tail of "all clear" after each short patrol of our overnight position.

"Beraal, tomorrow we must find water. The princess can't go much farther without it, and neither can I."

"Tomorrow I will find a place. With the princess's help, we may have success."

I let her strange assurances rest and told her to sleep and let myself follow, as well. With Apache guarding us, I felt confident we would not be taken unaware without his warning.

As the numbing chill became intolerable at first light, we moved out. When I asked how she was, the princess only smiled weakly, too exhausted with fatigue and weak from exposure to waste energy speaking. I cursed silently that I couldn't remedy her pain, and left Apache at her side to lean against as we trod. The gadron sensed her distress and slowed his pace to stay within her grasp. I caught up to Beraal.

"The princess is fading fast. I don't know if she can go much farther. What are our options, Beraal?"

"I am making way to a place where I think we can conjure sustenance. Just a little farther."

I wanted to inquire more, but my own fatigue favored me to conserve words. I droned on, struggling to maintain alertness as I put one foot in front of the other, every step pain. I was fading. We'd driven past even my endurance, and I wondered how the poor princess was still on her feet. She had an indomitable will, her fierceness and inner strength carrying her through like a good Ranger.

Beraal stopped many times to leave us to explore into tiny canyons and breaks in rocky faces barely wide enough to accept her form, only to return and start the search again. The princess rode on Apache's back now and I walked beside, making sure she did not fall. Beraal left us again to explore another blind path—what she investigated in each, I did not know. This time she returned hurriedly.

"I have found a suitable place for us to try. Bring her, Benjamin Colt."

Talis Darmon did not protest as I scooped her up and followed Beraal into the narrow passage. Apache trailed until a particularly narrow squeeze left him behind. He barked and whined as he struggled to follow.

"Stay, boy," I said. "We'll be back. I promise."

Beraal knelt where a collection of scree lay on the floor. Beraal sorted through rocks cleaved sharply from eons of punishment and selected those with dirty crystals in their fractured faces. "Lay her here, Benjamin Colt."

I eased her to sit beside Beraal.

"Princess, I think this place holds power. Can you feel it?"

Talis Darmon closed her eyes and extended her palms. "I'm so weak, Beraal. It has been very long since I have even tried."

"You must try now, Talis Darmon. You must reach within you to the Sylah blood that runs in your veins and try. Drink the last of the medicine first." Beraal pulled out the tiny flask the princess had touched to her tongue many times, and helped her upend the small container to deposit its last drops on her offered tongue.

"I will try. Make the form for me, please."

Beraal busied her many hands as I watched. She arranged the broken rocks with the face of the white dull crystal surfaces facing in a small circle and parted the fine gravel in the center until a tiny dish was created. Then she guided the princess's hands above it. Talis Darmon spoke in a whisper, but this time I could not understand a word of it. Strange sounds, musical and repetitive, came from her lips.

"Yes, Princess, yes," Beraal encouraged, and I stared at the spot, waiting for something to happen. Drops of water appeared from the crystals, at first a few, then more, until like turning on a faucet, water dribbled into the bowl. Beraal took a flask and lowered its mouth into the bottom of the dish. Water from a rock. This was a new kind of Ranger TV. Instead of a campfire mesmerizing my attention, the pooling water was like a water feature in a fancy house. I broke my reverie at the spectacle and furiously dug into our satchels for the other containers and passed them to Beraal. She handed back to me containers that sloshed as I gave her the last dry canteen.

"Drink, Benjamin Colt. Drink your fill and pass them back. Hurry."

"What about the princess?"

"You first. She must concentrate."

I did as Beraal ordered. Fresh water. The best thing I'd ever tasted. She insisted I do this several times until I refused more.

"You now, Beraal. And we must save plenty for the princess."

Beraal took a single mouthful before pushing another at me insistently. I drank a last time.

"Now her."

Beraal held palms to me and split her attention between the murmuring princess and the containers until the last was full.

"Stop now, Talis Darmon Sylah. You are a true child of your maternal dynasty. Leave your burden and rest."

The princess withdrew her hands to her lap. Her eyes remained closed and she wilted. I gently guided her head into my lap as Beraal took her perfect chin and touched a canteen to the cracked lips.

She took a little, choked, then took more as Beraal softly said, "Drink, Princess. Drink. You have saved all our lives as surely as if you had defended us against deadly beast with bare hands."

As I held her, her eyes opened briefly into mine, then closed. She went limp.

"What just happened, Beraal? How did she do that?"

Once after days on a sleepless patrol, I was plopped against a tree when I hallucinated a station wagon pull in front of me from out of the woods. The passenger door opened and the dome light exposed an elderly woman beckoning me as she held a steaming thermos cup. What I'd just witnessed was not that. That humid North Carolina summer night in the dark woods, there'd been no coffee. This liquid had been real, quenched my thirst, and life returned to me. More was in our canteens. Unless another explanation existed for how water came from dead rock, this was magic.

Beraal straightened with pride. "The Princess Talis Darmon Sylah is a sorceress. The last in the Red Kingdom of Mihdradahl."

✠ ✠ ✠

We remained there. I covered her with my cloak and rejoined a relieved Apache to keep watch outside the entrance to the craggy path. I leaned against Apache's side and stroked him as he lay still, eyes open and nostrils flaring as he sniffed for the whiff of danger. I stayed that way, until the cold forced me to pace the rest of the long night. It was windless and warmer here than our other rest stops, but my thin clothing barely sufficed to keep my skin from freezing hard.

The first dim light always strikes me as a figment of my imagination. I question whether it's a hallucination because it's the signal you yearn for that means night is over and the sun will be there soon to warm away the aches. Beraal's body was wrapped around the princess, and both were under my cloak. They stirred at my approach.

"I've cut off the pieces of meat dry enough to eat, and we have the last of the fruit," I told them. "We should eat."

So we did. I've always been amazed at the experience of breaking a fast, how even tiny bites of food transform into the energy of life you can feel travel with your blood and nerves to all parts of your body. Talis Darmon's almost red complexion returned, and I felt warmed by it.

"The worst, I believe, is over," Beraal said as she packed. "If we are near where I believe us to be, we will encounter actual paths soon. We may soon encounter Korundi, though it is not the season for the hunt. There may be Tarn scouting sign in advance of the time when the godahl descend from the highest passes to find new forage."

"I haven't seen anything an animal or us could forage, Beraal."

"True. Soon we will find where moss and lichen grow and the small life that feeds on them are found. All will be edible to us also." We had the large haunches of the gazraal which I draped over Apache. If we could find a source of water kinder than depleting Talis Darmon for the same, I knew we could endure almost indefinitely.

The princess rode on Apache's back and he was only too happy to have her, me at his side to rub against as I kept a hand around her waist and she an arm on my shoulder. The sloped cut we walked on noticeably widened and leveled as the day went on. Our trail curved around a bend at a rise, and Beraal waited there for us.

"Behold. The great Koga Valley."

Inverted triangles of valleys were staggered between impossibly tall blades of mountain chains on either side, making our way ahead seem obvious. Explorers often recorded moments of sublime peace, hope, and lightness filling their souls at such moments. I'd read of Shackleton, Livingstone, and Captain Sir Richard Francis Burton. Never did I think it possible there was a world where anything could be left to discover. Before me was a sheltering land I could never have imagined, and Karlo's revelation about gratitude returned to me. My eyes moistened.

"The worst is over, Princess."

She smiled, her own eyes misted. "Yes, Benjamin Colt. I feel it as well."

The lightness in my step carried me, Talis Darmon at my side, as we took the winding path. It was so wide that it had to have existed for many eons, trod by animal and Tarn alike.

Over her shoulder, Beraal said, "We can rest in a suitable place soon, then continue our travel in the dark as the footing is less perilous. Then we will rest by day in the warmth and travel by night."

We wound along until Beraal found another place to conceal ourselves for a rest break.

"This will serve," she said, leading the way.

Apache's growl rumbled deeply. I checked the path behind us. It was lifeless as a deserted museum. I snapped around as the princess shrieked, "NO!"

Both Talis Darmon and Apache were transfixed on Beraal's back as she disappeared into the passage. Vanished. One moment she was there between the craggy walls, then she was gone. Leaving only the path ahead visible. It was as though she'd passed through a mirror.

I sprang without thinking and thrust my arm through the illusion and grasped the crossbands of her leather harness. I pulled with all my might.

"No, Benjamin Colt, you cannot!"

I was snatched off my feet as if I played tug of war against a platoon of powerlifters. Talis Darmon's frantic screams faded behind me.

"The soul-eater has her."

22

A crushing, inescapable weight engulfed and surrounded me. I was in wet cement and blind though my eyes were wide open. I struggled, unable to find purchase with feet or hands. I fought the resistance that wrapped me. My thrashing movements were slowed the same way the flight from pursuit was suppressed down to a lead-shoe crawl, a child again trying to outrun the monsters of his night terrors.

I feared I would drown, but oxygen filled my lungs, perhaps even more richly than any time recent. But the panic that caused me the worst anguish came from within. It started as a whispering voice. My voice. And it grew to a deafening crescendo, suppressing all my own thoughts, until my skull split and the darkness exploded into burning pure white madness.

WEAKFRAILPATHETICDEPLORABLEWOEFULPUNYWORTHLESS.

The barrage gained momentum and danced in between the cells of my suffering existence until I was not whole but sundered and ripped into a billion pieces rivaling the number of stars.

I screamed and screamed with a mouth that didn't exist, a background score to the words that hammered endlessly in a vibrating earthquake of the splitting and joining and splitting apart of everything I was.

It stopped.

I looked at my tiny feet in the footed pajamas with the alternating pattern of Yodas and R2-D2s.

"Not again, Deacon Benjamin!"

It was my mother.

"Boy, I'm gonna whip your ass."

"Shh. Daniel. That won't help."

"He's just too lazy to get out of bed, I tell ya. Sleeping in it all night'll teach him."

I cried. Humiliated. I was cold and wet and stank of urine.

My mother bent to my ear. "You have to try harder, baby. No one likes a bed wetter. When you start school, if you wet your pants, no one will like you."

My father crushed his beer can. "Not to mention it's a sure sign you're a coward. The Army'll never take a bed wetter. How're you ever going to grow up to be a real man if the Army won't take you?"

The next day, my puppy bit me. I'd stepped on its tail by accident, and it yelped and bit my hand. I hollered. My father marched into the living room.

"What now?"

I showed him the tiny bloody scrapes on my hand from the sharp puppy teeth, and before I knew it, his knuckles rapped the top of my head. My skull rang with a hollow thump like a dull bell and more of my tears came with it.

"Be more careful around your puppy, dummy."

I was older, but still smaller than the world around me. I stood beside the wood desk at the front of the classroom. Mrs. Bishop swiveled to face me as her fingers dug into my shoulder.

"I've told you before, Benjamin. A cheater is no better than a criminal, stealing to profit by another's work. I told you twice to keep your eyes on your own paper. Now you must be punished. I won't let a child start the path down the road to delinquency. You'll thank me someday. Turn around and bend over."

"But, Mrs. Bishop! I wasn't looking at Sally's paper."

Sally had hair so gold, it shimmered, and I thought she was the prettiest girl in the whole third grade.

"Liar! A thief and a liar. I'll give you a swat for each. Bend over, Benjamin Colt!"

The swats from the giant paddle stung, but the tears I sniffed back up my nose stung more as they drizzled down the back of my throat.

"Go stand in the corner, Benjamin."

Giggles and snickers burned my ears.

My bike was gone. I knew I'd locked it in the rack. I was sure I did. I walked home with dread lodged sideways in my throat. I took the shortcut through the woods, just wanting to get home and hide in my room before Dad got home and I had to tell him about my bike. The narrow dirt trail widened, and I froze. The older boys were there. I was terrified of them. They were cruel and mean to me always, called me names and sometimes chased me and threw rocks. I knew they owned the woods, but I'd disregarded the danger.

Something popped sharply and the older boys all cackled with glee.

"Hey, it's the spaz. Hey, spaz, c'mere."

It was too late to run.

"Yeah, good idea," one of them said to answer their leader, Neil, who must've said something even nastier I couldn't hear.

Hands grabbed me and forced me down.

"Make him eat it, make him eat it," they chanted as I fought.

"It'll go easier on you if you just do as I say, weakling," Neil said as he straddled me. With two fingers, he held a tiny webbed foot barely attached to the rest of the bloody frog they'd blown apart with a firecracker. "You can't win, loser. Eat it and we'll let you go."

I dug my hands deep into my pockets and stared at my knees. My parents were seated on either side of me, and the officer sat behind the desk and talked about me as though I wasn't there.

"We know it was him, Mr. and Mrs. Colt. We've had a dozen complaints about pets missing. The complainant saw him kill her cat with a rock. We found him in the alley, poking it with a stick."

My mother groaned. "Benjamin, did you do this?"

The officer spoke to my father. "We can't ignore this. This is a very bad sign, as I'm sure you're aware. The judge'll most likely assign a case worker and order mandatory psychological counseling."

My dad lit a cigarette and coughed. "Babs, I told you a million times. We need to send him to the military academy. It'll do him good. He needs to toughen up. He needs to learn respect. My punishment doesn't do anything anymore and I'm worn out with him. I've done all I can."

My mom sighed. "Have you heard of that helping, officer? You've seen this before, yes?"

The officer shook his head at me then shrugged. "It's shipping a problem off for someone else to deal with, but honestly, it might be the best thing for him. I'm sure the judge will look favorably on a plan like that."

I had the new kid cornered. He was smaller and weaker than me, and I could feel his fear and it excited me. "I get your dessert. I get your dessert until there's a new kid to take your place, newbie. That's how it works. I'm the guy you gotta worry about here, not the teachers. If you go crying to them, they'll just make you do push-ups and run laps for being a snitch. Even if they don't, it won't save you from me. I'll get you when you're sleeping. Take it like a man, newbie. It ain't forever. And if you go along, learn how things work, and you toughen up—maybe I'll let you join my gang. First you have to show me respect."

Drill sergeants swarmed around me and Sergeant Knox was in my face. "You little piece of filth! You didn't say sergeant when you addressed me! You are a disgrace. Who do you think you are, maggot!"

It wasn't a question. I knew how the game was played. I'd used the proper address. He just didn't like me. I stayed locked at parade rest. A fist hammered my gut and I dropped.

"I'm going to make it my mission to recycle you as many times as possible before we toss you out of my Army, slimeball. Stay down! While you're down there, start pushing. I'll tell you when to stop. I'm going to make you do push-ups until you die. Knock 'em out!"

"One, Sergeant. Two, Sergeant. Three, Sergeant."

I'd never stop. He could beat me and make me PT until I puked, but I'd never stop. And someday, I'd get to be him. He was teaching me how.

The apartment door was ajar and I pushed it the rest of the way open. Coming out of the bedroom was some hairbag I'd never seen before.

"Where's Heather?" I yelled and I swung. I missed. He dropped me with a solid punch and kicked me on the ground. I struggled to breathe.

He stomped on my face with a steel-toed boot and I tasted copper blood. Heather appeared from the bedroom and laid an arm around the shoulders of the greasy zit-faced punk. Her robe came open and she glistened with sweat.

"What a loser you are. I can't believe I ever slept with you."

I was on a cold metal folding chair. My arms were behind my back and the manacles cut so deeply into my wrists, my hands were ghostly memories. My face rested on the desk. I was naked and shivered. They'd been working me over and I hurt everywhere. From behind, someone grabbed a handful of my hair and pulled me up as they slapped me to consciousness. Across from me sat Chief Bryant, his green beret on the table.

"How you made it into SF is still a mystery to me. Sometimes a selection process just selects a more elite piece of shit, doesn't it, men?"

Around me stood the team, fists clenched and blood on their knuckles.

"We don't tolerate a rapist. Or a murderer. You're a sick puppy and you're going to hang for this, Danny Deever. But we take care of our own. The MPs can't have you until we're done. We're going to leave just enough of you for them to court-martial and then place the noose around your worthless neck."

They stood me up and Mark pushed me against the wall. "I never liked you, Colt, but I never thought you were a dirty pervert. She was a child. A child, for God's sake!"

He smashed his fist into my nose, and the lights went out as they let me drop like a bag of wet cement.

Dave kneeled on my chest. "There are other missing girls, Colt. And you're going to tell us about every one of them."

He choked me as I entered the black tunnel, and I prayed this time I would die in its darkness.

In the fuzzy black void, a faraway voice buzzed in my ears. It was little more than a modulated hum. It repeated in a loop and always returned to the beginning before the same blurred sounds started their odd pattern of soft and hard, fast and slow. I couldn't escape the audible assault, and during the eternity it teased at me, it slowly grew louder and clearer, until finally I had confidence that what it said wasn't my imagination.

"Deacon Benjamin Colt. Come back to me. Deacon Benjamin Colt. Come back to me. Deacon Benjamin Colt. Come back to me."

I snapped awake. The door of the interrogation room opened, and a Tarn in camouflage wearing an MP armband entered.

"It's time, little human."

This wasn't real. None of the terrible things I'd lived in this life had happened. I'd never done any of the things I saw myself doing. I'd lived a life of honor and integrity.

"This isn't right! This isn't my life! This isn't me!" I pulled with all my might and the handcuffs snapped apart. I exploded to my feet and lunged at the MP. He showed his tusks and reached for his sidearm. I tackled him. The pistol was in my hands and I placed it between his eyes.

"THIS IS NOT MY LIFE." I pulled the trigger.

"Benjamin Colt, awake."

I was on the ground. My forearm burned like fire. Talis Darmon pried my fingers open to release the grip I had on Beraal's leather tunic. I gasped in pain.

"I called and called until my voice failed me. I never gave up hope. Oh, my brave hero. How have you done this thing? Only in legend has one escaped the den of a soul-eater."

Her tears flooded over my face and unlike those I'd swallowed, hers were sweet.

I was free. I won. But not without help.

"Talis Darmon. I came back from hell because of you."

23

When strength returned, I lifted a traumatized and stunned Beraal onto Apache. We resumed the trail to get away from the lair of whatever had ensnared Beraal and pulled me with her into its poisonous essence. Not much farther ahead, we took shelter beneath an overhang of rock set back far enough to accommodate us all. After receiving the seal of approval from Apache's nose, I helped Beraal onto the flattest spot to lay. It was fully dark now, and after several cycles of Apache perking ears and sniffing, he lowered his massive head on his front paws and we settled in. Beraal refused food or water, curled into a ball, and fell into a fitful sleep.

The princess put her rifle within reach. "I will take the watch, Benjamin Colt. Rest."

I lay back but was fearful to close my eyes. Would I dream of the sick things I'd done and have to see them again? Talis Darmon moved closer and I let her lift my head to rest in her lap. Soon she soothed my brow. As beaten up as I was, I knew I was going to be okay. Because she was real. Her scent, her warmth, her gentle caress. I'd felt nothing like it in the pit of despair she'd lured me from with the beacon of her voice. As tired as I was, I hoped she was acting as a woman easing her lover's burdens and not a mother comforting her sick child.

"How long was I in there, Princess?"

"Hours and hours, Benjamin Colt."

"Hours? To me, I lived my whole life over again. But it was all wrong. A nightmare." After some time, I relaxed and sank deeper in the comfort of her lap. I was about to succumb to its supreme perfection, when I tensed. If this was another illusion—if I believed I was free—I'd be defenseless again. I pictured this dream shattering like the two-way mirror I'd been pulled through and behind it, the cavernous labyrinth of the beast's deception, waiting to engulf me for more of its hideous mind games. I snapped to sitting and checked that my rifle and sword were close at hand.

Her hand was on my back. "You are here with me, Benjamin Colt. Safe from the soul-eater. I cannot begin to imagine what you endured. But your ordeal is over. The soul-eater was not strong enough keep you trapped. Your will was too great. There can be no other explanation. You not only saved yourself but someone dear to me. A truly selfless act."

I wanted to be her hero, but I couldn't lie. "It wasn't selfless. Had I known, I doubt I'd have had the courage to fight that thing."

I was unprepared for what happened. And being unprepared was a mortal sin in SF. But what could have prepared me for that kind of battle?

"I was small and weak. Powerless and at the mercy of everyone around me. I saw myself grow to become as cruel as those who'd hurt me." I shivered. "What was that thing? An animal? A machine?"

She held up a single finger and squinted in a way that made her seem like a wizened professor. "Soul-eaters are remnants from the very creation of the universe itself. An ancient race of Vistara who lived in the darkness of its deepest ocean depths made a pact with that last vestige of their presence left in existence. The Karnak experimented and sacrificed creatures of all manner and even their own kind in their quest for immortality. The oceans dried and by then our race thrived. Wars were fought as the dwindling numbers of old ones tried to conquer the world of the surface they'd ignored for thousands of millennia. They were defeated and driven away. Some left for worlds unknown. Those too weak escaped and took refuge in the deepest crevices of the Furrow of the Creator's Hand.

"Others sought safety in the many mountains of Vistara. Legend, but real. Myth, yet existing. Lore, yet danger true. They skulk in the remotest of places, far from man or Tarn. They suckle at the pain of whatever they ensnare—any opportunistic creature from whom they can squeeze fear. When a soul-eater is discovered, its lair is attacked by every means. But they are immortal, more phantom than flesh. The best that can be done is to seal one into the folds of Vistara itself. But eventually, it finds a way to freedom. Like all evil, it is ever existing."

"I've got the cure. A tac nuke. And I'll lead the patrol right back to its doorstep to make sure they've got the right address."

She offered her lap as my pillow again. I concentrated on my breathing and gradually accepted that I was not trapped in another deception. And if it was illusion and a setup for the big fall to come, then I'd enjoy this closeness while it lasted. Even an imaginary Talis Darmon was better than none at all.

"I know your torture was great, but so too was your fortitude. Only in the tales of mythic heroes has one escaped the grasp of an evil one. After ages of dominating the lesser minds of simple beasts, the soul-eaters are weakened and atrophied from their once malevolent might. Even so, their dark powers are too formidable for even the strongest Tarn to defeat. All battles take a toll on the warrior who fights them, even the victorious. If you wish to speak of what you suffered in the soul-eater's den, I will listen."

I knew what had happened to me. The soul-eater probed the soil of my mind for fertile ground, then cultivated and harvested the pain, fear, and self-loathing it needed for nourishment. I wouldn't relive the shame of it, even if it was all brainwashing from an even more diabolical version of a North Korean POW camp. "The most awful things that could twist a person's soul—I experienced them all as if they'd happened to me. But they hadn't. Some were vaguely like true moments of hurt—tiny pains from my real life the soul-eater distorted and warped. Most were nothing I'd ever experienced—the worst things. Things you read about that hurt because they're so awful to imagine."

"Then it is true—what is written of the fate of those entangled by a soul-eater. Only someone of great inner strength could win such a war. But still there is a danger to you."

"I feel fine, Princess. I'd feel better with a roof over our heads and cushions to rest on, but if wishes were horses, right?" I wouldn't trade all the comforts of all the palaces on Vistara for her touch.

She ignored me. I knew my idiom couldn't translate and chided myself to speak only in the formal manner I'd adopted.

"What you experienced, it now exists in your mind, much as those things you have actually lived. The danger that lingers is this—two types of experience now exist as your memories, both the genuine and those imposed on you. If you cannot distinguish between them, it will erode your soul and cause great damage."

"I know the things I lived in the soul-eater's den aren't real, Princess."

"Good, Benjamin Colt. Then you've taken the first important step to rebuilding your inner strength."

She massaged my temples and hummed a soothing tune. I relaxed even deeper. What prompted me to do so I'm not sure but, without fear, I revealed the secret skill that I'd never told another soul.

"I'm burying all those false memories. Pushing them beneath the surface of the black tar pit where I suffocate all the bad things from my past."

She promptly intervened. "No, Benjamin Colt. You must not do that." Her words were soft and soothing. "The power of them cannot be extinguished there. Like the soul-eaters themselves, they cannot be exterminated. They lie in wait for an unsuspecting victim, ready to snare you when you least expect and suck you down with them into their lair. Allow me to help you. Do you trust me as I have trusted you?"

There was no one I trusted more.

"Yes, Princess."

"Listen."

I met her upside-down face as she lowered it to mine. I wished there were light by which to see her beautiful eyes, but even had there been, as she chanted and hummed, my eyelids became as heavy a weight as any rucksack I'd ever borne. No matter how much I fought to stay awake, a pleasant heaviness spread to my whole body.

The sun was up. I rolled my head to where Talis Darmon made the same lulling chant she'd made over me. Beraal's head lay in the princess's lap, and I watched the princess at work like I were a naturist covertly spying on an animal in the wilds, scared that if I made a sound, I would disturb the doe and her spring fawn, and stop her ministrations to her injured friend. After a time, she eased from under Beraal, now in as deep a slumber as I'd been in. I made no attempt to disguise my stare when she met my eyes. Her smile was sweet.

"Good morning, Benjamin Colt. Are you well?"

I stretched and rose. "Never better, Princess."

Apache snored in the sunlight, his eyes darted beneath his lids and all his legs quivered as though he were chasing something.

"I think we should remain here today and rest, Benjamin Colt. If Beraal is well, then tonight we may resume our journey."

"I need a vacation, Talis Darmon, and that's the best offer I've had in years."

✢ ✢ ✢

After dark we struck out, Beraal back in the lead. She thanked me with a hug that drove the air out of me in a whoosh, all my vertebra cracking loudly. In mortal combat, I'd fought to keep a Tarn from getting four arms around me. She confirmed it was a fear I was right to harbor.

"Beraal! Careful! You're crushing me like a junked car!"

"I owe you my life, Benjamin Colt. For a thousand years, my clan will sing the tale of your service."

That was a bit much. I was mumbling something inadequate back when she kneeled and took my hands in hers. "We share together an experience of pain and desolation. Had you not the strength to save us both, we would have lived the rest of our lives in agony, and my dearest friend would be alone, without her protectors. And now, with the princess's healing, we move ahead to the promise of good things to come."

I was feeling better than I had a right to. All but starving, dehydrated, and everything that went with those conditions plus fighting creatures both eight-legged and psychic.

"Is that what she did, Beraal? Did she heal us?"

"Yes, Benjamin Colt. I told you, she is a sorceress. Her skills are great, especially those of healing."

Whatever the princess had done for me, it left me giddy. I had a new spring in my step as we set off. We marched and my mind floated. I watched the oblong moon trace a low path between gaps in the mountains, its smaller sister satellite overtaking the larger moon in the race across the sky during many kilometers of our night march. Finally, they both fell behind the peaks, and I lost sight of the winner. Talis Darmon walked ahead of me, and when I saw her tiring, I brought Apache with me at a trot to her side.

"Beraal says we have weeks ahead of us yet, Princess. Let us help you. Apache wants to carry you. And I want to walk beside you."

"Thank you, Benjamin Colt. And you, Apache." She patted his neck, and his entire body shook with his wagging tail.

I whispered, "Let's roll, boy."

It was chilly, but next to her I glowed like one of the amber light-stones. Without the moons to occupy me, the many questions that pestered at me became chigger bites that couldn't be ignored, and my curiosity demanded scratching. I found words to break the silence.

"Princess, are you a sorceress?"

"I am not a wizard, like those sung of in our ballads. I have no power to conjure or do anything truly powerful."

We walked in silence a bit before I tried again.

"I saw you draw water from stones. That's as magical as anything I've ever seen."

"That is as close as I can come to creating something tangible, and even that is not what it may have appeared to your eyes."

"The water is real and sits in our canteens."

"It is."

"Can Beraal do as much?"

"No. It is a crafting unique to my maternal dynasty, and I am unskilled in all but the simplest forms of science that they once possessed. My training was focused on matters of the mind. Communication. Diplomacy. Creating understanding between peoples. And healing."

"Hold on to Apache while I check behind us."

She removed her arm from around my shoulder, and I trotted back to the last bend of the path. I watched for a time, then bounded back to catch up.

"Tomorrow, Apache and I will hunt before first light returns. Beraal says soon enough we'll have makings for a fire. If we have Mydreen in pursuit, they're very far behind us. I think we can risk a small daylight fire if it doesn't smoke badly. I'll roast meat for us, to go with the other things she forages."

"That will be welcome, indeed. The dried meat has sustained our bodies, but the taste is difficult to ignore. Cooking will help."

"You've been a real soldier, Talis Darmon. I know many who would not have faced the challenge of our escape with the courage and determination you have."

"Thank you, Benjamin Colt. I am grateful every moment for your help."

After some time, I could hold back no longer. "Talis Darmon. I have great admiration for you. And great feelings. I wish I could wait until we reach safety, but if I wait any longer, I'll burst. Talis Darmon, I love you."

She sank in her bare saddle. "You must not say such a thing, Benjamin Colt."

"I'm sorry, my princess." I'd called her "my princess," partly thinking the words must be deeply meaningful, partly wanting to spark a response.

"Several times, I've ordered you not to speak to me so."

She hadn't scolded me with the same bite she had in the past, but she was distressed by my words, nonetheless.

"I apologize, Talis Darmon. I know I must be saying something ill mannered, but I promise it's not my intention. I don't know the proper way to tell you how I feel—to show you my affection."

She let me suffer in silence for some time. "It is natural for one whose anima is touched to have a feeling of attachment for the one who works to mend them. Especially for me, as I have been trained in the talents of my mothers. It is not proper of me to take advantage of such confusion. I would be no better than a soul-eater, imposing a false—"

I saw my opening and I took it. "Talis Darmon, you bewitched me long ago! From the first moment I saw you. Each day I've only become more certain that my feelings for you are true. I withheld them out of respect. Your situation was so dire, and I was your protector. I could never allow myself to take advantage of your need by offering my heart, ransoming your return affection as if I held power over you like your captors. I hoped to wait until there was an appropriate time. I'm sorry that I couldn't wait any longer. I couldn't live with my regret if—the worst happened, and we didn't make it."

Her arm found its way over my shoulder again. "And close to our end we have come often in such a short time." She sniffed. "Benjamin

Colt. We must wait. And wait more. As much time as is necessary for your inner self to be fully restored. And our circumstances returned to equanimity."

She was right. I knew she was right. To selfishly put her on the spot with my fevered passion was weakness on my part. We were on an E&E—escape and evasion. An alien planet with many dangers yet unknown to me surrounded us. I'd taken an oath to protect her. I had a duty. And I'd never let weakness interfere with the performance of my duty.

But I just had to have the last word.

"So, you're telling me there's a chance!"

24

In the Korund Mountains, I was as removed from whatever troubles bothered the rest of Vistara as I was from Earth's. Any matter not material to our sustenance and never-ending march had ceased to be of concern. The deeper we went through endless valleys bounded by impossibly tall peaks, the less I tried to plan for what would come after we finally found Beraal's people. There would be shelter, food, and comfort. That was all that mattered. What followed, I no longer cared to consider.

We were successful some days at hunting the goat-like godahl, and many days not. A small one didn't go far. It took most of a day to roast slices of a kill over a tiny fire, one piece at a time, sharing small bits as they were ready. Of the four of us, Apache was the only one to have a decent repast, raw godahl being perfectly acceptable to him. We ate the gritty plants Beraal taught us to seek, but hunger wasn't a driving force anymore. Energy was. We'd long since lost the pang of an empty belly—I'd learned it before after the first few days of survival school—but it was the listlessness that came with a starvation diet that had to be defeated. Without calories, it was feebleness, not hunger, that was the enemy. On a bountiful day, we took in much less than a half-thousand calories each, and the ratio of fuel to expenditure was always unbalanced toward a deficit. I feared our tanks would go empty before we reached our destination.

There wasn't a trickle of water from a rocky cleft nor a drop of condensation on a stone to lap at. Talis Darmon's conjuring saved us from deadly thirst—which unlike hunger only worsened, never abated. Several more times I witnessed her alchemy, and after she recovered strength, I asked for explanation.

"The math that describes the process is complex. I merely unbalance the equations as I join constituents together through the crystals and align the energies."

"But there's no instrumentality, Princess."

"Untrue. My mind is the instrument. It is just another kind of science, Benjamin Colt."

We hadn't had another threat from animal or other danger since the soul-eater—that was good. And we'd traveled so far that Beraal was certain we'd encounter help sometime soon—another item on the plus side of the list. Though weakened by our environment, I felt confident I could tap into the juice that made me a Jesse Owens among the polio-ravaged low-gravity residents of Mars. I wasn't my best self, but I could keep getting by.

There were too many items on the negative side of our list, but the only one that mattered to me was that Talis Darmon was withering before my eyes. And my heart broke as she did. With each of her mystical creation sessions, less and less water was produced. Her last effort barely filled half of one of our vessels.

"I feel the power grow stronger as we travel, much stronger than when you first helped me make the form, Beraal. But I can only drive the equation for a short while. I don't understand," she whispered, battling to keep her eyelids open.

"You need rest, Princess," Beraal said, always soothing.

In training for the tempo of combat operations—where food and sleep became rationed rarities—you see people become who they are. Pain, hunger, exhaustion. In no time, you find out if there's hardwood under the carpet or only rotten particle board.

The first week of Ranger school, I buddied with a guy who seemed solid. I mean, he looked the part of a tough guy. Bodybuilder. The proverbial brick outhouse. Confident. Affable. Funny, even. Someone who pulled his weight. A guy who knew how to keep his and your spirits up when the going got tough. By the start of mountain phase, he was already shirking. Hid when it came to trade-off on who carried the 240. Complained about being wet, cold, tired—as if everyone wasn't feeling the same. But it got to him. And the way he acted, his discomfort was supposed to be more important to you than your own. He snapped whenever he was woken for his turn on watch. He never volunteered for anything. Small tasks, like making the sand table for a patrol order, were done with the most minimal effort.

He stood next to me on graduation day. I got a black and gold tab pinned on my shoulder. He got a certificate of attendance. He had the minimum points necessary to graduate, but we peered him out. In the evaluation of his performance by his fellow students—including me—he was unanimously flunked. And in those kind of schools, if your peers say they don't want to go to war with you, you're blackballed. I saw him crying as he packed his duffel bag.

If I had to write a peer eval of how Beraal was doing on the first ever Vistara Ranger Class zero-one dash who-knew, she was an 11 out of 10. She was a merciful goddess sculpted from saintly jade. An indefatigable soldier. She was as different from the other Tarns I'd met as Karlo was from the false brothers who'd tossed me aside. Would I ever get the chance to reckon with them? Not if we couldn't find water.

Beraal lay her own cloak under the princess's head. "Tomorrow we can try again."

It didn't take an alchemic scientist to understand why the princess was failing where previously she'd succeeded with her magic. It was obvious. But to say it out loud would be acknowledging my deepest fear—Talis Darmon was fading like a battery on its last volt.

"I will find the strength. Just let me rest awhile."

All we could do was drone on like soulless robots. Slow ones at that. After the harrowing first few days of our evasion into the mountains, my obsessive-compulsive need to keep track of our progress kicked in. Back in Phase 1 of the Q course, I'd established my base pace count that's been hardwired into me ever since. In light gear, it took sixty-one of my even strides to cover a hundred meters. With every fall of my left foot, I counted. One to sixty-one. Bend a finger joint, first the small finger of my left hand, then continue right. After ten times and at bending the small finger of my right hand, a kilometer was reached. Then I'd think of a toe as a placeholder and start again on my fingers. A routine I multiplied ten thousand times.

This was uneven terrain, and our pace was necessarily slow and getting slower from our fatigue. Considering our winding, rising, and descending path, I adjusted my count tally and estimated we made twenty-five to thirty kilometers each night. Meaning since we started our flight, we'd maybe come five to six hundred klicks. A great distance.

Today, I stopped counting. What did it matter? Without a map, it changed nothing. It had just been a way to keep my brain working. The counting had become a schizophrenic voice, hammering at me and drowning out other thoughts both useful and harmful. The instant I stopped, I felt the beneficial effect of my self-prescribed medicine. In this case, the tonic was proof that nothing was in fact sometimes better than something. I felt alert. My throat was dry, my lips cracked, my feet throbbed, but my thinking improved. And thank God it did.

But when even Apache—an ardent survivor if there ever were one—failed as I did to react to a new danger, it was a hard slap of reality that our condition was even grimmer than I'd thought.

Rocks slid onto the trail between Beraal and us. Just a few, slightly bigger than my fist. Apache and I stepped around them, apathetic Walmart shoppers detouring our cart around a box of macaroni and cheese fallen off a shelf. It wasn't till it happened a second time that either of us reacted.

I murmured to the princess, "Someone's above us. Hold on tight. With me, boy."

I leaped twice to catch up to Beraal, who lethargically left her haze and took notice of me only when I touched her shoulder. I whispered, "There's a gazraal trailing us from above." One of the lions of Mars was stalking us, waiting for the right moment to pounce.

She squinted at the rock face. "Where?"

This time I had the better vision. Not a gazraal. Two legs, four arms. Leaving concealment just enough to spy down at us before fading back. It was a Tarn. I felt relief shoot through me.

"It's your clanmates checking us out, right? Should you hail them first?"

Beraal squinted. More dark shapes appeared in glimpses along the narrow escarpment, weaving out and dropping back behind projections like schooling fish swimming through a branching coral reef. Before she could reply, I stated facts like a detective revealing the murderer.

"They don't walk upright. They're a long way off but to my eye they're bigger than Khraal Kahlees. They're pale. Not Tarns." I raised my rifle.

Beraal sucked air through tusks and teeth. "No, Benjamin Colt. There are too many. If we fire on them, they will descend on us in a horde too large to contend with. They would overwhelm us."

I couldn't disagree. If I'd had an M4 in my hands, I would have. "What are they?"

"They should not be here," she said as a non-answer.

"Beraal, what are they?"

"The white apes. But that cannot be."

"Keep close and let's move."

In tighter formation we pressed on, and I kept my gun ready.

"We cannot fire unless we have no other choice," Beraal urged me. "The white apes are intelligent but are maniacally aggressive. They fear nothing. They defend their troop with a ravage fury if threatened."

"If they don't start anything, neither will I, but they're about to tickle the finger for my happy switch."

I knew she didn't understand me, but she got the gist.

"They will tear us to pieces until their last number if it comes to a confrontation."

I kept tabs on them as we hurried our pace. We were being shadowed. Twice now I'd lost sight of them and thought perhaps they'd lose interest, only to see their dark mirages reappear, to my disappointment.

"Are we in their territory?"

"I can't believe so. They are all but extinct and live far, far to the north in the cold northern mountains of the Sharpa. In the underworld, they guard the entrance to the Temple Farnest at the end of the River Blix. Soldiers of the White."

"Then the Endangered Species Act is working, 'cause they're making a comeback."

Talis Darmon spoke for the first time in so long, her voice was like a half-remembered song to me—so faint in the radio receiver, it was hard to recognize. "They have some purpose. Why haven't they attacked already if they mean us harm? Why haven't they departed if we demonstrate no ill to them?"

There was no complex reason. "They're animals, Princess."

Apache stopped short, sending the princess against the back of his thick, wrinkled neck. He sniffed the air rapidly, then growled as he lowered his chest, ready to charge. I hefted her off him to shield her behind me. Beraal and I had rifles up, and I strained to make out the danger just as Apache sprang ahead. A snarling war broke out in the darkness.

"Protect the princess!" I yelled and launched forward.

Our path had been progressing down a narrowing valley, two bluffs of tiered walls the boundaries. From the blackness, Apache's barks were challenged by screeching howls, and I expected to at last see one of the apes up close as I sped through the crevasse.

Apache was faced off with one, all right. It menaced him from a perch on top of a huge, flat boulder. The path had widened into a sheltered pit, a natural amphitheater. And in all the best seats of the craggy steps set in the walls, white apes crouched. I burst into the opening and my eardrums nearly shattered as the spectators unleashed in a unison of threatening hoots, fists pounding chests, tusks bared.

I'd followed Apache blindly into an ambush. I tried to call him back to me. "Apache, come. Let's get out of here. C'mon, boy."

Behind me, Beraal yelled over the animalistic fusillade, "Benjamin Colt, we cannot retreat."

"Back to back, Beraal. The princess between us."

The princess's other armed protector did as I asked. She spoke with ferocity, proving to me she was as ready as I was to die defending the princess. "The path of retreat was cut off by their horde. We had no choice but to follow."

No more of the shrieking, glass-shattering howls, now a coordinated hooting showered us from all sides. It was so dark, the rudimentary sights of the rifle might as well not have been there, but same as Apache's fixed attention, I aimed the muzzle at the chest of the one on the boulder.

Talis Darmon was at my ear. "Benjamin Colt, in there. Next to the pool. A cave."

Her finger pointed past the wide shallow pool of a stone fountain where cut into the rock face was the coal-tar black hole of a mouth into the mountain. The pool reflected the starlight, and I was reminded of a place like it that exploded out of memory like an airbag deploying in a head-on collision.

I didn't see a choice. "Slowly. With me. It's a better place to defend from than here. If they try to cut us off, I'm going hot. Don't leave me to have all the fun, Beraal. We'll burn as many as we can before it's swords and fists."

"They do not move to stop us," Beraal said as we took our first few cautious steps.

"This is what they want," Talis Darmon said. "They herded us to this place."

I called Apache. He fixed his tormentor in place with his fiercest tirade before finally trotting to my side, still foaming and barking at the opera of white apes all around us. I wish I'd had a bang. Or a flashlight.

"I'll lead," I said without looking back.

The intensity of the hoots diminished, but their echo pushed our backs into the tunnel like waves shoving a drowning man to shore. I came within an inch of running barrel first into a wall, halting only because a dim light reached my eyes at the last moment. The tunnel curved sharply and what I saw past that turn was like a missing sock pulled from behind the dryer. It hadn't gone to some fifth dimension. And like that mystery, I had the answer to what this place was. A dim amber stone glowed from a recess in the wall and around it, more pockmarks dotted the curvature of the walls. In the pockets, tiny stone figurines.

But no white apes.

"Do nothing rash."

My muzzle snapped to where a dried up shrunken man stood, his arms folded in judgment like one of the carved figures. His face, where not covered by long white whiskers, was sunken and coarse as though he enjoyed the same diet we did. His clothing, no better than ours.

The princess's gentle touch on my forearm guided my rifle away. "Water priest, we are in peril," she said. "I ask for your ancient and honorable guild to shelter us. The creatures outside mean us harm. We have been in the mountains for many weeks without help."

Like I somehow knew he would, the old man tittered—disturbed, mad, or malevolent. His sniggering changed pitch—amused at our plight. I wasn't so depleted to ignore the bad manners of some ancient tweaker after Talis Darmon's humble request for help. If he had any pearlies left in his wrinkled mouth, it'd be worth the brief joy of smashing them down his throat with my buttstock before a cyclone of gnarly white apes hit me.

Instead, my growl seemed to break the crypt keeper's amusement at our expense, and he recovered some manners.

"I have suspected for many days that Red royalty was nearby. The ninth ray told me you were tapping into its flow. The Hortha brought you to me. Whether I give you shelter or let the rightful masters of this realm sacrifice you to their god depends on who you are and why you are here."

25

I'd once seen a room of full colonels shrink into a bunch of cowed navel gazers when a command sergeant major ripped into them for lax security around their TOC. Every one of them made inspecting the color of their boots their immediate occupation until a staff sergeant took charge and corrected the deficiency. Churchill once shamed a woman who'd called him drunk by telling her she was ugly, but he'd be sober in the morning. Whereas one was a sermon at the fire-and-brimstone end of the spectrum of world-class rebukes, Churchill's was at the other end of the scale, a scolding disguised in pretentiously polite humor.

The princess's response made both seem like the reproach of amateur grievance holders.

"Filthy hermit! How dare you make threats! I am the Princess Talis Darmon Sylah, emissary of King Osric Darmon!" Had I feared her light was dimming for good? The fierceness I'd admired and frequently been the target of was not revived—it was resurrected like Lazarus raised from the dead. Her will, iron. Her presence, dominating. Her words, a condemnation delivered as lightning bolts cast from the heights of Olympus itself.

Her finger shot out, and for a moment I thought the metaphorical lightning was about to become real. "My king has long supported and protected you and your fellow recluses, despite your arcane guild's petulant manner towards him."

Was it my turn to stay *her* aggression? We were hat in hand, and she'd gone from begging to airing grievances like it was Festivus. And we didn't even have a proper pole to celebrate around. If this was her diplomacy, maybe Domeel Doreen had no choice but to take her hostage.

How do you one-up a tornado?

I loved her all the more for it. I'd back her play.

The old man startled at her response—as did I—his manner quick to deescalate, but in his words, both apology and accusation returned.

"Temper, temper, Princess. I promise no harm will come to you or your party. The guild swears it. Though the Red Kingdom of Mihdradahl is no more friend to the guild than are any, save the Hortha. Put down your arms. None of the races of Vistara save Tarn have passed this wellspring in thousands of revolutions around the sun. I had to act to protect the sanctuary."

"You trust only the Hortha because the apes do your bidding as slaves, priest!"

She was about to push this first hand of poker straight to the back-alley knife fight that usually takes till 4 a.m. to stir up. Now I had to intervene.

"We accept your oath, priest. In turn, I give ours that we will respect your house and customs while under your protection."

"He is not to be trusted," the princess growled.

"I don't see much choice for us," I said with as much subterfuge as I could for being in the close confines of a cave.

The hermit recovered, and with renewed fervor said, "You can trust this, Princess Talis Darmon—it was the ripple in the ninth ray that caused me to notice your presence in the Korund. My apprehension about the cause of the disturbance demanded I send the Hortha forth. What stayed my command for your destruction was the faint consideration I gave to the possibility that it was not the Necromancers of the air testing some foul science to pervert our guild's purpose. If not your gratitude, at least acknowledge that this old man holds sacred his duties of guardianship—to always investigate with science before allowing fear to counsel me. That it could be the blood of the Sylah dynasty at work was not high on my list of differentials."

The princess was grudgingly mollified, and her tone reflected at least a tiny amount of respect as she cooled. "Thank you, wise priest."

Apache growled at the passage behind us, the snorts and cries from outside reduced more to the noise of a half-empty pub than the riot it had been.

The old man bowed slightly. "Then I permit you entry. What I extend to you, Princess, is a courtesy not shown to the Red for an age. I hold you to your oath. Touch nothing unless I so permit. And mind your consort, White prince," the Gabby Hayes wannabe told me. I think he was fearful of another of her outbursts being directed at him. I'd been there.

"I am Princess Talis Darmon's guardian. I serve her," I replied, wanting to defend her strict sense of decorum. I didn't want him thinking she was my "consort" and whatever that might imply. But I was secretly pleased to hear him think so.

He rolled his eyes like an exhausted cop.

"The beast. Your gadron. He minds you well, yes?"

"Oh. That he does."

At least, I hoped he did. For the princess's sake, I gave assurance. He was my dog, but I didn't want to admit I had no idea if, when in someone else's home, he bit against orders. I didn't want the invitation rescinded and Apache was going with us, regardless. It'd be up to Gabby to mind his P's and Q's around him.

"Then follow." He waved a hand over his bracelet and a portion of the wall pulled back and brighter amber light escaped, suggesting great depth and breadth beyond the opening. I gave the okay and Beraal took to the old man's heels, falling into our order of march once again. The rock face closed behind me.

"Welcome to the Keep of the Water Guardian. Come. We will talk. First, your thirst must be quenched. There is no life without water and there can be no discourse without life. And discourse I desire. It has been long years since I've spoken with any but my own kind. The water flowing is proof enough that I stand my station. The guild needs no other confirmation, though still they test my loyalty, thinking me not worthy to be a master. My mistake? I thanked them for their diluted milk of kindness at breaking my solitude to ask every annual around the sun, 'Is the flow safe?'

"Well, come and see for yourselves. I break my vow of humility. Today Cynar the Younger boasts! See for yourselves the diligence of my dedication. I am beyond their judgment. Behold!"

Beraal gasped, dropping to her knees and four palms. "The River Blix!"

"Bah!" the hermit spat. "If anything, it is the River Cynar!"

✟ ✟ ✟

I reluctantly watched the princess go first to lay on the pallet and accept the healing light. When the priest offered, Talis Darmon saw my apprehension and explained. "The rays can be harmful if misused, but for severe illness, even the physicians in our kingdom prescribe its use. I think us to be so infirm that we must accept, Benjamin Colt."

Cynar the Younger—I still preferred to think of him as Gabby the old coot from so many Westerns—sniggered. "That the rays are harmful is false. Your so-called physicians are more like frightened children than scientists. The light of the third ray has sustained me for a thousand journeys around the sun and kept me vital so to attend the work of my commission."

I choked. "You're a thousand years old?"

Gabby was crazy alright.

He cackled in delight. "Hehehehe! The third ray has brought me no harm!"

I mumbled, "Dude, you're like a four-pack-a-day man saying smoking doesn't cause cancer."

"Hmm?" He let my gibe go unexplained. "The blood of royalty does not live in my veins, but the guild has secrets of its own. Let the princess be restored, then you and your Tarn. Your gadron needs no third ray." He cackled some more and placed colored crystals into different settings in a panel until a golden light appeared from above, spraying its warmth onto the supine princess, its borders oddly confined to her outline.

"Allow her to rest in quiet. Come." He waved Beraal and I to him.

"Apache. Guard the princess."

He dropped to his haunches, his back to Talis Darmon's prostrate figure, and eyed Gabby. He whined a little as we left, but did as commanded. He was an overgrown baby, but an obedient one.

"Good boy."

The priest led us back out into the main cavern where the plash of flowing water became strong again. The underground river was twice as wide as I was tall, and we halted on the esplanade where our host brought out cushions. His was threadbare while the others appeared unused. I took the offered seat and then the cup as he poured.

"When you are all restored, we will go to my garden and pick enough for a meal. I have more than I need. The water is sweet. Between it and the third ray, I need little food. There is much that I carry outside to lay by the wellspring for any passing creature to share."

I wondered if the fountain and cave combo near the crash site had a similar interior layout. "Cynar, I passed a way station like this in the Mydreen desert, a few days outside of the Tarn city. Some of my—" I almost said *friends*. They were not that any longer. "—companions saw one of your fellow priests, but he fled from them."

Cynar grunted. "Those outside the guild are a danger to our kind and our commission. Many mistrust us, thinking themselves more capable, more worthy to wield the craft. As though if they but controlled the science, they could restore the oceans of Vistara!"

Beraal was fixated on the flowing surface of the river, echoes of cool splashes of water lapping against the rocks. Locked on the river, she said, "You hide from the world you try to sustain."

"Indeed! Otherwise, the petty scientists of the atmosphere guild or others as badly misguided would try to take control of the source of water on this dead world, same as they hold control of the very air we breathe. But they would botch it! Same as they botch the stewardship of the atmosphere factories they so badly manage."

Talis Darmon had given me the basics behind the distrust between those who maintained the air and those who provided the water on Vistara.

"Cynar, the princess was negotiating with the Mydreen to allow her father's scientists access to the factory in their city, hoping to keep it running. She says many of the factories are falling into disrepair and failing, despite the scientists' best efforts."

"Best efforts! Likely so! A broken clock is still broken! The machinations of fools and idiots is still worthless, no matter how much sweat goes into their endeavors. If left alone, the factories would continue for thousands of years without attendants. It is their meddling which harms the factories. It is their failed attempts to duplicate the mechanisms which causes them to fail. Like all their philosophy, they think to create more, instead of living in the balance of that which has been established by those wiser. That is the peril they represent to the commission of my guild. They would destroy Vistara in the time it takes a hatchling to reach mere adolescence if we did not resist their intrusion."

I sighed. His explanation was cryptic, yet I understood resentment when I heard it.

"I don't pretend to understand your conflict with the air doctors, priest. But I'm amazed at what you've accomplished. The flow of the river is strong. Where does it come from? Where does it go?"

His bushy eyebrows shot up. "Curious, isn't it?" Then he laughed, amused I wanted to know the secrets of his realm. "From this station, the water I usher into form flows in two directions to service many other wellsprings."

He beckoned us again, anxious to keep his oath to boast. From the esplanade, a path led along the river and disappeared alongside the tunnel the current came from. Sensing I was not being followed, I turned to see Beraal hesitating.

"Coming?" I asked her.

My companion had displayed the fortitude and resilience of any Green Beret a thousand times over. But there stood the hulking green shield maiden. Frozen. I understood. What I'd thought had been her fascination with the river was instead her keeping a wary eye on a lion free of its cage. It was as though the waters might become discontented and spring from their confines to attack.

"It's safe. There's a path. Cynar doesn't expect us to swim, I'm sure."

"Swim!" Just the suggestion made Beraal take retreating steps.

"Hehehehe!" Her reaction delighted Cynar. "None have dared imagine a vessel so wide and deep as this on Vistara since the age of the Karnak and their fiefdoms at the bottom of the sea. To most, White prince, so much water is a reminder that there are ancient, unseen dangers that lurk on Vistara."

I understood his reference. "We met a soul-eater, priest. We know."

"A soul-eater? Impossible. If you'd met one, you wouldn't be here."

Beraal discarded her timidity. "Lord Benjamin Colt speaks truly, priest. We were ensnared by one of the ancient remnants, and he fought us free of it by the strength of his will."

Cynar wasn't laughing now. "I've never heard of such, but that does not negate it as a possibility. Well, if it was so, then you have my sympathy. Give no mind to similar danger while here. The only fear your Tarn friend may reasonably have, White prince, is drowning. Those of my guild alone know how to negotiate immersion in the life-giving waters. That is part of their mystery. In small measure, it is life. Unbound, it is death. A duality of nature the fools of the atmosphere guild are too blind to see."

"I remain behind, Benjamin Colt." Beraal had already retreated even farther away from the rim of the channel. "The princess may need me."

"I understand. We'll be back soon, will we not, priest?"

His wild cackles were back. "Indeed, hehehe, it is not far."

"Then lead."

The tunnel path continued, the curved ceiling dropping as we went until I had to bend at the waist to pass. The river became more turbulent as we went until the tunnel dipped to just above the surface and we seemed at the end of the journey. Before I had to bend much farther, he disappeared into another passage I hadn't yet seen. I followed him up winding steps, the roar of falling water growing louder as we climbed. We came upon a concourse where Cynar paused on a balcony, and as he yelled above the roaring pool below, I leaned out to see.

"The coalescence occurs within the very substance of the Korund. Here the product of the union comes together. Two trails they take from here. The one you saw, and another there." He pointed to a narrow channel like the top of a floodgate on the opposite side of the churning pool.

"Where do they go?"

"Here, we sit at the divide of the Korund Range. The tunnel passages flow to lower grounds in both directions away and toward the equator. Ancient and deep are the passages and the cisterns that mimic the groundwater that once were the circulatory system of a living Vistara. In places of power, other way stations lower than this contribute to the flow. Where there are no way stations, the water flows into the porous ground to feed wells, like those in the cities. First came the guild's plan to preserve the branches of these water paths. It was much later the cities of the surface moved to where they are now. Our guild determined the course for how the populations of Vistara would migrate and fix themselves. It was we who determined where such could exist to grow into what remains today. Every division of life on Vistara owes their existence to my guild, for without the thousands of years of our foresight, building, and stewardship, all would be dust."

"Where do you join the oxygen and hydrogen to make the water?"

Cynar scowled. "Eh? Nothing so crude occurs. I will show you."

Crossing the balcony into yet more tunnels and stairs, he held me back at the archway leading into the blue light of whatever lay beyond. "For lifetimes before I was hatched, none but my guild has seen what I show you now—not the kings of the reds or yellows, nor the Tarn chieftains from the time whence they first came to this starving land."

"Why do you allow me, Cynar?"

"Hehehehe. A White lord, a Red princess, and a Tarn travel together." It sounded like the setup to a joke, but he was right. A collection like ours was just that kind of thing. "You touch the ninth ray, survive a remnant of the evil that were the Karnak, suppress your fear to not throw your lives away by attacking the Hortha—if you meant harm to my guild or the great commission, I cannot sense how."

He removed his arm blocking the entrance. "And you've been most entertaining! It is a long forgotten light you ignite within this heart. So, come. Bear witness to my contribution to the great commission and be in awe!"

Awe was at least what I gave him.

"You see, don't you? My mastery is beyond what the guild suspects of one as young as I."

A cathedral as high as the mountains themselves rose in jagged columns, strata lined with veins of lapis lazuli, clear quartz, and mercurial metal shimmered their light like the rays of the sun, farther and higher than I could see their end. Beneath was the mechanism. Kilometers of glowing contrivances the likes of which didn't exist in the imagination of all the artists who ever lived, pulsing in a thousand colored lights.

"Dub me 'the younger,' eh? Refuse me the title master, have they? I've been busier and more successful than the stubborn old godahls would ever admit."

26

We sat together on the cushions, feasting as he'd promised. The healing rays had also delivered as he'd sworn. I'd never felt better. Most importantly, Talis Darmon glowed with new life. Her smile was a ray of its own that healed me as much as anything the priest's sick bay had done.

"How far do the river tunnels travel, Cynar?"

"They course to the ends of Vistara, until the force of the essence of the planet itself wanes."

I assumed his metaphor was to say that when there was no more elevation for gravity to carry the water, the tunnels ended. But where?

"Cynar, there's enough water here to make a desert blossom. It's as much water as one of the California aqueducts carries from the mountains to feed Los Angeles County. Do they pour into giant lakes? All this water must collect somewhere."

"Ha! Hahahaha!" That brought a genuine laugh. "For what purpose? To evaporate into the thin skies? No, the liquid dives deep into the ground to seep farther into the soul of Vistara to be stored. Deeper than could be detected by any science known but our own. When the guild decides the time has arrived to allow the surface kingdoms to know of the presence of our work, then can the whole of Vistara reclaim the planet."

Talis Darmon's mouth dropped open. Every shape of her face was a gift to me, even her exasperation. It wasn't caused by one of my failings, so at Cynar's expense, I enjoyed the new countenance she wore like it was a lost work of art discovered hidden in an attic. "What does the guild wait for, priest?"

"Eh?" Whether the monosyllabic response meant confusion or deafness, I wasn't sure. I thought it the latter.

She tried again. "If your guild has filled the deepest aquifers of Vistara to the ignorance of all, then why do they wait to reveal their presence?"

It had been the former. "Because it would be for naught! As long as the guild of the atmosphere sits in their councils. They would use the product to ease their laziness. You understand, sorceress! The dull—" he tilted in my direction, "—think we join together the constituents to make the water. You know it is the ninth ray that shapes the work. The fools of the atmosphere guild would take to the path of mental indolence and destroy our work in order to do theirs. They would use the basest of science to separate the essentials and render the precious water to atmosphere. They would waste our work and by it accomplish nothing. Science! Bah! They don't know the meaning."

I took his insult in stride. "So, until the atmosphere is completely restored by their guild, your guild won't share the wealth of the water you've made, is that about right?"

"You're not as dull as you look, White prince."

The gears of Talis Darmon's mind turned as she searched for the chink in the hermit's armor of defense. They seized to a grinding halt with her answer. A closed mouth. A face that dropped into hands. That alone amazed me.

Talis Darmon at a loss for words.

I thought I understood why. It was like finding out you'd spent your life like all the generations before you, pushing a plow over dust bowl ground, only to learn that if you'd spent the energy digging, you'd have long ago reached the gold deposits no one suspected were there all along.

"So, Vistarans have no idea that you've created underground seas," I said.

"Hardly seas, White prince. None to rival the oceans of the past, but significant nonetheless."

Beraal's shoulders shook with frustration, and I was ready to put myself between her and the hermit. With four clenched fists and clenched teeth, she said, "Priest, there is much suffering. There is much hardship. It could all be eased with the location of even one of the hidden cisterns."

Cynar tasted something sour. "Bah. We provide enough to sustain life through access to the ground water accessible under the cities and by the trickle of sustenance we give to travelers who pass the way station fountains. Without waste, without excess. We have done a better job than the atmosphere guild has ever done in providing for the kingdoms of human and Tarn alike."

Someone once said that the very rich were different in that they didn't see money as a representation of what could be owned or what things could be purchased with their fabulous wealth. It was love of the numbers themselves that drove their toil to make more money. I kind of thought it the same here. It wasn't what could be done with the water that drove Cynar's guild any longer; it was the pursuit of how much they could produce that empowered them. Especially him, the most prolific producer in the guild. The one that seethed in resentment for the lack of recognition and his exaltation at the fact.

"Cynar, you said it was the atmosphere guild's want of more rather than balance with what exists that you condemn. How is your hoarding of the water so different?"

"I had you right to begin with!" Cynar smacked his forehead. "All those muscles and nothing between your ears! Balance is exactly the issue. I told you—until they balance the needs of Vistara with sufficient atmosphere, to share the wealth of the water stores would result in a waste of all our work."

Now it was my turn to drop face to hands. "You make my head hurt, Cynar."

The old man grumbled and returned to chewing a leaf.

We ate in silence. Apache sniffed at his plate of white roots, licked one, nibbled, and rejected it with a very human sigh.

I mused out loud. "S'pose we need to hunt a few more godahl for him. We dropped what we had when we had to beat feet from the apes. The fountain outside probably attracts them. I bet it would be easy hunting for us. Beraal, do the Korundi raise the godahl, pen them like livestock for food?"

"We do. When we finally reach my people, Apache will not need to hunt, unless he chooses to, and neither will we."

I was wondering how much farther our journey would be once we departed from Cynar's hospitality when it struck me.

"Cynar, do you travel on the river?"

"Eh? Travel where? I do not leave my station."

"The river goes for a great distance, you said. And the way stations join the river where other priests contribute to its flow. Is the rest of the river channel like it is here? Large enough to float a boat down?"

Beraal choked on her veggies and coughed out in exclamation. "Benjamin Colt, you cannot mean to sail upon the river as if traveling the River Blix to the afterlife? What if that's where it leads?"

It was just simple physics, but also my general lay of the land told me their bus stop into the afterlife was somewhere uphill, not downhill. "Where does the river go, Cynar?"

I'd stymied Cynar. He had a far-off look, even considering that he was crazed like a paint huffer. "A boat. A boat?" He mumbled for some time, searching his memory for the meaning of the word. He puzzled and ruminated, his head tilting as his eyes focused on nothing until suddenly turning wild again. "Ha! Hahahaha!" He sprang to his feet and dashed away, leaving me again doubting his sanity.

"Crazy old coot. He's been here so long he's forgotten boats float on water. In fact, he doesn't seem to know anything about water except how to make it and maybe remembering once in a while to drink a little himself. Millions of gallons, and he doesn't even bathe in it, I bet. You're right, he's the poster child for the side effects of too much healing ray. We need to think about hitting him up for some provisions and after some rest hitting the trail again."

Just then the hermit returned, dribbling from the corners of a toothless smile.

"Boat! Boat! Boat! So long has it been! I had to refer to my register of all my many projects and laboratories before I was certain I had not imagined it. Come see, come see!"

A new maze of tunnels burrowed deeper and endlessly. Chambers full of dead mechanisms, tools, mounds of cracked minerals and crystals, walls covered in a language I could not read, symbols crossed out and rearranged in what looked like a copy of one of my high school chemistry examinations. I'd passed, by the way. Barely.

A curtain was pulled aside, and a cloud of dust billowed from its folds, causing coughs to intersperse with his perpetual "hehehe"s, mimicking the sputtering start of a hand-cranked Model T. With a final convulsion, he spat the last of the dust.

"I was once consumed by a fever of doubt. Nine hundred annuals ago, when they were truly correct to dub me The Younger. For a hundred annuals, a dribble was all I could manage, no matter that I correctly applied all I'd been taught. I recall my anguish at my inability to surpass the limitations of the equations, to rise to the greatness of my ambitions. In my fragile state, I planned to abandon my commission and flee. But in the construction of the method for me to skulk away, I found new strength. And with it, I worked even harder, the vessel I created shaming my back—a reminder of my weakness, a symbol of my fear and self-loathing. And when the new equations and transduction amplifiers proved out, it represented my graduation from acolyte to adept. I had forgotten it even existed. It has been hidden here since."

He waved a hand, and an amber stone came to slow life from within the dark alcove.

I wondered how long he worked on it. I'd seen popsicle stick sailboats that looked more seaworthy. Flat-bottomed, shallow gunwales, narrow. The hull was thin enough to see through, and the material it was made from was layered unevenly, folded over thicker fore than aft, like a bad papier-mâché job. It at least had a tapered bow which was the only thing that reminded me of a boat in his grand realization of what a watercraft should look like. He might be a master of water alchemy, but he was a dud of a nautical engineer.

"Your own design, Cynar?" A canoe, it was not. "It's not big enough." I ran a hand over the skin. Was it actually made from paper?

"Pfff! It will conform to support any burden against immersion." I must've made a face he understood as skeptical because he lit into me. "You've witnessed the greatness of my mind and my hands, and you doubt my genius equal when applied to a construct so simple? It is perfect for its task!"

"Cynar, it's not that I don't appreciate all you've done for us. It's just that I had something different in mind. This doesn't even look like it'll float. Did you ever test it? Maybe if you show me where you keep your materials, I can build a raft or something that'll hold all four of us."

"Aiiiiiyeee!" Frustrated, he pushed me aside. "Are you no different from the elders of my own guild? Is it this face that I've been cursed with that inspires disrespect from others? At least *you* I can embarrass into apology. Follow!"

It wasn't an invitation; it was a command.

The scrawny recluse hefted his creation overhead. It teetered and he struggled to keep it balanced. The ladies scattered to avoid getting bonked on the head as he seesawed wildly, his scrawny toothpick arms trembling like Apache making a pile.

"Let me get the other end, Cynar!" I ducked behind him and lifted my end. So light. It was the proverbial feather of resistance. It had to be made of paper.

This is a waste of our time, I thought, but I indulged the old coot. He grudgingly allowed me to help, and I let him set the pace as we wound a reverse route back to the esplanade.

"Time to erase your skepticism. I will hold the craft in place. Get in."

The boat lay on top of the water, dancing side to side in the gentle current. Should I trust him? He'd saved us. It didn't feel right to refuse. Worst case, when the darn thing sank under my weight, I could bail out and swim for the rim of the bank. I've negotiated much worse while dragging rucksack and weapon with me in the freezing winter waters of the Cape Fear River.

I eased in. The bottom gave way and sank to my weight as I'd anticipated. I expected water to spill over the sides and swamp the bottom, but instead, the hull formed deeper into a familiar rounded V shape and the beam widened with me.

"Not feeling so smart now are you, my dull white prince?"

I could see his gums, his mouth drawn open so widely in triumph.

I bounced a little to see if I could sink it. Water sloshed at the sides but never came close to the lip.

"It's still not big enough for three people and Apache," I told him. "We're going to need another one just to hold him."

"Gahhh!" I'd pegged his irritation meter to a new level. "Call your beast! You'll see! Then I expect the apology to make all other apologies since the goddess created the stars seem insult by comparison."

I hesitated.

"Still you doubt me?"

"No, Cynar. I don't know if Apache will get in. I'm sure he can't swim. Is there a way to make it bigger first so I can coax him in?"

Apache had been anxiously watching, me the subject of Cynar's frenzied derision and all.

"No. It conforms to the load applied. Is nothing I do good enough for you? The entertainment you provide is quickly wearing away. Try or do not. I am soon grown tired of this struggle against a will mired in ignorance. You defeated a soul-eater? More likely he spat you out because of your bitter taste!"

"Okay, okay. Apache, come to me, boy. Come on."

It took me several tries to get him to come close to the water's edge. I pleaded and pulled him by his muscled neck. Finally, one massive paw plunged into the bottom of the boat, then another, until he locked elbows and pushed back with all his might. The boat pushed away from the edge in response.

"Hurry it up," Cynar scolded. "I can't hold this forever. The seas dried faster than this."

"Ladies, give him a push of encouragement." I pleaded, petted, nuzzled, and pulled as the women pushed. Another leg, then another, and with a last lurch, he left the quay. With each step, the bottom deepened, the beam widened, and the boat grew in length. It was now to my fisherman's eye more of a properly shaped craft. Maybe something like a Boston Whaler but without the center console and the deep sea fishing rods around it.

"So, now you see!"

The bottom had deepened and the gunwales were now at my waist. The water line was well below the top edge.

"I do," I replied.

Apache looked nervously over the side and back to me, whining for my assurance that all was well. Cynar's boat was a miracle. I vaulted out and helped Apache follow, the boat shrinking in all dimensions in response with each ounce removed from its scales.

The hermit lifted the boat out of the water by himself and set it down gently without so much as a groan of exerted effort. "Well?" He was waiting for me to pucker up and kiss his bony seat.

"Cynar." I took a deep breath and spread my arms wide. "You are a master. The master of all masters. At seeing this, Leonardo DaVinci would commit suicide from embarrassment over his wasted life. Thomas Edison would race to patent this marvel and claim the credit. Jeff Bezos would pay to run banner ads on Facebook until Amazon shipped one by parcel post to the doorstep of every home. I stand in awe at your dominance in all fields of engineering and physics. Were I king, there would not be merely a single day on which to celebrate the genius of Cynar. Instead, every day would start with a parade held in your honor. Stamps would bear your likeness. Cynar would be the most popular children's name for boys and girls. Movies and TV shows would tell and retell your story. Only the most beautiful of actors would play you and would commit emotionally scarring acts of self-debasement to win the role. Why the very—"

He waved my apology away. "Gibberish. Who even heard of these nitwits you contrast me with? Humph. But one so dull can't falsify sincerity. Apology accepted."

27

Apache didn't need near the coaxing the second time as Beraal did her first. "How do we know the wizard speaks truly? That this journey does not end in our judgment and passage from this life altogether? I do not fear the afterlife. I welcome it. But the time is not yet right. There is much we have left to do here before volunteering to take the path to join our ancestors."

I'd failed to convince her. It was the princess's turn.

"I sense the direction of its course. It flows not to the north, but towards the western range of the Korund. The priest speaks truly."

Beraal still held back, a pair of hands fidgeting with her rifle, the other adjusting her satchel. "By his own admission, he has not taken the journey himself!"

I understood the problem. "You won't have to touch the water, Beraal. Even if you fall overboard, you won't drown. It's as Cynar said, the bottom of the channel is shallow enough you can stand up in it. Especially you. I tested it. It only comes up to my chest. Beraal, where I was raised, parents take their children to parks for experiences like this. Heck, if we had innertubes, it would make a nice float trip. We'd have permanently wrinkled butts by the time we got where we're going, but we'd be fine. Trust me, a boat is a first-class way to travel, and we'll be dry."

Beraal stroked her face with both pairs of hands. "The priest is right, Benjamin Colt. You speak gibberish. Sometimes." She winced. "Forgive me, lord. I allow my anxiety to quench the fire of my duty and my manners."

Then she said, as if to herself, "We must do this. I must do this. We will arrive at last in the den of my people and we will secure the safety of the princess and receive help to return her to her father." She gave me a thrust of her jaw and tusks. "All because of your courage and tenacity, Benjamin Colt. I am prepared."

"We've done it together, Beraal. We're a team."

Apache whined from in the boat, sensing he was being left out.

"You too, good boy," I told him. Some good firm claps of doggie-pats on his neck and he slurped happily. Beraal let me ease her into the boat, which deepened and expand farther.

"To do what has to be done, against fear, is the difference between the hero and the coward, Beraal. You're a hero."

She huddled in the bottom of the boat and spoke to her knees. "Most heroes die at the end of the song, Benjamin Colt."

Cynar let me take the boat as he fished around in his waist pouch. "There is a single way station between here and the western border of the Korund. It will take days for the force of the river to carry you there, but once you've arrived, you'll find the Korund Tarn are nearby." He gave me a small red stone. "Show this to Salkar the Rash. He will know it is from me and that he should accept you as a friend of the guild."

"Can't you call ahead and let him know we're coming his way? It would be better if he knows it's friends coming and not trespassers. Why is he called 'the Rash'? Does he have a skin condition, or a reputation for going off half-cocked?"

"Eh?"

I sort of knew my idioms wouldn't translate, but speaking thee, thou, thine all the time was a struggle—plus, I was feeling a little slap-happy about the prospects of putting in some real distance and soon.

He answered my question, though.

"Hehehehe, no, there is no way to communicate your impending arrival."

The princess was pained, but it was not from the same distress that afflicted Beraal. "Priest, I never imagined your sect to be as cruel as what I've learned of it from you. You've been the steward of this important work for the lifetimes of many men, without comfort or reward, without the succor of kindness from fellowship, and without recognition. Why is it necessary for your life to be so full of privation and needless suffering in order to tend your commission?"

For once, he did not act the part of the insane recluse, but soberly said, "I have given you cause to think this, but it is not so." Then he recited,

"The oceans dry, the air grows thin.
The way of cruel dissolve begins.
Duty, fealty, stewardship, all
To fight our fate, our single call.
We alone remember
The fields of Vistara's bloom.
Where others fail, we give our lives
To save our world from doom."

He nodded, as if this explained everything, then said, "I have let myself seem resentful toward my guild. Unappreciative of this life and the responsibility they have bestowed on me. We vow to allow no distraction, because only we can maintain the life of Vistara. There is no greater cause one could hope to have as their own. Our lives are solitary, yes, but the satisfaction that comes with this conservancy is reward enough."

Talis Darmon blossomed. I've never believed in things like auras other than as metaphors, but I swear, she flourished with a yellow-green energy that reinvigorated me in my own oath.

"Priest, I too am committed to the rescue of Vistara. I thank you for your mercy and for the gift our lives. I promise to use that gift in the service of our planet. I will endeavor to find a way to reconcile the conflict between your guilds for the good of all."

The wild eyes of the madman were gone. His bearded dipped and his hands folded over each other in the humility of a squire. "It is by more than your ability to touch the ninth ray that tells me the blood of the Sylah runs in your veins, Princess. Truly, you are royalty."

Why had I become a soldier? To escape a life of mediocrity? For the chance to do something adventurous? To have pride in myself? Most all professional soldiers hold a secret wish—a yearning for the chance to do something truly special, something unique, and to never be found wanting if that moment ever comes.

In the form of Talis Darmon, the chance to touch something noble had come to me—and I felt justified that I'd recognized it and acted. Dressed in rags, the luster of her raven mane returned. Though her hair was a matted nest, her feet caked with grime—she was the most noble person I'd ever met. I served her because she needed me. I served her because I loved her. Most of all, I served her because she was worthy.

The dignity of the moment was brought to an end like a catwalk model falling off her heels, finishing spectacularly with a head dive into the front row.

"Hehehehe, but the atmosphere guild are morons!" Gabby Hayes was back. "Not all the Sylah maternal dynasty gathered in one room could counsel those dolts into behaving like scientists!"

"And with that, we take our leave," I said and assisted the princess as Cynar again held the boat. "Goodbye, Cynar. Stay out of trouble, you crazy kid."

I pushed off, the current took hold, and the nose of our paper-thin boat found the middle of the channel. We drifted away and into the tunnel. The amber stone on the nose responded with life, revealing the walls and black water for a scant few meters ahead. Cynar's cackles followed us long after the light at our backs faded away.

"A White lord, a Red princess, a Tarn, and a gadron! Hehehehe! What was I thinking? What a calamity! At last, I can have some peace and quiet around here."

✤ ✤ ✤

There was no way to measure time. On the underground river there was neither day nor night. We bumped along gentle bends, the lapping waters of the gentle current against the boat a hypnotic sound. We took turns on the watch, though what we would do if the river boiled in capsizing rapids or a cascade of falls, I had no plan. But if we came to the way station and coasted by—sound asleep—it would be a lot worse than missing a stop on any train ride I'd ever taken.

With our energy and optimism restored, the anxiousness about our unknowns was a minor detractor from our greatly improved status. And it was a joy to speak with the princess, now her fully restored self again. She kept me company as I watched with Beraal napping against a snoring Apache, sleep the best medicine for her hydrophobia.

"Talis Darmon, I've been thinking about Cynar. For all his curmudgeonly protests, do you think underneath it all, he knows the water guild is wrong? Why else would he involve us, if at some level he didn't believe something had to change and that maybe we could help?"

She raised her brow. "He is a conflicted soul if ever I have met one. Professing pride in his silent sacrifice yet craving recognition. Boastful of his guild's colossal burden yet rejecting the worthiness of others' efforts to also save Vistara. It is more than the effects of the third ray. It is more than the product of isolation. Its roots lay in his earliest days as a hatchling.

"Little is known of the water guild, but it's said their priests are trained from birth for their purpose. Cynar is the sole water priest I have met. From his own words and actions, I see that beyond the great science he was taught, Cynar and his kind were indoctrinated to believe suffering is necessary for the achievement of their great purpose. Their commission is performed as a service but also as a punishment. For what? I cannot imagine. I suspect, their sect atones for some failure. Perhaps the failure to save Vistara earlier.

"So, were we entertainment? Were we a threat he must assess? Despite his protests about the ingratitude of his masters and the ineptitude of others, he reveals his misgivings about the exercise of the water guild's franchise to save Vistara. I think you are perceptive of our host's purpose, Benjamin Colt. I think we were a convenient means for his subconscious doubts to be transformed into action. How long had these questions formed inside him? How long had he waited for someone to air his grievances to? Imagine, Benjamin Colt! A thousand cycles around the sun."

She moved her hand to rest on mine.

"Alone."

Not even the tragedy of Cynar could subdue the electricity that surged from her touch.

✣ ✣ ✣

Apache stirred to check that I was nearby before laying his head down again and returning to a deep sleep. The river was soothing but rather than sedate me, the sounds invigorated me. The splashing tongues of swells on our hull were the sounds of action. Of a new odyssey. A literal voyage. Like Lewis and Clark, the French trappers, or the Jesuits—exploring the New World for the first time. I feared no danger. The princess traded places to lie against the world's largest throw pillow and Beraal sat the watch with me on the nose. She'd become less agitated about being on the water after a good sleep.

"Beraal, I don't wish to be rude, but you'd mentioned that we should trust Khraal Kahlees because—"

"We are comrades, Benjamin Colt. You may ask me anything without causing rancor. You wish to know why my father does not know his own daughter."

"I do. That you are called by one name when everyone else has at least two. Is that part of the story?"

"I have much to explain. I am Dosenie Beraal of House Pardoo. Dosenie is a title, not a name. I have no family name and as you suspect, that is because of my parentage. My mother was like me, Dosenie—a confidante and retainer to the court of King Osric Darmon. Her name was Lassa Laloo, from a proud line of Korundi who have provided generations of dosenies to the Red Kingdom.

"She fell in love with a young warrior she met on her travels with the royal counselors. He was low in rank, but she saw greatness in him. He promised that one day he would be a chieftain, and when he was, that he would send for her to sit at his side. Away from her people, she chose to bear his child. I was conceived and grew in the Red Kingdom, far from the Korund.

"The captivity from which you freed the princess and I was not my first at the hands of the Mydreen. I was a hatchling when once I traveled with my mother on a diplomatic mission to the Yellow Kingdom. We were attacked in our night's camp by a horde of Mydreen raiders who pillaged and murdered our party. My mother and I were spared by the desert Tarns, but were taken as slaves by a young Mydreen lieutenant named—Domeel Doreen.

"Domeel Doreen violated her in ways that I was too young to understand. Her last act before killing herself was to give me to distant cousins among the Mydreen—the same who helped us escape from Maleska Mal. Before she sent me away, she told me the name of my father. 'Khraal Kahlees is a great warrior. He will protect you.'

"I was smuggled to the Korund by a trading party and given to a family of House Pardoo. They raised me, knowing my mother was a dosenie, and when they could, eventually returned me to the Red Kingdom, who welcomed the hatchling of Lassa Laloo. There I was trained and educated and followed my mother into the service of the Darmon. The princess was a hatchling when I was assigned to her house, and I have been with her ever since." She rested, seeming to think her tale complete, only the sounds of the river's current and the whistle through a sleeping Apache's nose filling the silence she'd left.

"The water is not so fearful now, Benjamin Colt. I think it is a promise. A reminder that someday I will take a similar journey and at the end, be reunited with my mother once again, all the hurt and pain a forgotten memory."

I was dumbfounded. The snake Domeel Doreen was her mother's slaver and rapist! "Beraal, does Talis Darmon know all this?"

"No, Benjamin Colt, she does not. You are the only soul I have shared this with, and the knowledge must remain in your confidence. The princess bears a responsibility both great and terrible. To know so much would affect her diplomatic duties to regain access to the atmosphere plant in Maleska Mal and save Vistara."

"Oh, Beraal!" It was incredible. Words eluded me. "But I don't understand, why didn't you use your father's name and go to his house?"

"As time passed under the protection of my adopted family, I considered the name of my father and what it meant. It meant nothing. If Khraal Kahlees cared so little for my mother and I to leave us on our own, why should I look to him for comfort? I was content to be safe in House Pardoo, one name or no. In the service of the Red Kingdom, it mattered not. I heard the name Khraal Kahlees mentioned during my years assisting the princess. A rising name amongst the Korundi. If my mother loved him and he her, he must have some quality beyond that alone of ambitious warrior. It was this thought that I carried when I dared speak to him. After your intervention in our captivity and torture at the hands of Dormeel Doreen, I thought it would inspire him to aid us if he knew you were not a White lord but a warrior like him."

"Did you want to tell him who you were?"

"If loyalty to the alliance between the Red Kingdom and the Korundi wasn't enough to make him risk giving us aid, why should I reward him with the knowledge that he has a daughter! It was we who escaped our bonds, like my mother and I before—without the aid of Khraal Kahlees."

"And when we reach the Korund? What then? The princess knows Khraal Kahlees is your father, too."

"I have sworn her to my confidence as I have you. She knows all, save Dormeel Doreen's part of my tale. The Chieftain Jedak Jeraal will hear the princess and give aid. To the void with my father!"

Behind us the princess had joined Apache to snore peacefully as the river carried us in the dark.

"Thank you for your trust, Beraal. I know what it's like to carry pain."

"In the belly of the soul-eater, many pains untrue were conjured from my heart for its pleasure. But of those real, the rejection by my father and the humiliation of my mother were the worst. Though the princess has healed me, it has caused me reflection. She says that forgiveness is the way to wholeness. But I wonder, is revenge a better salve?"

I didn't know whom she meant to avenge herself on, Dormeel Doreen or her father. Had she told me all this, thinking that there might be a way for me to help? Like Cynar the Younger's doubts revealing themselves through our encounter, was Beraal subconsciously hoping that I would aid her plight, as well?

The river listened but kept its counsel beneath the rippling current.

✢ ✢ ✢

After what felt like a few days—but could've been less or more—it was Beraal who spotted the dimmest of light ahead. The tunnel widened and a similar but smaller esplanade than Cynar's came into view. I eased over the side while holding the top of the gunwales—all to the gasps of both women—found the bottom, and maneuvered us to the quay.

"Hold us fast, ladies." I propelled myself up and took a rifle, ready for anything. When all remained still, I waved everyone out. "Passengers may now disembark the *Bonhomme Richard*." I'd taken to calling our boat that for a very good reason. The fog from our survival flight was gone. My purpose was restored.

Like John Paul Jones, I had not yet begun to fight.

Beraal and the princess guarded as I pulled our craft out of the water. If this was not our stop, we'd retreat back and take our chances downriver.

Apache growled. A water priest stood at the mouth of an entrance, staring blankly at our arrival. Physically, he was Cynar's spitting image. He was a little more fashion conscious, wearing a pale lavender poncho with a gold belt at the waist. On a charitable day, Halston might've approved. I produced the stone that was supposed to be the token of recognition.

"Salkar the Rash, we are friends of Cynar the Younger. He gives me this as a token of the same."

He was as expressive as a turnip. Without a change to his glazed expression, he made a half turn and took a step aside, clearing the path for us.

I kept my rifle low. "Should we follow you?"

He didn't answer.

"Okay. We'll follow you. Lead the way, Salkar."

We ascended stairs and switchback inclines. "So, Salkar, how long you been in the water business? Cynar's doing some bang-up work up the road a piece. You should go for a visit sometime. It's quite impressive."

Not so much as a grunt from our pathfinder as we followed.

"Benjamin Colt," Talis Darmon whispered over my shoulder. "I know you think yourself humorous, but this is not the time for levity."

"Just remember, Princess, fun is something you have right now, not something you save for later." The disappointment carried in that sigh told me all I needed to know, and I surrendered. "Yes, madame ambassador."

We entered an anteroom, and the hermit waved a hand over his bracelet. The wall pulled back and to the side. He unceremoniously stood out of our way.

"Apache, to me, boy." If there was a passel of white apes in the sanctuary cave ready to pelt us with stone figurines, I wanted the big guy and me to find them first.

"Thank you for your help and for your service to all of Vistara, wise priest." The princess dipped her head to no response from the recluse whose skin was varnished in a grimy glaze. Beraal was last out and the secret door closed behind her.

"Anticlimactic, wasn't it?" I asked Apache.

He wagged his tail, sniffing the fresh air coming from around the exit passage. Dim light teased the stone walls with the rays of dawn. Our canteens were full from the river, we had two rifles—our third well destroyed and abandoned after the encounter with the lion—our swords and knives, and sacks full of provisions provided from Cynar's gardens. We passed by the gurgling fountain and followed the path out of the canyon.

For as far as I could see, the lower walls of the great valley were no longer the barren red rock of our previous trails, but had rich streaks of yellow and purple lichens, now common where before they'd been a rarity. I traced one of the draws up to where I saw tiny moving dots of the mountain goat-like godahl in abundance.

Beraal's excitement was contagious. "I know this fountain. I visited it once many, many cycles ago. We are near a village. We should reach it by day's end."

"Then we should be safe to travel in the daylight. Let's march."

Beraal resumed her rightful place in the lead. With Talis Darmon between us, Apache and I brought up the rear. I fell into my habit of checking behind us every so often, and despite Beraal's assurances that this close to a settlement there would be no dangers, I swept the ledges high above us for sign of ape or lion. The sun warmed my bones and the damp chill of weeks in the high mountains and days beneath ground finally left. At midday, we came on something new. A blind canyon left the path along the cliffs and opened into a wide bowl. Beraal halted at the mouth. Tiny mounds—the size of footballs—dotted the ground and lower walls. My eye recognized that the formations were not natural.

"One of the nesting grounds of the clan," Beraal answered my unasked question. I'd heard the term "hatchling" so many times in conversation and had taken it to mean any infant child. The Tarn women were as mammalian as the human Vistarans. It was only now that I began to suspect.

"Beraal, do the mounds contain—eggs?"

"Yes, Benjamin Colt. The young grow here in safety and warmth beneath the cover of their mother's mound until time for their entrance into the world."

It seemed indelicate to ask, but I couldn't hold my curiosity back. "Beraal, do Tarns lay eggs? Is that how you produce young?"

It was Talis Darmon that answered. "Benjamin Colt, all life grows from an egg."

A wave of mental images going back to my grandma's chicken coop flooded my head. "Talis Darmon, do you mean that on all of Vistara, for all people, this is how reproduction occurs?"

Beraal seemed anxious to explain. "Once per cycle, those of the clan who are ready conceive, each couple places their egg in the mound they have prepared together. When it is time, the whole clan gathers to await the joyous day we meet our hatchlings. It is three long cycles until they arrive full of life from the goddess. It is a most joyous day for the entire clan, not just the parents who have waited patiently to meet their progeny. This is one of hundreds. It is a sure sign we are in safety of the Korundi domain."

"But…" My confusion wasn't erased.

Now Talis Darmon took the reins. "Ah! I understand your puzzlement, Benjamin Colt. Human customs are different. Humans do not reproduce as a group all at the same time and only once per cycle around the sun as do Tarns. We choose when to reproduce. And our children mature in their egg under the protection of an incubator in its place of honor in the home, awaiting the child when it is ready to come into the world. Is this more familiar to you? Is this not the custom on Thulia?" She used the Vistaran name for Earth.

I was stymied. "No, ladies. On my world children are born of their mothers—alive, not from eggs." They both tilted heads in wonder. "I mean, there're eggs, of course, but they grow inside a mother, without a shell, and—" I didn't finish.

Talis Darmon's royal propriety took over. "Truly, it is different on Thulia. Perhaps it is best spoken of another time." She dismissed further discussion by resuming our march. I watched the princess's hips as she swayed in front of me and my imagination went to work. After distracting myself with patrol duties, I arrived at a conclusion. Whatever the biology was on Vistara, it didn't matter. I loved Talis Darmon. Whenever the time came, I knew everything would work itself out. I had faith.

"Hail ahead! Hail ahead!" Beraal yelled. I bounded to where she stood waving two arms overhead. Below us was a wide valley, smoke rising from huts. Arkall grazed, and Tarns worked busily. A pair of riders from the village trotted up the trail in our direction.

"We have arrived at last!" Beraal exclaimed with joy.

Talis Darmon's arm found its way around my bicep as we awaited our reception committee. "Thanks to you, Benjamin Colt." She kissed my cheek and squealed like a schoolgirl with tickets to see her favorite boy band. I felt taller than an arkall-mounted Tarn.

The riders slowed as they reached the crest of the pass. "Hail, Korundi. What house?"

Beraal made a gesture. "I am Dosenie Beraal of Pardoo, guardian and sworn servant of the Princess Talis Darmon Sylah, daughter of King Osric Darmon of the Red Kingdom of Mihdradahl."

The second rider had the nervous eyes of a driver pulled over for a cracked taillight, his trunk full of stolen merchandise. I let Beraal do the talking but kept both hands on my rifle.

"You are welcome, Dosenie Beraal, as is the princess and—the White lord."

"What can you tell us?" nervous boy asked in a high pitch.

"To what do you refer, fledgling? We have been weeks in the Korund."

The older, calmer Tarn said, "There is rumor that White lords from the Temple Farnest have traveled down the River Blix and sit now with Clan Chieftain Jedak Jeraal in Califex."

The second rider blurted, "And now another White lord comes! It is more than rumor. We are in the end of times."

28

The village of our two new companions was tiny, one of many that belonged to House Kull in this strip of the Korund. Beraal explained to the ranking elder that my presence did not mean that judgment day had come for the Korundi. Once he was comfortable that I was not the harbinger of doom, we told our tale.

"The Mydreen are offal eaters," the elder Tarn spat. "It is insult enough that they treat one of our clan so rudely, but to take hostage the only daughter of our ancient ally King Osric Darmon—it is an infamy. Domeel Doreen brings a curse on his clan."

The princess thanked him for us. "Your faithfulness brings honor to all Korundi."

We drank sweet water and gladly accepted the savory flat cakes of meal and meat—a welcome change from the gritty vegetables and roots from Cynar's subterranean garden.

"The lieutenant of our house has been called to join with all others to sit with Chieftain Jedak Jeraal. All were summoned to council because White lords have come to Califex. We await news, but if you say they are not of the Temple Farnest, it will ease many minds. We shall carry you to Califex to join them when you are rested, Princess Talis Darmon."

"The other Whites are not from the afterlife, elder father," I confirmed. "But neither are they friends. I have to learn their purpose with the chieftain. Their presence may mean danger to the princess and to the Korundi. We can't blindly walk into Califex."

Beraal put the icing on the cake. "Jedak Jeraal is the wisest of Tarns. But these visitors are as unpredictable as gazraal and have the morals of vereen. They are powerful at warcraft. They may well violate oaths of welcome by the Korundi to regain the princess as their hostage."

"Then we must bring such counsel to our chieftain," the older Tarn surmised.

For two nights, as the last rays of the dim sun dropped beneath the dizzying peaks, we journeyed once more in the mountain chill. Our new cloaks disguised us and warded off the cold better than what we'd set off with from Maleska Mal. During the days, we hid and rested in the home of a House Kull elder. At the last village before the capital, I left the princess in the care of Sarkan Sell—the mature warrior who'd accompanied us since our first meeting. With Apache assigned to the princess, I had no worries about leaving her among Beraal's mountain people while we scouted for sign of what could only be Chief Bryant and the team. As the sun vanished behind the mountains, it was time to depart on my mission to gather intelligence to form our next course of action. The princess could not accompany me.

"We'll be back as soon as we can, Talis Darmon. If we're captured, Jodal Jark will find a way to get word back to you." The youth had my orders to do so above all else.

The Korundi were stalwarts, just like Beraal. Sarkan Sell spoke with fortitude. "We will see the princess safely to her father if you do not return, Benjamin Colt. It is the oath of a Korund warrior and House Kull."

After Apache cautiously sniffed at the warrior's offered hands and allowed himself to be stroked, I knew Sarkan Sell was a good man. Apache had good judgment about people.

"Thank you, Sarkan Sell. I accept your word and give you my own. I will be cautious to not bring any harm to the Korundi by my actions."

"It is so," Sarkan Sell replied.

The princess walked with us to the edge of the village. She reached for my hand in the dark and held me back by the force of her grip, a vice of velvet. We were alone.

"I do not wish to be parted, Benjamin Colt."

"I know, Talis Darmon. I don't wish it either, but it's safest for you to remain here. Hidden."

"If it is the scoundrel Brandon Bryant, what will you do?" Before I could answer, she gave me my orders. "Do not kill him, Benjamin Colt. You must not try to win a war on your own. We will find another way." Her eyes were moist. "Return to me swiftly and surely. It is more than your oath of service that binds us."

"Yes, Princess. It is." I didn't acknowledge her command to keep my sword sheathed. I didn't know what my actions would be when I found my former teammates. My former brothers. I only knew I couldn't keep my promise to her. But the bloody thoughts that had been building at the prospect of finding Bryant were drowned beneath the waves of my feelings for her. It was time. Because another might never come. I took her hands in mine.

"Talis Darmon, I need an answer. When I've called you 'my princess,' why did it make you so mad? Calling you that has a very intimate meaning in your language, doesn't it?"

Her face was close to mine. "Yes, Benjamin Colt. To call someone 'mine' means just that—that they are yours and yours alone. To call someone 'yours'—without the oath of your heart accepted—are just the empty words from a drunken fool in lust."

"Princess, I am yours and yours alone. I am your Benjamin Colt."

"And I would be your princess, but for you asking."

I hesitated. "It should be under your moons-lit window that I tell you this, Talis Darmon."

She brought my hand to her cheek. "That doesn't suit you, Benjamin Colt. It's how a false suitor seeking a single night's passion would act. And it is not how I would want to hear the depth of your heart made known to me."

"I love you, Talis Darmon. I want you to be my princess forever."

"And I love you, Benjamin Colt. I will be your princess and you, my lord. From now until the end of time."

A woman's voice dripping revulsion—the one I thought had been silenced—came to me. Not the voice itself, but the memory of it. And what it reminded of was my greatest fear. That, of all the many skills I had mastery of, how to love was the least of them. I was unprepared for it. A child soldier, rifle thrust into hands and pushed to charge a hill. I'd passed my own tests for courage in combat. But the only test I'd taken at love had been at my own Waterloo, in a drab apartment, on a world that no longer existed.

"Talis Darmon, I know only how to fight. I know nothing about how to love you. I'd rather die than fail at that. You'll have to be my teacher."

She wiped her eyes with my hand. "Deacon Benjamin Colt, simply be the hero you are, and I will be filled by your great heart."

Then she said the words I'd always dreamed I would hear.

"I need you."

✠   ✠   ✠

Beraal strode beside me on the last leg of the winding trail leading down into Califex. Godahl bleated as we brushed past the foolish things, refusing to yield the path. We padded along until we broke out of the pass, and in the wide valley base below us lay Califex. Amber lights twinkled from a sea of low, flat huts, the rest a dark wall of the mighty mountains surrounding the capital, save the outline of the giant spires of the atmosphere works. I let Beraal and Jodal Jark lead, covered by the same cloaks as I—though I could never pass for a Tarn. At best, we hoped I would be mistaken for a visitor from the Red Kingdom, not uncommon in Califex.

"Where is the chieftain's hall?" I asked.

"Near the plant." Beraal pointed.

Showing maturity and tactical savvy for a youngster, Jodal Jark said, "We take a course through the markets and trade section of the city. It will be quietest there at this late hour, though not deserted. If questioned, a Red trader traveling with Korundi will not seem unusual. Just let us do the talking, Benjamin Colt."

"Allow me to do the talking, fledgling," Beraal corrected. "You are sure-footed, but not yet old enough to be sure tongued. I will indicate if I need your help."

Jodal Jark took the correction without umbrage. "Yes, auntie."

From the first, my observations about the Korundi were that they very different from the Mydreen. The casual cruelty and savagery that permeated life in Maleska Mal were absent in the people of the Korund. The Korundi were respectful to each other. They used family titles, treating everyone as if they were truly related. It kind of reminded me of how Dave talked about growing up on the islands. Everyone was a cousin, an uncle, or an aunt, even if they weren't.

From the first, the Army is an experience of cultural immersion better than watching a hundred foreign films. It's more like jumping into a mosh pit packed with guys from every corner of the country and beyond—grinding and grooving to music you've never heard before.

You grew up in the city? Your new buddy is from a hog farm. He teaches you how to butcher one. Never learned another language in high school? Your other buddy speaks just enough English to answer the drill sergeant correctly about half the time, and asks you to help him while he teaches you how to order a beer in three other languages. Don't know how to dance? Your Latin buddies teach you how to salsa, so when you come visit their hometown on leave, you don't embarrass them when they take you out to party.

I had a car my folks bought for me after I graduated jump school. It was held together with Bondo body filler and bailing wire, but it ran. For a private earning not much, it was an incredible gift. But as the owner of real transportation living in the barracks, you find yourself being an unpaid taxi driver for your buddies. One Saturday afternoon, I was lying in my bunk doing what I always did, reading. It was a book about the Punic Wars—all three of them. One of my favorites. I was well read but not well traveled. Though I was now a member of a whole new subculture—the Airborne—I was about to get an experience that I look back on as being one of the seeds that grew into my desire to be in SF. My imaginings about riding with Hannibal across the Alps to invade Rome were interrupted by a knock.

Gabriel, the giant Samoan private who lived across the hall, was dressed in a flowery lavalava, shower flip-flops, and a "Death before Dishonor" T-shirt with jump wings framing the words. He'd given me dead eyes my first weeks there as a "cherry"—being fresh out of jump school, a five-jump chump. Even after making my sixth jump and walking the gauntlet down the barracks hall to take my licks from the whole floor, though he longer gave me death glares, Gabriel never even grunted in reply to my "mornin'" or other minor pleasantries. I wasn't even sure he spoke much English. Here he was now at my door.

"Brah. You give me da kine ride to my auntie's."

I translated. He needed a lift to his aunt's. "Where's she live?"

"I show you."

His auntie lived in one of the family housing areas on Bragg.

"Dat it there. Tanks, huh," he said as we pulled up, and was gone.

A huge party was underway, the yard full of folks as brown and big—or bigger—than Gabriel. Everyone was dressed like my barracks mate in colorful lavalavas, a cricket game went on in the backyard, children played everywhere, smiles were on every face, the smells of a grand barbecue drifted unmistakably in the air.

The next day there was another knock at my door.

It was Gabriel.

"Colt, I get in big trouble wit my, auntie, brah. I no invite you in. She say you gotta come next week. Pig roast. I see you then."

Before I could say anything, he was gone.

The next week I drove us. I knew the way. No explanation. No foreshadowing of what was to come. It was another family gathering, the evidence of a great time going on.

His aunt crushed the life out of me as she kissed both my cheeks. "You good boy, Benjamin, you give rude boy Gabriel ride so he don' miss his family." She reached over and lightly slapped Gabriel's cheek as she pointed out his bad manners.

He looked at his feet in shame before he broke out in a big grin again. "You come, cousin. Auntie gonna feed skinny boy like you."

Suddenly, I was the object of attention and welcomed by Gabriel's whole family. I didn't understand but every other word of their pidgin and didn't speak Samoan at all. What I wouldn't have given for a decipher that day! But everyone, even Gabriel—who I'd thought didn't like me—smiled and slapped me on the back, made me play games with them, and fed me till I burst. I was "cousin" to everyone—though I wasn't—and his aunt sent me back to the barracks with a paper plate piled with so much tinfoil-wrapped pork, I didn't go to the DFAC the rest of the weekend.

I suspected—but never asked—he wasn't really related to anyone there, that he was "family" because it was part of the Samoan culture to be a big family wherever they were. And what did it matter? Was it really so different with my folks? If I'd brought Gabriel home, he'd have been treated like he was raised in a holler and hunted possum from birth. One of the family. An aunt is an aunt, a cousin is a cousin, whether the blood is the same or not. When the Korundi interacted, it made me think of Gabriel and his family.

It was a part of the drive of an SF operator to immerse in the culture of the people you worked with. To find the common values and the merits of your hosts and embrace them. To become that fish swimming in the same sea. The Korundi were winning my admiration as much as the Mydreen had made me cautious and uneasy. These were a people I felt a kinship with. I was thinking about how we would work together when I remembered that rose-colored glasses tint deadly vipers to look like garter snakes. The red-sashed Khraal Kahlees was Korundi, too. The one who'd cheap-shotted me and made me fight for my life. Beraal's unacknowledged father.

Maybe the Korundi character got a little diluted when in the company of their Mydreen cousins. After I'd whipped him a second time, Khraal Kahlees had given me a grudging oath of his protection in the Korund. If Bryant was offering alliance with the Korundi to join his renegade team and the Mydreen to face off against the Reds for the rule of Mihdradahl, where would the ambitious Tarn lieutenant's loyalties lie?

We weren't hailed or questioned as we passed the occasional group of warriors or lone Tarn about their business on the late night streets of Califex. I fought the oversized hood to stay low on my brow to conceal my face. Even at night, my deep tan was still not as dark as the Red of a Vistaran. None of us were sure what to expect and whether the general state of alertness would be increased with strange foreign visitors in the city. Would White lords ushering in the final judgment bring about revelry and drunkenness? Or solemn contemplation and repentance? So far, the atmosphere seemed calm and tranquil, as though no one here worried that the end times were approaching.

The base of the massive atmosphere plant peeked through gaps and above the flat roofs around it. We skirted well around those suburbs, not wanting to be caught in the wide avenue around the giant factory, staying in the narrow alleys between the groups of closed merchant stalls.

"The quarters and stables of the chieftain's vanguard are that way," the young warrior indicated. "And the chieftain's hall beyond."

"I want to veer close enough to see what's happening. Can we do it without causing suspicion?"

"I believe so." Jodal Jark guided us through another alley, and I eased ahead of my friends, skulking along in the shadow of a wall. At the edge of the breakout before the open area of the soldier's encampment, I froze. In the space between two barracks sat a GMV, the minigun just visible above the stabled horses shifting in place on eight legs as they slept. Six barrels stood out like a grizzly risen on two legs out of a stand of alders, announcing its presence to all interlopers that the biggest, baddest killer of them all was here. My heart skipped a beat before it started again with thunder in my chest. I pushed us back in the other direction.

"They're here, Beraal. One of our vehicles is parked out of sight."

"And your fellow Thulians?"

"No sign, yet. There's bound to be someone on watch. Come on." I let Jodal Jark take us on another wide route around the vanguard's cantonment and made the same careful approach to where I could evaluate from a different angle. We did this three more times until we'd made as careful a cloverleaf around the area as the layout allowed, then retreated back to the sparse traffic of the few wanderers in the market.

"I only see the one gun truck. Too dark for me to see if anyone's in it." If the guys weren't roving, it meant they felt comfortable. If it were me, I'd be in the driver's seat on watch, taking a nap, but ready to react if anyone tried to mess with our stuff. It was common thievery you worried about in a setting like this more than an attack.

"What will we do next?" Jodal Jark asked.

I'd been planning. Part of me wanted to return to the princess and make for the Red Kingdom. Part of me thought otherwise. I listened to the part of myself that wanted answers and a reckoning. "If there's just one, I can take him silently." If I found Marky in the driver's seat, I'd slit his throat on the spot. With his weapons, I'd kill the Chief, Chucky, and anyone else who needed it. We'd bargain with the Korund leaders for understanding later. When they heard our side of the story from Beraal and the princess, they'd see that these had not been friends. If I wasn't dead by then.

Beraal touched her knife. "If you must break your promise to the princess, then we go together, Benjamin Colt."

"No. You two stay here. If things go badly, you'll know it. I want you to leave me and complete the mission to get Talis Darmon home safely. That's an order."

Beraal dipped her head in acquiescence. "You've seen us far, Benjamin Colt. I will do as you command."

I moved out by myself, retracing my path to the farthest of the approaches I'd taken from which to view the camp. I selected the path for my stalk. I moved behind the open stables, the arkall asleep on their feet, occasionally grunting and groaning as I crept, bent and slow, past them. They didn't stir as I drifted by like a sailboat on smooth seas. It was perfectly dark. I paused and strained my senses to detect anyone ahead in the dark. After many minutes, the stillness was a green light for me to continue.

In my mind's eye, I saw through the walls of the quarters to where the GMV was parked in the narrow alley. More careful steps through open ground to reach the next building, then a pause to become invisible. I became a statue. After minutes of nothing, I slid along the wall and crossed the next open space to the next building. I took shallow breaths in and out of my nose as I neared the last corner, halted, and extended my senses again. A millimeter at a time, I sank into a crouch, then imperceptibly intruded around the sharp angle with one eye to find the dark mass blocking the separation between barracks. The GMV sat exactly as I'd imagined it. I slid onto my belly and slithered no faster than a worm.

Beneath the carriage, light reflected from a small watchfire tended by a pair of oblivious Tarns some distance away. The front of the GMV was well set back from their view. Tarns had good noses—like all soldiers—but distant from the danger of battle, surrounded by their mounts and acrid smoke, in the deepest den of their safety, I was a shark hunting in a placid fishing harbor. Only a faint flicker reached the front of the gun truck, but to someone under NODS, it would make them see things brighter than high noon. If they kept looking ahead, their enhanced vision meant nothing.

The windows of the gun truck were lowered. I reached the rear bumper and rose at the pace of a weed growing in the night until I crouched behind a fuel can. I sensed the purr of someone snoring gently inside. My knife was already in my hand. I became a dark phantom and willed myself invisible as I eased forward like rust beneath paint. I was serene and confident and my energy conformed to everything around me to assure the space that I belonged here.

In the driver's seat, head tipped back, the snoring came. In a smooth unerring way, like thick oil running down the edge of a bottle, I moved. At once my hand clamped the mouth and forced the head back into the seat with my knife edge at his throat, pressing, not yet drawing its deadly stroke. A nose sucked air and white eyes shot open in terror.

"Don't move or you're dead," I hissed and as I did, by the dark brows and the patchy beard under my palm, I recognized it was Dave.

His hands came up slowly and open, and a gentle verbal protest vibrated against my palm.

I pushed the knife deeper into his neck. "Don't say a word or I'll take your head off, Dave."

He nodded a single tiny dip—down and up, and I cautiously removed my hand.

In a whisper, he blurted, "Ben! Is that you? Oh, my sweet God! We never dared thought you were alive! Karlo and Mitch are here too! We split! We defected! We E-and-E'd from the rest of the team. Let go of me, brother!"

I let him out of the GMV and suddenly was engulfed in his embrace—once again my best friend. He lifted me off my feet as he laughed in nervous relief.

"I can't believe you're here. I can't believe you're alive." He held me at arm's length. "You look like shit! Ben-dog, everything's a mess. The Chief and Marky are nuts, brah. You gotta help us stop them!"

✤ ✤ ✤

At first light, Beraal and Jodal Jark left to retrieve the rest of our party. I was hugged out and my back sore from the pounding each of them gave me. My stomach squealed as though it had eyes when Mitch pushed an MRE at me. Chili mac was my favorite MRE, which is like saying a chair is your favorite place to sit. You don't know what you miss until it's gone, baby. I devoured it, struck by disbelief that I'd once thought it bland without at least a few drops of Tabasco. Cold and in plastic, it had richer flavor than all the meals I'd ever savored put together. Gourmet dining at its finest.

We sat together in their hootch as Karlo, Mitch, and Dave assaulted me with question after question. I took them through the full version of our escape—minus the soul-eater—right up until I'd almost decapitated Dave.

"If you'd shaved those patchy weeds off and been smooth like Marky, you'd never have to worry about wearing a hat again, brah," I teased him.

"Well, if there's anyone who deserves their throat slit, it's that son of a bitch Marky," Mitch fumed.

I started in on the jalapeño cheese spread, skipping the crackers and sucking it straight from the pouch. "It's your turn, bros. What happened after I got tossed in the dungeon?"

Karlo led off. "I was there when the Chief told you about his revelation that we were destined to rule Mars."

Dave shook his head. "Brah, the whole time he and I were out on that first patrol with the Tarns, he just got more and more worked up. The Mydreen are a huge clan with settlements all over—maybe twenty to thirty thousand mounted warriors. That got the Chief fired up. But when we saw our first Red city, Thoria, he got absolutely twitchy. We snuck in with a group of Mydreen disguised as Korund one night. Amazing. It makes Maleska Mal look like a dump. And it isn't even their capital. They say Shansara is tremendous.

"The whole way back, he was sounding me out about what if we organized the Mydreen and took on the Red Kingdom. I tried to calm him down, but when we returned to find out that Marky and the team had dealt a huge defeat to the Reds, his mind was made up. He and Marky-Mark had it all figured out. The past was gone. There was only us. The Reds were weak. With the Tarns, there was no way they could stand up to us. You couldn't be trusted. He threw his whole loyalty pledge play at us. Blah, blah, blah."

"Yeah. Got it."

"No, Ben, you don't," Mitch fumed. "Chucky and Doug fell in line in a second. Matty was a little slower to come around. All the while, Karlo, Dave, and I stood up against them and tried to get you out of prison. Once, we got close to drawing down on each other. We had to watch each other's backs for days. We were either on our way to the dungeons to join you or there was going to be a gunfight—until Karlo came up with a plan."

Karlo was the same calm voice of reason as usual as he told me about it. "I had to play along. I told Bryant that as long as you were safe, I'd keep Dave and Mitch in line, and I'd keep Baby Blue running. He agreed. And we waited."

Dave picked up. "Once we got the Chief and Marky's promise they wouldn't let Domeel Doreen have you, we just went to work. We started training the Mydreen."

"It's what we had to do, Ben." Mitch seemed quick to want my understanding. "It was that or be in condition red for the rest of our lives waiting for them knock us off, one by one. Karlo started cranking out basic M4s. We got a battalion of shock troops armed and trained—not well, but well enough for us to hit the nearest Red city. How it went down—we did what we could."

My throat tightened. "What happened?"

Karlo sighed. "We marched on Thoria. Domeel Doreen issued demands for their unconditional surrender. Bryant tried to parley an occupation. Promised them a peaceful coexistence under Tarn administration with a rebalancing of social justice to give the Mydreen what was justly theirs. Tribute for past injustices. The works. They refused, and the siege was on. The Reds don't have much of an Army posted around. The cities have guards—kind of a territorial police force. The flyers we shot down are about their most advanced platform. They ride arkall in cavalry like the Tarns. When they rejected the ultimatum and decided to fight, it was a slaughter."

Dave and Mitch looked away.

"The Chief told me, in his brave new world, he was going to enforce the law of land warfare," I said.

"We kept people safe," Mitch said. "When we could."

"But we couldn't be everywhere at once," Karlo said. "Once things settled down, Chucky and Doug led the effort to get the city ready for a counterattack, in case the Red Army came a-marching to retake it. Tarns can dig trenches, bro! The Chief and Domeel Doreen started planning the next phase of the campaign. I went to work with Baby

Blue outfitting more of Bryant's army. Marky got made vice-generalissimo and is de facto running the Mydreen Army."

Dave grinned. "I'd love to have seen Marky's face once he knew we'd split."

Mitch nudged me. "You should've been there to see Marky's face when we got word *you'd* escaped with the princess. Fit. To. Be. Tied."

I hadn't forgotten him or Chuck putting the boot to me. "I'd like to see Marky's face again. Real soon. And Chuck's."

"Their mistake was not trusting Mitch or Karlo to have one of these." Dave pointed to his armband. "Chucky, Doug, and Matt got them, so they've pretty much been independent. I had to be the go-between for these two whenever we worked with the Mydreen, so it meant we stayed together a lot. And planned.

"About three weeks ago, the Chief and Chuck split up. They'd both learned how to fly the air cars and took off on recons with a few Tarns for support. Whatever they planned next, they kept us out of the loop. Chief came back and took a GMV and a company of Tarns and split. Mark followed in the Stryker with Matt. They were going to send for us and the rest of the army when they'd decided on the next campaign. With the siege of Thoria being successful and us three malcontents staying in line, we were pretty close to being treated like we were all one big happy family again and followed orders to keep getting them ready. With Doug left in charge, we saw our chance had come and lit off in the last GMV."

Bryant was busy making plans for his next conquest. Maybe he'd be dividing his efforts and attacking more than one simultaneously. With enough Mydreen cavalry, he could. It sounded as if Domeel Doreen had gathered more of his tribe to him with the promise of brutal conquest, their army building larger and larger for the next campaigns, like the desert Bedouins drawn to Lawrence by the promise of plunder.

Karlo was grim. "We weren't going to help the Chief take another Red city. But, three men and one war wagon—we're no match for Chief Bryant and the whole Mydreen Army. We thought about making for the Red Kingdom, but there's no good way to get there overland without the obvious problems of Mydreen patrols and maybe eating a missile if we get caught. The lack of basic intel like good maps, real-time enemy troop movements, firsthand knowledge of the environment—it's crippling. Heading to the western range of the Korund was our best course of action to avoid the bulk of any of the Chief's army and to maybe find friends."

Dave smiled. "We've been doing your job ever since you left. Piecing together the puzzle here on Mars. The Korundi are allied with the Reds. That Khraal Kahlees character you told me about seemed like a potential friend. We've been here a week and the chieftain—Jedak Jeraal—he's only met with us twice. Once when we arrived and he gave us his oath of protection, and once since he's called his council of lieutenants. We've answered questions, but they're still hashing things over. It's hard to say which way the wind blows with them, but they've been very trusting and accommodating so far. Much different from what it was like getting to know the Mydreen. And when the princess gets here, I'm sure it'll cement things."

"If anyone can, Talis Darmon can," I assured them. "So, the chieftain hasn't jumped right in to saying he'll help us in the fight?"

Dave grimaced in a way that spoke volumes. "He'd be a helluva poker player. He's listened, but if he's ready to throw in with us and commit his Tarn cavalry to fighting the Chief and the Mydreen Army, he hasn't tipped his hand yet."

Both Karlo and Mitch sported silver bands on their biceps—no longer stuck in Babel without deciphers of their own.

"Notice you're finally in the club," I said. "That a gift from Jedak Jeraal?"

Karlo grinned. "Yes. The chieftain's wanted us all to be able to answer his questions. He's also allowed us complete freedom here. It's a relief to finally be able to speak for myself. I can't begin to understand how the decipher works, especially how it enables us to *read*."

Talis Darmon had taught me the rudiments of her language. The decipher helped me to recognize the patterns after just a single translation by her. How I wish I'd had one of the devices when I was trying to learn Spanish! I'd exasperated *mi professora* at the command language school. Thank God I hadn't had to learn Korean.

"Ben, did you know their written language is a mix of ideograms and logograms? I found a merchant who took an interest and I made a trade for his time to teach me."

"What'd you give him?"

Dave groaned. "He gave him his small Randall. The one with the stag handle. I've tried to buy that from you for two years, and you gave it a way for a reading lesson."

"It was more than a fair trade. I always use my Swiss Army knife when I have to cut something small, anyway."

I'd admired the knife, too, but it was too much of a work of art, the polish and sharp lines of the true and false edges mesmerizing in their perfection. I'd be hesitant to actually use it. I'd carried Ka-Bars for years, always with the intent to replace one when it got damaged, which rarely happened and only with the most abusive use. Proving one would hold up to puncturing a metal barrel was a good example. You never know unless you try, right? The guy who'd tried the same with his fancy Damascus blade—that had cost him two months' pay—cried when his blade chipped in a dozen places.

Such is the stuff young, bored soldiers do.

Dave didn't let up. "It's the principle of the thing, Karlo. It was beautiful. And I was willing to pay you double what it cost you. What's that guy going to do with it?"

"What I got in exchange for it is priceless, Dave."

Dave just exhaled. "Brah."

Karlo ignored him. "Ben, it's the greatest thing that's happened to me since I've been here. The decipher translates all speech, but I'm finding I can also *hear* the nuances in how humans and Tarns pronounce the different characters of their shared symbology. I think in a year I won't even need the decipher!" Karlo had found another thing to occupy his inquisitiveness.

Mitch sighed. "We're glad for you, Karlo. Really. I for one won't be devoting time trying to get by without it for a very, very long time. It's good to be able to skip the whole interpreter step. No offense, Dave."

"None taken, brah. It slowed things down for sure."

I was glad that everyone was on an equal footing in being able to communicate here on Mars, and it was a measure of how the guys had been able to earn trust so quickly on arrival in the Korund. The devices were a valuable commodity to the Tarns, who had to get them from the Reds. But we'd gotten off track. The gaping hole in our plan to fight the Chief was one as deep and just as real as the largest canyon in the solar system just a few hundred klicks away.

"You've done well, brothers. But there's one thing." I held up a finger. "What about Baby Blue? Where is it?"

Karlo shrugged. "Right where we left it. In Thoria."

That's what I was afraid he was going to say. "Did you at least break it before you split?"

Karlo made a distasteful shake of his head. "Ben, what are you talking about? That was never an option. Baby Blue is critical. Damaging it would be unthinkable."

I exploded. "Karlo! I know you're in love with the damn thing, but you left Bryant with the one tool that's going to let him take over the Red Kingdom of Mihdradahl."

The best brain on Vistara looked crestfallen. It was disappointment. In me. He was the sapient and I was the simian. It wasn't that I'd misjudged his reasons and actions. It's that I'd failed to see the big picture. He knew something I didn't. Like the shrill whistle of an inbound mortar round presaging the explosion, the deep breath he took told me a lecture was incoming.

"There's more than just the coming war with the Chief to consider, Ben. A lot more. It might very well be the key to a future here. If the atmosphere plants are failing and the Red scientists don't have the knowledge to repair them, someday Baby Blue might represent the only way to keep our new home a place where we can breathe. Otherwise, what's the point of everything we're doing now?"

He was right, but from where I sat—in a hut, wearing borrowed alien clothes, and eating Meals Rejected by Ethiopians—my current view of the coming red planet war hadn't changed.

Novices dealt in tactics. Masters dealt in logistics.

I slammed my fist into the ground. The problem was that we wouldn't be Napoleon in Russia, cut off from his supply train—we'd be every shortsighted loser of every war that had ever been waged. We'd be all the Axis powers of WW2 and the Cold War Soviet Union combined, outclassed by a system of production that ran on the economics of a quantum singularity. As a guerilla force, we could play hit-and-run and harass a larger army for years. But without the logistics to match the magic Blue Fairy, that's all we could do.

Dave intervened. "I know what you're thinking, Ben. As soon as we owned Thoria, Bryant wanted Baby Blue safe. It's in a hardened building with a dozen Tarns guarding it at all times. It would've taken a fight to get it out of there, and once we were on the road, we'd have had to go so slow to keep from damaging it that they'd have run us down in no time. There was no way we could've taken it with us, or we wouldn't be here now."

I'd been thinking about tearing into another MRE, but my appetite drained away faster than oil from a cracked engine block, which is suddenly how I felt. A knocking motor limping along on a prayer, hoping the next exit off the highway had the sign for the best garage mechanic ever born. I didn't know where the help would come from to fix this.

"Dammit! Even if we can field an army as big as Bryant's, it'll be spears and fizzle guns against everything Baby Blue's printed off for them. M4s for every Tarn. Enough 40 mike-mike, 7.62, and fifty-cal for endless campaigns. Unless the Reds have something we don't know about more deadly than air cars and souped-up fizzle guns, we're gonna be fighting a losing battle."

I saw Bryant's superior mug the day we rode the C-17 to our near fatal crash. Even then, in what were likely the last moments of our lives, he was a condescending prick.

"I'm not letting him win, not if all I've got left is a sharp stick to kill him with," I swore.

Dave and Mitch grinned like the Cheshire cat.

"What?"

They wouldn't budge.

"Show him, Karlo," Mitch begged.

Karlo reached beneath the neck of his shirt. Hanging around his neck on 550 cord was some nonsensical thingamajig made by a fourth grader who'd gotten into dad's liquor cabinet on his way to the Legos. The many angled pieces stuck out like thorns from a central branch and their surfaces shimmered like rainbows on oily black slicks.

"What's that?" I asked.

"The keys to the kingdom. Baby Blue isn't making any more boom-boom for anyone without this."

29

"Baby Blue has a key? I don't remember that being mentioned."

We'd all gotten an intro to Baby Blue, how to run the stored replicating programs and the like. That it had a master key hadn't been mentioned.

"It's not a key. It's a governor. The brain trust back at 51 had a lot of the same misgivings I did about how Baby Blue could be misused after our big skip into the future."

"But… I thought it was government black lab guys who built Baby Blue?"

Karlo shook his head. "No. The Caltech guys did. I got in pretty tight with the longhairs during my crash course on how to tame a wormhole in a box—you know, engineer to engineer. Skeptic to skeptic. Ours was the only stick without a dedicated GS-14 scientist to nurse their federation replicator. The gearheads and I got simpatico quick when I asked them specifically about how I could thwart some future Stalin. I wanted to know if there was a way to get out of a situation where I was put on the spot with requests like, 'Karlo, make us a nuke. Karlo, make some Sarin. Karlo, we need to gas a village of malcontents'—but without destroying Baby Blue.

"You see, they were just as concerned about the Beltway crowd as they were the hair-lips. They'd already considered the potential for abuse by some wannabe despot who dropped his sheep's clothing of a Thomas Jefferson reborn and put on the ermine robe of some Idi Amin pretender. Or a cabal of know-it-all PhDs and lawyers. I was the only one to ask about it, though."

He threw up his hands and grinned.

"They got to choose which matter mill went with us. Ours is one of the first three they built. The later Blue Fairies were mass produced by the first ones, and unlike the first few, the rest were made of sealed modular components to ease the diagnostics and repair by another mill when one broke down in the field. The first ones were not only built by hand, but they included a limiter."

He dangled the key.

"Without this, our Baby Blue won't make anything more complex than the organic compounds for foods, fuel, medicines—just sustainment stuff. This is what unlocks the potential of ours to make anything else in its inventory, or to take instructions to replicate new materials not in its storehouse of designs. And once one of the original three were interlinked with the rest, they could lock the others out, too. If you know how."

Those engineers were crafty characters, kind of like our own SF engineers—though they preferred tinkering with pocket universes and time travel rather than blowing things up. I was impressed. I thought we were the only subculture that planned for causing such chaos.

"Who else knew about this?" I asked.

"Can't say."

"But you kept it to yourself?"

Karlo frowned. "I know, I was taking a lot on myself. It may even seem like I was disloyal to the captain and Mike. But I told you—I was never going to allow myself to be used as an instrument to enable the suits to try anything nasty. Even if I had to be a one-man saboteur to any crackpot schemes by the provisional government *in absentia in tempus futuro*."

"English please, dude," Dave said. "My decipher doesn't do Karlo."

I thought I understood. "So, whatever the Chief's army has as of three weeks ago is all they're going to have from Baby Blue?"

"At least, for arms and munitions. Part of my plan was this—I had Baby Blue making JP-8 before we left. I figured if they saw Baby Blue was still working, it'd take some heat off our escape. If I'd wrecked Baby Blue on our way out of Thoria, it would've forced them to come after us immediately—and hard—to get me back to repair it. It probably took them a while before they figured out it isn't capable of making shoot-shoot anymore. It bought us more time to get away."

I understood why Karlo hadn't demo'd it. If we could recover it someday, he could put it back to being a perpetual taco machine for every gizmo we could ever want. In the meantime, if we could wear them down and get them to expend their stores of ammo, our odds were at least somewhat better of making that happen.

"So, you left Baby Blue to take the sting out of your defection, but it's stuck making MREs. How much pow-pow did it crank out for them before you left with the governor?"

"All total, about two hundred M4s for the Tarns, and enough 5.56 for a six hundred–round combat load for each. But their fire discipline is nonexistent. They burned half that much in the first skirmish against the Thoria defenses. Team stores are full up, though. Good news is we cut out of there packed to the gills and without so much as a sliver of room left in the GMV for even a single round. We are full up on ammo and then some. Plus—come look."

Karlo waved me to follow. In the bed of the GMV were six Javelins—anti-tank launch tube assemblies.

"We've only got the one command launch unit, but the other CLU sitting in the Stryker has only two missiles."

So, we had a three-to-one favor with our deadliest long-range weapon against Bryant. I was already planning a long-range vehicular ambush via Javelin to take out their GMV and the Stryker. Things were looking up.

Mitch was anxious to speak. "Think about this, too. No matter how good Baby Blue is, the M4s will still need maintenance. Gas rings go bad. Springs wear and extractors break. Gas tubes erode. Usual armorer level stuff to replace. As those components wear, with no more spare parts, it'll deadline some weapons eventually. And Karlo locked out the file for making lube. Once they run out and have dry guns, they might as well go back to using their fizzle sticks and swords."

"Lee–Enfields might've been a better choice," Dave said. No one argued the point. But none of that was going to render many weapons ineffective until thousands of rounds had been burned. There'd be some local substitute for lube, though it wouldn't be as good as machine gunner lube. But over time and with their ammo replenishment cut off, it'd drastically limit their training and fielding of the better battlefield weapons. It was all well thought out.

"I'm sure that's got Bryant and Marky furious. It's going to definitely put a hamper on their schemes. If they can't expend ammo, parts, and lube to get the Tarns proficient, it's really just the team who's the main threat."

"Other than being run down by thousands of mounted four-arm greenies wielding swords," Mitch added.

"There's that," I admitted. "How did the Tarns take to marksmanship and weapon maintenance?"

"Pfft," Dave spurted. "How do you think? I'd rate the Mydreen worse than the average illiterate third-world guerilla who's never had anything more complex than a machete to care for."

Mitch lifted the corner of a camo net. "And we have two of the four Gooses." The Carl Gustaf recoilless rifle had both anti-tank and anti-personnel rounds. It didn't have the range of the Javelin, but there was a lot of ammo for it packed into the gun truck.

I rethought my plan to go hunting for the Chief's war wagons. "You guys did good. But we need to think strategically—not tactically. We can't maximize our combat power if we don't get troops trained in how to use all this."

Mitch smiled. "We're making the inroads. If we secure the Korundi as allies, then we get hunter-killer teams trained in all this. The Chief and Marky were adamant to keep their toys for just the team. That means their biggest firepower will be concentrated to wherever they are. If we divide ours—bang! Advantage!"

"We saved the best for last, brah." Dave dug out a familiar kit bag stitched with both an 82nd shoulder patch and the SF arrowhead and dropped it at my feet. It was mine. "I got it all together for you. Maybe deep down I thought there was a chance we'd find you. Maybe I just wanted your stuff for spares. We're close enough in size. Anyway, here's your kit."

I tore it open. Boots, filthy plate carrier, and my M4 broken down into upper and lower. I pulled out my war belt and pistol and beneath it, on a bed of folded multicam uniforms, sat something bright and shiny. A blue and silver combat infantry badge. I picked it up.

"Where'd this come from? This isn't mine."

Dave spoke sheepishly. "Oh. Forgot I put that there. It was my uncle's, brah. He gave it to me after my first pump to the sandbox. I carry it in my ruck for good luck. When I packed up your stuff, I realized it was about the only thing you didn't have. I guess I kind of thought—"

"Posthumous award," I said for him.

Dave looked away. "Yeah, brah. Like dat."

Karlo took it from me. "Long overdue." Then he cleared his throat. "Attention to orders. For proven service during ground combat in the Mars Campaign as a member of Special Forces, Sergeant First Class Deacon Benjamin Colt is awarded the combat infantry badge." He pinned it through the thick material of the cape. "Job well done." The guys each shook my hand and pounded the CIB into my chest.

Did it matter? Did it really mean anything after all this time?

Yeah, it did.

Dave scratched at his own thin, scraggly beard. "Brah, I'm not one to talk, but you are looking rough. How about a shave and getting out of that oversize poncho? You remind me of that dude from *Saving Private Ryan* after he was stranded on that island. If you're going to help us convince the Korundi that we can do this, you need to look the part."

Karlo put a hand on my shoulder. "Welcome back, Team Sergeant."

Mitch dug in the back seat. "Christmas done come early, bro-man. I snagged this." It was the soft case with my MK 22.

"Oh baby! Come to papa!"

It was as sweet as Talis Darmon in my arms and our first kiss before we parted.

Okay, that's a gross overstatement.

But it was another special moment, so many stacked so quickly. My heart was full beneath the blue and silver badge, the cool of the backer pins on my chest reminding me it was there. I know it must've looked ridiculous, but I didn't care.

And with my rifle in my hands again, what it felt to be a dangerous god of battle returned to me.

Mitch had topped off my load of 300 Norma Magnum to a full two hundred rounds. Every copper pill a dead Tarn in waiting. And maybe, my crosshairs would settle on Bryant. They might have everything else, but I had this. The optic seemed tight and solid on the rail and everything else was with it, the same as I'd put it away before my last night on the team. My last night caring about being in uniform. My last night before I'd made the promise to kill men to whom I'd sworn allegiance against the universe.

It takes two sides to keep the promise of comradeship. Their promise was broken first.

✣ ✣ ✣

I went with Dave and a party of Korundi and waited on horseback until the forms of three Tarns, a curvaceous human, and a prancing eight-legged puppy the size of a steer came through the pass and descended the gentle road into Califex Valley. From a half a kilometer away, Apache saw me. Beraal tried to hold him back, but to no avail. The gadron made a burst of speed and I braced myself for the tackle, elated, but also anticipating my end would be similar to that of a car stalled on a railroad crossing. The mounted Tarns tensed, but Dave waved them off.

"It's his pet, Korundi. Not to worry. Just don't get between them. Apache doesn't like it."

With a quarter-ton puppy all over me, I had little choice but to pay attention to him, and it was a welcome distraction—because my composure strained like a dam to hold back the floodwaters as I longed to run to her, aching for the sun of her presence to rise and warm away the frost of the long winter of our separation. But I sensed her resolve to make her entrance into the city one worthy of a noble—her smooth, graceful stride perfect, measured, unhurried, yet purposeful. It wasn't until she was a hundred meters away—a gulf of aching distance still—when her royal demeanor gave way and she stroked her chin and laughed. She'd noticed. I was clean shaven and dressed as I'd been at our first meeting so long ago—in multicam and armed.

Weeks in the mountains together, starving, shivering, and almost dying, had not erased this fact for me—I was in love with Mars royalty. With an audience present, I had to act the part of one who knew proper etiquette. As an SF operator, I prided myself in being a quick study. I rose to my full height, spread my arms, and bowed. This brought an even bigger smile. I'd done right. We locked eyes as she crossed this last distance, resisting the urge to run to her and take her in my arms. Finally, she was near. I pushed Apache aside to take both of her offered hands in mine. Her smile melted me.

"I prefer you without the beard, Lord Benjamin Colt."

"I prefer you any way, Princess."

That brought a tremble and a blush, but the beauty I'd successfully flattered was replaced by the grave envoy of a kingdom.

"Is it true?" she asked, solemn. "Your loyal friends have abandoned the traitor, Brandon Bryant?"

"Yes, Princess. Karlo Columbo, David Masamuni, and Mitchell Crowe are here."

With a raised chin, Talis Darmon hailed Dave, still atop his horse. "David Masamuni, I trust you are well?" She did not smile, and her voice was cold and flat.

"I am, ma'am. And very relieved to see you."

Then, in low tones to just me, she said, "Is he truly your trusted friend again, Benjamin Colt?"

Dave had his lid on and his earpro sealed. I bet the volume on his ears was turned all the way up because he heard her.

"I am, Princess," Dave answered for me. I heard both shame and apology in his voice. "And I always was. We had to bide our time, Princess. There just wasn't much we could do without risking both your lives, ma'am."

"I see." She dismissed him and returned her attention to me. "Karlo Rinaldo Columbo tended me once while I was in captivity in the dungeons. We could not communicate as he had no decipher, but he was caring and did his best to reassure me. I do not know this other man, but you believe him trustworthy?"

"Yes, Princess. Mitchell Crowe is that. The reason I was not executed by Domeel Doreen was because these three held firm against Bryant. They all signed their own death warrants when they left his army. I trust them all, and they're committed to stopping him."

Then I told her.

"Thoria! Fallen to invasion by Domeel Doreen! I have many friends there. Oh, Benjamin Colt! We must get to my father. If the easternmost city in his kingdom has fallen, then the war has already arrived. From Thoria, it is next Clymaira that lies along the way to Shansara. We must reach him. He needs our counsel and our aid." She addressed the eldest of the mounted Korundi escorts. "Take me to Jedak Jeraal.

The chieftain of the Korundi will desire to meet with the representative of King Osric Darmon at once."

Beraal had been giving us space until then, allowing us as private a moment together in public as was possible. It confirmed to me that somewhere along the way, the princess had revealed to her closest confidante her feelings for me. As far as I was concerned, Beraal's comportment toward us was a gold stamp seal of approval. But now the sisterly considerations were done and the dosenie took charge.

"Senior, send word to your chieftain. Princess Talis Darmon will have an audience with him after she has had a brief respite."

A rider took the command as if from his own general. "At once, Dosenie."

Tais Darmon might be the princess, but Beraal was the strategist, logistician, and enforcer of all things proper. A sergeant major's sergeant major. But without the smugness. "Princess, the king's ambassador must prepare herself. Decorum demands it. I will quickly obtain what I can from the market. I will come to the encampment of Benjamin Colt's friends, and there I will properly prepare the princess before she represents her father in diplomacy."

Her cheeks flushed in a delightful deep magenta, darker than her normal red. "I see. Am I in such a state as to be unworthy of reception by an ally?" Her dark mane was as long and thick as any woman's I'd ever seen, a marvel from the creator of all things. Once we'd arrived among our new friends in the Korund, she'd taken to winding it tightly into itself to make a dense bulky bun that must've been as heavy as a helmet with attached comms. Her clothing was clean, plain, and ridiculously oversized. She was unadorned by the exquisite jewelry she'd worn in the apartment in Maleska Mal after Domeel Doreen paroled her to me.

I thought her perfect, and told her so.

She smiled, but Beraal rolled her eyes as if she'd learned the gesture from my mother—whose mastery of exasperated expressions on demand rivaled all Oscar winners. "You will bathe and I will fix your hair. I will find clothing as suitable as can be found and jewelry. At least a necklace to rest on your bosom. And wristlets. The fidelity of your father's treasury and the mark of a dosenie serving the House of Darmon will satisfy the merchants, unless they wish to incur the wrath of the king!"

"As you wish, Beraal," Talis Darmon accepted. "But do not sacrifice too much time. The hour for action is late."

Beraal rode off behind the senior Tarn, and I lifted the princess onto my own horse, then moved to lead the arkall and her back to the city.

"Benjamin Colt. Your place is to guard me. Mount, and I will ride behind you."

I knew an order when I heard one.

"Yes, Princess."

She scooted back and I vaulted onto the saddle, the arkall oblivious to the extra weight. It was now I who was Charlton Heston, she my Nova, the beautiful damsel—with no damn dirty apes to pester us. And I felt confident there wouldn't be a wrecked Statue of Liberty somewhere ahead. She wrapped her arms around my waist and our horse mindlessly sauntered after the Tarns while Dave brought up the rear, Apache waddling happily beside us. It was old times again for him.

She whispered, "I do not wish to be apart. I want my mouth to your ear and to feel your heart beat against my chest."

"And I yours, Talis Darmon. Now and for always."

If ever there were a perfect moment, this was it. And like all moments in time, it was fleeting. I vowed to record every detail of it.

She lay her head on my shoulder, rules of decorum not broken but at least bent, confident that she was not seen. "Benjamin Colt, there will be a time for us someday, but I fear it will not be soon. I steal this moment for us because, once prepared, I must entreat with Jedak Jeraal. Though he is a friend and has always been an ally true, there is never a permanent bond in politics. Peace is disrupted, and my father's kingdom is in peril. Be on guard, my brave warrior. I will use every skill available to me, but I fear it will be your gifts that are crucial to our task."

She squeezed my abdomen tighter, and I wrapped an arm over hers, silken and warm beneath mine. It wasn't merely my need to touch her. I wanted to shield every exposed part of her from the storm that gathered ahead, and I felt like I belonged. Here. With her. Always.

Somewhere buried deep within me were the memories of a man who was no longer me. The memories of a man who'd been humiliated. Shamed. Rejected. As strong as I'd made myself on the outside to repel the harms of the world, the soul-eater took the kernel of my innermost doubts and weakness and showed me their full blossom.

Now all that were left were echoes of memories of reflections of the man I had been before Talis Darmon. The white frothy waves of the storms that crashed around inside me had settled to swells, then to ripples, until finally the surface of my black pool of experience was smooth as glass and crystal clear. And when I gazed into the pool just now what I saw was myself. Capable. Strong. Fearless. Talis Darmon was with me, and as I protected her with my body, she shielded me with her compassion and her understanding.

I was healed.

And all it took was the end of the world to find my lovely physician.

✤ ✤ ✤

The princess was regal. Beraal did wonders in a short time. Gossamer blue fabric wrapped her in a gown as perfect as if it had been tailored by a dozen seamstresses. A gold belt gathered it all around her tiny waist. Her lustrous raven hair was full again and draped her head like the finest frame on the finest painting, complementing, yet never able to draw attention away from her perfect face. Gold and silver jewelry adorned her chest and bare arms.

"Let us proceed. You will announce me, Beraal."

"Yes, Princess."

I took my place at her left side, a step behind, my shield arm ready to defend as was the custom for all men-at-arms. What Talis Darmon may have lacked in grand finery and accoutrement from her father's kingdom wasn't noticeable to my eye. Instead, I saw only the statuesque powerhouse of the might that was her intellect. The aura of her command. The majestic presence of a born leader. I had seen her at the human limit of dignity. At her most disheveled and frail. Even then, she was always the picture of propriety and control. Now, returned to her role as emissary, she was every bit the queen I knew her to be.

And by whatever grace blessed me, I was hers.

The hall of the chieftain of all the Korund Tarns was a contrast to that of Domeel Doreen. The Mydreen Tarns lived as squatters in the decayed grandeur that had been Filestra but was now Maleska Mal. Whereas the Mydreen chieftain's audience chamber was as dilapidated as the rest of Maleska Mal, this hall spoke of strength and military order. Pride and history. Culture and tradition. I saw the same throughout Califex.

Aside from the atmosphere plant with its towering spires and odd shapes that spoke of mechanism and processes, Califex was splendid in its simplicity and cleanliness. None of it reminded me of the style of old Filestra, a gaudy remnant of human Vistaran hands.

The mountain Tarns possessed the skills of great artisans and builders, whose harsh domains and warrior culture were reflected in all they constructed with dignity and simple beauty. The mix of hewn stone and stretched animal skin roofs of the domiciles, the smooth columns and arched roofs tiled with red clay that defined the larger buildings, told me much about the Korundi—like all architecture should. Where the Mydreen resigned themselves to the drab colors of the desert, the Korundi borrowed the violet, yellow, and red tones from the mountain flora, colorizing the city in highlights to make it seem a living part of the landscape around it.

And like the Korundi, their chieftain was no less distinct than their capital city. On a throne of ancient ivory and femur bones, the skins of giant spotted gazraal lions draped over the tall back and four arms, sat Jedak Jeraal. He wore no crown. He needed none to demonstrate his kingship. An orange sash ran the diagonal across his chest. His tusks were yellowed and long. Even sitting, his mass and stature stood out among the warrior lieutenants seated below him. At his right hand was the red-sashed Khraal Kahlees. My antagonist and would-be host in the Korund fixed me in rapt attention as our procession halted before the chieftain.

I met his gaze and though I didn't mean to, my smile betrayed me. *I know that you know that if you try anything, it'll go badly for you.*

I'd once thought Double-K admirable, and it had almost gotten me killed. Desert or mountain or otherwise, maybe a Tarn was a Tarn? If K-K was going to turn this audience with the princess into another childish test of my worthiness, I was ready.

Beraal took a single commanding step ahead. "Jedak Jeraal, Chieftain of all Mountain Tarn and Protector of the Korund from foundation to the reach of the stars above. Your friend and ally King Osric Darmon, Father of Mihdradahl, sends his ambassador plenipotentiary, Emissary Princess Talis Darmon Sylah, to your court to entreat with you on matters urgent to all of Vistara." Beraal bowed deeply, four arms crossing her chest as she retreated.

The princess remained poised. Silent. Eyes blazing. The hint of her might was teased by the aura I was certain was not just my imagination, jade-green energy lighting her very being, her amber-red skin turned gold by the illumination of it. The chieftain rose and his lieutenants with him. For a moment, I thought to put hand on pistol, but arms crossed chests in a gesture of respect rather than menace. Jedak Jeraal left the dais of his throne and in two steps towered over us. Four hands touched his bowed temple in pause before he extended them open.

"Princess Talis Darmon, you among all of Vistara are welcome in my house. Your peril is at an end. I offer every spear and sword in the Korund in service to return you safely to your father's care."

I relaxed.

The princess blazed. "Now that I have reached your house, my peril is over?" she snapped.

Every muscle from my jaw to the soles of my feet firm sizzled in the electric current of her reply. The green aura was gone. Red fire flared.

"Peril true at the hands of your kin, Domeel Doreen! Peril that persisted as a captive for many cold revolutions of the moons. The conclusion of which was not brought through rescue by my father's ally, but by the divine arrival of a Thulian prince! Now that I arrive at no cost to you, you claim to declare for me and my father in Shansara? Where were the spears and swords of your tribe to aid me when captive so long in Maleska Mal, Chieftain? The cries from the dying lips of my father's councilors as they were tortured to death at the hands of the Mydreen were unheard by the ears of the Korund. What restrained aid to the daughter of your oldest ally then? Tell me, Jedak Jeraal, why now at long last would my peril be over?"

She pulled at the throat of her gown to reveal her chest.

"It would seem wiser to slay me now and declare to all of Vistara your favor for Domeel Doreen's war to rule."

30

Jedak Jeraal became a glacier as did not exist on all of Mars. His lieutenants froze with him. I froze. If there were a moment like it recorded in all the history of war and diplomacy, it escaped my knowledge. Cleopatra rolling out of the rug at Caesar's feet couldn't have been more shocking.

Far behind me, Dave whispered, "Et-gay eady-ray o-tay ight-fay."

His pig latin warning lacked detail, but perfectly translated my own telepathic projections to Karlo and Mitch. I eased my hand to my M4, presaging how we'd paint the throne room like the killing floor of a slaughterhouse, when it was erased from thought by a thunderclap heralding an end to draught.

A booming laugh like a coughing buzzsaw, so loud it knocked dust from the rafters, replaced visions of blood with the wonderment of a child on his first Christmas morning. I didn't know what would come next, but because it had been set into motion by Talis Darmon, I sensed it would be something wonderful.

The chieftain shook in a final tremor of laughter as he took a knee. "Talis Darmon Sylah! Your words strike with the temper of your father's steel and the fire of your mother's sorcery. As your mother's student of diplomacy for many years, I recognize your tactic. And recognizing such, I take no offense. First, because I know you believe your words are true—no matter you are misinformed. Second, because they justly arrive at the heart of the matter—no matter how unkindly.

"You of all people know that whether one is a king ascended by blood right as is your father, or one chosen to lead his people as I am, a leader cannot act on principle alone. There are many factors at play, but rest assured—my oath to you is true. Will you allow me to explain, my old friend and student of the same great professor? Before you shame me further in front of my clan leaders."

A smile spread across her face and the green glow of peace returned with her calm. "You learned from her well, Jedak Jeraal. The Korundi are a great and wise people to have chosen you as their chieftain. Your interpretation of my indictment and your own proper actions prove it. We will take all necessary time to reacquaint and have discourse. Long now on our journey to freedom I have suspected much has occurred that I am ignorant of due to my imprisonment and hardship in the wilderness. I accept your courteous invitation. Allow me to present my guardian and confidant, Prince of Thulia, Lord Deacon Benjamin Colt."

It wasn't time to be humble and spoil the tenor the princess had achieved. I knew that much. I snapped to attention and fired the chieftain a hand salute, held it, and returned to order arms sharply. "At your service, Jedak Jeraal."

"I know your name, lord. And of your deeds." He didn't indicate it was from Khraal Kahlees how he knew, but the lieutenant's proffered tusks meant someone had told stories from Maleska Mal. "There is a crisis in our lands. My most trusted advisors have scouted and confirmed that David Masamuni has spoken truly of what has transpired in Thoria and also what proceeds now. Lord Benjamin Colt, your clanmates have proven loyal to their oath while under my roof. I invite them to join us as we consult together. We will speak in comfort as there is much to discuss."

I let the princess take the chieftain's elbows and fell in behind as Beraal joined me in the procession. I whispered to her, "Did you know she was going to try to start a fight? And with the only friend we have between here and Shansara?"

Without looking at me, she said, "The princess always knows best. Have you not learned that by now, Benjamin Colt?"

✤ ✤ ✤

Instead of the cushions of the desert Tarns, chairs were brought, sized correctly to human frame. Califex was accustomed to visitors from the

Red Kingdom, otherwise we'd have been legs-dangling kindergartners in the principal's office.

The chieftain spoke kindly. "Princess, you appear to me as gaunt as a summer godahl. Though I know you to be a warrior trained in the ways of your people and mine, I see that your adversity was hard on you. Have the people of the Korund been hospitable since your arrival?" He snapped fingers on two hands to summon servants with trays of food.

"Most hospitable, Jedak Jeraal. I thank you for your concern, but please, we must speak of this now. When did you know of my imprisonment in Maleska Mal? And why did you not intervene on my father's behalf?"

The chieftain's brow furrowed. "Rumor of a disturbance in Maleska Mal reached my ear late some weeks after the craven assault by Domeel Doreen's clan on your diplomatic mission. I sent message to Shansara pleading confirmation and pledging support. I received answer from General Itkar Moline that if assistance were desired, the king would make request."

As if expecting this, he produced a document from a nearby table and presented it. The princess took the opaque sheet and swiped across it. Characters appeared in red. The angle was such that I couldn't see them clearly, and just as I started to make out some of the words, her arm collapsed from the weight of them.

Beraal spat. "Itkar Moline has always been a prideful fool."

Jedak Jeraal continued, "I dispatched my most trusted lieutenant and his finest band of warriors to Maleska Mal."

Khraal Kahlees dipped his head at the mention.

"I desired my own set of eyes amongst the Mydreen if your father's own general felt so insecure as to exclude me from his confidence. It was not an unusual visit, as we often trade and travel into the far eastern lands with our Mydreen cousins."

"Khraal Kahlees, pray tell, besides trying unsuccessfully to harm my protector, what was your purpose amongst the Mydreen? To observe my humiliation?" the princess coldly said.

"He did as I ordered, Talis Darmon," said the chieftain. "I did not send my best in order to act as a rescue party. The Mydreen and especially Domeel Doreen would have killed you had my Tarns acted prematurely, as well as precipitated a war between us. Tell the princess your tale, Khraal Kahlees."

Double-K spoke for the first time. "My chieftain allowed me latitude that if opportunity arose and I could guarantee your safety, I could free you on my initiative, Princess. You and your dosenie were all that remained of your party by the time I arrived. Domeel Doreen took me into his confidence as I worked to form a plan of action. Were you aware, Princess, that the king sent an envoy to Maleska Mal bearing treasure for a ransom? I was witness."

"I was not!"

Double-K continued. "Domeel Doreen had no use for ransom. His joy in humiliating the king was enough, and he shared with me it was a pleasure he intended to enjoy for as long as possible. Knowing he did not intend to kill you and finding my attempts at manipulating him to advantage were fruitless, I readied to return to tell my chieftain all I had learned. Then the Whites came.

"When Benjamin Colt made himself your protector, this was an unexpected development."

K-K met my eyes. "I did not depart after our last meeting, Benjamin Colt, as all were meant to believe." Our last meeting was where he'd tried to kill me. "And any Mydreen observing would think us declared enemies. Instead, I sent my squadron to bring word of all that had occurred to my chieftain. I remained behind, living in hiding in the abandoned parts of Maleska Mal. Listening. Waiting. Planning. True to the mission my chieftain gave to me.

"The attempted rescue by the Red warriors caught me by surprise, as did their sure defeat by the Whites. It was swift and merciless. Learning of your betrayal by your comrades was no less surprising, Benjamin Colt. But it told me that your oath to protect the princess was sacred to you, and that you too were a part of my chieftain's commission to me to provide aid to the princess.

"I learned rumor that Domeel Doreen accepted alliance with the Whites, and as I watched an army be raised and armed, I reexamined my duty and weighed my chieftain's commission to aid the princess against his need to be informed of this urgent news. I made plans to depart. First, I came in contact with Mydreen of Korund descent. It was they whom I sent to find you, Dosenie Beraal. I swore them to the fealty of their tribal roots to give aid to the princess and to one of their kin, as well as to conceal my presence from all on pain of their deaths."

Beraal gasped. "It was by your hand that their help came to me!"

Only the princess and I knew what that meant to her. A father who didn't know her had aided her in her time of greatest need.

"Blessings on your proud name, Khraal Kahlees."

The warrior dipped his head. "It was your hand that saw the rest done, Dosenie. I was readying to leave when I was surprised by the city alarm, and knew at once that your flight was underway. I apologize for having had no greater hand in it. I admit, it was by accident of location that I traced your departure on three arkall from the edge of the abandoned city. And late I was to that. I tried to follow but was waylaid by a party of pursuing Mydreen. They were quite correct—though accidentally so—and had me cornered as a conspirator, very desperate to locate you before they became the subject of Domeel Doreen's displeasure on his return.

"I killed them, but lost my mount and was wounded in the skirmish. I regret greatly that I could not aid you or spare you from your evasion into the mountains alone. It is a regret I carry as deep as any failure of my life. Please accept my apologies, Princess."

I spoke up. "Khraal Kahlees, I thought it was our luck that prevented a Mydreen war party from following us into the mountains. It was you who saved us. You have my thanks."

"And mine," the princess said. "No failure occurred on your part. Quite the opposite. It was your determination and honorable sense of duty that made our escape possible. Words cannot express my gratitude to you and your chieftain. Please forgive my rude tactic earlier. It was truly poor judgment on my part."

"There is nothing to forgive, Princess," the chieftain assured her.

"Your understanding honors me, Talis Darmon." Khraal Kahlees stood and bowed, then leaned back into the tall chair. If I could read a Tarn, I'd say it looked as though a weight lifted from his conscience.

The princess also seemed at ease, knowing she was not in the company of disloyal friends. "Then all is explained, and let us speak no more of things past, but of more urgent matters present. Tell me what develops within the sight of the guardians of the Korund Mountains."

Jedak Jeraal grunted. "Thoria has indeed fallen to this new Mydreen army and their Thulian warmasters. The siege of Clymaira builds as we speak. Lord Benjamin Colt," the chieftain broke with a sudden new direction, "what do you know of Tarns? You have spent time with the Mydreen, both as guest and as prisoner. Though Dosenie Beraal and Khraal Kahlees are fine ambassadors, you have spent little time in the Korund. Do you yet see that we are as alike and yet different to other Tarn as perhaps are the very worlds of Thulia and Vistara?"

His analogy was apt.

"Yes, Chieftain. I understand, and I welcome the chance to know the Korundi better. I think perhaps your people and mine are alike in many ways."

The princess nodded approvingly and held her words to allow the chieftain to continue.

"We live the way of the warrior. We suckle at the breast of Mother Vistara because there is no other way. We must live free. Korundi are made of the same clay as the Mydreen, though we are fired in different kilns. Of all Tarns, the Mydreen have always been the most belligerent in their ways. Theirs is a rebellious house. As for the house of my people, there will be opportunity for you and your kin to learn of us for yourselves." He ended his sidebar with me and turned attention to the princess.

"It is with the aid of the Thulians and their war machines that the ambition of the desert tribes has been made possible. Your father's army moves to relieve Clymaira and to prepare defenses for all in his kingdom."

"His army is so small!" the princess exclaimed. "I have seen the power of the weapons wielded by the renegade Thulians. They have armed the Mydreen with like. My father's army has little hope of success."

I was suffocating without the air of specifics. "How large is your father's army, Princess?"

"Including the constabulary of the Guard in each city? A few thousand total. The resources of the Red Kingdom have long been focused on preserving all life on Vistara, not at waging war with Yellow or Green. Our army is maintained for security. They patrol the outskirts of our cities and trade routes, mainly to deter the Mydreen from their raids. It has been ages since ours has fought another standing army.

Mastery of the air and more powerful weapons have always restrained the Mydreen from grander forms of aggression. The wars between Red and Yellow are generations settled and forgotten."

The Red defense force sounded more like the Costa Rican police than the Swiss Army. Focusing on basic self-defense was all well and good until someone saw your nonaggression as weakness, smacked you in the face, and took your lunch money.

"Three thousand? Dave estimated the Mydreen cavalry at twenty thousand," I said.

"The Mydreen have never been organized as a single army," Jedak Jeraal corrected me. "Not since the oceans and rivers first dried to dust. Not since the Korundi, the low country Vermeel, and the desert Mydreen warred with each other and also with humans."

"Chieftain, how many warriors do the Korund mountains hold?"

He bristled slightly. "All Korundi are warriors, Benjamin Colt, but I take your meaning. It is not a number equal to the Mydreen by half. But the Mydreen are spread far apart. They range to the south where they raid their cousin Vermeel in the grand desolation of the lowlands. They travel to the northern deserts where the ground never warms, raiding the unaligned city-states of Vistara. If Domeel Doreen called all the clans of the Mydreen to join in war against the Red Kingdom, it would take many months to gather them all."

Dave leaned in and raised a hand off his knee and waited to be recognized. "I have trouble understanding why communication is so difficult on Vistara. Is there no means of contact over large distances?"

The princess sighed. "Forgive me, David Masamuni. I forget how things that must be so common to a Thulian are difficult to understand about Vistara. I have seen how you communicate with your technology, but you have told me yourself it is very limited here as compared to your home, yes?"

"It is that, Princess," Dave admitted.

"Vistara is a shadow of its once great self, David Masamuni. Though you have not yet seen the grandeur that is Shansara, the sublime harmony found in the nexus of design that joins every corner of Pyreenia, nor the high towers of Thoria, the Vistara you find yourself in is not the Vistara of our ancient ancestors. We simply do not have the science or means to connect great distances together as was once taken for granted. Communicating across a city by voice and transmitted image is done. But across the deserts between us, no such ability remains."

Dave mumbled, "Not one friggin' telegraph line on all of Mars. You're telling me it's all pony express?"

I frowned and was ready to give him a stiff elbow. My brother was a stud. An operator among operators. But a commo man was a commo man. His disbelief at the lack of it here didn't excuse rudeness. He and I would have words later.

The princess soothed away my irritation. "While I do not understand your meaning, David Masamuni, I understand your frustration. It has long been one of the many burdens that we on Vistara accept as our heritage of greater knowledge lost. We live on a dying world. While many of us work daily to secure a future, we live accepting that there is only today, and that to pine for what we do not possess is futile."

Dave's face showed I wouldn't need to scold him later. With regret, he said, "I'm so sorry, Talis Darmon. If we can win this war, someday it would be my honor to try to solve that dilemma for the betterment of all."

I gave him props for a good recovery. The princess's heartfelt smile caused Dave to blush.

"I'm certain your talents match your bravery, David Masamuni. I hope we can use both to build that Vistara together."

I could see by the swell of his chest that Dave was full of the same grace she'd given to me. She had that way with people.

The chieftain grunted. "We have accomplished much. The air is clear. Much remains yet unknown. Especially so is the will of your father the king, Princess. I have sent courier after courier. No word returns to me. Neither does message arrive by your father's hand from Shansara. I have grave fears as to the cause of his silence. We must then decide our next action with only what knowledge is available now—to act as we see fit, regardless of the chasm of our intelligence. Princess, though I feel for you like a Red sibling, you see the truth of what I am about to say.

"I cannot march the might of the Korund to Shansara."

Her poise was great, but her sorrow could not be concealed. "I do understand, Jedak Jeraal. And I would not ask it of you."

"But fear not, my friend." A fierceness returned to his manner. "I also cannot allow the Korund to sleep while roamaks mass to take down a mighty predator. We will find means to aid the Red Kingdom without charging blindly like a fledgling gazraal into a pack of gadron thinking to steal a kill."

As the sole representative of gadrons everywhere, Apache made a slurping sound as he raised his head off the floor in recognition. It had been impossible to keep him from trotting alongside, but he'd obeyed and laid at my side this entire time.

"Let us plan."

31

The largest of all Tarns again offered elbows to the princess. Attendants parted animal skins to reveal a courtyard, where a fire blazed and tables awaited stacked with food. "But first we must see to your nourishment, Princess. Your intellect and wisdom will be best cultivated in the soil of a strong body."

I held back until they passed and made a beeline for a man I'd judged, misjudged, and now judged again to be admirable. Like everything and everyone on Vistara, they were the tall hedges of a garden maze that I charted a path through, sometimes falling through hidden trapdoors along the way. But like the grand treasure that was Talis Darmon, there were other treasure chests on this journey. And this one I didn't want to leave unopened.

The red-sashed Tarn awaited my approach. I halted and we stood apart, appraising each other.

"Khraal Kahlees."

"Benjamin Colt."

I had to make the first move. "My gratitude alone is not adequate repayment. In my army, you would receive a medal of the highest distinction for your bravery and cunning."

I'd puzzled him.

"Medal? What is this thing? A mount worthy to ride in battle? A weapon?"

Apparently, there was no direct translation. "A medal is a device worn to display a record of valor and give recognition of the same, awarded for acts of great bravery on the battlefield."

Jaw and tusks thrust to one side as he considered this. "Hmmm. The Reds have such devices. To a Tarn, they seem distasteful."

So much for my hands across the water.

Before I could take another swing, he said, "For any Tarn—to challenge another in contest, to make claim of fighting prowess—cultivates the spirit of the warrior. But should I wear a boast so that more may be thought of me than by my word or deed? For a warrior, valor and rectitude are rewards unto themselves. Their presence is apparent in the bearing and acts of the soldier, not in jewelry. You wear no such devices. I sense it is not a custom important to your band. One warrior knows these things about another, as you and I know it about each other, Benjamin Colt—Thulian and Korundi—or were we any other. What use is a declaration of acts past?"

What he said touched me in a way I hadn't previously considered. I didn't want to explain the when's and where's of medals and insignia, and that I had a lot of them, but settled for my first thought on the subject.

"We have a saying. 'Every day is selection.'"

"Hmmm. I see the essence of its meaning, Benjamin Colt. The simplest maxims hold the most truth. It is good."

"Khraal Kahlees, what I mean to convey to you is simply—I am in your debt. I recognize the great danger you faced and the fortitude with which you performed your mission. I would have others know it as well."

His jaw protruded in a display of Tarn mirth. "No debt was incurred, except perhaps mine. There was a moment when you halted the flow of life to my skull, and I briefly touched the waters of the River Blix. It is I who thank you for having the nobility to not answer my assault on you with death! My foolish plan was to drive you to exhaustion and take the role of merciful victor. How close to disaster my plan came!"

Disaster was right. Had I killed him, where would any of us be now? I caught Beraal looking at us. Would her opinion of Khraal Kahlees be changed knowing he had in fact worked to save her—an unacknowledged, unknown daughter? When the time was right and we were alone, I would broach the subject. Life was short. Too short to hold grudges. Too short to let love go unspoken. Too short to let evil go unpunished.

We both heard it. The vibrations of a pulsing hum leaked from the courtyard, and I dashed to the princess. If our opponents had taken to the air, we'd been caught flatfooted.

"Make for the GMV and get that minigun up," I called out. The guys were bouncing away when the chieftain halted our actions.

"Hold!" An aide spoke in his ear, and Jedak Jeraal said, "It is but a single airship, bearing the crest of the Red Kingdom." He pointed to Khraal Kahlees. "Retrieve the visitor. It is fortuitous timing."

In a short time, Double-K returned escorting a human dressed—well, he was hardly dressed at all. For a Tarn, the costume seemed somehow appropriate. For a human? I'd call it a mix of beachwear and cosplay. He wore little more than a loin cloth, the only other clothing a cape attached to the shoulders of his matte-gold chest plate. His armor appeared more ornamental than functional. Vambraces covered his forearms. Greaves covered shins. He wore a helmet with a noseguard and carried both sword and blaster rifle. Otherwise, he had a lot of exposed skin.

A terrible choice of kit with which to fight a war against a horde of green warriors armed with M4s, courtesy of Baby Blue.

"Princess, you're safe! This is a welcome surprise!" The Red soldier bowed deeply before recovering. "Chieftain Jedak Jeraal. I am First Shield Kleeve Hartus of the Clymaira Guard. I bear grievous dispatch from General Den Gillead. Thoria has fallen to attack by an army of Mydreen led by White lords of the underworld." The new arrival noted the presence of more White lords. "I see. Of course, we have learned the belligerents are not of the White, but Thulians arrived on Vistara to make war against us."

"These are friends, First Shield," the chieftain announced. "Not here to make war against any save the Mydreen invaders. But we save introductions for later. Tell me your report."

"As they felled Thoria, so their army masses against Clymaira. The king's army have met the invader on the field of battle. While they have deterred their advance, the cost to the Red Army continues to be dear. The enemy has issued demands while still engaging the king's forces, as though their victory is inevitable. I am sent to request aid of the Korundi in halting the siege that comes to my city."

The chieftain placed upper hands on the swords at his side. "At last, we know the king moves to action. Tell us all."

All the while, the four of us in multicam crowded closer while we listened to the first shield's brief. He spoke in the formal, yet vague way that I found tiresome as I struggled to put together a tactical picture on which I could formulate a plan. Finally, I took a step back and pulled the guys close to me, the chieftain and the princess oblivious to our minor retreat.

"Mix of old news and not a lot of useful new," I mumbled. "I was expecting to hear Clymaira had already fallen. But it seems like taking over a world with an army on horseback is slow work."

"Get a load of Flash Gordon," Dave muttered, unable to restrain himself.

I couldn't fault him his prejudice, and my own wall of propriety crumbled. "Please tell me the Reds have another army outfitted for war. Not a real army of camouflaged young enthusiasts to be found here, just beefcakes dressed for cosplay gladiator week. Sweet ghost of Jean Lartéguy." That quotation about "two armies" hung on the wall of every first sergeant's orderly room I'd ever been in.

Mitch mumbled to Karlo, "Pathetic."

Karlo's eyes were fixed on the first shield, like a father revulsed at the sight of his daughter's prom date. He just gave a slow, pitiful shake of his head.

The Red soldier was a fine-looking specimen, I had to say. They grew them fit here. Of course, other than the princess, I'd not met a single other human. I don't count Cynar the Younger or Salkar the Rash. Putting together my earliest impressions of what Vistara fashion must be like based on how Talis Darmon dolled herself up when she had access to all her royal finery—where skin revealed or teased was clearly the norm—and now how this character was outfitted, I was forming a picture of what the streets of a Red city must look like.

A combination of bad movies about the Spartans and soft porn, with a hint of martial costume jewelry thrown in to add flavor.

Mitch sighed and spoke in a trance-like state as he stared at the new arrival as the dandy continued to brief the chieftain and the princess, all bent over a map. "My grandad fought with loincloth-wearing, crossbow-wielding Montagnard in the Central Highlands of Vietnam.

I had visions of us leading Tarns on horseback to the relief of a siege. Commandeering levitating airships so we could strafe Mydreen on horseback with our 240s. A mighty army of Red soldiers in desert camouflage, maneuvering to contact, laying down volleys of suppressive fizzle-fire. Maybe it'd be like *Dune*. Instead—"

Karlo finished for him.

"Looks like we go to the relief of a bunch of Gucci He-Men."

✤ ✤ ✤

Dave and Karlo were in the GMV. I rode with the vanguard next to Khraal Kahlees at the head of three hundred of the chieftain's best cavalry. There was no time to organize more, nor to formulate much of a plan other than to move out. It was going to be a five-day ride to Clymaira, on a route skirting north around the lost bastion that was Thoria. I would develop a plan as we rode. The lieutenant led the Korund contingent, but I would try to influence him as much as I could to let us direct the fight.

All of my years of troop leading procedures and planning assaulted me as we rode. From one side of my brain, there was a gong sounding in the notes of METT-TC and other acronyms, as Napoleon's words consoled me from the other. They weren't exclusive to him—as no truth learned in war ever had been—but I liked his version.

"Take time to deliberate, but when the time for action has arrived, stop thinking and go in."

My hero Patton came to my rescue, too.

"A good plan, violently executed now, is better than a perfect plan next week."

What we most lacked—besides superior firepower and numbers—was information. So rather than concentrate on what I didn't know, what started to occupy my mind as we trotted along—the canter of an arkall the perfect rhythm by which to contemplate your navel as well as if you chanted a Buddhist mantra or listened to the classical music channel—was killing. Not killing in general.

Killing in the specific.

Chuck, Mark, and the Chief—I would kill on sight. Doug and Matt? I wasn't sure. I thought they deserved the opportunity to prove they weren't the same kind of lowlife the other three were. But how?

The rubber was very close to meeting the road the nearer we came to Clymaira. The inevitability that it was going to be them or us was no longer theoretical. It wasn't "what if?" It was now "how soon?"

A deadly confrontation was coming and with so much time on my hands as we rode, it got me thinking.

Young soldiers are blasé about killing, or at least the concept of it. Really, it's much worse than that. You're not indifferent to the idea of taking the life of another human—you're curious what it will feel like. You're a little thrilled at the idea of breaking that societal taboo—and being rewarded for it instead of ending up in prison. You run to a cadence call, singing about how napalm sticks to kids. I'm not negatively critical of that. It's necessary. Beneficial even, I think. You can't train teenagers for war by avoiding those things, or making them seem awful, or regretful.

As a youngster, I may have been as silly about the subject of killing as any of my other fellow neophytes. And yes, some guys you could say live the unexamined life, no matter their age, because they're not that bright. But it's not the norm. The infantry is stuffed with very smart people, despite popular opinion.

Certainly, as you mature into the role of soldier, the subject becomes deeper. A soldier's business is bloody. But you do it all in defense of your country and to keep the wolf away from the doorstep of your loved ones. There's no other way.

But somewhere in between the stupidity of the action movie—the one where the hero ex-Green Beret kills a few dozen bad guys then walks off into the sunset without a care in the world—and the mawkish saga of the veteran tortured by his wartime acts lies reality.

Older soldiers who'd walked the path of war and mentored me weren't indifferent to their acts of killing. But they had the confidence that they'd acted as professionals. That what they'd done was by necessity—by design, even. If you planned correctly. And their righteous outlook that it was just so was backed up by a culture that reinforced the same. If they carried guilt, it wasn't apparent to me.

Sure, there are those who do. Some of the causes being bad luck, truly bad acts, or bad coping mechanisms. Having been guilty of the latter, I had a lot of sympathy for those who suffered from it. But according to the number of books and movies about the guilt-wracked vet, popular culture would have you believe that what a soldier does in war only creates a ticking time bomb that counts down a lifetime of simmering self-destruction until it ends in the saddest of all kabooms.

I call bullshit on that.

Not just because of knowing such professionals most of my life, but because I was one now, too. I'd always had that tiny curiosity about what the two-way shooting range would be like. What the experience of combat would be. How would I feel when it came time to break that ultimate taboo and take a life? The answer was—I felt nothing. It was just another day at the office. I was the McDonald's employee who'd worked his way up to running the shake machine. That guy didn't get nervous every time he had to pull that lever. And neither did I. Plus, unlike theirs, my shake machine never broke down.

You might think it was because so far, I'd only taken the life of an alien race—the Tarn. Nope. A Tarn life was no different to me than a human's. Sure, they might be the ultimate example of indigenous forces or a foreign enemy—depending on whether they were with me or against me—but they were people. I'd killed by necessity—from the very personal view of a sniper scope to as up-close-bad-breath range as you can get. And I felt fine about it. To paraphrase however the actual Shakespeare went, my cause was just.

Talis Darmon had somehow healed a part of my psyche that had for a lifetime eaten away at me from the inside. How she did it, I don't know. She'd admitted she was a sorceress, so I guess it was white magic. And to go along with her brainwashing, I'd proven to myself I was worthy to be called a soldier. And a man. Which hadn't taken combat or witchcraft to prove to me—other than the magic of her affection.

But as I considered killing men—human men—who'd been my comrades, I wondered if I reflected on what was to come for this reason: some part of my upbringing was telling me that I should feel something dreadful about this situation. And I didn't. Maybe I'd need to unburden myself about it to my physician someday.

Maybe not.

My earpiece buzzed.

"Coming in from your ten at three hundred meters, how copy?" Mitch's voice came over the MBITR, which meant he had to be just a few klicks away. He'd been gone two days, left with Kleeve Hartus in his air car to scout the route.

"Good copy, Mitch. Meet you at the GMV."

I told Khraal Kahlees and the word spread. Now the hum grew loud enough that all could hear, and arkall snorted as our tiny battalion of horse soldiers and a single war wagon spread into a defense. After a few days and nights with the Tarns, I'd learned they had a well-developed tactical sense and methods of patrol that were much better than the horde of Mongol riders I'd anticipated.

The air car raised no dust as it came to rest, the method of its haunting propulsion very unclear. Karlo had given the air car a once-over, shrugged, and said, "FM."

The M stands for magic.

Mitch and the gaudy Red hopped off and trotted to the GMV where Double-K and the rest of us waited.

"What's the good word?" Dave said as he thrust water bottles into their hands.

Mitch pulled a laptop out of his daypack and rested it on the hood of the war wagon.

"Mostly bad, but some good," he replied.

He clicked and spread the drag pad to enlarge a photo taken through his MK 22's clip-on, the Christmas tree reticle of the scope a dark lattice of right angles and small numbers over everything. The green night vision image came alive, and a short MPEG ran several times in a loop.

"So, they're airmobile now," Karlo narrated. A trio of air cars patrolled from a few hundred meters above the desert, the lead flyer sweeping the ground ahead with an infrared illuminator like a searchlight. "Looks like your intuition was right on, Ben."

"One of us is behind that Hellfighter on NODS," Mitch said. "Has to be."

"One of *them*," Dave corrected.

I let it go. It was no time for semantics. "Obviously, you weren't detected."

"By sheer luck. First Shield Kleeve Hartus and I were just getting ready to start our night patrol when we spotted them. If they hadn't been running with that IR headlight broadcasting their presence, things mighta turned out differently."

"I am masterful at aerial gunnery," Kleeve Hartus said. "I have had much practice against Mydreen raiders. But against three air cars in flight, and with the greater range of the Thulian guns? It would not have ended well for us."

"They're daring anyone with NODS to take a shot at them," Dave said. "Are they getting complacent with their tactics?"

"Maybe." Mitch shrugged. "But who other than us has NODS? Kleeve Hartus tells me they don't. Our tech outclasses the locals in about every way, except the propulsion for these magic carpets. Now it looks like the OPFOR have recovered the best of Vistara tech from the Thoria siege and are putting that to good use. Why wouldn't they feel invulnerable?"

"Where was this contact?" I asked.

"We ran into them the first night, after a full morning flying low and fast before the sun got high and we lay up till dark. That patrol we encountered about here." He pointed to a spot on the map, one of the illuminated sheets of Vistara tech, the opaque smooth surface alight with the contours of the Korund Range running to its western edge, the cities of the Red Kingdom laid out between it and the great abyss of the Valles Marineris sprawled diagonally across the equator.

"So about halfway along our route," I estimated.

Even zoomed in with a tap at the edge of the sheet, the scale was useless except for general orientation. Lacking topographical detail, it was little better than an animal skin map sketched by a Bronze Age explorer.

"Here's the best we could get without risking compromise." Mitch ran a few more vids. "This was last night. We risked a few high angle runs. There's not a lot of resolution, but it looks like the delaying force the Red Army sent got wiped out on the plains west of the city. We watched small skirmishes all around Clymaira."

"The guards fight bravely," the first shield said, "but against such numbers, they cannot be victorious. The Thulian weapons make our air cavalry useless. I led one of the early stands against the Mydreen advance. Their ranged weapons suppress our movements. General Den Gillead ordered the construction of armored sleds and air cars, but the fabricator's efforts produced only a few dozen by the time the invader massed. The city engineers constructed barricades, trenches, and berms here, here, and here, along the best avenues of approach to the city center." He pointed out the barely visible shapes on the screen. "They work tirelessly even now, but it is too little, too late, I fear."

"How did you get out of the city to deliver the call for help, First Shield?" I asked.

Even in the dim blue light for our conference in the open desert night, his face told me the tale. "Five us departed the city with the goal of reaching the Korund. I alone arrived."

I didn't press him for more.

"The OPFOR don't have a big air wing, Ben," Mitch told me. "At most I've seen two patrols of three air cars operating together. Kleeve Hartus says the Mydreen don't like to fly. I've piloted this one a little. They're not difficult to fly, but it's probably been very limiting to Bryant's plans that he can't get many volunteers to take the job of pilots."

"Tarns are scared to fly?" Dave asked.

Khraal Kahlees took umbrage. "No Tarn warrior lets fear interfere with duty, not even the Mydreen. But—" he hesitated. "Only a fool or a human leaves the ground in a mechanical contrivance. It is unnatural."

It sounded like the sentiment of many guys I knew who'd survived crashes. Hell, I was inclined to think that way after riding our bucking bronco of a C-17 piled up in a heap with four broken legs, needing to be put out of its misery.

Kleeve Hartus smiled. "None doubt the ferocity of the children of the Korund, Khraal Kahlees."

"Nor do the Korundi the honor of the Guard, First Shield. Your warriors comport themselves with honor, as do you."

I agreed. Once again I was guilty of making a faulty judgment based on what I deemed the ridiculous appearance of the Red Guards. Mitch seemed comfortable with Kleeve Hartus's soldiering after their time spent together on the very dangerous task I'd assigned. Maybe someday I'd get it right and learn to reserve judgment until I had something worthy to judge by.

But if I had anything to say about it, I'd still be seeing about getting desert fatigues for his army.

"So, that's part of the good word," Mitch said. "They don't have total air supremacy. And against our 134, they're as susceptible as the Reds were to them. Plus, we have more Javelins."

"A Javelin's not a Stinger," Dave fired back in his own version of air defense artillery to bring down Mitch's suggestion.

Mitch dodged Dave's warhead and spurted back, "Yeah, but I've spent a couple of days on an air car. I don't know what makes them tick, but they put off heat. Think you couldn't hit a chopper with one in a pinch? Wanna bet that I couldn't get a lock on three of them massed in one of their patrols? From a few klicks away? A top-down kill? They'd never know what hit 'em."

Karlo made a pursed lip noise. "Humph. If they're moving slow—you never know unless you try. A sure thing if we found them on the ground, though."

I ended the discussion. "Okay. All good options to consider. We have to choose our moment to use the few Javs we have. Then we're settled. We move to relieve the siege of Clymaira. Did you get a fix on where the Stryker and the GMV are?"

"No. Without spending days or weeks on the ground on a recon. My sense is, they're on the other side of the city, blocking a retreat and set to engage any more forces riding to relief of the defenders."

Kleeve Hartus was concerned. "The invaders made demonstration of their superior war implements to break our spirit. Do we truly have the means to fight such a force?"

Dave squinted as he looked at the still shot of the glowing city on the computer. "You're thinking about a stealth probe with anti-tank teams to hit their armor before they know we're here?"

"Great minds think alike. Right in one."

32

My bent-at-the-waist creep through the labyrinth of draws between the sand drifts was tiring. I carried my MK 22 and a Javelin missile. Mitch carried his semiauto sniper rifle and an extra missile as well. Khraal Kahlees carried a missile ready to go with the Javelin command launch unit. On his back, it was no more than a carbine, but I could tell he was uncomfortable with the load. He had to stoop even lower than us to remain below the line of sight to the city we skirted. We tested his camo drape against our thermals. Like the ones the Mydreen wore to infiltrate our lines back at the C-17, it wasn't as good as our ghillies at concealing his body heat, but it was better than going bare.

Where we could, we trotted. Hard. Where we couldn't, we crawled like animals on all fours or sixes. We'd ditched the arkall many hours ago, sending them back with Double-K's guards.

Mitch balked when the Tarn leader insisted he join us. "Don't you need to stay with the cavalry? You're their commander."

"And as leader, I take responsibility for the most vital mission. If we do not locate and destroy the armored war machines of the Thulian invaders, will not all else be in jeopardy?"

It was hard to argue otherwise.

Midway through the night, I halted us to take another cautious creep to where we could scan for the wheeled metal dragons. I guessed we were on the back side of the metropolis of Clymaira by then. I focused the huge night vision optic weighing down the front of my MK 22 while Mitch fired up his thermal imager. The dense blanket of stars and double moons made the scene no less bright than a noon painted in shades of green and black.

"Negative," Mitch whispered.

"No wheels, but plenty of Mydreen." I passed my handheld thermal monocular to Double-K. I'd let him use it before. The first night on the trail from Califex, we'd figured out that the Tarns didn't see colors in the same band of wavelengths we did. Unlike many animals but just like humans, they didn't see IR at all—something very good to have confirmed. Without night vision devices, our infrared devices like our lights and aiming lasers were invisible to them too.

The color discrepancy between us was a challenge. What we saw as blue was all but invisible to them. We found that out when I demonstrated to Khraal Kahlees the different color palates available on the thermal for indicating an object radiated heat and appeared "hot" to the device. After hearing his hum of approval at the white = hot mode, I clicked over to blue ice = hot. Nothing.

"I see only gray. All is the same."

I toggled on to the full color digitized mode. The stoic warrior couldn't suppress his gasp of surprise.

"Such colors. It is like a fevered dream."

We were testing the thermal by scanning a company of herded arkall, dunes behind them, the mountains far in the background, a few roving soldiers on watch.

Karlo's curiosity was piqued and he brought up his own thermal. "Can you describe it? Tell me how you see the mounts."

Double-K held on to one. "By daylight, the arkall are bland. A solid brown or gray, much as the mountains. I see them now in a dozen shades of red, yellow, and orange. The neck and chest the brightest, limbs and tail darker."

"A dozen shades? Hmm," Karlo said. "I see them evenly red through mine. I'd say Tarns are blue-blind but have extremely enhanced cones for red and yellow. Of course, the digitized colors on the thermal aren't true. It makes me think what we see as the dull colors of the vegetation around the Korund are much more colorful to the Tarn eye than ours. Fascinating. What about IR image intensification?" Karlo spread apart a pair of dual tubes and handed them over.

"I see shades of blue and orange."

Blue and orange? I thought. But Karlo just said they were blue-blind? Plus NODs only showed the world in shades of green and black. That couldn't be right.

Khraal Kahlees scanned around. "The image is much more distinct than the heat-seeing device."

"Yup. You got it," Dave said, ignoring the strange color combos Double-K saw and instead rewarding his observation about the image quality. "Which is why we use both. They each do different things better. Thermals detect targets better, NODs see them in better definition, especially at greater distances."

"Why cannot one device see both?"

Dave laughed. "They can. We have them, but not in quantity. And if you have to ask why, the answer is always money. Money, to reduce friction, or to increase surface area. Isn't that right, Karlo?"

The degreed engineer had taught us all that those three things were the correct answer to most all of life's questions as to why something was the way it was.

"Go to the head of the class, Dave. With your knowledge of circuits and electromagnetic radiation, you and Mitch will be my first engineering students when I open my university here. But first you have to learn calculus."

Mitch chuckled. "No thanks. Dave can be your star pupil. I already know trig. At least, all I need to know to be a sniper."

Karlo ignored him. "Khraal Kahlees, try this." He took the NODs back, turned on the clip-on thermal imager, and handed the tubes back to him. "Try them now."

"There is a glow around everything hot. So, this is thermal and starlight amplified, as seen together?"

Karlo nodded. "You are a very quick student, sir. If you are willing, I'm always available to demonstrate our equipment and teach you how to use it."

"The Korundi say that when the student is ready, the teacher will come. I am ready, teacher."

Karlo's smile reflected the stars. I'd never known anyone who loved teaching more than him. If not for his need to jump out of airplanes and shoot at bad guys, he truly did belong in an engineering department at some grand university. It was cool to hear him hint that he already had plans for one on Vistara. Dave broke my moment of inspiration.

"Karlo, how come Tarns see blue and orange where we see green?"

"Green is a very wide band of visible light, Ben. Tarns apparently see it in very fine gradations, much more than we do. And what does the name we give to the radiation we call a color mean anyhow? Colors are just perception in your brain. What it really means to me is that the Tarn can be trained to be very good observers with night vision. Something we should keep in mind in case Bryant and Marky have figured that out, too."

Double-K handed back Karlo's NODs, though somewhat hesitatingly. Once you've made the night daylight, it's hard to go back to living in the dark.

"So, why are the Tarns called Greens by the Vistarans?" Dave asked.

"It is an inaccuracy of language of the humans that we live with, David Masamuni. They see us all as their green. We see each other in blues and purples. When our mates come to estrus yearly, they glow a lovely orange. It is a wonderful sight."

"Hubba-hubba," Mitch murmured.

"I bet." Dave frowned. "What color am I to you, Khraal Kahlees?"

"White, of course."

"Humph." Dave was always very proud of his naturally bronze skin, which had become even darker as of late. We were all getting dark. Karlo said it was because the lack of an ionosphere not only thwarted our radio wave propagation, but let more unfiltered radiation from the sun bake our skin. Maybe the healing ray treated cancer? I hoped so.

Where were the damned GMV and the Stryker we'd come to ambush?

Mitch lowered his thermals. "If the war wagons aren't here, maybe we should chance breaking radio silence to let Dave and Karlo know." We were encrypted and the commo men had keyed our MBITRs for a very narrow transmission band, one the team didn't use.

"No," I said. "We save it for absolute emergencies. If they pick us up, it's as good as shooting up parachute flares to tell them we're here."

A dull hum pierced the night air. I scrambled and pushed my NODs down, craning my neck up to search the skies.

"Ten o'clock, heading straight for us," Mitch said. He tossed netting over the front of his rifle. "Cover up."

A trio of air cars left the aurora of the city glow and, as Mitch said, seemed to be on an intercept course for our position. No telltale IR flood preceded their path, unlike the patrol we'd seen previously.

"It might be coincidence," I said, even as I knew that in combat, there were no coincidences. "Freeze and let's see what they do."

They grew closer.

"No good," Mitch said. He pulled a mag from his chest and exchanged it for the one in his rifle. He'd switched to black-tip, tungsten-core armor-piercing ammo, the same as we'd use against any vehicle.

Behind his gun again, he asked, "Waste a missile on them?"

I'd already settled on that course of action. "No way. We need them too badly. You've got the right idea. Remember where the power plant is on them?"

"Rear third."

"I've got the one on the left. You get the lead bird and the other. If mine doesn't drop, give that one some love, too, alright?"

His semiauto was made for just this kind of task—multiple targets at medium ranges. My big gun—best at bringing the good news to those that needed it at the greatest distance. Everything weapon system is a trade-off between requirement and capability. If Karlo could figure out how to make the fizzle guns better, maybe I'd finally have my one gun for all uses. Until then, this one suited me fine.

He took out another mag and laid it beside his gun. "Say when."

They were coming straight at us. Slow, cruising at a few KPH. Slow flying ducks.

"Stand by."

We waited. They didn't veer off. They descended as they flew, until they were only a couple hundred meters off the deck, and when they were about a thousand meters away, they sealed their fate. I placed my reticle about halfway back on the underside of my bird.

"Ready. Ready. Now." I pulled the trigger and immediately worked the bolt. Mitch's gas gun spat. *Pfft. Pfft. Pfft.* One after another. I sent another, my suppressed gun slightly louder, but still producing no flash from the small hole at the end of the long cylinder at the end of my gun.

Double-K was at my side, the thermal to his face. "The entire planet knows we attack. The cavalry move. Finish the sky riders off!"

The cadence of Mitch's fire increased until a bright flash blinded me, a small erupting sun causing my night vision to shut off. The autogate had never cut in before. The flash had to be incredible to cause it to trip. I clicked the knob off and on again, ready to pull the trigger as soon as my vision returned. The unmistakable sounds of falling debris crashing to the ground filled me with joy. Fireballs and showers of hot sparks shot into the sky from the ground. I dropped my NODs down and took the wide view. Nothing moved in the sky, but Khraal Kahlees had reported correctly—the cavalry were on the move straight for us.

"The good news, we smoked them." I could hear Mitch's grin. "The bad news, we've got about a hundred riders on the way. The nearest are two klicks off, but heading fast. What's the play?"

"Time to call for help." I hit my PTT. "We've made contact. We just knocked down an air patrol, but we've got riders inbound for our position, how copy?"

Dave came back. "Hold one."

"Observe," Khraal Kahlees said forcefully. His face was bare, holding the thermal at his chest. I looked where he pointed to the far side of the city. Fiery lines rose into the sky and the sound of a chain saw buzzed from far away, trailing the fury of the minigun by several seconds after each burst. Bright flares lit the sky on the far side of the city in more violent sunbursts before they fell beneath the towers of Clymaira.

Dave was back in my ears. "Ben, we just knocked down a trio of air cars. We've got our own problems, brah. We've got cavalry on the move. Beat feet, man. We can't come get you. I'll send who I can as soon as I can, over."

"Understood. Charlie Mike, Dave. We'll keep you informed. Out."

"What does that mean?" Double-K asked.

"I told them to continue their mission. They got their hands full. It means we're on our own."

"We knew this is how it would go down," Mitch said as he locked a new mag in place. "What say we at least find another place to start work again? No sense making it easy for them to find us."

"Let's boogie," I agreed. We were on our feet and running. I spoke aloud as we ran. "We find a new firing point and we keep them pinned down where they are. Even if they have M4s, we own them past five hundred meters. Probably closer, even. You said they don't shoot worth a shit, right?"

Mitch grunted as he landed beside me. "Good plan. At least until we run out of ammo. There's a metric shit-ton of them."

We took another two-legged bound to the top of the next dune. Double-K was close behind. What he lacked in the distance we covered so easily in a few hops he made up for in speed. I pointed to a tall dune.

"That's the Alamo."

We were already there and prone by the time Khraal Kahlees arrived, winded. He set the launcher down carefully as he joined us.

"I'm little more than a pack animal. I must learn how to utilize the new weapons. At first, I thought the idea of fighting from such a distance a cowardly act for a warrior. Now I find I am envious. I do not like it."

"I'll teach you, Double-K," Mitch said as he snaked forward on his belly to adjust his bipod.

The Tarn's voice raised to a new octave. "Double-K?"

Mitch settled behind his gun as he spoke. "It's your new name, Khraal Kahlees. It means you're one of our clan now."

I risked lazing the distance rather than guessing, and dialed my elevation. I would wait until the advancing horde were crossing the imaginary line from where I could practically guarantee a hit for every pull of the trigger. There was an open expanse from which they would be no escape to defilade. I'd schwack the first rider who arrived there. 1300 meters. Child's play in the low gravity of Vistara.

"I'll start off, Mitch. You spot for me until they get close enough for you to play, too."

"With pleasure."

We watched as the cavalry halted near one of the burning air cars, still glowing brightly as the remnants of its powerhouse slowly dwindled, circling the drain in pale fury at the end of its life. It was too good an opportunity. I hit the button to the range finder perched on the top of my scope mount, dialed my turret up, settled, let my breath out as I whispered, "Sending."

I recovered from the recoil with time to spare and was rewarded with the sight of a rider toppling in the light of the flickering flames. Heads on horseback snapped in every direction, looking for the source of the silent lightning that had struck.

"1836 meters," I bragged. I settled my reticle on another rider and went back to work.

"Too easy with the big gun, man," Mitch said. "Spot for me. Sending."

His gun coughed. I counted one-one-thousand, two-one thousand, and watched a giant arkall stagger and fall, his rider thrown.

"I'll count that as a hit, Mitch."

"It's what I was aiming for, bro! You better."

His smaller gun was doing just fine. I'd underestimated both of our functional effective ranges. Sometimes it's good to be proven wrong. Besides, I play by *Price is Right* rules. Always bid under.

A group of riders took direction from a wildly gesturing Tarn, and I aimed in on him next. He toppled, but his riders were already speeding away out of the kill zone and toward us. "Let's work them at 1300. Let them get there and turn loose."

We gave them a brief respite, and I took a drink before settling back in. When they reached the flats, we both resumed our labor of joy. Mitch tapping out a steady muffled bark every few seconds, me following just a second behind his.

I only had five loaded magazines and inserted my last.

"Loading," I said to let Mitch know as I fumbled for a box of ammo from which to load loose rounds into my empty mags, high with the thrill of the buffet of plenty we fed from. Back on my optic, I dropped another rider, racked the bolt, and stopped. A few dozen mounts and more Tarn bodies littered the plain. A few hundred meters behind the remnants of our massacre, the burning wrecks backlighting them, more riders were trapped in the cement of fear.

"It takes some folks longer to learn than others," Mitch said. From my peripheral vision, I saw him dial his turret. "Let's work the back of the classroom some more. Sending."

A rider at the front of the halted mass fell spectacularly, four arms snapping out, his head mimicking a melon hit with a sledgehammer.

Their line broke, arkall wheeled in a cascade, and then all we saw were fleeing backsides.

"We did it!" Mitch rose to his knees and dropped his NODs down to survey downrange. "Who'd ever believe it? We grounded their air force and broke their cav assault. Two snipers against a battalion. Tell me who's ever done better?"

"To our right!" Double-K cried. A volley of bees buzzed past my head, the report of M4s behind them, and Mitch toppled backward. I crawled to him as another volley landed around us, dirt kicking up in angry eruptions.

Mitch had a hand on his throat; blood poured from between his fingers. Another volley rained down on us. I grabbed Mitch's rifle and drove it to where cracks of flame came again. The flashes of their muzzles betrayed them, on a mound only a few hundred meters away. I dialed down until the turret stopped and unleashed. I didn't stop until it was quiet.

"Khraal Kahlees, are there more?"

"No. I see no more." He was at my side as we both pulled until Mitch was with us behind the crest. The Velcro of my IFAK made an obscene sound as I pulled it free, lay it open, grabbed a dressing, and flung myself at Mitch's head. He was limp. I collapsed onto him and put my ear to his mouth. My face was wet in warm blood, and the last few odd pulses of the fountain from his neck settled to nothing. He was gone.

"Benjamin Colt, the riders mass again."

"Where?" I asked as I marched up the rise.

Khraal Kahlees lay on top of the dune. "Another unit has arrived, and they mass near the fires."

A swarm of little green bees and large black ovals gathered. My fire demanded fuel.

"Too easy."

I grasped the Javelin, pulled the front cap off as I kneeled.

"Don't stand behind me."

I didn't wait for him to respond. If he did, I couldn't hear him over the blood pounding in my ears, my heart a machine singing "kill them, kill them," with every pump. I'd loaded it with a multipurpose warhead before we left. I sighted in on the burning heap with the densest collection of greenies around it, squeezed the seeker trigger, toggled over to down attack mode, waited for the lock, then hit the death switch.

The explosion, the concussion, and the reverberation that followed, riding to me from across the field like the Valkyries come to carry Mitch home, rattled deep in my chest. I dropped my NODs down and stood to watch, daring the Mydreen to try to take me down. I held the power of a god. If they doubted me, I was ready to spend the other missiles as if I had an unlimited supply.

Later was later. This was now.

Khraal Kahlees gasped. "By all that is sacred! By all that is pure! How is this possible?"

More hot forms than I could count lay like so many felled trees after a hurricane. Those that could, rode. Others ran. What few there were. All retreated, back, back, back. Away from the city. Into the desert. Away from their doom.

Finally, they'd learned.

I detached the CLU and stood. Khraal Kahlees remained fixed on the image through the thermal held to his eye. He lowered it and turned to face me, mouth open, awaiting my explanation. I had only this.

"Because I am death. And before I'm through, the Mydreen will understand that it is time for them to flee to the River Blix and join their ancestors willingly, or I'll send them all to Hell."

33

I carried Mitch in my arms. Without being asked, Khraal Kahlees brought everything else. He followed behind me and I kept my pace slow, like a funeral march, oblivious to the ache in my arms as mile after mile, the sand dragged at my feet, my friend's lifeless body making my biceps burn to numbness. Limited resources be damned! I should have used the Javelin earlier. I should have brought a whole company of Korundi. I should have done something other than what I did. Mitch was proof.

"Ahead. Riders come!"

Khraal Kahlees's warning snapped me out of my reverie. I lay Mitch down and reached for his rifle slung on my back.

"Stay your hand, Benjamin Colt. It is my company, come to our aid."

We rode silently as the sun rose, making best speed as the sands allowed. The noise of automatic fire in the distance was rare now. I only had to look for the GMV to know where Dave and Karlo waited. At the entrance to Clymaira the war wagon sat, our cavalry noticeably small in number around the truck. The nearer we rode, the echo of fizzle guns and the rare M4 told me the sweep through the city to rid it of the Mydreen was underway. There was scant traffic on my radio. I'd half heard it, half ignored it. Other than to let them know I was on my way in, I said nothing else. I couldn't.

Still, I wondered. Where were the Stryker and the other GMV? Poised somewhere within, ready to appear and counterattack?

"Oh no!" Karlo yelled at the sight of us riding into the early morning shadows cast by the glass-like spires of Clymaira. He ran to meet me, the portrait of the toll we paid to walk the road of war painted vividly by the body of our friend still in my arms.

"Give him to me," Karlo said as he reached up to take Mitch. Dave was there, too, the anguish on his face too much for me to bear.

Khraal Kahlees rode beside me. "I go to receive report from my men, Benjamin Colt. I will return," he said and he cantered off, leaving me with my brothers.

"What happened?" Dave asked as Karlo examined Mitch's limp body on the cool morning sands. I told him. Karlo tended Mitch until finally, he pulled a wrap from his large aid bag and spread it gently around the body, the light breeze gently tugging, until he finished tucking the fabric under him like a blanket for our brother to sleep beneath.

Karlo was first to speak. "You did all you could, Ben. That and more. We're too few. That's all there is to it. We're just too few."

Dave laid a hand on my shoulder. "If you'd found the war wagons, this thing would be over. It was the only thing to do."

I understood, but I couldn't admit it. No matter how I'd examined and reexamined it all while holding Mitch on the long ride back, I understood that. But I had to leave it all for later. "What's the situation?"

Dave broke it down for me. "Kleeve Hartus and the Tarns are working through the city. He has Karlo's radio. The Mydreen are gone. There may be some more holdouts in the city, but what resistance they've routed out so far's been lightly armed. Only a few with M4s, like the ones who got you."

Karlo rubbed sand over his hands to clean the dried blood off. "Bryant and his army took the city and left a token force. Come look."

I followed them around the GMV, and next to it in the shade was another wrapped body. I eased the green plastic down off the face. It was badly burned, but I knew who it was before Dave told me.

"We pulled Matt's body out of the wreckage of the air cars we shot down. No sign anyone else from Bryant's crew was here. Guess he was left in charge of the occupation while the rest of the team went elsewhere."

I'd wanted it to be Bryant. Or Mark. Chuck's body would've made me feel less awful. Doug I would've felt bad about. But Matt? He was the most tortured of us all. When I thought about the day before we disappeared through the gate, I couldn't help but remember how I'd talked him out of sending his wife and kids to that Iowa farm.

Replacing the tall green corn, red barns, and gentle people I'd imagined was Bryant's laughing face. The rage I needed was there again.

"We have to get after them."

✣ ✣ ✣

First, we mopped up. We took patrols out to police the battlefield. We recovered a few M4s, including the three that had done so much damage in such inexpert hands, and let Kleeve Hartus reorganize what was left of the defense forces of Clymaira.

"The administrator was executed," the first shield reported when gathered in the city center after three sleepless days and nights of searching the city for the last of the Mydreen. Buttoned up in the GMV, we patrolled the streets, leading the way for our dismounted troops. We were attacked only once. Ineffective fizzle fire rained down on us from a balcony, and a few bursts from our door-mounted guns and a single 40 mm HE ended the fight.

The Korundi were good. Very good. I watched them work with little direction from us, efficiently and effectively clearing structures building by building, letting the local guides Kleeve Hartus assigned assure the residents that these were the good guys, here to help.

Clymaira seemed wholly undamaged. The description Talis Darmon gave didn't do it justice. The city was one giant crystal cathedral after another. Rich translucent blues, purples, and greens blending harmoniously. In any other setting, it would be a marvel to explore and admire. If Talis Darmon and I walked these streets in peace, I could do just that. With her. But the anger I held made it a cruel art gallery of soothing colors and impossible shapes that only made me hate their beauty.

The residents stayed hidden, despite Kleeve Hartus's pleas for them to come out of their homes. The first shield had taken charge and was trying to prepare the city defense for another attack. So far, the people of Clymaira seemed to believe it would be accomplished without them. The large screen at the end of the conference table held the face of an elderly man dressed in a crimson toga. The chief counselor to the administrator remained in his home. In the background, an equally mature woman sat in a white upholstered chair, wringing her hands.

"We must resume the functions of the council," the first shield argued. "General Den Gillead is dead, as are all ranking officers of the Guard. I am assuming command and will begin reorganizing and calling volunteers. I cannot run the city, nor is it my task. It is up to you to gather the elders and take charge as you see fit."

The older man balked. "I am master of the treasury. I am no politician, and I am no leader. I've never sought appointment higher, and I refuse it now. Find someone else."

Khraal Kahlees grunted, but kept his repugnance unspoken.

The first shield carried on as though their ages were reversed. "I suggest you find your sense of civic virtue. I'm sending a squad of Korundi allies to your home to escort you here in safety. They have orders to bring you in chains if need be. Your people need you. We will work together to find who on the council remains and who can be appointed to replace those seats necessary to help restore order and function. Whether you remain as the administrator of the new council or not, for now, you will take charge of the process."

"Wait until the king hears of this!" the chief counselor warned, and the screen went blank.

"Ass!" Kleeve Hartus yelled at the vacant screen. "They conspired together to undermine the guards for generations, to use us as a vehicle of favoritism, and now it is a cost born by all of Clymaira." He kneaded his forehead. "Forgive me. I do not wish to sound disloyal. General Den Gillead was my uncle. He was a fine man with many rare qualities. But he was a politician, not a soldier." He sighed heavily before his dark face turned sallow.

"The barbarity and savagery of your fellow Thulians could not be more evident. I have a clear picture of how things transpired soon after I departed for Califex. When Domeel Doreen's terms were rejected, the Thulians led the invasion. The combined forces of the king's army and our Guards did little to deter them. They mercilessly cut down what resistance remained. Executed those who surrendered to prevent them from later rising against them. Then began a systematic campaign to identify and remove the mechanism of the king's governance, executing all the leaders they could find. It happened within the rise and fall of a single sun. Yet they left the city intact, with instructions that if there was defiance, any who acted against them would be brought to justice. They intended to rule here. As they do over all Vistara."

There were tears of hatred in his eyes. "That you brought such men with you to our world was a curse visited on us for all the past sins of my ancestors."

I had no counter. Bryant had taken all the worst lessons from Earth's history and put them into action. Everything we'd been trained to work against, he'd adopted as his methodology for swift, total control. A blitzkrieg of terror.

Khraal Kahlees cleared his throat roughly. "First Shield, nothing that comes to us is blessing or curse. There is only what is. And what has come packaged to us with this burden is the twin of the evil that befalls us. These Thulians. They spill their blood on the sands of Vistara to quench the steel we forge together. Without them, you would be alone to stand against this storm."

He dipped his head to where I sat and crossed all arms.

"A warrior now walks with his glorious ancestors in the underworld."

I returned the gesture.

Kleeve Hartus also made the sign of respect at mention of Mitch's passing. He took a deep breath. The wind he filled his sails with I expected to power another attack at us. Instead, the clouds parted from his brow.

"My words were spoken in haste, friends. I am grateful for your bravery and courage, as I am of the whole of the Korund. I am fatigued. The cowardice of the coin handler vexes me, though I understand. Only in the tragedies of our ancient history have any seen the horrors of war laid at their doorstep. Our war has been one of science, not arms. And in this war, we have become indolent and selfish. We concern ourselves with matters of comfort, accepting that eventually this world will die. Perhaps we are already dead."

I wasn't the physician Talis Darmon was, but I recognized the symptoms of his illness. And I could offer the only relief I knew to give. Truth.

"Kleeve Hartus, whatever decay you've seen infect your society, you do not suffer it. If you've been born in a time of political expedience and deficiency of purpose, you've stayed true to what is right and good.

And now that your people need someone with that character, they have him. On my world, we're taught that the word *soldier* is both noble and ancient. That it means *here am I*. And by what you do, you prove that you're a true soldier."

The change in his bearing made me think I'd given him the tiny dose of medicine he needed.

"Thank you, Benjamin Colt," the first shield said. "I appreciate your confidence. I hope only to do what is proper. But I say to you with honesty—I know only that I do not know how."

He was overwhelmed. And who wouldn't be?

"First Shield, there have been many great generals on my world. Some were great fighters. Some were great organizers. But the most successful ones won the day because they knew they couldn't do it alone. I can't take responsibility for the war we've brought to your world. We didn't choose to come here. But I can tell you that as soldiers, we promise to do what is right. I've given my oath to the princess and I give it to you as well—if I can help save your world, I will."

A youthful member of the Guard entered the chamber and stood at attention waiting to be recognized. Kleeve Hartus let him wait. "I believe you, Benjamin Colt. I only pray there is time." He turned to the Guard. The soldier was one of the few dozen members of the force that remained. His bruises and the many dressings binding his wounds spoke for him. He was a fighter. "Report, Guardian. Have the wizards of the atmosphere guild responded?"

The man bowed. "I regret they have not, First Shield."

"But the plant appears unharmed, does it not?"

"It does, First Shield."

"That is good news. The king's tinkerers no doubt cower in their citadel still. No matter. Their order deserves to be informed, but if the learned men of the guild choose to live entombed in their works, I will leave them until they tire of living in the darkness and seek the light of the outside world. What we do next, I doubt they can influence."

Karlo spoke. "Kleeve Hartus, we've seen the atmosphere factory in Mal Maleska. It seemed impregnable. You make it sound like the scientists who maintain the works live like the hermits that run the water guild." I'd told the guys about our experience with Cynar.

"Hardly. The head of their guild here in Clymaira holds a seat on the council, though he rarely occupies it. The scientists live in comfort as though they were kings themselves, in the grandest towers of the city, unlike the hardship of those once assigned to tend the plant in old Filestra. When Domeel Doreen banished them from his capital, the rest of the guild took note. At the first sign of the troubles here, they retreated to the safety of the factory."

"Isn't there a door to knock on?" Dave asked.

"If only it were that simple," the first shield griped. "None but they know how it is accessed. Theirs is a secretive cult. And powerful. They control the future of Vistara!"

I was about to move our meeting forward to more important matters—our next course of action to locate and annihilate the Mydreen—when a commotion started outside the hall. My hand went to my pistol.

"Allow me to pass, Korundi, I have urgent news for Khraal Kahlees," someone cried.

"Let him through," Double-K yelled.

The red-sashed Tarns stepped aside and another rushed in.

"Khraal Kahlees, I need to speak with you. I am sent by Parkus Laan with urgent news."

"Speak."

The messenger hesitated. "It is for your ears alone, Lieutenant."

"Speak, I say. You stand in the presence of our bonded war kin. I command it."

The Tarn blurted out his message, almost too fast for my decipher to translate. "Califex has been attacked. Our chieftain is murdered. The senior clan leaders call the Korund to the war council. You are to return at once."

I sprang to my feet. "What of Talis Darmon? Where is the princess?"

The messenger's shoulders dipped and his arms folded over his face to conceal his mouth, a Tarn habit when giving ill news.

Khraal Kahlees shouted. "Stand tall, warrior, and speak!"

The trooper popped to attention. "It is unknown on which side of the Blix she lies."

34

I stood on the bow of the air car with a MK 46 SAW at my feet, next to as many boxes of belts as I could toss into the air car with both hands before we took off. M4 on my chest and a grenade in the pipe of the 203 beneath it, I searched ahead through my binos, looking for sign of movement or anything out of place in the rolling desert sands. We were not playing it safe. We cruised at an altitude I guessed was around 5,000 feet above the ground, about where I'd be checking my wrist altimeter on a freefall in preparation to deploy my parachute.

Our pilot was the soldier who'd reported to Kleeve Hartus. I countered his protest when I directed him to fly us as high as we could possibly go.

"The atmosphere is too thin at this altitude!"

He was young, younger by far than Kleeve Hartus, who assured me that the junior guard was an excellent pilot.

"Can the air car stay aloft?" I asked, remembering a C-17 that couldn't.

"Yes. The issue is that we may not be able to remain conscious."

"I've been higher than this in the Korund. Get tough, kid," I told him. "It's that or eat lead from a minigun." Cruising this high I hoped would make us very near impossible to hit with their M134, but the trade-off was that we were visible for many, many miles around.

Khraal Kahlees manned the fizzle gun at the waist. Like me, he was trying to stay occupied. The weapon was more powerful than the light model the Tarns carried, but it was still little more than a prop at this altitude. If he was perturbed by flight, it wasn't apparent by the scowl of his bared tusks. He was ready for a fight. Two of his vanguard manned the starboard gun, looking less sure about the gravity we defied as we flew at the fastest speed I could badger Avril Mysteen to push the air car.

The sun was set to drop behind the Korund Range at any moment. I set my binos down and picked up the thermal, vainly hoping it was more than just my futile attempt at distraction to keep the twisting in my guts from dropping me like a deer hit by a car. If Talis Darmon were dead… I erased the image. I knew just where to put it. The familiar tar pit bubbled, the arms of drowned monsters took the image down with them, and I pulled the white carpet over it all.

Our pilot yelled past the console windscreen, "Benjamin Colt, soon I will not be able to navigate. We should put down until the moons rise and there is light to safely steer by."

I'd already planned for this. I gave Double-K the high sign to come forward and I handed him my NODs.

"I know every ripple of the sands and the location of every crevice big enough to hide a godahl. On belly or from the air, I can guide us safely anywhere in the Korund," he said. He'd assured me that he could follow the terrain to a good spot where we could land and make inquiries.

We both agreed that landing in the capital was ill advised.

"Return to your den expecting your throne usurped by predators," was the saying Double-K shared. So far, every bit of Korund wisdom he laid on me, I agreed with. Despite the assurances from the messenger that the White lords and their war machines had departed, that had been almost three days ago—the time it had taken the messenger to ride day and night to Clymaira. Anything could have happened since then.

What had been reinforced to me over and over on Vistara was that without long distance communication, actionable intel was rarer than an honest politician.

Leaning over the side of the air car, Khraal Kahlees coached the young Avril Mysteen.

"Aim for that tallest peak and maintain this distance above the ground. We pass over low foothills, and on the other side, the Dragahl Valley will be apparent as it leads east. Then we will slow and descend by half our current height. Do not fear. The valley is wide and there will be ample time for you to respond to my directions."

"I have no fear," the kid spat back.

"Take no offense, Guardian. It is clear to all that Kleeve Hartus selected you for your fortitude. But tell us with candor, will your wounds prevent you from combat?"

"Hardly, Tarn!"

Double-K pulled his jaw back in amusement and nodded to me. "He'll do."

The two Tarn soldiers made no such protest about their fitness. They'd left their spot on the waist and assumed the same position I'd seen Beraal take when we first loaded onto Cynar's boat—hugging knees and burying faces. Double-K guided us as we veered east and up the valley, veering gently into new passes every so often, yet continuing the path higher and eastward.

"There!" he was first to shout.

The dim flickers of amber indicated the small village Khraal Kahlees meant us to halt at to taste the air of the Korund for the scent of danger.

"I just today returned from Califex," the matron of the house reported. "We went to the relief of the capital when called. My husband and eldest remain. I returned to defend our village until I too am called to war. We all await the horns to sound."

A dozen Tarns gathered around us, making similar pledges.

"The Mydreen will pay for killing our chieftain under a light of peace!"

"The Mydreen are vermin! They always have been."

"They show their true selves at last."

"They've always been craven in their skirmishes. But now they abandon the acceptable way of challenge and bring true war!"

"They couldn't have done it without the Thulians!"

An old warrior, bent and thin, stepped up. "Tell us, Thulian, we are told you fight against your kin. Where is your war machine? We've heard they came with two! Many warriors died! The will of the Korund alone cannot stop them!"

"Yes, we can," a small boy with short tusks stepped forward. "I'm ready to take the warrior challenge now and join my sister in the fight. I won't wait another year!"

Khraal Kahlees calmed them. "We go to Califex now. Do as you have been bid and prepare. That is your task. When the council calls, all the Korund will join to answer this slight."

More of the villagers shouted questions at me. Where had we been when Califex was attacked? Why didn't we rush to their aid as we'd done to aid Clymaira? Were humans all we cared about? Was Jedak Jeraal foolish to have trusted us?

"We'd best go, Benjamin Colt. Pay them no mind. They will soon know of your people's dedication to all Vistara, Red and Korundi alike."

We lifted off, this time with the amber light of a large stone surrounded by a reflector to light our way, and Khraal Kahlees resumed navigating us. We skirted many villages, rightly unsure if we might draw fire, until the bowl of the Califex Valley was ahead. We circled over the central square where a perimeter of warriors guarded the great hall of the chieftain. A squat dark shape danced between the warriors and my heart jumped at the thought that it might be Apache.

I leaped out, and a Tarn I recognized from the council approached with a contingent at his side.

"Hail, Khraal Kahlees!"

"Hail, Parkus Laan! I answer your summons and bring Benjamin Colt to council."

The ranking Tarn lieutenant thrust his jaw and tusks forward. "And much we have to discuss."

The gadron pulled free of the Tarn restraining him, and I shouted for joy. "Apache! Where's the princess, boy?"

My companion through so much hardship dropped to his back to show me his belly, his ears flat, whimpering as though he understood and asked my forgiveness.

"Where were you, boy? Why weren't you guarding the princess?" I patted his belly. The Tarn who'd been restraining him came forward. He limped and had an arm in a sling across his stomach.

"Your gadron was penned, Benjamin Colt. Dosenie Beraal entrusted him to me whilst you were absent on your mission. He was distraught and underfoot and the dosenie asked for my help. I could not care for him at all times, so I kept him with our own companions. If he had been present when the attack came, he would be dead now, like so many others…"

"Is Talis Darmon dead?" I asked, hoping against hope.

Parkus Laan was subdued in his answer. "She has not been found. Nor has her dosenie. Come. There is much to tell."

My heart was in my throat. She wasn't among the dead. Had she escaped? Was she captive?

Khraal Kahlees nudged me. "This must be done." He gestured the rest of our party by the air car to him. And pointed at one of his Tarns. "Take Avril Mysteen to the physician and see to his comfort. You need rest, young warrior."

The Guard protested, "My place is with you to represent the first shield."

"No. First you must restore yourself. You will join us later."

The kid was firm, but wrongheaded at the wrong time.

I put a hand out. "Do as Khraal Kahlees says. You're letting pride confuse your duty. We will need you ready for what comes next. Go and rest. That's an order."

"But—"

I cut him off. "If you're going to lead someday, you must first follow. Your honor isn't in question, Guardian, but I can't waste any more time to teach you how to be a good soldier right now. Until I learn to pilot the air car, I need you sharp. I expect you ready to fly when I call you. Go."

"Yes, lord. I obey."

Apache fell in alongside us as we walked.

Khraal Kahlees said, "The Guard were never as fierce or capable as they believed themselves, but if there are more like Kleeve Hartus and this youth, they can be made so."

"But it's always time that's against us," I said sadly. Dave and Karlo already had plans to get the Guard built quickly. The guns and ammo we'd recovered were finding their way into the hands of Khraal Kahlees's vanguard. It wasn't much, but it was a start.

The great hall was lighted by torch and stone. The chieftain's grand perch of ivory and bone sat empty. I took a seat next to Khraal Kahlees in the circle and accepted a cup. I couldn't remember the last time I'd eaten. I could go without sleep or without food, but not both. My stomach growled, and I followed Double-K's lead and took one of the offered plates. The urgency of the situation didn't prevent the Korundi from being practical, and the more time I spent with Khraal Kahlees and his clan, the more I felt this to be true.

Theirs was the culture I'd always dreamed I'd someday be immersed in. As bad as things were, the thrill of our future together warmed me like the fires around us. Every meeting of soldiers should be by firelight, with meat and fresh water, swords and animal skin chairs.

A stab of shame jolted me from my silly musing. Because my eyes had become accustomed to the flickering light. Bullet holes riddled the walls.

Enough delay to my question.

"What of Talis Darmon?" I asked.

Parkus Laan spoke. "I was not in Califex when we were attacked. I ask Draal Silva to tell all."

I'd seen the Tarn take his seat with us. His head was bandaged across an eye. He was missing a middle arm, freshly amputated and bound at the elbow. He held his pain back with a gritted jaw as he spoke.

"Your party had been gone but two days, Khraal Kahlees. I was here when the air car came. It was piloted by a Thulian. He brought Domeel Doreen and a small contingent to the hall to entreat with Jedak Jeraal. The princess was there to receive them as well."

I kept silent, but my head swam as I waited for him to continue.

"What he said were the words of the Mydreen we know so well, not those of a cousin Tarn bound by treaty."

Khraal Kahlees growled, and I felt the same rumble in my throat.

"The Thulian with him spoke words of subtle threat. He said that Clymaira had fallen, as had Thoria. That their army was poised to fell the Red Kingdom. Domeel Doreen then made his ultimatum. The Korund could join or be counted enemy, but we could not stand silent.

"The princess cursed them. Jedak Jeraal laughed, and told them, 'The Korund does not tremble at the empty desert wind.' It was then they attacked."

I could see it all.

"The Thulian had been acting suspiciously, speaking softly into the device at his lips. I could not understand the words, but I knew it portended treachery. The Mydreen army had already entered the city." He stood on shaky legs and steadied himself against the chair as he pointed to the empty seat. "Without challenge and like an animal seized by fever, the Thulian shot Jedak Jeraal as the Mydreen guard cut down all in this hall."

I could wait no longer. "The princess? Dosenie Beraal? Out with it!"

Parkus Laan's posture told me all. "I do not know if they were harmed in the violence here in the hall. I was left for dead. Everything is a blur. But until I cross the Blix, I will remember that day."

Khraal Kahlees roared as his fists pounded his chest.

"What did the Thulian look like?" I asked, my nails biting into my palms.

Draal Silva thrust tusks forward. "He was foul. White. Smooth of face and dark of mane."

He described Mark.

Parkus Laan continued. "With so few warriors left in Califex, the city fell quickly. The Mydreen and the war machines of the Thulians killed all indiscriminately, and left. I came from Halosa with all my riders to find Califex in chaos. But that is not all."

I was blank. "What else could there be?"

"The nesting grounds of Califex were ravaged. Hundreds of eggs, destroyed. Not one was left. They mean to end our line for all time."

Khraal Kahlees covered his face with four hands. It was genocide.

"Our path is clear. Is it not, Khraal Kahlees?"

My friend had composed himself. "The way is set. We kill all Mydreen. Then we leave no Mydreen egg in nest undefiled from which they can spawn their filth again upon Vistara. It is time to call the might of the Korund to war."

✣ ✣ ✣

As the sun rose, we were still in the council hall. Talis Darmon and Beraal had certainly been taken prisoner. As much as I wanted to leave and take the air car on a desperate search for the Mydreen army, certain the princess and Beraal were again captives, I knew my hopes for a rescue were delusions. Khraal Kahlees spoke quietly to me as the discussion waged on.

"I know you are greatly troubled, friend. She lives, Benjamin Colt. Of that, I am sure. She is a valuable hostage. They will use her as Domeel Doreen has already—to strike at the king. Dead, she is of no value. Now they will use her to force the king's surrender. It must be so."

I tried not to think of her. Would Mark harm her? Would Bryant? Would Chuck or Dougie be brave enough to protect her, despite their turn away from sanity?

"What we do now can be the only way to bring her to safety, Benjamin Colt. And to do so, we need your service."

I took his meaning. It was time for me to get into the fight.

"Thank you, my friend. My despair is over. I promise. Now there is only what we do next."

"Good. Doubt not, we will transform that despair into victory."

I fought an internal battle. Did I break a confidence and tell Khraal Kahlees that he had a daughter now in the clutches of the Mydreen? I decided no. If there were a time and I felt it was my place, that it would do some good, I'd revisit the question. For both of us, the actions taken next were more important than the reasons behind them. Right was right.

While the decision to call the entirety of the Korund to gather in Califex was agreed upon, the question as to where to march them troubled us all.

"To Clymaira, then," was suggested by one of the lieutenants. "If Khraal Kahlees has upset the enemy's plans and retaken it, then it is where we can next rally while we search for the Mydreen army."

Another waved him off. "No, we must waste no time in garrison. Directly to the Red Kingdom we must go. It is the aim of Domeel Doreen to have it. It is there we must reach, before the Mydreen take it as well. They are days ahead of us. And by the time we gather, many more will pass. It is on the fields of Shansara we must be before they begin their next siege."

Parkus Laan spoke. "If Shansara is locked in siege, it is there where we can best gain advantage. The forces of the king no doubt are prepared for such by now. We can best aid their relief and avenge ourselves on the Mydreen by allowing them to begin. It will force them to fight on two fronts—the Red defenders ahead and our army from behind."

There were grunts of approval all around, and mine was one of them.

Then someone cried, "Parkus Laan, Master Haran Koze of the atmosphere guild presents."

I turned from the map table to see a trio of green-robed and gold adorned humans with long red beards of a color too bright to be natural. It had to be some clownish dye job. The front man seemed every bit the pampered boor the scientists of the atmosphere guild had been made out to be by everyone I'd heard describe them. If Cynar were here, I'm sure his invectives against them would spark a brawl. What a welcome sight that would be—the rangy Cynar against the ostentatious buffoon of his enemy, an atmosphere scientist. I bet Cynar could take him.

The leader tapped his staff on the stone floor three times to announce his presence. "Who now speaks for the Korund Tarn? Who will affirm the oath of the Korund to King Osric Darmon to shield our guild from harm? I demand assurance of such, as it is evident that Jedak Jeraal has failed in his duty."

I hated him already.

It was Khraal Kahlees who stepped forward. "We have pressing matters of war to attend to, Master Haran Koze. The matter of chieftainship will be settled later. For now, we speak as one. And as such, I assure you that the oath of the Korund outlives any individual. Our service to the king and to your guild remains as always, and we are grateful for the future you provide for all Vistara."

Parkus Laan crossed his arms on his chest but did not dip his head. "Does that satisfy, wizard?"

"It would, if you had but protected the hallowed grounds of the atmosphere works during the criminal assault by the children of the desert. Our sacred citadel was violated."

"Of what violation do you speak?" Khraal Kahlees asked.

One of the junior scientists stepped out of the trail. "An air car came dangerously close to the dispersal fractionator columns. The harmonics of the field were disturbed by the ray of the repulsion engine. Besides the catastrophe of a collision, it is for reason just like this that there is a sphere of exclusion around the works! Why, the cursed thing was there so long, it exposed every alignment field to its emissions. I've toiled for three days and I'm still uncertain if it will be balanced this cycle. Why did you not restrain whatever fool ignored the law? It exists for the good of all!"

Parkus Laan sighed. "Is it not clear that a battle raged, wizard? Is there any other damage to the works, scientist?"

"None that we can find," the grand wizard said with disdain. "No thanks to your neglect. It is only fair to warn you that we must inform the head of our order in Shansara. He sits on the king's council and has his ear. Do not be surprised when remonstration from the king arrives. Whomever you choose as next chieftain of the Korund will bear the responsibility for correcting such deficiencies as allowed this to occur."

That brought a grunt from many. "Then it sounds as though you have the situation on its way to resolution," Khraal Kahlees said to dismiss him as he turned his back, the others following his lead, but not me. There was something amiss.

Someone mumbled, "Where were the wizards when Califex was attacked? Hiding in their factory, no doubt."

"Perhaps the guild needs to provide for their own defense if they have such concerns about traffic around the works."

"The Mydreen are no better pilots than any Korundi. It is miraculous that they did not crash into the factory while they were at play in the air."

A pit formed in my stomach deep as the Valles Marineris.

I asked aloud, "Why would an air car invade the airspace around the works?" I already knew the answer to my query but, before I could give name to my fear, a rumbling earthquake shook the ground and screams filled the air. I bolted past the scientists and sprang outside.

I'd seen this a hundred times in documentaries. The towers telescoped down into themselves, clouds of dust and spikes of purple lightning rising. The precision with which the atmosphere works crumbled onto itself spoke of the mastery of a demo man.

Chuck.

A stampede caught up to me.

"This cannot be!" A guildsman with a fire-engine-red beard gaped.

Khraal Kahlees was transfixed by the billowing mushroom clouds of ash, still climbing as it grew to block the early sun. "Was this the work of the Thulians?"

"They're shaping the battlefield," I said. "They had a time delay on their charges. They wanted as many witnesses as possible to see this."

The guild master wept, "The savages! They mean to hasten the end of this world. Why would they do this thing?"

I felt sure I understood.

"They're telling us all. If they can't rule this world, they'll kill it."

35

"Show me how to fly this thing."

We were high over the desert speeding back to Clymaira. I worked a compromise. Khraal Kahlees would stay and help the Korundi assemble as quickly as possible and move for Clymaira. It was not so far out of the way on the route to Shansara to make it a bad waypoint. Our objective was the capital of the Red Kingdom, but without additional intel, we faced the possibility of marching the army to its demise. If the Stryker caught them on the open plain, the Mk 19, .50 cal, and MGs would coat them like soft butter on white bread.

Being undergunned sucks.

Bryant's scorched-earth campaign had outmaneuvered us at every turn. Yes, it was because we were so badly outnumbered, outgunned, and out-strategized, but—his plans had as yet gone virtually unchallenged by us. That was going to change. I burned to get back to tell the guys what I wanted to set into motion.

It was time to disrupt Bryant's decision-making loop by doing something he wouldn't anticipate.

Apache had his head hanging over the side of the air car, his drool coating my arm. The moment just missed being the kind of Sunday drive on the way to the DQ, my favorite gal by my side, and my second favorite companion in the back of the truck enjoying the breeze. It was the dread hollow in my heart caused by the missing piece of our trio that made it joyless. If I broke contact with Apache's hide to watch over Avril Mysteen's shoulder, the big baby whined fiercely.

His soulful eyes said, *I'm sorry, Dad. I feel terrible. Don't leave me behind again. I'll do better next time. Promise.*

"It's okay, boy. It wasn't your fault you weren't with the princess. I don't blame you."

He received my assurances with a wag of his stubby tail.

"But I have work to do. Stay and be good."

His tongue went back to its role as a drool-streaming wind flag.

The air car was operated by a standing pilot. Like much of the technology I'd seen on Vistara, it looked to me like cheap Hollywood props—glowing crystals arranged in raised geometric patterns over the flat console. Avril Mysteen sporadically traced a finger over the patterns in meaningless action. At least the joystick he held represented something concrete to my eye.

How hard could it be?

"I don't need the how behind things, but I need to know the basics. Start me off."

The youth was even more serious than normal, his brow troubled. "That is fortunate, because I don't know the science of the ray. I've not taught another to pilot, so if I am unclear on anything, please let it be known. As you know, the repulsion drive is located behind us. The controller is simple. To maintain level flight, all you need do is not disturb it. An easy hand is all that is necessary. A sudden movement can produce severe consequences. Take the control. Gently."

He moved aside as I slipped my hand where his had just been. I'd heard it said that when learning to pilot a helicopter, the aphorism they taught new pilots was that you held the stick as gently as if it were the female breast in your hand. I said as much.

His eyebrows shot up. "Indeed. As the first shield taught me."

By the time we'd made several trials of descents, landings, and takeoffs along our route, I had the fundamentals. The rest would be cemented by repetition. It wasn't harder than driving a bass boat or a Zodiac, except for learning to correctly read the intensity of the central red jewel to indicate the power needed from the drive to counter the abundance or lack of the

"ray" that provided our levitation and thrust. Bright red meant I had plenty of available power and could back off to keep my present speed and altitude, or raise the amplification of the ray to make the drive hum louder and power the pilot's wishes. It was like learning to anticipate how much pressure to apply to the accelerator of a car when going up or downhill.

The air car was not highly maneuverable. I asked Avril Mysteen to demonstrate what he thought of as grit-your-teeth aggressive maneuvers. None of them produced responses that made the air car seem much different from how my grandad's big Caddy floated through a tight turn. These craft were built for stability and a smooth ride, not for air-to-air combat. By afternoon, we were over Clymaira, and I landed us smoothly in the courtyard beside the council building.

I'd made a slow turn as I descended, just like I'd seen many choppers do to allow the crew to check the landing zone for obstacles. Dave and Karlo were waiting.

"I thought you didn't care about flying, Airborne," Dave teased when I hopped out from behind the console.

"I don't, but it's time we all started expanding our wheelhouse of talents. You guys are going to learn how to fly ASAP, too. Let's get inside and I'll bring you up to speed."

"I see you found your best friend," Karlo said as Apache plopped onto his hind end to allow the flat of his massive head to be massaged by both men. Then Karlo asked, "The princess?"

I shook my head. "She's alive. I think."

I left it at that for now.

Inside we found Kleeve Hartus at work directing someone on the viewscreen.

"You're the new director of works. I'll expect a working solution at tonight's meeting," the first shield said. Then he turned to acknowledge me. "You're back much sooner than expected. What news?"

He looked a little more rested and confident. I was about to test that impression. I'd saved the awful news until we were all together. I had no way to cushion the shock and just told them.

"Madness. Madness." The first shield shook his head in disbelief. He could never have seen the old movie, but the words were as apt here as it had been when the doctor said it after viewing the aftermath of the destruction on the River Kwai. What was the point of it all?

Karlo was equally astonished. "They've gone insane. They know the atmosphere plants are all that's keeping this world alive. It's terrorism on the grandest scale. How could they?"

"They're dead-enders." Dave nailed it. "Bryant's leading a death cult. They don't care if they live or die. And Domeel Doreen's too much of a dumb thug to care about the future beyond the next conquest."

"Or they know something we don't," Karlo said. "I can't believe they've become this desperate."

"Have the scientists of the atmosphere guild come out of their hole?" I asked. "I've got questions. The wizards in Califex clammed up. They were ready to slit their wrists. I tried, but got nothing out of them. We need to talk to someone who has answers. Now."

The first shield raised his head out of his hands. "What do you need to know?"

"Everything. I'm sick of the secrecy. If there's something the guild can enlighten us about, they need to do so. Maybe this will shock them out of the idea that they're somehow exempt from the war the rest of us are engaged in."

Kleeve Hartus was on his feet. "I know where the entrance to their labyrinth is. I will take a squad and hammer on their vault until they either grow deaf or respond."

"Shh!" Dave shushed us, his eyes wide. "Listen." He pulled the comm cable out of his radio and placed it on the table.

The speaker squawked.

"I know you can hear me, so don't play dumb."

It was Bryant's voice. Superior and annoying as always.

"Bryant!" Karlo spat. "He's got to be close!"

Kleeve Hartus opened the viewscreen and a solid-looking Guard responded.

"First Shield, I was just about to contact you. We have reports of an air car hovering on the horizon. Our patrols report no enemy ground forces in sight."

The first shield looked to me. "What shall I tell my men?"

"Tell them to wait."

From the radio speaker, Bryant growled, "I know you're monitoring the net. Come back to me, Dave. You guys will want to hear what I've got to tell you, over."

"Let's go burn that flyer down," I said. The GMV was just outside.

Through thin air, Bryant seemed to sense my desire. "I'm not in the air car you've undoubtedly seen by now. But I do have a repeater in it. I've got a chain of them running. I sent one airborne near Clymaira to parlay with you. I'd appreciate it if you don't shoot it down. Come back, over."

"Think he's telling the truth?" Karlo asked.

Dave tilted his head. "I'd wanted to set up a chain of repeaters between Thoria and Maleska Mal. I s'pose he just used my same commo plan from wherever he's making his FOB now. He wasn't an Echo, but he's had enough cross-training to know how to do it. Doug could've, for sure. I've cross-trained him. Do you want me to answer?"

I thought. "Talk to him. Don't give him anything. Especially, don't let him know I'm alive."

"Here goes." Dave grimaced. Then said, "I got you, Chief. Good copy, over."

"Good to hear your voice, Dave. Karlo there with you?"

Dave looked to me and I gave him the negative.

"Nope, Chief. By myself."

"Sure, sure." He didn't buy it. "Well, listen up. Knock it off. I don't want to come after you guys, but I will if you get in my way. I'm going to have Shansara wrapped up soon. I don't have the Korund Tarns on my side, but they know to stay off our back now. You want Clymaira for yourselves? We can talk about it. I just want to know you don't have some kind of bullshit in mind. You decide to get greedy and try for more? You pissed about your buddy Colt dying in the mountains? Make a move against us and I'll crush you. You read me, over?"

Good girls! The princess and Beraal had Bryant convinced I was dead, and he was buying it!

I made an intuitive guess. "He thinks you guys went rogue and stole his kill of Clymaira for yourselves. He's assuming you got the same idea as him. Keep him talking, let's see what we can get him to give up."

Dave hit the PTT. "What's your suggestion then, Chief?"

"I get it. You guys want a piece of this world for yourselves. You, Karlo, and Mitch. I understand that you were pissed about Colt. There was no avoiding it. He had to go. Sorry he's dead. Sort of. But you guys and I can work out a deal to divide things up once we've won. And that's gonna happen soon. I'm not holding a grudge. I'm just saying, don't be stupid. Set yourselves up in Clymaira if that's what you want.

We'll find a way to work things out later. Just don't get involved any further. Agreed?"

Dave looked to me for a response. Before I could give him one, Bryant came back.

"Where's Matt? I left him in charge."

I told Dave what to say.

"No, Chief. We lost Matt, and Mitch. Like you say, it was unavoidable."

There was a pause.

"Sorry to hear that, Dave. They were both good men."

"We're sorry, too, Chief. We didn't know Matt or any of the team were here when we hit the Mydreen. It's all been a bad dream."

"But that's just it—it doesn't have to be. I'm sorry things got heavy-handed back in Thoria. I'll make it all worth your while once we're through. I'm just asking you to stay put. That's all. But you should know, the situation's different now. Baby Blue is just about dead."

Dead? That was different from being limited to making basics. Karlo looked like an arrow pierced him.

Dave acted his part. "What do you mean, Chief? It was fine when we left."

"Yeah, well, I was there and checked. Dougie's coaxing it along, but it's not producing much except MREs, and not even good ones at that. We wondered if Karlo messed with it before you guys left. It was going along fine, cranking out POL, then it conked out. Doug says Karlo'd never mess with Baby Blue because he was married to the damn thing."

Karlo's voice raised an octave. "He doesn't know!"

I was unsure. "Is he playing us?"

Karlo shook his head. "I don't know."

Dave kept him talking. "So, no more boom-boom?"

Bryant chuckled, "That's about the size of it. Maybe when things settle down and I can prove to you I'm not holding any grudges, Karlo can take a look at it. But Doug says he doesn't think even Karlo can get it going again. It's out of star juice, or whatever it runs on. But it means we've had to accelerate things a bit."

"Ask him about the atmosphere plant," I urged.

"Chief, we know you brought down the atmosphere plant in Califex. A runner just told us. Why'd you hit it? We all need air, Chief!"

Bryant's voice patronized. "Dave, Dave, Dave. If you guys hadn't gone off half-cocked, you'd understand. But I'll get you up to speed now. We grabbed one of those air factory scientists in Thoria. It took a little encouragement by Marky, but we got the old wizard to tell us the truth."

"What scientist?" I asked.

Dave and Karlo both shrugged.

"Marky-Mark and the Chief were busy in Thoria. They were up to a lot they didn't clue us in on," Karlo said. "We were on the 'no need to know' list."

Dave picked right up. "What'd he tell you, Chief?"

"Those bearded goofballs are pulling the wool over everyone's eyes to keep themselves in the lap of luxury. The atmosphere plants are already about petered out. The one in Califex hadn't been making oxygen in years. The one in Thoria and Clymaira are just puttering along. It's the ones in the Yellow Kingdom that are still producing, and even they're not doing that great."

It seems the curmudgeonly water priest had been closer to the truth than he knew.

"Cynar told me the atmosphere guild are incompetent," I said. "But I doubt even he suspected it was this bad."

Bryant continued. "So, nothing lost, get me? It was a chance for good psyops. Even on this backward world, the word will have reached everywhere by now—don't mess with us, because we'll burn it all down. But here's the other thing—the atmosphere guild has worldwide instant commo with every other factory. They're holding that back from the rest of the planet, too. They're a bunch of snakes, manipulating everyone on Mars for their own benefit. As soon as we take Shansara, I'm going to set things right with the king and let him in on how his own scientists have been deceiving him."

Kleeve Hartus growled, "I'm going to hang the first wizard I get my hands on."

I waved him down. "Ask him about the princess."

"Chief, do you have the princess as a hostage?"

"We do. I'm going to offer her to the king for a chance to negotiate our terms. That and the knowledge of how his own scientists have been hoodwinking him—at least about the communication tech they've been secreting away. And if I have to drop another air factory to let him know we mean business, I will."

Bryant had it all figured out.

"Ask him if he knows what happened to me?" I suggested. "I'm betting the princess lied about me surviving."

It seemed the Chief was in a talking mood.

"Colt died in the mountains. Got eaten by some kinda monster. She's telling the truth. Without her boyfriend around, she isn't as proud as she was in Maleska Mal, I can tell you that. It's made her see the light, too. She's ready to help me get her father to see reason."

Karlo burst out, "Good for the princess! She's playing chess while Bryant's stuck on checkers. How much you want to bet she doesn't tell her father to lay down for the Mydreen army?"

Bryant started again.

"So, I hope I'm helping you guys to see the light, too. If you just lay back, everything's going to be okay. Once I've got this under control, we can figure out the long game here. Maybe the Yellow Kingdom is our next target. Maybe Karlo can use that big brain of his to get the atmosphere plants going again. Maybe there's a way for him to fix Baby Blue. He's there, isn't he?"

I gave Dave the nod.

"Yes, Chief. He's here."

"Good. See? A little trust right now will help us all. So, do I have your word you guys will stay out of it?"

I nodded.

"You got it, Chief. Karlo and I both agree."

"Let me hear it from him, Dave."

Karlo took the radio. "I agree, Chief."

Bryant belted out a triumphant laugh. "Karlo, you're a wise man. No doubt you're telling Dave how to play it. I knew you'd see reason. It's a big planet. We can all have a piece of it. Listen, men, all is forgiven on my end. No hard feelings. We've all been pushed to the limit. And if we look back, I could have gone about things differently. What's done is done. But this is my only warning. If you crawfish on us, I won't hesitate to kill you."

Dave took the radio. "We understand, Chief. We're looking forward to finding a way for us all to live here together."

"When I've got things set and have access to the atmosphere guild's comm system in Shansara, you'll know. Then we can figure a way forward. That's all for now. Bryant out."

Dave turned the MBITR off. "He thinks we're the same kind of Genghis Khan he wants to be. So, what do we do?"

She'd told me it was harmful. That how I coped with my anxieties and doubts was a slow poison. But without her, I didn't know any other way. The old me knew what to do. How to bury pain. To halt its effect. To harness its energy. Talis Darmon's face was pulled under the tar as it seeped past her screaming lips to drown her. And there she would stay until I had the means to bring her to life again. I'd decided how from the moment I saw the atmosphere plant demolished.

"We go for Baby Blue."

36

"How do we know Baby Blue's still in Thoria?" Dave asked.

I played back in my head several times what Bryant said and ran it past the guys. Karlo agreed.

"How he talked sure made it sound like it was right where he walled it in. He put it in the Guard's garrison next to their operations center. There's an underground garage where they park their flying carpets. Air cars. Whatever they are. I'm calling them flitters from here on out."

"Flitters, it is," Dave agreed.

That settled, Karlo continued. "I think Doug's still in Thoria to run both the occupation and matter mill production. Doug's a smart guy. Next to me, he had the best grounding in its general operations. Bryant must've flown back to Thoria after they took Clymaira, hoping to stock up on more class three and five, only to get the bad news about Baby Blue only cranking out class one. It's a big assumption, but if I were a real O&I guy and had to put the links of the chain together, that'd be my analysis."

"Nice touch limiting the menu to crappy MREs, brah."

Karlo's dark brow wrinkled. "That's what's got me worried. I didn't. It should be limited to fuel and rations, not just bad menus. Maybe it actually is breaking down."

"Oh, boy," Dave said. "From bad to good to worse again."

Kleeve Hartus had remained. "What is Baby Blue?"

I had Karlo tell him the what and why of the matter mill's importance to us all. "Besides being our best option to arm ourselves with weapons to give us a better advantage in the coming fight, I'm hopeful I can use it to bridge the gaps in ancient and current technology on Vistara."

"How can I be of service?"

"I'm through flying blind," I told him. "You were on your way to pounding down the door to the air wizard's lair? Let's do it."

Soon enough we were on the other side of the city, Kleeve Hartus crowded in the back of the GMV and Apache trotting alongside as we wound through the still deserted streets. Occasionally a curious head would poke out of a window, and we would all wave and smile to let them know we were the good guys. Who could doubt it? We had a dog with us. When do bad guys have doggies? The shocked faces didn't seem to pick up on the message we tried to lay down, and quickly disappeared back into the comfort of their homes.

The walls of the massive atmosphere plant were in sight, and Kleeve Hartus directed us to a building close by, one as grand as the council chambers. Translucent jade green arches supported many storied spires and tall crystal windows that defied the physics of the thin columns that ringed the ground level like toothpicks holding up an engine block. It didn't seem possible.

"This is the library. Below are the catacombs and storehouses of knowledge. It is there that the entrance to the atmosphere plant lies. They think it secret, but it is only because none have an interest in the workings of their guild. All this time, we have thought them dedicated to the betterment of our world. I admit I am not surprised to learn that the scientists are selfish deceivers. They are unlikeable in their conceit. I look forward to confronting them and hearing them admit the truth at last."

Dave stroked the pack on his shoulder. "They can open up, or we have a doorbell they can't ignore."

A gathering of Guards waited.

"No response yet?" the first shield asked his men.

"No, sir. None have emerged. They remain entombed."

Karlo smirked. "Not for long."

Where were the books? The vaulted concourse was not endless shelves and dusty tomes but a garden of mineral sculptures, an art gallery. Row after row of trees with branches like drooping willows dangled crystals for leaves. Karlo was entranced and halted to hold one of the hanging gems.

"To call it art's an insult. I've never seen anything like it. It's more than sculpture, isn't it?"

Kleeve Hartus took a small boxy device from the base of one of the trees and placed it under the garnet in Karlo's palm. A hologram appeared and our guide stroked his finger across the hovering apparition. An index of pictures and words scrolled past like a roulette wheel, too rapidly for me to read.

"The library contains knowledge from the entire history of Vistara. It sits unused by all but the most curious."

Karlo spoke with the reverence of a priest. "I could spend the rest of my life in here."

"Later, Karlo." I nudged him. "Game time."

We followed the Guards through the crystal grove and made an abrupt turn into one of the many dark recesses we'd passed, alcoves that reminded me of where figurines sat watchfully in the caves of the water priests. But here, winding columns ran from floor to ceiling around which spiraled cubes, polyhedrons, pyramids of all colors and sizes, waiting to be plucked and tasted for the knowledge they must contain within. Karlo was about to exercise his curiosity when a guard stepped out from a hidden wall, a sallyport angled in such a way it would be missed by any who didn't know it was there.

Kleeve Hartus ignited an amber reflector. "This is one way in and out of the works. There are others, to be sure. Follow."

We entered a short hall dimly lit by amber stones, and at its end, a narrow staircase wound downward.

"My spidey-senses are tingling, brah. These bozos may not be relying on just a hidden door for security, know what I mean?"

"Big time. Where does this lead?"

"It is the path we know the wizards to take. It is a part of the library used by only the wizards. My uncle, General Den Gillead, once told me of its existence. He knew only the entrance location. Perhaps he was preparing me for this very day."

"Wait." I pulled my respirator on my goggles down, indicating everyone should do the same. Kleeve Hartus hesitated to copy, the gear we'd given him still around his neck.

Karlo explained, "We're going underground, First Shield. By the time you need a respirator, it's always too late to benefit from wearing it."

We expected trouble. A few strings of gunfire could contaminate the air in any confined space. Even fizzle guns probably ionized the air and made it toxic. Hacking and coughing was no way to win a fight. Kleeve Hartus reluctantly followed suit.

I yelled at the Guards, "We're going down. Don't follow us. Without respirators, you'll choke. We'll call you up when it's time. Keep holding my dog back. Apache, STAY!"

My puppy looked hurt, but obeyed as I took the first step.

After many dozens of meters, our descent ended. There was one passage and it was dark. I brushed past Kleeve Hartus's cloaked shoulders and hit the switch to my white light. A thousand reflections returned.

Karlo's respirator thwarted his attempt at a whistle. "As above, so below."

"It's a hall of mirrors," Dave said, muffled. "Freaking carnival's what it is."

A maze of white minerals lined the walls, rougher and coarser than the polished smooth surfaces of the city. The angular path ahead was indeed maze-like. I took a step forward, and the walls blossomed in white around me, like motion sensors on an outdoor floodlight.

By unbreakable habit, I softly swore, "What the hell?"

"Burglar alarm, brah. We're toast. Let's power through."

"Wait!" Karlo's eyes drove me in the direction of his gaze.

In this first jag through the passage, the way widened briefly. Set into a rim of polygonal cuts of white quartz, a mirrored surface as big as a Tarn reflected our images. Then the silver shimmer faded to gray. A mist swirled and became—a violet ocean, white frothy waves splashing on the hull of a silver craft. Sails of glowing golden energy rose off the decks covered with red and yellow Martians dressed like Kleeve Hartus, the sharp bow of the ship slicing through the sea smoothly and at great speed.

"Amazing," Karlo gasped.

The first shield placed a hand on the image as if to feel the sea spray. "It must be the time of Oceania, the Amethyst Sea, alive and full!"

"C'mon," I said. "Charlie Mike. No time for a history lesson."

At each jagged bend, another portion of the walls came alive and images were set into motion, triggered by our presence. Green and purple forests. Beast, bird, and fish that reminded me of the fossil record of Earth, strange yet almost familiar. Cities like Clymaira, grander and larger. Massive metallic ships defying gravity to disappear behind moons-lit clouds and into the starscape of the night. Battles raged. Cities burned. Dust blew across ruins.

It was impossible not to stare at each, at least for a second, as we moved ahead.

"How our world once must have been." The dizziness in Kleeve Hartus's voice betrayed his wonder. "Are these records of things past or conjured fantasy? I cannot discern."

Next to me, Dave scolded him. "Don't get distracted. Looks like it dead-ends ahead."

We'd wound footfalls through the hall of mirrors. Here the path widened where three could stand abreast. A blank metallic door waited ahead and in the last alcove before it, a final mirror swirled gray. I tucked in to give the guys room to work. Near my left hand was a small hanging plate, a tiny hammer beside it. Was this the door knocker?

"I'll watch our six. Go to work, guys. First Shield, I bet they're listening. Give it a try."

Kleeve Hartus aimed himself at the blank metallic door as Dave and Karlo busied themselves beside him. "Master Aldor Farkus, it is the commander of the Clymaira Guard who addresses you. I have implored you for a day and a night to respond. The whole of Vistara needs the help of your guild. I know you are aware of the danger and what has befallen your brothers in Thoria and Califex. Open and greet us as your protectors. We seek your assistance. The time to act is now."

A disembodied frail voice answered.

"You answer to the king, as I do to the head of my order. I have been commanded to remain secluded until the emergency is past and to resist all attempts at intrusion into our sanctuary. I warn you, do not attempt to breach our domain. You have been warned."

Karlo and Dave ran hands over the vault door.

"Might not be much tougher than a class two metal door," Dave said with the returning hollow ring at each knuckle tap.

Karlo humphed. "ECT, then a LSC if that fails?"

Explosive cutting tape of the 1200-grain variety would more than do the trick if the door were as thin as it sounded. The linear shape charge with its metal "V" bed would cut anything, but it made for a lot of frag and might bring down the house. It was undoubtedly what they'd used to bring down the works in Califex. Chuck'd probably made a perfect target analysis of the plant in Thoria when he considered how to drop the one in Califex.

"ECT, guys," I said. "Make it quick."

We'd already laid out a door charge for each explosive big enough to let us pass, and Dave pulled the rolls of ECT from his pack and started peeling the backing as Karlo applied it. My elbow brushed the plate. It was heavier than it looked. I put a hand on it to keep it from swinging and then for no reason, fascinated by the surface, scaled like flakes of mica, I flicked it with my middle finger. It made a tinny, musical gong.

I spoke loudly to be heard through the respirator. "C'mon, Kleeve Hartus, time to get back. The overpressure is going to be fierce in this tunnel."

But as I was about to pull him back from the door, behind me the swirling vortex in the mirror accelerated and now took shape. The image settled and I gasped.

It was me.

Not a reflection. A picture of me.

And I wasn't alone.

I felt a humid mist against my skin. It settled on my goggles, blurring my vision. There was no time to gawk, but what I saw, I saw. Only the new hazard made me abandon the mystery.

"What's this? In the air."

Kleeve Hartus seethed. "Death somnolent. They mean to send us up the Blix to Temple Farnest."

"Will it absorb through our skin?"

Kleeve Hartus's outfit left a lot of exposed hide.

"No," he said. "Well, I don't think so. I've never been exposed to it."

"Run. Go. We'll be right behind you."

Dave attached the cap to the main line. "Ready to burn."

"Do it."

Dave pulled the ignitor.

A pop, then smoke.

We ran.

"Two minutes on the time fuse," he made a muffled reminder. It was long enough of a burn to let us get clear, short enough to keep the wizards from monkeying with the charge. If they were brave enough. I doubted they were.

"I hope we don't destroy the hall," Karlo fretted. "Even with the ECT, the N.E.W. is maybe too much to keep from—"

"Screw that," Dave fumed. "They're trying to kill us. If the net explosive weight breaks every mirror in the joint, who cares? Now they get what's coming to them."

We wound out of the maze and paused at the base of the stairs, just as the charge blew in a *snap*, a column of dust and ejecta billowing at us overhead.

"Let's go," I said.

I'd been last. About-face, I led. Our carbine lights pierced the gloom. This time the crystal lights did not respond as we raced past them to the door. Dust hung high against the ceiling until we reached the last bend. The door lay in mushroomed pieces.

"Positive breach! Amateurs," Dave yelled. "That's a shitty security door."

Fast, but not too fast, I took a hostage rescue pace, as though we were heading for the crisis site, ignoring anything but a human. The fog cleared and we hit a wide ramp up, Dave on line with me as we plowed up to burst into a huge chamber. Three scrawny, red-bearded, and purple-robed old men coughed like Doc Holliday.

"On the ground! Don't move. Keep your hands in front of you," I yelled.

Karlo knocked the nearest down, and in a flash, we had their pencil-thin arms flex-cuffed.

"You!" Karlo rolled the first onto his back. "Tell me how to clear the air in here or you're probably going to die."

The dust and whatever they'd pumped into the hall of mirrors was putting them in the hurt locker. I wanted them alive.

The man coughed. "Take us to the courtyard," he hacked. "Through there. I can't breathe."

Kleeve Hartus ran up a skeleton staircase to a landing and activated a sliding portal letting daylight and air rushed in. We carried the old men like grocery baskets and deposited them in the daylight. The ring of the walls we'd only seen from outside curved high around us. We stood in the hidden perimeter courtyard on a wide band of red polished stone, the towers of the factory piercing the sky above us.

The first shield removed his respirator and took the chin of one of the collapsed men and held it to his own face. "Was that what you expected, wizard?"

Dave bumped fists with Karlo. "Gets 'em every time."

We let the old men sip water as they coughed the last of the dust from their lungs.

"Whatever they tried to gas us with must not've been forced into the sanctuary in a strong concentration because they seem to be doing better."

"It was not deadly," one wizard gasped. "A gentle sleep is all you would have suffered."

Dave spit. "Likely story, you old geezer. The gun wasn't loaded. I didn't mean for anyone to get hurt. I'd never hurt a fly. Tell me another one."

Kleeve Hartus returned to the courtyard. "I have the air exchangers on full. The tunnel should be clear soon."

The oldest and baldest of the wizards scowled at us from his cross-legged seat, his back against the outer wall as he sipped at a plastic bottle with cuffed hands. He squinted at the sunlight. The dark skin of the average Red Vistaran made me doubt this one got out much—pale pink face and arms. He was still defiant. His manner reminded me of Bryant. Superior. Conceited. Irksome.

"This is a grave violation, First Shield. You will suffer judgment and a living death in the tomb of the sacrilegious for it. The punishment for this violence is known to all. You forfeit your life by such wanton—"

"Shut it, gramps," I said.

His empty threats annoyed me. Not quitting the fight when you're the loser was one thing. Shooting your mouth off like a gang banger cuffed and stuffed and acting tough for his homies is another.

"We know that you know that we know you're full of roamak scat. Your lodge brother in Thoria spilled his guts to our enemies. Your guild's a bunch of con artists."

My grammar had gone out the window along with my respect for these buffoons. Still, his pained squint told me he got the gist of my accusation, acting as stunned as if I'd struck him. I preferred the power of words when I could use them, but I didn't mind the fist when it suited.

There's a tool in the toolbox for every task.

Kleeve Hartus squatted to put his face on level with the old man's. "I am greatly displeased, Aldor Farkus. All of Vistara is taught to venerate your guild for your tireless service. Instead, we learn the truth. If great evil has befallen us, then I am grateful that our blindness to your crimes is at last at an end before this world perishes."

The lightning in the old man's eyes faded, revealing he knew he was defeated. Like a guilty man who knew he'd been caught at last, he let the tautness of his resistance drop, and surrendered.

"What do you want?" he sighed.

I knelt. "You're going to raise your brothers in Thoria, and we're going to ask them some questions about the situation there. Then we're going to lock you up—somewhere deep and dark for you to think about your betrayal of Vistara—until we turn you over to the king."

✠ ✠ ✠

The old man on the screen had the same bad dye job, but not the same petulance as Aldor Farkus or the other air wizards. Not that I condoned it, but it might have something to do with Marky torturing his station chief in a very, very grisly manner that was responsible for his improved manner.

Marky always was one for expediency.

When I laid eyes on him again, it would be to put a bullet through his brain.

"We've been left alone, with instructions by the Thulians to tend our work," the air wizard said. "The fall of the Califex works is a tragedy that rivals our dried seas. The master of the guild in the Yellow Kingdom of Annameria has alerted their supreme ruler, but moves only to prepare their own defense should their kingdom become a treasure the Thulians try to steal. They send no aid. They are no friend to King Osric Darmon. Never have been."

Beside us, Aldo Farkus was subdued. Finally, he said, "It is as I told you, is it not? You may tell them all, brother."

"Thoria is occupied. There is but one Thulian here. There is no need for more. No resistance remains. The Mydreen army killed hundreds, nay, a thousand. There are but a handful of Mydreen left guarding Thoria compared to the hordes that lay siege to our city. But who would dare stand against them? They've promised they would return in full force and execute women and hatchlings in revenge if we took up arms to expel their occupying army, as small as it is."

Historically, it was pretty much SOP for an occupying army to threaten the invaded in just such a manner. Americans had done it. In the invasion of Iraq, the Marine General Mattis was reported as telling the local leaders in his area of operations, "Do not cross us. Because if you do, the survivors will write about what we do here for ten thousand years."

Good quote. And if he really said it, it was sure justified in my opinion. But in Special Forces, we didn't think too much of that man. Not because he didn't say some cool stuff—he did. It was because he flat out refused to send Marines to support a wounded SF A-Team fighting in southern Afghanistan, bringing with them the future president of that country.

The A-Team and their force got hit by a friendly JDAM, injuring three Americans and scores of allied Afghans. Mattis refused to send a casualty evacuation. Stated the ground situation was unknown. The Air Force didn't think the situation was too volatile. They sent help from much farther than the Marine base only forty-five minutes away. But six hours passed for that A-Team with three wounded Americans, who all died. Not to mention the Afghans.

Bring up Mattis around anyone in SF and see if you don't feel the temperature rise in the room. No man leads a blameless life but, for a guy who talked a lot of hard-ass warrior stuff, refusing to come to the aid of other Americans is what spoke loudest to SF.

I wanted hard intel about how many Mydreen were left in Thoria. "What's a handful? Fifty? A hundred Tarns?"

The old man shrugged. "I have not personally counted."

Dave cursed him. "For a scientist, you're not very science-y."

"What of the happenings in Shansara?" Kleeve Hartus demanded harshly.

"The Supreme Master of our guild, Tyreen Sorell, informs us that a great battle wages. The king's army and the Guards fight fiercely to defend Shansara. As yet, the invader has not triumphed. But no aid comes. Not from Aetheria and the Yellow cousins, not even from the king's own son, Prince Carolinus Darmon. His exile in Pyreenia has not made him regretful for his insolence, but instead made him resolute in his hatred of the king."

Dave was close by, interrogating one of the wizards about the comm system while we questioned the others. I tried to tune him out, but his probing of the scientist was also important to our future.

"How does it work? Is it transportable?"

"No. It cannot be moved. The stations are as old as the atmosphere works themselves. The alignment that allows the tenth ray to link with the other stations is fixed, not variable."

Kleeve Hartus overheard. "Tenth ray? There is no tenth ray."

Karlo begged understanding. "I don't understand the concept of the 'ray.' Is it a description of different bands within the electromagnetic spectrum? Is it a metaphor? It's a strange translation, whatever it is. There's no equivalent I can assign."

"You have no hope of understanding, Thulian," Aldo Farkus sneered. "Nor you, First Shield. The manipulation of the essential rays is the purvey of science, not warcraft."

Pushing aside my frustration, I focused on the man in Thoria. "Describe the Thulian in your city to me," I asked.

He gave a good description of Doug. As big as a Tarn, but easy like Sunday morning.

"I'm directing you to remain silent about what you've heard," I told him. "If the Thulian asks, you've had no contact with anyone. Understand?"

"Yes. I have not seen the Thulian in many days. He is otherwise occupied, is my sense. I have instructions to retrieve him if contacted by his compatriots from our sister facilities."

"Have you had reports that there are Thulians or Mydreen in Shansara or Pyreenia yet?"

"No. I have had communication with the masters of both works within the past day, and they report no such thing."

"Do not speak to them about us. If they get the same treatment your master received at the hands of the enemy—if they knew about us—it would work against what we're hoping to accomplish, understand? I'm not threatening you. I'm telling you our interests are aligned. We're trying to help."

"Do you come to our aid in Thoria to repel the invader?"

I wasn't about to tell him anything.

"We'll be in touch."

I motioned the nearest wizard to close the communication. I was ready to be rid of them.

"First Shield," I said, "perhaps you can pass our esteemed scientists to your men so they can begin their meditations on all those things the rest of us peasants can't hope to understand."

"With pleasure, Benjamin Colt."

After they'd gone, I told the guys my plan.

"We're going for Baby Blue. Kleeve Hartus is going to muster every air car and pilot and we're making for Califex. We'll pick up Khraal Kahlees and his best men, and then it's on to Thoria."

But I had a stop to make along the way.

Dave spoke through gritted teeth. "We can do this. The Korundi are capable."

Karlo grinned. "They'll never expect it. We'll hit them blind. Sounds like there's only enough Mydreen left behind to act as a token defense. They're maintaining control by terror. When you ignore ethics, you can save on manpower. But we have to be careful. Doug's smart. What they lack in numbers, he's made up for in defenses."

"That's right," Dave said. "They started working on it shortly after we took the city. The west side is all trenches, fougasse, and firepits."

"POL we were *not* short of," Karlo reminded.

Foo-gas was an expedient flame defense for a camp. It was effective against tanks throughout many twentieth-century wars. Baby Blue had cranked out plenty of liquid petroleum, and I'd have been surprised if it hadn't been used. Against Tarn cavalry, it would be devastating. In the language of warfare—very asymmetrical. Like Welsh longbows at Agincourt kind of asymmetrical.

"So, we don't go through the front door."

"Good idea," Dave said. "Who knows a better way in? We gonna build a big hollow wooden horse?"

"I've got a friend we need to visit along the way."

"So, we meet Cynar at last?" Karlo asked.

"We're going to try," I said. "He could help us unravel more of these mysteries."

"Speaking of, I want time here and in that hall of mirrors. Incredible. Hey, Ben, what happened right at the end before you figured out they were gassing us? It sounded like you were about to say something?"

I blew him off. "I don't remember. C'mon, daylight's burning."

I looked forward to seeing Cynar's withered face and toothless grin. Just as I had news for him, I was sure he'd have answers for me. Whether he did or not, we would still be on our way to Thoria. It was a stepping-stone. An island that would give us our next foothold on the way to Shansara.

And Talis Darmon.

Action had a way of inspiring hope. And that hope brought Talis Darmon up out of the black where I'd had to hide her, the oily surface parting to reveal her perfect face. Not a speck of filth remained there, her light repelling and overpowering the dark void around her. She smiled.

And just as I freed her from the tar in my mental dungeon, I knew I'd soon do it for real.

Because I'd seen the future.

37

"Cynar, open up. We need your help."

I'd brought Apache into the cave and left everyone else outside. An ante room full of Tarns would put anyone off from opening the front door. There was only room for two air cars to land beside the fountain. I stood where I knew the hidden door to be and made my case again for Cynar to open up.

"I know you can hear me. I wouldn't be here if it wasn't necessary. A lot's happened since I was here. Things you need to know about."

My radio squelched.

"Checking in, Ben. Any progress, over?"

Dave was with the Korundi, wherever they could set down their air cars on the angled flats in the passes feeding the fountain way station. It took us two days to reach Califex and then Cynar's labyrinth. Khraal Kahlees knew the place and guided us in single file flight through the treacherous caverns of the high eastern Korund Range.

"Still at it," I said. "Any sign of company?"

Karlo was outside. "Negative visual, but I'm on the ridge above the fountain and there're plenty of tracks and marks by something with two-legs that's not human or Tarn. A lot of somethings. Big somethings."

Double-K was with him. Khraal Kahlees had been skeptical when I'd briefed everyone on the likelihood that Cynar's security contingent would make an appearance at the earliest sign of our intrusion. If there was a delay in getting Cynar to call off his hairy troop of protectors, I wanted everyone to withdraw to the air to avoid having to smoke check Hortha and irrevocably alienate the hermit from our cause. Khraal Kahlees scoffed at my concern.

"The Hortha do not haunt the Korund. Surely you know they cannot be this far south."

Amused that Karlo found evidence to contradict the Korund native's beliefs about the Hortha's range, Dave leaped at the opportunity it presented. Khraal Kahlees was a teammate, and whenever you could, busting balls was good for morale. If not the bust-ees, at least for the bust-ers.

"What's Khraal Kahlees say about all that sign you found? He think it's not made by Ben's albino gorillas?"

"Just a second." There was a pause. "He says he'll believe it's them after he has one skinned."

"Tell him you can lead a horse to water. Out."

Apache was unnerved, and growled at every breeze that whistled its way into the cave. He looked at me with mournful eyes.

"It's okay, boy," I assured him. "No nasty white apes are going to sneak up behind us. Everyone's got our backs. But I've got to get Cynar to come out of his hole. Cynar," I called out, aiming my plea at the blank wall. "Things are bad, buddy. It's only Cynar the Great who can help us."

Then I made my soliloquy of all that had happened, unsure that anyone beside Apache was actually listening.

I told him about the fall of Thoria at the hands of the Mydreen Army, and the barbarity that had occurred there.

I told him about the fall of Clymaira, and how with the help of the Korundi, we'd retaken it.

I told him about the attack on Califex, the capture of the princess, and the destruction of the atmosphere plant.

I told him about how we'd breached the works in Clymaira and how we'd learned about the duplicity of the atmosphere guild.

And I told him my plan.

"Cynar, we have to retake Thoria. If my matter mill is there, we can use it to build weapons to defeat the Mydreen and save the Red Kingdom. I need your help to get there. I want to use the river system to infiltrate the city. If we can't, then the Mydreen army will roll over the Red Kingdom and smash everything that remains. How long until they come after the water guild?"

My audience of one plopped on his hind end with a grunt. Apache had grown tired of waiting too.

"Cynar, is any of this convincing you? It has to be you who steps up to do the right thing. You can't hide anymore. I know your guild is detached from everything that happens aboveground, but I also know that you're not the same as them. You know that your efforts to save Vistara only matter if there's someone decent left to live on this world. Don't leave it to the robbers and the predators."

Silence.

If we breached the sanctuary like we'd done to enter the atmosphere works, Cynar would rightly become our enemy instead of an ally. But it was quickly looking like our choices were dwindling like the very air of Vistara. I hit my PTT to tell Karlo to bring in the demo. Then a crack appeared in the wall.

"Hehehehe!" The old hermit stood in the opening.

"Cynar! Why'd you make me wait so long? Are you going to help us?"

"Hehehehe! Tell me more, White lord, tell me more! Hehehehe! I knew it! I knew it all along! The oafs. The fools. The liars! Their science is all a hoax. The air wizards are frauds! Tell me more!"

Cynar bent over in a fit of coughing, then slapped his knees and hopped around the cave, laughing maniacally as he celebrated. Apache cowered at my feet. I'd never seen him act like such a baby, but Cynar's mad dance was unnerving. Even the gadron thought the hermit had finally bought the big ticket for a straitjacket and a padded cell.

"This is the greatest day of my life. The air wizards are frauds!"

"Cynar, of everything I told you—the war, the kidnapping of Talis Darmon, the destruction of the atmosphere works—my revelations about the air wizards are what made you open up?"

The old hermit grasped my shoulders. "I've never had a friend such as I have in you, White lord. Never did I think that permitting you access to my sanctuary would result in this. Kindness returned a hundredfold. I feel a thousand annuals younger!"

"So, you'll help?"

He stopped abruptly. "I heard your plea. It is the half-baked plan of a dullard. If you wish the help of Cynar, it is his intellect you require, not his highway. Come. Bring your friends. I feel like showing off. Twice in one annual… I must be mad."

✠ ✠ ✠

Khraal Kahlees was dumbfounded, but too proud to break his stoic guard. It was Kleeve Hartus who gasped at the sight of the river.

"I thought your tale fanciful as a tale for children, Benjamin Colt. There is much we do not know about the secret workings of our world."

The first shield took a step closer to the edge of the quay and peered into the dark waters, the tunnel, and the gurgling river that disappeared into it.

"Benjamin Colt, you traveled this path like the ancient mariners of Oceania?"

"We did. Thanks to Cynar the Great. And I want us to take the opposite course to arrive as close as we can to Thoria."

"That's some Trojan horse, brah," Dave said as he knelt to test the waters. "Cold. But we've swum worse."

Cynar grumbled, "It is not possible. You assume incorrectly, blindly applying one observation in hopes that it models many phenomena. It is an error of the scientific process. The course of the water does not travel east from the Korund by the same system it does west. The aqueduct east is steep and of high velocity, White lord, and the tunnel would not permit use of a floating craft such as I gifted you. Unless you can hold your breath for days in total darkness, it is not a means of travel. Dullard."

Dave's compounded expletives I'm sure wouldn't translate, and I was a little glad. The probability of the old man having that kind of flexibility was unlikely.

"Then we go with plan B," I said. "We infiltrate the city and hit them as we find them. We take the war to them with the army we have, not the one we wish we had."

I rolled out one of the maps, the crude representations of the major features and cities above the great chasm of the canyon we'd appeared in so long ago. I guided the image to the east. Maleska Mal lay at the foothills below the eastern Korund Range. Farther east and south by a large gap was Thoria, marked by a caricature of tapered towers as tall as the line drawings of the peaks of the Korund.

"Khraal Kahlees, can we fly through the passes of the mountains to a place where we can approach Thoria unobserved? Maybe from much farther east, where they'd least likely expect an attack?"

He stroked his chin with an upper hand as his lower arms tapped his abdomen. "I have not done so." He looked to Kleeve Hartus, who made a two-handed approximation of the same intense process.

"Benjamin Colt, would it be so much better than skirting south of Maleska Mal to approach across the wastes from south and west? At low altitude, our seven air cars could travel far and safely. Or, do you think their rolling war machines positioned in those locations to intercept us? If so, then at all costs we must avoid a route near them."

"We don't know what we don't know," was my inadequate answer. "The air wizard in Thoria said none of our big guns were there, but that source is unreliable at best. If we can't sneak in by the underground river, I want us to consider all options for a secretive approach."

Karlo hummed. "None of us are air planners. In every successful raid, how the special operators gets to the target is as much a key to success as what they do on the objective. Without good maps, we don't know which route's superior to the other. But Dave and I have been in Thoria. From Maleska Mal, the terrain would mask an approach better than the flats around Clymaira would."

Cynar had been quiet for longer than usual. It had been in minutes since he'd last insulted me. Instead, he groaned while he watched two Tarns cautiously approach the river. They encouraged each other until the first got splashed by the waters lapping the edge of the quay, and retreated.

"Since reality denies you the path you vainly hoped my works might have provided, it seems I may return to my labors in peace," he absently said. "Depart then."

"Cynar, tell us how far west the aqueduct can be traveled? We made it by boat all the way to Salkar the Rash and almost to Califex itself. Is there a way to Clymaira through the tunnels? To Pyreenia? How about to Shansara?"

The old hermit cackled. "Yes. There are channels flowing westward to those stations that are quite similar to the one you traveled."

He took a finger and drew on our map. He made a wavy line connecting his way station to the one east of Califex by putting an *X* where

Salkar the Rash had greeted us in a living coma. He traced farther west where he made another *X* in the southwestern foothills of the Korund.

"Karvell the Patient is priest there. If he still lives, the superior oaf. Him I disdain only half as much as the air wizards, which is to say still a great amount."

There he made radial spokes south. One took a minor angle eastward toward what I thought was the way station near our crash site, one coursed west-southwest in the direction of Pyreenia, and between them a line went straight south, stopping just short of Shansara.

"So, it's possible?" I said.

He grunted with disbelief. "Physically, the aqueduct would permit you to do as you envision. But who would travel the rivers with you? Them?" He thumbed at the two Tarns who now had their backs against a wall, treating the river as though it were an enemy ready to attack.

"We'll cross that bridge when we come to it."

"What are you thinking, Ben?" Karlo asked. "That if we get Baby Blue and I can get it working, we crank out as much munitions as we can? We ferry it all to the grand central station, and infil our Korundi army by underground river to Shansara? Then what? We won't have the GMV and the big guns. We won't have mounted Tarn cavalry to attack with. There are a lot of holes in this plan."

"I'm thinking about a coordinated air-land link up. We take the minigun and the door guns off the GMV and mount them on air cars. It'll divide our firepower over more platforms. We move the majority of the force by river, and bring in our air cav to support us when we're ready to attack."

"Our lack of comms is killing us, Ben-dog," Dave said. "There's too much to go wrong with us all separated. It's like one of those Civil War battles, where it took months to mass troops. Weeks to figure out where your order of battle is actually located. Days of miscommunication to get them all moving to the objective in some kind of coordinated fashion. It's blind man's bluff, brah."

Cynar got even grumpier. "I cannot assist you in this grandiose delusion. I'll ask you to take your leave and your small brains with you. Carry all the water you can. The fruits of my genius are my offering for your success. Goodbye." He gestured us toward the exit.

"Cynar, wait. I think there're other ways you can help us. The air wizards have a secret system that lets them communicate across the planet from one atmosphere works to the others. The rest of Vistara has nothing like it."

He shrugged. "Eh?"

It was another case where I was unsure if he'd heard me or didn't understand me. If he was a thousand years old, even with his life-prolonging light treatments, deafness had to be a thing.

Karlo intuited how I was failing. "We've seen the device, Cynar. It transmitted a live image from Thoria to the station in Clymaira. The wizard told me it was some manipulation of the tenth ray."

The old wreck threw back his head and laughed. Here was the Cynar I knew. "Hehehehe! Tenth ray indeed." He laughed till he coughed, then recovered. "Those dolts. Their knowledge of science is rubbish. There is no tenth ray. They do not understand even the simple manipulation of the fifth ray to pierce space. Instead, they invent some nonexistent force to explain their inadequacy. Hehehe. I tried to chase you off too soon. What other amusing insight can you give me into their idiocy? I've not had such entertainment—ever!"

Dave looked about to burst with excitement. "Cynar, do you have a communication system like the air wizards?"

Offended, Cynar said, "Like the air wizards! Do you think my guild as feeble?" He turned to me. "Did you not tell your fellow dullards of the great science you witnessed here? You have seen for yourself, White lord, there is no manipulation of science that escapes me."

I tried to calm him. "I apologize, Cynar. I don't remember you showing me anything of the sort."

"True, I did not demonstrate it! But I told you, my guild communicates with us. It is our vow to work in solitude that denies us the distraction and reliance on human interaction, not a lack of science to enable useless bantering. Bah!"

I thought back. "But when I asked you to call ahead to let Salkar the Rash know we were coming, you said it wasn't possible."

The ancient wreck slapped his forehead so hard in frustration, I felt the concussion.

"I never said such. You assumed. Salkar is so named 'the Rash' because he once initiated communication with the masters of the guild without proper cause. The story of his indiscretion was a lesson drilled into all initiates of the temple. He refuses to receive or respond to communication as a vigorous demonstration of the renewed fealty to his oath—the one he broke in weakness by seeking contact with the guild masters twice in two hundred annuals. I told you, I am in communication with the heads of our order! How did you think that occurred? By magic? You may be a great warrior to have survived beast, Mydreen savages, a soul-eater, and the very Korund itself, White lord—but you are the poorest of wits I have ever known."

Karlo frowned. I knew it was at mention of the soul-eater. He wouldn't know what it was, and I'd never mentioned it. If he brought it up, I'd claim ignorance. It was too painful.

You've heard of a person's reason for being? With fervor Dave ignored both the mention of the soul-eater and the insults thrown my way in pursuit of his *raison d'être*. "Cynar, can you help us with communication? We need very much to be able to speak to each other over all distances. It's the difference between life and death."

"My order would never permit it. I've given too much help already to this one." He threw hands in my direction. "I did what I did—yes, it was my own vanity that drove it—and I have castigated myself for it ever since. It was a calculated boast, one I knew would never be discovered, because Salkar would not utter 'offal' if he had a mouth full of it!"

I begged. "Cynar, you were right about everything. The atmosphere guild are phonies. Vistara is a car with a rusted out frame and they're the used car dealers painting the fenders gold. The Mydreen are poised to take over the Red Kingdom. If they control the atmosphere plants, the whole planet's going to die. If you don't stand up and help us, who will?"

Cynar frowned. He didn't seem ready to throw in with us, but he wasn't firmly on the side of "no" yet.

"You say the corrupters of the atmosphere works have allowed the most basic manipulation of the fifth ray to fall into legend on Vistara? Impossible!" Cynar's head dropped in despair. "Vistara has fallen dark while my order has toiled in silence to maintain the very source of life itself. What degeneracy the fools of the atmosphere guild have manifested over this world!"

I wished the princess were here. Her ability to make someone see the truth within them would persuade him. But she wasn't. There was just me.

"It's all the more reason for you to help us, Cynar. I know how much you've suffered for all of Vistara. You told us the oath of your guild. The princess understood. She reasoned your order chooses a life of service and sacrifice because of some great guilt you all blame yourselves to hold."

Cynar froze. It seemed the princess had intuited correctly. Rather than lash out at me, the deep well of his eyes told me I'd struck a chord.

"We're willing to sacrifice our own lives for the greater good of all Vistara," I pressed on. "But we don't want to waste our lives and fail. We cannot hope to win a better world without your help."

Khraal Kahlees spoke. "From the time I was an egg, I was taught to be a warrior. I was taught to protect life. To respect life. To never turn my back on a wrong. Even if one must stand alone. Now I know the truth. The atmosphere guild has perpetuated ignorance to gain position and power for themselves. If you swore an oath to save Vistara, then whether you have dispensation from your guild or not, it is time for you act. One does not require a sword to be a warrior."

Cynar cringed. A battle waged inside his ancient skull. His eyes clamped shut. He vibrated like an off-balance washing machine, his fists hammered the air in tiny strokes like he was powering the engine of his conscience. Just as quickly, his convulsions ceased and his bloodshot eyes opened like a roller-blind.

"I am the only intellect alive that can aid you, eh? Is that it? The fate of the world rests on these shoulders?"

I knew what he needed to push him over the edge. "Yes, Cynar! Yes! The whole of Vistara needs your genius."

"Hehehehe! Then who am I to deny an entire world! Come, my dull friends. I have gifts for you. I have but one set of transmitters that you can have, but it is the thing of simpletons to make more. That I will do. As for the rest—ask and it shall be given. And if you succeed, perhaps I can get some peace and quiet again. There are many scientific discoveries yet to be made and life is short. If the boobs of the atmosphere guild are at last outed as frauds, then it will be Cynar who sends them on the Blix beneath a clouded sky!"

✠ ✠ ✠

Karlo gawked at the many lab spaces and the plethora of devices. Cynar stopped in one and began digging. Things metallic, crystal, earthen. Rough and smooth. Modular and monolithic. Some seemed like I could guess their function by their shape.

Hands on his hips, Dave surveyed the room. "The big urn-thing has to be for making sun tea," he guessed. "That twisted shrub with all the tubes and glass filaments? Home nuclear reactor."

"Shh," I urged. I felt the frown of Talis Darmon haunting me. Now who was the adult in the room? "Don't set him off," I whispered.

"These will serve. You," Cynar pointed to Karlo. "Benjamin Colt says you have some knowledge of science."

I was shocked. Cynar hadn't used my name before. I was usually dullard, or muscle-bound idiot, or any combo to indicate I was the terminal direction of his disdain the same way a JTAC wielded a laser target designator.

Karlo introduced himself.

"Take this, engineer," Cynar replied. Karlo accepted the two silver necklaces while Cynar cackled to himself, "Engineer, hehehe. *Engineer*."

Karlo examined them. "They appear similar to the deciphers." Karlo held a necklace up to me, but I waved it to Dave who'd been patiently waiting to be included.

Cynar grunted. "The principle is not entirely different. They will find each other over any distance save separation by the great ether you crossed to arrive on Vistara. Touch the facet here to skin and it will transmit voice directly to the mind of the other wearer. By the time you return, I will have this ready." He held up a bracelet. "This will transmit image as well as voice—but not as clumsily as those crude anachronisms you saw. I perfected all these uses of the fifth ray along ago, but—I can't place where the twin to this is just now." He frowned as he searched his inventory as if sorting through cards of a mental Dewey Decimal System. Then he blew away the dust from hundreds of years of disuse and returned to us.

"No matter. What is this device you go to rescue?"

Our engineer swelled a little, sensing he had a colleague at last. "It harnesses the properties of a black hole to transform matter. It's an engine of creation."

That was a new euphemism. Minecraft Box was what the Rangers at Area 51 had called it—whatever PFC had come with it should've gotten an ARCOM for improving efficiency—and Doug had coined Baby Blue from the scientists calling it the Blue Fairy. Karlo's "engine of creation" was much subtler to describe the physics of the universe fit into a single machine.

If I'd have said it, Cynar would've berated me for the same condensed summary the way an intelligent child would irately challenge the explanation that it's dark because "the sun's asleep." Instead, Karlo's description sparked the vibes of a collaborative attitude.

"Curious," Cynar mused. "We will develop the language together to evaluate that summation once I see it. The crude noises of our mouths cannot express what is the motion of the universe itself."

Karlo took in Cynar's lab, the foreign symbols coating the walls, and the heaps of constructs created, piled, and forgotten. There were dozens of labs like this—larger, deeper, more mysterious in what must lay within them.

"I want to learn it all," he said.

Cynar didn't cackle. But he did throw a jab at me.

"So, not all White lords are oafs. Why are you senior and not he? Humph. Why should it be different among Thulians? There is no meritocracy by intelligence."

I shooed everyone off and waited until it was just Cynar and me. I had his interest with a few words. "Beneath the library and the atmosphere works of Clymaira—" I started, then I told him about the subterranean hall of mirrors and the vivid scenes we'd witnessed from Vistara's ancient history. "Either they were images captured of history or re-creation, but they were so perfect in detail, it's as if we were watching it as it happened. Even Kleeve Hartus was amazed."

His eyebrows shot up. I don't think I'd ever surprised him—just annoyed him or amused him. I'd never intrigued him. Here was something new.

"The mists of time. The fools use their energies there."

"Hold up right there, Cynar. You make it sound like I was looking across time itself."

"If it was as you say, then you intuit correctly. You viewed things through tunnels into the past. A powerful implement for examination—which I doubt they use properly. It is a tool for academics who live to study the past, not a tool for science."

"Only the past?"

He frowned. "What did you see, White lord?"

I told him what the last mirror showed me. He became pensive.

"The self-righteous, deluded fools. They see only what they wish to see. Blind to their own ignorance. Driven by deception."

"I don't understand."

For once, he seemed to have sympathy, as though he pitied me. "The mists can open tunnels into the past as well as the future. The past has created permanent etchings that can be touched and amplified—but not the future. Though the mists can conjure images of probabilities, that is all they can do."

He could see I needed more.

"The manipulations that allow the future probabilities to be viewed are a useless expenditure. It is a misuse of both science and intellectual capital. Humph. It does not surprise me that the atmosphere guild would rely on such. They use the mists like an oracle to guide their weak intellects. The fools. Used this way, the mists will deceive. My guild abandoned the research long, long ago. Probabilities and possibilities are infinite.

"The mechanism will guide to the probability the subject desires, not the future itself. It is a drug of the worst kind."

"What I saw wasn't real?"

"Benjamin Colt, I must impress upon you how dangerous this was—an encounter as perilous as your trial by the ancient evil you stumbled upon. The princess helped you overcome that trauma. I can only tell you that you need no such narcotic as what the mists showed you. Do not give it mind. Do not assign it importance. It was a delusion."

I wanted to believe it was so. Still, I persisted. "But Cynar, it was so real. No different from the other panels. I was looking at something that *had* happened. You said it was a manifestation of a desire, but I've never considered, never imagined, never given thought to anything like it.

"It was a place I've never seen, a hall with walls of polished jewels, light filtered through the prisms of a crystal ceiling. A great throne sat above a thousand heads. Talis Darmon stood to one side. Khraal Kahlees on the other. It was me on the throne between them. And all the people below shouted in unison, over and over—*Warlord*."

38

The route through the mountains had been another treacherous, slow trek. The mood of the Tarns eased noticeably—the boasting and rivalry at who would kill the most Mydreen began again—when we broke out of the last jagged peaks. Kleeve Hartus piloted our lead flitter and dropped to glide a few meters above the ground to the terrain-following course we would maintain for the better part of a day to reach Thoria.

The rest trailed behind like a formation of pissed off geese. Ever been chased by a mad goose? If so, you know what I mean. Geese armed with M4s? That would make for some deadly feathered infantry.

Double-K stood with me next to the pilot station as we rode the deck on our gently bobbing course. Young soldiers yearn for the fight, and I was one of them. The exhilaration caused by the ground rushing past made our blood lust surge in time to the pulsing hum of the engines.

"The Korundi are becoming less anxious about flying," I offered. I enjoyed his opinions and was trying to draw him out. "Low altitude does seem to make a ground-pounder less anxious, but it's a false comfort. No recovery time for a pilot if they get distracted. But there is something about rushing along at treetop height to make you feel ready for war—even if we have no trees."

Double-K had vacillated between berserker and philosopher since I'd known him. He took the measured role of a mix of both. "We do not fear heights, not like the childish Mydreen. It is the lack of control we detest when riding in a craft controlled by another. No Tarn would ride arkall reined by another unless carried as a corpse. It is distasteful."

"Then we'll get you and your men trained to pilot."

He squinted. "That would not improve our dislike of these unnatural contrivances. The ships should not resist the pull of the ground. That they do seems a perversity. And is a crime not always punished? You say you attack from the sky by floating to the ground beneath a trap that holds the air. A parachute? This would seem worthy to the Korundi. Pouncing onto an enemy like gazraal from a perch. That at least seems to expiate the sin of fooling nature by taking flight."

Airborne Tarns? I hadn't considered the possibility. Would the thin Martian atmosphere be offset by the low gravity to allow the use of a standard T-11 canopy? I'd ask Karlo.

Kleeve Hartus let me spell him at the controls but remained close by to coach me. Double-K and I had this in common—I didn't love flying either. But I'd steeled myself that I had to learn. Independence and capability were more important than my comfort.

"You have a good feel for this, Benjamin Colt," Kleeve Hartus said.

"Thank you, First Shield. I had a good teacher in Avril Mysteen."

"He was a fine student. But he is not ready for war."

"No one ever is, Kleeve Hartus."

"I suppose you are correct. That such times should come to us... Well. We should see the towers of Thoria by midday. They will be as the Korund themselves in height."

"But you're sure we won't be spotted from them?"

"The grand heights are not occupied because the air is thin there, but they are a magnificent sight, nonetheless. They are an anachronism, I suppose. Our ancestors had abilities we cannot match today, and Thoria is testament to that. Nothing lies to the east of the city. With desert mirage and masking terrain, our chances at being undetected are excellent. It is a good plan, Benjamin Colt."

"Terrain serves the one who knows how to use it best, First Shield. We're just matching circumstances to tools."

We rested, then when night fell, made the last leg to come in over the eastern horizon, the wonder of Thoria visible across the dry sea like guideposts that never seemed to get closer until at last, we could see the hint of their terrestrial origin. As the guys had told me, the rough grounds around Thoria were advantageous—sandstone channels that looked like they'd once been cut by rushing waters let us keep below an observer's line of sight. Unless they had O2 tanks to breathe out of from a higher vantage point. We grounded and I pointed to our commo man.

"Ready," Dave said as he fiddled with the screen on his chest.

"Do it."

"Done. I've jammed every band. If there's more than one of us in there or they have any repeaters set up, they're cut off from each other."

I wore one of the necklaces, Dave the other. I made a loop overhead and knife-handed to the city. "Move out."

Our two elements split and we headed out. I'd sent Karlo with Dave, Double-K, and the Tarns. I took Kleeve Hartus and the Guards. We were a small force, but if our limited intel was correct, we'd be enough. We'd slither in, search and kill silently—or we wouldn't.

There were few other options.

But once we were in the city, we would have an advantage. They'd be trying to pick ticks off a thick coat; the only way to get them all would be to poison the host. I liked being that kind of invisible threat.

We were the plague that would bring their demise.

"Let me know when you're at your ORP."

I heard Dave in my head but had to speak for him to hear me. It wasn't telepathy.

"Roger, brah. One hour estimated movement. If you hear from me earlier, it'll be important. Out."

There were no outskirts to the city. From the nothing around it, the towers sprang. I made a careful view of what seemed the most direct path between the nearest of the giant columns, passing my thermal and my night vision monocular to the first shield and around to the rest of the troops to get eyes on what lay ahead. It was cemetery still.

"Dave, we're set."

"Gimme fifteen, Ben. We've sighted a small roving patrol just inside the city. Khraal Kahlees has two guys moving in to take them out. I'll get back to you."

The wait was an eternity. I expected shrill alarms and piercing amber lights to disrupt the silence at any time. I'd prepared everyone to rush at my command. Finally, Dave's voice squelched my inner thoughts through the speaker in my skull.

"We're clear. Good hunting."

"Let's go," I whispered.

To walk slowly through the night air toward an enemy is a feeling as contrary as relaxing into an arch when in freefall. Tense, become rigid, fight it, and in a millisecond, you're spinning out of control. Instead, relax. If the job was stealth, running flat out to cover open ground was the same as fighting the air you fell through. Worse, it was shouting, *Look at me. We're coming to kill you.* Even though every fiber of your being made the muscles in your thighs ache to run, run, run—at night, slow, methodical movement was camouflage.

"We're in the city," I reported to Dave.

"Good copy," he said, using a language that seemed suddenly out of place. Dave's voice was as clear as my own thoughts. Clearer. It was as though he was speaking in my ear, right next to me. The necklace needed skin contact to work. It was like his words traveled through my dermis to reach my brain. "We're moving to the city center. It's going to be a long one."

I motioned the men to spread apart and to stay in the shadow side of the linear path we followed into the city, the smooth walls and right angles as different from the desert as the water was from dry land.

I foundered for something pithy to say. "The journey of a thousand miles begins with a single step."

Dave let me get away with it and just groaned, "Out."

Our new walkie-talkies were working, but we heard each other give quiet commands—no way to avoid it. The necklaces were a kind of hot mic that gave us a running commentary about what each other was doing, but as we moved deeper into the city, there were fewer and fewer distractions as we said less and less, the Guards responding to hand signals and the natural environment of the echo chamber that was the city. Being in the belly of the beast has a tendency to do that—make even the uninitiated take a whiff of reality cologne.

The moons had not yet risen and Kleeve Hartus knew the way. The oddly shaped atmosphere works were a silent guide to the city center, the curving puzzles of strange tubular twists and projections distinct in the starlight. The city was laid out in a radius, the streets orderly spokes from the axle that was the atmosphere works.

Apache sniffed the air at each halt. After an hour of careful patrolling, we'd not encountered a Mydreen patrol or even a human on the streets. The closer we came to the central hub of Thoria, the indication that the population remained within was betrayed by their shadows dancing in the dim green light filtered through the glass of the translucent walls above.

"We change course here to reach the civic headquarters," the first shield whispered into my ear.

"Dave, we're moving to the west side of the city guard's station. No contact yet."

"We're still moving from the east. All clear." I heard immediacy in his voice, and could practically feel the moisture in his breath as he hissed, "Hold."

Fizzle guns echoed through the streets.

"Dave's in contact. With me," I said aloud. "Move!"

I told Kleeve Hartus earlier that when the time came, I would bound off and he and his men would have to keep up as best they could, just like Apache.

Through street and narrow passage, I flew. Taking dozens of meters with each stride in a dead run, a foot contacting the ground to propel me ahead to each corner where I landed with two feet and arrested my momentum to make a lightning-fast shoulder check in each direction before I leaped to the next funnel of thoroughfare. There were no roofs to bound onto in the towered cityscape, and each intersection was a blind discovery.

The fight was around the next corner and as I came to a crouching stop, a dozen Tarns burst out onto the open road beside me. I brought the SAW to my shoulder just as they noticed my movement. Too late for them. I worked them with short bursts from flank to flank. They dropped as if hit by lightning bolts, the stunned confusion of those farthest away almost comical as they sent fizzle fire in all directions, searching for the source of muffled thunder from the suppressed MK 46.

Apache was there, barking madly. Guards appeared at my side and sent white bursts into the bodies on the ground. I'd left none standing, but they were doing as I'd ordered. You don't stop shooting until there's a reason to stop.

The dead ones can kill you. And they aren't dead until you see their souls leave their bodies.

Dave came back to me. "Ben, hold tight where you are. They've got two fighting positions outside the ground entrance. Sending grenades now."

The close interval of 40-mm whumps from a pair of 203s came, followed by the sharp report of explosions bouncing through the streets like the Doppler of a high-speed train. Cynar's magic commo necklace had no decibel cut-off, and Dave's shouted command did the same echo in my skull. "Assault, assault, assault." He was so close, his words reflected around the tower a second after his order to move was in my head.

"Block these roads," I said and pointed to Kleeve Hartus. "Take three men. Rest of you, with me."

I led to the far side of the tower. The nearer we got to our other element, the more demanding I had to be. When the shooting starts and the kill-switch has been engaged, it's easy to get disoriented, forget where friendlies are, and use your trigger finger as a replacement for your brain. Small unit movement on the two-way shooting range is an improvisation more complex and dangerous than any known to man. A great jazz musician can only go on a tear if his band keeps the rhythm. If everyone starts in on their own improvised solo, it's musical slaughter. I had to make sure each of these players followed the sheet music. I took each by the shoulders to aim them where I wanted them to cover the encroaching avenues. It was infantry on-the-job-training for my gladiator cosplay cops.

My job to make sure they did it right.

"Hit anything that moves, but NOT in *that* direction." I indicated where Dave and the Tarns were busy working. "Dave-Dave. Talk to me." He was the only one who could receive my transmission, but saying someone's name twice to make sure they knew who was being called over the radio was a habit. And with some names, it became a natural to use full time. Marky-Mark wasn't the first Mark I'd known to be stuck with that moniker, but on this world, he would be the last.

"We're in. Baby Blue is here. Right as the mail, brah."

"How many you need to babysit? It's time to finish up."

"I'm leaving Karlo and three Tarns. We'll link up at your location. Moving."

He kept a running commentary, and in a few minutes yelled, "Blue, blue," from around the tower. A quick leap to where I was, and we were ready to push west toward where I thought the bulk of the Mydreen would be—with their backs turned to us.

"You take the Tarns and run this street. I'll take the Guards and we move up this one. We'll bound block by block. First to make contact is the base of fire. Give me my signal team."

It was time to call up our air support.

Khraal Kahlees selected the two soldiers. I couldn't remember their names and it was a case where in the dark, all Tarns looked alike.

Handing one of them my pin flares, I said, "Remember what I showed you. You know the plan. Once you're at the edge of the city, fire three of these. Once you're loaded, lead them here, then follow this lane west into the city. That way you'll be behind us when you move up."

"Yes, lord."

The two trotted off just as Dave spoke to me from a street over.

"We're posted at the next linear danger area. Let me know when you're at your overwatch, and we'll start our next bound. I'm thinking if there are more Mydreen holding the western city perimeter, they'd be—"

My answer to Dave's speculation that the defenders would pull troops off the hardened city defenses was my SAW chugging out a couple of quick bursts.

"Troops on the ground, twelve o'clock, three blocks down," I told him.

That he had faced something similar was obvious. The unmistakable *whoosh* from an AT-4 came from Dave's position on my right front. The massive burst ahead produced terrible animal howls and Tarn screams. Dave was having all the fun.

"On line. Move." I prodded my squad ahead. These guys were not infantry—yet. They'd been patrol cops. Figureheads of authority. Cav scouts even, riding on their flitters over the desert, trading potshots with renegade bands of Mydreen. But they were getting the hang of it.

We fought this way for many blocks, pushing back the Mydreen response to our intrusion. Too little. Too late. We were deep behind their front line. Arkall moaned and wheezed where they lay. They ate up a few rounds or frag before dropping, and though massive, they weren't like the tanks they approximated in size. We couldn't leave wounded Mydreen behind us as we pushed ahead.

Yes, it was brutal.

The hum of air cars came behind us. The lead flitter landed, and the young Guard Avril Mysteen dismounted and ran to us at a crouch with the two Tarn guides I'd sent to retrieve the flitters.

"We followed the sounds of battle. What now?"

"I'll show you." I called to Dave. "We've got air support. Come to us."

Once we were together, I laid the plan out quickly.

"Dave, go airborne. Take a Guard with each flitter to run the waist guns. Get us eyes on the western boundary and be ready to hammer them there. We'll work to you. If they hunker down in their trenches, then we hammer them—you from above, us from the ground. If they try to leave the city, get them on the plains. Either way, this ends before sunup."

"Air cav, it is," Dave said.

The flitters lifted off, leaving Kleeve Hartus with Khraal Kahlees, the Tarn element, and me.

"Let's go. Keep them spread out, Double-K, and be ready to maneuver to support whoever makes contact."

Speed, surprise, violence of action—all the dicta soldiers mouthed as if the words themselves were a talisman for success—those terms were generally used the way a hack chef tries to pass off a freezer-burned steak. If the meat's no good, you can't disguise it with fancy spices. Just like that bad steak—bad plans, bad tactics, bad troop employment weren't improved because you used velocity like a spice. Those words weren't synonyms for going faster. They were the stuff that made for momentum. We had it. They didn't. We were a fifty-ton freight train flattening pennies on an iron rail.

There was a ticking clock hanging over us, counting off the minutes when a small force could succeed against a larger defender. If it could achieve surprise. If it could unleash sudden, explosive force. If it didn't get bogged down. What I was trying for was a violation of a known tenet of warfare. It took armor and divisions of men to take and hold a city. We were a raiding force with delusions it could be an occupying force. A ninety-pound weakling on steroids was still only ninety pounds.

What I was trying was possible only because of the weakness of Bryant's plan to hold Thoria with a token force of Mydreen—powered by terror and a Maginot Line.

The weakness in the man yielded the weakness in his plan.

"Ben-dog, I've got more Mydreen moving off the perimeter and into the city for your location. I'm going to make some runs on them. Wish us luck."

I relayed what was happening.

Khraal Kahlees made the intuitive tactical leap. "We move then to halt their advance, cut them off, and let the fire rain on them from above." His tusks glowed white in the moons. "The Mydreen know to dig deep when an air car sings. Let us aid them in their chorus of pain."

The Mydreen were probably decent cavalry. As raiders, they'd harassed commerce and vandalized the great cities of Mihdradahl with varying success. As infantry—they were disorganized, ineffective, pitiable. Dave directed Avril Mysteen and the other air cars overhead, raining blaster fire down on the Mydreen we pinned down from altitudes where the Mydreen fizzle guns couldn't counter. If any of the defenders had the new weapons from the Thulian factory machine, they went unused. I'd been worried that at some point we'd come under fire from a 240, but it never happened. Bryant had left his occupying force with nothing more than swords, spears, and pop guns.

Dawn teased the sky when Dave said, "They're breaking. The last of them are taking paths between the fighting positions and trenches and heading for the desert."

"Keep them pinned there, Dave. I'm going to finish it."

We moved to the site I'd been searching for. The few holdouts inside the command bunker dropped to our fire, and I found what I knew was waiting. A Red Devil igniter sat on a crate lid, shotgun primers next to it. The shock tube led to a series of more thin lines, a family tree mapping the genealogy of pain to come.

"Get everyone inside or back, Khraal Kahlees. It's going to get hot," I said.

I checked that Apache was near, loaded the igniter, and thumbed it. At the speed of light, the ignition carried. The concussions and distant screams told me it had all worked as designed. Just not as intended.

"Let's see." I exited the bunker and climbed on top. The trenches and berms around the city were flaming pits of black, sooty smoke. Walls of fire and thick fumes danced over the ground. Apache whined to be comforted and pushed against me.

Dave's voice was in my head. "There were a hundred or more of them trying to evade through the perimeter defense, Ben. They're cooked."

"It is done," Khraal Kahlees said with satisfaction.

Kleeve Hartus clutched fist to chest. "It is too cruel by far."

The Tarn laughed. "Perhaps. Perhaps not. But is better them than us."

I pointed at a clear egress where a small band of Tarns ran, having barely evaded the inferno. I brought up my SAW and sent a burst at them. They zigged to my zag. *If at first you don't succeed* is the saying. I sent another, just as an air car swooped overhead and a blast from its waist gun finished them off.

"Now, it's done."

39

We rode flitters into the city center as the sun rose. The detritus of our assault against the defenders was evident—the pockmarks of spall and shrapnel, the singe marks of explosives—all peppered over the glass walls. Dozens of Tarns littered the pavement in parts and pieces. Karlo stood outside waving an arm overhead as we circled over the landing area.

We followed him underground to find Baby Blue. I blew out an anxious breath I didn't know I'd been holding in. It was intact, on its trailer, surrounded by barriers of thick sheets of the glass-like material, bunkered beneath the ground level to serve as a factory for Bryant's war.

"What's the word, Karlo?"

"I'll know more soon. It's running a self-diagnostic. I'm almost afraid to ask, but… did you find Doug?"

I grimaced. "We haven't had time to comb for bodies, but I don't think so. We never came up against a single one of our own weapons. Just fizzle guns."

Dave shook negatively. "We better find him. Sun's up. If it were me, I'd have plenty of surprises ready. Claymores, IEDs, gas bombs. Engineers are vicious. If he's alive, he's going to hurt us, brah."

Khraal Kahlees turned to one of his men. "Bring the prisoners." Two bound Mydreen, both wounded, were pushed into the underground space and knocked to their knees.

"Where is the Thulian left in charge here?"

Both Mydreen remained silent. With the single motion of his draw, Khraal Kahlees removed the head of the nearest. Severed cleanly off the shoulders, it rolled on the floor. The body fell limply next to it.

"I ask you the same."

The other Mydreen made a sucking sound through tusks and pled, "Do not send me to Farnest on my knees, Khraal Kahlees. It is no death for a Tarn."

"Then it shall not be so. If you speak truthfully."

"We have not seen the Thulian for many days. I can show you where he has taken lodge."

"Do so, and there is a chance to walk in honor with your ancestors."

With eyes out and waist guns ready, our squadron of air cav fanned out and we took a course high and north to where the prisoner indicated. This section of the city spoke of leisure, art, and culture. Sculptures of poised humans, wide staircases, concourses around covered seating and stages spoke of high society, all undisturbed, as though at any moment a festival might break out.

"He is in this building. I accompanied my elder here to report to the Thulian shortly after Domeel Doreen and the army departed. That was some time ago. Little has happened since and the Thulian is rarely seen. We have been contented. Thoria is rich with plunder."

Khraal Kahlees thrust tusks forward. "Honor has been served." He drew and toppled the Tarn's head and Apache howled. "On your feet you crossed the Blix."

Karlo threw up his hands. "Killing prisoners! No! We're not the Mydreen. Ben, do something!"

The muzzle of my M4 was aimed at the entrance. "We will, Karlo. Later."

Up the spread of stairs and into the open entrance of the main floor we spilled. "Clockwise, then up. Room by room. Dave, with me." We led. There were few rooms on this ground level, reception and sitting areas, all empty. But the tower was like all in Thoria—it practically reached the stars. How many levels above could there be to search? Hundreds?

"Before you killed him, it woulda been nice to know *where* in this building Doug was holed up. Double-K, you've gotta be a better interrogator, brah."

"Next time I will allow you to question the prisoner, David Masamuni," Khraal Kahlees grunted. "I am content to remove the head."

"No more killing prisoners, Khraal Kahlees," Karlo said behind us.

Double-K patiently answered, "The way is known, Karlo Columbo. Until the defeated invoke surrender and accept submission, protection is not granted. The Mydreen prisoners could have made surrender. They did not. They retained their right to resume hostility. This one desired honorable death. It was granted. All is as it should be."

"Leave it, Karlo," I chastised. "How do we go up?"

"Here," Kleeve Hartus directed. "The ascender."

"Where?" I strained to locate anything that looked like a mechanism. "This bright patch of floor?"

The first shield waved upward and the floor beneath us rose. Apache, left behind, barked and lunged up on his hind legs as if to reach us.

"What the—" Dave gasped. "No handrails. Where's OSHA?"

We were many meters up and nearing the ceiling without sign of slowing down. I involuntarily started to duck when the ceiling above opened and the ascender slowed. Facing out, we brought guns up as we passed through the floor and glided to a halt. At light speed, Double-K was first off the platform.

"Most egregious, First Shield. Unpleasant in every way."

"Kleeve Hartus, there must be another way to get to the higher levels. That was damn dangerous. If there were someone waiting for us—" I left the rest unspoken.

"Where are the stairs, brah?"

Karlo was the only one not perturbed. "Wonderful. How does it work, I wonder? It must utilize the same technology as the air cars." His gun came up. "YOU! Hands up. Don't move."

A naked woman stumbled from an arched doorway. Her eyes glazed, her hair disheveled, her adorning jewelry her only costume. She saw us, paused, then disregarded Karlo's instructions to take a weaving unhurried course away, veering into another room and out of sight without a word.

It was the first human life I'd seen in Thoria. I placed a single finger to lips and made slow thrusts with my rifle at the doorway she'd appeared from.

"Deep sleepers, here," Dave said in a murmur which came through loud and clear in my head. "And they don't worry about dressing for company, either."

I made a tiny "uh huh" of agreement.

Beyond the half-open doors, the dimmest amber glowed. I made a barrel release to tell Dave I was going and drove forward, moving along a curved wall, the surface beneath giving way to my steps and unbalancing my glide. The floor was one giant cushion. Thorians were strewn across the entirety of the room like randomly oriented red brush strokes on a canvas. A soft grunt below made me change directions before I stumbled and almost fell, and changed course again as another curved form squeaked and rolled to get out of my way.

Our lights joined to flood the floor and walls as we painted white over the scene through the thin curtains of gossamer fabric draped from the ceiling to divide the room by wispy dreams. Karlo grabbed a handful and pulled violently, the material tearing and rending as it floated down.

A slurry feminine voice scolded, "Heyyy. Watch it."

There was no one who could've been hiding a gun.

"What's that smell?" Dave asked aloud. "It's like burnt sugar. What is this?"

"Sparkle dust." Kleeve Hartus spat the taste from his mouth. "Courtesans. The depravity of Thoria." He said it like a bumper sticker history lesson.

A woman made a half-hearted shriek as she rose to run but was cut off by the first shield's hand against her face as he drove her onto her buttocks.

"Be still," he told her.

"Here," Karlo bellowed. His light rested on the back of a tan-brown back, almost as tall and wide as a Tarn, concealed by a half-dozen curvaceous human blankets with flowing hair. "Help me get him on his back, Ben."

The blond man-bun was the right color, and as I rolled him over, saw the same color beard filling in the rest of the face that had been smooth when last I'd seen it. Doug's head dropped to a loll in the small of a girl's back like a boulder coming to rest at the bottom of a cliff.

Karlo took a light off his side and spread an eye apart. A gush of air. A cough. Hands waved across the face to ward away the poison-white beam.

"It's him," I blew out. "He's doped."

"Ya think, brah?" Dave exclaimed. "He's fried like a clam."

"Get up, Doug."

Both eyes opened when I spoke. He lifted his head off the girl, his elbows finding purchase on the same rest to produce an irritable protest beneath. Doug's baby blues came to a glassy kind of awareness. He broke into a huge white grin.

"Ben? Ben-dog! You're alive! Hey, Karlo. Hey, dudes!" His smile persisted and I lowered my gun. "You made it. Welcome to my end-of-the-world party."

✣ ✣ ✣

Sitting on a crate, draped in more of the gossamer stuff we pulled off the ceiling for an expedient robe—Doug's clothes and weapons being nowhere in sight in his crash pad—he was less euphoric but still not firing on all eight cylinders.

"Who's your friend?" Doug asked. He and Apache eyed each other cautiously.

"Our mascot. Here." Karl passed him a cup of MRE coffee. Baby Blue's whirring sound of production sparked him to awareness, and he took a long look over his shoulder before turning back to make a tin chuckle into his cup.

"Knew it. Knew it all along." Doug took a slurp. "Good stuff."

"Knew what, Dougie?" Dave asked.

"That Karlo'd futzed with it." Doug emptied the cup and smacked his lips. "I told Bryant it wasn't possible. It couldn't be done. But I knew." He laughed out loud. "You're the real deal, Karlo."

I frowned. "Time to start talking, Doug. I mean all of it. Now."

"Yeah, yeah." He waved me down. "Cop a squat, Ben. All you bros. You're gonna dig this. I pulled off a real psyop on ole Bryant and Marky. Douche-nozzles." He drooled and wiped his mouth with the back of a hand.

Settling down by my side, Apache eyed our recovered teammate, still wary of the new presence.

"What the hell, Doug," Dave started in. "You're a mess."

Doug exploded. "Hey, Dave, like you never partied back in your surfer days? I'm just hunkering down for the end of the world, man."

"I knew you were from Long Beach, Dougie, but you're an NCO. Act like it, brah."

"Screw you, Dave! I saved your asses and kept Bryant from hunting you guys down when you ran for it. They flew back for a visit after they took Clymaira down. When they found out you three had split, and that I didn't stop you? And Baby Blue was on the fritz? Marky put a friggin' gun to my head. Think he couldn't have found your trail? They wanted to, too. Believe me. Till I convinced them you had nothing to do with our horn o' plenty going south of the border. How about a little gratitude, *brah*!"

"All right, all right!" I motioned everyone to cool it as I pushed Apache back down and smoothed his hackles. "Just pick it up from there, Doug."

He sighed, blinked a few times, then coughed. "You guys are a real buzzkill. Don't get me wrong," he focused his bloodshot eyes on me, "I'm glad to see you. Glad you're all alive. Especially you, Ben. You got a raw deal. It was only a matter of a time before the rest of us got the same from the three musketeers. I just wish you'd clued me in you were splitting this bad scene, Dave." Doug was all over the place, still under the influence of whatever he'd been in to.

"You mean Bryant, Mark, and Chuck?" I clarified which trio he referred to.

"You know it. There isn't a team anymore. It's just those three. They left me here because I told them I could get Baby Blue going again, even though I knew what had happened." He winked at Karlo. "How'd you do it, bro-man?"

"Never mind, Doug," I tried to get him back on track. "Tell us what happened."

"Things got rough here when we took Thoria, Ben. Rough. You guys weren't any happier about it than I was. Am I right, Dave?"

Dave and Karlo had told me about the siege on Thoria. "True, Doug," Dave admitted. "But we weren't sure about where you stood on things."

"You seemed pretty content with how it went down, Doug," Karlo added.

"Chuck had me under his thumb. So'd Marky-Mark. You know how bad it was. Loyalty oath and all that BS. But I promised Chuck I'd play cool. Then he split to go do the advance work on Pyreenia, then Matty split with the Chief and Mark to hit Clymaira. Then you guys split, I was alone. Hey, where's Mitch?"

I told him about our two latest losses.

"Poor Mitch. Poor Matty. You know, Matt didn't like things any better than I did. I was hoping maybe in Clymaira, he'd be able to lie low like I was doing. I don't blame you guys. Guess other than wait for the whole planet to suffocate, going out in a gunfight's the only way out for all of us." His face dropped into his palms.

I shot Dave and Karlo looks.

Dave rolled his eyes and mouthed, *drama queen*. Always the protector, Karlo made a sour face back. I nudged Doug to take a bottle of water. He took a swig.

"Marky worked that atmosphere wizard over good. He got him to tell the truth, though, and I believe what he said. The atmosphere plants in the Red Kingdom are putting out zilch. It's only the Yellow Kingdom and a few others that are keeping this whole place in O-two."

I steered him again. "Chuck's in Pyreenia? Who did the job on the works in Califex?"

Doug made a guilty face. "I made the charges, but Marky did the deed. I s'pose it brought the house down, huh?"

"It did at that," I admitted.

"He'd have killed me if I'd refused, Ben. Without Chuck to watch my back—" He let the rest hang.

"What's Bryant's plan, Doug?"

"You mean, other than to be king of Mars?"

Dave refined the question. "How's it going down?"

"The Chief isn't too concerned about Thoria. Or Clymaira. You guys taking both back isn't going to slow him down. Chuck's been in Pyreenia. He took the Mydreen ultimatum to them and found a receptive ear. I guess the king's son is a real piece of work. Hates the old man. Chief said that we weren't even going to have to make them fall in line—just the promise that we'd back Prince Carolinus as the new king was enough to get him to sign off on the big plan.

"But you can't trust a traitor, know what I mean? I bet the Chief's got something for his ass. Eventually. Guess that means Chief and

Marky'll have the Mydreen in residence in the capital soon enough. Well, game over then. We might as well get back to the party."

He stood up as if to leave.

"Sit down, Dougie," Dave said.

"What for? Domeel Doreen has all of the tribes of the Mydreen headed for Shansara. From there, it's on to the Yellow Kingdom. They don't need Baby Blue. They've got twenty thousand riders. They can do it. And if I know the Chief and Marky, they mean what they say. If they can't take it all, they'll burn down Mars on their way out. So, if that's the way it's going, then I aim to make the end as pleasant as possible." He winked. "Did you check out the local talent? Makes Malibu Beach look like a dog show."

"Dude," Dave drew out in exasperation. "What happened to you?"

Doug was on his feet, fists balled, the thin fabric over his shoulders falling off to leave him naked. "You gotta ask, Dave? We're stuck on another planet! Everyone we've ever known is gone. There's no America. There's no Army. Mike and the captain are dead, and Bryant's a fricking Napoleon with Marky-Mugabe as his hatchet man. There's no way off this desert island. We're going to run out of everything. Even air! So, what's the point?"

I was so mad at Doug's fall into uselessness my face must've been red enough to pass for a Vistaran. Karlo put himself between me and Doug, picking the fallen gossamer off the floor and resting the cloth on him again, as gently as if he was dressing a frail, dying man instead of a hulking killer. "Okay, okay. There's nothing more to be gained right now. Let's get Doug bedded down and let him sleep it off. I found your quarters, Doug. Let's get you to them. We'll talk later."

Doug made a stupid drugged smile of surrender. "Yeah, Karlo. Sounds good. You always have the best ideas." He pointed to Baby Blue, which had churned out another case of 5.56 since we'd been talking. "Don't know how you did it, but I know you did, man. I fooled 'em for you. Lied. Said it was just how the guys at Area 51 told us the machine would eventually break down. But I also told 'em I could nurse more out of it. That you'd showed me how. So, they let me stay. Chief told me to keep tabs on the Mydreen. Keep them from doing anymore ultra-violence on the locals and while I was at it, do some civil affairs and get the Thorians to be chill with us taking over. Make friends."

Dave frowned. "And?"

Doug grinned proudly. "Well, some of them are friendly, don't you think?"

"C'mon, Doug, you can tell me all about it on the way," Karlo eased one of Doug's thick arms over his shoulders.

"Go with him, Dave. Toss his hootch and make sure there're no weapons."

Doug shook Karlo off, offended. "I wouldn't hurt you guys for nothing. I did what I did so you'd be safe. Don't you believe me?"

"Sure, brah," Dave took his other arm. "Of course we do. You did a great job. DOL. Aaron Bank's looking down on you with pride. Let's get you bedded down."

"Wait," I said. "Dougie, do you know where the entrance to the atmosphere works is?"

"Sure thing, Ben-dog." He smiled. "If I tell you, will you go retrieve a couple of my friends to keep me company, buddy? I've got friends for you guys, too. You'll see, it's a whole 'nother level of sweet around here. This place is the best."

"Sure thing, buddy. But tell me where the entrance is, okay?"

He did. "I feel a nap coming on. Doesn't a nap sound good, puppy, puppy?" He made a smooching sound at Apache, who perked his ears before growling. Doug let himself be carried off, regaling us with his exploits in cross-cultural communication all the way out of the garage.

With pity, Kleeve Hartus watched the escorted Doug stumble, laugh, and weave away.

"The intoxicant will be with him for some time. The benefit is that in the throes of its effect, I doubt he could manage a deception. The sparkle dust renders its host open to suggestion."

Khraal Kahlees had kept his judgment to himself until now. "I doubt there is more he can tell us. What are your plans, Benjamin Colt?"

"We go to the atmosphere works and seek out the wizard for news from Shansara. Then we seal his mouth."

"With great pleasure!" The first shield grinned.

"Metaphorically. We reiterate it's in his best interest to conceal our activities here."

Double-K tapped the handle of his sword. "And if he has blundered and made our presence known to his brethren, we must know as we prepare for our next battle. Our destiny awaits in Shansara."

✣ ✣ ✣

The wizard was anxious and agitated. I tried to calm him, but understood. The last time one of us was in their secret clubhouse was probably when Marky had beaten a confession out of his lodge president, not stopping until the old man died. That would leave anyone a little gun-shy.

"I swear I have not revealed what has occurred here to the guild master. Please, do not hurt me!"

"No harm will come to you, wizard," Kleeve Hartus assured him. Better coming from him, a Vistaran, than me. "But what news from Shansara have you received?"

The man cowered and shook like a beaten dog. He was withholding news he thought we may not wish to receive.

"Speak!" Khraal Kahlees barked.

The man released. "The king is dead! All is lost!" He turned as if to run, panicked.

Kleeve Hartus grabbed a fistful of the absurd red chin whiskers and brought the man's face to his. "What do you mean?"

"Shansara has been paralyzed for weeks repelling the Mydreen siege. But two days ago, Prince Carolinus Darmon entered with his army in relief, finally answering his father's call. But just as hope returned, it has been destroyed! The king was murdered. The throne seized."

"Tell all you know from Tyrell Soreen, wizard," Khraal Kahlees demanded. The first shield released the man's beard. The wizard seemed to settle. At least, he knew enough not to give in to his panic and try to run again.

"When the rescue of Princess Talis Darmon from her captivity in Maleska Mal was repelled by the Thulians, the prince set into motion a plot that seems long in the making. Conspirators within the king's own council and the Guard made it possible. By the prince's own hand, he felled his father and took the crown and placed himself on the spectral throne."

Karlo got my attention. "You think Bryant's army's going to meet open arms in Shansara? Is the prince a Neville Chamberlain, ready to lay down and show his belly for some scraps from Bryant, or is the new boss going to put some steel into his army where his old man failed?"

Kleeve Hartus frowned. "Hah. There is no steel in Prince Carolinus Darmon. He is a shadow of the man that was Osric Darmon, may he walk with his ancestors in honor."

I saw the gears that had to mesh for this to happen. "Chuck was in Pyreenia. This is no coincidence."

Dave shook his head. "Damn."

Karlo saw it now, too. "Chuck found a royal exile, ready to step in, no doubt with a promise from Bryant to be his best friend if he did. That. Is. Masterful."

I could admire the exercise of such a grand strategy. The conventional war, carried by the downtrodden alien minority against the humans, bolstered by the team's knowledge and superior weapons, topped off by the subterfuge of a fifth column invader to undermine the Red Kingdom from within.

"Masterful," I agreed. "Even if it's been done by Bryant. I've underestimated him."

"No, Benjamin Colt," the first shield said. "The prince is a craven opportunist. His only desire has been the throne. For the promise of a crown, he would conspire with any enemy. But if he now sits in the Hall of Spectral Light, my instinct tells me he will remain there only as a puppet. Fight the invader? He is a coward. How he mustered courage to face the king, it amazes me. It was only because the promise of reward was so great."

"Then it is as I said, our destiny is in Shansara," Khraal Kahlees rumbled, his hand on his sword. "Wizard, I would silence you permanently if I thought you would betray us. Instead—" He drew the sword and smashed the panel of the communicator with the pommel, over and over, until the dust of the crystals showered the floor.

Dave winced. "I guess that's the move. Still, would've liked to get more intel first. We need to know if Bryant's in Shansara."

Khraal Kahlees sheathed his sword. "Rest assured he must be by now."

What I said only to myself was that Talis Darmon was the destiny I had to reach. I tried not to imagine what she was enduring. I prayed that Beraal was by her side. If Bryant and the prince were in Shansara, she wasn't any use as a hostage anymore.

We left the wizard and returned outside. As we moved to mount up for our return to start our planning, I was overwhelmed by a fierce impulse, one I was powerless to resist. Whether it was correct, whether it would bring us closer to victory, I didn't know. But I felt the time had come.

"We'll be right behind you, guys. First Shield, will you lead the return? Leave a flitter. Khraal Kahlees and I need to speak alone."

Kleeve Hartus raised his eyebrows. "Of course. We await your return at the Guard's headquarters."

Karlo and Dave were puzzled, but accepted my instructions.

Khraal Kahlees sensed there was something unusual in my dismissal of our companions, but waited by my side patiently as we watched them fly away.

"What transpires, Benjamin Colt?"

Whatever guilt I would feel for it, I'd gladly bear if it brought Talis Darmon to safety. "Khraal Kahlees, I risk our friendship at a critical time by breaking a confidence. I do not do so lightly. Do you remember a dosenie of House Pardoo, a woman named Lassa Laloo?"

40

"Laze the rock outcrop halfway up that slope, Ben. The one that looks like Snoopy at attention."

"327 meters. I guessed 300."

Karlo scrunched eyes. "I thought it looked closer to 350."

"*Price is Right* rules, I would've won."

Dave scoffed, "You're telling me, with that gizmo hanging on the end of a fizzle gun, it'll reach that distance?"

The new attachment looked much like a suppressor except it was rectangular, and fizzle guns didn't make much noise to begin with.

"Let's find out." Karlo shouldered the Tarn rifle.

"Whoa!" Dave looked for a way through the wall of Double-K and Kleeve Hartus to step off the peak of the sand berm we all crowded on. "Lemme get behind the line. Have you tested this yet, Karlo? You sure it's not just a fancy muzzle obstruction? I mean, no offense, but you aren't a weapons man."

"None taken, Dave." Karlo gave him a one-finger salute. Karlo was a master-class shooter and weapons smith, and Dave knew it. "And, yes, I've already tested it for safety."

"Ignore him, Karlo," I said. "Let's see this." I stayed where I was, right next to Karlo and the gun he shouldered, a teensy bit of apprehension lingering after Dave's comment, enough to make me flinch and twist my face slightly away as Karlo fired.

327 meters away, a puff of dirty vapor materialized under the beam's impact, the *crack* and noise of the gravel shower a second behind.

Karlo reacted. "Nice!" Whether it was the solid offhand hit or the proof of his design that made the genius grin, I only knew it was a rare sight.

Double-K and the first shield were stunned.

"Take a spin, gentlemen," Karlo offered. The two took several shots each at the same rocks, marveling after each shot the way anyone would if a BB gun somehow got juiced up so it could knock over an engine block.

Dave's ears were pinned back in amazement, too. "When'd you come up with this, Karlo? Today?"

"Ha! I should tell you I did, that'd get you back! Hater!"

"No, really, Karlo. This is incredible, brah. In a month, we couldn't crank out enough M4s and trained Tarns to make a difference. This'll make up-arming the Korundi instantaneous. How'd you do it?"

Karlo waved him off. "I started working on it back at the crash site. I figured out almost immediately it was a collimation error that made the fizzle guns so weak. I don't get to use it much, but I have a lot of optics engineering in my background. Particles are particles. Light or electrons—which is what I think the fizzle guns are hyper-accelerating. Protons would be too dense and do a lot more damage. I think. Anyway, I worked a design out back then, but didn't get a chance to turn it into a prototype until just now."

It was hard not to be impressed. I pounded his shoulder. "Proof of concept? Check."

Karlo watched as the Vistarans took more shots. "We should rename our upgraded weapons to distinguish them from their weaker parent. How about—blasters?"

Dave rolled his eyes. "For such a genius, you got no imagination, brah. Slaughter ray. Slicer. Hammer beam. Eradicator. Intruder stream. Sun gun—hmm. Not that last one. There was a Swedish K. How about Italian K? K for Karlo. Italian for… Karlo."

"Special-K," I said.

Dave snapped his fingers. "K-Special, so it doesn't sound like a short school bus kinda thing."

"K-spec," I said. "It's just the sort of name no one could figure out if they weren't in the know, but they'd know it was so cool, only the cool guys would have 'em."

Dave showed his approval by making the horn sign overhead with his index and pinky finger like a metal head. "Ben gets it! That's how you name something as badass as this, Karlo. K-spec it is, brah."

Our master tinkerer pretended he didn't hear. "I had to design better sights for it to take advantage of the new range since the mark-zero model was just a spray-and-pray kinda weapon. Its trajectory is the same as the line of sight. The offset between them is nil. Maximum range? I'm guessing on soft targets will be about 400 meters. I'll get Baby Blue cranking it all out ASAP."

Khraal Kahlees traced a finger over the flats of the barrel extension like he was testing the edge of a sword. "How many can be produced?"

Karlo considered that. "Five—" he paused. I was waiting for him to say five a day.

"Five hundred a day. Three thousand this week, give or take. They're very simple."

Now my jaw dropped. "Karlo, that's—incredible."

"You just made our M4s obsolete, brah."

Karlo sucked air though his teeth. "Be cautious, Dave. Baby Blue can't make the whole gun—yet. I may not even be able to improve upon them anymore. I don't know the power source for a fizzle gun. It's sealed and self-contained. It runs dry in about fifty shots, then it's junk. There's one source of manufacture—Shansara. This is a great solution, for now." He made eye contact with our Vistarans. "Anything wrong in what I said, gentlemen?"

Kleeve Hartus seemed to grow taller as he spoke. "What you have said is true, Karlo Columbo. Mayhap you will learn the secret intricacies of the weapons fabricators, and more. But do not undervalue what you have accomplished. It is monumental. I worried that honorable defeat was the best we could hope for. Now I see a way to victory."

Khraal Kahlees had been sullen since I'd told him the truth about Beraal. For the first time in days, he broke his sullen mood and offered one of his erudite thoughts. "The villainy of Domeel Doreen and the Thulian renegades cannot stand against the rectitude and honor of our cause. Especially so, Karlo Columbo, because your skill and knowledge are fueled by a heart of justice. Thank you, friend."

I'd never seen a man with so much in his head be caught so blank, like a laptop frozen in an update as he considered how to respond. Karlo was a genius, but sometimes, like all of us, he lacked words to match a moment. Karlo crossed his arms over his chest in the Tarn manner of solemnity. This was a good custom. It spared words when words could only come up short to return honor given.

With the rifle at his side, the Tarn raised three of his arms above him. "But with only these left with which to fight, I would spend the last drop of my own blood to see our enemy's equally spilled, and turn the deserts a red sea before I let the Mydreen rule over Mihdradahl. With this weapon or without, I swear this pledge. I will not fall before his people feel the fury of Khraal Kahlees and see Domeel Doreen's head separated from his body."

Selfish. Manipulative. Cruel, even. The effect I'd wanted had been achieved. This was war. I could forgive myself for manipulating Khraal Kahlees, but if she knew, would Talis Darmon forgive me?

The green throat roared to the red Vistaran sky.

✤ ✤ ✤

"What do we do about Doug?"

We couldn't put it off. Like a huge credit card bill, just opened then tossed in the pile because payment wasn't due for weeks, the decision waited. Time had slipped away and the account had to be settled, no matter how our checking account was lacking. It was just the five of us in the underground den, around the massive sand table we'd built of our continent-spanning theater.

Double-K had been as puzzled as the Tarns we'd enlisted to haul in dirt, rock, and colorful items heisted from the empty offices to build our map. With the newfound zeal of a convert, he understood its utility. Now he moved a finger from Thoria across the desert as he thought out loud.

"From Califex, we will begin." He traced a finger down the Korund to the last way station. "There we will make departure to arrive beneath their nesting grounds as if invisible. I promise ancient fears will not stop my kin. They've learned to accept the discomfort in taking flight to carry the might of our war. They will do so aloft on a river if at the end of it there will be blood. The waters will not quench the fire in my people to see battle brought to the doorstep of the usurper and Domeel Doreen."

I dreaded splitting up our band. Together our strength had brought us the kind of invulnerability I'd once felt on the A-Team we were supposed to be, instead of becoming a promise lost the day we landed on Mars—with Mike and the captain paying the price for our naivety. Had they not been killed, I doubt we'd be where we were now. How could we have known? How could we have better prepared? I'd already answered that question and accepted the forgiveness that came with the answer.

We couldn't have.

I could blame the ineptitude of the planners of Task Force Elon Musk, the scientists who built the gate, or the Guests. I might as well hold a grudge against my parents for bringing me into the world, for all the good it would do.

But Bryant. Bryant, I could hold accountable. And Marky. And for the choice we had to make now, they were also responsible.

Khraal Kahlees and Kleeve Hartus were full members of this team, and their opinions mattered on what to do with Doug. I already knew what I thought best. Karlo and Dave had known our adrift teammate longer than I, but from the way they talked about him, it was like they were memorializing a dead man.

"Doug and I went through RASP together. We went to selection together," Dave said. "I gave Mike the word to bring him on the team. They used to call him Thor."

Karlo summed it up. "True. You might not think so now, Ben, but when he came to the team, he upped us. Guys started calling us the Avengers. He was invincible. But now—he's broken."

We'd tried to involve Doug. He was free of the drugs, but a dull, shell of himself. He offered no opinion. Took no initiative. Whenever Karlo would leave to check on Baby Blue, he would use it as an excuse to wander away and return to his bed where we would find him sleeping fitfully.

Khraal Kahlees was impassive. "If he has lost the will of a warrior, he is a liability. We will leave him in Califex."

The first shield spoke up quickly and with urgency. "I will take him with me to Clymaira." He was departing on his own to check on the council's progress before linking up with us in Califex. "No offense given, Khraal Kahlees, but he may not fare well amongst the Tarn. If he were known to be damaged… if what I understand is true, when a Tarn warrior puts down the sword…"

"No offense is taken. What you say is true. Among us, a warrior lost to the way permits his closest friend to end his life standing. There is no shame in it. It is how a Tarn can cross the Blix with honor."

"No!" Karlo objected the same time as Dave and I did. "I don't want him somewhere where he can get the idea."

Kleeve Hartus was firm. "Then he comes with me. The wizards are untrustworthy, but I believe what they say is true, that Clymaira remains unmolested by the attempt of the Mydreen to regain her. He would be safe there."

I'd made my decision. "We're going to leave him here."

The first shield's rejection came out as an indictment. "Under the influence of the Thorians? He would return to the state of debauchery we found him mired in."

Karlo's face wasn't that of the logical engineer I'd seen probe the mysteries of the universe in holy reverie, but the face of the physician torn by how to save his patient. "There aren't enough antidepressants in my bag to repair him enough to make him functional. He's found a way to kill his grief, even if he's just burying it. I'm at a loss for what else to do."

I was relieved Karlo'd made the same leap I had. "Leaving him may be the best way to keep him alive. If he can hold on, I think Talis Darmon may be able to help him."

Dave was baffled. "How's that, brah?"

Do I tell them? If it meant the difference in saving Doug, I'd explain, but I trembled and swallowed sour vomit at the thought of sharing my secret.

"I've seen her work. There's a kind of therapy. A way to heal minds. She—she helped me."

"What do you mean, Ben?" Karlo frowned.

Do I tell them about the pit of ugly fear and self-loathing I'd carried? That she took it all away?

"She is a sorceress," Khraal Kahlees said, stepping in. "She has the knowledge of her maternal line, the last of her dynasty to hold the power. It is so, that she has healing powers. Perhaps she can someday help repair your friend to remain this side of Temple Farnest."

Karlo looked at me with understanding. I think he knew, but let me out of the trap I'd almost sprung on myself, the steel jaws I'd forced open, held so by a tiny disc, just waiting to be stepped on by the unasked question, *What was wrong with you before, Ben?*

Our medic looked like it was he who bore the weight of Doug's fall. "I learned from my best teacher that inside every man is a universe of his own creation. His own heaven. His own hell. Doug was our strongest. Mars broke him. Even him. We've made it because we're together. He didn't because we left him. I should've known. I'm guilty of leaving a comrade behind. I'm as sorry for it as anything I've ever done."

Dave closed his eyes like armor to repel Karlo's self-recrimination. "You're not guilty of anything, Karlo. Not your fault. Or mine. Or Mitch's. We did the best we could, brah." He opened his eyes. "I think you're right, Ben. If he can hang on, maybe when this is over, she can help him. He was happy when we found him. If it's just a bandage, then it is what it is. I say we leave him, for now. But we won't forget him."

"No, brothers. We won't. Splitting up is the best of bad options, but no one will be alone. Not for long. Not even Doug."

Baby Blue would move overland by arkall power, protected by the bulk of our ground forces and a detachment of flitters for air cover. The factory would keep producing as it rolled. We'd considered sling loading Baby Blue underneath a trio of air cars, but ruled it out just as quickly. Never tried, no time to experiment, maximum potential for disaster. A wagon train was slow but safe.

Khraal Kahlees would fly ahead to Califex to prepare the assembled army. Dave would go with him and start the process of up-arming our soldiers with the new ranged weapons and begin the mass movement to our departure point.

I was on my way to revisit Cynar. I could stay connected to Dave while we were on our separate journeys. If Cynar had perfected our new commo, it meant we'd never be out of contact with each other again.

We each took a grip with Kleeve Hartus before he mounted his air car. "I am responsible to Clymaira to ensure the council has acted responsibly to return the city to function in my absence. I will join you with as many able Guards and air cars as is possible. Until then."

Double-K took to another flitter with a Guard to pilot, checking the waist gun as he waited. Dave joined them.

"Keep me in the loop, brah," he said. "I'll have the Tarns shooting the center out of bull's-eyes in no time. Double-K says his troops will take to movements to contact and bounding elements like kids to candy. We'll be ready to bring the smoke show to the Mydreen in no time. It's all coming together, brah, thanks to you."

"We did it together, bro."

"That we did, Ben-dog." He hesitated. "Hey, it might be nothing, but keep an eye on Karlo, huh? He's beating himself up about the Doug thing. Never seen him this down on himself. Ever."

"Will do. Catch you later."

I gave Khraal Kahlees a salute as they lifted off, the Tarn raising his rifle overhead in reply as they levitated, and they were gone. I went back to helping Karlo organize the last items for our caravan. We had ten mounted Tarns. Two to pull Baby Blue on its trailer. Three flitters with Guards for pilots and a Tarn each to man the waist guns, newly outfitted with collimators. The more powerful deck guns were now the equal of our fifties—maybe better. With no drop to compensate for, they were aim-and-kill weapons out to practically the distance where you could see impacts—a thousand meters or more of white lightning death. Until they ran dry. How to get more of them was a problem we'd deal with later.

I loaded my kit into my own air car, Avril Mysteen my pilot and a Tarn to man the waist gun with me. Apache loved flying. He laid on the deck, gnawing at a bone. I tried not to think about where it had come from. None of the Tarns seemed put off by it.

"I'll find you on your route in a couple of days, Karlo, bearing gifts from Cynar."

His goodbye was lackluster and abrupt. "I'll have the rest of our combat load-out ready by the time we hit Califex so we can hit the ground running. I better get back to it. See you." He hesitated before turning away.

I dropped the last of my kit into the air car. "I'll be right back, Avril Mysteen." I wandered over to Baby Blue where Karlo checked the carriage. Even if he didn't, I at least had things that needed to be said.

"Thanks for letting me off the hook earlier, Karlo. I know you got that I had some deep stuff I didn't want to talk about. Anyway, thanks."

He waved me off. "Everybody's got baggage, Ben. Not just you."

I thought back. Dave had tried to tell Karlo once how much he admired him, as I did. He'd blown us off, like an android reminding us that though he looked human, we shouldn't be concerned for him because he had no emotions. What I heard for the first time, was that he wasn't a Mr. Data.

"If I've never told you, you're the most incredible guy I've ever known," I said. "You know so much about everything, how the world works, even people. You make me realize how much I've slacked all my life, bro."

"Not so." Karlo stopped checking the cable he'd already checked twice to avoid looking at me. His shoulders sank. He spoke, facing Baby Blue. "There was a time I thought I'd reduced the world and everything in it to formulas and equations, structures and microstructures, materials and properties. Thought I could navigate life because I knew how *things* worked. I learned I was wrong."

Karlo, wrong?

"How'd you come to think that?" I asked him.

"I had a mentor. A man I respect, who opened my eyes and taught me that people were more complex than any circuit board I'd ever designed."

It was as much personal insight into his inner world as he'd given since that day in Maleska Mal when he revealed how he coped with our new future.

"Who?"

"His handle was Kato. He was maybe the biggest influence in my life. A real legend. Deserved. He bounced back and forth between 75th and SF his whole life. He was teaching at medlab when I went through the Q. He took an interest in me being an X-ray, not even a year in the Army and already in the Q-course. And it wasn't because I was brilliant that I got his attention, Ben. It was because I was an asshole."

Dave was right. Karlo was down. I knew about beating yourself up. Not wanting to spook the rare creature I hunted for, I stayed still to give him the ease to let him come out of his den, to tell what he wanted to tell me.

"I was prideful, Ben. Arrogant. Here I was, in the toughest course in the world, and I was smoking it. PT? I was always at the head of the pack. Barely had to study while other guys spent every second in a book. And sometimes, I was loud about it. Boastful. He'd smack me down more than once when I'd flex my mental muscles and throw my education around. Or the same when I'd talk about how an eighteen-mile ruck was nothing compared to an Ironman. Yeah, I used to do that. I know I'm not that way now. The reason is because of him. He made me see myself for the first time. The harshest mirror I ever stood in front of. Made me see how I really was, not how I thought I was.

"He's the one taught me that just because I was smart, it didn't make me special. Instead, it meant I had responsibilities. I was going to be an SF medic. That a team was going to need me to be more than a guy who could stop the bleeding and treat malaria. He taught me there was more to people than anatomy and physiology. He told me, 'You've got a gift for knowledge, but it's not enough. Fixing people isn't fixing machines, young medic. There's gonna be times when you've got to try to find the hurt you can't see, and keep guys from losing what's more important than their blood. You gotta keep them from losing their hearts.'"

"You have, Karlo. You've done that, and so much more."

Now he met my eyes. "Thanks, Ben. Sorry, man. I don't mean to be down. It's not just Doug. It's—you ever wonder where the others ended up? I hardly ever think about it now. And I feel bad about it. I don't want to forget them, just like we're not going to forget Doug. Or the world. I just know, whatever comes next, I'm not going to forget Kato's lesson. I'm going to do better."

We were silent for a while.

"We've got to take care of each other, Karlo. I want you to talk to me. I'm not the smartest guy, but I know how to listen. I got lucky, having you and Dave at my side. And I got lucky to have Talis Darmon in my life. She's very special. I not only fell in love with her, she helped me. Maybe you need her help, too?"

"Yeah, maybe. We're all messes, dude. Except Dave."

That made me laugh. "Yeah. He's the real rock, don't you know? Whatever keeps him chugging on, they need to figure it out and bottle it."

"It'll have a taste that's a strong combination of hate and a freshly lubed bolt carrier group with undercurrents of making commo, whatever flavor that is." He laughed just enough at his own joke—practically a guffaw by his standards—to let me know he was back on track.

"I'm not kidding about talking, Karlo. We've got to keep close tabs on each other. And Dave, too. Even if he seems like he's even-Steven."

"We will."

"See you in a few. I'll be back with presents. If Dave's been hiding a sack of sorry's better than the rest of us, what Cynar's promised to have for us will make him the king of the Echos. For him, it'll be better than a Thorian sex club with a 'Dave Only' sign."

That brought another chuckle.

As I turned to leave, he caught me. "Ben, we'll get Talis Darmon back. Whatever else comes of this, you deserve to be together. Don't lose hope. We're close. I feel it."

"I do, too. Hey, you know what you just did?"

His forehead wrinkled and he shook his head. I pounded my chest, where inside, the same kind of certainty grew, just as Mike had once inspired in me. The optimism that the future was not something to be dreaded and endured, but something to long for, a thing to wrap myself in like a comforting blanket, an impenetrable armor of hope.

"What your hero Kato told you. You gave me heart, brother."

41

"I remember the course to the Fountain Way Station, Benjamin Colt," Avril Mysteen said as we pitched and rocked gently. We flew fast, youth coupled with competence bolstering my pilot's velocity and easy hand on the controls. We crossed borders of wide shadows separated by narrow corridors of bright beams of morning rays and back into the chilled shade of another high peak. Except for our weaving motion, it made for a perfect illusion that we were in the stationary center of a merry-go-round.

"Almost there," I said as I extended my arm. "It narrows ahead. Ease back as we slide into this valley and follow that trail in."

Movement caught my eye. A not-quite white figure shambled between rocky crevices.

"Throttle back," I snapped. "There's something below."

More blanched shapes of Cynar's ape-guardians were apparent, strewn through the crags and tiny flats above the bottom of the pass. Even from hundreds of feet above it was obvious. The coats of the Hortha were mottled with dark splotches, their pure white coats ruined by a camouflage pattern of blood. The lone ambulator that had caught my eye dropped without even turning eyes skyward.

"The enemy must be near! We will shock them with our sudden appearance overhead and have the advantage of surprise." Avril Mysteen moved to bring us back to speed.

"Throttle back, I said!" The kid loved velocity. If he lived long enough, I'd teach him that sometimes it was a trap. He took my command with frowning disdain. Flyboys were all alike until they got shot down the first time. We rounded a sharp corner to finally view the knot of our destination nestled at the bottom of the sharply angled pass. Three air cars were grounded around our destination.

"Bank and get us some altitude," I yelled. I pointed to the waist gunner. "Light them up!"

It was a teachable moment. Avril Mysteen kept silent and took direction, focused on his task to maneuver us higher. I crowded next to the Tarn as our pilot deftly rotated us to port. Both red human and green Tarn scurried to action as fizzle guns flashed below like erupting sunspots. Churchill once said there's nothing quite so exhilarating as being shot at without result. He was right. They were too far away to have effect with their weaker arms. It doesn't take too many simple facts to spur intuition into a tactical decision. I was right to have told the waist gunner to have at.

Apache's tongue wagged in the wind, oblivious.

With renewed vigor, I slapped the Tarn's middle shoulder. "Make 'em pay, son." The Tarn's tusks thrust forward told me he understood it was truly okay to action. He lowered his face and leaned sharply to depress the muzzle and went to work.

Our arrows flew farther. Our stick was bigger. Our hammer was heavier. At the third burst, an air car exploded and the "YES!" of success came with it for successfully bringing the pain to them, gift wrapped with a big red bow. Bodies flew. A flaming man weaved away in a parody of a waltz until he succumbed and collapsed, draped by his cape as it too caught fire. A grander exit, I'd never seen. Did they have Viking funerals on Mars? He just got one.

Without need of my encouragement, the Tarn walked white bolts toward the next grounded target, grunting his pleasure in a solo orgy of superior firepower.

There's no sound in the world like a minigun. People liken it to a chain saw or a dirt bike, but that's only saying your mystery meat tastes like chicken, but ain't. Steak tastes like steak. An M134 burping out copper death pills has its own unique signature that can't be described except by bad comparison. And just like the roar of an F-22 taking off from Eglin, you don't need to see it to recognize it's the trumpet of an invincible guardian angel, materialized to shield your fragile life, pride racing comfort to reach your spine with its sound.

Except when its flaming sword is slashing at you.

A burst ripped past our nose.

I dropped with the Tarn falling on top of me as we both slammed into the deck. I tried to grab onto something firm as the air car lurched and dove. Bees traveling at hyperspeed punched through the deck and my arm felt the pricks of metal spall. The flitter rocked and yawed wildly.

Avril Mysteen was loud, but calm. "We're going down." Centrifugal force from our tight circle of descent pushed me and the Tarn hard against the gunwale, Apache the same ahead of the console. It was better than the bucking bronco we'd been on, but I winced. Not because of the burning in my arm, but against the pain I knew was to come at the end of our fall, presaged by the cliffs speeding upward around us.

Avril Mysteen paddled both arms violently down across the control panel and a repelling force pushed us suddenly from below, like an upward freefall. We bounced. Once. Then a second and final time as the air car came to an angled halt in a cloud of dust. I slid across the deck, the Tarn toppling after to crush me against the opposite gunwale. Apache crawled over and slobbered kisses on my face.

I pushed him off and spat grit. Had I just survived another crash? Better than the alternative, I suppose. My arm worked fine, but was numb.

"Get that waist gun free and let's move," I said.

I looked about for Avril Mysteen. The deck was bare. My own M4 and a spare K-spec was where I'd lashed my kit in front of the control console. I hopped off and landed awkwardly on the slope, sliding down on the loose scree like it was ice, until I bounced against the flitter.

"Get to that flat spot," I yelled to the Tarn gunner. "I'm right behind you." I saw a bare red leg behind a jutting boulder. I crouched and leaped, landing on top of the rocky column. Wrapped around it, like a noodle on a fork, lay the broken body of Avril Mysteen. Beside him now, I rolled him to me. Parted lips bubbled red. I scooped him up and slid down the slope and laid him against the air car in the shade.

"Apache, come, boy."

The gadron peered over the side, then obeyed.

I spoke to him like he could understand. "Stay here and protect our friend."

The Tarn manning the K-max—the up-powered waist gun—sent more electric sizzles of fire. I had to win the fight. I left the youngster in Apache's care and took two bounces then crawled to my gunner's side. He was busy sending careful blasts ahead. We overlooked the trail leading from the bowl of Cynar's way station.

"They've got an M134 mounted on an air car. I can't see it now, but if anything lifts off, give it everything you've got."

A Tarn moved into the pass. I got my M4 up and blew out a breath. I pressed the trigger. The upper arms dropped a weapon, the lower reached to cover the hunched midsection, then the Tarn fell away.

"Yes, Benjamin Colt. If they bring it to bear on us again, it will be bad. I have seen the revolving death at work. I made an offering to the ancestors to never be on this end of its wrath. Next time I will make an offering of something truly dear so it is better received."

For the moment, the gap ahead was bare of threat.

"Tell me your name again, warrior," I asked the Tarn beside me.

"Garlak Ranz."

"You were with us when we visited the water priest before, yes?"

"I was, lord."

"Listen, Garlak Ranz. In a minute we're going to assault through. Keep on the objective. I've got to make a call." I touched the swelling of the necklace against my skin. "Dave-Dave, do you read me, over?"

To my shock and relief, his voice rang in my skull. "Got you, Ben-Ben! Isn't this amazing? Man, I can't tell you how much I've missed—"

"We're in the shit, Dave." I quickly told him the essentials.

"If their only minigun is there, you know what that means, Ben? One of the team's there, too. What the hell brought them to Cynar's hideout, though?"

"Yeah, ditto on all. Dunno why they'd be at Cynar's. It must be coincidence. There's no way anyone could know I was headed to the way station."

"Benjamin Colt, do you receive my voice?" It was Cynar's croak.

"Cynar! I hear you. I'm in the pass west of the way station. We flew into an ambush by soldiers outside your lab. Are you okay?"

"Never again will I curse your intellect, White lord! The invaders appeared without warning from the sky. Tell me you've avenged the Hortha killed defending me!"

"Cynar, have they breached your lab?"

"No, they have not. The Hortha responded to my call and held the curs at bay. My noble friends gave their all! Had you not arrived to halt the intrusion—wait. Are you yet engaged with the enemy outside my redoubt?"

"Yes, Cynar."

Dave's voice filled the space between my ears. "We're mounting up, Ben. Help's on the way, but it's going to take the better part of a day to fly there. Get to a defendable position. Keep in touch. Out."

"Your army comes to our aid, White lord?"

"Yes, Cynar, but it's going to be many hours from now."

"Benjamin Colt, why does this enemy bring war to my doorstep?"

"I don't know, Cynar, but I'm going to stop them. How did you hear me? Have you been able to all this time?"

"Eh?" he preambled in his familiar and annoying way. "I have been too busy to listen to your babble. It is by welcome accident that I heard my name carried by the seventh ray while in my lab at work. White lord, I have no defense with the Hortha all but massacred—my poor, pure friends. If the enemy gains entrance here, they can do great harm to us all. I beg of you, my friend, stop them."

"Stay put, Cynar. The cavalry's coming." I'd both rogered and dismissed Dave's advice to lay up simultaneously. My decision to take the fight to our enemy had been made the second I'd scooped up Avril Mysteen and processed that somewhere on the other side of those cliffs, there was a man or men in multicam who I wanted to kill. Whichever one or all of them it was.

I patted the shoulder of Garlak Ranz. "We're a two-man team. You stay put until I make my way to that spot on the other slope. It'll only take me a few leaps. When I'm set, I'll wave. You move on this side to that next spot higher up the slope on this side. If we take fire, whoever's moving, get prone and get to killing. That's your thirty-second lesson in bounding overwatch. Ready for the practical application?"

He growled with tusks moving side to side. He was ready.

"All I've got to say is don't watch me, watch those ridges. I'm depending on you."

Without waiting for his assurance, I bounced down the slope. One, two, I was at the bottom of the valley. I sprung off the flat of the trail, up and forward, landed, and slid a little until I recovered on firm ground, then sprang a last time to reach a cluster of rocks. I'd covered fifty yards farther forward in seconds. I paused to look over my gun. All calm. I made a big wave behind and waited just long enough to see Garlak Ranz begin his course. It was four hundred meters to the ridgeline. I prayed that at any moment heads would pop up, letting us outclass the puny fizzle guns our opponents carried.

We moved like this, my bound taking a scant minute, my partner's bound clumsy, slow, fighting the slope as he used legs and free arms to navigate from rock outcrop to rock outcrop before settling in. We were halfway to our phase line when a *CRACK* whizzed over my back and the impact of a very large projectile peppered the uninjured side of my body with tiny rock fragments. I heard the dull report of the muzzle. Suppressors worked. I couldn't tell where the shot came from.

Someone had me in the crosshairs of their MK 22. It had to be Marky-Mark. I sprang low and another shot whizzed overhead, no doubt landing where I'd just evacuated a millisecond ago. The sniper wasn't on the ridgeline ahead, unless he'd made one hell of a slow stalk and I'd missed the change in the scenery. He had to be up on a slope farther away to get the angle on me, which meant he was at least seven or eight hundred meters from me. To my right, the K-squared fired. It fired again. I was too low on the slope and too busy avoiding being the recipient of a competent sniper's attention to see the impacts. I came up behind the biggest protrusion of the most beautifully solid rocks I'd ever seen and plopped down.

Garlak Ranz was on the move. I cursed, and eased myself to a spot where I could get a gun up to cover him. I was too low to see much but the sharp outline of the mouth leading to the last bend into the bowl ahead. I no longer had a high vantage. Defilade; check. Overwatch; negative. I spotted another rock outcrop up the slope, maneuvered myself to where I could get two feet onto firm ground, and sprang. I went high and silently prayed a 230-grain copper pill didn't shatter me like I was a clay bird. I landed and scrambled behind cover.

"White lord! Here!"

On the same level directly across the valley from me, Garlak Ranz waved. "I saw the foul Thulian fall to my second shot. He tumbled down the slope. I am certain."

I yelled in joyful abandon, "I think I love you!" Just then I meant it. I should be dead. "Sorry, dude. Stay there and keep at it until I bring you up." I saw where I wanted to end up. I took three deep breaths, coiled, and released. One bound, two bounds, three. I needed a new *I'm up, he sees me, I'm dead* mantra to time my bounding rush ability. I knew just where I landed, below the last rise. On the other side, I pictured the reverse of what I knew was below—the commanding view over the bowl of the ape amphitheater, the fountain pool, and the entrance to the cave.

The most audacious and unlikely plan is sometimes the one most likely to succeed. I laid two frags beside me. In quick order I sent each from my back, tossing them overhead behind me. Three bass *crumps* and I was already rolled over. I popped up and took quick aim to the far side of the bowl to where I would be if I were them and lobbed my first 40 mic-mic there, followed by a second to where I knew the trail widened before entering the bowl. I deftly swung my carbine on my back and filled my hands with my K-spec. The burning flitter was on the ridge above. By the fountain, another sat unharmed. Only bodies lay around, bare white fur stained with blood, scantily clad red and green skins in tatters, none showing life. I waited. I waved overhead and motioned Garlak Ranz. He waved in return and I pumped my fist in the universal sign language of haul ass.

I stayed on my K-spec and waited patiently for my partner to huff and puff up the slope to me. He plopped next to me. I had a water bottle ready for him. He took it and sputtered as he sucked deeply several times. "Nice work, Garlak Ranz. I owe you a life."

He passed the bottle back and I took a swig. "I am reborn anew. It is with new eyes I see the world behind this—" he patted the K-squared. "There!"

I heard it, too. A flitter rose and whined away, below our line of sight. Someone was escaping.

"Get to that air car by the fountain. We have to go after them. It's got to be the air car with the 134. We have to kill it."

Over we went. I reached the air car first. I was behind the controls and spinning up the drive by the time the Tarn threw himself and his big gun in.

He waved a pair of arms at me. "Go." He was on his knees and pushing to the nose as we cleared the bowl. My MBITR crackled. I had it on, always curious if it would come to life as it had back in Clymaira.

"Dave, Karlo, I thought you guys agreed to sit this out. I thought we had an understanding. The Chief's going to bring hell down on you. And so am I."

The voice was harried. Strained. Pained, even. But I'd heard it in my dreams whenever I thought about the fierce beating I'd taken, berating myself all the while for forgetting Talis Darmon's wisdom to leave the past in the past.

It was Mark.

I pulled my radio free. "Not Dave, dickhead."

"Colt! You traitor! If I'da thought it was you—you son of a bitch."

"You're going down, Mark."

Garlak Ranz turned to me. "For Malesak Mal they flee."

"Stay on the gun!" I yelled. "Bring him down."

I concentrated on flying. I pushed our velocity and tried to anticipate the curves of the trail as it wound up the narrow valley of jagged peaks. "He's got a head start on us, but I'm going to run him down. Be ready!"

In reply, my partner placed a cushion beneath the barrel and settled in as we swerved.

"If he's grounded, yell out. He can be waiting to nail us with the minigun. We'll only have a second. Stay sharp."

The Tarn gave a raised fist. He knew how to ride down a fleeing quarry. He was worth his weight in the rarest gems on Vistara. It was as if I'd hit the lottery with an easy pick. It couldn't be random chance. Mike and the captain were looking down on me, blessings for my revenge their supernatural gift.

We pursued. An hour of flight and I began to have doubts we were on the right trail, when in a flash, I saw the tail of a flitter disappear behind a peak. The blast of the K-squared told me Garlak Ranz had seen him too. I pushed the flitter faster and swerved, the edge of a mountain so close I could almost taste scraped paint off our air car. Too close.

A surge of speed and we were in a straightaway. The flitter hung in front of us, a thousand meters away. He'd gunned the air car, and I did the same. The K-squared fired. Fired again. And again. I thought I saw a flash of impact.

Garlak Ranz threw the gun to the deck and brought his K-spec up. "It is spent, White lord. Get closer."

I cursed our first bad luck.

But just as fast, my anger turned to joy. The flitter smoked. It dove and disappeared behind a rise.

"You got him!" I slowed. "We're going to take our time." I eased us down to a spot on the trail just wide enough to accept our flitter.

Garlak Ranz moved to the console as we landed. "Why do we halt?"

"I think he's alone. If he's down, he can bring the M134 to bear against us. We're not going to give him the chance. Let's roll!"

We moved at a trot up the winding trail. A few hundred meters ahead was the top of its rise. When my eyes were even with the peak, I dropped to a crouch and waved the Tarn low. In an unconscious shift to the whisper of the hunter I guided him.

"Low and slow. Let's find him."

The last few meters I dropped to my belly and crawled ahead in the lead. I cautiously raised my head. The flitter was smoking, dark billows rising above flaming vapor to shroud the air car in a screen.

"He must be gravely injured. Let us wait. Let him expire and we will find our prey a trophy on the ground, awaiting our gutting and feast!"

He was probably right. I knew he was right. Wait for Dave and the cavalry. We could run him down by air when they arrived. If he was still alive. But I had a score to settle, and the red of Mars burned in me like a branding iron. That sun would never be quenched unless I saw him. I put my radio to my mouth.

"You're done, Mark. Lay down on the trail spread-eagle and I'll let you live. Karlo will fix you up."

I could feel the spittle form his mouth as he sucked air in and out with each halt. "You sold out your team for a piece of tail… you… weakling. Mike made two mistakes." He panted. "Not killing the first Tarns we met… and bringing you to the team." He strained like a wounded man on the move.

I stood. "Stay behind me. If he gets me, finish him."

"No, Benjamin Colt. Let him die slowly. The day is ours!"

I shook his arm off my shoulder. "Not good enough." I set out, the plod of heavy legs right behind me. The fire raged. I took a breath and ran through the heat wave around the air car and to the other side. I pulled ahead to make room through the narrow pass for my partner and wiped soot off my face. Whatever cancer the toxic stuff from the burning power plant would give me, I'd worry about another time.

"Watch ahead." I pointed.

On the nose was the M134. The pintle mount had been taken off the war wagon and welded to the bow. I pulled the pins to release the gun, fighting panic to abandon my efforts as flames scorched and blistered my exposed head and neck. The gun came free and I dove with it.

A pair of Tarn hands pulled me away from the oven. "Benjamin Colt, this is madness."

I patted his hands away. I coughed. "I think I saved it. Get behind me. Let's go."

I eased us around the next corner, and the next. I recognized an overhang where Talis Darmon had once nestled my head in her lap and soothed my brow as I gazed into her eyes. A burst of M4 fire danced around me and I collapsed back behind cover. The Tarn shoved his K-spec around me and fired blindly around the corner in three quick bursts, then sprang past me.

I protested, "No. Stay back. He's mine."

I was gripped in madness. I pushed around his wide back to take the lead again.

"Look at the spoor on the trail. Blood. He is dying, lord. Leave him die."

"I know what I'm doing."

I risked a sliver of a peek around the next bend. Mark was crouched, singed multicam standing out like neon in black amongst the jagged rocks. He posted himself just behind the opening to the canyon I remembered so well.

I eased back but yelled ahead, "What really happened in Venezuela, Mark?"

"You know dick, Colt. The Chief is always ready to do what it takes, you weak-ass pussy. Not like you. If we'd stuck together, we'd already have this whole planet rolled up. But no, you've got to think with your Johnson. What a loser you are. Didn't you get enough attention from your mommy?"

"What lie do you and the Chief tell about happened? Did he knife some unarmed woman and claim she was a secret policeman ready to compromise your mission? Or did he just see the chance to be a savage? Just like you? You two were made for each other, Marky-Mark. You ready to die?" I sent the round from the 203 long, down the trail, close enough to sting him, but far enough away not to kill him.

I stuck my head out with my rifle up, ready to hammer him if he was still there. He'd faded back. I burst ahead. I pounced, I sprang, at the last I ran. I skidded around the mouth of the narrow canyon to see Marky was already snared. An arm and leg had disappeared into the invisible barrier, making him look like a sectioned carcass, but his mouth and wild eyes told me he was very much alive. He pulled against the unbeatable foe on the other side, his terror and fear too great a prize to ever let go.

"How's it feel to be beaten, Marky? No one's going to have your back in there. In there, you're going to see me laughing at you for eternity. Enjoy."

Terrified eyes met mine.

"What's happening?" he shrieked. His fear swelled into a tsunami as I felt the pull of the soul-eater, as surely as if it were me in its grip again. For a second, I felt regret, and as quickly, it passed.

At my side, Garlak Ranz was witness. "A soul-eater!"

Like one of the zombies sinking beneath my black tarry pool, carrying with it my worst fears, Mark sunk into the soul-eater's den, slowly, slowly, slowly. Away, away, away. Fading, fading, fading. The evil of the place throbbed and radiated waves of malevolence until with a last pull, my enemy vanished, his scream fading behind the gateway to endless nightmares, a puff of dry breeze in his wake. The surface was still, only the jagged canyon scene left to lure its next victim into the safety of its haven from the harsh mountain pass.

I yelled into the abyss, knowing he could still hear me, "Have a nice stay in hell, Mark. It's everything you deserve."

42

I STOOD OUTSIDE THE ENTRANCE TO THE CAVE AND TOUCHED THE necklace to my chest. "Cynar, we're coming in. It's just me and my Tarn companion. It's safe." We'd cleared the grounds and dead checked every body, white, green, and red. I found a ruined Carl Gustave and the remains of some unused AT-4s, the tubes fractured. If they'd had some fire in their bellies, we'd have died. We'd caught them unsuspecting, unprepared, and unwilling to do what it took to win.

Too bad for them.

Garlak Ranz puzzled over one of the Red soldiers, the chest plate a shot up tin can. "These men are from the king's army. How they are aligned with the Mydreen, I cannot fathom."

Cynar thundered in my head and I turtled my neck down as if it were a volume button. "Quickly, Benjamin Colt, your female friend lies in the sanctuary! I move to unseal the door."

Talis Darmon!

I ran into the cave blindly, fumbling for my flashlight. A Tarn lay in the dark, alone. My heart sank, but I found my voice as I knelt beside the tragic heap. "Beraal, it's me." Her hands were bound. She didn't stir as I cradled her. The door slid open and Cynar appeared.

"Bring her and follow."

Garlak Ranz cut the restraints as Cynar and I positioned her gently on the bed, the rich warm light of the third ray enveloping her in its radiance. The grizzled priest ignored my inquiry as he concentrated on the display until he seemed satisfied with the settings. "She will recover. I regret I could not risk opening until certain that all danger had passed." Cynar looked truly ashamed. "I am no warrior. She was in distress, and many times I struggled to open the seal, but my hands would not obey my command—do you understand?"

"I do, Cynar. If the third ray can heal her, then it will be fine, my friend."

His voice trembled with his hands. "The Hortha answered my call. Never in all of eternity did I think I would be calling them to their death. I pray some of my friends yet live, but I've called and called for them. I sense them few and far away. Oh, calamity, never did I believe war could arrive here!" Cynar shed tears.

My Tarn partner surveyed our surroundings. This time he did not seem to shrink from the river gurgling in the dark beyond the esplanade, marveling at the sound and scent of the water, the golden light that bathed the sleeping Beraal and the shrunken man.

"I yet find it hard to believe I am not asleep, living in the fantasy of a hatchling's tale," Garlak Ranz said.

Cynar cried, "The beauty of all I have suffered to build, all I have endured in the name of preserving life—all may as well be fantasy. It only serves to mock my helplessness as I cower here deep in Mother Vistara, chilled beneath the great shadow of violence cast onto this sacred place. Never ever did my guild instill in us the fear that we could be treated so! We live in seclusion not out of fear, but out of duty. Oh, that I had made mighty weapons to defend this sanctuary! One less cycle spent exploring the mysteries of science, one more spent delving the depths of malice in the heart of Vistara, and this would not have come to pass. How false our belief that reason would prevail in the world we abandoned to toil in solitude."

His grief consumed him and he collapsed.

"But I cannot do harm. I cannot."

I lowered to console him. "It's terrible to feel helpless, Cynar. There's nothing you could have done. If your labs were damaged, the harm to the whole world would be immeasurable. Don't doubt yourself. You are a good man. I don't understand why your guild forces you to live so cruelly, but it hasn't made you cruel. It's not your nature to harm. That's our job. We fight not because we hate our enemy, but because we love the good in the world. We're going to make it safe again. We're going to build a better world. We're its protectors now. Take heart, Cynar. With your help, we're going to win."

The old man looked every bit the thousand years of his age. He allowed me to help him stand. "It can only be that one force counters another. I cannot harness the ray that would quell evil in men. But I will strive to work for your enablement to be that sword for our justice."

I'd done a Karlo. I'd helped him find heart. And for it, I felt dirty. Like the seedy political class back at Area 51 that Karlo and I shared such disdain for. It was the lie I'd told Cynar hidden in my words of consolation for his cowardice.

I did hate.

For her I wanted to be the very ideal of the pure warrior. The noble knight. The gentle hero. But as long as Talis Darmon was in danger, as long as Bryant lived, I'd bring my hate to bear on every one of my enemies until I doomed them all to hell as I had Mark. Forgiveness could wait. First, I wanted total victory. And with this first great taste of my revenge, I had an unsated appetite more.

"It is not the sword that makes the warrior, priest," the Tarn said. "I learned this from Khraal Kahlees, and a mightier warrior never lived. He and Benjamin Colt prepare the way. Do not grieve longer. But I ask you, what has Dosenie Beraal suffered? Come look."

I stood next to him as he surveyed my gentle, maternal friend bathed in gold.

"She heals before our eyes, but do you see? Insults blanket her skin. These are marks of torture. These are the ways of the Mydreen."

She'd been burned. Repeatedly.

"Embers were held on her skin. Her nails have been removed. She has endured a trial of great suffering."

My rage returned like a summer storm, the thunder in my chest booming the name of the one who I knew directed this atrocity. "These might be the methods of the Mydreen, but I sense the hand of the Thulians in this." It may not have been until this moment, but by calling my former teammates Thulians, I made my declaration.

Vistara was my world.

I regretted nothing. Mark was getting everything he deserved. And there were at least two more I'd gladly see keep him company.

✠ ✠ ✠

Apache howled to me as I bounced down the path. Next to the flitter where I'd laid him, the young Red remained. I searched up and down the notch in his neck, over and over, forcing my finger pads to be gentle and relaxed. I questioned if it was there, or just the deception of hope, until I was finally sure I sensed a pulse.

"With me, boy. Catch up."

I scooped the broken body and sprang. It was the whole experience of Vistara condensed into a moment. It wasn't the high of my bloody victory I felt as I flew like a superman towards the cave, it was hope that Cynar was a real magician. Because, it's true. What is magic but science unexplained? Vistara was the clash of violence I knew as a man, but hidden beneath the carnage, she was also a wonder that made me feel childlike and ignorant in understanding.

Avril Mysteen lay on the healing pallet now. On a bed of cushions with Apache at her side, I helped Beraal take a gentle sip, her dry lips making a request she was still too weak to voice. Dave's voice startled me.

"Ben-Ben, you got me?" Dave called again before I could ease her head down. Her eyes closed as I placed her head on the cushion. Her smile told me she understood she was safe again.

"I do, Dave. We're secure here. I'll send Cynar and Garlak Ranz to bring you in."

"We're not there yet, but soon, Ben. What went down?"

"I'll fill you in when you get here, but it was Mark. He was here."

"And?"

"He's never going to raise a hand to anyone again."

The long break told me Dave was processing what I'd said. "That's good. We're over the way station now." The whistle was sharp in my head. "You had a tussle, brah. Be there in a sec. Out."

✣ ✣ ✣

Soon enough, we stood together, the warm light of the healing bed reflecting off our faces.

"You look like you need some time in there, brah," Dave seethed as he followed the trail of red behind my collar. "Nasty. Your arm, too."

I felt my neck. There were no blisters, but it was hot to the touch. My arm was an even dull ache from the spall peppered over it. "I'm fine, maybe later." Cynar thought the young Guard would pull through, but it would take several sessions. I could wait.

"How'd it go down, Ben-dog?" Dave patted Apache's hind as the gadron wagged in ecstasy.

The blow-by-blow I made routine, like a mechanic reciting his list of repairs. I came to the confrontation with Mark. "We brought down his flitter. I saved the M134. You should send a party to retrieve it. We wrapped it up, then came back to make pick up on Avril Mysteen." I deflected. "The kid did good."

It didn't work. Dave stopped his attention to Apache's needs. His forehead tilted, eyes squinted, lips pursed. Two sets of fingers drummed a rhythm on Khraal Kahlees's folded arms. Not even a four-armed alien did I fool when I gave no details to Mark's end. I couldn't tell a believable falsehood to save my life, or my dignity. It wasn't a skill I had, and consoled myself that I didn't need to be ashamed for that. I prepared to tell the truth at last.

Garlak Ranz spoke for me. "The Thulian met his end in the maw of a soul-eater. I did not know there was one in the Korund not accounted for and destroyed, but I witnessed its evil with my own eyes."

Beraal groaned lightly and I moved to her side, grateful to escape the center of attention. "Do you want to sit up?"

"Please, Lord Benjamin Colt." It was Garlak Ranz's words that had brought her strength. "First, tell me, is it true what you said, the Thulian beast has met his end? He suffers now in the pit of the soul-eater?"

I shushed as I helped her to sit cross-legged on the cushions and eased one behind her back. I'm no Mother Theresa, but I remember being in a dark cell, alone, naked, and wondering if I was even alive. That minute of kindness from Karlo made me understand forever what it was to be helpless and dependent. You never forget.

"What are they talking about, Ben? Is it that stuff the Chief said about you getting eaten by some monster in the mountains? I thought that was just some bullshit story he'd been fed."

My Tarn battle-buddy went on. "The White lord drove the Thulian like a master tactician, driving him to his own demise like herding an animal to the slaughter pen."

"Cease, Garlak Ranz," Khraal Kahlees said, as gently as I'd ever heard him speak. "It is not for you to tell."

Beraal raised her palms to me as she dipped her chin. "Praise to you, Lord Benjamin Colt. To suffer as we suffered together in the monster's belly is justice, if ever such exists this side of the Blix."

Dave persisted. "I still don't understand."

Cynar took my silence as a cue. "When these two came to me with the princess, they had survived the ordeal of a soul-eater, the remnant of the ancient evil beings who are responsible for the destruction of Vistara. Benjamin Colt fought the wicked phantom from within to rescue himself and the dosenie. When the princess told the tale, I knew I had acted correctly when I broke my vows and admitted the strangers to my sanctuary, so incredible was the unlikelihood of it all. It confirmed for me that there was yet one more thing unique in the odd party disturbing my solitude, something I could not account for by logic."

It was time. The sharp knife cuts the quickest. I wanted to bring an end to the discussion. "It's a prison, Dave. A living hell. The creature makes you relive all your worst fears and experiences. Puts bad thoughts in your head. Lives off your pain. I survived it. Beraal and I. Afterward, the princess used her powers to heal our minds. And I put Mark there. Right now, the soul-eater is torturing him, making him live a whole life of shame, fear, pain, and suffering. Each day a lifetime. And it'll go on forever." I shuddered as I remembered.

"Any way he could escape, too?"

Only the beacon of Talis Darmon gave me the strength to fight the soul-eater. Without her, I couldn't have done it.

"Not a chance," I said. "Now you know. I won't talk about it again. We have to move on."

Beraal's voice was pained, but urgent. "There is much I must disclose. Much I must atone for. My failures are great, and I beseech your help to make amends for my weakness."

She and I had shared more than anyone in my life besides Talis Darmon, and together we had her spirit in common. I placed a hand on her shoulder, but she ignored me. Her eyes fixed on the giant Khraal Kahlees. I wondered what they each were thinking? She didn't know I'd broken her confidence, that the man before her knew she was his daughter.

"Dosenie Beraal, do you have strength to fulfill your duty and speak? How came you to be here?"

"I do, Khraal Kahlees. And I will. It was by torture that the secret of this place was pried from my lips." She stroked her arms. Though no longer there, the memory of her wounds remained. "When the Thulians killed Jedak Jeraal and the Mydreen laid waste to Califex, we were taken prisoner. The princess and I were held in seclusion from one another, caged once again as animals by the Mydreen. Some encampment in the barren wastes between Clymaira and Shansara. A great battle waged nearby for many, many days. Such was to our advantage, as Domeel Doreen and the Thulians were too busy to molest us.

"The Mydreen and the Thulians fought the king's army to a standstill, but not to defeat. It was not until Prince Carolinus Darmon answered his father's plea for help that the tide turned in favor of the enemy. Come from Pyreenia with his men to bring relief, the prince instead carried out his coup, then welcomed the Mydreen into the city."

"So it's happened," Dave said. "Shansara's fallen."

"I was there when the prince gloated to his sister that he now ruled in Shansara. It was then that our situation worsened. With the capital taken, the Thulian Brandon Bryant and his henchman, the dark one—Mark—had ample time to turn attention to us. The story of our escape from Maleska Mal troubled them. Especially your part in it, Benjamin Colt. Domeel Doreen felt certain we could not have survived the Korund without aid. I heard the princess's screams, yet could do nothing but weep in agony, pleading that instead I was the one they took. And they did.

"I knew by their persistence that she never revealed to them that you remained alive and defiant of his evil, White lord. I as well refused. But I grew weak as they tortured me. I was ready to die, but they would not let me travel the Blix. I had to tell them something in hopes of giving you time to act. I told them of the aid we received here, insisting it was only the princess and I who made it to this sanctuary which saved our lives. But they did not believe you dead, Lord Benjamin Colt. The madness of Brandon Bryant and his foul henchmen to discover if you were truly dead led to this. Great Cynar, it is my fault your kindness brought his tragedy. I beg forgiveness." She wept and a flood of tears ran from her.

Everyone eventually gives in to torture. Everyone. Holding out as long as possible, then giving an interrogator just enough information to satisfy them, is a proven strategy. I wanted to tell her how well she'd done, but I had a building sense Double-K was firmly in the driver's seat. Propriety is a kind of ESP, and I was glad I had a little. I held silent for Double-K to remain her focus.

"Do they know of the rivers beneath Vistara?"

"No. A thousand times, no. Not in my deepest madness of pain did I reveal such. But the existence of the water priest and his aid to us I could not keep inside, not matter how I fought, no matter how I vowed to not let them win the knowledge from me."

"Leave us," Khraal Kahlees commanded harshly. Then, softly. "Leave us. Please."

I motioned us all to depart.

Khraal Kahlees caught my shoulder with his giant grip. "Remain, Benjamin Colt."

When the others had departed, Beraal stood. "Release me with honor, Khraal Kahlees. I cannot bear my shame any longer. I would kneel if you so demand. It is what I deserve."

The mighty Tarn warrior betrayed nothing, a statue of martial might, his hand on his sword, and for a moment, I thought he would draw. I poised to leap. His hand relaxed, as did I. "No, Beraal of House Pardoo, daughter of the Korund and Lassa Laloo. I know you. And your honor remains intact, and great it is."

Beraal looked at me. At once, she knew I was responsible for betraying her secret.

Khraal Kahlees wrapped himself in his great arms and bowed. "There is no way to return to the past and erase my own failings. Had I only known. Instead, it was my own weakness and selfishness that made you an orphan among our people, as I vainly sought position and prominence. It is you who must forgive me, daughter."

He moved to embrace her.

At first, she tensed, a taut rope about to break, then softened.

"You must live. You serve House Darmon and the princess. You did more than a hundred warriors of the Korund in your battle to serve her. I ask you to find the strength to go on. She is in need of you now, more than ever."

"I will try—Father."

"And I have given oath, Domeel Doreen will die slowly. And you will hear his pleas, as will all Vistara."

Beraal pushed back from the embrace. "Lord, there is more that I must tell. To make his ascension to the throne complete, Carolinus Darmon moves to cement the loyalty of all in the Red Kingdom."

Khraal Kahlees's eyes shut as he nodded knowingly. "I foresaw this, but dared not speak."

Beraal's eyes held even greater sorrow. "The prince forces his sister to wed."

My blood turned to ice such as did not exist on Mars. "You don't mean—"

"Yes, lord. It is an ancient custom, long unexercised. Carolinus Darmon forces his sister to wear the crown of his queen to unite the kingdom behind him."

✣ ✣ ✣

We left Beraal to rest, Apache instinctively remaining to guard. Khraal Kahlees gazed into the tunnel, the echoes of the current softly lapping the walls. "The Red soldiers that litter the ground outside with the Mydreen filth are not the king's men, but Pyreenian traitors under control of Carolinus Darmon. Yet there must have been elements in the king's confidence complicit in his betrayal."

I was still astonished at Chuck's advance work in Pyreenia. He'd found a leader in exile with an army, exploited the prince's flaws, and delivered a fifth column to Bryant to end the siege of Shansara. It was only a matter of time before Bryant moved to regain Thoria and Clymaira to make the Red Kingdom of Mihdradahl whole again.

Then who would rule?

Even if he sat on the throne, it wouldn't be Carolinus Darmon. It would be Bryant. More likely, both he and Talis Darmon would ride the River Blix. I'd seen the throne, though I'd never been there. But it wasn't Carolinus Darmon who sat on it, nor Bryant.

It was me.

Cynar had assured me the vision was nothing, that it held no truth. Yet—

"We have to rescue her. We have to get her out of there before our attack. They'll use as a hostage against us. Or Bryant will kill her outright. Cynar, is there a way into Shansara itself through the aqueducts?"

The priest's brow furrowed with even more wrinkles. "The time for secrets is at an end. Yes. I know of it."

"You have to come with us."

"Eh?"

"Cynar, you have to come with us. We need a guide. There's no other way."

It was as if I'd electrocuted him. He shook until a tetanus seized him.

"What you ask of me—I cannot. I am bound to this place as the very bedrock."

Khraal Kahlees scowled. "Is there some magic that holds you here, priest? Would you turn to dust in the sun of Vistara?"

Meekly, the priest croaked, "No."

"Then it is settled. You come with us. Your oath to save this planet is not fulfilled unless you do. Fear not. Our courage will lend you strength and the honor of doing what you think you cannot will make you whole. This I swear to be true."

"I'll see you back here again, Cynar. If it's the last thing I do. I'll see you returned to your labs, where you can spend another thousand cycles investigating all the mysteries of science you haven't yet begun to delve. But unless we win, your days here are numbered. You know I'm right."

At first, I thought it a new seizure, brought on by the inevitability that we were taking him with us into a world now as alien to him as it had once been to me. Then, I recognized it. The cough. The heaving of the rib bare chest. The throaty song.

"Hehehehehe! Tell me that I will see the smug faces of the air wizards turn to anguish when I repair what they could not, and I will travel with you to the Blix! Cynar will avenge himself on the red-bearded fools at last!"

It took a lot to impress Dave. And Cynar had done it.

"Bitter much? I run on hate, but daaamn! Way to make lemons into lemonade, brah."

43

Holograms floated above my wrist.

"Dave, what's your ETA to Califex?"

It looked like the caravan was halted, and the weeks I guessed it would take for the slow moving mule-train to reach us weren't getting clipped shorter by a standstill. I'd sent Cynar with Dave and all but one flitter to find the caravan, hoping between Cynar's and Karlo's geniuses, they could get Baby Blue producing Cynar's boats. Lots of boats.

Khraal Kahlees, our two WIA, Garlak Ranz, and I landed safely in Califex the day before. It was post-war Europe, the wreck of the atmosphere works tainted black and white to my perception just like those old photos. It was no less a reminder of the stakes of our war than it had been as I watched the towers disintegrate.

"Karlo's got something to tell you, brah."

Karlo occupied the other holo cloud, the different view behind showing I'd been correct. The flitters packed with Cynar's junk and as many Korundi as could ride atop were grounded around the caravan.

"Cynar says he'll have us flying to Califex by the end of the day," Karlo said.

My head swam. "Sorry, what?"

"He no sooner landed than he took a look around, called me a dunce, and started tinkering with the air cars. I'm rigging for a sling load now."

I pictured Baby Blue freefalling then shattering on impact into a million pieces like Grandma's china on tile. Baby Blue was twice the size of one of the flitters.

"We can't risk it, Karlo. Don't do it! Cynar's crazy."

"Dullard! Moron! After all I've done, you doubt Cynar!" The grizzled priest pulled Karlo's wrist to his face, displacing him in the cloud.

"What must I accomplish to end your ignorance? Must I make the heavens cry flood over Vistara? If the help you claim only I can provide isn't wanted, return me to my sanctuary, fool!"

"Hey, I seem to remember someone swearing to never insult me again!"

"You swore you needed the greatness of Cynar!"

He had me there.

Karlo muscled back his wrist against the pull of two scrawny arms. "Give us some credit, Ben. We'll get a solid test run or three before I let us take off. Cynar says one can handle the load, but we're rigging a two-flitter rig to split the payload."

Cynar's voice screamed at me through both clouds. "An intellect hardly more advanced than your own knows to trust the science, Benjamin Colt. What this one achieved aligning the second rays of the crude weapons is evidence that even you could someday grasp basic science."

Dave raised a hand in surrender. "They got it handled, brah."

"At least cross load all the K-spec conversions and other stuff you've cranked out into different flitters in case the worst happens."

Dave rolled eyes. "Yes, Dad. Thanks for the lesson."

"Okay, okay. Uncle. Buzz me when you're inbound, otherwise I'll leave you alone. Cynar," I yelled to the priest, visible in neither cloud but who must be close by, ready to hurl more insults my way. It energized the relic in the same way a soul-eater feasted off his prey. If it kept him happy, I could take it. I've been called much worse and all of it true. Being thought a son of a bitch can be high praise from both friend and enemy. "I need you to make it here in one piece. You. And Baby Blue. I need you to guide us, remember?"

His face reappeared. "I value my own life, as well as this new mechanism. I will bring both great entities to your feet, White lord."

White lord? His words. And Baby Blue was "great." What could he and Karlo accomplish working together with Baby Blue as their plow mule?

"Thank you, Cynar the magnificent!" I waved off the communicator, but not in time to miss hearing his victory cry.

"Hehehe!"

✤ ✤ ✤

I didn't just open my eyes, I snapped upright like I'd been stung by a scorpion. Apache sensed me stir and rolled to eight feet. It was pointless to try to sleep again. I'd toss and turn, and probably just wake the guys, then none of us would be rested for the big day. I grabbed my clothes and snuck outside, shushing the gadron as he followed, ready for him to doze again as I paced away in the moonlight. Maybe I'd join the night watch and stare at their fire, and try not to see her face in the flames.

Instead, I found Karlo and Dave were on camp stools, as surprised to see me as I was them.

"Dang it. Sorry we woke you, brah. Thought you were out cold." He slid to a cross-legged seat on the ground. "Join us." Apache trotted to him and lay his massive head near to be scratched, Dave taking the cue and supplying.

I pulled my shirt on as I eased down. The little three-legged stools always made me visualize a comical collapse. I shook off Karlo's offer of the steaming cup he held.

"You went down hard, Ben. What got you up?"

I might've been awake, but I was still fatigued. I deflected by firing right back with a yawning question. "What kept you two from going to sleep?"

The gadron was already making nasal snores beneath Dave's hand. "Apache was farting up a storm. Plus, I couldn't stop thinking about the idea of dying in the ridiculous getup we gotta wear, brah."

Courtesy of Kleeve Hartus, we had full costumes for our rescue mission. Cape, breechclout, decorative armor, and shiny matching helmet. Swords and daggers. But at least we'd have our K-specs. Our skin was deeply dyed, and Dave had shaved smooth.

"If I buy it—aah, who cares, brah. If I buy it, there's no one I know who'll see my corpse, anyway."

"I'm mad I'm not going with you two tomorrow," Karlo said. "But I understand." I was making Karlo remain behind to get the army moving and finish the last of the preparations for the big campaign to come. Apache would stay back with him no matter how he protested, and I'd given instructions to kennel the gadron once it was time for Karlo to depart and join us with the rest of the army. Where I was going was no place for a pet, not even a war hound.

There were still some hard feelings between Karlo and I, not yet erased. We'd nearly come to blows over it. In the end, he understood the necessity, and bowed to the inevitability of what I'd had him create with Baby Blue. He didn't like it, though. Neither did I.

Karlo was the bigger man, leaving everything we'd said to each other in anger back where we'd decided to bury the hatchet, agreeing to disagree. He reverted to friend and medic. "Your turn."

I said nothing.

"We agreed we were going to talk more, 'member?"

I sighed. "I saw Mike."

Dave groaned. "Dreams are just dreams, brah. Don't mean nothin'."

Most of the time, I'd agree. "It wasn't anything bad. It was the day he came to see me back at Bragg and asked me to the team. It was just like that day, too. How good it made me feel."

"That woke you up?" Dave asked.

"Nah. It was that dumb thing after. You know the kinda dream. I was walking from Bragg—I think to Eglin, excited to get on the team. Everywhere I looked, I saw a glimpse of the princess. I'd call her name and run after her, she'd be gone. Then I'd see her again. She'd disappear behind a corner, a car in a parking lot, a tree. I just kept running faster and faster to find her, but when I got there, she was always gone." I stopped from saying more. In the dream, I'd resigned looking for her, reaching a lucid state at the end, knowing I'd never find her. The pain of it woke me up.

Whether it was the hour or our fatigue, Dave was unusually sincere. "*That* means something, brah."

Karlo sighed. "You know what it means, Ben."

I let the night speak for me, Apache sawing away until exhaustion forced us all to sleep.

✣ ✣ ✣

We flew to the far Korund, where the peaks were reasonably small, only as tall as the Rockies I once tried to clumsily ski down. I've never cared for snow and didn't miss it now, not even on a world without it. Cynar fiddled over a gadget as he directed Kleeve Hartus through the passes. Khraal Kahlees confirmed that the course was correct and would lead to the way station.

"Long ago I visited the fountain and the shrine within. We've always known the fountains were built by your guild, but all thought your kind absorbed by time and legend, priest. How odd it is to know your guild lives, and works, and of the lifeblood that courses beneath the desert of Vistara. Will you make such known to all at the end of our journey?"

"Eh? We are thought extinct?"

"Yes, priest."

"Hmmm." He laid the glowing device down. If it was a Cynar GPS, I wanted one. "Ahead it lies."

"Will your buddy welcome us, Cynar?" I asked again. "He's not going to unleash the Hortha on us, will he?"

Cynar was hurt. "No. The Hortha do not live here, nor perhaps will they return to any part of the Korund. I may never have their trust again. But there may be other… guardians. We must be wary."

"You did not prepare us for such danger, priest!" Kleeve Hartus said as he slowed our flight. Below was the way station nestled in a flat, rocky valley, terraces in the jagged roughness on one side suggesting where the cave would be. Light caught the surface of the fountain in a familiar way, out of place here, yet like a lighthouse promising safe guidance to lost sailors.

"It is hard to recall. I am not certain. I have distant recollections. There is much this mind contains, and my retrieval of all is not what it once was."

"Well, get him on the horn and chill him out," Dave said over wrist communicator from the flitter behind us.

I stayed on the nose and had the first shield make a slow racetrack over the valley. "Seems quiet. Let's land."

We touched down in trail near the fountain, its waters bubbling calm music in the crisp air.

Cynar accepted my hand to the ground. "I go alone. Wait until I call to you." He limped off into the cave. I'd not seen him so discomforted before, and wondered if there was something to Double-K's taunt about the old priest turning to dust. Dave was off the other air car and met me, seeming to read my thoughts.

"Dude's older than dirt. I'd probably be limping, too, if I were that old."

"The princess thinks he's a thousand years old." I sighed as I watched him disappear into the mouth of the cave. "I'm amazed we're here. Finally."

One of Clymairan Guards alerted us with an uncertain tone. "Something approaches."

A Korundi raised his rifle. "The stones move!"

First one, then another. Shambling. Undulating. From piles they rose, columns of stone moved as though alive. They closed like a slowly closing noose from a hundred meters around us, one gliding step at a time.

"Stone men," Khraal Kahlees said. "More legend proven real."

"Cynar," I yelled. "We've got trouble."

"No!" Dave yelled, too late to stop the Tarn as he fired. The flash of the K-spec hit the mass of oblong and irregular stones. The hulk only increased its pace, as did the others.

"Hold, Korundi," Khraal Kahlees ordered. "Fools! Did I tell you to fire? You've made threat!"

"Cynar!" I yelled again into the cave. Nothing.

"What's the play, brah?"

"Grab everything and make for the cave!"

Khraal Kahlees objected. "Inside, the stone men will trap us. Crush us. Tales say they cause panic, force their victims to where they cannot escape, then grind their enemies to meal. Let us take to flight before it is too late."

"Mount up and get airborne!"

I took Beraal's offered hands and let her pull me aboard. One of the stone men collapsed from a collection of boulders mocking an upright bear into one great ball. From shuffle to sudden burst of speed it came at us, accelerating, a rolling dreadnaught of animated rock. We lifted just as the mass passed below us, missing by mere inches. Behind us a Tarn stalwart yelled in defiance as he fired repeatedly, not giving his ground, until another of the rolling forms plowed over him. Our second flitter lifted, narrowly escaping as we had.

"Brave fool!" Khraal Kahlees moaned. "The tales say the stone men menace, but give chance for escape from their territory to any who flee. Who has failed to credit the stories of our nurse maids? Are they not all proven true? Blast the priest for his failing memory."

We circled and I called for Cynar.

After a few minutes, his face appeared. "Did I not tell you to wait?"

"We were about to be flattened by a bunch of rock men, Cynar! You never said anything about—"

Khraal Kahlees crowded in. "Priest! A fine warrior has joined his ancestors! Did I not listen to your lament that you had not made weapons? What are the stone men but weapons?"

"Like the Hortha, they serve to deter. I failed to gain Karvell's attention in time. The stone men were brought to action by a presence more threatening than mounted Tarn. The way is safe now. Return."

I looked down. The stone men in all their forms were retreating, dissembling into the piles we'd first seen and ignored.

"Are you sure it's safe?"

"Karvell is willing to listen. He is not yet convinced, but accepts we are not a threat. For now."

"I'll come in. Alone. I'm not letting anyone land until we know it's safe."

"Come then. And be quick. He must see that we mean no harm."

"You heard the man," I said to Kleeve Hartus. "Take me down."

"I accompany you," Double-K said. "If there is more treachery, this priest Karvell will not live to profit by it."

From a hover we hopped off and ran into the cave as the flitter levitated away. In the sanctuary, Cynar stood. On his own wrist floated the cloud of Karvell the Patient.

"The White lord I spoke of is here, as is a battle lord of the Korund," Cynar said.

If there was a hidden entrance to the underground, it was still sealed.

"Karvell, you are my elder, but do not dismiss me as your younger. I appeal to your science. Do not ignore the elements of fact I have exposed. Analyze and find a model that fits. We have slept while Vistara turns its last to become naught but the dust we have vowed to prevent."

Cynar turned. "The phantom that is Karvell struggles with speech, so long it has been since he has uttered sound."

I understood why. What I saw wasn't human, but a mummified shell. The lips writhed, but no sound came out. With a great effort finally, he croaked.

"You. Break. Your. Vows."

Our priest was a youthful lad compared to this skeleton. "Our vows! I have tried to contact our order. I believe them vows to men long turned to dust themselves. When last did you know them to be this side of Farnest?"

The skin stretched even tighter over a skull that strained to speak, easier now, but still with great effort. "I... do not recall."

"Think, and you will see what I say is true. They have gone to the underworld and left us in ignorance and without guidance. We are all that remains—Salkar and Tarnis and a few others. They acknowledge my hail, but cower in their dens, afraid of the truth."

"There is... only our great... task."

"Yes, Karvell, our great task. But how will we stay true to our oath, to atone for our collective guilt, if we allow the end to come to the world above? Examine it all as the great scientist I know you to be!"

This went on. Cynar told the withered wreck all that had happened. And again.

"I for one have chosen to act. I only ask you to have faith, as you once did when young, and I learned at your feet how to ignore all but science and the manipulation of the rays of all essence."

"The binding rays. The penetrating rays." The vision left its dream state and focused its eyes for the first time. "Cynar... the Younger."

"Yes, Karvell the Patient. My wise elder. Open and accept us. Do not pass away in regret. You will not walk in peace in Temple Farnest if you turn us away."

I stepped aside and waved Double-K to my ear as I whispered, "If Cynar can't convince him, we've got enough demo to get in. Last resort, but I'm ready to do it."

"We watched the atmosphere works fall. Will it not be a disaster to use explosives? It would hinder us greatly if by unintended consequence we destroy the pathway to our objective." I was about to say we'd take that chance when the wall slid back and aside.

"Thank you, Karvell," Cynar said. "The logic of your science is flawless. We come to meet you, elder brother." The cloud holding the dried face dimmed. "Bah. He's as arrogant as ever. Come. Bring all. I tire of the anticipation of our journey." Cynar took off.

I looked to Khraal Kahlees. "What do you think?"

"Our priest seems sure. I will bring our party. I too tire of the anticipation. Let us rescue the last of the Sylah dynasty."

44

The channel was as wide as that we'd traveled to reach Salkar the Rash's station above Califex. Then we'd rode the brisk current. Like he'd adopted as icon the *Enterprise*'s chief engineer, Cynar complained and protested when Karlo suggested a propulsion system for the boats, but nonetheless had one produced in mere hours. The stone cavern rushed past us as we cut the water. I drew the ridiculous red cape around me but still shivered. Our velocity was so great it made for a chill wind at our face. Kleeve Hartus and the other Guards seemed unbothered. Running around mostly naked all the time was a kind of conditioning I didn't have, I reckoned.

After a day of darkness with Cynar glued to his GPS—never sleeping, never seeming to tire—he slowed us. "We come to the vein that will take us beneath great Shansara."

"How much farther?"

He spoke as if to conserve breath. "Today."

I'd become concerned. "Cynar, shouldn't you rest?"

He coughed. "Sleep is a long forgotten need, White lord, and the simple sensations of the unfamiliar energizes me."

"Cynar, couldn't you have just taught me how to navigate by the device? You could have remained in your sanctuary after all."

He coughed again, but then like an old boxer, proved he could still jab. "Karlo Columbo, mayhap. But you? Ha!"

Though not the skeleton of Karvell, he was getting frailer before my eyes. "Karvell seemed on death's door. Can he live much longer?"

"It seems unlikely."

"Will we be able to use the way station if he dies?"

"Karvell understands his part in this as correct, and I have secured access. And yes, he may very well have passed whence we travel against the aqueduct flow to his station again."

"I'm sorry, Cynar. I know you had your differences, but he seemed to really respect you."

Leaving the safety of his sanctuary had many consequences for Cynar. When was the last time the thousand-year-old man had considered mortality? He sighed. "It has been a long life. One of serendipitous joy in exploration. And solitude. If he travels on before we are victorious, I believe he will take this satisfaction to the underworld."

"Are the elders of your guild really gone?"

"I am sure it is so. And I am angered by it. Not because they have come to their end, but that they failed us. We loyal acolytes have been abandoned to our own ends. I now judge their arrogance, their secrecy, their abuse of us all, was manipulation to disguise their inadequacy. If they had vision with which to guide us into a future without them, it is unknown to me, as it is to Karvell."

I shouldn't have said it, but I did. "Were they so dissimilar from the atmosphere wizards, then?"

To my surprise, he didn't explode. "Karvell said much the same. Beneath the heads of our guild, he was our most senior to toil in the great task." He changed from somber to playfully sardonic. "Hehe, though he accomplished but a fraction of my own greatness. If there is time, I will show you and let you judge for yourself, having witnessed my mastery. As if the very flood we travel upon is not evidence enough."

"If you're most senior, won't you become head of the order? You've advanced the work more than anyone. Can't we go to the master's lab and set you up to build the guild again?"

He scoffed. "And where is that? The location of our training grounds and the halls of the guild are a secret from even Karvell. No. The time for our order has ended. But do not fret, my young friend. I will find a way for me to complete the commission of our order before my time is over. Of that, I am sure."

"Thank you for this, Cynar. And I am your friend. And so is the princess. When she's queen, she'll engage the resources of her entire kingdom to see you succeed before—"

He brushed me off. "Bah! Don't think me ready to ride up the Blix yet. Dullard."

The amber lamp illuminated a passage, the rush of the current pushed into it stronger and louder. He guided our tiller to send us down the tunnel, barely wider than the beam of the expandable wonder we floated in. Cynar released the steering column.

"Now I will rest."

✣ ✣ ✣

We made a brief stop at another underground terminal, where a timid priest waited, a watchman filled with dread anticipation. He retreated as if about to run, but held at the corner of his escape route as we coasted to a gentle collision with the quay.

"The last way station nearest the wastes above Shansara. I will be brief." Cynar moved with calming intent and spoke quietly to the withered soul there. It was only a few minutes before he joined us again, guiding us from the wide channel to the leftmost of the three narrow tunnels leading away.

"Lemuel the Novice is the youngest among us. He was the sole one to acknowledge my call with true response. Though he is greatly guarded in expression of it, I believe he has already intuited much of what I have confided to him about the state of our order. He will not resist us, but I think he believes this some kind of test of his loyalty, as though he will be called betrayer and embarrassed by the elders, as once Salkar and I were. Such lessons long remain, even when learned through the trials of others."

"Glad at least he's not fighting us with some other surprise. Electric eels? Flying spiders?

You just be sure and warn us if you suddenly remember there being any other deadly surprises out there. How much longer?"

"Soon."

It wasn't an hour before we came to the end of the line. The esplanade was tiny. We unloaded our gear and crowded onto the narrow landing. Cynar was certain that at the top of the smooth sandstone switchbacks we would enter into Shansara.

"Children, first turn the craft and finish securing the lines," he said. "I will await your return."

Kleeve Hartus was unsettled. "I know the palaces of Shansara well, as does Dosenie Beraal. Where does the passage let out, priest?"

The glowing crystals arrayed on the curved slate were no kind of map, not that anyone but Cynar could decipher.

"There is a grand fountain in this city, is there not?" Cynar said.

Beraal adjusted a dagger beneath her cloak. "Yes, Great Cynar. The Waters of Persidia are a wonder of the Red Kingdom and Vistara."

"There will be a way through the secret works from which the city feeds. Long before the aqueducts were tunneled, this fountain stood. Our precious product is carried to the fountain and its works in perfect concealment. Different from the others, even that of oldest Filestra, where with even deepest excavation all that would be discovered are the natural springs from the ground itself, never the deep channels that feed them."

The revelation brought an outburst from one of the Clymairan guards. "The monument to the seas of our history is but one more falsity of our world. The fountains do not spring forth as symbols of Vistara's sustaining goodness—they are as empty as the promise of the atmosphere works. The times I spent kneeling at the fountains, contemplating our past and my service to our future—wasted."

I remember the reactions of Task Force Elon Musk when the earth opened up and swallowed them with the news of the mutagen plague. Though he objected in Mars-proper Victorian grammar as opposed to the expletive-laden banter of the typical nineteen-year-old Ranger, his disillusionment was no less fueled by anger. All of the Red Kingdom would be having a similar experience. How it would be dealt with would be another battle as important as the one we prepared for now—and I was glad it wouldn't be me trying to bolster the confidence of the masses.

But a soldier, him I could encourage.

"Not wasted. Cynar's science is real. The waters are real. The future you help to secure for Vistara is real." I knew where he was coming from. I'd had my reality screwed with. The sting of learning your worldview was a lie doesn't get erased with a snap of the fingers and a pep talk from a coach with dyed skin in a cape. He seemed unconvinced, but I hadn't made anything worse.

Garlak Ranz stepped forward. "I have seen his works and heard his honesty. Where the water priest guides, I follow."

Cynar pointed up the stairs as he held out a peculiar object, a tiny sphere surrounded by rings that floated around it like a miniature silver Saturn. "Here there is passage through the works. When this glows, a response it will bring, and the way will be made."

I took the little planet and placed it in my belt.

"We'll be back as soon as we can, Cynar," I said, fighting a premonition that the hermit I'd grown so fond of would become a fossil like Karvell before we returned. A team I'd always wanted, and a team I now had. He was a part of that now.

"What are you waiting for? A kiss? Why are you all still here?"

For a water priest, he was a fast study in grunt goodbyes.

Dave blasted white light up the stairs, a K-spec in his other hand. "You heard the man. Don't let the door hit us in the ass, brah. Lead off."

I took his light. The way up was much like the passages in Cynar's lab. Switchbacks leveled out onto landings where accesses led to deep excavations not meant for travel but were filled with tangles of piping that wove in chaotic directions to disappear into bedrock flecked with crystals that returned my light. I kept checking the tiny planet, expecting some indication of life, but it remained a cool, metal heat sink in my palm. Up and up we went until for several rises until the passage forced me sideways like walking between pews. The last glimpse of the exposed works had been many switchbacks below. A level course made me think we must be nearing the top of our ascent.

Kleeve Hartus reached to put a hand on the wall. Moisture sweated from the rock and tiny channels in the floor collected the drippings. "The curving radius of our path gives intuition that we course around the grand fountain."

Dave's voice came from behind. "Are we gonna pop out into the middle of the Las Vegas strip here, brah? That is, if we can even find this secret exit. I'm holding a grudge at Cynar for not having a better brief for us. What the hell are we looking for?"

I had the little token in my palm and held it ahead of me like a compass. It was 2 a.m. Zulu time local-Mars. "He said this thing will let us know. It's got to be soon or we're stuck here for another day."

The passage widened around the curve, and I expected to come into some kind of obvious chamber, when ahead was just a blank wall as frustrating as her dad on the porch when you brought your date home. My grudge against Cynar's exasperating memory gap was about to leave Dave's in the dust when the tiny orb did as described and glowed.

"Check it out!" Dave had been looking ahead while I stared instead at the light in my palm. A section of the chamber dematerialized into an arch and on the other side, a pair of Guards roamed in the starlight. My gun came up and I was about to smoke them when they inexplicably walked on. I had guns up all around me, all which lowered as with me we realized that we'd been unseen. But how?

It was Dave who moved to explore the threshold with outstretched hand. His stretch halted at the fingertips, then his palm flattened as he pushed. "Two-way mirror?" he muttered. "Not a way in. Hmmm." He searched around the arch.

I pushed against the mirror, but my arm didn't stop. I staggered, and hands behind pulled me back.

"What manner of thing is this?" Khraal Kahlees said as he let go of my shoulders. Without restraint he reached to the portal, only to be halted as Dave was. Jaw and tusks tilted sideways. "It cannot be that only the bearer of the device can pass?"

"Time to find out." I braced myself. Holding the device ahead of me like a lantern, I let my arm disappear. I panicked for a second and flinched back. Then shook it off. I wasn't being pulled into this event horizon, I had to push through it. With a deep breath and the conviction that Cynar wouldn't set me up, I entered. I was out the other side and standing between two pedestals supporting massive statues on either side of me. The fountain was a two-acre pond, set in a bowl like an amphitheater of more of the gargantuan statues around it. Footfalls sounded in the dark. Behind me was only a face of relief carved stone. With the device in front of me again, I tested. And back through, I pushed.

"I made to follow, but was repulsed," Khraal Kahlees said. "How will any but you proceed then?"

The footsteps I'd heard before were the two roving Guards, returning on their patrol. I knew what to do.

"I'll block the way. Now let's get some answers. Go."

I stepped into the archway and paused to be a gentleman holding the door to invite my guests to the party. The race was on to see who would be first to action in enemy-held Shansara. The two Guards were dog-piled, pummeled, and dragged like bags of wet cement back through the portal in seconds. With my own retreat, the wall turned solid again and I returned the device to my sash.

A Tarn kneeled between the shoulder blades of the nearest. The man fought to look over his shoulder.

"What is the meaning of this, Mydreen scum?" he cried.

Dave tightened flex cuffs with final clicks on the other man's wrists as he growled, "King Carolinus Darmon made all swear the allies' pledge. He will hear of this!"

Kleeve Hartus took the man's face in hand. "You wear the brassard of a subaltern, virgin with lacquer from stores if ever I've seen one. Are you newly promoted in the ranks, you traitor to the murdered King Osric Darmon? Is this a reward for treachery, little vereen?"

"Who are you to—" the man began until Dave applied a wrist lock. "The Shansara Guard are under orders of the army. Who are you to accost your superiors? Ghaaa!"

Dave torqued his wrist harder.

"Where is the Princess Talis Darmon held?"

The other Guard strained a breath under the crushing weight. "Where do you think? The new queen is in the bedchamber of her husband the king, made bride today, fool!"

"Silence," the senior tried to command as the first shield placed a knotted gag in his mouth and pulled it tight.

"Get this guy up." I pointed as Dave and one of the Korundi snatched the talkative one to his feet. I drew my knife and held it to his throat. "If you want to keep your head, nod."

Dave smirked. "He'd rather cut your throat than ask you again."

The Guard complied with wide eyes.

"Question and answer time, junior."

✦ ✦ ✦

Beraal hesitated as I had at the portal. "I know," I said and patted her through. Last man, I followed, securing the little planet in the pouch under my sash. Two of Kleeve Hartus's Guards exchanged their gold cloaks for the army red of our prisoners and positioned to lead us through the dark streets. The first shield between them, they looked the part of official detail. "It is not far to the Spectral Hall and the king's palace. Beraal, guide us on the path to reach the service entry and the bedchambers."

I shook the bad thought out of my head.

Beraal's tusks gleamed in the dim night light. "No, Benjamin Colt. It will not be as the vile soldier says. Such marriage is not joined; it is ceremonial. The princess will be held as captive, not queen. As hostage, not bride."

We knew this part of our infiltration would be dicey. Talis Darmon might not even be held in the palace grounds.

"These two didn't have much to offer," I said. "The sand's running out of the hourglass."

My plan was to make opportunity as we went with as many snatches and spot interrogations as necessary for success.

"We'll never enter the palace grounds, much less the inner chambers," Khraal Kahlees said as he sent Garlak Ranz ahead to scout. "We are exposed and weak, in the very heart of the kingdom's seat. Who close to the court can give intelligence?"

Beraal was insistent. "My proposal is unchanged. I recommend seeking the chamber of the court dresser. She is loyal to the princess beyond question. Her quarters are with the other courtiers. If we can trust anyone to give aid, it is the spinster Dureen Zell. Alone, I can best travel. I will return with news soon."

Once before I'd vetoed her offer. "No, Beraal. You're well known. If you're recognized, the rescue's over before we start. We all go."

"Boldly, and as if we are masters of this city," Kleeve Hartus said. "I know the way. Make formation and let us march calmly." He placed a hand on Beraal. "We make escort of lady comforter to the princess, as ordered by the king. I have witnessed many such details carried out by the court guard of Shansara when undergoing my training. Is it not done so, Beraal?"

"It is so, First Shield."

"Who dares, wins," Dave said. "Like Kleeve Hartus said, we walk around like we own the place."

The first shield was firm. "And I will abuse any who try to halt us. The power of commission by the king carries with it the implication of danger to any who question it. I'm sure that is especially perceived under the reign of Carolinus Darmon."

Khraal Kahlees laid a hand on his knife. "And we kill any who fail to cower. Silently."

Tusks revealed to their base like sharp mountain peaks in rising moonlight to join human grins in approval.

45

It was a truism that if you looked like you were on important business, you got treated that way. Once, in SERE school, an old man in a wheelchair—he could've been a water priest—lectured us on what it meant to be audacious. In the cobbled together uniform of a German officer and with little language besides curses, he'd gotten through multiple checkpoints to make his way to help and eventual escape—all with little more than pure testicular fortitude and confidence. I'd never forgotten it.

The sprawl around the central palace held multiple sections. Our path was short from the fountain to reach the border of what was an area meant for public use and the naturally repellent entry into the functional, duller part of the palace district. None of the intricate woven filigree that decorated thresholds and windows like frost were to be seen in the simple architecture here. Not until we arrived at the channeled path leading to the repository of the palace workers did Kleeve Hartus have to play the role of annoyed taskmaster.

Two Guards stirred to stiff posture and crossed spears to block the way. "The king's orders. We escort the lady comforter to bring forth the queen's favored dresser."

Before they could question us further, the first shield put the cherry on it. He leaned in as if to share a confidence.

"The new first shield awoke me himself. Order came directly from the king. Seems her brother has need for the new to queen to be disarmingly radiant at early court tomorrow. Visitors from the Yellow Kingdom. No doubt she needs many hours and much coaxing to be at her best so early."

Privates were privates. They both chuckled.

"Talis Darmon needs little primping to bowl over those Yellow bastards," one said.

The other man relaxed as well. "The king's already showing wisdom, putting his best weapon up front. They'll be coming to a fencing match unarmed."

Kleeve Hartus played along. "Perhaps she'll tempt them to invade, eh?"

The men stood aside. We were on our way.

The cottages of the courtiers and servants lay down a narrow alley. The threshold of each apartment was lit by a small amber stone.

Beraal pushed her way to the front. "That one."

A door opened across the way and a woman's head protruded out before retreating like a rabbit sniffing coyotes. The sight of Mydreen soldiers had to mean trouble.

Beraal knocked lightly. Three times she repeated before the door cracked.

"Dureen Zell? It is Dosenie—"

I pushed past, covering the old woman's mouth firmly and gently as we forced our way in, the door closing behind us. The old woman was nude. It surprised me, though it shouldn't have. And in the moment of my reluctance, she got me. The amber stone she held fell as teeth bit into my palm, her growl as fierce as Apache tearing into a steak, and she kneed my groin. I rolled my thigh to miss her strike and bit my lip. The last time I'd suppressed a similar sound it involved a zipper.

Beraal came to her rescue just as my other hand reflexively moved to apply pressure to a windpipe hidden beneath many chins. I didn't want to strangle an old woman, but I would. There aren't many parts more sensitive than your hand.

"It is I, Beraal! We mean no harm, Dureen Zell. We seek your help to bring aid to Talis Darmon."

Her bloodshot eyes were the size of saucers. The mouth shot open and I removed my throbbing palm. I was shoved out of the way by a wide green back as the two women embraced.

Even in a whisper, her voice was gruff. "Dosenie! I'd heard you'd been taken away by the Thulians." She spit the taste of me out. "Who are these vermin?"

Dave sniggered as I massaged the marks away. No blood. The crone rose with the stone in her hand. She was as gummed as she was sagged. She came back with the feistiness of a kicked Chihuahua. "That's no way to enter a lady's chambers unless you have rape on your mind, beast!"

"The hour is late, dear Dureen Zell. These are true friends to the princess, come to her rescue."

"The queen, thou meanest?"

"Talis Darmon will sit on the throne alone by the time we are done," Kleeve Hartus said.

"Then let an old woman dress, because the dosenie has chosen well. I prayed for this moment. I will guide you—make no attempt to dissuade me, hatchlings! I've served three generations of Sylah. I didn't get to be this ancient in the service of the court without making many a self-inflated guard regret attempting to hinder my path. By reputation alone, Dureen Zell commands obedience of those who would otherwise think themselves above me in station."

Dave gave an amused cough. "Wanna bet who was a role model for the princess?"

Her garb was somewhat more modest than my princess's, but not by much. She saw me massage my hand as we prepared to leave. "No man lays a hand on me, child. I apologize for nothing, though hope not to have damaged you irreparably if your purpose is to save our princess." Her subdued cackle reminded me of someone.

"No, madame. I am fit to fight. I apologize. No offense meant."

"None received, hatchling. Do you know the way, warriors, or are you pretenders to the streets of Shansara as you are men of this traitorous alliance?"

She directed us farther down the narrow alley from Beraal's side in the center of the formation. "The queen—I mean, the princess. Oh! Unsettled I am by this. Our Talis Darmon—she is in seclusion in the dowager's keep. There are many sentries in her gilded prison, all men from Pyreenia. None have even a hint of loyalty to any but the foul Carolinus. Oh, but that a rock had fallen from the heavens and crushed his egg! How will you free her?"

Khraal Kahlees was the one to answer. "By blood."

"I take you through the entrance reserved for the maids. The back stairs lead to the common ascenders of the residences. See the Guards posted ahead? That is our destination. Heads forward! Do not look about as if you do not know the way. March right in front of them and tell them to move!"

Beyond, the very tops of the palace towers loomed in emerald.

I pushed between the two women. "This is going to happen fast. When we move to take them, stay with Beraal and let her shield you, then we'll let you show us the way to her suite."

The old woman had to put me in my place. "I could not be stopped from doing so by a thousand Mydreen."

The Guards snapped to attention as the first shield came to a sharp halt and faced.

"Make way for the escort of the queen's attendants," he said.

At once, the men flanking took action. Just as I'd coached them and with the proper aggressiveness, they drove their blades into the soft notches beside the neck and down into their chests. They were dead on their feet as their chest cavities filled and they drowned in the gush of their own blood. Multi-handed bodies moved smoothly and swiftly and we flooded in, carrying the struggling corpses with us.

The entry gave way to stairs, and we were up them in a thunderous stampede. On a couch sprawled two dozing Guards, hazily alerted at our sudden presence. I was on the farthest, my knife finding that same sweet spot. The other Guard gasped and gurgled, tasting someone else's steel at the same time.

We were in a vaulted chamber with multiple entrances. A young woman stepped into the room and dropped a tray in fright. The loud clash of the tray and the gritty roll of the ribbed vessels across the smooth floor were sirens. Dave reached for her as she sucked in air to scream.

"Be still!" the old woman barked. "Be not a ninny for once, Celes Drake, lest you betray your queen! Go to your cot and remain there!"

Three discs of light came to life across the floor. Kleeve Hartus poised between them as other Guards moved the bewildered servant out of the way. "Which?"

"The center. It comes to rest at the common entrance to the suites. Hers is at the far end."

"How many Guards?" Khraal Kahlees asked as he moved onto the illuminated circle.

"Too many," the old woman cried. "Be swift. They carry orders to kill her!"

"Wait," Beraal pleaded. She bent to the dropped tray and arranged the vessels on it. "Allow Dureen Zell and me to go. We will proceed to the correct door and engage the Guards until you make appearance on the ascender."

"Yes!" The old woman moved to push armored bodies many times her size off the platform. "It is the way. Allow us three long breaths, then ride quickly behind."

Kleeve Hartus and Double-K surrendered to the old woman's manhandling, but looked to me for approval.

"We'll be right behind," I told them. "Drop to the floor when we come, because it's going to be a shitstorm. I don't want you getting shot by accident."

"Do whatever you must, Lord Benjamin Colt."

The old woman flashed a wide, gummy grin. "A proper fight and at its end, freedom for our Talis Darmon. Stand away now!"

The ascender lifted the distance of the chamber and the floor above opened, then closed silently behind them. The blank floor lit anew into another white disc and we crowded on.

Kleeve Hartus barked. "Count of ten for them to reach the end of the hall, and we go. Ten."

Dave nudged me as the first shield counted down. "This is it."

"Seven."

Khraal Kahlees practically sang, "Battle calls and we answer."

"Three. Two. One."

We rose. I craned my neck up, ready to drop my muzzle from its high ready position and drop on the first red cloak I saw. The floor parted at our arrival just as below us, the crackle of fizzle fire erupted. It was too late to stop. The last I saw below was Garlak Ranz firing. I readied. Through the floor, my new vista was of a hall lined with Red soldiers.

A shrill shout came from ahead. "For the princess!" The nearest soldier's back was to me, looking at the distraction. I fired. Off the platform and advancing, I hammered the left side. Dave matched pace on my right, and two more streams of lightning joined. I snapped to the end of the hall as red capes dropped. I ignored the fallen and took a horizontal bound to where Beraal straddled a man, her dagger plunged to the hilt in his chest. Next to her, the old woman lay at the feet of a Guard, hands at his throat, blood pulsing between fingers into a waterfall. I shot him.

I blasted the lockwork and was through. In the middle of the sitting chamber floor, a strange woman lay curled up in a ball, whimpering and pleading not to be killed.

"Where is she?" I demanded, then rushed past her and chose the most obvious door. Ornate and closed. It surrendered to my shove. I yelled with all the thunder stored in my chest, saved for this moment.

"My princess!"

A blur of danger at my peripheral and the dread of a corner uncleared filled me—a trefoil dagger point was aimed at my face. I was barely able to arrest the arm that held it, as an avalanche of lustrous raven hair parted to reveal the most beautiful face in the universe. The stiletto dropped from her open hand to fall between us.

"Benjamin Colt!"

My arms were full of her. She gasped and cried. She pulled away and took my face in hands to kiss me over and over. She threw herself again into my chest and crushed me like the mightiest Tarn.

I broke her embrace. The joy in her eyes turned to fearful storm.

"If ever you leave me again, I shall drive my dagger into your breast with a might that will split asunder the very ground beneath your feet!"

✤ ✤ ✤

"We aren't out of this yet, my princess." I pushed her behind me. Dave blocked the door to shield us both. I caught a glimpse of Kleeve Hartus and Double-K disappearing down the ascender, bodies piled in the corridor like knocked over bowling pins.

"They went to clear the way. You catch the fight breaking out just as we cleared the ascender? We're made. Let's move. Behind me."

Beraal remained outside the door, kneeling at the side of the fallen Dureen Zell. "She is wounded, yet lives. I will carry her. She is but a tiny thing."

"Get her and let's go," I said. I pushed the princess behind me, confident she'd be between me and Beraal, cradling our wounded friend.

We waited for the ascender to appear. Talis Darmon stroked Dureen Zell's face. "The brave, fierce, grand old thing!"

The floor opened and a Guard leaped off to give us the platform.

"Take this one down, White lord. I will follow once certain none pursues."

As we lowered, I surveyed the room from above. One of our Tarns was on the ground, a gaping, bloodless hole burned in his chest. A pair of Red soldiers lay dead at one of the passageways. At the top of the stairs, Kleeve Hartus waited, Garlak Ranz at his side. I was relieved the dead Tarn was not him.

The first shield waved us forward. "No alarms sound yet, but this scene will be discovered soon. Make haste."

"Lead us out."

On the street outside, we slowed to form up. Khraal Kahlees placed Tarns to ring the princess in green armor. "Let nothing pass between you, Korundi. Not blade, not bolt, not wind itself."

I knew how a bank robber felt. I wanted to run at full speed, but I fell into the marching pace of our group, trying to appear as stoic and unconcerned as we had on the way in. At the checkpoint leading out of the borough, a shrill alarm pierced the air from the tallest tower of the palace. K-specs combined to make a sunburst as two Tarns rushed ahead to drag the bodies into the alley from the main street.

Through a gap between bodies, I sprang and yelled, "Time to gallop like a herd of arkall!"

A patrol stumbled into our flank from a narrow street, and before they could offer the challenge of the night guard, we cut them down. Behind me the Tarns plowed ahead like a Brink's armored car carrying the Hope Diamond. We cleaned up the last of them, reflexive spasms of fingers sending a few fizzles chaotically into the air as they succumbed.

Khraal Kahlees was carrying out my orders. He drove the contingent with the princess ahead. A few bounds and I was at the lead again. We reached the avenue of the fountain memorial. To our left, the way to safety. From the right, a blast of white electricity cooked the air over my head. I hammered away where I'd seen the blast momentarily expose the shooters, more firepower immediately joined at my sides to send a wall of unyielding supercharged electrons that broke their line. Those that could pulled back, leaving their dead and wounded behind.

Kleeve Hartus pushed me away. "Go, Benjamin Colt. Only you can open the portal." I didn't argue.

I took one bounce and another. Between the statues of a sword-wielding goddess and another emptying a vessel into the pool, the Tarns were a circle of impenetrable flesh around my princess. "Make a hole!" I yelled. I caught the barest glimpse of the princess, just enough to make my heart sing, and reached into my pouch to find—nothing.

Curses flew from my lips as I tore at my sash and the belt beneath. Behind me fizzle fire surged again.

Khraal Kahlees was not the dispassionate Tarn I thought. "Benjamin Colt! The key! Produce it!"

"I can't find it! I'm—" I noticed a fullness. Then a searing pain from deep in my nethers. I dug uncouthly into the bottom of the loin cloth to find where the ball had come to rest, directly beneath two similarly shaped objects near and dear to me. My finger pads pulsed with heat as they closed on the tiny thing. I held the glowing orb in my flat palm like a venomous insect. I made a fist and thrust it into the wall and the barrier melted to nothing.

"GO!"

I held as the last of the Tarns passed through. "Guards! Let's go!" They did not turn and run. With a disciplined aggression that is all but impossible to teach, the three Guards kept up a wall of K-spec fire as they walked back. Dave posted opposite me in the portal, both of us screaming over the firefight for them to fall back, until, grasping the shoulder of the last man—Kleeve Hartus—green hands dragged us all. On the other side of the portal, Mydreen and Red soldiers poured into the gap made by our absent firepower. Confused faces gawked at the place of our impossible exit, until flashes erupted again. We flinched aside, but to our amazement, the impacts flared harmlessly off the barrier, the portal finally fading to solid until the fizzle fire squelched to relieved silence.

"Wha'ppened, brah?" Dave took a few heaving breaths. "What was the friggin' holdup?"

I held out the Saturn, cold and silver again, while with my other hand, I rubbed a very tender spot. I was the focus of every red and green face. The princess shared in a body language apparently common to races with and without tusks—teeth gritted, faces scrunched, recoiling in pained empathy. Garlak Ranz absent-mindedly rubbed his own loincloth with two lower hands. I found Kleeve Hartus in the crowd. Harsher than I meant to, I let my courageous friend have it.

"This goddamn army's getting pants if I have to sew them all myself."

46

We bobbed fore and aft in coursing surges against the current, each dip of the bow misting us. I pulled my cape around her shoulders and renewed my embrace each time it loosened with the bounce of each trough. Dave shielded us ahead—once again—as he spoke to the floating cloud of a cheering Karlo.

"Yes! I've got an airmobile company headed to meet you at Karvell's." Every air car from Clymaira and Thoria had been brought to Califex for our use.

I raised my head. "Dave, tell Karlo we're launching as soon as we get back."

"Hear that, Karlo?"

"Tell Parkus Laan the princess is safe," Karlo said to someone out of sight, then turned back. "It'll be shouted across the Korund in no time, Dave. It's going to be hard to hold them back from charging straight for Shansara."

I leaned forward while still holding her. "Then we don't hold back, Karlo."

"Roger that, Ben. Troops are already headed for the marshaling area at Karvell's and should start arriving today. Let me know your ETA, guys. Just about finished with the last mods to the air cars, and I'll be there at the way station to meet you. Out."

Talis Darmon rested her head on my chest. "Whatever may come, promise to never let me go again, Benjamin Colt."

I squeezed her harder and made clumsy assurances I wouldn't. "I know you were hurt. Is there anything you want to talk about? Anything I can do?"

Her head nuzzled deeper. "Just let us be still together while we may."

Though it no longer tortured me, there was a scene in my head that still remained—transformed from painful regret into a lesson I'd chiseled into the granite foundation of my new self. A commandment.

It is impossible to translate fear of loss into the language of a loving heart.

If I had mastery of my emotions during combat, what better cause was there than her to which I should be as disciplined? If I truly wanted to be deserving of her, I had to always remember that. I made myself into a bearskin rug. Soft and comforting. My stillness, her order.

We blew past Lemuel's way station, and Cynar gunned his propulsion system with the turn of a yellow crystal knob and we shot into the wide channel of the main aqueduct.

"Hehehe, now we make real progress!" he cried.

After a time, the princess shrugged the cape. In the boat behind, Khraal Kahlees was next to Beraal who still cradled the wounded Dureen Zell. Seeing them together, she shook her head in wonder.

"How did Beraal find you?" she asked. "I knew her gone only because I no longer heard her anguish. I feared her dead, but the Mydreen unwittingly gave comfort by their boasts that she was leading them on an important hunt."

"It was by accident I found her."

I told her all that had happened—except how Mark came to his end; that would wait—everything until the moment she almost plunged a square blade into me. "I got sucked into the room and made the biggest rookie mistake of all—not clearing my corner. You almost got me, Princess! Wouldn't that've been tragic?"

She shivered. "I feared I was being readied for execution! Bursting such into my chamber and in your disguise—I believed the end was at hand. Your speed was great to catch the blade, Benjamin Colt. I have not had the chance to prove to you otherwise, but I am skilled at combat. Trained to defend myself from the time I was a hatchling."

"I believe you, Talis Darmon. But, executed? I thought he needed you as queen?"

"Not a queen to rule at his side, not a regent. Though supernumerary for men, with the Sylah name bound to his, consecrated by marriage law, it means legitimacy to his claim. My mother's line is the oldest royal line of Vistara. By both her blood in his veins and marriage to one who holds the maternal dynasty name, he meant to make himself above derogation. As if it would erase the stain our father's murder by his vile hand! He is ill of mind and spirit—even more eroded than when sent away."

She scoffed. "There are others with royal bloodline besides the Sylah dynasty whom he could have made his queen—perhaps some even willingly. It was done as much to aid himself as it was to punish me for our father's favor. King Osric Darmon was a great man. His sobriety plus his union to the Sylah dynasty maintained the Red Kingdom in a placidness of stability. After the Sylah name was bound to Carolinus Darmon, it would be forever recorded. He could dispense with me and still have the connection."

No matter how she answered my question, it wouldn't matter, but I still had to ask it.

"You're married to your brother now?"

She scowled. "It is not a marriage of man and woman. Do not think of it as so. It is a thing of tradition and politics."

"Was there a ceremony?"

"Witnessed by many conspirators and traitors to my father, yes, curse them."

"And you're queen now?"

She it shook away. "I am not a regent. By law, one must be crowned so." She took my face again. "I am your princess, Benjamin Colt. Not his queen. I know this distresses you, but—"

I blurted, "The only thing I'm distressed about is what you endured. What happened?"

She became dark.

"It will do neither of us good, Benjamin Colt, to relive that."

"Not good enough. Beraal told me you were tortured."

She pleaded, "Do not hold on to these things."

"That's what people do. They hold on to things."

"And when you did, it brought you only pain."

"This isn't about my pain. Please don't put me before you. You've shared my pain. Let me share yours."

She surrendered. "You are my true love, my true protector. Brandon Bryant and the Thulians were rough, but not more so than the

Mydreen. I was caged. Bound. But I've experienced the indignity of imprisonment before, and survived. I knew what to expect."

She paused.

"Carolinus used my gifts against me in ways very cruel. From Pyreenia, he brought a witch to invade my mind."

I cringed.

"Do not suffer on my account, Benjamin Colt. It was a trial, but much of what I did for their benefit was theater. She tried to attack me with destructive auras. To warp my mind. To convince me I was abandoned, forgotten, weak. Sleep and food deprivation used to weaken me—all the tools a captor would use to undermine the resistance of one being interrogated. She used her skills to touch the empathic part of me and work from within to erode my will."

"Like a soul-eater?"

"Ha! The witch aspires to that power. She could project only the tiniest portion of the malevolence under which you and Beraal suffered. But her dark science is taken from the same well of evil that sprouted the phantom souls of the Karnak. In exile, Carolinus found her. In Pyreenia, there is an evil which flourished under my brother's aegis and my father's ignorance. She has influenced him, and he her. But her sorcery is weak. It was a simple matter to act the fear and pain she worked to create in me. I was able to make them believe I had succumbed to her spells, while concealing from them what they wished to know."

"So, they went to work on Beraal to see if your stories were different."

"The Mydreen are cruel."

"I punished them for it. Mark is dead. Beraal is safe. Cynar healed her body and now you can heal her mind again."

The princess shifted to find Beraal. Our friend was engaged nursing Dureen Zell. "In this world, hers is a soul as pure as the hidden vessels of darkness are evil. And we must find and rout them from the kingdom."

"We're getting closer to that day, my princess. Our army is on the move."

Even in the dim light of the aqueduct, nothing escaped Talis Darmon's vision. "Khraal Kahlees is very attentive to Beraal."

While I wasn't ready to muddy our reunion by revealing I'd sentenced Mark to hell, I had to admit this.

"Khraal Kahlees knows. I told him. He's made contrition to Beraal, too."

I didn't stop.

"I betrayed even more of her confidences." I told her what had happened to Beraal's mother under Domeel Doreen. "I thought deeply about what you and I discussed in a place just like this. That perhaps Cynar had subconsciously wanted our help. I remember it like it was yesterday. Just the three of us, floating away from the suffering that joined us, thinking we'd left the worst behind. I feel ashamed, my sharing Beraal's secret with him. Justifying it to myself that she subconsciously hoped I would mediate a reunion. But I also hoped it would benefit our cause. That it would fuel Khraal Kahlees to full commitment. It was selfish by all accounts. But I did it with you in mind, however wrong it was."

She raised an eyebrow, considering how to scold me. Prepared to take my just punishment, I waited her embrace to disappear and my soul to wither. Instead, she gripped me tighter.

"Nothing is as simple as we would like it to be, except that there is good and evil. What I see happening between a father and daughter is a great good. The rest… I must put it to you this way.

"I was taught by two wise teachers. My mother taught me the ways of connection. My father taught me the ways of governance. Both taught me service. To be a leader, means to accept that there is a greater good to be achieved. The leader exists as a necessity to guide all to that end—otherwise, barbarity reigns and civilization crumbles. As a warrior, I know you already understand this.

"There is never a justification for evil means to be used to achieve good ends. You did no evil. But there are times when a burden must be assigned. Remember that, and know it is by burden of leadership that you must by necessity burden others. And forgive yourself, as I forgive you. And as you may someday need to forgive me."

"I always will, my princess. Whatever needs may be."

I felt lighter. For a fleeting moment. Because in my arms was the reminder that I had a burden to discharge. Bryant. Chuck. Domeel

Doreen. An army waiting to be crushed. An unnamed witch and a cabal of evil that helped undermine a kingdom. Knowns and unknowns.

She distracted me with a kiss. "I've died for want of hearing you call me your princess. It does me well to see you smile, Benjamin Colt. Do I make you happy?"

"You're the source of all happiness, my princess."

"And when Shansara is won, we will live that every day."

"But first, Talis Darmon, I'm going to make you a widow."

The only waves to make music on Vistara since a time forgotten were jealous of her laugh.

✣ ✣ ✣

Karvell was dead when we returned, his long watch ended. Cynar was unmoved. When I left them, Vistara's oldest living water priest was speaking collegially to Karlo as the wounded Dureen Zell lay bathed in the third ray. I could've told Karlo the sky was on fire and he wouldn't have heard me.

Those of us who'd witnessed the metamorphosis eyed the piles of boulders with suspicion, but they never moved. A fleet of air cars and many companies of arkall-mounted Korundi milled about. Some had already taken their brethren's invitation to peer into the way station and see for themselves the great river they would soon ride. Dave and I found Parkus Laan in contemplation while considering the fountain.

"It's time to move the Korundi to war, Parkus Laan."

He lifted his wrist with the comm bracelet, one of the ten Cynar had made for us. "Khraal Kahlees prepares to lead our floating caravan. In two days' time, he will be staged to commence the attack on the defenders of Shansara. When the attack is launched outside the city, his vanguard will appear from within to cause chaos."

I'd passed the key off to the appointed leader of the task force. He'd fought with us in the city—the capable Garlak Ranz.

"I must show you how to secure items in your belt so they do not go astray, Benjamin Colt."

I was back in my MCs. A velcro tear and I pulled the key from my chest pocket. "Pockets are better," I said.

He gingerly took the silver Saturn.

A thunder of feet rushed to us. Kleeve Hartus and Double-K came to a hurried rest.

"Benjamin Colt, I have report from Clymaira," said the first shield.

He raised his wrist and a cloud appeared again. Linked through the atmosphere wizard's device, I recognized the Clymairan lieutenant, who gravely said, "An army moves on us. The Mydreen advance to retake Clymaira."

Dave glanced at me. "That's what the Chief's truce was worth. Nothing."

✣ ✣ ✣

"This is what we know," I said loudly to get everyone's attention. All the leaders crowded with us on the esplanade. "While we were on the way to rescue the princess, the Mydreen army was already on the move for Clymaira. They're still several days away from reaching the city. The scouts also report this—one of the war wagons is on the march with them. It means their forces are divided. It's an ideal situation for us to carry out our attack on Shansara."

A Guard barked, "So Clymaira falls! Again!"

Kleeve Hartus fixed the man with a frown. "Hold and listen."

Clouds of grumbles erupted into storms of discontent.

"We left our homes undefended to aid you, Thulian."

"Hang Shansara! Clymaira has already suffered a hundredfold worse."

"Time for us to protect our own."

Dave yelled, "Shut your face-holes and listen up!"

There were only a handful of Clymairans numbered among our total force, but they'd been fiercely loyal to our cause. The pilots of our fledgling air force were vital to our success—so far and to come. I was not about to betray them.

I lowered my own voice. It was an old trick. Rather than yell louder, it forced them to quiet further. "We do no such thing. We destroy their army on the open plains below Clymaira *and* attack Shansara."

A pilot challenged me. "We cannot win in a two-front war against the thousands of the Mydreen hordes, even with our improved weaponry."

It was best to keep my plan under wraps for a little while longer. Was it possible there were spies in our midst? I'd be a fool to think otherwise. Not until we were committed would I reveal the full scope of the plan. For now, just the broad strokes would have to do.

"We can't win if we fight on their terms. We will not."

47

"You cannot ask me to remain behind."

I'd been dreading this. Before I got my hands up, she slipped an uppercut in on me.

"The last time I was abandoned in Califex, things did not go so well."

Low. Blow.

I shook it off and didn't pull my punch. "You're a liability. I'm leading us right into a fight. No matter what we do, no matter that we're better than our enemy, I can't change that people are going to die. Them and us. I have to go into harm's way. I won't take you with me to that place."

"It is not your choice to make for me, Benjamin Colt. I will not allow others to fight for my kingdom if I would not risk all for it as well."

"No one is asking you to risk your life, Princess. Your part in this is different from mine."

"That is so. But it doesn't excuse your logic."

It was our first fight as a couple.

"My logic? I'm being perfectly logical. You're not a soldier. This is a war."

But in a contest of wits against Talis Darmon—the diplomat, the scholar, the sorceress—I was a paper tiger and heavy rain was in the immediate forecast.

"If you are defeated, staying behind would but delay my demise. If I die with you in battle, it is still preferable. Though neither is the outcome I believe we have to look forward to, it is ignorance to not account for those possible results. We have reached the time of total commitment. If this army fails and you fall with it, there is no future I care to live in."

Then she threw her right cross over my guard.

"Do not allow fear to govern your life with me."

Like a perfect feint, she drew my eyes to the distraction of the commandment I'd made for myself. Then she finished me.

"Besides. You promised."

Knock out.

Now came the gracious victory speech. "There is much we have yet to learn about each other, Benjamin Colt. I do not know your notions about such things, but in my depths I think you must believe as I do. We found each other by purpose of cosmic tragedy. What the cataclysm of two worlds brought together did not occur by pure chance or without greater purpose. What tragedy has joined I will not allow to be separated ever again. My place is at your side, and yours at mine. Forever."

If I had to lose every disagreement with her for eternity, then I'd gladly stack up a record of all losses. But I'd always get on my feet to take another swing. "Yes, my princess. But a diplomat knows when it's time to compromise. Out there, you'll do as I say."

She smiled the smile of a benevolent conqueror who wasn't insisting on an unconditional surrender. "Yes, General."

✣ ✣ ✣

She covered her mouth with the back of her hand and coughed. "Bleh. It smells of arkall sweat and rotting carcasses." We flew in formation, ten flitters. Half of our air force. But not even flying on an open deck flitter could disguise my exertions soaked into the armor. I'd worn the plate carrier practically day and night for so long that during my time without it in the Korund, it was like being separated from an identical twin.

"It's as close as I can get it to fitting you. If you're going to make this a habit, I'll get something better for you. When we get near, you won't take it off again until I say so. Period. That was the deal."

She removed the helmet and recoiled after examining the interior. It's best not to see how the sausage is made. Beraal helped lift the stripped plate carrier from her shoulders and held it at a distance. "Is it dead or a living thing, lord? Will it remain where I lay it or must I chain it to something to prevent its escape?"

I wore my chest rig, a shingle of M4 mags, and other pouches stuffed with items transferred from my kit. "It's not silk and gold, sister, but be careful how you talk about my rig. You'll hurt her feelings."

The dosenie was outfitted as any Tarn warrior, bronze toned armor and helmet, ready to protect the princess. I knew better than to start another argument by trying to leave her behind, too.

I had Mitch's bucket. It would've been more comfortable to wear my own rather than give it to the princess but, holding both in my hands, it was his that I held onto the tightest.

The first shield's voice came from my wrist. "Aircraft ahead." I grabbed binos and steadied against the pilot's console.

I squinted and painted the empty sky with a search. "I don't see them."

Avril Mysteen pointed. Pilots had good eyesight. Better even than snipers. I tested 20/15 acuity. I supposed it was trained sight rather than vision that let them pick up things so well. Now I had success with the binoculars. Two dots at our one o'clock and our altitude, veering away.

I brought my wrist up. "Anything in the air is hostile! Knock them down!" Communication between elements was still a hindrance. When we had that licked and everyone had comms, we would truly be a superior mobile fighting force. It just wouldn't be in time to help us in this battle.

We still were only a little better than a wooden ship navy. After an exchange of flapping signal flags, three flitters peeled away to chase down the enemy air cars. There was nothing for the rest of us to do but to keep on course. I maintained anxious watch until meteors streaked in the daylight. Three air cars returned and swooped close to our flitter. Gunners grinned and slapped the tops of their waist guns and waved at me. I gave them the double thumbs-up of their big brother's approval. It was the first kill of the big battle. And for these crews, their first one with the new guns.

My corollary to Churchill's proverb was this—there's nothing so exhilarating as a confirmed kill. It proves your guns have real death power. *That* was a confidence-builder better than any rousing speech given by any general ever. The only kind a real warfighter cared about.

Talk's cheap.

"Both of the enemy aircraft are downed, Benjamin Colt."

I keyed the communicator and let the visual cloud form to bring to life a picture to go with the words. The first shield ducked lower behind the wind screen as he piloted.

"We remain undiscovered," he said. "Two subtracted from their dozen ISR platforms." I'd taught them the acronym.

"When your man makes commo again, I want an update on all enemy compositions," I told him, "and I want to know where that Thulian war wagon is. Emphasize it's critical. No excuses. Not unless he wants to have another Mydreen occupation."

"The captain's next contact is soon. He knows this, I assure you, but I will make emphasis again."

"I leave it to you to choose where we ground for the last rally point. Whatever intel we have then, is what we'll have."

"Then we attack. Understood, Benjamin Colt. Out."

The vagaries of rates and distances made everything a seat-of-the-pants operation, which I hated now more than ever. We'd ground, I'd give my final operations order, and in the dark, we'd start our air offensive.

I had much more planned, but there were two pairs of ears in our flitter that I kept out of the loop. I'd apologize later. If there was a later.

The landscape dimmed enough that stars began their shine. Our altitude decreased and after another hour of low-level flight, flags passed the order to assume a landing formation. The horizon hinted at the peaks of Clymaira.

Gathered around the lead car were Clymairan Guard pilots, Tarn deck gunners and infantry, and us. I stood at Kleeve Hartus's shoulder to let his cloud hold us both. The captain had a lighted slate behind him, the city perimeter in outline, the figures of enemy troop positions laid out at its southwest.

"They betray position now by the air cars above their formations," the captain said. "My men report they leave convoy to make for battle formation and have increased their speed. They will envelope our border before midnight at their current rate."

"And the Stryker?" I asked the first shield.

"Last seen it was with the westernmost band."

"What's the description?" I crossed my fingers.

"It is large and has as many wheels as an arkall legs."

It was the Stryker.

"Bring your people in, Captain," I said, glad at the news. "We won't need them anymore. Tell them they've done well and prepare to defend the perimeter. You may be in for a fight, and we'll have our own hands full. It's the best we can offer."

"We have the defenses prepared. Good luck to us all then."

The cloud faded.

On the deck, all eyes were on me. Internally, I cursed for the millionth time. I was a one-eyed man in the kingdom of the blind. It was because I knew there was a better way. A way in which warfare didn't have to be so disjointed, chaotic, and uncoordinated. Yes, there was such a thing as too much central control, too much communication, initiative paralyzed by micro-management on the battlefield. But if a general in the grand Napoleonic Army had been whisked forward to my time, learned how even a thing as simple as radio communication could revolutionize warfare, would he be content to return to his own time with only quill and parchment, smoke and flags, bugles and drums with which to communicate?

Hell no. He'd feel as crippled as I did.

I ran through the plan, then had each pilot and deck chief recite back their responsibilities and actions. There's nothing new under the sun. This was a ritual probably dating back to King David. It was simple—prove to the commander that an order given was an order understood. Rituals become so for good reason. And violating the liturgy of the service for battle was a sin.

I supposed this was the time to make some great speech, like Aragorn before the last battle for Middle Earth. I was about to launch into something ripped off from what I remembered of it—none of them would know—when Talis Darmon appeared from behind. I'd lost sight of her in the gathering. At some point, she'd mounted the air car, waiting patiently for her opportunity.

"General, may I speak?"

I almost looked around to see who she'd called general, but acted like I'd known it was me all along, bowed and stood aside.

She'd fixed her hair. A shimmering gold cloak which she whisked back with great flourish was received by Beraal who smoothly bowed and retreated.

The princess knew what a red carpet moment was.

"Our world stands on the brink of two possible futures. One, a path to its certain end. The other, the road to glory and a new hope. By your bravery, you secure for all of Vistara a chance at redemption. A moment that comes only once in the history of a world. What you do today will become the first day of a history that will mark the rebirth of this dying world. You do this not for your kingdom. You do this not for me. Not for tribe nor family. You do this to prove to an uncaring universe that we will not fade away in pathos. We let the stars know that we choose to remain. To fight our fate with a roar. To let our might shake the very foundations of creation."

She spread arms wide.

"You do this for all Vistara!"

✣ ✣ ✣

The cheers went on. Kleeve Hartus took charge and dismissed crews to their vehicles. I lowered the princess to me on the ground, lighter than the air of Mars itself. She raised to herself full height. Chin proud. Aloof, dignified, and regal. Ready for the official photograph to be taken. She was the cat that ate the canary.

"You learn that from your mother or your father?" I mumbled as she acknowledged another crew's bows of farewell. She remained in pose as Beraal draped her, arranging her hair over the collar.

"You above all know that our princess has a gift, Lord Benjamin Colt," the dosenie said.

The last of the crews departed. It wasn't until then that Talis Darmon broke poise. "I only wished to give service to you, General. I hope you are pleased with the results."

I offered her my arm. "Time to armor up and hunker down, Princess."

Avril Mysteen looked up from attending his console. "We are ready, lord."

The princess let me heft her onto the deck.

"Help the princess, Beraal," I said.

The princess made her sour face. "I will do as you wish, but there will be a time when you must sleep and Beraal will scrub the uncleanliness from this Thulian repository of disease. Or better yet—when you are properly donned in armor fitting for a general, she burns it."

I saluted the young pilot with a fist to chest, and he returned it, but winced. Not in residual pain caused by his healed injuries but because he was about to take another beating, worse than his last.

"Good lad," I told him. I'd never called anyone "lad" before. It just came out.

The flitter lifted. I watched it rise and as it did, her helmeted face popped over the side. Shock turned to realization, then fury, but before the princess could tear in to my shrinking form, the air car sped away north into the darkness.

I picked my kit off the ground and bounced into the last grounded flitter. The mix of chuckles and Tarn snorts made for the grand sound of fighting spirit. Green hands took my gear. Jodal Jark and Sarkan Sell volunteered for the mission before I finished asking. I'd trusted them since the moment they protected me and the princess in the Korund. Youth and experience combined to make them just who I wanted with me.

"Ready to have fun?"

The young Jodal Jark kneeled to pat a long bundle next to his ruck.

"I've dreamed of nothing but, Benjamin Colt."

48

We skimmed low and slow on a dead reckoning to take us west and around the city. I flew us. My PVS-31s made the world day, and I chose the best path possible between dunes and rises to keep us below the enemy line of sight. "I'm betting their air scouts have gotten used to seeing the Clymairan Guard out and about trying to keep tabs on their advance, but this near we're going to get a reaction."

"We travel lightly," Sarkan Sell encouraged.

Jodal Jark balanced as if on a surfboard, clearly enjoying the experience. "He is long in the tusks, but still able to keep up with me, lord."

The older Tarn groaned. "It is not too late to replace this hatchling with a seasoned warrior, Benjamin Colt. One speaks by competent action, not from gaping mouth and empty head."

They both made sounds that, if you didn't know Tarns, you'd think was how one dog warned another it was too near its home turf. Mirth was a fierce coughing growl. Real ferocity was a roar. These guys were having fun with each other.

"Just keep up with me, and don't drop anything. We've got to move fast and far. If you fall behind, I'll leave you both."

The time to put on our game faces was at hand.

The Mydreen flitters patrolled over the advancing army, satellites in the night sky, lower than they'd been. They were shifting from aerial reconnaissance to aerial fire support, readying for the attack. When they did notice us—not if—they could be on us in minutes. I grounded. "Take over," I told the pilot as Jodal Jark and Sarkan Sell readied. On the second false insertion, we leaped off and the ship gunned away. It would make one more brief touchdown a few klicks in front of their main body, then make for the link-up where the squadron was masked behind the city.

We hit the ground at a run. I slowed my pace, which meant the Tarns were at full haul-ass to keep from losing sight of me. During our time together in the Korund, making our way from one village to another, they'd told me about life in the mountains. Both were of a tribe that practiced mountain running not only as discipline, but as the traditional means of communication between settlements—a Tarn pony express. I hit another patch that left me no choice but to cover open ground, dropped and high crawled. I paused at the next decision point to find a best course, and by the time I felt them behind me, took off again.

After an hour, my fifth-grade failure to master the impossible story problem wasn't an issue any longer. Train A traveling at eighty miles an hour was now in sight of train B at sixty miles an hour. Solved with my feet, not my head. Simple.

I dropped the ruck and was pulling out the Javelin CLU when my loaders arrived. We had three missiles. I was going to use them all. Loaded, I crawled over the berm, ready to hunt. The Stryker should stand out like a sore thumb. If it was there. I got my answer as the *chug-chug-chug* of the .50 cal caused geysers of dirt and the 660-grain M33 ball told me to get out of there.

There was no beating thermal. My ghillie suit and the Tarn desert capes were as useful as nose glasses at a costume party. The *whack-whack-whack* of the Mark-19 barely reached me before 40-mm HE rained clouds of shrapnel. They weren't dead on me, which meant I had one shot at it, because if it were Chuck or Bryant in the gunner seat, the next would be. I fired.

I yelled, "Load!"

Arms flew in hurried action around me. I settled behind the sight and didn't wait to see what the first had done before I sent the second.

You know when you know.

"Pain is brought, lord."

"Enjoy your ride on the Blix."

I don't know who said which, but they were both right. The Stryker burned furiously, both missiles had hit. Back on my NODS, I searched the skies. Their only way to reach us now was from above.

"Save the last missile." I rolled down the slope, dropped the CLU in the ruck and shouldered up. "Run!"

I took off, reversing our course. Behind us, fizzle guns and M4s fired. At what, I didn't care. They might as well have been sending rough language our way for all the good it did them. Oh, how I ached to dig through the wreck and see which of them I'd cooked, Bryant or Chuck. Could I have gotten them both? No chance, that, I figured. If Mark had been in the gunner seat, we'd be dead now.

Instead, Marky-Mark was reliving his worst memories a thousand times a day.

We reached a good spot to hunker down.

"Get up top and keep an eye out," I said.

The Tarns pushed up behind me, their K-specs peeking ahead.

I keyed my wrist. "Task Force, you're clear. Good flying. Good hunting."

Kleeve Hartus came back, "Get out of there, General. We carry the fight now."

The buzz of K-specs sang the warning. I crawled up between them and thrust my M4 ahead. I tipped my NODS back and dropped behind my optic, the clip-on already warmed up, making a green world magnified to 4-power come alive. A mounted patrol was maneuvering on us. Arkall were trotting away without riders. Wishful fizzle fire and cracks of M4s came from a wide base, a few hundred meters away. I got on my elbows and blooped my first grenade at the closest.

While my friends sent good shots at whatever dark patches presented in the distance, I took a moment to smell the roses as our air force appeared above. "Keep it up. You're doing fine." I took another scan around, saw nothing moving in our sector, and blew out a glad breath.

MacArthur had a nervous stomach. He threw up before every major operation, and it didn't stop until the battle was underway. The historical precedence for my own episode over the side of the flitter before we left made me feel I was in good company.

Thanks, Douglas.

Say what you will about the man, but for not having that little bit of history erased from the books, I was grateful to him. Because I felt great.

Until I saw the flitter headed our way.

"Aerial target headed our way. Priority. Shift fire."

The Tarns didn't respond.

"Knock that air car down. Now!"

I raised my M4 and started a slow cadence of fire, a single pull of the trigger with each sight picture. My night vision flared with the shots that joined mine from either side. One big flash, the air car veered. Maybe it was my imagination, but I swear I heard the same sound a downed prop-fighter made in a black and white dog-fight movie. It crashed as one of our flitters passed well above us, just the buzz of its propulsion a trail behind it. I picked it up under bare eyes as its waist guns peppered the ground and skies ahead.

It was as sweet as an A-10 to me. The Guards had boasted about their gunnery prowess. They no longer had to prove it to me.

"Not our kill, guys, but I'd say we helped the flyboys boys locate it. So, fifty percent our kill. Stay on the dismounted troops and keep them off us."

Jodal Jark was on a combat high. "You promised amusement, lord, and you delivered."

"Yeah, yeah. Stay in the game, junior. We can end up dead yet."

Our air force went to work. I had to encourage both of my Tarn team to keep on their sector, but it was near impossible to ignore the air war part of this campaign. From high altitude, the gunners raked the enemy lines. Low altitude air bursts heartened me that it was enemy air cars being sorted out by our flitters as K-max deck guns hammered the skies and at the troops in the open.

For good measure, I sent another grenade lobbing into the defilade behind a dune a hundred meters away. No screams rewarded the effort, but if there were any Mydreen who still had the bright idea to assault our position, it was a cheap deterrence. Grenades, I had plenty of.

This kept up for another hour. The columns of troops we'd ambushed pulled away, moving to the center of their front, herded by the gun runs. It was impossible for the Mydreen to touch them. All thanks to Karlo.

The action was now out of sight. Our corner of the world had become a boring vista of black and green, the noises of the battlefield telling me good things were still happening. I'd held off bugging Kleeve Hartus—because he had to be a one-legged man in an ass-kicking contest—but I couldn't hold off any longer.

"Flight leader, report in."

A flitter made a pass many kilometers away, raining dragon fire down on invisible targets. A 249 spat in longer bursts than I would have allowed. Some of the teams' remaining firepower had been divvied up for use by whoever had been able to make the leap, Tarn or Red. Whoever'd been trusted with the precious resource, they were using it like amateurs. But if I were in their position, maybe I'd do the same.

Because our slaughter proceeded like a hurricane. Spinning faster, winds howling, rain stinging.

Sarkan Sell relaxed in prone, his chin resting on the gun. "How long will they continue the massacre from above?"

"Not much longer. The guns will run dry soon."

No matter how we outclassed the Mydreen, there weren't enough K-max or K-spec to win the day. Ten to fifteen thousand Mydreen couldn't be beaten with the number of guns we had. Not if they all bunched up in a football stadium and held hands singing "Kumbaya" while we worked them over.

The eagerness and abandon Jodal Jark had going into this mission was evolving. With reverence and cautiousness his next question came. "Has the time arrived?" He lowered his rifle. The infantryman's familiarity of ground and gun, kill or be killed, win or die, wasn't life philosophy adequate enough to prepare him for the next.

"Back on your gun," I scolded. Not even I was sure what to expect.

The first shield's voice finally returned. "We have lost a crew to ground fire, General."

The flitters weren't fast movers—a jet was all but impossible to hit with most any ground fire. The flitters were hardly that. Had they lost altitude awareness and gotten sucked in to their targets? Risk ignored so the pilot could soak up more of the thrill of the kill? I'd prefer to imagine it was just bad luck. And on the two-way shooting range, luck favored the persistent. As long as the Mydreen had someone to press a trigger, anyone could die. Getting killed by an incompetent stung worse than buying it from a master. But, that was war.

"Are the enemy troop formations optimal?" I asked.

There was a break and my mouth went dry with anxiety while I waited his answer.

"I am satisfied."

"Then start your runs with the payloads and get clear."

"Yes, General."

Jodal Jark softly said, "Will we see results from here?"

"No. And because none of the flyboys can tell us apart from anyone else on the ground, it's time we get moving. Let's not be test subjects, okay?" I pushed us back off the slope. "Expect to run into enemy patrols. This will be a slow movement. I'll lead and we'll be making frequent security halts. Silence is the order for the rest of the night. Questions?"

The younger Tarn took a last look into the direction of the distant melee. "I am curious about what will occur."

Sarkan Sell grunted. "Hatchling, have no concern. You will have your fill of death before this is finished."

The two fell in behind me, and as I'd commanded, we set out. We walked for some time, each of my halts and careful scans from each security perimeter yielding nothing, even the sound of our flitters now long absent.

As we patrolled, the eerie desert silence invited my inner playback of the fight with Karlo.

"Hannibal had elephants," I'd reminded Karlo. "He used the tools at his disposal and created an asymmetric advantage. No one looking back thinks he played unfairly because of it."

Scoffing, he'd said, "This isn't near the same, and you know it. Don't try to justify it by some grand academic analysis. And don't go telling me about the Trojan War or the first time iron blades fought bronze ones, or Agincourt, or any other bullshit, Ben."

Dave was on my side. "Yeah, well, how about the way we ended the war with Japan, brah? You think that was a bad idea, too?"

"They have the numbers, Karlo." I stuck to the simplest, most important fact of the matter. "We're outnumbered. Thanks to you, we have a relative advantage against their superior numbers with our better small arms. But it's a limited advantage. It only puts us ahead in small engagements. One big, protracted fight, and all our Christmas toys are out of batteries. Then we're no longer ahead in the calculations, we're not equal, we're behind. If it comes down to us fighting on *their* terms like two massive cavalries, it's obvious we can't win. You know that's what it comes down to. So, can you do it?"

Dave made it clear which side he was on. "Karlo, you ain't gotta like it, but you do have to do it, brah."

Even I knew the chemical formula for the alkylating agent. Hydrogen cyanide was simpler, but history showed on the open battlefield, it was too vulnerable to the atmosphere and dispersed quickly. In the thin air of Mars, it would be even less effective over a large area. I'd stared at those slides with every basic training class. Had all the classes myself, since the first days of my own military training. I wrote the formula out on a page from my sniper data book with one of our last barely wet sharpies and forced it at him. He snatched it from me.

He took the pen, corrected my mistake, and turned it to show me. "You were close, Ben."

"Not my strong suit," I mumbled.

"Can you do it, brah?"

Karlo had cursed, exempting Dave and singling me out for his disgust. "Yeah, Kaiser Wilhelm. I can make mustard gas."

✣ ✣ ✣

Another hour into our patrol and my wrist buzzed. I took a knee and risked the light. The magical communication cloud materialized. "General, it is done."

I dropped my atlas stone.

"Come get us. Tell the crew when they're near, I'll fire a pin flare and have them identify, then pop a chem light to home in on."

"I'm coming to get you myself, General. Out."

He wasn't alone.

In my life, I've known great elation. I've known great dread. I can't recall having ever experienced both at the exact same time. Was there even a word for it? It was being handed the keys to an Italian supercar for a sunny coastal drive, transported from Planet Poverty into the lifestyles of the rich and famous. Then, past the bend, the cliff road is washed out by a mudslide. The way back, blocked by brushfire mountains.

But at least you're in a Ferrari.

On the prow, she wore my plates and helmet, my thrill and my natural disaster in a single package. We jumped on and I grabbed the console edge as the first shield coughed "sorry" and lifted. Hands on her hips, she balanced expertly and gracefully, the force of the flitter going airborne negligible against her greater will. Contrasting her goddess-like poise, my Tarn companions lurched to find handholds and ease to the safety of the deck.

The princess took bold steps, our yaw and pitch inducing zero weave in her course straight for me, when a guttural roar got all our attentions.

"The enemy's greatest weapon! The impregnable beast! The White lord crushed it with his own hand! I saw this thing myself! Benjamin Colt! Benjamin Colt! Benj—"

Sarkan Sell double-elbowed the youth. "Not now."

Later I'd find the time and place to thank junior for giving the princess yet more ammunition against me. I'd been the same boisterous kid once. And like a good squad leader had done for me, I'd educate him as I'd been. Wall-to-wall counseling was underrated.

She stopped so close, she almost pinned my feet in place, then bobbed her head toward Jodal Jark. "I know I do not have to ask if this is true, Benjamin Colt. You kept from me your intention to seek martial glory. I've made myself clear that your obligation must come before such needs." She thrust two digits up. "That makes two promises you have broken to me in but a single day."

"I'll never fail you, Princess. That was my promise. As for leaving you behind—let's agree to disagree that qualifies as breaking a promise. There was a chance the poison would kill us all."

But I froze. Had the gas worked? Had it in fact killed anyone?

"Kleeve Hartus, what was the effect of the agent? Did the packages deploy as we anticipated?" We'd had no time to really test them.

"The containers deployed easily. I led the first pass then stayed above to direct the rest of the sorties. I counted them all. Not one failed to detonate on contact."

"And?" I wanted him to tell me he saw panicked roaches scatter like it was exterminator Tuesday at the mess hall dumpsters.

"I believe there was effect. Ground fire diminished greatly with each pass, but… I cannot give a more precise report."

It had been only starlight before. Both moons were overhead and the ground was bright as if covered in a light, red snow.

"We need an assessment. I'm dropping you all off in Clymaira and going for a damage assessment. Alone. No need to risk more people than necessary."

We leveled off and set course for the city when Kleeve Hartus countered, "No, Benjamin Colt. You may be general, but I am flight leader. You have already risked more than any to bring us a chance at victory. I will be dropping all of *you* off and making an observation flight alone."

"We go now, and together," the princess huffed. "There are things we must know and time is critical, is it not? First Shield, take us over the battlefield at the altitude you believe safest to minimize risk. Don't look to him for permission! I order it." She huffed when he did not look away from me.

I didn't have a respirator even for myself, much less any real MOPP gear. I checked my chrono and did some finger-counting math. "It's been several hours. I might be a little overly cautious, but not even Karlo had a solid on how long the stuff might linger or if it would disperse in any kind of significant concentration into the atmosphere. Okay. But I'll be up front, sniffing and waiting for my skin to tell me if we're in trouble. If I give you the high sign, get us the hell out of there." I gave the princess an eyebrow. "Good enough?"

There was no reason to flip my NODs down. If there were survivors, they were doing a good imitation of fruit arranged for a still life. Not a laced tablecloth with a bowl and shiny apples, but an orchard as large as a Montana county. Larger blots of arkall, smaller spots of Tarns, and the smaller yet of men. I made a fist to indicate I wanted us to hover. I tried to count the dark spots. Too many. I dropped my NODs down and searched again. After another minute, I gave up, and made an overhead loop. The gunwales were crowded with everyone searching as I had.

Kleeve Hartus gasped. "How many thousands, do you suppose?"

"All of them."

I'd taken a chill I hadn't noticed until the princess placed a warm hand on my bare arm.

"On to Shansara. It is time to finish this as you have finished them here. Well done, my general. My true hero."

Saddam and the Kaiser had to take the lower podium steps. I'd won the gold medal for mass murder.

And because she'd placed the ribbon around my neck, I felt fine.

✽ ✽ ✽

I was on the call to Dave as we headed back. "These guys need some refit time, then we'll be wheels up and screaming to Shansara. A day and a half, at least." Helmet off, the princess dozed on my ruck, still wearing my plate carrier like it was one of my old T-shirts. If there were ever a sexier gun bunny to model it, I'd never seen equal on Soldier Systems.

Dave waved me off. "We'll either be mopping up by then, or they'll be doing the same to us."

"Sorry, brother. I wish there was another way. Out of all of us, you're taking the biggest bite from the shit sandwich."

"Nah. So long as I don't eat one their Javelins, it'll be smooth. They've only got two. First one they get off, everyone else will be on them like white on rice. I'm running a minigun myself *and* directing the air campaign. We won't let up until we're Winchester on the bullet launchers and stone-dead on every K-max. Shock and awe, brah."

With all of our heaviest firepower on flitters—134s, the 240 and the 249, plus a few dozen K-max—our air force would bring even greater pain to the defenders than they'd wreaked here. Dug in or not. But unlike the battle for Clymaira, an air campaign alone wouldn't be winning the day. Ground-pounders had to evict the squatters. In my mind, it was a foregone conclusion. In a day or so, Javelins or no, the enemy would all but cease to exist around Shansara.

It would be over. This mad episode on this mad world would be ready for the history books. The real mission to save Vistara could start. And Talis Darmon and I could discover who we were together, without the looming darkness of Bryant and Domeel Doreen hanging over us.

"I tried Karlo earlier. He didn't answer."

Dave waved me off again. "He took the canoe trip with the Tarns. Don't worry, brah. He knows we're right. He'll get over it once he's free to solve all the mysteries of science Cynar's got him revved up about. I talked to him earlier. He and Double-K have the assault force formed up, ready to roll. By this time tomorrow, I'll have something to tell you." He mimicked choking with both hands around his throat. "It work as advertised?"

"It's not quite daylight yet, but from what I saw, yeah. We did it."

"Then it was worth it, brah. Hey, gotta go. Time to play air force. Out."

While the others slept, Kleeve Hartus and I took a solo flight in the early morning light, no argument from the princess as Beraal coaxed her away to a bed. I half expected to see dazed troops rising off the ground to shake off a forced slumber, ready to take up arms again. Maybe Karlo had substituted the mustard gas formula for some nonlethal sleep gas as a big screw you to me? I hated myself for holding even a tiny doubt about Karlo's commitment. But as we cruised over the battlefield in the red light of morning, that mistrust was wiped away as surely as if those concerns had been on a dry erase board, made clean again with rubbing alcohol.

Nothing but nothing moved. In every direction. Judgment day had come for them. We made a swoop to the west until we located the far left edge of their formation and the wreck of the Stryker. "Take us lower."

The shell of it sat in the center of our tight orbit as we descended to within a few hundred feet and leveled off. The hatches were blown open, the top deck rent and twisted. I kept a waist gun on it, ready to hammer away in case it rose again from the dead. I wished for a multicam body to pop out and shake a fist at us in defiance, Chuck or Bryant—preferably both—cursing our total victory. *"I'd have gotten away with it too, if it hadn't been for you kids and your pesky matter mill!"*

I was ready to end it like Scooby and the Mystery Gang never had. *Here's some K-max as the cherry on the cake of your day, you bastards.*

But it wouldn't happen. What was left of the war wagon wouldn't be fit for a Benning live fire range. It was… unsatisfying.

Kleeve Hartus read my mind. "Were the Thulians in there?"

Nothing less than their mutilated and blistered bodies was what I was willing to accept as confirmation. "I don't believe in the tooth fairy, the Easter Bunny, or body counts without corpses. Your Guard's captain is getting another mission from me. I want that battlefield swept.

Especially that Stryker. If they have to wrap themselves in garbage bags and peel it apart with a can opener, I want it done."

"I've come to understand some of your idioms, my friend. I understand the essence of what you say, though I do not have equivalent translation. The means are available. I will make it clear to him, Benjamin Colt. It will be done."

I checked the time.

"We won't be hanging around, though. Best speed, First Shield. Time to make troops wakey-wakey, drop their snakeys, and get to flying. There's a kingdom needing its queen."

49

She told me we had to talk. You know—*the talk*.

The long flight to Shansara was a passage through a stasis as blank as limbo itself. There was nothing to occupy my mind except the pregnant what-ifs we'd be dealing with a full day or more away. Big what-ifs. The biggest. So, when she brought it up, it was actually welcome. Because until I heard from Dave, there was nothing more I could do. I'd already checked three times that my M4 bolt was lubed. That's the OCD of a grunt with idle hands and an anxious mind.

About weekly in my only adult relationship with she-who-will-not-be-named, she'd hit me with a "we need to talk." It was an exercise in existential angst to which I never had the right answer for her. *What are we doing together? Where are we going to be in a year? Why do you want to be with me?* The biggest plus of our break-up—besides stopping the bleeding of my life force—was we never had to have that discussion again.

When Talis Darmon sat beside me and said, "We need to talk," I wanted the same thing.

Her hair was pulled back into one of the intricate hairstyles Beraal helped her create. A masterpiece of feminine macrame and line-rigging so intricate a salty sailor would wonder how such knots were formed. Functional for flight, high-art for display.

"Benjamin Colt, I think it is time we speak of important things." Her preamble was more refined, but I heard it as the relationship OPORD of all OPORDs. I just knew there would be more than five paragraphs to it.

We were as close to being alone as you could get on a flitter. Avril Mysteen was at the controls and a pair of gunners were the only others awake, everyone else racked out on the deck. I took turns spelling him, the work easy as all I had to do was follow the leader—Kleeve Hartus—at the arrow point of our flight. I'd tried to nap but couldn't. I can sleep standing up if need be. Rest evaded me on this trip, the same way a ghost–Talis Darmon couldn't be reached in my dream. At each hint of it, unconsciousness fled from me.

She let me take her hand, a check that this wasn't any fashion of illusion. She was right here. "Please, Princess. There's a lot I'd like to say. We may be going straight into another battle. Since the Korund, we've barely been alone. I almost miss those times."

"Or the many quiet hours in my gilded cage in Maleska Mal, just you and I."

I was right on track. She hadn't wanted to talk about something worldly like the coming fight.

"As awful as my captivity was, I would not trade our deprivations and trials together for anything. With every step we took together, I learned your true heart. Which is why I must be tell you that I release you from your vows to me."

That's not what I expected her to say.

"I must ascend to the throne of the Red Kingdom as sole regent. With that will come responsibilities and a structure you cannot be expected to grasp. Though you have fought as a true son of this kingdom, you are still a stranger in a strange land. The passion of our circumstances has delayed the consideration of those realities, but soon we will not be able to ignore them."

I sloughed it off. "I know who you are, Princess. And I don't care. I know who I fell in love with, and that being with you will be a package deal—you and your throne and the whole ball of wax that goes with it. I know we're not headed for a little cottage where we'll raise kids together and play cards on Friday night with the neighbors. If my role is going to be to hold your scepter and offer you my shield arm, I'm ready for it."

Her eyes were wells of pity. "It is my destiny to rule from the spectral hall. It does not have to be yours. You may live your own life, free and unencumbered, with all my love and gratitude—with no trace of malice or resentment in a single cell of my being. You do not need to answer now. I do not wish you to. I am telling you that when that time comes, when the strictures of Shansara threaten your happiness, I release you with a thankful heart."

I loved her more than ever.

She'd rather see me happy than chained. But they were shackles I'd wear with joy. Her empathy, her beauty, her kindness. The way she'd made me a better man, given me a purpose grander than any man's, had healed me. One moment she scolded me like a naughty child, the next, made me feel like Achilles ready to charge the beach.

"Talis Darmon, I'll give you my answer now and forever. I love you. And whatever burden you must carry, I'll be there to carry it with you. You are the only home I ever want or need. The only adventure I ever want. My place is with you, however and wherever."

I took both of her hands in mine. There was always going to come a time when I'd ask her to cement our relationship. I just had no idea it was going to be now.

"Will you marry me?"

She gasped. Her hands pulled from mine to hide her face. Then her shoulders shook. Tears came with sobs.

This was not how I'd fantasized it playing out.

I knew what it had to be. A commoner couldn't marry royalty. Wasn't that always the drama in every romance about this very thing? I knew it! I should've talked to Beraal first. She'd have counseled me, set me straight, let me down easy. Talis Darmon couldn't marry me. And now I forced her to tell me herself. I was the dummy who'd sprung the ambush before the enemy patrol was in the kill zone.

When would I ever learn? It was Davy Crockett who'd said it, and while it wasn't one of Roger's Rules of Ranging, it should've been. First be sure you're right, then go ahead.

Shit.

I backpedaled as her sobs wracked me in guilt.

"I should've known. There's a law that says we *can't* marry, isn't there? Please don't cry. I'm sorry I brought it up. I don't care. I'll be your boy-toy. I'll be your… whatever. If we can't be married, we'll still make it work."

My stomach fell like the first moment of freefall.

"Please, forgive me."

I was ready to join her sorrow with my own when she launched and threw her arms around me in a tackle. She showered my cheeks with kisses, then squealed like a little girl with a birthday pony. The deck came alive with startled soldiers reaching for K-specs.

"Law? There is no *law* that binds Talis Darmon from choosing her husband," she scoffed. "YES! Yes, I will be your wife!"

I kissed her and held her and we both laughed and cuddled, ignoring the world like it ignored us as irritable men rolled over and went back to sleep.

✣ ✣ ✣

I piloted, Talis Darmon at my side through an endless night of stars and meteor showers, moons and spiral arm galaxies. I imagined us flying to another planet like the ancient explorers of Vistara, speeding through the ether of the solar system on our way to another mysterious world, just her and I. The sun rose and broke and brought me back to reality. Shansara teased ahead. Signal flags cautioned to prepare for the cautious velocity we would assume as we waited for word to come in. Getting no reply, I feared the worst. Dave was either very, very busy, or—the other thing which we left unsaid. His voice teased the mirage of the future into an oasis of cool shade and sweet water with his laid-back tones.

"Ben-Ben, you got me?"

"I got you, Dave. Talk to me."

"We smoked them like cheap cigars, brah."

I cheered. The princess squeezed me and the deck echoed with protests until I got a steady hand back on the controls. Avril Mysteen hurriedly nudged me aside like a driver's ed teacher taking the wheel, and I brought the cloud to life to see a frazzled, smudged-face Dave and his irrepressible grin.

"It's safe to come in at the concourse of… what's it called?" his fatigued voice asked someone out of the cloud.

"The Concourse of Diasemony," Kleeve Hartus filled in as he joined from his own cloud.

"Yeah. That's the one. The LZ's cold. Clearing's still going on in the city proper. We'll give you a sitrep on the ground, brah, er, General. Ha ha. I'll pop a red smoke to mark the LZ. Out."

"It is nearly over, Benjamin Colt."

"Princess, is there ever a time when we just use a single name?"

She shook the sound away. "Thulians are so—inelegant. Your name is a beautiful song. I am not content to sing it out of tune."

"I have a song to sing for you, Talis Darmon, and I'll sing it to you every day for the rest of eternity."

She beamed. "Inelegant was the wrong word. Brazen is correct."

"You have no idea, my princess."

Last time I was in Shansara—the only time—it hadn't been a sightseeing tour. Its colors do not live in a palate I knew how to describe. The towers of the palace I'd perceived as illuminated green in the night were anything but monochromatic. The entirety of the metropolis shimmered in a pearlescence that shifted from whatever angle viewed between purples and blues, whites and greens. They combined to make every mystical construct appear different yet unified, bound in harmony by wonder.

The rapture of Shansara in the day was made vulgar by what surrounded it. The morning discovery post-Clymaira was of cataclysmic extinction. This was poignant devastation. This unveiling was like the aftermath of an earthquake with its fires and carnage, the plains a vista recording our wrath.

Bryant bragged he was going to rule Mars. He only proved he couldn't lead a cub scout troop in a game of capture the flag. Not with thirty thousand committed savages.

When we found them, I wouldn't pity his remains. I'd mock them. Then I'd bury him. The perfect literal after the figurative.

A wafting trail of red smoke guided us to an avenue wide enough to accommodate a tank division. Titans of Vistara's lore lined the way in opposing columns. Mythical or perhaps once real creatures were represented in the turquoise mosaic of the highway.

The princess solemnly said, "The artisans of our time will leave their own mark on the concourse. It is a new chapter in the history of Vistara."

At what had to have been a control point, a football field length section of the way was rubble. More of the mixture of red and green flesh, animal limbs and mangled weapons, all made for another kind of mosaic. The princess cast her arm across like a spell. "And they will be commissioned to restore what has been wounded to beauty again."

Dave and Khraal Kahlees waited together as we grounded. Both made obeisance to the princess, Dave's bow as sharp as a parade ground salute. Maybe he'd practiced. From distant and scattered directions the rattle and bark of firefights answered my hanging inquiry.

Dave knew what I wanted. "Still some barricaded-up dead-enders getting dealt with. It's a big place."

"Parkus Laan is joined by Karlo Columbo to sweep the city of the Mydreen. They cannot hide themselves. But more than one of our patrols have taken severe casualties when deceived into an ambush by traitorous Reds."

Dave added, "Problem we're encountering is telling good Red from bad. Those two prisoners we snatched from the fountain park gave up some good information. At least some portion of Osric Darmon's army turned traitor when the Pyreenia contingent arrived. Some may just be playing along to avoid a cell. Some of the city guards too."

"We have found execution grounds." Khraal Kahlees bore tusks. "Some at least were loyal to the king, and must have resisted with courage."

I understood. "Nothing brings a middle-of-the-road guy to heel like shooting a few of their leaders."

"It is not a few. There are many in shallow graves. They were not given a warrior's death."

Dave closed the matter. "I've given orders that any Reds who don't throw up their arms at the first opportunity—it's gotta be make 'em pay. We'll sort out shark from sardine later. Like Mike always said, they ain't friends until they are."

I fired off the HVI list. "Bryant and Chuck? Domeel Doreen?"

Dave shook his head. "Nah. Not yet. Maybe croaked out in Clymaira?"

"The search is on. It's hard for me to believe they handed the Stryker and the last of their big firepower over to their indig."

"I tried to tease them out over their radio net after the air campaign was underway, brah. Nada. It was worth a try, but they're probably zilch on juice. I was looking forward to making Bryant eat humble pie. I guess whether or not he was around to figure out it was us who fed him his own ass, the result's the same. Hey! It's Karlo."

The cloud appeared. "I need close air support. Southwest city grid. We've got heavy resistance. Someone's got one or more of our gooses. Ate our lunch from so far away, it took me a minute to figure out what it was. They're good, too."

"You think it's Chuck or Bryant?"

"Who cares? They've got us stalled."

Dave groaned. "We knew it was a risk. We're double Winchester. We burned out every K-max and there's not a round left for a gun. I've got one AT-4 left. It ain't much, but I'm on my way."

Kleeve Hartus next to me brought his wrist up and joined from his own cloud. "I recognize the section of the city behind you, Karlo Columbo. It is the Golden Hub. I will be airborne immediately with a flight. We have much firepower to bring to your aid. Guide me to the source of your troubles and we will end it."

"Good copy. I'm moving to a forward spot where I can direct you. I'll try to mark with my laser, but I've also got a mag of tracers. I'll mark what I can, and talk you in for what I can't. Let's try to do this without leveling the place."

The first shield departed, and Karlo remained on visual. "Ben, the Tarns aren't honoring surrenders. They're killing every Mydreen, even the unarmed ones who've proned out. Parkus Laan won't intervene. He didn't even order it. The Korundi are just at it like business as usual."

"I hear you, Karlo. Nothing you can do. Just finish up and stay safe. No heroics. Marking targets works both ways."

"Yeah, yeah." He ignored me. Then he asked, "Clymaira?"

I nodded. "Done. Thank you, brother."

He was close to processing what that meant when the sound of flitters drew his attention away. "That was fast. I gotta hustle. Time for some JTAC work. I'll update you, Ben. Out."

The princess was distressed. "The Golden Hub is a center of production and commerce. It will be costly in ways difficult to calculate if the damage is widespread. That Karlo Columbo is so concerned to minimize the destruction despite the danger—he is a paragon of martial virtue."

"He's a jackass is what he is, Princess," Dave spewed. "If he draws fire from a pair of gooses to save the pretty architecture, he better hope he gets vaporized because I'll choke the shit out of whatever's left of him, stick him in the golden third ray gizmo, then do it again."

The princess recoiled. She'd never heard one of Dave's tirades. If anything, he'd held back in deference to her. Enough of it translated to get a reaction out of her.

I moved us ahead. "There's still a war going on, Princess." To emphasize that, the sounds of new battles echoed, channeled through the artificial canyons of the metropolis streets.

"We must save what can be saved, General. There may be a way to bring about a cessation of hostilities without toppling Shansara around us just to rid it of its vermin."

✣ ✣ ✣

Like a Roman *testudo*, shield-bearing Tarns formed a shell as we marched under cover to the palace grounds. We took no fire, though more gunfights broke out—distantly—but the number of them was concerning. Through brief cracks, I saw the colossal statues that ringed the fountain. We were near. Khraal Kahlees called a halt from the lead. The center parted at his command, and walls as thick as a fortress waited, already forming a path. Tarns made up the balustrades of the grand stairs, upper arms crossed from shoulder to shoulder like bannisters. Middle arms held K-specs at the ready, facing outward. More and more, I appreciated four arms as an enviable evolutionary adaptation.

Khraal Khalees waited at the top of the stairs with more troops, the expanse of the chamber and each grandiose way in and out sealed by Korundi. "We have held the palace grounds and the interiors for many hours. There is but one place to which we have not gained entrance. Out of reverence, I have ordered it unmolested, but guarded."

The princess approved. "Take us to the spectral hall."

Black crystal doors as tall as the ceiling were sealed like a vault, fierce Korundi at guard. Talis Darmon parted them with gentle hands.

"It would be impossible to breach these doors by any means save that which would shatter the palace itself. They will open at my command, the blood in my veins an order that must be obeyed. Stand ready."

She placed palms against each door and chanted. The sounds didn't translate to anything in my head. Was it a magic spell? Was it a secret phrase? Was there a difference?

The sound of a glass stem breaking accompanied the crack of doors parting. I pulled her aside and behind me and like a flash flood into a dry riverbed—and no better organized—in we went. I was caught at the front of a wall of rushing water, boulders of Tarns pushing me from behind like station masters on a Tokyo train platform.

When you're in a flood, start swimming.

And though I'd never been there, I knew it for what it was. Walls of polished jewels formed the massive hall. Light filtered through the prisms of a crystal ceiling. A great throne sat above a bare floor of shining amethyst. And on the great seat, a lone man waited. Beside him, a dark curvaceous figure hovered.

I ran to maintain my position at the front for fear I'd be trampled. Dave at my side, we dug in together to force a slow. Finally, our flood spread out to fill the canyon, and our tidal wave wall threatened to engulf the tiny island in front of us. The two figures atop the dais did not flinch, did not move, did not threaten. All sensed the danger I did, and without command, we halted as one. It was with relief that Talis Darmon's voice spoke from directly behind me.

"Hold, warriors! By your honor, do nothing until I so command!"

The elevation cap of my red dot optic sat just below the feet of the still seated man. He draped the armrests with cape and largely muscled forearms, a match to any Red warrior I'd yet seen. If he twitched, I'd fill him in.

My princess's voice was strange to me, frightening in its deliberateness and hissing malice. "Betrothed. Kill the woman. She is a witch. Do it. Now."

The dark woman reared and her dark gossamer gown parted, a mist of evil emanating from her center like a plague of locusts. The malevolence of it made any hesitation of mine vanish. The trigger precisely responded like the tiny clicking ratchets of gears meshed in a perfect mechanism and my suppressor barked in staccato. Red blood and dark organ meat ejected behind her. She was not ether, but viscoelastic as any life. She fell.

The man on the throne was a statue transfixed, his gaze focused over my shoulder at the one who commanded us all. From beside me, her arm raised to rest on mine and willed me to lower my weapon. She glided ahead like a lioness stalking her prey.

"Carolinus Darmon! False son! False king! False husband! Did the mists of time foresee for you your end? Why do you not fall to knees and beg for your pitiful life? Or have you succumbed yet further to delusion that you may triumph still?"

With a speed I did not believe possible, the princess moved as a blur for the seated Carolinus. Did time slow, or had she become mist herself? Caught in the void of surprise, my voice and action were matched in their paralysis. Holding a long dagger I'd not seen her conceal, she reached the top of her parabolic trajectory and fell on the throne.

I was freed from my suspended animation and on the move at last. Her ice pick grip stabbed downward at him in revolutions of chopped circular arcs. With each return, a spray of blood, a pressurized red oil, spurted in growing fountains. Only when she leaped back from her target did his massive arms raise, a warding come too little, too late.

My concrete-laden boots shed, I was finally at her side. She stood over Carolinus Darmon as blood gushed from a dozen square punctures perforating his chest, neck, and face. A death grimace and rigor captured him; blood pulsed strongly from each wound and his twisted mouth.

"Nothing to say, brother? In death, you show the dignity you never had in life. I silence you forever, our father avenged! No royal barge awaits you for your journey up the Blix. Only the darkness you embraced."

His lips parted and a final guttural expulsion came in frothy bubbles and two barely heard syllables.

"Kar… nak."

The dais was a stampede of thundering green bull moose. The princess wiped her dagger on the robe still draped over the seat, sheathed the blade within the filmy clothing flowing from her waist, then cast the robe from the seat and onto the floor next to the grisly corpse.

Dave prodded the dead woman with a foot as his muzzle menaced her still.

"She is gone, David Masamuni. A threat no longer. She thought herself master of her craft, but she could not secret away from me her mistress's plot. There is great evil yet in Pyreenia. And their coven knows I am coming."

She smoothed her garments and smiled at me, beatific and placid again. "As you say, my betrothed, one problem at a time."

I stood at the shore of a bottomless sea, pondering the depths of the woman I loved.

Who was my Talis Darmon?

She raised herself grandly and with a sweep of her arms, her garments settled gently on the throne she mounted. Beraal was there at her side in supplication. Grasping the dazzling crystals on the armrests, she closed her eyes and chanted again in the mysterious voice. The ceiling parted. Stone and crystal grew like living trees straining to reach the light and pierced the opening above. She continued her incantation until a beam of all colors ever imagined shot into the sky. A single sustained note, pure and angelic in its siren, penetrated everything. Living and inorganic. Each and every thing.

It was a hypnotic no soul had ever experienced. I was captivated and could not look away as the sound and the sight united in harmony. My heart pounded out brief seconds from its metamorphosis until its death. The splendid tone silenced and with it, the light of every color retreated. I came to. Around us, every knee bent.

Her smile was more powerful than the prism of all color that had filled the sky over Shansara. And it was aimed at me.

"*He* could not do *that*!" She laughed.

"It is done. There will be a ceremony to herald my ascension, as there always must be. Tradition is tradition. But my regency cannot be challenged. If *that* does not signal to all that this kingdom is again rightfully ruled, then kill any who resist the truth of it, betrothed.

"For I am Queen Talis Darmon Sylah."

50

Those first weeks together in Shansara are one indivisible conglomeration of days and nights to me now. I stayed true to my word at last. I never left her side. A promise was a promise.

When she saw me swoon from the mental fatigue signaling my relief at crossing the finish line of yet another marathon of endless councils and meetings, she took pity on me. "Betrothed. All is well. Go exercise. Go be with your brothers. A general's place is not as a bodyguard. Your promise to me is intact, even if we are not in sight of each other. I do not hold the execution of your oath to the limit of your sanity."

Beraal was, as usual, indefatigable and renewed in vitality to be at her side. A brace of Korundi surrounded her at all times, even outside the door of our private quarters. I'd tapped on every wall, checked behind every tapestry, probed every crack. Talis Darmon assured me that there were no secret passages from which an assassin could appear, but I still slept with one eye open and many nights slid silently out of our bed to test the air and strain for the sound of padded feet or catch the current of a hidden breath.

"Do not have concern. You are my hero, and the mightiest warrior on all of Vistara, but you are not the only one capable of protecting me. You know I think the precautions too much."

I was conflicted. I was dreadfully stiff and bored, but I'd worry nonstop away from her. "Talis Darmon, I don't trust these clowns. Most of them made it through your brother's purge. That goof with the pointy beard—the treasury minister? He argues with you like it's an obligation."

"He makes an appeal for restraint in all matters, much as he did for my father. His manner is always abrupt and unpleasant. Numbers have displaced his empathy, which makes his sobriety a constant. Only if it were otherwise would I doubt his loyalty."

"Good to know. But I wish you'd have slowed down reforming the council until we'd vetted all these functionaries. We still don't have a full accounting of who did what in Shansara after you left for Maleska Mal. All these people are at the top of my list of potential conspirators and enablers. They should not have such close access to you."

She disagreed. "The mechanism of the kingdom is not like a military organization, Benjamin Colt. There's much I will teach you about government and its dispensation. These are all bureaucrats. As you say—pencil necks. They would not dare harm my person. Even if they harbored any malice, they have not the ability. Their loyalty is to the kingdom and to its people. They serve whoever sits on the throne, sworn to exercise their duties for the good of the people. It is a strength of our system."

"So, the bean counters and street sweepers are robots not capable of subterfuge. Got it. It's another agree to disagree. But what about the ranking Guards and Army officers? The ones we believe were complicit are either dead or missing, but the new first shield and that General Marviel Lanconin—they don't seem capable. They flail and flap at every meeting as if they could fly, but they've got penguin wings. I've asked for tables of organization and equipment at every meeting. Nothing. How can we organize and rebuild if they can't produce something as simple as that?"

"Put yourself in their place, betrothed. You are a foreign general thrust into their midst. No matter you did what they could not, theirs are positions of heredity and tradition from long lines of officers."

"Talis Darmon, the Korundi are providing most all the military presence around the city. At some point, they have to return home. Neither of these new guys are making me feel like the security of any part of your kingdom is a priority. They're not taking any responsibility for what happened, and they're acting as though the war is over. Pyreenia is the source of something bad. You won't say more about it, and whether it's voodoo happening there or a sanctuary for any of the Mydreen warriors who escaped—I can't protect you if I don't have the means to do it. I may be your general, but it's just a title. I have no place in the chain of command. No authority. I'm not asking for favoritism just because my fiancée is the queen, but…"

"Be patient, betrothed. When we are wed, you will assume title of Consort Supreme. Then, assigning you authority of office will follow. Of course, you will be in charge of defense matters for the kingdom."

That wasn't really what I wanted. I wanted to be a free-roaming problem solver, like I had been. It's where I could best help her. Me and Dave and Karlo, with some of the Korund Tarns—an A-Team. We'd get the army rebuilt. Properly. Then we'd go to Pyreenia and sort them out. When that was done, we'd go from city to city, reestablish the standards for all forces, get them trained on the new weapons, improve tactics, go on patrols.

Hey, you love what you love, right?

You yearn to do what you're good at.

But I couldn't bring it up. I was just barely keeping my promise to her—no matter that I took it seriously. The heart wants what the heart wants.

I wanted her *and* my vocation.

"Can we please at least talk about that pompous ass, Supreme Guild Master Tyreen Sorell?" I couldn't wait for Cynar to come and take the starch out of his purple collar. "Why aren't the atmosphere wizards in a cell already? We've proven they're con artists."

I knew the look. And the smile. She crossed her hands over her waist just like a patient kindergarten teacher.

"Endure, betrothed. The great value of martial decision and the action it produces is not a virtue in the realms of government. I wish it were possible to treat all as if it were a battlefield—with clear enemies and abrupt solutions applied with full determination. I could take such a course of action as regent, but it would fracture institutions and disrupt the confidence of the people in our traditions. If these men or their institutions are corrupted, their intentions will be made clear soon enough. Best to leave them in their positions. For now."

The woman who'd ordered me to execute a witch and who'd Jack-the-Rippered her own brother had chilled out.

I cracked my neck. "All right. I think I'll take a break. I do need some exercise. I'll catch up with you back in our suites later. A quiet dinner? Just you, me, and Beraal? Like the old days?"

She was reading a slate and didn't look up. "No, betrothed. Tonight is the dinner for—"

Beraal filled in. "The public works and agriculture ministries. And their wives."

"I need you there at your most handsome, charming self. It will be an excellent opportunity for you to learn about how our great city's works are accomplished. It is also an opportunity for you to impress them with your own knowledge. It is important that everyone gets to know you as I do, betrothed. Er… I mean no criticism, but as of late, some of your speech has become… undisciplined. Perhaps you will adjust that, for me?" She made a kissy face.

"I'll be as proper as a royal should be," I winked, "my princess."

It was good to see I could still make her blossom.

"Now, go attend to your physical hygiene and give my regards to your brothers."

But Dave and Karlo were gone to the Korund, as was Khraal Kahlees. Baby Blue would soon return with them to Shansara, secure in its new redoubt, ready for Karlo's ministrations and plans for endless research and investigation into solving every crisis on Vistara. Apache would be coming back with them. I never had a dog before, always gone and never consistently able to care for one. I missed the big lunk. I hadn't broached it yet with Talis Darmon, but if I couldn't figure out a diet that had less unpleasant results, then he probably wouldn't be sleeping in our quarters.

Kleeve Hartus and Avril Mysteen were in Clymaira. I waited expectantly for word from the first shield that the bodies of Bryant and Chuck had been found. If there were a splotch of multicam goo or a bone to found, I wanted it piled in front of me. When they returned for the coronation ceremony, I was certain they'd bring with them some evidence that would give me the peace that the wicked had in fact received their punishment.

Domeel Doreen? The crafty chieftain had eluded discovery as well. There were credible reports that when Dave's air campaign overwhelmed the defenders of the city, a multitude of air cars had taken flight from Shansara. With the entry of our assault troops, there were also reports of overland escapes of many packs of mounted Mydreen.

A watertight cordon had been beyond our ability.

Had the Chief and my former senior engineer been in Clymaira or Shansara? Had D-D escaped? If so, I knew Khraal Kahlees would mount a search through the wastes of the great canyons to the peaks of the white mountain wastes to find the Mydreen thug. Just as I was prepared to do if evidence failed to materialize to burn away the last dangling thread of doubt with two members of my ODA still unaccounted for and alive out there somewhere.

Of my other comrades, Garlak Ranz remained on as part of the queen's Guard, as did Sarkan Sell and Jodal Jark. And while I saw them almost daily, there was never a relief from the decorum of the throne, much less the hope of comradery around a campfire.

I wandered the halls of the palace, alone, as I thought about my situation. I was still coming down from many months of living at the tip of the spear. A few good hours of hard exercise and my mind would be clear again and let me see that now was not forever. Better days were coming. It would just take time.

I was rescued from self-pity by a pair of henna-dyed beards detouring to skid past me.

"Hey! You two! Where do you think you're going?" I had a hand on the sword I now wore on my left side, my pistol always on my right, ready to have some fun at their magisterial expense. I hated them nearly as much as Cynar did. They really were unbearably conceited ass-clowns.

"Communication from our brothers in Pyreenia comes for the queen. Do not deter us on our task."

I froze one with a finger and I pushed the mouthy one against a wall with a hand. "At least you're smart enough not to pretend you don't have a communication device anymore, beardy. Who is it?"

"It is for the queen's ears alone!"

I rotated my thumb over his suprasternal notch and pressed firmly onto his trachea. "Try again."

He coughed. "Savage! It is one of the Thulians."

✠ ✠ ✠

I knew how to patch through from Cynar's communicator to the rays of the atmosphere wizard's device. My heart pounded as Talis Darmon cued and the cloud materialized.

Brandon Bryant was alive.

He and I had the simultaneous realization about each other. But whereas I raged to get my hands around his neck, he first turned pale—then slowly to a red like the sands of Vistara as he fought to find words. I pounced.

"Not expecting to see me, Bryant? When you've stopped having your coronary and can find words, why don't you tell me where you're hanging your beret these days so I can come and end your miserable life? Because it's coming, asshole. How's it feel to see your old O&I sergeant still upright and pissing on your face from the top of the mountain? You useless prick."

Okay, not the most eloquent thing for posterity to record, but I really hadn't prepared. The Talis Darmon of orators, I was not. The queen took over.

"Brandon Bryant, by what mad and brazen delusion do you make communication with the throne of the Red Kingdom of Mihdradahl?"

A scarred and barely recognizable Chuck was at Bryant's elbow. At seeing me, he wheezed and collapsed into a fit of coughing like Doc Holliday's understudy, then disappeared from the cloud.

Bryant's silver hair was no longer held in place by whatever sticky substance he'd once had to keep his vain mess slicked back. "Colt! Somehow, I knew you were out there. When Marky never made it back, somehow I knew. I should have—"

"Should've what? Your mouth's still the only part of you that works." Talis Darmon took over.

"Brandon Bryant, you and the Thulian outlaw Charles—"

"Simpson," I whispered.

"—Charles Simpson are under a death warrant. Better you had crawled into a hole and pulled it in after you than make your presence known to the throne."

Bryant affected the smug laugh and golf clap that made me wary of him from the first. "Bravo, lady. Bravo. I was calling to give you a fair shot at a peaceful negotiation, despite knowing it'd just waste our time. Offer retracted before made. So instead, I'll just say, be seeing you both." The cloud went blank.

The room erupted.

Talis Darmon was the color of a pale pink rose. "Betrothed, what does he mean? Has he the ability to wage war against us? It cannot be!"

"He's all talk," I seethed. "He doesn't have a pot to piss in. It's time to go to Pyreenia, flush him out, and bring you his head." I tapped my wrist and got Dave and Karlo in one cloud.

"You'll never guess who just called me out of the clear red sky."

✢ ✢ ✢

Apache lay at my side between me and the queen at the head of the table. The full complement of my closest comrades were seated near us, royal ministers pushed farther down the long table to their visible dislike. With Talis Darmon's consent, I'd taken charge of the conversation and asked the obvious. Dave had the low down.

"We're Winchester, brah. We got nothing to go to war with."

I'd already figured as much.

The queen was impassive. "Please elaborate, David Masamuni."

"Ma'am, our high-volume weapons are all pretty much deadlined. If all three of us go to work and we get Baby Blue printing new barrels and internals, Karlo says we can be up again in a week."

Karlo seamlessly followed. "I got us back to a minimum load of ammunition before we moved Baby Blue, but I can't do everything at once. It's always a matter of prioritizing, programming, doing QC on the products, refining the output. It's not the perfect factory we wish it was.

"As for fizzle guns, the well is dry. I can make as many compensators as we have troops, but we have no guns to mount them on. The factory's been cleaned out, and it turns out they've been at a trickle of production for a generation. Most of what's been in circulation is old stores."

He took a long look at the minister of production. The man was fixed on what must've been a captivating spot on the table. "Until I can figure out their workings, I can't make duplicates with Baby Blue, either. It's going to take me time, and there's only one of me and one matter mill."

Kleeve Hartus spoke up. "The armaments from my air detachment have the most reserve of any of the weapons in our inventory, but it is doubtful as to how much that is. Enough for an offensive against Pyreenia? Not with the same level of overmatch as we have previously experienced." The first shield was a fast study, and had absorbed on first exposure anything we'd exposed him to regarding military subjects.

Khraal Kahlees interjected. "I have dispensation from our chieftain to maintain our army here as long as necessary to provide for the defense of the kingdom."

The queen dipped her head. "I thank Chieftain Parkus Laan for the friendship of the Korund. It is an alliance that I hold most dearly."

"The might of the Korund is at your service, Queen Talis Darmon."

I'd not had the opportunity to ask Double-K how he'd come to be here instead of taking the chieftainship of the Korund himself.

I took over. "I doubt Pyreenia has any serious offensive capability. What Red Army they had, they brought to Shansara, and we wiped them out. But I'm not willing to risk a march on them just yet. We lack the intelligence we need to make an accurate assessment." Bryant may have been shooting off his mouth, maybe not. I wasn't about to say in an open meeting that we were working on getting the intel we needed.

"So, for now, it leaves us in a defensive posture until we are better prepared. And we *will* mobilize every resource to make that preparation."

Talis Darmon rose, signaling an end to the meeting. "My coronation is the day after tomorrow. My betrothed and I will consecrate our marriage soon after. When he is made Consort Supreme, he will be named arbiter of defense for the kingdom, and leave his role as tactical general. Until then, you will follow his direction as though given by me."

After she left, there were plenty of grumbles from the ministerial bullpen and more than a few side glances of contempt. Khraal Kahlees showed his tusks, which had the effect of moving them out quicker. It left me alone with my core of friends.

"I'm sorry this is what's bringing us together, brothers, but here we are."

"Do you really think Bryant's got something to back up his boast?" Dave asked.

"We're going to find out." I nodded to Kleeve Hartus.

"Avril Mysteen is leading an intelligence gathering mission to Pyreenia. He takes two trusted Guards with him. It will take much time to perform such a covert task, but he has the training of an investigator, is one of our most accomplished pilots, and has learned military skill. If it can be accomplished, he will do so."

"How'd Chuck and Bryant get away?" Karlo asked. "Do we know?"

"Chuck was covered in enough scars for a whole burn ward. He must've been commanding the mission to retake Clymaira, but he wasn't in the Stryker. If he had been, I wouldn't be here. Whoever they trained up was just competent enough, but not a pro. Chuck probably had a respirator, but it wasn't enough to protect him fully. He was smart. He knew what was happening and made his escape."

"And the Chief?" Dave asked.

"Either he was here in Shansara and got out, or he never left Pyreenia. With there being only two of them, multiple fronts, no solid leaders to delegate to, their grand plan was never going to pan out. Not against us."

"They can't hide in Pyreenia, brah. If not tomorrow, then soon, we'll go clean their clock. It's just one final theater to mop up. Like Japan in W-W-Two. Operation Downfall. One last beach, and it's over."

Karlo frowned. "Don't ask me for a nuke. Ain't happening."

"Okay, not a perfect analogy, brah, but you get me. The end is still in sight. C'mon, it's going to take all day to get the miniguns stripped and figure out what you need to print. You coming, Ben? I mean, before you become the civilian secdef and all… Gotta nab you for armorer detail while it's still okay for you to get some grease under your nails."

I gave him our favorite salute and he returned it.

"I also must depart, Benjamin Colt. Will you join me later to review Avril Mysteen's operation order?"

"I'll be there for his brief back, First Shield. Promise."

Khraal Kahlees and I were left alone. "I too have duties, Lord Benjamin Colt." He moved to leave.

"Please, Khraal Kahlees, don't go. I—" I wanted to tell him I missed his company. Ugh. Too needy. "I'm glad to see you here, but what happened in Califex? I was certain you'd be taking the chieftainship. You led the Korundi in every battle. Surely, that should have secured your ascendance."

He was a friend, and a good one, but while he considered an answer, I feared I may have been too abrupt with my question. If he'd lost the vote of the elders, it was probably a blow to his pride.

"In the council hall before all tribal lieutenants and clan heads, I withdrew my name from contention and led the cry for Parkus Laan to take the chieftainship."

"Why?"

He made the gruff throaty chuckle of his kind. "I asked myself that as I led the chant to throw in for Parkus Laan. Does even a warrior as accomplished as yourself truly think before acting? Or does your heart tell you what is just and to take the correct action in the moment?"

"I suppose the latter."

"I remember a Thulian who stood against a hall of Mydreen and even a brace of Korundi to defend a helpless hostage. If ever was action without thought of consequence, 'twere *that*."

Pot, meet kettle.

"From you alone, Benjamin Colt, my reasons I would not conceal. There were two that weighed on me as I returned to Califex. You know the first. She has become like a sister to you. And I wish to make amends and fulfill what role I can while time remains. Without consequence have I ever considered conflict. In life and death, there is no choice. I choose death, ready to give all without fear. And while I accept such gladly, if I am to fall, I would know I have left nothing undone this side of the Blix. If I can repair what I can with Beraal, I would have it so.

"And then there is you, clansman."

I made the silly gesture of pointing to myself.

"My heart tells me you have need of me yet, and that my path to martial perfection lies in step with yours. The way is not a destination, but a journey. I choose to take it with you as far as it leads."

I was touched. "It sounds like my path is going to be behind a desk. That's not where you belong, Double-K."

His forehead wrinkled and tusks jutted to the side. "Do you truly think that is how things transpire for your future, my friend? I break confidence for your benefit as you once did for me. Those closest to you see things differently." He winked, something he'd learned from us.

"As David Masamuni said, I believe it was, 'He'll be tall in the saddle and on the trail again.'" As an afterthought, he added, "Brah."

✣   ✣   ✣

I'd just dozed off, comforted and relaxed by the notion that maybe I wasn't destined to be a chained bull. A commotion outside our bedchamber startled me awake, pistol and dagger in hand. Talis Darmon was safe beside me. She'd fallen asleep with a slate in hand, still pouring over reports after I'd extinguished the stone by my side of the bed.

I was at the door in a bound. Outside, my Korundi stood over a woman, the tray she'd been bearing scattered on the floor beside her. Her comely face was locked in painful rigor and as I neared, estuaries of dark coarse veins coalesced to turn her red skin black.

"Poison," I said, master of the obvious.

Jodal Jark stood over her, sword in hand. "Benjamin Colt, this servant made entrance past the outer cordon."

Sarkan Sell appeared from outside. "She has somehow silently killed the two Korundi standing first position. They appear as she does, mutilated from within."

Talis Darmon was at the threshold to our bedroom. "Do not touch her. It is not a poison imbibed. It is the weapon of the evil ones." She pointed to the bracelets. "She conjured the rot and killed herself to avoid capture."

"I knew her not, Queen Talis Darmon. At first, I feared I'd erred grievously, and I would disturb your rest. But her intrusion, though peaceful, was out of place. I held sword to her breast as she dropped her tray, and her hands roused a foul mist. I ran her through."

"You did well, Jodal Jark." The elder Tarn sheathed his own weapon. "You outraced me to action."

Alone in our bedroom again, I comforted my betrothed, but it was time for her to speak plainly to me. "My love, this was an assassination attempt. You see the truth of this."

"As clearly as the hurtling moons."

"It's time you told me."

Her strength was a natural part of her aura, but now, it gave way. She wilted. "I suffered the ray of their power when the witch set upon me. I saw its malevolence in her mind, and from her I know it is strong in Pyreenia. When alert, I can detect it, fight it, neutralize it. I have not sensed it since you destroyed its vessel in the woman at my brother's side. His aura was tainted by it as well.

"Its essence is the same as that of the soul-eater. It is the Karnak. They live."

✣ ✣ ✣

We did not sleep. She insisted on having council the next morning as scheduled, but I ordered the Korundi that anyone who tried to enter the queen's sphere be run through—no warning, no questions. She left with a double layer of Tarns around her, and I promised to join her soon.

The guys were as disturbed as I was when I told them. Khraal Kahlees detailed himself to remain with the queen at all times until I returned to her side. Karlo worked intently on Baby Blue as it produced that last of the spare parts and assemblies for all our weapons. Dave and I finished replacing the last of six barrels on an M134 and were function-checking the gun when one of the Guards appeared.

"Lord Benjamin Colt, the queen summons you and all. She has urgent news."

I processed he wasn't telling me there'd been another attempt on her life, and my heart started again. Dave and I ran out of the armory, Karlo lagging behind long enough to secure the vault door that now sealed Baby Blue and our gear. Only the three of us had access to the hyper-critical means to our dominance on Mars.

The council chambers were buzzing. In her hand, she held a slate glowing its dim fluorescence. She locked eyes with me.

"It is brought by envoy from the south, across the great gap of the Furrow of the Creator's Hand and into mine. It is from the supreme magnate of the Yellow Kingdom of Annameria."

I remembered her lessons to me in our apartments in Maleska Mal. The other great kingdom lay so far to the south as to be on another planet, as distant as our time together with me, her overwhelmed apprentice.

"The Yellows send proclamation of the illegitimacy of my throne." She read from the message. "*Osric Darmon, temperate and wise... Carolinus Darmon, true son and heir supreme... Usurper* is used three times. *Breaking of sympathetic bonds... hostilities long held by your person towards the line of the Magnate... Misbegotten Sylah Dynasty*, et cetera."

Marviel Lanconin had once been a long-serving aide to her father's head of the army, General Iktar Moline. Moline had cautioned the king to do nothing when the princess's mission to Domeel Doreen dragged on. To let the princess use diplomacy. When finally cornered after so many months of impotent stalemate, he planned the first and the second botched rescue of the princess from Maleska Mal.

He'd done no better with the relief of Clymaira.

His student now sat at the head of the Red Army.

The new general slammed his fist on the table. "They sense weakness. The sooner we can organize a display, the sooner we will send a message to the Yellows that we are not to be trifled with. Before their spies depart, they should be availed of the opportunity to witness the splendor of our soldiers in full dress and on parade. I will organize and lead it myself. With your permission, Queen Talis Darmon?"

She flitted him away. I tried to be helpful by not shooting the man before he'd made it out the door. "Thank you for your restraint, Benjamin Colt. He's not wrong that the Yellows sense an opportunity created by the turmoil in Mihdradahl."

I imagined an army flying for Shansara, and us nowhere near ready to repel much more than a herd of arkall-mounted Mydreen. And beneath it all was the faint hum of a mosquito, buzzing in and out of my subconscious, whispering the warning of an irritating sting. There was a master of chaos at work. And Bryant revealing himself was enough to prove the adage to me. There are no coincidences.

"What does the Yellow Kingdom mean to do about it, Tails Darmon?"

"This missive is a preamble to invasion."

51

From our balconies, I marveled at the migration of red and green skins flocking into the city center. Scanty silk clothing of rich colors mixed with equally sparse bronze armor to leave Red skin exposed in abundance. They were schools of colorful fish swimming over rare reefs of tiny jewels glinting in the morning sun. It had started before sunrise, all of Shansara alive and vying for places from which to witness the day's events. It was a sign that with the sealing of the promise made the day Talis Darmon lit the spectral song of the throne, normalcy would return.

The palace was opened to the public, and an aide appeared to tell us that from the Spectral Hall to the Waters of Persidia, it was standing room only.

"I guess it's time to go." I offered her my arm.

She gave Beraal a nod, and my Green sister shooed out all the attendants and dressers, closing the doors behind her. My queen was every bit the vision of perfection I'd been struck by that first time she greeted me on her feet, only partially recovered from her captivity, and dressed by Beraal in only what she could scavenge, so long ago in the Mydreen city. I'd become accustomed to—but never immune to—her beauty and the immodesty with which she and the people of her kingdom dressed.

She gave me a once-over. "My betrothed, you look as regal as I remember my father being on the day he was crowned. I wish he had known you. He would have been proud to have you as a son, Benjamin Colt. I know you would have come to love him as a father as well."

"Our tears for the departed and for the future they could not share with us are dried now, my love." I'd thought carefully about my comportment and practiced every verbal contingency I could think of in order to make her day perfect. "Our future is a grand adventure, and I'm the most blessed man who ever drew breath to live it with you."

Still, she did not reach to take my arm when I offered it a second time. And instead of the joy I'd hoped to inspire in her, she wiped at her eyes.

"I know, my princess," I said softly. "It's a terrible thing that's come to pass, having to rise to the throne this way."

She shook away my presumption. "My love, my heart, do you remember when once I tried to explain that there are times when a burden must be assigned? The burden of leadership by which one must by necessity burden others. And to forgive."

"Of course, my princess." She let me hug her. "But there can never be anything for me to forgive of you. Have I done something wrong? Do I need to ask *your* forgiveness? If I've been crude, or brash, or impatient, I'm so very sorry."

"Never, my love." She took a deep breath and with the ebb of her chest, her aura returned to radiate a calming glow. Strength, peace, and beauty. "Will you escort me now, my brave hero?"

Through palace halls lined by stalwart Korundi, a way parted wherever we traveled, until at the end of our lengthy path, the spectral throne sat.

I took my place standing in the front row beneath the dais, next to all my comrades. Dave and Karlo were dressed like I was. Kleeve Hartus had directed the tailors. He'd inspected, corrected, tweaked, and fussed over every detail himself. A command sergeant major insisting on absolute perfection in attention to 670-1.

"S'pose we'll have to get in these costumes again soon for your wedding, brah. I'll hang mine up just like it is, soon as we're done. I can't stand to be dissected again like I was back in the NCO academy. I'm too old for that stuff."

I suppressed a laugh and nudged him to be quiet, though if he hadn't made some of his covert small talk to me while in formation, I'd have been secretly disappointed.

The spiral horn of some strange beast sounded. Without prelude, Beraal appeared from behind a curtain, herself trailing a flowing robe. She took deliberate, careful steps one at a time to the throne. She placed the dazzling crown on the queen's head, bowed, and descended to fill in the space reserved at her father's side next to us. Talis Darmon broke the silence.

"Mihdradahl is restored. The Spectral Throne seats its regent. The peace of our kingdom and its prosperity is assured by the promise of my dynasty and its blood. A lineage will issue from my body. The chain will remain unbroken. This I swear."

A Red Guard thrust a gold spear into the air. "The throne and crown proclaim the truth. Queen Talis Darmon Sylah rules in Mihdradahl. Long may she reign."

The city joined to make the chant three times, each more deafening than the last.

Talis Darmon perched tall from the edge of her seat, erect and grand. "This is a time when we ensure that tradition is consecrated, stability ensured, assurances of fealty sealed. But," she paused, "the peril of our times insists that it is challenged properly, soberly, mightily."

My head spun. I knew, but I didn't know. I was thrust into a dream. A haze. A fugue.

"First Shield of Clymaira Kleeve Hartus. Step forward."

My head cleared, relieved.

"I name you First Shield of all Mihdradahl. You will remain in Shansara. You will yield supreme power in my name in all matters of internal security. Do you accept this burden?"

My friend bowed, stepped out of our rank, and took a knee. He dipped his head then raised his voice with it. "Until the River Blix, Temple Farnest, and the underworld hereafter." He stood and returned to his place.

"Khraal Kahlees, Battle Lord of the Korund. Step forward."

This surprised me. If his stoicism was ever capable of breaking, it came close now as his jaw went briefly slack before bulging muscles firmed it closed again.

"I have obtained release by the chieftain of the Korund to name you general of my army. I offer commission to all Korundi to join their Red brethren in service to Mihdradahl, for the necessary concern of all Vistara. Do you accept this burden?"

The giant did as Kleeve Hartus had done but from a knee, and crossed four arms as he recited his oath.

"Cynar the Magnificent."

The old hermit had been too overwhelmed to say much when I welcomed him to Shansara. He'd lived in a cave for thousand years! Now, surrounded by more people that he even knew existed on Vistara, he was catatonic. Dressed in a green toga and as cleaned up as he'd probably been in centuries, he was still attended by Dureen Zell. Dave had told me on their arrival, "I could be reading it wrong, but I think those two have a love connection going on."

Now she took him by the elbow and led him forward, remaining by his side.

"Cynar the Magnificent, Supreme Master and Priest in Residence of the Revered Guild of the Life-Giving Waters, I name you Supreme Scientist of Mihdradahl, with commission to restore all function to the machinations of every life-giving property. Do you accept this burden?"

He made an attempt to kneel and thought better of it. To his credit, an "Eh" didn't pass his lips. Instead he said, "I do so accept."

The queen smiled and winked at him. It was a gesture that was spreading.

"There will be more appointments and burdens to come. It is a time for all the kingdom to consider their talents, their abilities, and their call to serve."

I relaxed. She was done shaking up the power structure of Mihdradahl.

"This is an auspicious day. One that will be recorded for the ages as the first day of the resurrection of our kingdom, and all of Vistara. It is but a start. I speak with all candor to every ear in the kingdom. Our future hangs on the precipice of disaster. The air we take for granted disappears. An enemy of great might rallies to see us erased from a future Vistara. Old treaties have turned to dust. Diplomacy has failed. It is a time as grave as the cataclysm of wars past, when all of Vistara fought, and marked the beginning of our end.

"I have struggled to continue as we have, maintaining our long-existing institutions and traditions. I have come to this realization: they have failed us. To blindly revere the ways of the past is our doom. But history also provides us guidance.

"There is one man who shows us the way, who can lead us, bind us, encourage us, teach us."

My hands shook. I became lightheaded. Like the time I locked my knees in Division Review and almost passed out. I flexed ever so imperceptibly and rapidly as I could to move blood from my quads to my brain.

"Lord Deacon Benjamin Colt, step forward."

I didn't feel as confident or powerful as Kleeve Hartus or Double-K had looked in their perfection, but I did my best to copy them.

"Not since the Amethyst Sea first receded has the mantle of Warlord been weighed upon shoulders. In my name and answerable to none but the regent, I delegate to you supreme power concerning all matters existential to Mihdradahl and Vistara. This is what it means to be Warlord. Do you accept this burden?"

What if I said no?

If I'd known the oath and practiced it for a week, I wouldn't remember it now. I filled my lungs slowly like I was going under for a crossover in the widest swimming pool, and prayed my voice wouldn't crack. With my drill sergeant command voice, from my diaphragm, I bellowed, "I vow to serve this world and see it thrive and blossom, her mighty queen our inspiration. By my life, or my death, and beyond, this I swear."

I bowed and stepped back.

"Warlord, your place is here beside me—the arm of my will. Ascend!"

My high-laced boots clicked across the floor, echoing in the absolute still as I joined her at attention.

It was like my vision.

Khraal Kahlees roared, "Warlord!"

The Tarns joined, and then Reds. Spear butts struck stone in tempo. Arms raised, fists pounded chests. The chant continued. Over and over.

I fought to keep the force of the cheers from bowling me over, but their power did not distract me from this—the glares, the arms folded in disapproval, the sneers of raised lips. The elites, the ministers, the functionaries. Even those who were aware of their conspicuousness and succumbed to join the madness of the moment were insincere and reserved in their mimicry.

Talis Darmon had exposed the enemies within.

✠ ✠ ✠

The party afterward was, as they say, off the hook. Tables for a thousand filled the courtyard. Braziers of amber stones in their brightness diminished the shine of a trillion stars and the red moons above.

My queen sat at the head of course, but this time, I was seated beside her. Her guard was dismissed, but like dorsal fins cutting through ocean swells, they circled and hunted the lanes between our hulls.

We feasted on course after course such as I'd never experienced before. I'd been promised a personal tour of the farms and factories where food was produced. In vats and with minimal water, from science, not from the sterile soil. I knew it would fascinate and capture Karlo's imagination, and wanted him to join me to see the mystery of how they sustained such on our dying world.

Our world.

Karlo did not look well. He'd taken to the dark green syrup the servants continued to fill our cups with, and drained another only to pull the arm of a servant back to refill his cup, the staining liquid sloshing onto the tablecloth and his cape.

It was sweet, dry, had a sour aftertaste, and was most certainly fermented. A few sips were enough for me. My princess beamed at me and giggled like a little girl as she chatted with the young ladies of the elite, who bowed and took audience with her from her seat. With hands concealing lips and furtive glances, it was Dave who was the subject of their secretive exchanges.

"You're a hot item, man," I teased him from across the table.

He kept eyes on me but tipped his head sideways at the number currently hush-hushing with the queen. "Hubba-hubba."

I'd never been a drinker. But I'd been around them my whole life. Sometimes the most stolid soldiers became like playful children. Some held their drink well and almost seemed to function better as old aches and pains were temporarily quelled. Sometimes the most reserved and disciplined became wild and unruly and had to be subdued for their own safety in their abandon of all sense.

And some became mean.

One look at Karlo, whom I'd never seen drink in our time together on Earth, and I immediately knew what type of drunk he was.

A mean one.

He slunk, scowled, muttered curses just below audible range. Every so often, I'd catch him curling a lip and casting a glance. At me. I caught Dave's eye and mouthed, "Is Karlo okay?"

Then the explosion came.

"You know what a Judas goat is, Ben?" Karlo said it loudly. Our end of the table got quiet.

Dave tried to head him off. "Hey, Karlo, can I get you something more to eat? Nice break from MREs and the local field rations, huh, brah?"

"I was talking to Ben!"

I smiled back, hoping to set the tone. "Sure, brother." He was getting ready to accuse me of being the one to lead others to the slaughter.

"I bet you do! You know, I spent a lot of time with goats." It was not well known, but the Special Forces Medical course used goats for live tissue training. The students had to treat the animals like people. Name them, ensure their health, diagnose their ailments, draw blood and other samples from them, just like a hospitalized human. They learned surgery on the animals, and trauma treatment under extreme conditions, where only by mastery of the most advanced lifesaving procedures would they prevent their patient's death and graduate.

"Well, there's a worse kind of goat than a Judas goat." He slurred his words and didn't bother to wipe the drool from his lips.

"Goats are the nastiest creatures I've ever seen. They smell bad. I've eaten them. They taste just like they smell, too. Once you've spent months in the pens with them—nursing them to health, trying to keep one of the dumb things warm while it's shivering with pneumonia, praying to a god you don't believe in it'll live so you don't flunk out and get sent to 82nd, all the time while it tries to headbutt you—you can never get rid of the memory of their filth in your nostrils. They're a constant green-on-blue." He meant a deadly attack by a local whom you thought was a friend.

Dave tried to help. "Everyone knows how bad you medics have it going through the Q, Karlo. Great story. Maybe not a dinner topic, but—"

"I'm speaking. BRAH." He took another slurping drink. "I was saying, there's another kind of goat, even worse. I saw it one day when

I was cleaning the pens. I hadn't slept in days. I had a trauma scenario that afternoon and just knew I was going to flunk. The sun was shining through the pines, and there were two of the cutest little goats you ever saw. Playing, just like little kids. Kids—get it?"

He slurped another sip.

"One little goat would jump over a log. And his little buddy would follow him, doing the same stunt. Simon says. The one would dash behind a tree and peekaboo the other one. And his little buddy would do the same. I couldn't believe it! The damn things were cute." He belched.

"Then I saw it. The leader got an all fours and shimmied on his belly under a bar. He came back to other side, waiting for his playmate to do the same. The little guy wagged his stubby little tail, got down, and did the shimmy.

"And *that's*," he hiccupped, "when Simple Simon jumped on his back, pinned him, and went to town like only a real billy goat can. To his own little buddy. Made him his bitch."

Cup thrown to the ground, on his feet, his finger punched each syllable at me.

"That's you, Ben! That's you! And I ain't gonna be your little buddy. You ain't doing it to me. I'm not following you. I'm not making any WMD for you. I don't care how you justify the flood, like you're some kinda vengeful god. Go solve all the shit problems of Mars yourself. Warlord!"

He staggered off, pushing a minister out of the way and upsetting the old man's balance to trip into his wife.

Dave's eyes shot to the size of the moons. "Holy guacamole! Ben, he doesn't mean it! I've never seen Karlo drunk. That's all it is. I better go after him." He dashed off.

A hand touched mine. "Is Karlo Columbo ill? I understood little of what he said, but he seemed in great distress. At you."

I clammed hers with both of mine. "Don't give it another thought, my love. He doesn't do well with strong drink. He'll be fine."

But the sparse camo net I'd thrown over Karlo's departure didn't conceal the potential of my new fear. When the sun rose again, would he be the Karlo I trusted and depended on? Or would he have transformed like the other lycanthropes from my original team? Twisted into a new form by the dual moons of Mars, thirsty for my blood.

52

Dave came to get me to tell me he'd located Karlo, diligently at work on Baby Blue.

"Did he look like he was, you know, sabotaging it?"

"Nah, he's just cranking out more ammo. I tried to talk him into getting some breakfast with me, but he waved me off. Wouldn't say a word. Lemme go first, Ben, and feel him out, okay? Just hang back, brah."

Like a spy, I did. It would've made me feel dirty and deceitful, but the pounding in my head blocked it. Khraal Kahlees and Kleeve Hartus introduced me to a tasteless liquid they drank from tiny thimbles—which should have been the red hourglass on the back of the spider warning that the venom was there—then Talis Darmon and I celebrated until the moons set. Outside the vault, I leaned against the crystalline vault door, the cool of it soothing the back of my neck.

"Yo man, brought you some breakfast, just in case you changed your mind."

There was no reply.

"Y'okay, brah?"

At last, his voice. "I gave myself an IV. Yeah, I'm okay. I'll be good tomorrow. Man, that sno-cone syrup has a kick. Now I know. Ugh. Never again."

"Hey, Karlo. You remember that movie? The one where the Diehard guy finds out he's indestructible."

What a non sequitur! How was this feeling Karlo out about last night?

"No."

"Really, Karlo?"

"Never had a lot of time for movies. I was always too busy."

"Too busy?"

"Busy. Differential equations, Fourier transmission, machine learning, CAD, material science, computer language, printed circuitry—you know? Busy. Learning. Not killing my brain with pap." Karlo tapped at something lightly, like he was cutting a diamond.

"Okay, okay, Karlo. Geez. You worked while the rest of us slacked. Got it. I surrender. But you at least have *heard* of the movie I'm talking about. Mace Windu is the bad guy who owns the comic book store. Wearing purple like Prince back in the day."

Sigh. "Kinda busy, Dave. Maybe. Why?"

"Well, been thinking about it. Kinda applies."

Karlo stopped what he was doing. "The one about the guy discovering latent superhero powers?"

"No, Karlo, the musical. Yeah, the superhero one. Ah ha! Busted, by the way. You *have* seen it."

Bigger sigh. "Dammit, Dave. What are you wasting my time about?"

Dave feigned hurt. "Just came to bring you breakfast, brah."

Karlo was regretful. "I'm sorry, Dave. My head's hammering me after last night. I'm just tired. Really. Please, what did you want to ask me about?"

"It's just this. Doesn't all this seem just too familiar in a weird way? I mean, it's all a total head trip. But doesn't it all seem like something you've seen or read before?"

Karlo stopped his tinkering noises. "It does, Dave. We've been too busy surviving to sit around and braid each other's hair while we talk about it, but I admit you're right. It's all familiar in a collective unconscious kind of way."

"Exactly, brah! In that movie, the villain had this theory that the comics about superheroes were really just an expression of that. Memories of abilities and occurrences of things that once existed in human history. And as mankind advanced, those things just faded into myth."

Karlo hummed deeply. "Yes. I remember that from the movie. It was the only thing really interesting about it. Wasn't even an original plot device. I've read similar done better. But... hmm."

I was growing tired of waiting for Dave to give the all-clear that the blasting cap was grounded and it was safe to enter. But Dave's strategy was bearing fruit. Hitting Karlo with his theorem was just the smelling salts our genius needed to shake off his haze. When he spoke again, he did so with a refreshed spirit.

"Dave, I truly apologize. The idea that a multiverse or alternate dimensions exists because it exists in our subconscious, that we have a bridge to those realities through memories, or that they spring to life from thought itself—it might explain how the slipstream deposited us where it did."

"Weird, huh?"

"Dave. I'm sorry. I was short with you and a little judgmental. That was wrong of me. You're a very smart guy, brother. I mean that."

"Nothing for it, brah. Whatcha cranking out?"

The steady pulse and hum of Baby Blue made me think it was fine, and my fear unfounded.

"Making sure we have a deep reserve of all our ammo. If I can't get the fizzle guns figured out, I'm going to have to start up the M4 production line. The Korundi will be better than the Mydreen with them, but you remember what a slow process it is. Last time it took a month to get a few hundred made. That's not a lot. The math says if I do a run of all components and we do the assembly, we can increase production compared to letting Baby Blue do single unit construction. But it's a lot of work. I'll get on more armorer tools and vises, and the three of us—"

"Say, I hate to bring it up, but you were kinda rough on Ben-dog last night, brah."

A longer pause. I inched closer to hear.

"I was?" Perplexity.

"Dude, do you not remember?"

The emphatic shaking of a head was transmitted by his bewildered denial. "No. Did I say something to him?"

Dave sucked through his front teeth. "Brah, you told him this story about Medlab, and how this one goat roo-roo'd another, and how he was just like—"

Panic. A metal tool dropped onto the hard floor. "Tell me you're messing with me, Dave!" The sharp thud of a palm slapping smooth forehead followed. "I thought I dreamed that. Oh shit!"

"Brah, you're Italian. I thought you guys could hold your liquor."

"RRRRRR. My mom's from Oklahoma. Cherokee. Mostly."

"Isn't that a stereotype?"

Another heartfelt groan and a drawn out exasperated bellow. "I don't knooow, Dave. Daaaaave. What am I gonna do? Tell me no one else heard me at least."

"Ha!" Dave was enjoying this. "Right at the head table, dude. In front of Talis Darmon and all of Mars. Classic! Like that time the Charlie company commander wiped his nose on the host nation flag at the dining-in."

"Banishment, here I come."

That was my cue. I strolled in like the proverbial ghost of Christmas past, present, and future to Karlo's Ebenezer Scrooge.

He stammered, "Ben, I—"

I didn't let him dangle on the hook. "Forget it, brother. In vino, veritas. It's okay."

"No, Ben! Not true! I don't even remember how I got to where I did with all that. I didn't mean any of it." He plopped onto the bench top and sank, not meeting my eyes. "I'm sorry, Ben. On Talis Darmon's big day." He folded. "I'm so messed up."

I took the spot next to him. Dave crossed his arms and just looked at his feet. After a silent eternity, I pulled the pin. "Tell us, brother. Whatever it is, don't hold back. Just say it. Save yourself, and just say it."

He let the spoon of the grenade inside him fly.

"I don't want to be in the army anymore."

It was no surprise.

"Your wish is granted. Poof. You're a civilian."

"Huh?"

"I am the grand poobah of the loyal order of the water buffalos and I say, you're discharged. Job well done. Thank you for your service. We don't have a plaque for you, but we'll figure something out. A party, too. But without the MD 20/20. I always thought you were pure east coast Italian stock, Karlo."

He shrugged. "No. I'm half Native American. My mom was doing her graduate work at MIT when she met my dad."

Dave tried to help, but as usual, came up short in the empathy department. "I get the red face flush when I drink 'cause both my folks are Japanese, but, wow. That was something. We didn't even know who you were, brah."

I waved Dave down. "Dude. Enough."

Karlo made a contrite face. "Won't happen again. Promise." Then he frowned, as if he needed clarification about what I'd told him. "Do you mean it, Ben? I can be a civilian?"

"Of course."

"You don't want to know why I can't do it anymore?"

"I know why." Karlo had already revealed his secret, even if he didn't recognize it for what it was. It was different from the one I'd held—never believing myself worthy. His was that he feared he'd stagnated—that his potential was being smothered in the army. That he served lesser men.

Then the world fell apart.

Baby Blue was a lifeline for him. And I'd made him use it in a way he'd sworn never to.

It didn't have to make sense to me. A rifle. A K-spec. A mortar. Mustard gas. Total victory was what I believed in. Me and the black-and-white generals I carried around with me. In a war, what did it matter which weapon you used if the goal was to win?

To Karlo, it did.

Dave tepidly tested the waters of our new association. "You aren't going anywhere, are you, brah? You're still going to doctor us and Baby Blue, right?"

Karlo was hurt by the question. "Yeah, of course. I'm not quitting on you guys, or the mission. I just have to do it a different way. A gun in my hand isn't going to make as much of a difference as what I can do here."

"Damn straight." I slapped his shoulder. "The queen'll name you minister of research, production, and whatever else. You and Cynar can run wild together."

That brought a tiny smile.

"Can we go get Dougie? He needs us."

It was time to tell them we had one last mission together as a team. "We will. On the way back."

✻ ✻ ✻

I had to ask her permission. And to do that, I had to admit what I'd done.

"Then you must, Benjamin Colt. Atonement and the seeking of forgiveness are rituals for a reason. I know the pain you lived with. You have identified the way to exorcise this one. It is as important as the grand task you lead for me. Do you wish me to accompany you? Because I will. The kingdom will not collapse in a matter of days without me as the focus of the endless complaints and petitions."

But there was a hint of inconvenience in the offer, I could tell.

So many weeks of hardly being parted had eased the potential anxiety of a separation for both of us.

"I know you would, my princess." I still called her that, and it still made her blossom. "And that's what means the most. But—stay. I only ask that once I'm out of your sight, you don't override the security measures I ordered."

"I will live and sleep surrounded by an impenetrable shell of Tarn warriors until you return to be my shield, my betrothed. But do hurry back. We have a wedding day approaching."

✣ ✣ ✣

Kleeve Hartus let Dave and Karlo take turns, correcting and coaching in the finer points of piloting. Apache loved flying, loved the constant attention from everyone, loved the never-ending supply of treats Karlo had for him whenever he sat like a good boy. We flew straight through and dropped Cynar off at his lab. When our task was completed, I was prepared to retrieve him, jam-packing every square inch of the flitter with more of his gizmos.

I knew the way as if I steered it every day of my life. In my mind, I had. We touched down far enough away for safety, hefted rucks onto the crawler Karlo'd whipped up, and I set off in the lead.

"How long did you three wander through these mountains?" Dave asked from behind as I led our march.

"More risings and settings of the moons than can be remembered, David Masamuni." Beraal walked beside me as a sister. A protector. A friend.

I'd never forget the barren rock and winds of the Eastern Korund. Sometimes, even with Talis Darmon's heat to warm me, I felt its chill at night. Just as I'd never forget the mouth of the soul-eater's lair. After many bends, rises, and dips on the trail, a pair of hands restrained me. "With care, Benjamin Colt. Such devious evil has surely moved to deceive us of its boundaries."

Khraal Kahlees had been on guard the whole way, alerted for all manner of myth and magic. "Is that its lair?"

Both Beraal and I confirmed.

The rubber tracks of the flatbed mule skipped once, then found traction. Dave fed out a spool of shock tube as Karlo drove it by remote. All but Beraal and I gasped as the robot disappeared through the mirrored plane.

K-spec gripped tightly, Khraal Kahlees was entranced. "One has not been found in the Korund since the time of my mother's egg."

"Back it up." I pushed everyone down the trail, the last to follow, until I reached the gathering at the end of the long green thread. Dave held the device up to me.

I was still terrible at speeches.

"Mark Wayne. Whatever you've done, I hope you find peace now. You've suffered enough. How you acted—it wasn't all your fault. You lost your family, your world, and everything in it. I've hurt you worse than you deserved. For my part, I at least, forgive you."

I passed the igniter to Dave. "I remember the good times, Marky-Mark. How you made us howl that time we hit the water instead of the DZ, and you put a dead mackerel in Mike's ruck for him to find a week later. I'll try to remember the thens—not the laters—all the times when you were a good teammate. We've got the watch now, brah."

Karlo took the black metal box. "I'm sorry I didn't find a way to save you from him, Mark. I wish I'd shot him myself. If I'd known where he was leading you—I'm not Mike. I wish I had been. *De oppresso liber*, Mark. We can be the ones to free you from oppression now."

He passed it to Beraal. She held it while I pulled the ring to remove the safety pin and checked the red indicator. I nodded. The flash traveled at the speed of sound, and the earth shook. We'd used every bit of demo Karlo could make in a day. A lot.

There was no phantasm to accompany the destruction. No specter of evil smoke rising away. No eerie screech of torment to match the pain it had inflicted on others.

Kleeve Hartus asked the unasked. "Do you know he did not escape, as you were able?"

"He did not," Beraal said with certainty. "I heard Mark Wayne's torment within." She put fingers on head and chest. "Inside me. As though I were with him. But I know it is so because of this—he was no Benjamin Colt."

I disagreed. "No, Beraal. It's because he didn't have someone like Talis Darmon to call him back. But he was in there," I said. "When I'm near whatever it is, it's a scent. A vibration. I felt it with the witch in the throne room, and the one that tried to kill us in our quarters. It was strong here. But it was Mark inside it."

I sensed the malevolence of the soul-eater—the remnant of the Karnak. And from inside it, a scratching. Ragged fingernails against concrete. A sound felt in your spine.

"Both are gone."

Perturbed, Khraal Kahlees said, "Enough of rays and mists, foul essences and magic. We will finish the Mydreen and their Chieftain, and a kingdom of Yellow enemies if need be. I will set the course of Mihdradahl's might to bleed that which can bleed. The sooner we depart, the sooner we end this." He looked back to the dust rising above the peaks. "But it was a thing well done, clansmen." He was first away, then thought better of it until Beraal was joined at his side.

"C-4 has a nice way of solving life's problems, brah. Feel better, Ben-dog?"

"Once we're out of here, I will."

Karlo ticked off on his fingers. "A night at Cynar's, a day to Thoria, then home. What, three more days at most?"

"Then what?" Dave asked.

Karlo grinned. "The rest of our lives."

"I meant, what's the first priority for work, brah."

"Dave—" Karlo was a little exasperated. "Don't you want to take a moment to think about your life and what it all means?"

"Nah. I'm good."

"No issues, Dave? No concerns? Nothing building up inside you that'd feel good to get off your chest to your brothers?"

"Bummed I'll never surf again. Other than that. I'm solid, brah. Don't fret about me, Karlo. Worry about Ben. Did you catch what Talis Darmon said about 'issue from my body'? He's got to be a daddy as well as big kahuna. He's the one under pressure, not me, man. I just roll with it."

Kleeve Hartus and I let them go, their back-and-forth just barely started. I took a final look behind us.

"There is not legend to match what you have done, my friend," the first shield said.

It was all impossible.

"I did nothing. I was just—there. The guy who showed up and didn't quit. And I'm only here because of all of you." I suddenly wanted nothing more than to be with Talis Darmon. "Do you care if we leave right away? I've got the urge to fly tonight. Makes me feel like we're sailing across an ocean of stars, headed for a perfect shore I've never seen."

It was that song "Tales of Brave Ulysses," come into my head. It had been there for me at my lowest. The fantasy I fooled myself with that if I persevered, I would yet see turquoise waves lapping a white sand beach. And I would find my Aphrodite. Now the words of the song returned to me, a wish fulfilled.

"Not at all, Benjamin Colt."

Apache rubbed against me, his wagging an earthquake. He knew we were going for another ride.

"C'mon, boy. Let's sail."

✠ ✠ ✠

I've spared nothing. Told all. The truth of it. Whether it reflects well on me or not.

I'm no hero, though she calls me that. I've made mistakes. Done terrible things. I'd hurt myself and in turn hurt others. I'd countenanced opinions of flawed men and almost succumbed to their poison.

And some of it was in me still. From the depths of a tarry pool, a face refused to stay submerged. Black goo sheeting off silver hair, viscous drips from his mouth, laughing.

But I wasn't alone to fight the zombie of Bryant.

When I thought of Talis Darmon, the black pool in me cowered and evaporated in her light. Brighter than the explosions that turned the Nevada Test Range to glass. If there was once a woman who'd made a fool out of a man, she'd made a man out of a fool.

I wasn't the same person who'd flown into a malfunctioning maelstrom of time and space. She'd remade me.

My name is Deacon Benjamin Colt.

I am Warlord of Mars.

ABOUT THE AUTHOR

Doc Spears is a veteran of the United States Army and works as a consultant and trainer in the defense industry. Writing has been the worst vice he's found yet and doubts he'll be able to stop even with help, which he refuses to seek. When not offending the sensibilities of all decent peoples everywhere, he can be found with Nick Cole and Jason Anspach plotting to infiltrate all realms of sci-fiction.

To be notified about Doc's upcoming books, including the sequel to this title, visit www.WarGateBooks.com

Made in the USA
Coppell, TX
22 November 2022